Dr. Neruda's Cure *for* *Evil*

Dr. Neruda's Cure *for* *Evil*

RAFAEL YGLESIAS

WARNER BOOKS

A Time Warner Company

This book is a work of fiction. Certain real locations,
products and public figures are mentioned, but all other
characters and the events and dialogue described in the book
are totally imaginary.

Warner Books, Inc., 1271 Avenue of the Americas, New York, NY 10020

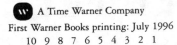 A Time Warner Company

First Warner Books printing: July 1996

10 9 8 7 6 5 4 3 2 1

Library of Congress Cataloging-in-Publication Data

Yglesias, Rafael
    Dr. Neruda's cure for evil / Rafael Yglesias.
        p.   cm.
    ISBN 0-446-52005-5
    I. Title.
    PS3575.G53D7   1996
    813'.54—dc20   95-46461
                                        CIP

Book design by Giorgetta Bell McRee

For the cabal:
Susan Bolotin, Ben Cheever, A. J. Mayer, and Paula Weinstein

SEALED

This manuscript has been sealed at the request of the author, Rafael Guillermo Neruda, M.D., until fifty (50) years after his death. Authorization from the Director is required for handling. All examination, including for the purpose of preservation or cataloguing, is forbidden.

Joshua Black
_____
Joshua Black
Director, Prager Memorial Library

August 28, 1994
_____
Date

Victim Psychology &
the Symptomatology of Evil

———————

AN OBJECTIVE CASE HISTORY OF:
GENE KENNY AND HIS THERAPIST

———————

by

Rafael Neruda, M.D.

A Note on the Organization of the Text

This study is divided into three parts. Part One is an account, in memoir form, of my own psychological history. Part Two is a case history, covering fifteen years, of one of my patients, Gene Kenny. Part Three is a record of my investigation into the cause of the catastrophic failure of his therapy, the results of that investigation, and my radical alternative treatment.

—RAFAEL NERUDA, M.D.

PART ONE

Psychological History

of the

Therapist

CHAPTER ONE

Magic Thoughts

I AM GOING TO PRESENT THESE TWO CASE HISTORIES IN LAYMEN'S TERMS. Perhaps that will render them useless to psychiatrists and psychologists. It shouldn't. If I have learned anything from the ghastly tragedy I must explain, it's that life is lived in laymen's terms.

The dirty secret of analysis is that for the collaboration to succeed the doctor has to be gifted. Not only with the ability to decode a patient's unconscious. Not only to have an illuminating and healing insight specific to that patient's experience of psychological trauma, thus inspiring civil disobedience against his illness. The above are certainly necessary— yet they are insufficient. The therapist must also supply insight at the right moment; when, as it were, the security police are asleep. A talking cure succeeds only partly because it aids self-awareness; most of the work is accomplished through a sensitive and precise management of the healing relationship. What the analyst feels is as crucial as the analysand's sorrows. Thus it follows that there is a fatal flaw in all scientifically presented case histories because they are solely concerned with the patient's life and character. To understand why the treatment proceeded the way it did one must also know about the doctor—his brilliancies, his mistakes, and his own psychology. The true story of a therapeutic exchange begins not with the patient's present problem but with the healer's past.

I, Rafael Guillermo Neruda, was born in New York in 1952. My mother, Ruth, was Jewish; my father, Francisco, what sociologists now call Hispanic. For the first eight years of my life we lived in Washington Heights, a working-class neighborhood at the northern extreme of Manhattan. In those days the Heights were predominantly Jewish. So much so, my father had to show the landlord Ruth's birth certificate to prove she was Jewish before he was allowed to rent our modest apartment. Although I was accepted by my mother's family, my Jewish friends and their families, they were quick to remind me that I was half alien to them.

I spent summers with my father's parents in Tampa, Florida. My father's people were the children of Spanish and Cuban immigrants who moved there in the 1880s to earn their living as cigar-makers. Although my grandparents were American born, they had been raised in an insulated Spanish-speaking ghetto of Tampa called Ybor City (pronounced E-BORE). They spoke English with heavy accents and were distrustful of the white and black Americans who surrounded them. My grandparents were too timid and superstitious to travel to New York, thus I had to be sent down to Ybor City during summer vacation for them to admire and display me to a seemingly endless parade of cousins, aunts and uncles. While summering—baking would be more accurate—with the Latins of Florida, I was accepted as a beloved object of pride; yet there were frequent reminders that I was half alien to them.

Interestingly, neither the Jews nor the Latins made an overt play for my loyalty. I stress *overt*. There was one notable exception. Samuel Rabinowitz was seventy-five years old when I was born. My mother was his youngest daughter. She gave birth to me at the age of thirty-six, late in life for a woman of the 1950s. I have a single vivid memory of Papa Sam, an encounter at my Uncle Bernie's on the first night of Passover in 1960, in which he claimed me as a Jew and defined my fate. I imbued this event with the magical thinking of a child, a magic that after all became real, because it called into being the ambition of my life.

That morning my mother and I took the train out to Uncle Bernie's Great Neck estate to attend the Rabinowitz family Seder. Bernie was Papa Sam's oldest son. He was a multimillionaire thanks to real estate ventures that had taken advantage of the postwar boom in New York City for low- and middle-income housing. Bernie possessed the capital for these investments thanks to the profits he made from selling powdered eggs to the government to distribute to our troops during World War II. My uncle was able to make a huge profit because the eggs he powdered for our boys were the rotten throwaways of upstate farmers and thus Bernie's only cost was the processing.

By 1960 Uncle Bernie was worth nearly one hundred million dollars. His great wealth was regarded with awe by my mother's side of the family and indeed the world—with the exception of my mother. The rest of the Rabinowitzes did not agree with my mother's analysis of her brother's moneymaking, namely that Bernie had lived through the best two decades to be in business in American history, that anyone who entered the war years with substantial capital trebled it, that the riskier and more foolish the investment made then, the greater the return. Even if they *had* shared my mother's interpretation of economic history, my uncle's staggering accumulation of wealth beyond the status of mere millionairehood would have convinced them his success was due to more than just good timing. But the abundance did not persuade my strong-willed mother of her brother's genius. Quite the contrary. To her it was a proof of his lack of character. Among many explanations for her attitude I should note that she was a member of the Communist Party. (My training analyst once noted in an ironic mumble, "Your family history is a little complicated." Here's another taste of its strange flavor: my father hadn't come with us to the 1960 Seder because he was living in Fidel's Cuba, doing research for a book sympathetic to the brand-new revolution. He hoped to help forestall an economic boycott by the U.S., which he believed would soon prove fatal.)

Uncle Bernie was also admired for his generosity and philanthropy. And with good reason. From the age of eighteen on he supported his parents, two brothers and four sisters with direct gifts as well as jobs for them or their spouses. He contributed millions to Israel, Brandeis, two major hospitals, and the Metropolitan Museum of Art. He virtually paid singlehandedly to build a new temple near his mansion in Great Neck. In 1960 and '61, for example, Bernie gave away more than ten million to various charities and causes. All praised him; all believed he was great; except, as noted, for Ruth, my artistic mother, the youngest sibling, and also the only one who did not live off Bernie's largess. She refused her brother's offers to employ her freelance husband, just as she had refused years before when Uncle Bernie offered to support her if only she would give up her intention to marry my Latin father.

Ruth's unwillingness to accept her brother as a paragon did not begin when Bernie opposed her marriage to Francisco Neruda. No, it originated (what does not?) in childhood. She felt slighted by their parents in his favor from infancy on; and she felt slighted by Bernie her entire life. Her gift for music and acting wasn't taken seriously and was sometimes actively thwarted by their immigrant parents. Later Bernie himself, when he was father pro tem, insisted Ruth give up the dance and music lessons she was taking after school and get a part-time job. Of course, Bernie received nothing but praise and encouragement from their parents.

My mother believed that she and Bernie battled as children because he had usurped the role of their father. Bernie believed paternal responsibility was thrust upon him. The rest of the Rabinowitz siblings believed Bernie had saved them from a family calamity in the midst of a national disaster. The event in dispute was Bernie's assumption of the role of breadwinner following Papa Sam's non-fatal, but temporarily crippling heart attack. His coronary was blamed, in those days, not on Papa's relish of chicken fat, but the failure of his third grocery store in the Bronx. It was the trough of the Great Depression. Bernie, accustomed to putting in long hours after school at the family store, was sent out to work full-time. He was thirteen. For four years he was to be the household's sole support—until his brother was old enough to help. By then, although only seventeen years old, Bernie was well on his way to making his first million. All their lives Ruth and Bernie considered each other opposites; everyone who knew them thought they were as different as could be. As early as age eight, I would have disagreed. I think their natural conflict was intensified because they were so much alike. It was simply unfortunate for my mother that she was born into a society that discriminated against independent and innovative women while Bernie was born into a culture that favored men who were bold and determined.

By 1960, Uncle Bernie had led the Rabinowitz Seder for more than two decades. That year, after the ritual was over, as two uniformed black women began to serve the real food, he shocked the assembled parents with an announcement. He said the reward for finding the *Afikomen* (a piece of the blessed matzo hidden by the Leader during the early part of the ritual and then hunted for by the children later on) would be twenty dollars. In previous years it had never been more than five—already an extravagant prize.

"Twenty dollars!" Aunt Sadie exclaimed. She covered her mouth with a hand; whether to stop a criticism or to express shock, I couldn't tell.

I didn't know much about the relative value of money at eight. Anything over twenty-five cents was a lot. Anything over a dollar was infinite. My older cousins (whom I envied and loved and wanted to impress) cued me that twenty dollars was in the upper range of the infinite category. They made a collective sound of their longing to win—a chorus whose parts were gasps, giggles, wows, and one piercing whistle from my cousin Daniel. He was two years older than I, Aunt Sadie's youngest. I admired Daniel. He seemed to disdain me; he delighted in besting me, especially at such things as football or tennis, sports which, coming as I did from a working-class city neighborhood, I had never played before. Earlier that day we had competed in both games on Uncle's grounds. I was so bad at them, particularly tennis, that Daniel said I was a spaz— short for "spastic." This hurt my feelings and my pride. Not only because I knew it to be unjust (I was good at the athletic games of my class: handball and stickball) but because I longed—with the passionate heart of a child—for Daniel to like me.

"Well," Uncle Bernie said. He pushed himself a little ways from the long Seder table. The gold wedding ring on his left hand, fashioned with twists like a sailor's knot, rested on the shiny white tablecloth. The yellow metal called my attention to his fingers. The skin was dark. Above the knuckles were long tufts of black hair; the same thick black hair covered his large round head. When he smiled—bright teeth against olive skin—his wide features stretched and gave him the friendly appearance of a well-fed baby. Not that his nose or eyes or mouth were infantile. On the contrary. But there was an oval beneficence to the general shape. The deep brown eyes, however, were keen with authority, calculation and a gleam of mischief. "I have a reason for making the reward so high," Bernie said. He played the table with the fingers of his left hand. Not an impatient drumming, but a pianist's melody. That kept his ring in motion. I was fascinated by how the gold encircled the finger's tuft of hair. The fine silky hairs were gathered into a knot underneath the ring; once free of the band they fanned out. I tried to remember if my father had that much hair on his fingers. Francisco had been away in Havana for only a month, but to an eight-year-old a month is very long. At that moment I couldn't remember my father's face that well, much less details of his fingers. The answer happened to be no; my father's fingers were virtually hairless. In fact I have never met a man whose hairs had such length and thickness as Bernie's. Again, I don't mean to suggest there was anything ape-like about my uncle. Rather the tufts were cropped and handsome in appearance. I wondered if they had been intentionally groomed to be decorative.

"It's a test," Uncle said. He surprised me by looking right at me.

Surprised because, during all the time I had been in his presence that day—from the gathering in the den for the adults to drink cocktails and fuss about the children having messed up their clothes playing, to the transition to the table and the start of the Seder—Bernie hadn't looked at me. I was glad because there was too much of him. His voice was too resonant, his head too large, his gray suit's fabric too thick, especially on that day, an unusually hot April day. (In fact while playing tennis with Daniel I took off my shirt. "You sweat like a spic," Daniel commented.) Bernie's stare at me, as he told Aunt Sadie the hunt for the *Afikomen* was a test, seemed to be the first time he noticed me at all.

I lowered my eyes immediately. I was annoyed at myself and quickly looked back. Too late—I had lost his interest. He had shifted his intense gaze to Daniel. If I knew a harsh curse to abuse myself with, I must have used it then because I can still remember the sharp disappointment I felt that I had failed to hold my rich and powerful uncle's eyes. I vowed not to make that mistake again.

"Aren't you going to negotiate with them?" Uncle Harry asked. That was the tradition in our family and in many others—namely, that the Leader hid the *Afikomen* and bargained the amount of the reward with the child who found it. This is a fractured version of the correct tradition: in Europe, Jews did not have the Leader hide the *Afikomen;* rather the children (males only, of course) stole it and refused to make restitution until the Leader paid a ransom. *Afikomen,* by the way, means "dessert" although it is a symbolic treat, another Seder reminder of the deprivations of the Hebrew slaves of Egypt, since it is in fact nothing more than a piece of plain matzo. I find this change in the Passover ritual interesting because it reflects the shift from the harsh demands made upon Jewish children in the ghettos of the Old Country to the comfort and dependence of their lives in the United States. The original tradition placed a value on initiative, independence and ability to earn a living—even to the point of larceny. That must have been necessary to a Jewish family's survival in Eastern Europe. The revised tradition is a hide-and-seek game created and controlled by adults, symbolic of the prolonged childhoods of my generation of Jews in the New World. (The stereotype of the overprotective Jewish mother is, I suspect, an American phenomenon.) I'm sure my uncle preferred the old *Afikomen* ritual and that night hoped to restore a little of its former character, to once again make it a test of manhood. Bernie, remember, had had to go to work as a child. (Thirteen, in spite of puberty and Bar Mitzvah, for the majority of boys is still essentially a time of childhood.) He believed, as do most unanalyzed people, that the misfortune of his life—his premature role as family wage-earner—had been good for him. He argued that all children should be responsible and self-reliant as early as possible. He often quarreled in public with his wife that their children—in college by 1960—were spoiled. I, of course, did not know that, or anything else about the inner life of my uncle. All that mattered then was his challenge, "It's a test," followed by a stare right at me. Then he looked at Daniel, and one by one at my other male cousins. He skipped the girls, although they would also be searchers.

"A test of what?" my mother asked. She snapped the final *t*, whipping the sound scornfully. I cringed because of a fight my mother had had earlier in the day with her oldest sister, Sadie. Aunt Sadie had picked us up at the Great Neck train station to drive us to Uncle's estate. Conversation had been pleasant until we pulled into the driveway, and then she said to my mother, "Don't make trouble today with your brother."

My mother laughed. "It's a non-aggression pact. If he doesn't fire I won't shoot back."

Aunt Sadie warned her again, repeating in different words that Ruth shouldn't fight with Uncle Bernie. "Even if he does shoot first," Sadie added.

My mother lost her temper. I was startled. I had seen her angry with my father, but that was only once or twice, and never with anyone else. Her thin face and smooth white skin were quite different in color and shape from her dark brother's oval head. Enraged, her high cheekbones lifted, pulling back her lips to expose her small bright teeth, and her green eyes narrowed. She might have been a big cat in a furious fight for her life. She bobbed her chin at Sadie and said, "Don't tell me how to behave! I'm not a child! I'm not on this planet at Bernie's sufferance! I'm not living off him like the rest of you! You're terrified I'm going to blow up the Bernard Rabinowitz gravy train—well, don't worry, it won't be me who cuts his throat. It'll be the working class. It'll be people like those workers down South. Those poor people he brags he brought to their knees."

"Shut up already," Sadie said, both scared of the cat's angry motions and also conscious of my presence. She indicated me with a nod to my mother.

"I'll never forget him gloating about how his paid thugs drove a truck over one of the strikers!"

"All right, I'm sorry I said anything!" Sadie opened her door and fled.

My mother panted, angled at Sadie's vacated seat as if her prey were still there. From my back-seat view, I saw a single green eye in profile. That eye seemed to find me, with the spooky myopic stare of a bird. "Come on, let's go in," she said to me. She added, without irony, "We'll have fun."

What I got from all that was that my uncle was a powerful man, a dangerous man, an important man. If he had devised a test for me, then I wanted to pass it: to avenge my earlier defeats at tennis and football, to win my cousin's love, to please my mother, to represent my alien father well, and also, finally, to hold the gaze of my terrible and handsome uncle.

"A test of their character," Uncle Bernie said to my mother. He continued quickly to us children, "I've hidden the *Afikomen* somewhere in this house." His fingers continued to play a silent tune on the white cloth.

"You haven't left the table," Cousin Daniel said. "You still have the *Afikomen*."

As Leader, at the beginning of the service, Uncle Bernie had broken off the *Afikomen* from a plate of matzos on display at the table. He wrapped it in a thick napkin with a shiny white satin border and put it in his lap. As he did, I overheard my cousin Daniel whisper to his older brother, "I'm gonna watch him this time." I didn't know what Daniel meant. At eight I didn't remember the previous year's Seder. He meant that he would keep an eye on Uncle, waiting to see where he slipped away to hide the *Afikomen*. Bernie hadn't left the table during the Seder and therefore, Daniel had reasoned, he must still have it in his lap.

Bernie's mouth widened into his beneficent smile. "You mean this." He lifted the napkin from his lap. "Very clever, Daniel."

"Yes!" Daniel got to his feet. "I win!"

"Not so fast," Bernie said and raised his hand like a traffic cop. There was something comic, not mean, about Uncle's expression and tone. Most of the adults chuckled and commented on Bernie's wisdom and Daniel's greed. Uncle ignored his grown-up audience and continued to address us children. "This year we'll do it differently. This is only the symbolic *Afikomen*. I hid the real one—"

"Call it what it is," my mother interrupted. "A door prize."

She was shushed by the grown-ups. The children, including me, ignored her. But my uncle didn't. He flicked a glance in her direction and the emotion in his eyes amazed me. It was contempt and hatred. But only a flash. Immediately, his eyes were friendly again and he continued in his smooth deep voice, a resonant cello, "I hid the real one while you were playing outside. The child who finds *that Afikomen* will find it not only because of his intelligence and his perseverance but because of the strength of his character."

My mother made a rude sound with her lips. Daniel got out of his chair to leave the table. His father restrained him; Uncle Bernie hadn't signaled us to begin our search.

Bernie ignored my mother's contemptuous noise. Instead, he smiled generously at Daniel. "You stand like greyhounds in the slips," his cello vibrated. "Straining upon the start." Bernie raised his right hand, decorated with tufts above the knuckles. "The game's afoot," he said and waved his arm like a racing flag.

Daniel and the others bolted. I made my move as well, running behind Uncle's chair and passing four or five other adult relatives, until I was caught up short. A hand had taken hold of my left arm. The sudden yank caused me to stumble. I fell against the chair of the person who had stopped me. It was my mother.

"You stay here," she said and she sounded angry. I assumed she was angry at me. "You're not playing this stupid game."

"Mom," I complained and tried to wriggle out of her grasp. My struggle for freedom proved how much I wanted to win that contest. I was not a bold child. In fact I suffered from acute shyness, especially in front of adults, and although these grown-ups were my people, some were totally unknown to me, thanks to my mother's role as the family black sheep. I was shy and I was not defiant of my parents. Normally, if my mother grabbed me in public and forbade me from something in an angry tone I would obey her injunction silently, if unhappily. Indeed, my attempt to get away so surprised her that I easily freed my wrist from her loose grip. For a moment we exchanged a look of mutual shock at my action—and then I ran.

Uncle's formal dining room had a wall of glass, allowing a panoramic view of his unblemished lawn sloping to the water—the pool and tennis court were placed discreetly on the ground's perimeter. I ran from there into a huge living room, itself the length of most people's homes. It too had a view of Long Island Sound; only here it was provided by four windows with small panes of leaded glass, a kind of latticework that distorted the manicured lawn and tranquil water into a moody Impressionist painting. Two cousins were in there, one on his knees checking the wall cabinets, another on his belly peering under the sofas and love seats.

My mother pursued me. She caught me as I reached the large central hall, painted a light yellow color, and dominated by a sweeping dark mahogany staircase. My cousins' feet thudded and trampled on the second floor; occasionally they raced across the landing in their movement from one bedroom to another. They were having their chance at glory while I was under arrest. This time Ruth's grip on my arm was tight and painful. She was incensed. Today, I suspect she was more humiliated that I had defied her in front of her siblings than infuriated by my contrariness. At the time I was baffled by her. "Don't ever run from me like that again!" she shouted. Her words hurt, too. The violence of her tone hurt. "You're not going to play this ridiculous game! You're not a performing monkey!"

"I wanna!" I protested and pulled at her grip. This confrontation changed my understanding of myself and her. I was shy, I was obedient, yet I was willing to fight her. And, although I was not to understand why for many years to come, I discovered that day that this inner self, the adult growing so far undisturbed in an unilluminated corner of my child's soul, was a person my mother didn't want to meet. She only wanted to know the sweet, bashful, compliant boy. (And why not? Such a child was a great compensation for the abrasive and selfish personalities who had been her lot in life. One of the first practical lessons of psychology is that neurotics aren't fools. Typically, they are clever people whom the world has thwarted.)

"No, you don't!" She shook my arm so hard my entire body trembled. She was shaking all the intransigent men in her life; she was trying to dislodge the stubborn materialism of her family and her nation. So she had to shake hard. She had to shake as hard as she could; and yet she could never shake hard enough.

Daniel, of all people, came down the staircase like Errol Flynn playing Robin Hood, dancing, leaping, using the banister to propel himself three, four steps at a jump. His wide face, the characteristic Rabinowitz oval, was flushed. *He's found it,* I thought, heartbroken.

Daniel raced around us. "I figured it out!" he bragged as he disappeared down the narrow side hall that led toward the kitchen. But he was empty-handed, not carrying the heavy white napkin which would be wrapped around the *Afikomen.*

He hadn't found it! I was thrilled.

"Look at me!" My mother wanted to shout; shame suppressed her demand into a maddened whisper. My head had turned to follow

Daniel. Why the kitchen? What did he think: it was still in the matzo box?

I was convinced of this suddenly. My uncle was a businessman and he had probably thought of matzo's production: returned the *Afikomen* to its box, stashed the box in a kitchen cabinet, in the working section of the house, tended by the black cook and maid. The lesson would be clear: a reminder of work and service. Obviously, at eight, I couldn't have articulated this reasoning, but that, more or less, was the logic I theorized. Had Daniel? Was that what he meant when he cried "I figured it out" and ran toward the kitchen? Or was he headed to some other room? There were many others in that direction: the family den; the back stairs to the finished basement; the pantry; an office for my uncle. The house was huge, more than twenty rooms; I hadn't seen most of them.

First, I had to get free. I sagged against my mother's hold on my wrists, a premature sit-in protester, becoming a dead weight.

"Stand up!" she ordered, trying to hoist me to my feet. But she wasn't especially strong—this was more than two decades before women of her age pumped iron. I felt a malicious pleasure at her impotence. She frowned and complained, "Stop it! Stand up!"

My legs bumped her shins. "Ow," she said and kicked the heels of my Buster Browns, first one foot, then the other. Not hard. Now we were both behaving like frustrated eight-year-olds.

I drooped, ass hanging low, arms stretched to the limit. I thought they might pop out of my shoulder sockets, but I didn't care. "I know where it is!" I shouted at Ruth. "Let me go! I can win! Let me go!"

She quit trying to lift me. Instead she pulled me toward her face, a face distorted by rage and frustration. "Stop it right now or we'll leave this minute! I swear to God I'll drag you by the neck all the way to New York."

I pictured the humiliation of such an exit. As yet there were no sixties images of noble passive resistance to inspire me. To be dragged out by my angry mother in front of all my cousins, the pretty aloof girls in their dresses, the self-confident and athletically skilled boys with their rougish shirttails hanging out, seemed to me to preclude any chance that they might one day respect and like me.

When Ruth began to carry out her threat, twisting toward the door and yanking me at it, I straightened. "Okay," I said, head down to avoid her eyes. I was angry and I was ashamed of my anger. She was my mother: I loved her; she was the god of my universe; to hate her that much was painful and confusing.

I began to cry: choked sobs of thwarted anger and disappointed love. A beautiful cousin—Uncle Harry and Aunt Ceil's daughter, eleven-year-old Julie—stopped in her progress down the mahogany staircase. Her long straight black hair draped her narrow face, the ends curling inward, nearly touching under her chin. I was ashamed and quickly looked away, but not before a glimpse of her told me she was sympathetic. The quizzical tilt of her head—perhaps it was merely her beauty—convinced me she understood I was the victim of an injustice.

"What's wrong?" she called down to my mother. Julie had a sweet and yet confident voice. Later, it served her well in business. When she challenged you, there was no challenge in her tone.

"Nothing," my mother said impatiently. She pulled me to her, covering my face and muffling my tears. "Calm down!" she whispered. But it was an order.

Of course, it was my attempt to quell the anger that brought on hysterical tears. But I accepted her injunction and fought them.

"He can search with me," Julie said. She finished her descent and walked over. Her alert brown eyes scanned us with curiosity and maybe (perhaps this is a later imposed memory) a hint of condescension.

In any event, at her offer I cried louder. Ruth pressed me tight into the smooth fabric of her skirt. "This is a family discussion. Could we have some privacy, please?" Ruth's tone was unpleasant.

Julie was brave. She answered in her unchallenging and bold voice: "Well, if you want privacy you're in the wrong place. This is the foyer," she added and let go of a short volley of laughter.

"I know this is the foyer," my mother said, and added sourly, "We'll get out of everybody's way." Being at her brother's mansion drained Ruth of her sense of humor. She walked me—still hiding in the slippery fabric of her dress—toward the narrow hall where Daniel had disappeared. We moved awkwardly, like a mother-and-son team in a three-legged race. I was coughing at this point, coughing from the tears I had swallowed.

"Calm down," she said again, this time tenderly. She stopped and rubbed my back.

"I'm trying," I said in a pathetic way, coughing and choking. At least we were alone in the narrow hall. It was dark. The only light came from two doors leading to adjoining rooms.

"Try a little harder," she said, but again tenderly. She bent over and kissed my wet cheek.

It occurred to me Daniel might come by any minute. The thought of him witnessing my babyish behavior stopped my tears.

"I want you to understand," my mother said. To be on my level, she knelt on one knee. Her tone was anguished. She had made me the victim of her dissatisfaction with the world; I could hear, although not comprehend, her regret. "Your uncle has made a lot of money and he thinks that getting money is good. That it shows how smart and great a person is. Well, most geniuses, most of history's great men, never made any money at all. And they certainly didn't care about making money. Looking for the *Afikomen* is just supposed to be a fun game—it's not supposed to be a test. When my father—when Papa used to lead the Seder—" she stopped. I couldn't see her face that clearly. Besides, I was distracted, furiously wiping away my tears, to remove the evidence should Daniel happen by. Meanwhile, Ruth had reminded herself of a neglected duty. "Come," she said and took my hand. "We're going to visit Papa Sam."

I was leery of seeing Grandfather. I remembered from my visit to Great Neck in December that he was confined to a wheelchair. There wasn't much substance left to his body, a body that was once, especially for an immigrant from Europe, tall and muscular. Indeed, his athletic figure had been the cause of his initial success in life. At seventeen, Papa Sam was chosen for the Tsar's personal guard. The men selected for that honor were picked because they would look strong and handsome on state occasions. Papa Sam was the only Jew to wear the bright red uniform with gold buttons and a fur collar. His fellow guardsmen regularly abused him for being a Jew. They would form a circle, put him in the middle, and take turns kicking his legs with their hard-tipped boots while they called him kike. He couldn't fight back. To resist meant a court martial, and a sentence of at least twenty years' hard labor, if not death. That was the story he liked to tell about his life. Papa Sam would bring out a photograph of himself in the honor guard uniform, standing at attention in front of a palace, and then show us his scarred shins.

One day Papa Sam informed his colonel that his mother was ill; he asked permission to visit her in the small town of his birth. In fact, the news he had gotten was of her death. He was granted a leave. He walked all the way to Paris and eventually made his way to London, where he met my grandmother. The emigrated through Ellis Island to the United States seven years before my mother was born.

Unfortunately, by the time I met Papa Sam, heart disease had shrunk and warped his tall frame. In December, his big head looked precarious atop a skinny torso that scarcely filled his wheelchair. His bony shoulders were hunched forward; they carved a bowl in his chest. His skin was loose and bloodless; his eyes dull and hopeless; the mouth slack and stupid. He probably smelled as well, but I don't remember that. In any event, the prospect of going to see Papa Sam didn't thrill me or compensate me for missing out on the *Afikomen* hunt.

However, this time I was obedient. Ruth led me toward the kitchen. I could see into it. The black women were cleaning and readying the real dessert. The cabinets were closed and there was no sign of Daniel. I heard the hilarity of the grown-up relatives through the service door to the dining room. They were raucous. Some sang, "Chad Gad Ya! Chad Gad Ya!" Others teased the singers about their lack of musicality. My young cousins, of course, raced above, behind, and below—full of their own energy and happiness. Only my mother and I were glum non-participants. Just before we reached the kitchen, Ruth turned into another hallway that was new to me. It led to a short addition to the mansion, built to accommodate Papa Sam and his nurse after my grandmother died. It consisted of two small bedrooms and a bathroom, a kind of motel for the sick old man. During the December visit I had seen him in the living room and I had assumed he lived elsewhere, probably in a hospital, since his nurse looked and behaved like a nurse, with a white uniform and a crabby manner.

Papa Sam was in bed, covered up to his neck, his arms outside the blanket. He appeared mummified. His nurse sat in a chair by the door, reading. Her tensor lamp provided the only light.

"Is he asleep?" my mother asked the nurse in a whisper.

"No . . ." Papa answered in a groan. He lifted his huge hand—it looked large because his wrist and arm were now so thin—above the plaid blanket and gestured for us to come close. "Is that the Little Gentleman?" he asked.

In the shadows he was a gloomy, dying presence. The nurse got up and turned on his bedside lamp. Its light cast shadows across Papa's wasted face.

"You remember," my mother said as we approached. She kissed him on a gaunt cheek. Papa hummed with pleasure at her touch.

"Of course." I am not reproducing his classic Yiddish intonations and accent. They were very thick. I had to concentrate to understand him, often not realizing what he had said until a few seconds after he spoke. That made me shyer than usual. "You're the Little Gentleman," he said, rolling his great head to the side. His lifeless eyes didn't seem to focus. I wasn't really sure he could see me. In December he made a speech to my mother that I had always, even as a toddler, been a perfect little gentleman. Ruth explained to me later he was impressed that I had not only sat quietly and listened while the adults talked, but contributed to the conversation. Papa also commented with admiration—the significance of this wasn't clear to me—that I seemed to be very tall. He was vain about his height and considered mine (I was in fact tall for my age) to be a genetic achievement that was to his credit.

I nodded and looked down. Again I couldn't meet the eyes of a Rabinowitz elder. I was scared by the old man's physical deterioration. And, as professionals among my readers already realize, I was no more of a Little Gentleman than any eight-year-old. The polite role I had once played accidentally seemed too difficult to repeat on purpose.

"We just wanted to say hello. We'll let you go back to sleep," my mother said.

"No!" Papa croaked with as much energy as he could. "I can't sleep. Stay and talk for a little."

I kept my head down, staring at the carpet. I wasn't seeing it, however. I pictured Daniel, standing on a stool, reaching with glee into the kitchen cabinet to find the *Afikomen*.

"How are you?" my mother asked.

"I can't get a breath." He made a gurgling sound in his lungs, whether to illustrate or involuntarily, I didn't know. He sounded bad. Death was in the room with us; I felt my mother's dread in her moist hand.

"You relax, Daddy. Don't exert yourself." Ruth talked softly over my head to the nurse. "Would you like to take a break? We can stay here until you come back. Is that all right, Papa?"

"Sure," he said.

"All right. Thank you, ma'am. I could use a cup of coffee." The nurse's voice was loud. She wasn't afraid of the implacable presence waiting to take my grandfather. "I'll come back in fifteen minutes?" she asked.

"Take your time," my mother said. And yet she was uneasy; I heard tension in her voice. The nurse left quickly, as if worried that Ruth might change her mind.

"Fifteen minutes is probably all I've got," Papa said and tried to laugh. The strangled whine he made sounded like a balloon leaking. It raised my eyes from the carpet. Papa's face turned a strange color, not red or white, a sort of greenish pallor. He struggled to quell something and ended up coughing. "That'll teach me not to make jokes. So where's your handsome husband?" he said in a hoarse voice. Papa sounded relaxed. He seemed to feel no bitterness about his condition. At the time I didn't know his attitude was exceptional. Perhaps he had avoided so much death during his life—the Tsar's punishment for desertion; America's Depression; Europe's Holocaust; and three attacks from his own heart— that this peaceful finish seemed to be good fortune. Anyway, I never forgot his pleasant humor and bravery.

"He's still working on his book," my mother said.

"His book? About that guy with the beard in Havana?"

My mother smiled. I did too. It was amusing to hear the great Fidel, a man who was spoken of by my father as the embodiment of strength and virtue—the bull whom all the women of Cuba wanted to, or had, slept with; the gourmand who ate a dozen eggs for breakfast; the military genius who had defeated a dictator's army with a band of untrained peasants; the Cicero who could hold a nation rapt for three-hour speeches; the Cuban George Washington and Ben Franklin and Thomas Jefferson all wrapped into one—to hear him called (in a Yiddish accent) the guy with the beard was funny. "That's the one," she said. "Fidel Castro."

"He likes cigars, too," Papa said. His dull eyes were on me; the blank look of a blind man. "Like Groucho," he added. "Think maybe Castro is Jewish? Sephardic? Could be. Now that would be something to write about. You know there are people in Spain—" He stopped. The punctured balloon whined again. His white color changed to green and he coughed.

"Relax, Papa," my mother said nervously. She reached out to touch the plaid blanket covering her father's chest. It trembled with each cough.

"Can't—" he said. The green changed to a duskier color—purple. "Can't—" he tried to say again. He looked as if he were being flooded with blood under the skin, drowning from the inside out.

"Get the nurse," Ruth said to me. Then she changed her mind. "Wait," she said, holding my arm. I don't know if she saw fear on my face. Perhaps it wasn't what she saw; she could have realized an eight-year-old was a poor emissary. Leaving me alone with the sick man wasn't acceptable either. Both choices were bad. She decided not to spare me, but to find help for her father as quickly as possible. "I'll get her. Stay with Papa," she said and ran out before I had a chance to react.

I was alone with a dying man. Grandfather couldn't produce any sound other than a gurgling struggle to speak. His eyes were wild with fear. He reached for his constricted throat and pulled at the invisible strangler's grip.

His chest jerked as if he were being electrocuted. I put my hand on top of the plaid blanket, at the epicenter of his torso's earthquake. I didn't look at his choked face. I stared at my hand and thought very hard: *Get better, Papa.* I wished for a healing bolt to flow through my arms and into my palm; I willed it to soothe Papa's wounded chest. *Get better, Papa,* I thought, beaming the magic power, wishing with all my heart to heal him.

After a moment, Papa's hands covered mine. The long bones of his fingers, although they looked fragile, pressed down hard on my palm.

Get better, I sung silently to his hand.

Papa pushed harder and harder on my little hand. I was horrified at what he was doing. I thought he was going to push it right through his chest. I pictured my fingers falling inside and touching his blood and heart and my vague idea of what else would be inside a human being.

And then he released the pressure.

"Oh, that's better," he said in a clearer voice than I had yet heard from him.

The nurse, my mother, and Uncle Bernie appeared. I looked at my grandfather. His skin was back to normal. His eyes were no longer dead; they shined at me. And he continued to hold my hand against his chest; but now lightly, the way someone would caress a favorite object.

The adults fussed and questioned him.

"I was dying and the Little Gentleman saved me," Papa said, but in a lilting, jocular intonation.

My mother, in fact, took Papa seriously. She hugged me, asked if I had been scared. I said no. She explained to me almost apologetically and fearfully, as if I were a stern boss, that she had gone instead of me because she could find the nurse faster.

"No, no, I'm fine," Papa was saying to the nurse, who hadn't accepted his reassurances. "I couldn't get my breathing for a second. It was nothing. Forget it. Go away." He waved energetically and struggled to lift himself higher on the bed.

"You want to sit, Mr. Rabinowitz?" the nurse asked. She arranged his pillows so they would prop up his head.

When she tried to rearrange his blanket, he held it down firmly and said, "Stop. I want that—leave me alone. Everybody but my grandson—go. Right, Bernie?"

Uncle agreed with a nod. He took my mother's hand affectionately. She reacted with a startled look and then smiled. Uncle tugged her toward the door.

"Go," Papa said to the nurse. "Have your coffee." He encouraged my mother, "Go. I'll send your boy out to you."

"Okay?" my mother asked me softly.

"Yeah," I answered honestly. My fear of the old man's decay—and of the relentless presence waiting for him—was gone. Besides, I liked being called the Little Gentleman. I preferred to stay in the ordinary room (much more like the rooms in Washington Heights) with this relative who approved of me. Who had, moreover, some use for me other than as a hostage to his ideology. Or so I thought.

Papa waited until we were alone before speaking. He nodded at an untouched plate on a folding table by the foot of the bed. "There's a piece of cake. You want?"

I went to see. It was plain pound cake. "No thank you."

Papa smiled. "So polite." He waved for me to come close. I obeyed. This time I noticed that my assumption he would smell bad was wrong. In fact he smelled of talcum powder. His eyes were still bright from the struggle he'd just won. "Do you know you're Jewish?" he said. The Yiddish pronunciation made a whooshing sound out of "Jewish"; it was comical to me. I guess I didn't react. "You may think you're half-Jewish." Again, the swishing sound he made saying "Jewish" tickled me. He nodded no. "According to Jewish law, you're Jewish." This rapid repetition of the word almost had me giggling out loud. I didn't want to offend the old man so I kept a solemn face. "The reason is: your mother is Jewish. Now, if it was the other way round. If your father was Jewish and your mother a . . ." he hesitated. "A . . . well, not Jewish. Then you wouldn't be considered Jewish unless you converted."

Naturally, this seemed preposterous to me. I suspected he had made up this law to convert me into a whole Jew. (In fact, he was accurate.) Obviously, I reasoned, he was disappointed that I wasn't completely Jewish (in the same way that it bothered my Latin relatives that I wasn't completely Spanish) and he had concocted this sophistry to dispose of my Jewish deficit. But I admired him for his direct approach, for his honesty in admitting that he wanted me to belong entirely to him. And I was pleased. Why shouldn't I have preferred being wanted? It was flattering.

"It's true," he insisted. I must have looked dubious. "Israel will take you just as you are under the Law of Return. But they wouldn't if it was your father and not your mother who's Jewish. It's true. It's in the Torah."

All that, to my eight-year-old ears, was gibberish. I nodded yes to mollify him. I already knew how to behave in these situations: with Jews I was Jewish; with Latins I was Latin; with Americans I was a New Yorker.

"Come," he beckoned. He squirmed to sit higher. "I'll tell you something else." I had reached the side of his bed. "Raise your hand. Your right hand." I did. I felt as if I were at an assembly at P.S. 173 and I was about to Pledge Allegiance to the Flag. That is, I felt foolish and grave, embarrassed and awed. "I saw it while I was dying—" Papa lowered his voice to a whisper. "I'm serious—I was about to go. And then I saw your hand on my chest. Do you know what you were doing?" Papa illustrated with his own hand. He raised it, palm out, fingers together. He gradually moved his pinky and ring fingers away from his middle and index fingers while keeping the separated pairs flush together. He was able to separate them quite a lot: he made a broad V in the air. "That's what you were doing. Can you do it again?"

I looked at my fingers and waited as if the volition to act belonged to my hand and not my mind. Indeed, they seemed to move on their own. Sure enough, I could separate my fingers in the same way as Papa.

Papa still had his hand up in the symbolic position. He said, "Not everybody can do this. Know what it means? It means you are a Cohen." He pronounced it CO-AIN. "The Cohens were the best Jews of the old days. They were the wise men, the healers, the generals. Of all the Jewish people, who were God's chosen people, they were the highest, the best. I'm a Cohen. You wouldn't think it to look at me. But I am. And you are too. You have my blood in you."

Years later—much to my amusement—I saw an actor named Leonard Nimoy on the *Star Trek* television series make the same sign with his hand as a traditional greeting for his character's alien species, the Vulcans, who seemed to have been thought up as a kind of crude version of a Jungian archetype to combine with the equally crude archetypes of Captain Kirk and Dr. McCoy. [I used *Star Trek* as the subject of my paper on Jung's theory of the Collective Unconscious. Not as a joke. I didn't intend disrespect. As readers of my books know, I like to use modern popular culture to test the viability of psychological theory. For one thing, Freud and his disciples thoroughly mined the classics. For another, since contemporary culture is often a reaction to theory as well as a confirmation of it, the ore it yields, although perhaps corrupted by self-consciousness, has greater practical value to a therapist. And practicality, after all, is the great challenge that faces analysis in the next millennium.]

But I'm sorry to have broken the spell that my grandfather created at that moment on his deathbed. I didn't know Leonard Nimoy would make the gesture foolish; I didn't know that my grandfather hadn't reproduced accurate Jewish lore in what he told me. All I knew for certain was that he had been dying moments ago and that I had wished him back to life while holding my fingers apart in that mysterious V.

We held up our hands in the sign of our genetic bond. Papa nodded toward the door, presumably to the house full of cousins, aunts, uncles. "None of them can do it. None of them have the Cohen blood. You're the only one I know about." My aristocratic V pressed against his. His palm was warm, and his eyes glowed, the same eyes that had looked so dead before.

For a time we touched like that. Finally, he folded his long fingers around my hand and pulled me close. He hugged me, squeezing my head awkwardly next to his while not rising from the pillows. There was something stiff beside his chest under the plaid blanket. He whispered into my ear, "Who gave you your name?"

Papa let me go to answer him. One ear was irritated from his embrace. I rubbed it while thinking. "My parents," I said.

"Which one? Do you know?"

"My Daddy. It's a Spanish name."

"No, it's a very old name. It's a Hebrew name. Do you know what it means in Hebrew?" I shook my head. "It's a good name for you. Rafael." He almost said it the way my Latin relatives did: RA-FIE-EL. I preferred that pronunciation. The usual accent given to it by my friends, teachers or other non-Latin adults was RAY-FEEL. Papa said, "Ra-fie-el," again. Slowly, lovingly, he said a third time, "Rafael. It's a good name. And a very good name for you. I'll tell you what it means. It's a promise from Him." Papa pointed to the ceiling. "It means: God will heal." He stroked my head. "You're a good boy. You will keep the Lord's promise, Rafael."

I was impressed by the intensity of his gaze, of his expectation. I wanted it to come true.

"You should go back," Papa said as he withdrew his petting hand. "But first I have something for you." He lifted the plaid blanket aside and revealed the stiff object I had brushed against a moment before: the *Afikomen* lay next to his frail body, wrapped in its satin-edged napkin.

Papa extended it to me. "Your uncle said I should give this to the child who came to visit and showed me he deserves it. Do you know what it is?"

The look on my face must have been transparently happy; I can still hear Papa's chest laugh at my reaction.

That was the last time I saw him. He said, "Go!" and away I ran. I ran wildly into the entrance hall, splitting a knot of cousins; I jumped over a startled Daniel as he inspected the living room cabinets; I dodged the seated, exhausted figure of my mother in the dining room, still talking about the scare over Papa; I bumped into Uncle Harry, who said, "Whoa!," and kept going, right up to the dark round face of Bernard Rabinowitz.

This time, when my uncle's clever eyes focused on me, I held them without flinching.

"I found it," I said.

He smiled: bright teeth against olive skin. "Good for you," he answered.

CHAPTER TWO

The Triumph of Oedipus

TAMPA, FLORIDA, IS AS HUMID AS A STEAM BATH FROM LATE SPRING TO early fall. Even in winter the air is heavy. It is no accident that it was chosen by the cigar industry as a location for its factories. Tampa is an open-air humidor, as an eminent American writer pointed out. No need to fear the long green tongue of the tobacco leaf will dry out.

My mother and I traveled to Ybor City for the July 4th weekend in 1960. Papa Sam had died in May. Ruth didn't take me to the funeral. Indeed, she didn't tell me Papa Sam had died until late June, not until she could promise me that my father was returning from Havana and that he would meet us in Tampa in July. Years later, Aunt Sadie explained that my mother delayed informing me about Papa Sam's death because she didn't want to upset me while the next occasion for seeing my father was still uncertain. According to Sadie, without the reassurance of an upcoming meeting, my mother feared I would imagine my Daddy was dead since hers had died. Of course she was projecting her own worry about Francisco onto me. But it was not entirely fanciful on her part. She had reason to fear that her husband might be killed.

My father returned to the States before finishing research for his book because of the excitement generated by an article he had written for *The New York Times Magazine* about the Cuban revolution. The article provoked interest from publishers who wanted to buy my father's book before its completion; he was to meet with the editors who had made offers. Meanwhile, *Esquire* had commissioned another piece that was due on the stands around July 4th, and some sort of primitive early media tour developed, mostly on radio.

Francisco was scheduled to do a radio call-in show in Tampa on July 2nd. He was to do two such programs in Miami on the 1st. More radio programs were set up in New York for later in the month. There was also talk of an appearance on the Dave Garroway show. I suspect, but don't know, that Dad's media appearances were encouraged by the Cuban government, which was desperate to counteract the mounting anti-Castro propaganda emanating from the White House. (Building support for the coming Bay of Pigs invasion, of course.) In any event, whether my father was or was not directly encouraged by Fidel's government, the anti-Castro community in Miami, New York, and New Jersey had decided he was. There were threats both by anonymous letters to the *Times* and crank calls to the radio stations in Miami.

I should pause here to note that many people have strong feelings about politics and are made uneasy when they cannot identify someone's ideological bias. In case you are experiencing strong reactions to my parents' activities and opinions, or to Uncle Bernie's equally convinced behavior and ideas, and wonder where I stand, I must confess that I do not have an answer to satisfy you. I have known many brilliant people and read many more. Certainly I was lectured by experts. I grew up surrounded by dogma: political, philosophical, and scientific. What I can say with conviction is that no one is stronger than, or independent of, the people and things that surround him. Ideas are objective, but their truth is not the glue that makes them stick to us.

Nevertheless, I recognize there are times in history when one must choose one side or the other, when there is no room for doubt. In the summer of 1960 I had no doubts. I was eight years old. My father and mother told me that Fidel Castro was a great man and I believed them. They said that the United States was an imperialist country responsible for the degradation of the Cuban people, that our government had supported a cruel dictator (Batista) in order for American corporations, such as the United Fruit Company, ITT, and the like, to make huge profits and I believed them, just as millions of American children believed their parents when they were informed that anyone who called himself a Communist was evil and that Fidel was an absurd, strutting madman. My parents instructed me that anyone who said the Cuban revolution was bad, including the President of the United States, was wrong and I believed them. At eight, those were my politics.

However, at eight I was not passionate about politics. I was passionate about the New York Yankees. Unfortunately, even that commitment wasn't free of ideological scrutiny. My grandfather Pepín was a Dodger fan and a Yankee hater. I didn't understand the reason why until years later when I learned the sociology of baseball for his generation. The working class rooted for the Dodgers and Giants (or the Sox or the Indians) while the middle and upper classes were Yankee fans. What I saw as virtues about the Yankees, namely their wealth of talent and consistent success, made them symbols of privilege to Grandpa Pepín. Sure, they won more games than anybody else, he conceded, but they had bought their championships, not earned them. Besides, they were a racist franchise, unwilling to use "the colored ballplayers." I didn't argue with the old man. After all, the reason I became a Yankee fan wasn't so highfalutin: in 1960 they were the only baseball team in New York City.

Anyway, Grandmother Jacinta didn't allow Pepín to bother me about my team for very long. If Grandpa berated me for more than a sentence or two, she would mumble at him in rapid Spanish, too fast for me to understand. I heard the word *"chico,"* indicating me, and I saw the dismissive wave of her hand, which meant he was to shut up, an order that—to my surprise—Grandpa obeyed. Standing beside his small wife, made smaller by her hunched back, Pepín looked able to step on her, but she ruled him and everyone in her house without contradiction or even fear of it.

This dictatorship was to my liking: Grandma seemed to think I could do no wrong and that everyone else was too hard on me. She was fiercely demanding of the others in her family (and their friends, too) but all she required of me was that I eat the delicious food she cooked. Even that demand was flexible: if I didn't like what she cooked, she would make something else. Freud, in one of his rare optimistic moods, wrote that "happiness is a childhood wish fulfilled." Grandma Jacinta managed to fulfill many of mine while I was still a child. In that respect she fit the only generalized description one can make of good parenting.

My mother and I arrived in Tampa midday on July 1st. That evening we listened to my father on a Miami radio station whose signal was powerful enough to be heard in Tampa. He sounded happy and smart. I moved close to the speaker of my grandparents' old-fashioned receiver and felt his voice resonate in me. The house was full of relatives and friends. They mumbled their agreement with my father's arguments; they talked aloud their approval the way the parishioners of Martin Luther King Jr.'s church amened and called out, "Teach it, Martin," as he sermonized.

[Remember, these Latins were not the exiles who now dominate the Cuban-American community. These 1960 Tampa Latins were not middle- and upper-class refugees from the terrors of socialism, or fleeing officials and officers of Batista's government and army, but the children of poor 19th century immigrants. Their parents had fled the inequities of Spain's monarchy. They had been wounded by Franco's defeat of Republican Spain and had to bear the ongoing heartbreak of his facism. In the United States—their adopted country, Franco's ally and Fidel's enemy—they were regarded as only slightly more respectable versions of niggers. These Cuban-Americans believed that Castro's army consisted of people like themselves, oppressed workers and peasants, whose only motive was to rescue their beautiful ancestral island from its status as the premier whorehouse of the American rich and a lucrative gambling franchise of the Mafia. To understand the passion of their loyalty to Fidel's Cuba—or blindness, if you prefer—think of how the American Irish of that generation felt about the IRA, or, better still, think of how immigrant American Jews felt about Israel.]

The radio show host took phone calls from his listening audience. Two of them had to be cut off because the Spanish-accented voices were obscene and belligerent toward my father, insisting he was a Commie and he should go back to Russia where he belonged. I was slightly confused by my father's and the radio show host's reaction to this accusation. They seemed amused by the notion that my father was a Communist. Francisco did not really contradict the host when he said in a fatuous tone, "Well, I think most of us understand that Mr. Neruda is a journalist and that when he reports for such newspapers as the *New York Times* or magazines like *Esquire* he is trying to give an objective account of what he's seen and heard. Telling what you saw doesn't make you a Communist. Isn't that right, Mr. Neruda?"

"I don't really believe anyone can be truly objective about anything," my father said in a soothing tone. "But, yes, what I wrote for the *Times Magazine,* the strides being made in health and education, the closing of the casinos, the elimination of prostitution, can all be confirmed, and have been reported by news organizations throughout the world, whatever their editorial position on the revolution is."

But my father was a communist. Why didn't he say so? I wondered. Not strenuously; I understood that he wanted those mistaken Americans to pay attention to the facts about Cuba and not fall back on their automatic rejection of an ideological label. I understood that and yet I didn't really understand all of the denial. Several of my relatives complained about the callers who accused my father of being a Communist. Grandpa said it was disgraceful. An aunt said it was, "Red baiting." I asked what that meant. I listened to the answers without protest, but I didn't agree: if my father was a communist why should the accusation be disgraceful or unfair? (Of course, I did not understand the distinction between Communist and communist.)

This disquieting moment passed quickly. My father charmed all of them, including the angry callers. He told funny and credible anecdotes about how the Cuban peasants took control of their lives; trying to repair the harm done by years of economic inequity the results were sometimes not brilliant, but always sincere. Maybe Francisco was wrong to dodge the accusations that he was a communist, but he knew how to win over an audience and make his points. Eventually I fell asleep on the rug right next to the speaker: I heard my Daddy in my head and pictured how he would smile at me as I lost consciousness.

The next morning, while I finished a second helping of pancakes and my Grandpa Pepín finished a second cup of espresso, Grandpa said, "You don't want to go pick up your Daddy at the airport, right?"

Grandma Jacinta agreed that I didn't. "He wants to watch the ball game," she said.

My mother seemed surprised. "You don't want to come to the airport?"

"I do," I said. In fact no one had asked me. When my grandparents wanted me to feel a certain way, they simply ascribed their desires to me and then graciously agreed to accommodate themselves.

"That's nice," Jacinta said. "But your Daddy will come here. Right from the airport. You won't miss him."

Pepín said, "Your Yankees are on *The Game of the Week*. You don't want to miss them."

"I'll make you *biftec palomillo* and *plátanos*," Grandma said. "Oh!" she cried and went to her refrigerator. We were eating at a round yellow Formica table in the kitchen. She never sat down, however. She was continually on her feet, feeding herself from a plate on the counter while she brewed more espresso or grilled another pancake. This time she hunched over, peering into the refrigerator; she did something inside it, probably testing the firmness of her vanilla pudding with the tip of her pinky. "Yes. The *natilla* is almost ready. You can have *natilla* for dessert."

"But not the *biftec* for lunch. I'll go get you a Cuban sandwich," Grandpa said eagerly to me as if the problem of keeping me at home was that Jacinta's bribes of food weren't sufficiently tantalizing. "You like the Cuban sandwich—they press it flat." He held an invisible iron in his hand and ran it over something. "You like the Cuban sandwich, right Mickey Mantle?"

"No, no. He wants the *biftec palomillo*." Grandma had moved beside me. She stroked my forehead, lifting up my bangs. The palm of her hand felt cool. "The Cuban sandwich is so greasy."

"I'm going to get some, woman!" Pepín stood up and waved his arm. "Frankie is going to be hungry from the plane and he loves the Cuban sandwich."

Of course it was my grandfather who truly adored the Cuban sandwich. This delicacy consisted of nothing extraordinary to my boy's palate, merely glazed ham, a slice of fresh pork, cheese, and sliced pickles in a light Cuban bread that was then flattened and heated by the final step in its creation: smashing it in a hot press.

"If Rafael wants to come, he can come. His Daddy'll be thrilled to see him waiting at the airport." That was my mother talking. She wasn't eating and she had refused a second cup of espresso. She smoked a Marlboro with the openly indulgent pleasure that people used to display before cigarettes became a symbol of moral turpitude and death. Above her head, illuminated by the bright Florida sun beaming through a window over the sink, the smoke swirled into a brilliant yellow cloud.

Grandpa appeared in the cloud. He leaned over and whispered in my mother's ear.

"Shh, shh . . ." Jacinta created white noise to cover Pepín's talk with a mischievous smile. She made no attempt to disguise her desire to keep their conversation a secret from me. She also moved to block my sight of Mom and Grandpa.

"Oh," I heard my mother say loudly over Grandma's sound barrier. There was dismay in her tone. "You think so?" she added with a tremble in her voice.

"I don't wanna go," I called out, to interrupt their heavy-handed conspiracy to keep me at home. I was sensitive to their feelings, although I didn't understand what worried them. I still don't know for certain why they didn't want me to go to the airport; presumably, they thought there was danger because of the crank calls to the Miami radio stations. "I wanna watch the game," I said, which after all was partly true. I had never managed to last for an entire nine innings, but I liked to try.

"I told you," Grandmother said. She resumed lifting my bangs off my forehead, soothing me with the cool compress of her approval.

Mom and Pepín left early to go to the airport. In fact they departed before my father's plane took off in Miami. This was a tradition of the Neruda family—always at the airport two hours ahead of time.

The Game of the Week wasn't due to begin for another hour. I took a pink rubber ball and my baseball glove outside. Pepín and Jacinta's home was a two-bedroom one-story clapboard house with a patch of lawn stretching no more than seven or eight feet forward and hardly any wider than the structure. Only a child would consider it a lawn at all. Their street had duplicates of my grandparents' house up and down the block. It was paved, of course, and they were off a busy avenue, but there was hardly any traffic. Therefore I was allowed—not without many warnings—to stand in the middle of the street and throw my rubber ball against the three concrete steps leading up to their porch.

This was another example of my grandmother's indulgence of me. She kept precise and immaculate care of her house. Nothing was allowed to be soiled for more than an hour. Dishes were done immediately. Dirty clothing was washed by hand daily and hung on the line in the back-yard—a space no more generous than the front. Her kitchen floors were swept after every meal or any invasion in force. They were mopped at least once a day and waxed once a week. The living room, which had a green carpet, was vacuumed every day although it was used only when company came over. And the company mostly stayed outside on the wrap-around porch, furnished with many wicker chairs and rockers. (The porch was the true social room of the house, overflowing during the humid nights with friends, brothers, sisters, nieces, nephews.) It would be difficult to overstate my grandmother's obsession with cleanliness and order. For her to allow me to throw a ball at the front of her masterpiece, when a mistake might tear the screen door or break either her bedroom or living room windows, when relatively accurate throws might hit the front edge of the porch floorboards and smudge or chip its gray paint, was a remarkable act of generosity.

I doubt I appreciated it at the time. But I enjoyed my game. Pitching the ball against the steps helped relieve the tedium of having to spend so much time without a playmate my own age. Although a cousin only a

year older than I lived nearby, he attended a day camp or had other activities (Little League and Boy Scouts on the weekend, for example) and
thus I had to amuse myself.

The previous summer I had invented a solitary version of stoop ball, a
city game. In New York, my friends and I stood beside the street curb
and threw a rubber ball against its edge hoping the ricochet would send
the ball beyond an opponent attempting to catch it. Landmarks were
chosen to establish whether the thrower had hit a single, double, triple,
or home run. Being alone I couldn't play that game, but the three steps
to my grandparents' house suggested something else. I stood in the middle of the street and aimed at them. If I hit the flat of the steps, producing a dribbling grounder, I considered that a called strike. If I missed the
steps altogether, I considered it a ball. If I hit the edge of the step, which
resulted in hard grounders, line drives, or fly balls, I considered that the
hitter had put the pitch in play. I would try to field these "hits."

That day I decided to turn this game into a full-fledged World Series.
I got the idea as I emerged from the shadow of the porch and felt the insistent Florida sun on my face. I sneezed at the pinching scent of the
flowering bushes Grandpa had planted around the edges of the house.
The aftermath of the sneeze seemed to inspire the notion: I would enact
the Yankees against the Dodgers in the World Series. I would assume the
roles of both Whitey Ford and Sandy Koufax. Never mind that they were
lefties and I threw right-handed. I was thrilled. I felt sure that whatever
happened with my rubber ball and the steps would be an accurate prediction of the coming 1960 finale.

In fact, the game I had invented was hard work. I had to throw hard
to make the ball rebound with force. And since the steps were a small
target, the combination of throwing hard with the need for accuracy
made it a tough couple of innings for Whitey Ford and Sandy Koufax.
Within minutes my shirt was soaked through, a sheet of water, flopping
away from my skin as I ran for the ball, then sticking back onto me with
a clammy slap that made me shiver. I got light-headed, probably from
dehydration, and that made me stubborn. I didn't want to give up. The
score was Yankees 4, Dodgers 3, and it was in the third or fourth inning.
I had a long way to go and already I was so tired I could hardly keep track
of the hitters or the count.

Whitey Ford was facing a bases-loaded situation. I revved up and
threw with all my exhausted might. I heard the unmistakable—and satisfying—resonant sound of the rubber ball hitting the edge of the step

squarely. It produced a powerful drive, a deep fly ball over my head, well beyond the curb to the house across the street, sure to reach its small lawn, a hit that, if it landed safely, would count as a grand-slam home run for the Dodgers and give them a formidable seven-to-four lead.

I got a great jump on the ball because I had become so attuned to the sound it made on the steps. I ran sideways, watching it over my shoulder. The ball soared in the air, into that endless tropical blue sky, a sky so high it seemed to whiten out at its peak from proximity to the sun. Up there the ball appeared to float, hardly moving. I felt I had all the time in the world to catch up to it. Nothing existed but its flight and my pursuit. What a happy moment of absolute concentration! That is the immortality of athletics: in its sensual freedom there is no ego and no death.

Unfortunately, in my case, in this athletic moment of absolute concentration, there was misjudgment and a hard surface. On the downward arc the ball picked up speed. I wasn't gaining on its forward movement as readily as I thought. I leaped, without any conscious decision to do so, my left arm fully extended. When I landed I was surprised. I caught the ball all right, a brilliant diving save for the Yankees, but my right arm hadn't hit the soft grass. It flopped against the paved walkway to the neighbor's door. I heard a bone snap; the sound was as loud and clear as if I had stepped on a stick in the woods.

I didn't feel any pain at first, but my stomach contracted and I was nauseated. I was humiliated also. I had made the catch, but who would believe me? Only the clumsy injury would be remembered. Then the pain started—a stabbing inside my right forearm. And yet I didn't let go of the glove and ball in my left hand. I wanted to prove that I had in fact made the catch and saved the Yankees.

I pulled up my knees and rolled a bit onto my side. Moving my broken arm scared me. I imagined the loose bone would poke out through my skin into the air. I threw up.

At the end of my grandparents' street you could turn right or left—but straight ahead stood a large church. Lying on my side, askew on the neighbor's lawn, I saw a pastel blue car parked by the church's curbside. Three men were seated in it. The two in front, both wearing hats, didn't see me. But the man in back looked right at me. He had on a baseball cap and aviator sunglasses. The roof of their car was white, a satin white that made a brilliant contrast with the car body's pale color. It looked to me as if the vehicle was also wearing a hat, a broad panama like the one my Grandpa put on when we went out to a restaurant.

I called to the man in the back. I was scared to move my arm and anyway I had no energy left: no water in my body, no food in my belly. I doubt that I managed to shout loudly or say much more than a feeble, "Help." Evidently he didn't care I was hurt. My mother and father were atheists and at eight I had a suspicion of churches and the people who liked to go to them. The indifference of these parishioners didn't surprise me. In fact I gave up on them, suddenly afraid to accept their help.

I removed my hand from the glove. Although scared to touch it, I put my left hand underneath my broken right arm and raised it gingerly. The block of small houses and palm trees blurred as I sat up. For a moment I thought I would retch again.

"Rafael . . . ?" My grandmother had noticed the cessation of my ball throwing. She appeared on the interior side of the screen door. Because of her position, I saw only her white hair floating, a disembodied wig.

"I broke it," I croaked.

She didn't hear me. She opened the screen door and came out onto the porch, carrying her dust mop. I called to her again, but a nearby car started up and drowned out my plea.

I struggled to my feet. My legs were wobbly; holding my arm across my stomach also defeated an attempt to balance. I managed to stand for a second and then sagged to my knees.

"Rafa!" Grandma cried out. She dropped her dust mop and rushed across the street to me. Within a minute, other elderly Latin women—two were lifelong neighbors—appeared and they surrounded us as I walked gingerly toward the house. Grandma, I'm sorry to report, was not her usual commanding self in this crisis. She was frightened and helpless. She didn't drive, and she didn't want the one friend of hers who did to take me to the hospital. In fact, she didn't want me to go to the hospital at all, but preferred that her GP see me. I suspect what she really wanted was to wait until my grandfather returned and then my parents could take me. Twice she asked if I was sure that my arm was broken. The other women argued with her—very gently, I noticed—that whether it was broken or not, I was in pain; that something was wrong with my arm since I couldn't move it; that it might be hours before Grandpa appeared, and so on. This distrust of the outside world and relegation of duties to certain family members (only Grandpa drove; only he was fit to deal with doctors; and anyway only their Latin doctor should see me) was characteristic of my Tampa relatives. My grand-mother loved me very much, acutely in fact. To see me in pain must have hurt, but leaving her house in a strange car (even if it belonged to a life-long friend) to go to a strange hospital and allow strange people to take care of her grandson's broken arm was an overwhelming series of unusual decisions and tasks, all outside her range of expertise and security.

The conflict brought a flush to her pale cheeks (she almost never went out in the sun). She looked discombobulated: her apron was askew; she had a smudge of dirt on her forehead from when she helped me up off the lawn. Her neatness and self-possession had fled.

I wasn't feeling well and I was frightened. Both were exacerbated by the absence of my mother. Grandma's unusual hysteria was also worri-some. They led me to Grandma's porch where I sat in a wicker chair, my limp arm laid across my lap. It was throbbing from the inside out, a pe-culiar reversal of my normal experience of injury. Grandma gave me as-pirin and a Coke. She put a straw in the glass bottle and held it to my lips while she and her friends argued about what to do. I understood their dis-cussion in bits and pieces, since it was played in the almost musical hys-teria of their Spanish; had they spoken in English, the interruptions and speed of their argument still would have made it difficult to follow them.

At first the soda's sugar was helpful. The nausea and light-headedness were relieved. But with the recovery of my blood sugar came fear. It was vague, appropriately enough. I knew that eventually my parents would arrive, I knew that my arm was going to be all right sooner or later, but I was afraid that somehow it all wasn't going to work out, that I was going to be crippled forever and that I would never see my mother or fa-ther again.

"*Miralo,*" one of the women said. They stopped talking and watched me, heads tilted sympathetically. I had collapsed into uncertainty and fear. I was crying. "*Pobrecito,*" another said and stroked my cheeks. They were wet with tears.

That settled it for Grandma. She would accept her friend's offer to drive us to the GP. She told me later that she hadn't seen me cry since I was a baby; she explained in detail that I wasn't crying when she first found me on the lawn or moved me to the porch; that I didn't cry when I had the measles, or a painful earache; that I . . . and so on, making a myth (a flattering myth) of me as a stoic and thus this exceptional mo-ment of weakness proved the intensity of my agony. (In fact, I believe that I cried as easily as most children, maybe more easily. Anyway, the tears weren't caused by physical pain. I was disoriented and there was much in the air, understood imperfectly by me, to provoke anxiety and fear. Just the simple fact that I hadn't seen my father for more than four months increased my vulnerability.)

Jacinta refused her friend's advice to phone her GP before we left to ask if we should to go the hospital instead. Having hesitated for too long, now she was in too great a rush. She insisted we leave immediately. She removed her twisted apron while her friend ran off to get her car.

Her friend was Dolores, a woman with a very wrinkled face, a brassy voice, and an arthritic skinny body. I can still easily summon the image of her elderly form hobbling across the street in a rushed and yet crippled walk.

I also remember that the gray roots of Dolores's hair were visible, particularly from the rear. Riding in the back, I got a good view of them during the drive. Grandma Jacinta sat alongside me en route. I was fascinated by Dolores's two-tone hair because the explanation for the gray's weird stoppage and sudden conversion to pitch black was unknown to me. Sometime during the drive I tried to point out the phenomenon to Grandma. "Look at how her hair—" I began.

"Shh," Grandma interrupted. She kept her eyes on the road and called out turns to Dolores, who knew them anyway.

"Honey, I've only driven to Dr. Pérez a million times," Dolores answered Grandma's prompts in English, with that odd juxtaposition of accents typical of my Tampa relatives and their friends. Their English was spoken in deep South and Spanish tones, not within the same word, but alternating, one word with a Southern drawl followed by another with a Latin accent.

"Look at her hair," I started again and this time my grandmother put a hand over my mouth. I was astonished and looked to her for an explanation. She shook her head from side to side with brows furrowed: a stern no.

I was impressed and fell silent. Only then did Jacinta drop the gag from my mouth. She also allowed herself a smile.

"What did you say, honey?" Dolores asked in English.

I didn't reply. "He's fine," Grandma said in Spanish.

There was a brief silence. Jacinta said, "Did you miss Seventh Avenue?" She had asked this twice before.

Dolores ignored the question. "Are my roots showing?" she asked me in English.

Grandma leaned forward and pointed emphatically at Seventh Avenue as we passed it. She shouted something I didn't understand in Spanish. We had missed the turn and now we had to double back. That took no more than an extra couple of minutes, but it exacerbated my grandmother's anxiety. She berated Dolores for not paying attention. Dolores defended herself—for a change. By the time we pulled up to Dr. Pérez's clinic, Dolores was screeching at my grandmother, who returned the abuse in a deeper, softer and yet somehow much more furious tone. Meanwhile, I was distracted by Dolores's question. What roots? I knew about tree roots and that the part of the carrot you eat is a root and I wondered if women, or very old women perhaps, grew roots, and where or what they might be for. In the mild state of shock that I was in, this dream-like notion took hold and I imagined all sort of grotesqueries emerging from Dolores's thin and buckled body.

I was so entranced by the question that as Dolores joined my grandmother at the curb to help me get out of the car, I said to her, "Your roots don't show."

Dolores smiled. Her severely wrinkled face became all lines and cracks, as if the whole facade of flesh were about to shatter. "Good, honey," she said.

"But I would like to see them," I added.

"Some other time," my grandmother said, already preoccupied with the task now facing her, namely entering the doctor's office and managing this unfamiliar situation—overseeing the care of an injured grandchild.

The doctor's waiting room was very cold and dark, because the air-conditioning was on high and heavy drapes were drawn across a wall of windows. I shivered while Jacinta explained the whole story to the doctor's receptionist in Spanish. I could see the woman trying to interrupt, but Grandma needed to delineate everything about the accident and her decision to bring me. She also said that my parents were at the airport and that she was concerned they would be frightened if we weren't back home by the time they arrived. I trembled so from the cold that my teeth clicked together. Dolores put her hands on my shoulders and gently rubbed them to warm me up.

When the receptionist was at last permitted to speak she said she would check whether the doctor could see me right away.

My grandmother's trust in Dr. Pérez was well-placed. He came out immediately and painlessly inspected my broken arm at the receptionist's desk. He said it was probably fractured; a simple one he thought. He said it was pointless for him to take an X-ray, that she should get me to an orthopedist and let him make the determination as well as treat me. He gave the name and address and said he would phone ahead to make sure we were taken care of.

But, at the orthopedist's, although we were expected, there was a long wait—at least it seemed long to me. The discomfort and debilitation of the shock were having an effect—I felt sad, tired, and irritated. It must have taken a long time before my arm was X-rayed and the cast fitted because Grandma sent Dolores back to the house to greet Pepin, Francisco and Ruth and tell them our whereabouts.

Grandma sat next to me, except during the X-ray and fitting of the cast. She was too timid to insist on following me into the examining rooms. But, during the intervals, she placed my head on her chest and stroked my cheek while she kept her eyes fixed on the door, anxious about my parents' arrival. I was uncomfortable in the position, and I didn't like the worry and possessiveness of her petting. But I didn't have the energy or nerve to tell her to stop. I felt weak. I felt I had failed: I had upset my Grandma; I had ruined my father's return; and I would never play center field for the Yankees.

My mother came into the examining room while the cast was being set. Unlike my grandmother, Ruth was not only unawed by the doctor and nurse—she seemed to be their boss. She hugged me awkwardly—because of the wet cast—and immediately fired off questions about the fracture and its treatment. Mom had left the door open and I could see a sliver of the waiting room between her body and the nurse's.

My father was out there, talking loudly and cheerfully to his mother in Spanish. Jacinta hugged him with abandon. The difference in their sizes made it appear she clung to him, calling up for his attention the way a dog greets his master. Her usually composed face was animated with emotion. She looked younger. Her eyes shone and she smiled joyfully. She loves him so much, I remember thinking. I was surprised. I thought Grandma only loved me that way.

"Frank," Ruth called to my father. "Frank!" she called a little too loudly for my taste. "Your son's in here."

The cast had begun to harden and I had my first experience of its rigidity as my father entered. I tried to shift my wrist beyond a certain point and my thumb was stopped. There was a twinge inside the arm. When I attempted to touch it, I was distressed to find not my soft living flesh, but the unyielding hollow plaster. I got a hint of how frustrating and tedious wearing it for six weeks was going to be.

"Hey, my boy," Francisco said, brushing past the doctor, the nurse and my mother. Although I was elevated by the examination table, he was so tall he had to bend down to reach me. He hugged and kissed me on the cheek. Remember, this was no physically frozen father of the Eisenhower years. Francisco was a proud Latin *Papá* who saw me as an extension of himself. That meant he was often very warm and loving—and, by the same logic, sometimes very careless.

The orthopedist and his nurse weren't Latin. When the doctor began to examine my broken arm by moving it about in a painful way, he told me that little boys don't cry although I hadn't made a peep. My father's hug and kiss of me provoked the doctor into nervous reassurance: "He's fine. It was a simple break. Snapped it clean. I don't think it even hurt him."

"A simple break!" my father teased. He took my nose between his index and middle fingers and squeezed hard. So hard it made my eyes water. "That can't be. We Nerudas don't do anything simply." Francisco looked great. His hair was long and almost entirely black. Only a smudge of white appeared above his ears, like racing stripes on the side of a car. He was tall, six feet three. His stomach was flat, his shoulders wide, his posture vigorous, his chest so proud it almost invited an attack. The setting for his eyes was deep and wide apart, a characteristic shape of the Nerudas. The jewels that peered out were a warm brown; they seemed insistently friendly, despite a gleam of mockery. His eyes were highlighted by thick brows that curved up and away at the corners, emphasizing his profile and intelligent forehead. Francisco was obviously handsome, almost a cliché of the Latin lover. When women got their first look at him, they invariably smiled. Indeed, the orthopedist's nurse, a blotchy-skinned brunette with a harsh Southern accent, a sour woman who had disdained to address my bowed grandmother, who had barked at my mother when she first barged in, and who had told me several times to sit still although I was in pain and not really moving that much, broke into a smile at the sight of my father and roared with laughter as he continued his joke. "Maybe we should break it a few more times," Francisco said. He put his arm around me, engulfing me into the crook as he squeezed. For a moment he shut out the world. He let me go. "Right, Rafael? Twist it into a pretzel. Make it into a Neruda fracture, a Cubist arm. After all, it was a Spaniard who began Cubism."

"Cubism," my mother mumbled with disgust, as though naming a social travesty. "He's a glorified cartoonist," she added to Francisco.

"No, he's a genius." My father hadn't disagreed; he cheerfully wiped Ruth's opinion away. "And loyal to the Republic," Francisco added with a laugh. My father noticed that the doctor, the nurse, and I were all baffled by their discussion of Picasso's politics. "Thank you, Doctor," he said and clapped the physician on his back. The orthopedist was startled not only by the force of the contact, but by the fact of it. "My only question is: can the patient have ice cream?"

My father's reaction to my injury was to treat it as a triumph. He announced we would stop at the Dairy Queen on Seventh Avenue and buy me a chocolate dip cone, my favorite. Grandma protested weakly that I shouldn't have ice cream on an empty stomach. Normally Grandma would have been ferociously negative and stopped him, but she was still too enfeebled by the embarrassment of my injury occurring while I was in her care to argue with much conviction. Typically, my mother would also have overruled Francisco, but she had fallen into a moody silence since we left the orthopedist. She kept her arm around me and twice kissed my temple; otherwise she was disengaged, staring ahead at the Tampa streets, apparently bored by my grandmother's account of events.

But Francisco was cheerful. He told me I was the first Neruda to break a bone in thirty years. "You know why it's taken so long?" he asked me as we got out of the car to go up to the Dairy Queen counter. He grabbed my head again with his arm and squeezed. "I can't get over how big you are! You're a giant! I think you're going to be taller than me."

"I don't think so," I said.

He laughed at that, squeezed my head hard once again and let go. The embrace of his arm made me deaf and dumb for a second and its release just as abruptly restored the bright world. It is no fanciful metaphor for me to say that my father could make the earth appear and disappear at will. "You're a Gallego all right," my father said, referring to the province of Galicia where Grandpa Pepín had been born. "You've got the hard-headed common sense of your peasant ancestors." We had reached the counter. Behind it was another Southern woman who beamed at his approach. My father referred to the white Southerners in private as "crackers," an insult, like so many ethnic slurs, that seemed utterly meaningless to me when I looked at its target, but he smiled back at the waitress with welcome. "We're here to spoil our appetites for dinner," my father announced.

"Well, darling," the Dairy Queen waitress answered, "that's what we're here for. To spoil you men silly." She might call him a spic or a wet-back or God knows what in private and Dad would say she was a red-neck or a cracker in Grandma's spotless kitchen, but face-to-face they seemed to see other possibilities in each other. Dad chatted with her a bit before giving our orders. He told her he was going to be on radio that evening and she promised to listen. Eventually he ordered us both choco-late dips and watched her retreat to the stainless steel soft-ice-cream ma-chines with careful interest. Then he returned the full glare of his attention to me. "What was I saying? Oh yes, you're the first Neruda to break a bone in thirty years. You know why?" He didn't bother to pause for my reply. (Sometimes I catch myself responding today to questions my father asked long ago without waiting for my answer.) "Because you're the first Neruda to do anything physical in thirty years. We've turned into decadent intellectuals." He grabbed my head and repeated the blackout of light and sound. He let go and continued, "I broke my leg sliding into home when I was twelve playing with the cigar-makers. I used to love playing ball in West Tampa on Sundays. You know there are a couple of Tampa boys in the major leagues. In fact, Al Lopez—he managed the Cleveland Indians to a World Series—was responsible for breaking my leg . . ." I knew. I had heard this story several times. My fa-ther was a natural celebrity. He had the knack of making conversation with strangers that suggests intimacy and yet didn't truly expose him. He had a colorful fan of anecdotes that were amusing, credible and sub-tly self-aggrandizing. He spread it gracefully and with apparent spon-taneity: like a peacock's feathers, they were impressive and they distracted from the frail body at the center of all that brilliance. Unfortunately for members of his family, Francisco sometimes forgot that we weren't strangers; we had already been seduced by his plumage; we didn't need to be dazzled anymore.

When the Dairy Queen woman returned with our towering cones—she seemed to have given us twice the usual portion—Francisco was al-most done with his Al Lopez–broken leg anecdote. She showed interest in it and he repeated the story for her. I bit off the tip of hardened choco-late syrup at the top, sucking up the interior cream. There was throbbing inside my hard cast. I wanted to touch my arm where it hurt. The pain was deep inside my forearm, unsoothable, an awkward ache that couldn't be eased by any position I assumed. And it seemed to be getting worse.

I sucked up more of the ice cream, determined to enjoy myself, to follow my father's lead.

This was my favorite ice cream cone. But having it while I hurt was worse than not having it at all. I had the pleasure in my grasp but I tasted only discomfort. The soft ice cream leaked out of its chocolate cast and down the edges of the cone, streaking my hand.

"Eat up," my father said as he finished the broken leg story.

The cone fell. I hadn't let it go, but I hadn't held on either. I watched its graceful somersault and crushing splatter onto the concrete with morbid fascination. I was glad to see it destroyed.

My father and the waitress exclaimed with dismay. I looked up at Grandpa's car and saw my mother staring at me. Grandma Jacinta was talking to her, again with an unusual animation and uncertainty. My mother's curly flop of black hair, parted on one side and covering half of her brow, was still while she listened. That too was unusual. She always seemed to be in motion, especially her hair; it would tremble from her nervous energy. Her green eyes were wide as she stared at me. But she wasn't seeing me. She didn't react to the ice cream cone's death.

I sagged. I didn't keel over. I slumped against my father. I felt weak and exhausted. There was commotion. My mother came out of the car. Grandma called my name in a faraway panicked tone: "Rafa! Rafa!" The waitress said she'd get me water. Francisco picked me up.

"Ugh," he groaned at my weight. "What a big boy you've become."

"What's wrong!" my mother said in an angry shout.

"He's tired," my father insisted. "You can lie down in the back, Rafael. We'll go home and you'll take a nap."

I was horizontal in my father's arms as he carried me to Grandpa's car. The low Tampa buildings bounced. A blue car with a white hat bobbed up and down. It was across the avenue, stopped at a gas station, but not at a pump. I didn't notice the occupants before my father turned away from them to angle me at the Plymouth. I wondered if the man with the baseball cap and aviator glasses was inside that blue and white car. I thought about mentioning the men and the car to my parents. Ruth had lectured me around Christmastime about strangers watching us. She told me to let her know if I saw men hanging around outside our apartment building. I asked why they would. She didn't really answer. She said that some men had been questioning our neighbors about us. When I pressed for a fuller explanation, she was vague. (I had no idea that for a decade my parents had been subject on and off to harassment—some might prefer to call it surveillance—by the FBI. They had been members of the Communist Party until 1950 and then there was my father's friendliness to Fidel's Cuba.) She made me promise I would report any men lurking about. I wondered if these men in the blue and white car qualified.

I didn't get a chance to bring it up. When Francisco maneuvered me to the rear door, a disagreement started between Ruth and Grandma about who was going to sit in the back with me. At first, they expressed their desires passively.

"Jacinta, you sit up front," my mother said. "You'll be more comfortable."

"No," Grandma said, "there's not enough room for you in the back."

"There's plenty of room."

"No, I'll be fine. I'll put Rafa's head on my lap," Grandma insisted.

"I can put his head on my lap," Ruth said.

"It'll wrinkle your dress," Grandma objected.

"For God's sake," my father said. "Somebody open the door!" He was still holding me. It was hot. He shifted me in his arms, weary from the weight.

Jacinta opened the rear door and slid to the far seat.

"No!" my mother protested. Francisco put me in and Grandma eased my head onto her lap.

"*I* want to sit with him," my mother insisted to Grandma. The sharp tone she used on Jacinta was rare—in fact, unique. She was always solicitous of Grandma. "Why aren't you paying any attention to what I say? I'm his mother. I want to sit with him."

"Take it easy," my father mumbled.

"You take it easy," my mother said loudly. She was angry, but she wasn't hysterical. She had confidence. "It took over two hours to get Rafe treated. He hasn't had anything to eat since breakfast and he threw that up. I think he's dehydrated and your great solution is to give him ice cream and pinch him and shove him around like he's some chum in a bar—"

And then something extraordinary happened. So extraordinary that I completely forgot about my pain. My grandmother began to cry. She talked through the tears, saying in English to my mother, "It's my fault. I know that. You blame me. I know I was stupid. I got so nervous. I know I ought to take him to the hospital right away." Big tears rolled down the old woman's face. One splashed on the bridge of my nose and rolled into my left eye. It stung a little. To see my dignified and reserved Grandma cry was amazing. Also her tone of voice was amazing. She sounded like a little girl pleading to be forgiven; oddly, she spoke with much less of an accent than she usually did. If I were to shut my eyes I couldn't have recognized that voice as hers. "I'm an old fool. I know. But he was not hurt by my stupidity. He's okay." Grandma looked down and stroked my face. More tears fell on me. She wiped them off with her fingertips. "I would never hurt my only grandson."

"Oh Jesus," my mother moaned. It was her turn to cry. She put her hands to her temples, rubbed them and then covered her eyes, pushing the tears back. "I give up." She opened the front door and got in. "I'm never right about anything!" she shouted at the windshield.

I fell asleep. I wakened somewhat as my father carried me to the guest bedroom. I heard voices greet Francisco with enthusiasm and quickly modulate to whispered concern about me. I kept my eyes shut.

The air in the room was still and hot. Ruth and Jacinta each brought in a fan. They argued over which one was more effective. They didn't convince each other. After an ominous silence, my mother said they should keep both fans going. Ruth took off my sneakers and Jacinta lifted my head to slip a pillow underneath. I pretended to be asleep. In fact, with the heavy cast lying across my chest, I wondered if I could ever sleep again.

The guest bedroom was right off the living room and had a window looking onto the porch. Wide horizontal venetian blinds covered the screen, but the window was up and I could hear my father hold court out there. Judging from the chorus of exclamations, questions and laughter that punctuated his storytelling, a crowd as large as what one would expect in the evening had already gathered, although it was still midafternoon. Twice my grandmother complained to the group that Francisco needed to rest from his flight, especially because he was due to be on the Tampa radio show at eight o'clock. My mother joined with Jacinta on this issue and said to my father that he had to stop talking by five so that he could get himself ready and eat some dinner.

"Let Frankie finish about the shoes!" a cousin complained. "Then we'll go home and warm up the radios so we can listen to him tell those anti-Communists what true socialism is all about."

My father told them that for decades Cuban children had been undernourished because they suffered from tapeworms. It was the primary cause of Cuba's high rate of childhood mortality. Many died from opportunistic diseases made possible by the wasting effect of the worms. My father described how the worms grow in the stomach. (He told these stories in English, repeating key information in Spanish, evidently because he feared a particular relative wouldn't understand.) He said the worms wound themselves around and around in the intestines and got to be as long as six feet, sometimes twice as long as the child is tall. Under Batista's rule medical treatment was never free, even if the illness were life-threatening. Drugs existed that would kill the worms in a matter of weeks. American children could get a prescription from their pediatrician and have it filled for a moderate cost or for free through various agencies or clinics, but the price of the medicine was ten times higher in Cuba thanks to Batista's profiteering. Anyway, even at the lower American cost, the pills would be more than a Cuban peasant could afford.

Since the revolution, my father asserted, not only were the affected children receiving medicine at no charge, but the spread of the parasites had been stopped. How? Simply by handing out free shoes to each and every Cuban child. Evidently the worms entered through cuts on their feet. "You know how we've all seen pictures of happy children in tropical countries, running barefoot?" my father said. "It isn't because they're so carefree. It's because their parents have no money to give them shoes."

That wasn't his last anecdote, despite the promise to my mother. But I didn't hear the next one. I dozed off, thinking of those insidious worms, picturing them crawling into my feet. I didn't know they got in as microscopic eggs; I imagined fully developed creatures puncturing my skin. I saw them slither up into my stomach, winding around and around, ropes of quivering slimy robbers, eating me alive.

There was one sitting on my chest as I slept, crawling toward my face. I woke up screaming.

Once my mother calmed me, I was hungry. My arm didn't hurt at all. Grandma cooked *biftec palomillo* and *plátanos* for my father and me. We ate dinner side by side at the yellow kitchen Formica table. Grandma, Grandpa and Mom watched us. Grandpa was full from snacking on the Cuban sandwiches he had bought coming back from the airport; Grandma ate at the counter while cooking; and my mother refused any food. She touched her flat stomach and insisted she had gained too much weight.

"You're very beautiful," Grandma answered. "But you're too skinny," she added in a friendly tone.

"I love you Mama," my mother said to her. They hugged at Grandma's post by the stove with as much feeling as if they were saying goodbye for a long time. "I need to have you with me all the time," Ruth said as they let go of each other.

The fried bananas were sweet and, thanks to my Grandma's technique, weren't greasy. I ate as many as my father did. He was silent. His eyes were alive with internal conversation and speeches. I understood that he was rehearsing for the radio program. I could see his lips occasionally part and seem to whisper something. When his mother touched the back of his head lovingly he didn't react. After he finished his dinner and was waiting for his espresso, my mother reached over and took his hand. He squeezed it but still looked through and beyond her.

Outside, the sky—blue all day—was now being churned by black clouds. I saw lightning flash, cutting across one of the dark masses in the sky. Huge drops of rain followed. They splattered noisily against the windows. Thunder cracked above us. The noise was clear and terrible: as if God had broken the sky across His knee.

I wanted to run and hide in the bedroom. I was too embarrassed for that. But I did slide off my chair and hide under the table.

The grown-ups laughed good-naturedly. The room had darkened so much from the black rain clouds that Pepín turned on the kitchen light. I stayed under the table. I took hold of my cast with my free hand; for the first time I was glad to feel my new armor.

"No Pepito," Grandma protested about the light. She believed it was dangerous to use electricity while there was a lightning storm.

There was a clap right above us, ear-splitting and awful. All the lights went out. My mother shrieked in surprise. I must have screamed. The next thing I knew my father was beside me. He had folded up his tall body and crawled under the table. He winked at me. I was so scared by the thunder that at first I didn't get his joke of a performance of boyish fear. I thought he was as scared as me.

"*Mira,* Francisco!" my grandmother said, chuckling.

Again the sky split open. This time Grandma exclaimed at the boom.

"I'm getting under there with you," my mother said. She kicked off her high-heeled shoes (she was dressed up for the radio show) and scrambled next to my father and me. She gathered me in her arms and snuggled Francisco. I smelled his aftershave and her perfume. The rain came hard and fast and straight; peering up at the window, it was as thick as a curtain. I could no longer see the palm leaves of the backyard tree.

Literally we huddled as a family, sheltered from the storm. I was eight. That was the last time my mother, my father and I embraced.

Overheated afternoon Florida storms rarely last for more than thirty minutes. It's as if the weather were a toddler, exhausted and frustrated by the long hot day, letting loose a tantrum of rage and tears that is gone as suddenly as it begins. An hour later there was no sign of the cooling rain, except that the suffocating humidity had been slightly ventilated. By then it was time to go. I asked my father to take me with him to the radio show. Ruth, Jacinta, and Pepín all said no.

Francisco overruled them. He put his arm around me and said, "I have to take Rafe with me. He proves to those *Yanquis* I'm no crazy radical. How could I be? Look at him!" He hooked me with his arm and squeezed my head. "He's a real American boy. That radio host will take one look at Rafael and he'll believe everything I say."

He insisted Grandpa stay home to keep Grandma company. "I'll be my own chauffeur," he said. I sat in the back seat of the Plymouth; my mother rode in the front with Francisco. I can't recall (and there have been many concentrated attempts at recovering all the details of that day) what stopped me from remembering the blue car with the white hat and mentioning it to my parents. I can summon a vivid memory of pressing my face against the rear window to see if there were any cars behind us. Why did I do that, if not to search for the blue and white car? Maybe I was uninformative because I didn't have a chance to look very long. Francisco, tense while he searched for the radio station's building, snapped, "Sit down, Rafe! I can't see out the rearview mirror!"

The radio station was in a beige four-story building beside a highway overpass. The street consisted of office buildings and had a spooky deserted look, although it was early evening. We parked across from the entrance.

The host signed my cast. So did his producer, a young woman. They were friendly. The producer gave me a Coke and brought my parents coffee. The host was especially cheerful and welcoming. Until airtime.

"Aren't you a Communist sympathizer, Mr. Neruda? I've read your article in the *New York Times*." He said New York as though it were contemptible. "You make every possible excuse for Fidel Castro's crimes of robbery and murder. It doesn't matter that he has destroyed countless family businesses, grabbing the money they worked hard for, supposedly to spend on the peasants. My bet is it's all going into a Swiss bank account. But you and the *New York Times* tell us it doesn't matter. It doesn't matter that Castro has firing squads working round the clock killing people whose only crime was that they were soldiers following orders. You call these understandable excesses. Some excesses. I wonder how you would feel if some foreign reporter called it an understandable excess when the Communists take all your money and shoot you in cold blood."

Ruth and I were in a room down the hall from the studio where we had been graciously invited by the producer to make ourselves comfortable. We could listen to the show over a speaker mounted flush into the ceiling.

"My God," she whispered, shocked. I glanced at her and worried about the beat of silence. My father didn't answer immediately. If he was feeling anything like the way my mother looked, then it was going to be a quiet program.

Francisco's voice finally did come down from on high. He sounded calm and amused. "I'm not sure I know what your question is, Ron. I didn't write that murder and robbery is understandable. I *did* write that there aren't revolutions without people being killed. There were lots of killings on both sides. As for these family businesses you mentioned—I don't know what families you're talking about. Ninety percent of Cuban assets were owned by foreign corporations. They weren't mom-and-pop operations. I've heard ITT called a lot of things, but never a family business."

My father's first cousin, Pancho, taped the broadcast on a reel-to-reel machine. His daughter, Marisa, sent me a copy a few months ago and, listening to my father refute the seemingly endless stream of anti-Castro questions and arguments from the host and his callers, I'm not surprised that I admired my father as much as I did while listening in the station's waiting room. Francisco was funny, he was full of facts, he told stories that made the Cubans and their struggle real. No matter how alone he seemed in his convictions, no matter how angry his opposition, he sounded serene. I think his perfectly sincere account of Cubans as a people who love American culture, from baseball to movies to rock music, was the most effective. Certainly it made an impression on me since Francisco used me as an example of the contrast between an American boy's opportunities and a Cuban's under Batista.

"My son Rafael broke his arm today. He was able to find treatment within a short distance for a modest cost. Under Batista a Cuban peasant boy might have had to travel for miles on foot and could easily have had his arm set incorrectly by an unskilled nurse. Here there are no shortages of doctors, no scarcities of antibiotics in case Rafael's fracture should infect. When we return to New York this fall Rafael will go to a well-equipped school, a free school, whose teachers and facilities would be the envy of Havana's most expensive private schools under Batista. The illiteracy rate at the time the revolution triumphed was over ninety percent. The Cuban government has announced a goal of one hundred percent literacy in five years. I spent two days in shacks in the sugarcane fields, shacks with no windows, no desks, just a few hard benches, where people of all ages and sexes were squeezed together as they were taught to read and write. And, after the lesson, everyone, including the teachers, went out to work side by side in the fields, converting the acres of sugarcane— profitable to the United Fruit Company, but unbalanced economically for the Cuban people—to useful crops that can lower their import costs and improve their nutrition. Of course all these wonderful changes would be undone by a U.S. embargo of Cuba. Cuba is a poor country. With our markets closed to them, with all their imports having to come from much farther away than the industrial giant only ninety miles off their shore, that Cuban peasant boy who roots for the Yankees like my son Rafael, who'd like nothing better than to go to the Saturday morning movies at the Loew's on 175th Street along with all of Rafe's school friends, may not, in spite of Fidel's reforms, have enough food, or the antibiotics he needs, or the books to learn from. You say, Ron, that Cuba is an ally of the Soviet Union and therefore our enemy. I'm not sure that's true. Yet. But it we continue to cut off Cuba from our resources, they'll have no choice but to be Russia's friend. Their lives will depend on it."

My happy life was an accident of geography. I saw myself, poor, my broken arm twisted, walking barefoot across a desert (I pictured lush Cuba as a wasteland) to a shack presided over by a sad-faced nurse who cried out, "I don't know what I'm doing," as she wrenched my arm this way and that. Tapeworms crawled into cuts on my feet. I was so badly educated I didn't have the vocabulary to tell the frantic nurse about my stomachache.

Absurd, no? My Coke was suddenly tasteless. The red velvet seats of Loew's theater in Washington Heights seemed a monstrosity of waste. Did Francisco have any idea what it meant to associate all the commonplaces of my life with inequity and injustice? And yet what my father said was perfectly true. That poor peasant boy did exist and he still doesn't have the medicine or food or the learning of his middle-class American equivalent. Of course, thirty years has made a difference—nowadays that deprived child can also be found in New York City. (Please bear in mind,

I don't approve or disapprove of any particular bias as to the solutions of these social problems, including the bias that nothing can be done.)

We left the station in high spirits. By the end of the broadcast, even the hostile radio host seemed won over. There were so many phone calls the producer ran the show for an extra hour. She followed us down the stairs alternately thanking my father and asking how long he would be in Tampa. She wanted to do another broadcast with him. They agreed to be in touch in the morning.

Grandpa's Plymouth was alone on the street. It was dark, after ten-thirty, and humid again. Tampa out-of-doors seemed as close as a room with all the windows shut.

We started home, my parents in front, me in back, leaning forward to peer over Francisco's shoulder. My mother sang his praises. She reminisced over particular rejoinders he had made; she laughed at his jokes; she teared up as she recalled his account of the Cuban peasant woman learning to read at age sixty-eight. She made love to him with her admiration.

We stopped at a light a few blocks from the radio station. We were still in a deserted commercial neighborhood. There was only one other car on the road. Its lights came up behind us, getting brighter than they should, like a big wave set to engulf us. My mother turned toward it. Her features were bleached by the intensity. And then we were hit.

I smacked into the vinyl and tumbled into the ditch of the car floor. I rolled over my cast. In fact it punched me in the stomach. My first thought was that I must have broken it.

I heard furious male voices. There were snatches of obscenities and words in Spanish. Doors opened. My mother shouted, "No, Frank!"

The cast wasn't damaged. I didn't move, though. My nose was pressed into the hump that divided the back. I was terrified. Outside something horrible was happening and I was too frightened to look.

I heard my mother scream. It was unlike any sound she had ever made. I raised myself to see. Her dreadful cry had summoned me from my cowardice and would, I'm sure, have summoned any mother's son.

The impact of the rear-end collision had pushed us completely across the intersection. My mother was on the hood of the Plymouth, her face cut and bleeding. Her dress—I know she looked beautiful and young in it, but I can't remember its color—had been torn apart down the front. Her bra had also been cut or pulled off. I don't know about her panties—I assume she had been stripped of them as well. At first I thought her condition had been caused by the accident.

I saw the man in the aviator glasses off to the side. He had my father's head in his hands. It seemed, in the glare of the shattered lights from both cars, that he was holding Francisco's decapitated head. Actually, my father was on his knees, bleeding from a head wound caused by the collision. He was conscious but woozy. The man with the aviator glasses had him by the hair, pulling to keep my father's head up so he would see what his companions were doing to Ruth.

They had thrown her across the hood like a slain deer. Her vulnerable skin trembled in the light of their car. One man climbed up and knelt above her chest, his knees pinning her arms. He urinated on her bloody face. She screamed in pain. I never looked to see what his friend was doing to the bottom half of my mother's body. These snapshots of what I remember were difficult enough to process.

I was abruptly outside the car. I don't remember doing that. I don't know why the men in the white and blue car had left me alone. Perhaps my collapsed body in the rear was presumed to be unconscious. Certainly the force of the crash could have knocked me out.

What I did may seem strange to someone who isn't knowledgeable about behavior in such situations. I didn't rush to my mother's aid. I couldn't accept that the abused body on the car was my mother. I ran at the man holding my father's head. I didn't see that in his free hand he had a gun.

I smashed into his arm with all my eight-year-old body. My cast led the impact.

His gun went off. There was a howl from one of the men assaulting my mother. Presumably he had been hit. I fell against Francisco. I expected my father, now that I had freed him, to take over and rescue us. My head was near his. The man in the aviator glasses, who was cursing in Spanish, came at us. I heard my father whimper something in Spanish. I still don't know what he said, but I know the beginning of the phrase was, "Don't . . ." and I know from his tone that he was pleading.

I was kicked in the face. My head whacked into my father's. I saw bright flashes of light that people sometimes call seeing stars. After that, there were shouts around me and sirens in the distance.

My mother's horrible screams stopped. I told myself to keep quiet as well. My father was still beside me. I thought he was dead. I didn't want to think about my mother. I just wanted to pretend to be dead so they would leave me alone.

As it turned out, my mother was badly beaten, but alive. My father had a gash on his forehead, and seemed incoherent but was otherwise un-hurt. My cheekbone was broken and my cast had to be refitted.

I thought that I was playing possum, lying on the ground, silent and still. I wasn't. The police found me standing beside my mother's naked body, clutching her right hand. My eyes were shut and I was screaming.

CHAPTER THREE

The Basic Anxiety

NO ONE WAS ARRESTED. BOTH MY PARENTS WERE ABLE TO IDENTIFY THE attackers as Cuban. My father was convinced that, because of their accents, he could specify on which part of the island they had been reared. But they weren't caught by the Tampa police. I don't know how thoroughly they searched. I know they checked the hospitals for someone who had been shot. From a trail of blood at the scene, evidently one of them had been wounded thanks to my collision with his confederate's gun.

My mother later insisted that I had saved our lives. I assume she said so to my father as well, but I don't know. He returned to Cuba the day after the attack, presumably to escape another attempt on his life. If the purpose of the assault was to stop Francisco from continuing his radio and television appearances, it succeeded.

My mother was hospitalized for two days because of the beating and rape. (Of course, at the time I didn't know she had been raped; and I'm not sure who, besides my father and the police, knew that she had been.)

In the early morning, my father came to my bed and woke me to say goodbye.

"I must go, Rafael. You understand? That way you and your mother will be safe."

I remember his words exactly. They are oddly phrased for English. In fact they translate naturally into Spanish. But I know he said them in

English. He kissed me. He hugged me. My lips did not answer. My arms stayed at my side. He embraced a lifeless body.

I had retreated into a schizoid state. Forgive me for that term, but it is a good specific description. I mean I sat mute in front of the television, with no outward evidence of a mood, not seeing the shows, absorbed by fantasies that denied the existence of the attack, or replayed it in literal horror, or rewrote it to an ending in which my father killed the three men. At night I didn't sleep. Grandma kept me company in the television room, gently rocking in a chair beside the sofa bed where I was supposed to sleep. She would nod off and startle awake. I honestly can't recall having slept at all. The hot nights, the suffocating feeling that I lived in a world with no ventilation, became a new terror. I lay still; but my heart beat furiously. I saw those men and the images of what they did to my parents and I struggled to breathe. But there were no tears or sobs: nothing to cool me off or give me air.

My mother returned on the third night. I clung to her. Literally. I held her hand without permitting a break. A couple of times she tried to let go, but I protested immediately and she resumed the contact. My relentless grip through dinner didn't inconvenience her too much. She wasn't eating any solid food. Since her jaw was swollen and bruised she was limited to my grandmother's *natilla*. I ate well that night. Grandma had to cut up the food since I wouldn't let go of Ruth, leaving me with just one hand to feed myself.

I got my first full night of sleep sharing a bed with my mother in the guest room. I woke up only once.

Ruth was out of the bed. She stood in the doorway, on her toes, attentive and still.

"Mom . . ." I called sleepily.

She rushed back on tiptoe. She sat against the headboard and pulled her legs under her. Her attention stayed focused on the open door.

I put my head in her lap. Because of the hot night she wore something thin and satiny. The warmth of her belly, her sweet smell, proximity to the origin of my life, were all a thrilling comfort. Is that sexual? Is that reassurance? Is that regression? Am I being unintentionally trained to confuse sex with comfort? Or *are* they the same? Does the interpretation matter? Is it more or less important than the fact of the action? Would I have been better served by the touch of my father's strength than my mother's consolation? Is that sexist? When I am done answering these questions will I be improved?

How silly introspection can seem or be made to seem, and how silly it is in fact, until self-examination becomes a matter of life and death. Whatever you make of this tableau—a frightened boy atop the heat of his mother's belly—it restored me to the world.

"He feels better when he's with his Mama," was how Jacinta put it as she watched me eat a stack of her pancakes the following morning.

I started talking again. My cheek ached when I did and that's how I knew I had been silent. That night, when my mother and I were in a train heading for New York, if you had stopped me as I squirmed by you in the narrow passageway (Do you see me: the little boy with a swollen and discolored cheek, a deep tan and a cast on his left arm?) to ask how I had gotten hurt, I might have cheerfully told you it was playing baseball. I had begun a repression of the direct memory of the attack that was complete by week's end. I do not mean traumatic amnesia. I knew the assault had happened. But details faded and only a knowledgeable interrogator would have been able to summon the unwholesome creature from the dismal basement where it skulked.

[It is an interesting question to me (obviously) whether immediate psychological intervention in a case such as mine could prevent the distortions and deformations that seem inevitable after an overwhelming and terrifying experience. Some of the great theorists of my profession are convinced of human resilience, especially a child's. Not to become bogged down in arguments between "schools" of psychology, but I refer to those who deemphasize the absolute significance Freud and his many revisionists place on infancy and early childhood as the real crux of our drama, with adulthood more or less the predictable final scene, or perhaps something duller, merely the cup of coffee one has after the show to rehash its highlights. In fact, to be fair to poor overscrutinized Freud, it is an overstatement to attribute such pessimism about mature life to him. His championing of the talking cure itself shows he thought more of adulthood than that. But where would he, or does any psychologist, stand on this question: should there be trauma psychologists rushing to scenes of tragedy, like paramedics of the mind, giving mouth-to-mouth to prevent further damage? Of course, I am ignoring those neurologists who believe traumatic events trigger biochemical changes in the brain. They *do* want to rush in with stupefying drugs whose exact effects they admit we do not understand. I am grateful they have no mandate to experiment on us, beyond their already sweeping powers. But, if they are right, why not? Shouldn't an immediate chemical prophylactic be administered? And as for the behaviorists, if they are correct, shouldn't they too be on the scene, able to prevent engineers of self-defeat from digging deep tracks? There are of course the beginnings of such a response with support groups and the like. My point is that psychology is the only branch of medicine that has no systematized emergency procedures or established preventative care. We wait until the problem is full-blown. Perhaps none of the various "schools" can honestly claim "cures" because we have all waited too long to begin our work.]

Sometimes merely the image of my poor mother and me, alone in our terrors, shuddering side by side with the train's movement, believing the worst was over while really the damage had just begun, brings heartache and sorrow. When I shed tears for my mother (and I do) I cry for her because of those apparently quiet months of the summer and fall of 1960. Although it may seem she could have been saved later on, that was the Ruth I wish I could have had as a patient. Though they were dull and uninteresting days to a casual observer, that was when her accident became an illness.

My lay readers are probably more interested in why my raped and beaten mother traveled alone with her terrorized child to New York. Why she did and why she was allowed to. My father's stated reasons have already been given. Jacinta and Pepín were too timid to travel to New York under normal circumstances. I know they believed we would be safer in New York; I suspect they were also overwhelmed by a reaction to the events of that night which was informed by 19th century attitudes toward sexuality and moral strength. I sensed their disapproval of Francisco and their embarrassment about Ruth.

My mother's desire to flee the scene of the disaster was natural and typical of brutalized women of that time. The assault was shameful to her. I know she never told any member of her family about the rape. She told her sister Sadie a sanitized version of the attack after we were back in Washington Heights. And she requested that Sadie keep even that bowdlerized account to herself.

We returned to 585 West 174th Street for the rest of the summer. Of my four friends, three were away. That left Joseph Stein, who, at eight years of age, well before the groundbreaking work which earned him worldwide fame, was an intellectual. He looked the part. Indeed, with his thick black-framed glasses and pants belted above the navel, Joseph seemed much more like a brilliant scientist than when he made his important discoveries. There were no pleated tailored pants; his cuffs hovered above the ankles, showing a pale skin, until black socks appeared below and completed his retired old man's look. Joseph was careful not to reveal much about his past to the press and I am sorry to expose him in a way he would not like, but again, as will become clear, to explain the terrible events of this narrative requires the exposure of many secrets. (Besides, secrets are a psychiatrist's deadly enemy.) Joseph was the only child of a couple who had survived the Holocaust. I should say he was the only living child. His mother's firstborn died en route to Buchenwald, as did the father, her first husband. Another baby, the result of a rape by a German guard, also died there. Mr. Stein's parents, his wife, and two little girls were killed by the Nazis. At the time, neither Joseph nor I were aware that his parents had previous loves and families. As a child, Joseph only knew that his mother and father met in a repatriation camp run by the Allies, emigrated to Washington Heights (as did many other survivors) and created Joseph.

They lived in our building, two floors below us. Mr. Stein worked in the diamond district as an assistant to a wealthy merchant. Mrs. Stein stayed home and took care of Joseph. Her surveillance of him was the closest of any mother in the neighborhood, and in Washington Heights, she had a lot of competition. But she was the clear winner. Joseph was not allowed to play at the apartments of his friends because of his wide range of allergies. If you had no pet, he was allergic to your rug. (Mrs. Stein's carpeting had been especially treated by a mysterious process.) If—as was the case with us—you had no pet or rug, then he had to be in an air-conditioned room because of his asthma. (Joseph had never had an attack of asthma; Mrs. Stein claimed that their pediatrician declared Joseph's lungs to be susceptible to developing the syndrome.) Requiring air-conditioning excluded our apartment, but I know from Joseph that those who did have air-conditioning and met the other conditions (no rug, no pet) were found wanting for some other reason. Joseph told me that on one occasion Mrs. Stein was confronted by a mother who appeared in person to guarantee she had no pet or rug, that all her rooms were air-conditioned, swore she was prepared to serve Kosher food (although Mrs. Stein didn't keep a Kosher home), and had removed all the pillows from her son's room because Mrs. Stein was on record that their down filling would cause Joseph to choke to death. Despite these assurances, Mrs. Stein refused to release her son on the basis that the accommodating mother's perfume—Mrs. Stein sniffed it out on the spot—was considerably more dangerous to her son's respiratory system than an apartment overrun with dogs and cats. The truth, it became obvious to the least observant person and the most naive child, was that Joseph had to stay home, always within his mother's immediate physical realm.

This cost him a lot of friends. Not only did you have to play at his apartment, but you had to stay inside. Joseph was not allowed to go out unless the weather was perfect. The temperature had to be above seventy and yet below eighty. The sky could not have a single cloud or a hazy look; only the kind of clear blue that one sees on postcards from the Caribbean. Such a day is quite rare in any locale. Besides, many of the other mothers—including fellow Holocaust victims—felt that such a crazy woman could not help but raise a strange child, a child who would not be a good influence on their, if less delicate, no less precious progeny.

They were right. Joseph was a strange child. He was also a sweet and lonely soul. For the remainder of that sad summer, my mother, who had once allowed me free rein to play in Fort Washington Park, or on the sidewalk in front of our building, didn't want me wandering outside unescorted. Anyway, with my arm in a cast, I couldn't have played most outdoor games. Sending me two flights down to Joseph's air-conditioned cage, something she used to discourage, had become attractive.

Each day, I arrived so early Mrs. Stein would offer breakfast. I always refused. Her bland lunches were enough of a discouragement. Thanking her, I walked on the plastic runner that guided you from room to room, careful not to step off onto the deep green carpet, and proceeded through their petrified forest of a living room into Joseph's cooled cell. I would hurry through the spooky living room; Mrs. Stein kept the drapes drawn day and night and protected the furniture with fitted plastic covers. At least Joseph's room was well-lit by a standing lamp, a desk lamp, and a red tensor lamp next to his bed. Those lights had to be on all the time since the windows had blackout shades *and* venetian blinds. There was more of the deep green rug, although here we were allowed to walk on it—not with shoes but our stocking feet. Everything was kept clean and neat. No object lacked its special place. A hardware chest, consisting of small drawers, was converted to a multi-level garage for his Matchbox cars. There were several boxes to organize different shapes of his wooden blocks, and coffee cans separated the colors of his Legos. In his clothes closet, an arrangement of shelves on the inner door provided room for Monopoly, Risk, and other board games, including, of course, Joseph's impressive chess set. Not the plastic pieces and flimsy folded board that belonged to most kids. Joseph owned an expensive Staunton design: classic black and white weighted wood and a thick maple board.

Usually the chessmen were set up, waiting for my arrival in the morning. A folding table and chairs for playing board games (this seemed to me the most remarkable of his room's organizations) was under the standing lamp. So that we could continue our competitions while eating, his mother would bring into his room a metal tray with adjustable legs and there serve us our late morning snack of fruit, our lunch and our afternoon milk and Oreos. "Want to play?" Joseph would say instead of a greeting, and incline his head seductively at the chess pieces.

I didn't, because I was going to lose. And I did, because I wanted to improve and beat him. Once or twice, I insisted we do something else. No matter how satisfying the other choice, however, Joseph would tempt me to play at least one chess game a day.

The contests followed a distinct pattern. Within the first few moves I would unaccountably find myself in trouble: due to the outright loss of a piece; or a congestion of pawns that choked my position; or defending an awkward configuration surrounding my King. No matter what I tried, at the start I always suffered a disadvantage. The first few times we played I lost quickly. But I am willful, if nothing else (sometimes I think that's the only talent I possess) and I struggled hard, refusing to concede.

We settled into a new pattern. I learned to avoid the more disastrous moves and stave off quick defeat, thereby forcing Joseph to prove his advantage was a winning one. Half the time he would give back his early gains, or I would liberate myself from the confusion of my pieces. But then, seemingly exhausted by my long struggle up the hill to equality, I would blunder again in what is called the endgame of chess—positions with only a few pieces on board. Joseph's confidence, high at the beginning, strained in the middle, would soar at the end. His quick decisions about what and where to move—typical of his play at the beginning— would return and he would smash me. Our games became marathons with thrilling reversals of superiority, although the final result was always the same. We played every day until school started and I never won, although I came closer—it seemed—each time.

My arm healed by the beginning of school and that interrupted our new intimacy. I preferred, with my arm working again, to play handball against the side of our apartment building with my other friends or to go with them and their fathers (mine had still not returned from Cuba) to Fort Washington Park to play touch football or softball. I invited

Joseph to join us; unfortunately the neighborhood lacked a domed stadium to protect him from the elements.

I didn't reject Joseph because of this impediment. I tried to continue our friendship at P.S. 173. It is a measure of Mrs. Stein's belief in education that she allowed her boy to wander its halls. True, he brought his own lunches and there was no carpeting. But even I believed the school's atmosphere was poisonous; at once dusty and scented by ammonia, the rarely ventilated air could choke healthy lungs. I remember well Mrs. Fleisher's daily struggle with the painted-shut windows; the metal-reinforced glass cast prison shadows of gloomy webs across her face as she worked to force them open.

When I was elected captain of the class softball team, after making the obvious selections, I called Joseph's name to be on the team. One of the better players groaned. Joseph looked pleased, but he refused. I assumed he had been discouraged by the groan. I stopped by his apartment after dinner to urge him privately. I was convinced he could be at least a competent player. Certainly I knew from chess that he was a determined competitor. Besides, I wanted to free him from his airless green prison.

Mr. Stein answered the door. He greeted me as if I were a delightful surprise. He was short, very thin and almost completely bald. Unlike his son and wife, he didn't wear glasses and he had almost no eyebrows. In fact his left eyebrow didn't exist; the right one consisted of a thin line of hair. Today, I assume that this was the result of some torture or calamity at the concentration camp. At the time it seemed merely an organic part of his overall appearance. He was like a friendly human mouse: white and small, he squeaked, "Hello!" when he saw me. He called back, also in a high semi-hysterical voice, to the interior of the apartment, "It's Ralph!" as if that were great news and eagerly waved me in. (I didn't react to his mistake: it was common.) "Come in. Come in. We're having some cake. You want a piece?"

Gently, but insistently, he pushed me to their kitchen table. It happened to be the same model yellow Formica table, with a band of ridged metal around the edge, that I had hidden under in Tampa. I hadn't noticed it before; all our meals were served in Joseph's cage. Mr. Stein guided me into a chair. Mrs. Stein, beaming, approached with a mustard yellow plate. On it was an enormous slice of sponge cake whose color was almost the same hue as the china. Her glasses were fogged, her hair was covered by a scarf and she seemed, to my ignorant eyes, to be dressed for bed. What looked like a hideous pink nightgown to me was in fact a housecoat. Joseph sat directly across, wearing the same old man's button-down white shirt he wore to school, and smiled at me proudly. Of his parents? Of himself? Of the sponge cake? I didn't know. I was uneasy, however. I felt captured.

Mr. Stein told his wife to give me a glass of milk, told me to eat the cake, and asked me to explain about the softball tournament that Joseph had said I was in charge of. He delivered these orders in his squeaky voice, which somehow made them inoffensive.

With my mouth full of sponge cake, I told Mr. Stein I was merely captain of our class, not in charge of the tournament. I explained that each class was to play against the other classes in their grade until there were six school champions. (P.S. 173, typical of the city's public schools then, bulged with baby boomers.) The winners were to go on and play representatives from other Manhattan schools. Eventually there would be a borough champ for each grade. All that was true. I said there would be a citywide championship, a state championship, and then a competition that would end with national champions. All that was invented. Why make it up? I wanted to persuade them to allow Joseph to play. When I noticed Mr. Stein widen his narrow eyes and raise his one eyebrow with the mention of each championship I naturally thought the more the better as far as he was concerned.

I was right. "Mimi," he said to Mrs. Stein, "this is a very good thing." He added a quick order, "Joseph, you should play."

"Great!" I said, spewing crumbs. "Sorry," I mumbled and took a sip of milk. It tasted awful. Mrs. Stein served skimmed milk.

"You don't like milk?" Mrs. Stein said.

"Yes," I said and forced myself to drink more.

"But Joey doesn't know how to play baseball," Mrs. Stein said.

"I can teach him!" I cried out.

"I know how!" Joseph complained. He blushed. He took off his glasses and rubbed his eyes. Probably to avoid looking at me. I knew he was lying: how could he know how to play baseball if he had hardly ever been outside?

"Doesn't matter. He'll learn," Mr. Stein said.

"But where do you play?" Mrs. Stein asked. "You know, he's allergic to grass."

I told her Joseph would be safe from nature, playing in P.S. 173's concrete yard, a yard he went into every day. Mrs. Stein was able to point out that if our team was successful and went on to compete against other schools, that Joseph would be dragged to strange locations, probably places with lots of grass.

All of the city games would be played on concrete yards in Manhattan, I assured her.

But what about this state championship and the national championship? she pointed out, shaking her head sorrowfully. "They have grass in Albany and Washington. And Joey can't be going all over the country. He'll get asthma."

Joseph had left his glasses beside his half-finished plate of sponge cake. With them off, his eyes had an unfocused look. They trailed over the ceiling, as if he were searching for a way out.

Mr. Stein also nodded sorrowfully, in harmony with his wife. "That's true. And I can't get time off to travel with him."

"I can't go," Mimi Stein said. "You know I can't travel."

"Of course not!" her husband squeaked, outraged. He smiled at me and pressed the table once with his index finger, as if making a selection on a vending machine. "Well, I'm sorry," is what slid out of him. "Best of luck. I'm sure you'll win."

"I lied," I called out, tossing the truth onto the table. I wanted it back when I saw how they reacted. The mouse face lost its humorous grin; Mr. Stein's small mouth pursed as he tasted the bitter flavor of my betrayal. Mrs. Stein leaned back, retracted her chin, and studied me as if I had just entered the room. I rushed on, hoping to soften their reaction. "There aren't any other tournaments. There's just a borough champion. We'll never leave Manhattan. We probably won't even win the class tournament. Everybody thinks 4-6 will cream us."

"Joseph," Mrs. Stein said in a deep tone, almost a man's register. "Go to your room."

"No," he moaned. Not so much as a protest, but as a pained recognition of the approach of disaster.

"You know you get too upset," she added. "We have to have this out with Rafael." She pronounced it the way I disliked—RAY-FEE-EL.

I was terrified. He gets too upset about what? Have what out? What were they going to do to me? Run, I urged myself. But I was paralyzed.

"This is very serious," Mr. Stein said, also having lowered his voice at least one scale.

Mrs. Stein stood up and touched Joseph's arm. "Go to your room."

Joseph pushed his chair back abruptly, its feet squealing on the linoleum. To my ears the sound was a shriek. Don't leave me alone with them, I pleaded. But no words came out. (I'm not sure I ever truly forgave Joseph for leaving, silly as that sounds.) He grabbed his glasses and rushed out.

Run! I begged myself. But I couldn't move.

"Liars can't be trusted," Mr. Stein said. He opened his hands to me, as if he were helpless. "Isn't that so? How can you trust a person who lies?"

"Leave him alone," Joseph wailed from the distance of his room. It was a ghostly cry. I felt doomed by the futile tone of his plea.

"I didn't mean anything!" My throat closed on the words, sounding shame and fear, not protest. "I just wanted you to allow Joseph—"

"You didn't mean anything?" Mr. Stein said in an utterly cold tone. His small eyes, the once bright twinkling eyes of a cartoon mouse, were unreflective now. They had the black color of disdain. "I wonder what you did mean? What else are you lying about? What did you really plan to be doing when these games were supposedly played?"

"Nothing! I only lied about the championships!"

Mr. Stein frowned with disgust. He waved a hand at me. "When are these games supposed to happen?" he asked as if this were my last chance.

"We play right after school." I looked at them and felt sure I was going to be killed. Literally. There was no voice of reason, under my fright, assuring me I was perfectly safe from harm. I was convinced I had to plead for my life. "In the north yard!" I added this detail, hoping it would help.

"Why hasn't the teacher written us a note about this?" Mrs. Stein asked her husband. She was still on her feet. In that puffy pink housecoat she was too enormous a blockade to circumvent. "She always writes notes. I'm sick of her notes. But about this? Staying after school, who knows how late, she writes nothing?"

"Maybe there is no tournament." Mr. Stein grabbed hold of my wrist. His fingers felt as if they were made of steel. I had to struggle not to cry out. He didn't appear to strain. His eyebrow—malignant and solitary—lifted, but otherwise he was expressionless while increasing the pressure on my arm, the same arm that had been broken. "Tell me what you were really up to. What did you plan to do with Joseph?"

I tried to pull away. I couldn't answer. My panic left no air in my lungs to power the words. Anyway, I didn't believe it would help to say anything. Unless I could get free and run home, I was doomed.

"You have nothing to say!" Mr. Stein demanded and squeezed harder. My bone felt ready to collapse.

"Where is your father really?" Mrs. Stein said. Her voice came from an unidentified location. She was probably behind me. I had been drawn closer to the mouse's face. I was fully occupied by Mr. Stein's small black eyes and hovering half of a brow. "He's somewhere in South America, Joseph tells me," Mrs. Stein's interrogation continued. "For this long? And what does he do down there?"

"He's a writer," Mr. Stein said. He was suddenly thoughtful. "We're going to talk to your mother and get to the bottom of this." He stood up and pulled me out of the chair.

Cool air passed through me, right through me, as if I were suddenly incorporeal. I was going to be free. I could breathe. I was going to survive. We were going home and I would be safe with my mother.

Mr. Stein dragged me all the way up two flights of stairs. He didn't release his handcuff—the skin on my wrist felt raw by then—even when Ruth answered the door.

For a moment Mr. Stein didn't say anything, surprised by Ruth. My mother must have looked odd to him. I had become accustomed to the slovenliness of her appearance. She was wearing one of my father's Brooks Brothers shirts. She wore them wrinkled, usually with nothing else on but panties, since the shirts trailed down to her knees. Thankfully, to answer the door she had pulled on a pair of chinos, also belonging to my father. These clothes were spattered with paint because she was redoing our apartment room by room, usually during the night. Often I found her in the morning asleep in a chair or on the couch, the brushes resting on the lips of opened cans nearby. Apparently she drifted off while taking a break. She had decided to use a different color for each room. In the case of the master bedroom she changed her mind twice, from faint pink to bright yellow and finally to light gray.

For a moment, we three looked at each other in silent confusion.

"Rafe?" she asked me in an uncertain tone.

I made one more great effort and yanked to be free of Mr. Stein. He let go. I touched the bruised spot. It felt as if my bone had been softened. I hurried into the apartment and stood behind my mother. The back of the blue Brooks Brothers shirt she had on was torn. Exposed by the billowing opening of the tear, I saw a line of gray paint crossing vertically on the bare skin of her skinny back. Where it intersected her spine, the bone rippled the line, so that it seemed alive. How had she painted a line on her own back?

"I wasn't lying!" I said or something like it, forgetting that I *had* lied somewhat. I meant I wasn't lying overall, that my intentions had been honest, that I was in fact a good person.

My mother dropped her arm around my shoulder. Her hand snaked around to my cheek and softly, but insistently, pulled the skin taut, distorting my mouth. "He lies a lot," she said to Mr. Stein. Her tone was loving, not critical or disappointed. Her fingertips tugged at my cheek. I could easily have spoken despite their spidery hold on my face, but they communicated her wish that I keep quiet. "He's very imaginative. I'm afraid my whole family is. I used to tell lies all the time. Fantastic lies. They were really my way of making myself more interesting. He's probably told you all kinds of things about why his father is away. He misses him and I think he may be a little bit angry, so he makes up stories about why his Daddy can't come home. The truth is he's a reporter for the *New York Times*. He's on assignment in Latin America, and he's constantly moving around so there's no point in our joining him down there. We don't know when we'll see him next. It's hard on Rafe."

"That's not—!" I wanted to explain that it had nothing to do with all the secrets I wasn't supposed to tell, about my father being in Cuba, Mom and Dad being Communists or the rest. But her web of fingers tugged a warning and I shut up before she interrupted me.

"That's not what you were lying about this time?" she said, again with no hint of anger, in a sweet understanding tone.

Mr. Stein, back to his mouse-like squeak, finally spoke. "He told us a long involved—a whole thing about a softball tournament in school. Supposedly he's the captain and he wanted Joseph to play. He was going to take him all over the city . . . supposedly to these baseball games."

"I see." Ruth pushed me away from her. "Go to your room. Go straight to your room. Don't go poking around looking for your toys. Go straight to your room, shut the door and stay there until I come in. Go!"

I went. I heard the start of her apology to Mr. Stein.

"There's probably some truth to it, but of course it's a lie. You'll have to forgive him—"

As I passed, I noticed that the door to her bedroom was closed. That was unusual. I didn't think about it. I was enraged. I slammed my own door shut and hurled myself onto the bed. I pressed my face into the pillow. Wild anger pulsed in my head, the kind that makes you feel will explode your skin and scatter your character into unrecoverable bits.

Worse than the fury, however, was my confusion. Why had she done this? Why had she told such a diabolical lie, a lie that left my character in ruins? She had heard from Mr. Stein himself that his worries had nothing to do with Dad or Cuba and yet she had made me into a living paradox, someone who would be believed less and less the more he told the truth. I was in quicksand; my end would only be hastened by resistance. How could I free myself from what Mr. Stein would tell Joseph and, by extension, every friend of mine, their parents and finally (Washington Heights was a small town in this respect) my teachers? Even the candy store man who sold me baseball cards, Milky Ways, and Pinkies would hear of it eventually. I would be Rafe the liar to them all.

I couldn't stand it. Longing for justice, I opened my door and walked out. My bedroom was the third in line off a narrow hall. A small bedroom, which my father used as a study, lay between my room and the master bedroom. All three shared a bathroom at my end of the hall. A strong smell of paint lingered in the windowless passageway. I took one step out of my room and stopped. I didn't proceed into the living room and foyer to confront my mother and Mr. Stein because a strange man stood at the study door, looking at me.

Shocked, I inhaled sharply and held the breath.

The stranger whispered to me in an intense voice. When he was done, he put his finger over his lips. He spoke in Spanish but I knew enough to understand. He said, "I am a friend of your father's. Be still."

He was Latin. He looked a little like my stout, black-haired, round-faced Cousin Pancho. An Asturian, my father would say, referring to natives of the Spanish province of Asturias. "Pancho, you have the Asturian sturdiness," my father liked to compliment his cousin. "You're built like a thoroughbred bull. The one that gores the matador." But I knew that my father preferred his own build, which he would praise using my body as a mirror. "You have the broad shoulders and narrow hips of the Gallego," Francisco told me almost every time we were alone. "Women like that shape in a man," he would add and smile into the distance. This strange Asturian moved on his toes toward the hall entrance. I remained stuck in place, holding my breath, watching him. I could hear that Mr. Stein was talking, but not the words.

"'I understand," my mother's voice was loud, so loud I was startled. The Asturian also. He stopped in his tracks. Mom sounded strained and angry. "No further discussion is necessary. I'm sorry if any of this has caused trouble for you, although I don't see how it has."

"You don't!" We could now hear Mr. Stein as well. The Asturian looked silly—he was stuck in mid-stride—arms out, heels off the floor. He settled back on his heels and sure enough, a loose floorboard groaned. We both gasped. But the sound of the front door shutting with a bang drowned out all those noises; and then Mom was there, staring at us with a look of surprise.

Surprised at what? Didn't she know the Asturian was in the apartment? For an awful moment, I was scared I had made a mistake in keeping quiet.

"Rafe, I told you to stay in your room," she said, thoroughly annoyed. "God damn it, don't you listen to me?"

"Who was the man?" the Asturian asked in English. "A police?"

"No," my mother frowned in disgust. "A nutty neighbor," she dismissed him. "He lives on another floor. Wait a few minutes, then take the stairs. He's nothing to worry about, anyway. He's got nothing to do with the police."

The Asturian turned to smile at me. "Your son," he said in Spanish to my mother, "is very handsome. And intelligent, too," he added. "He didn't give me away."

My mother walked over and hugged me. She ran her hands through my hair and pressed my face into her cleavage. She smelled of paint, turpentine and sweat. "He's a good boy," she said.

"I'm sorry to bring bad news."

"It could be worse," my mother said. She kept my face tight against her. My lips were parted by one of the Brooks Brothers buttons. It was as smooth and hard as a pebble.

"I'll go now," the Asturian said.

My mother released me.

"Let me check the hallway first," she said and left us.

As soon as she was gone, he came over and whispered in English, "Your father gave me a message only for you. He said"—the Asturian paused, eyes on the ceiling, then recited the message—"'Remember, Rafa, remember to yourself always, that you have the hard-headed common sense of the Nerudas. If trouble gets in your way, use your brain.' No, no," he corrected himself, " 'If trouble finds you, use your peasant brain.' " The Asturian tousled my hair, smiled and then rushed off after my mother in a comical way, a hurried waddle.

Of course I forgot my anger. When Ruth returned, I didn't confront her about the ruination of my character. There was a calm look of concentration in her green eyes, a strange and beautiful contrast to the wild tangle of her black hair. Her posture, often defeated and wary since our return from Florida, was erect and alert. "He brought a letter from Daddy," she said to me, but also not to me, speaking over my head and scanning the hallway intently, as if trying to decipher something on the wall. "He didn't want me to read it to you, but I'm going to. I'm going to have to destroy it and I want you to know it really existed. It's too important for you to believe on just my say-so."

She had no letter that I could see. She walked up and down our little hall, first peering into my room, then the study. "No!" she said decisively. "Certainly not here." She put a finger to her lips and said, "Keep quiet." She wasn't talking to me. She took my hand and led me into the bathroom. It's a bathroom that I sometimes see when I visit friends on the Upper West Side. But that's rare. Those who pay today's prices for New York apartments usually replace the characteristic black and white web pattern of tiles, the milky porcelain sink and faucets, the toilet whose flush sounds like an explosion, and the narrow frosted glass window, permanently stuck in a position not fully closed, so that, especially on a winter night, a breeze shocks the bare behind of its user.

Ruth pushed our blood-red shower curtain open and bent down to turn on the bathtub faucet. A squeal, a shudder from the pipes, and then a burst of water made thunder. She moved to the sink and both its faucets were wrung open to add to the storm. She tried and failed to shut the frosted glass window. The split in my father's shirt billowed as she did and I saw all of her skinny back. There was more than a single line on her; another intersected it. She had an X painted on her back as if she were a target. She finally settled on the closed toilet seat, reached into the deep pockets of my father's chinos, and pulled out a letter written on two sheets of unlined yellow typing paper, a kind of cheap foolscap that I can no longer find in my local stationery store. Today the pages are so brittle that the edges break off if any pressure is applied. Looking at them as I write this I see that the coarse paper absorbed the blue ink of my father's pen unevenly. Some words are fat, others faded, a few almost illegibly blurred. She patted the rim of the bathtub near her, inviting me to sit. I obeyed.

"'My dear, sweet Ruth—'" she read in a cold matter-of-fact voice. Then she stopped and seemed to skip ahead. "Well, for a while he writes about how much he loves me," she said and sighed, not with longing, but a kind of exhaustion. "Here, this is the part I want to read to you." She was at the bottom of the first page. Its top drooped like a flag in a dying wind. "'I dare not explain how I know about the danger I'm in, even though a reliable man will bring this letter to you. It is certain that the CIA is out to silence me. My life isn't worth a nickel if I return. I have spoken with what they call in the spy movies a double agent and he showed me proof of exactly how determined the Kennedy administration is to prevent me from bringing home the truth about the Revolution.'" She looked at me. The utter loss in her eyes was scary. Her cheeks were hollows. "I'm sorry, Rafe," she said in a mumble and lowered her gaze to the floor. She let out a huge sigh, an exhalation that was part moan. "We're terrible parents," she whispered and I heard tears in her voice, although there were none in her eyes.

"No, you're not!" I answered as if a stranger had made the accusation. "I love you, Mommy," I said. I reached for her right hand. The left one still held my father's letter.

She squeezed my fingers for a second and then let go, sitting up to read from the second page of foolscap. "'Obviously it would be crazy for you and Rafe to join me in Cuba. An attack could come at any time and should the U.S. bring all its forces to bear nothing could stop the devastation. I certainly don't expect any mercy at their hands, not even for the innocents. You're safer in New York. But still, I'm sorry to have to alarm you, and I don't think you should repeat any of this to Rafael, but I'm convinced that you are in danger so long as you are associated with me. I've let it be known in Havana—especially in the presence of those I don't trust—that our marriage is troubled and that you don't care for my politics. If things become too uncomfortable for you, maybe you should consider talking to a lawyer about a divorce. Do whatever is necessary to make it seem we're on the rocks. I know this is a hard thing to ask, but we've both known since Julius and Ethel the kind of people we're up against, and certainly what happened in Tampa has proven they'll stop at nothing. Don't worry about me or the fate of the world—think of yourself and Rafe only. Pretend you've given it all up, especially politics. You should get a divorce—I'm sure an American court will grant it once you tell them where I've voluntarily chosen to live. Think of me as being in prison, a prison you can't visit, but a prison from which I will soon be paroled, not broken, but stronger than ever. I couldn't protect you and Rafe once. I must stay here to prevent you from being hurt again. I must stay here and help defend the Revolution. If Cuba goes, then true Socialism will exist nowhere. If it fails then I fail and I will be worthless to you and to myself. You know whom to contact to get a message to me. Be sure to destroy this. Hug and kiss Rafe for me. I don't know if he'll ever accept me as his father again. I hope to make it up to him someday. Without your love I am lost. Without the hope that I will see you both again, I am desolate. *Un fuerte abrazo. Te amo.*' " She recited his words in a consciously controlled tone, fighting her pain. As a result, she sounded angry. "That means, I love you," she said in a grim tone.

"Daddy's not coming home?" The rim of the tub was a precarious and uncomfortable seat. I braced myself with my hands. The porcelain was cool and massive. "Is that what it means?" I asked. I seemed to feel nothing. I know my mother expected me to be upset. Obviously, I didn't really understand what was going on. "Use your peasant brain," to choose just one example of my confusion, seemed like an insult to me. I understood peasants to be primitive people, only a cut above Cro-Magnon Man; indeed, peasants were less impressive since they were alive today, demonstrably inferior to other human beings, whereas Cro-Magnon was the peak of intelligence for his time. And what trouble was going to find me? More men who wanted to pee on my mother? Those terrifying Cuban anti-Communists (they were called by my father *Gusanos*, which means worms) and the CIA, deadly agents of the most powerful government on earth, were going to be defeated by an eight-year-old's peasant brain? Or by my hard-headedness? And why was my father proud of our primitive ancestors? I didn't want to emulate them: I wanted to be like him, a handsome intellectual.

But I knew even then, had known since that night in Tampa, that there was a part of Francisco I didn't want in me, and I also believed, although I immediately shoved it out of sight, down below into the damp and unlit basement, that his reason for staying in Cuba was more cowardice than self-sacrifice. I knew what I felt and believed and then in an instant, I never knew that I had ever thought such a thought. O, miracle of miracles from the creature that thinks: we move inexorably toward truth, and on arrival, shut our eyes.

"That's what it means, honey," my mother said. She had no warmth in her tone, hardly any coloration. She could have been a recorded phone company voice, explaining that the number was disconnected. "Daddy won't be coming home for a while. But he's fine and he loves us." The letter went back into my father's chinos. "Don't be frightened," she said and stood up. She extended her hand. "It's bedtime."

Oh no, I was certainly not going to be frightened. Of what? What was there to be frightened of?

Poor woman. She was lost. I took my mother's hand. To me she was beauty, sustenance, comfort. Even in the torn shirt, with the target on her back, swimming in my father's pants, I put my hand in hers with confidence.

My room had only the nude ceiling fixture, a triangle of three bulbs that spread a yellow light, a sickly glare, as if the sun were dying. Ruth had taken down my shelves of books, comics, baseball cards, and games in order to paint the walls blue. She had done one wall and then decided the color was wrong, that it ought to remain white as before. But it was still undone, since painting a room white bored her. I had one wall of blue, three of peeling yellowed white, and my possessions were in a disorganized heap, sometimes covered by a sheet and sometimes not, depending on whether Ruth had vowed that morning to do the job. I looked at this wreck while I undressed and Ruth turned down my bed. No wonder Mrs. Stein wouldn't allow Joseph to play at my house. Maybe it had nothing to do with her nuttiness. Maybe it was us.

I had never seriously considered that we were the weirdos. Despite our political unorthodoxy, my father's lack of a typical job, I had a heroic image of my parents and I trusted their assertion that I was strong, fast, smart and good. It was gracious on my part to be friendly to boys like Joseph, wasn't it? But now, as I put on my faded Superman pajama bottoms (I didn't wear a top), I saw that we were the oddballs. Everyone else was a happy American, not enemies of the government like us. Everyone else's mother wore dresses and cooked dinners. Everyone else's father went to work in the morning and came home at night to talk about the Yankees, not Dostoevsky or the Third International. I wasn't the envy of my friends, the delight of my teachers, the wonderful exception. I was the unfortunate kid, the geek, surrounded not by genuine regard, but the kindness of pity.

I don't remember when my tears started, whether I was already into bed and had been tucked in, or whether it was just before. My mother said, in that flat voice, "You're crying," and got into bed with me, gathering me into the warm hollow of her curved body, her head arching over me, her legs covering and entwining with mine. She no longer had the chinos on. Perhaps she had gone out for a while and resumed painting, perhaps this took place in the middle of the night, and I had woken weeping. I don't remember exactly. The Brooks Brothers shirt I can recall. Its fabric, smelling faintly of my father and faintly of my mother and strongly of paint, was somehow both soft and coarse. My tears wetted a large circle on the upper ridge of her left breast. Her nipple emerged, a truncated pillar, rising in the soaked material.

After a while I stopped crying. The room was dark. Harsh light from the street's amber lamps spread through my venetian blinds. They undulated with the breeze; shadows of their thick latticework moved over the wall, the partly open closet door, and the naked unlit bulbs.

Lying on the damp of my tears became uncomfortable. I tried to turn away from Ruth and the shirt, but her arms locked and wouldn't let me.

"Stay!" she implored in a whisper. She pushed at me with one foot, digging under my legs, and, claw-like, used her other foot to gather me, pressing my legs, pelvis and hips against her. She undulated like the shadows, and her big lips, dry and hot, manufactured soft kisses on my forehead. Moans—I mistook them at first for sobs—escaped between her caresses. I felt the looseness in her sex. At least I remember I did. She rocked and kissed and shuddered until her body went rigid. Her muscles clenched and she jerked a few times. The bedsprings squealed violently; yet her embrace felt gentle, only a breeze that moved the shadows across my unpainted room. After that, she lapsed into sleep. I slid out from her relaxed embrace, found the chinos in a lump by the bathroom, and stole my father's letter.

Chapter Four

Transference

DURING THE REST OF MY EIGHTH YEAR RUTH'S STATE OF MIND WORSENED. Most of the time she communicated with me by writing messages on a yellow legal pad. I had to answer in kind with the red pencil she offered or simply nod my agreement. (I never disagreed: you don't talk back to a mute.) When our written conversation was over, she tore off the sheet from the pad and methodically folded the paper into a square. She stared intently, pressed her lips tight, and ripped the square into smaller squares. Her face had a look of fury and concentration. She gathered the litter of yellow pieces into a cup made by her palms, carried them before her as if they were holy into the bathroom and flushed them down the toilet. While the water rushed out, she checked under and around the bowl to make sure none had fluttered onto the black and white web of tiles.

The messages weren't worthy of secrecy. They were: "Put your dirty clothes in the hamper in my closet." Or: "Don't forget to close the re-frigerator door." Or, every woman's favorite injunction to men: "Don't leave the seat up after using the john." It was absurd, heartbreaking and scary.

One winter night, at bedtime, she wrote, "Painting your room. Sleep in mine." While I got into pajamas, she pushed my bed away from the wall and covered it with an old sheet, streaked by colors she had tried out elsewhere. She moved brushes, cans of paint, a ladder, and other paraphernalia into my room. But no painting was ever done there; and she had finished the rest of the apartment.

My parents had a king-sized bed, so huge that our sharing it for a few nights might not appear odd. Besides, we had no visitors. Ruth deliberately quarreled with her Communist Party friends, presumably as part of the need to separate publicly from my father. She had a nonpolitical friend, the mother of one of my buddies, but she fought with her as well, on some pretext—I never heard that detail. I was allowed to play outside with my friends for an hour after school and some weekend mornings but I was forbidden to visit at their apartments or invite them home, because her paranoia was galloping. She explained on her yellow pad: "Adults are dangerous. Keep everything secret. Go to school and come home. Keep quiet around grown-ups. They could put me in jail." She didn't bother me every night; not often, in fact. And was it bothering? How I long to use the jargon that would clothe my nakedness for those of you lucky enough to be shocked by it: I was glad of the security of my mother's bed and I enjoyed the warmth of her body. And I did my best—believe me, it was my best—to ignore it when that body, swishing the sheets and creaking the springs, became too animated for comfort alone. I nestled deeper into the pillow, reaching for unconsciousness. In fact, sometimes I did nod off while she moved against me with that insistent, furtive rubbing.

And what did I feel? Or rather, what was I aware of feeling?

I was the two-sided boy: the marred downcast face of a geek I saw in the mirror and the outward beam of a happy boy shown to teachers and friends. Sometimes my performance of normality and happiness even fooled me. I would forget for hours at a time, while with the children at school, that I was not a child. I was the revolutionary-traitor, the fatherless-father, the boy-lover, the terrified-strongman.

My prison was not without parole. I did captain the softball team; I was allowed to play in the schoolyard after class in the various pickup games of stickball, touch football and so on. Contrary to what you might expect I did well at school. My grades were excellent. I was elected to the student council. I was considered to be an exceptionally mature and responsible boy. The explanation is widely understood by child psychologists today, although that does not necessarily make a sufferer easier to spot. Back then only a few specialists (and not all, by any means) would have suspected my imitation of harmony. A truly unhappy child, the child whose parents do not play their roles, knows best how to mimic the behavior of responsible grown-ups and has the greatest motivation to do so. The particular abuse I endured was that my mother cast me as father and lover. She didn't attack my ego: her abuse wasn't that active. She ignored me, refused to nurture the real me into manhood, forced me to be an adult-manqué and take care of her, in every sense of that word. For long periods of time children are capable of this fakery. (Usually they become incapable as adolescents or adults, when something more difficult than precocity is asked, when real maturity is demanded by friends and lovers.) Eventually, of course, the facade cannot be supported; cracks and stresses on the flimsy supports multiply, and sooner or later it collapses. But that doesn't happen right away and, I'm convinced, it is this phase—the cover-up—which does the most harm.

My mother would pull herself together from time to time. We visited Aunt Sadie and Cousin Daniel occasionally. I was especially enjoined to tell them nothing. I obeyed gladly: the last person I would have admitted my situation to was Daniel.

And, by the way, when I speak of my situation, I mean the facts as explicated to me by my mother, namely that my father was a revolutionary in exile, a defender of Cuba, preparing for the day when the corrupt government of the United States would be overthrown. I was unaware that my mother's nighttime embraces were wrong, in the sense that they were the hurtful actions of a traumatized adult for which I bore no responsibility. Nevertheless, I also knew I wasn't supposed to talk about them; I knew they made me uncomfortable . . . sometimes. Even if Ruth had released me from my vows of secrecy, I wouldn't have spoken. In my mind I was a full participant. I didn't pull away; I made no fuss about sleeping in her bed. I wanted to stay. I kept the secret for my own reasons. The thought of losing her, including what I didn't like about her, filled my head with panic and resolve.

We did not attend Seder in 1961 at my uncle's, although by April Ruth seemed to be improving. She was grooming herself again, circling ads in the newspaper, going on a few job interviews. We were broke. The money my father had left behind in the bank was used up. I believe—I'm uncertain about this detail—that Ruth had been offered part-time administrative work at Columbia Presbyterian Hospital and planned to say yes.

On April 15th, 1961, my ninth birthday, Ruth didn't throw a party. She wrote on the legal pad: "We'll go to the movies and have a cake. But no friends. Children are good but can't trust parents."

It was a Saturday. She took me to the Museum of Modern Art where, in a narrow, stark white screening room they showed Charles Chaplin movies to serious-minded film lovers. My mother enjoyed herself. For the first time since Tampa, I heard her laugh long and loud. And she cried, of course. That was almost as unusual as her laughter. She whispered to me again and again, "He's a genius. Isn't this great?"

I hated Chaplin. I thought the pathetic tramp grotesque, the absence of dialogue a dreary reminder of my home's inarticulate misery. I wanted to see a James Bond movie—I think *Dr. No* was playing then. Friends of mine had been given the 007 attaché kit for their birthdays. It included a plastic copy of Bond's Walther PPK that fired red bullets. My friends let me play in their hide-and-seek spy games, but I had to hide all the time, since I had nothing with which to defend myself. Worse, I had nothing to shoot at them.

I told Ruth I thought Chaplin was great. I watched her out of the corner of my eye and echoed her laughs, smiling when she turned her head to confirm that I was enjoying it.

"You have such good taste," she told me over my birthday dessert at Rumpelmayer's. "Is it good?" she asked about the piece of dark chocolate cake she had ordered for me. She had vetoed my request for Black Forest saying it was vulgar. (I liked cherries—still do.)

"Yes," I lied. The dark chocolate was too rich and too bitter for my unsophisticated child's palate. (Still is.)

We crossed the street to Central Park. Ruth found an empty bench, in an odd spot, near a stone bridge. (I can't find it today.) Occasionally a bicyclist went by; once, a couple walked past. She fell silent each time until they were gone. She took my hand, looked toward the trees, not at me, and made a speech.

"You're nine years old today. It's amazing to me. It's absolutely amazing. I can remember how you looked the day you were born. You had a full head of black hair. You weren't one of those wrinkled old men. Your eyes were the shape of almonds. And they were so bright. The nurse said you couldn't really see yet, but you seemed to look right into my heart and I swear you knew who I was. The nurse showed me your full head of hair and then she straightened your fingers to show me how long they were." Ruth gently lifted the tips of my fingers away from their curvature toward my palm. " 'He's going to be tall,' " she said. She was right," Ruth commented with a note of surprise. "I don't think her method was scientific. Well, she had seen Francisco. So it wasn't that brilliant of her, was it?" she chuckled. She must love Chaplin, I remember thinking. Her mood hadn't been this gentle and easy since the attack.

"That was the happiest day of my life. Not the day you were born. I was too scared and too foggy from the anesthesia to enjoy it. The next day, when I got to hold you and feed you and everyone came—" she narrowed her eyes, "even people I hated were nice and so impressed by you." She stopped here, I think because of a passerby. When she resumed, tension had returned to her voice. "I had lots of days when I was happy. I don't want you to think I was always like this. I wasn't. I wasn't always angry and scared." She glanced at me. Her eyes were wet. I hoped she wouldn't cry. "I was happy when I used to dance. Before Bernie put a stop to it. Put a stop to it quickly. Put a stop to that. And to a lot of other things."

She rapidly turned her head as if she were going to catch someone hidden behind us, eavesdropping. When she saw no one she turned back and resumed. "But there was always something that turned things sour. Not the day after you were born. Everything was gorgeous. I didn't feel sore or any pain. I did the next day. But not your first full day on earth. I remember everyone saying how well I looked. I looked well because I was happy." She didn't glance at me. She squeezed my hand for emphasis, but her green eyes nervously scanned the trees and nude lawns. She raised her voice, abandoned the hunted whisper of her paranoia, and spoke clearly above the distant surf of traffic on Fifth Avenue. "I want you to know that. No matter what happens to me, remember the day I got to see you, really see you for the first time, was the happiest day of my life."

We returned to our apartment building around five o'clock. As we were about to go into the lobby, a voice called from a window. It was Joseph. Outside of contact in school I hadn't played with him since the day I was branded a liar to his parents. (I was wrong about the label becoming general throughout the neighborhood. Either the Steins had no credibility or they didn't talk to anyone.) He called down, "Rafe!" and then glanced back furtively into his apartment. Something appeared in his hands. "Happy birthday!" It was a package. He indicated he was going to drop it. "Catch!"

I moved under his window. He let go. He had wrapped the present in brown paper and written "Happy Birthday" in Magic Marker on both sides. His handwriting was as neat as a girl's. Inside the wrapping was a paperback book. Not new; very well used, in fact. And on the inside cover there was a sticker with Joseph's name. The title suggested the book would solve a mystery: *How to Play the Opening in Chess*. Upstairs, I got out my plastic pieces and tested my assumption. Sure enough, the dramatic advantages Joseph used to gain at the start of our games came from that book. My opponent for the openings had been the advice of generations of chess geniuses who had explored the first twenty moves or so and recorded the best options. Joseph had never let on. The rest of Joseph's books were on the shelves for all to see, but this one hadn't been on display. Indeed, I suspected (I was correct) that he must own more than one chess book. I noticed an advertisement on the back jacket that said there was a companion volume, *How to Play the Endgame*. I wanted to thank him. And I wanted to play chess again. I tried to think of how I could convince first my mother and then his mother that neither the CIA nor the Nazis would gain anything by Joseph and me playing together. I guess it's a sad indication about my life that I didn't laugh at this summation of my obstacle but seriously began to compose speeches to surmount it.

My attempt to puzzle out a convincing brief for parole was interrupted by Mother breaking the radio silence of our apartment. She shouted my name, "Rafe!" with urgency and horror.

I ran to her. She was in the hall off the kitchen. In happier days my parents used to serve meals at the long pine table in this room to argumentative Communist and ex–Communist Party members. For large groups they cooked Cuban peasant food: Francisco prepared great pots of black beans and rice; Ruth had learned from my grandmother how to make *ropa vieja*. Truly huge crowds were sometimes invited for dessert. Ruth baked delicious blueberry and apple tarts. She explained how she kept their crusts flaky during the brief lulls of political debate. And in the corner, sometimes to illustrate the subject of their discussions, was a small black and white television. Not the huge consoles of my friends and certainly not a hypermodern color set. It was the kind of portable television that soap-opera addicted women kept in the kitchen or indulgent parents bought for teenage children to watch in their bedroom.

I found Ruth kneeling in front of it. The news was on. Probably Walter Cronkite, but I don't remember.

She said, "They've bombed Havana." Havana was where I understood my father to be living. At my local public school there had been atomic bomb drills, later satirized or solemnly re-created by many works of the anti-war culture of the late sixties. We practiced getting under our desks.

I saw my father under a desk. I saw him under my grandmother's kitchen table winking at me.

They were showing file footage (I guess) of Fidel's troops taking Havana. The report (which turned out to be false) was that the Cuban air force had revolted against Fidel and bombed the capital. In fact, U.S. planes had dropped some bombs and a lot of leaflets to weaken morale in preparation for the invasion of CIA-trained Cubans at the Bay of Pigs. That was not what my mother knew, however. She heard that Havana was under attack from a Cuban counterrevolution. She knelt before the news bulletin, but her hands weren't in a prayerful pose; they were clenched fists poised to strike at the image.

The phone rang.

"Oh, my God," Ruth said. She stood up. She was still in the clothes she had put on to take me out for my birthday, a cheerful yellow and white dress that billowed prettily when she walked. She was forty-five years old but looked younger. Her eyes were bright, a pale green at that moment, although they could look darker, almost brown. Her brows were black, hardly plucked, expressive arches that emphasized her alert eyes. "You answer. Say I'm not here." She covered her mouth and stared at the ceiling as if someone were hanging from it. "Shit. Of course they know."

The phone continued to ring, insisting on our attention. "I'll get it," I said. Ruth called out for me not to, but I was in the kitchen and had lifted the phone from its cradle before she could countermand me.

Grandma Jacinta was on, talking in rapid Spanish, almost hysterical. We had spoken earlier, when she called to wish me a happy birthday. This time I couldn't understand her. In the background I heard a relative of mine shout: "They say it's an invasion!" Jacinta calmed herself enough to say, "Listen, honey, don't worry about a thing. Put your Mama on, okay?"

Talking with Grandma, Ruth sounded tough. She said, "Those bastards." A long pause. "It's all a pack of lies. I'm sure they aren't Cuban. There is no Cuban air force—they only have six planes. They must be ours." Another pause. "No. We're fine," she said. And again, "Fine. No. We're okay." She sounded angrier and angrier.

I wandered into the kitchen. I wished I were anywhere but home. Our kitchen had one large window which was half open. Its view was of the narrow courtyard, a tunnel of windows that revealed identical structural interiors but surprisingly different interior decorations on every floor. I leaned out and glanced down two levels to what I knew was Joseph's room.

He was there! Looking right up at me. He smiled and waved. I called down, "Thanks for the book! Now I can beat you."

He said something.

"What?" I yelled.

Joseph raised his window higher and stuck his head out. "I know a way we can play like this." He produced a flashlight, turning it on and off. "Morse code and chess notation." He abruptly attempted to pull his head in, whacking it against the window. He shouted, "I'm coming," back into his apartment. "I'll show you in school," he called. "Gotta go." He withdrew into his shell.

I was smiling when I turned around and discovered my mother confronting me, smelling sweet, but staring with rage. "They can put me in jail." My throat went dry. I don't think I could have talked if I knew what to say. "They killed Ethel. They electrocuted her. They didn't care that she had two beautiful little boys. Do you understand? You're killing me." She said this in a calm sane voice: the steadiness was unnatural and all the more terrifying. "You talk to people and you're killing me." I expected her to hit me. She had never done so; but I heard it in her tone, like a hard slap across my cheeks. Instead, she turned on her heels—her dress billowed as if she were dancing—and walked out.

I cried. I cried hard, hysterically.

Ruth appeared when I was winding down, or when I had run out of tears might be a more accurate description. She had tissues in her hand. She wiped my nose. She had changed into slacks and had her raincoat on. Her head was covered by a scarf. She certainly looked surreptitious, if not subversive. "I'm going out, honey," she said in a gentle whisper. "This is Aunt Sadie's number. Call her if there's an emergency. But there won't be. I'll be home by the morning. There's milk and cookies and peanut butter and bread if you get hungry. You can watch TV past your bedtime." She had finished wiping my nose. She kissed my eyes one at a time, then my forehead and said softly, without irony, "Happy Birthday." She left. I listened to her retreating footsteps all the way to the firestairs. I could make out the sound of her going down and then she was gone.

I was excited to be able to watch television at late as I wanted. But when it grew dark the big apartment sounded empty and vulnerable as I listened to New York's night music: sirens, the raucous shout of a drunk, the taunts of a gang of teenagers. They were noises I had heard all my life, but they used to be a harmless background, the churning surf of a tempest whose waves couldn't reach me. I tried to fall asleep in my parents' king-sized bed with no success. I was too little and the sounds crept closer and closer: ambulances coming to pick up dead bodies; killers shouting they were looking for little boys to stab.

Don't be weak, I told myself. If you get scared and call for help, you'll have failed her. *Use your peasant brain,* my father reminded me. I hunched my shoulders, stuck my tongue over my upper teeth, and grunted like an ape. I did feel stronger as a brute; as a thoughtless animal, I wasn't frightened.

I lay sideways in a fetal posture on the huge bed, with all the lights on, held my penis and made savage noises. They would have seemed silly and pathetic to an observer, but for me it was salvation. I escaped into a fantasy of power and fell asleep.

Ruth wasn't there in the morning. I felt confident at first. The sun was out, there were Cheerios for nourishment, the Rocky and Bullwinkle cartoon hour for entertainment, and later, when I heard the noise of the weekly adult fast-pitch softball game across the street in my schoolyard, I got up my courage, dressed and went outside. I remember the day was clear, sunny and cool; and the game was thrilling, especially because I was able to get close, perched on the ledge behind the fence. I had been limited to watching from the more distant view of my bedroom window since I had been forbidden to go out on weekends for a year. Some of the men, flattered by my attention and applause, talked to me. I felt heartbroken when the game ended.

I was hungry. I returned to the apartment intending to make a peanut butter and jelly sandwich. That was when I discovered my error. I had no key to get back in. I guess I expected my mother to be home by late morning. She wasn't. I rang and rang until a neighbor appeared. She asked if anything was wrong. No, no, I insisted, horrified at the thought that I might have revealed Ruth was away, information which could lead to her imprisonment and electrocution.

I ran off to the stairs, down a flight or two, sat on a step and wept. I had made a bad mistake. I couldn't figure out how to correct it. A different neighbor appeared to see who was crying. I fled to another landing. That scare got me thinking long enough to make a decision.

I would ignore my hunger and wait outside until Ruth returned. I stood near the building entrance, trying to appear casual and not let on that I was expecting someone.

An eternity seemed to pass. Probably no more than a few hours, but while enduring them I felt more and more abandoned and helpless. I had vivid fantasies. I imagined my father dead in the rubble of Havana. I pictured a malicious laughing Cuban pilot as he landed at an airport in New York to celebrate his destruction of Fidel's revolution. I saw Ruth step forward in her James Bond outfit, pull out a Walther PPK and shoot him.

One of my friends appeared with his father. They carried baseball gloves and a softball. My friend asked if I wanted to play catch in Fort Tryon Park. I answered that I didn't, although I desperately wanted to. I couldn't risk not being there when Ruth returned. I would be in enough trouble for having left the apartment. I had been trying without success to think up a noble reason for having gone out. I think my friend's father was suspicious. He asked several times if I was okay.

I remember those three or four hours on the sidewalk vividly. I could write hundreds of pages on the compensating fantasies, the despair I saw in New York's mottled sidewalks, the breathless anxiety when people I knew happened by and interrogated me, the heart-stopping fear when I noticed a police cruiser on the corner and I hid between parked cars. I lived a lifetime in a few hours. I felt as if my entire character had been changed. And yet nothing happened. In the real world, outside the terror and longing in my head, the afternoon was dull. But inside me World Communism struggled for its life and lost—and I was orphaned.

Joseph rescued me. He spied me from his window and called down to ask what I was doing. I didn't tell him the truth but I made it clear that I was on my own. I was cold; my stomach hurt. He sensed my desperation and told me to come up. I hesitated for all the obvious reasons, namely his parents and my mother. "I'll answer the door," he said. Somehow that reassured me. Maybe he meant to sneak me in.

But no, Joseph had too much respect for his mother to do that. He greeted me at the door and asked in a whisper, "Where's your Mom? What's wrong?"

"I was supposed to stay inside. I got locked out. I don't know where she is."

Joseph nodded in his old man's grave manner and said, "Follow me. Keep quiet and say you're sorry when I tell you to."

We walked, much to Mrs. Stein's surprise, right into her kitchen.

"Mom, Rafe is here. He's come to tell you that he's sorry he lied. His mother has punished him by not letting him go out or see his friends for six months. He doesn't tell any more lies and now she lets him go out. We'd like to play chess, just one game and then he'll go." Mrs. Stein stared open-mouthed throughout his speech and stayed in that pose when he was done. Joseph nodded to me.

"I'm sorry," I said. I almost burst into tears. I had to fight to keep them to a trickle. "I'm really sorry. I won't do it again."

"That's all right," she said, trying to be stern-faced, but melting to me. "You did a bad thing, but if you're sorry and you don't do it no more, then it's all right. Go ahead. Play." We turned, ready to move fast. "You want something to eat?" she asked.

I was never so glad for bland food. I told Joseph a truth, namely that my mother had left me alone all night, but not why, and I explained that if he told anyone, he was putting me at risk of being grounded forever. Joseph said I shouldn't worry about my mother finding out I was at his place—he had a plan. We moved the chess set so we could look up to see the windows of my apartment. If Ruth turned on a light we would notice. Since it was daytime, I had my doubts she would, but I might spot her moving around. Anyway, I didn't care if this precaution was fallible. Out on the street my fear and hunger had overwhelmed me. I was too relieved by my rescue to care if I was punished for it.

The next obstacle loomed with nightfall. Joseph's father and mother appeared and looked at me as if I should be leaving. I had tried to beat Joseph using the Sicilian Defense, gleaned from the little learning I had gotten out of his birthday present the previous day. But I was quickly trounced twice—Joseph didn't tell me he owned a new book with more variations. I tried a different opening for the third game and seemed to be winning. I was about to attack him King's side when I saw the mouse's one-eyebrow face, squinting at me unhappily. "It's late," he said sourly.

I had an inspiration: "I'm sorry, Mr. Stein. I lied to you. I'm very sorry. I'll never do it again." This humbling of myself, this lie of an apology, an unthinkable abandonment of my pride only six months before, was a relief to me. I wanted to give myself up, to crush myself if I could, to be remade from top to bottom. I stood. "Thank you for inviting me," I said to Joseph, who looked so astonished by my formal manner I thought the lenses in his glasses were going to pop out. I walked toward his parents, resigned that I had to go.

"Ma," Joseph asked, a pleading note in his tone, "can Rafe sleep over?"

Mrs. Stein glanced at her husband. He blinked at her. The fierce man with steel fingers who dragged me to my mother's had disappeared down a hole and come out a mouse again. "It's a school night," she said uncertainly.

"We'll go to bed early," Joseph said. "No talking after lights out."

"Sure," the mouse said in a faint squeak. "If it's all right with his mother."

Joseph opened his eyes wide and stared at me. He spoke these words with slow significance: "Why don't you go upstairs and ask her?"

Bless him, he concealed his new chess books and pummeled me all night—I lost that third game and then two more—but he made sure I was cared for. I rang my bell a few times, without much hope. Mostly, I tried to think of a reason why I wouldn't be returning to the Steins with pajamas or school clothes or schoolbooks.

I told Mrs. Stein all my pajamas were dirty—that shocked her and gave her a pleasant feeling of superiority. I said my mother wanted me to go home early in the morning to change for school.

I woke up in the middle of the night, worried and scared. I cried. I thought I was doing it silently. Joseph turned on the tensor lamp. He squinted at me myopically. "Are you crying?" he whispered.

"I'm sorry," I blubbered and let out a sob.

He put a finger to his lips and then whispered, "Don't cry. You can always stay here. My parents think you're very smart. And, you know, by Jewish law you're Jewish."

"I know," I said and stopped crying. I remembered Papa Sam. I saw Uncle Bernie's round face smiling as he presented me with a twenty-dollar bill.

In the morning I left. There was still no answer at home. I decided to go to school in my dirty clothes. It was April 17th. That morning roughly fourteen hundred Cuban exiles, trained and backed by the CIA, invaded at the Bay of Pigs. They were easily and quickly defeated. But in the interval between the first report and the final result there was, at least among supporters of the Cuban revolution in the United States, a conviction that American troops would follow up, that this was the forerunner of a U.S. overthrow of Fidel. To this day it isn't known where my mother spent Saturday night and Sunday. By mid-morning on Monday she was arrested. She spat on Adlai Stevenson as he entered the United Nations (at the time he was the U.S. ambassador) and then fought violently with the guards who dragged her away. She was carrying a gun and a can of gasoline.

I didn't know those details for many years. Aunt Sadie found me in gym on Monday afternoon. She walked across its varnished floor with a look of horror in her eyes, a look that belied the account she gave of my mother. She said Ruth was going to be okay but that she was sick and had to stay in a hospital for a few days. (In fact, she was undergoing psychiatric observation at Bellevue.) Huge tears rolled down Aunt Sadie's cheeks while I explained that I had been on my own for two days and nights. Aunt Sadie used her key to my parents' apartment, packed a bag for me, and we went to her house in Riverdale.

Cousin Daniel looked through my things while Aunt Sadie left us to phone first her husband and then Uncle Bernie with the report about me. Daniel made fun of my schoolbooks. He said he had learned all that in first grade—I was in fourth.

"Well, it's because I go to a private school," Daniel said. "It's much better. We're years ahead of you."

This remark didn't wound as deeply as it would have a year earlier. I knew that I was a geek compared to Daniel, a monstrosity to his normalcy, but I also knew much more about life. I had faced killers and saved my parents' lives. I had stayed alone in my apartment and lied to grown-ups. I knew how to please my mother better than he could ever please his. I knew the secret that real men knew, the secret that women become loose and groan if touched in the right way. And in my Indian wallet, I had a special letter (that spies from the CIA were looking for) from a revolutionary, a man who had unselfishly given up being my father to make a just world. Besides, when I challenged Daniel to a chess game, thanks to Joseph's tutelage, I mated him in fifteen moves. Danny got so mad he picked up the board and scattered the pieces all over his beautiful carpet. He was a sore loser, but I wasn't. I worked hard until I learned how to win. I was a geek and I was an outlaw, but I was a man and he was a boy.

Aunt Sadie came in as Daniel threw the pieces. She casually rebuked him and told me that Uncle Bernie wanted to talk to me on the phone.

"Hey fella," his cello voice greeted me. "What a brave boy you are. Your Mom told you to keep what she was doing secret, is that right?"

"Yes," I said.

"Well, it's good to obey your Mom. But you don't have to keep secrets from me. I'm family. We don't have secrets in a family."

"Is Mom in jail?" I knew from Sadie's nervousness that her account wasn't accurate.

"Uh . . . Didn't Aunt Sadie tell you she was sick?"

"Yes," I said. *Use your peasant brain.* "But I don't think she told me the truth. If Mom's in jail, can I come live with you, Uncle?" I couldn't be a burden and a worry to my parents anymore. My uncle was rich. He was the great capitalist, the overwhelming force that had defeated my parents. Maybe I could get his help, get his power, and avenge my father and mother.

"With me? You're gonna stay with Aunt Sadie and Max and Danny. That'll be more fun. My kids are in college, you'd—"

"Mommy says you're a genius, Uncle." That was true. She said he had a genius for using power. "Daniel hates me. He says I'm a spic. I don't want to live here. I want to live with you. I want you to be my father."

There was a long silence. Then, in a choked voice, Bernie's cello sang low: "I'll come get you, boy."

He told me to put Aunt Sadie back on. I rushed to find her and grinned at Daniel as she went. He challenged me to another game. I mated him in ten. He threw the board against the wall so hard it split in two. I was triumphant. Aunt Sadie returned from her second conversation with Bernie. One side of her hairdo was stuck up in the air and her eyes were red. She kissed me and then wheeled angrily at Daniel. "You and I have to have a talk, young man."

Uncle Bernie took me away in a black limousine. I leaned against him and fell asleep on the ride to Long Island. I was nine years old and I was in charge of my life. I thought I was doing a better job than my parents had. After all, I was on my way to live in a mansion, on my way to help them win their lost cause.

CHAPTER FIVE

Overcompensation

I WAS MOVED INTO PAPA SAM'S OLD QUARTERS. EILEEN MCELHONE, A young woman (she seemed quite grown-up to me; but she was only twenty-eight) was hired through an agency to supervise me. Aunt Charlotte had no interest in playing mother now that she had sent her children off to college. She spent most of her time fund-raising for various museums, hospitals and Jewish organizations. Three or four nights a week she stayed in Manhattan. My uncle expected to be busy as well, supervising his real estate interests and preparing for an expansion into retailing through the purchase of Home World, then a foundering Northeast chain of appliance stores. He was frequently on trips or working late in Manhattan, not to mention the events he attended because of his charities and art collecting. It fell to Eileen to keep me company, ferry me to and from school and various athletic activities.

She was very beautiful, an Irish stereotype. She had light blue eyes, thick red hair, and high cheeks that alternated between bloodlessness and bright embarrassed flushes. Her speech was a melody. She had the natural literacy of a nation that puts Yeats and Joyce on their paper money. Her white and red colors, her gay moods and teasing speech, were so different from the dark, brooding Jews and Latins of my family that I was sometimes slow to answer her conversation, mesmerized by the spectacle of her exotic appearance.

Eileen lived in what used to be the nurse's room, only a step across the hall from mine. We shared a bathroom. She was kind, but too convinced (as Freudians and Catholics tend to be) of the inherently bad nature of humanity, especially as evidenced in children. She could not distinguish between the natural egotism of a four-year-old and the pathological narcissism of a forty-year-old. She believed sex was unspeakable, savage and dirty. We got along well; at nine, I held similar opinions. I believed all my desires to be evil. But I had a comforting rationalization: I wanted money and power as weapons in the good fight, to save the miserable and the poor.

Eileen was critical of American children. She thought my fellow Great Neck schoolmates were spoiled, whiny, rude, and arrogant. So did I. She praised me lyrically. "Oh, what a good boy you are. What a joy you are to take care of. Why you hardly need any attention at all. You're practically taking care of me. Not like these others, the little monsters they call children. Ordering their mothers about like servants and treating the servants like they were still slaves from Africa." She had no respect for my parents and wasn't shy about speaking ill of my mother. "What kind of a woman leaves a child alone for two days and nights? And in New York City, which is no better than a jungle, or even worse than a jungle, if you ask me. As a mother she was a good Communist. I have no use for her kind. I don't care that they want to make things better for us poor and us workers. I know what happens to their hearts once they get the power. Then they don't care about the poor anymore. They're not so sentimental about workers when they're the bosses. I know about Communists, yes I do. I don't have much use for greedy capitalists but the Communists are even worse. Under capitalism you can have nothing to eat. But under Communism there's nothing to cook your nothing with."

Other adults avoided the subject of my parents. I mean my uncle, his wife, Charlotte, Uncle Harry and Aunt Ceil, and Aunt Sadie. Since Bernie employed his brother, and all his brothers-in-law, I saw more of them, especially on weekends. My status had changed, of course. My cousins, except for Daniel, were more friendly. They played with me; they praised me if I did something well; they encouraged me to try again if I failed. Daniel continued to be sullen. He tried to beat my brains out at anything we played, from Monopoly to tennis.

The latter was to become harder and harder for Daniel, although he was an excellent player (he had entered and done well in several junior tournaments) because after my first two weeks living with him, Uncle

Bernie took an active interest in improving me. He arranged for a group tennis lesson at the nearby racquet club and had the same pro come over to teach me privately on Friday afternoon. He also hired a swimming instructor, "to work out the kinks in my strokes." I merely knew how to stay afloat, not cut through the chlorine with the grace and speed of an Olympian. "I want you to be a strong athlete for camp," Bernie said with his characteristic frankness. "The popular kids at camp are the good athletes. If you're just smart, they'll pick on you." I wholeheartedly shared his worry. I was a geek and a half-breed: with so many tender spots I needed all the armor I could lay my hands on.

A math tutor appeared after my first two weeks at Baker Hill Elementary School because a teacher commented to Bernie that, although I was very bright, I wasn't as well prepared as the other students in that subject. My father, being a writer, had encouraged me to read books above my age level; as a result, Bernie received glowing reports from the English, history and science teachers. Especially the latter. My mother had pushed science on me. In addition to her belief in communism, she felt the future of humanity would also depend on our ability to conquer space. She encouraged me to read lots of young adult books on earth science and often took me to the Hayden Planetarium where she plied me with pamphlets and later quizzed me, pretending I was a contestant on *The $64,000 Question*—only I wasn't being slipped the answers. I got Hershey kisses instead of money.

How do I know what the teachers said about me? Bernie was direct. He called me into his study after my first two weeks at school, pointed to the deep red leather armchair opposite his oak desk, and beamed. "Your English teacher says you're reading at a twelfth-grade level. Your history teacher says you know more about the Civil War than she does. And your science teacher thinks you'll make an excellent candidate to try for a Westinghouse. He's a little concerned that the local public high school won't be strong enough in the sciences for you. He says that what he's struggling to get the rest of your class interested in is like kindergarten material for you. Oh," here Bernie looked up from his notes, "and he says you beat everyone in the chess club. Not the school tournament. You arrived too late for that. But he said you beat their best player." Uncle grinned and added, "Easily."

I nodded casually, preoccupied by my survey of Bernie's study, a room that was usually kept closed off.

"You didn't tell me." Uncle sounded accusatory.

"I'm sorry," I said.

The study was all deep colors. Recessed shelves were filled with sets of leather-bound editions of the Great Books (they were never read, of course); the carpet was maroon; the curtains were another shade of dark red. The furniture was heavy and square. The theme was blood and history. It was my uncle's throne room. His dark round face had the serenity of a king's. He wore bifocals to read from his notes, but he looked strong and his cello voice sounded omniscient. "You're apologizing for not bragging?" he said.

"I'm sorry," I said again.

He removed his bifocals and leaned away from his notes. "No, boy, you don't understand. You didn't tell me anything about school when I asked you. That's why I made a special trip to talk to your teachers. I assumed you were having trouble adjusting. You know your aunts predicted that you'd have difficulties coming from a public city school and competing," he grinned, "with our brilliant Great Neck students."

I nodded; I thought I would too. I was, in fact, not doing well in math, mostly because all year they had been studying other base number systems than the decimal and at P.S. 173 we were still working on simple multiplication. "They're pretty smart," I said. They were certainly articulate. And sophisticated: they talked almost like grown-ups about sports, television, music, movies and theater. But, oddly, almost none of them seemed to know how anything was made or why it worked the way it did. And politically they were babies: they believed President John Kennedy would never lie and that racism only existed in the deep South. "I can catch up," I said, worried that Uncle thought it was too hard for me because I was behind in math.

"Catch up?" Uncle rubbed his forehead, exasperated. "I was being sarcastic. I keep forgetting you don't know me very well. I was kidding you, boy. The children around here aren't smarter than you. You're smarter than them. You need a little tutoring in math, but even your math teacher thinks you're very bright. She said you've almost caught up on the whole year in these two weeks. The other teachers think you're the brightest kid they've got. I sent for your records—I know you're tracked into the special progress classes at P.S. 173—but I wanted to get a look at your IQ. Can you believe it, I had to call—?" Uncle waved his hand, saying goodbye to this detail. "That's not important. I got it today. You're at the genius level."

That startled me. The word genius had a special significance. My mother used it as the ultimate compliment. She told me there were merely a handful of geniuses in all of world history. In conversation her list of geniuses was brief: they were Marx, Einstein, Mozart, Tolstoy, and Ernie Kovacs—the only one I knew of who appeared on television.

"I don't understand why your mother didn't tell me. Or your father. He was always proud of you, I have to give him that. But what were they thinking of? Letting your brain pickle in that . . ." Bernie shut his eyes and gently rubbed them. "Solidarity with the working class," he mumbled.

Rise with your class, not out of it—my Daddy's phrase. He had beaten those *Gusanos,* beaten them quick. Uncle Bernie himself said that someone he knew—a very powerful man in the Democratic Party, I overheard Uncle Harry explain to his wife—believed Kennedy was going to lose in '64 unless he did something to overshadow the humiliation Castro had handed him. Bernie had said, "Jack has to prove he can stand up to the Communists." (Bernie usually called the President by his first name; I naively assumed they were friends.) By the time I had this audience with Uncle I felt more encouraged about my future. My parents weren't defeated. Hang on, I thought. Wait for me. I'm coming to help.

"My school was okay, Uncle," I said. I was pleased Uncle realized I was smart, but I didn't take the IQ test seriously. I knew my mother had worked in the PTA to stop that testing because it wasn't fair to the poor. Made sense to me. After all, I knew more than other kids because my parents read books. They weren't rich, exactly, but they had the education of rich people and they didn't have to work in what my father called mind-numbing jobs. (With apologies to the current rage in psychology for testing, although modern culturally neutral IQ tests are based on different criteria, they still have a conventional standard of what intelligence is, and I take their results no more seriously than the older clearly biased versions. So do, I believe, the more thoughtful educators and child experts of today, who know that such tests measure only one piece of the puzzle of human capacity and achievement. However, in Great Neck in 1961, a high IQ was regarded as a sacred fact, almost an obligation.)

"But you prefer your new school, don't you?"

I nodded without much conviction. I didn't. What I had liked about school in New York City was the company of other children. The learning and studying was uncomfortable. My parents had showed me on many occasions that what my teachers told me, or what was in the books (especially history books), were simplified (and in some ways incorrect) versions of grown-up knowledge. I wanted to get right to the grown-up learning.

"Aren't you happier with children who are as bright as you?" Uncle laughed at himself. "I mean, at least closer to being as bright as you."

I thought of them as brighter, I really did. They knew what clothes were cool. They knew sophisticated expressions. One girl said ciao instead of goodbye and I remember how impressed I was that she knew Chinese. And, most of all, they were brimming with what I interpreted as self-confidence. They believed they were right even when they were dead wrong. Sometimes they convinced me I might be wrong when I knew I couldn't be. And when finally proven wrong, they showed no embarrassment at their previously mistaken confidence. But I didn't like them, because what they respected were all the wrong things: they were interested in me because of whose nephew I was; they were nicer if you got A's than if you got B's; they were mercilessly derisive if you messed up in athletic games and slavish if you were expert. These were bourgeois values. I knew that much from my father and mother, I knew these children were overwhelmed by bourgeois qualities—competitive, acquisitive, and snobbish. I didn't blame them for their faults. Ruth had often told me people were inevitably going to be hard-hearted and materialistic in a society whose mechanism depended on inequitable rewards. (Stalinists have a behaviorist view of humanity.) Despite my disapproval I was attracted to my schoolmates' smarts, beauty and wealth; I wanted their respect and I wanted to best them at everything. But I didn't like them. After I wiped out the top chess player in the school I accepted warm congratulations from kids who had been disdainful of me only an hour before, walked down the hall to the boys' room, found the stall farthest from the swinging door, flushed the toilet, cried, banged the door and cried some more. "I hate them," I whispered into the rushing water. But I dared not complain to Uncle. I couldn't risk being sent to live with one of my aunts. After all, I had been raised by Marxists and I knew about the power of Capital—Uncle Bernie was the Tsar of the Rabinowitz family and I meant to stand beside his throne.

My uncle's domestic routine changed. He arranged to be home more often. The weekend after the IQ revelation he took me to his country club to show me off. He provoked a chess game between me and the grandson of the owner of a chain of New York retail stores. (Bernie and this Retail King were soon to be competitors.) Bernie stood behind me throughout the game and watched, although he didn't know anything about chess. His presence dried up my throat and knotted my stomach. Pieces blurred, diagonals wavered, and I felt doomed. But I couldn't surrender to the pressure. I reminded myself how much was at stake, that I had to win to keep Bernie's favor.

My opponent was tough, as tough as Joseph. He was familiar with the opening I tried; I couldn't remember the right moves because of my nerves, and I got in trouble.

The Retail King gloated. He said something to indicate he was sure of his grandson's victory. From behind I heard my uncle's cello rasp: an angry and guttural scrape of his bow. "It ain't over yet," he said. His hand spread over my head, fingers massaging my skull so that the skin shifted like the loose fur of a dog. "Never give up," he whispered. I remembered Joseph telling me while we lay in bed my last night in Washington Heights that he thought when I fell behind I was too quick to counterattack. He said I was so good at defense he might not be able to beat me if I simply dug in and forced him to prove his advantage was a winning one. I tried that this time, adopting passive tactics, working to relieve my positional congestion, and overdefending the obvious point of attack. My opponent hesitated to go for an all-out King's side assault and gradually his advantage began to stall.

The Retail King became impatient with his grandson. "This is going on forever and nothing's happening," he complained in a mumble. "I thought you said you were winning."

"He *was*," I answered. Uncle and his friends laughed heartily. (There were two or three other club members who took an interest in our match.)

"I still am," my opponent said. "I'm up a pawn."

"So what?" I said, contemptuously. "You don't know what to do with it." I had seen a winning attack for him half a dozen moves ago, a line I would have been glad to try if our positions were reversed. I learned a lesson about defense that day, namely search with an enemy's eyes for your defeat and then decide your strategy.

He attacked at last, only now it was rash. My overdefended position recoiled at him. In a few moves he was destroyed. There was something magical and tragic about the turnaround. Yet I felt unaccountably sad at the devastation, the rageful vengeance of my cramped pieces once they were liberated. I had never enjoyed a win so little.

Uncle, however, was gleeful. I was surprised at the childish way he goaded the Retail King. "Told you it wasn't over. That's always been your problem, Murray. You take things for granted."

"Come on," the Retail King said to his grandson. "We're late." He yanked his heir out of the chair. I was disturbed by so harsh a reaction to failure. After all, they were in a direct blood line, not the more distant relationship I had with Bernie.

Uncle rubbed my hair, put an arm around my shoulder as we walked to the valet parking, and said loud enough for the Retail King and my foe to hear, "You're a born winner, boy." Once in the car he asked if there was a special toy, some treat he could buy me on the way home. I said no. I didn't feel deserving. There was something ugly to me in my victory. I couldn't identify what and that also bothered me. Uncle said, "Virtue is its own reward, eh? I'll say this for Ruthie. She didn't spoil you. She didn't make the mistake I made."

He asked me to explain what had happened in the game. I told him about Joseph and his chess books and the principle of overdefense. The next day, when I got home from school two boxes were waiting for me. They contained almost every chess book in print as well as a handsome wooden set and a wallet-sized travel set that could be folded flat. The latter was made of black leather with my initials in gold. Inside the wallet were bright red and white plastic pieces fitted with magnets so they couldn't slip.

As soon as Bernie showed his pride and interest in my intellectual abilities, my aunts, uncles and cousins (including grouchy Daniel) were more than friendly—they became attentive to and somewhat worried by my opinions. Wearing the robes of Uncle's favor and approval I was treated with a miniaturized version of the deference and awe accorded him.

The exception was my cousin Julie, beautiful twelve-year-old Julie, Uncle Harry's youngest. She had reached an early maturity, with breasts and hips, and a gleam of subtle mockery in her eyes for her older male cousins. She had treated me as an equal when I was the family alien. She continued to treat me as an equal in my new role as Uncle Bernie's Special Project.

My first full experience of the new family attitude to me was a gathering on May 19th to celebrate my uncle's fifty-fifth birthday. I used to move among them without being noticed much, except for the occasional remark that I had my father's Latin looks, a comment made in a dubious tone and that, then and now, I associate with racism. In fact, my black hair, brown eyes, thick eyebrows, and tanned skin could have been inherited from Papa Sam and Uncle Bernie as easily as from Francisco and Grandpa Pepín.

That day, all during the afternoon athletics and the dinner, I seemed to be the focus of my aunts' and uncles' interest. The racist undertones remained, however, in spite of the newfound admiration. After the birthday dinner we gathered in the living room. The adults sat on couches and wing chairs, arranged in a semicircle facing the latticework of leaded glass windows. Teenagers and children stood or sat on dining room chairs that had been brought in by the maids and placed in a row behind the heavier permanent furniture. Uncle Harry reminisced about the doubles match in the afternoon. He made much of the moment when I threw my tennis racquet down in disgust at missing an easy put-away. He said it showed my Latin temper. Actually the other Rabinowitz players had raged louder at their mistakes. At one point Danny threw his racquet over the fence and out of the court. But his ill humor went unremarked while Harry noted mine.

Another indication of its racist content is that Bernie didn't enjoy hearing my anger characterized as Hispanic. When Uncle Harry said in apparent good humor—"That's his Latin temper"—Uncle Bernie frowned.

"That's his will to win," Uncle Bernie corrected his brother in a stern tone. "And a good thing too, because he can be a great man." He proceeded to tell the room about his investigation into my academic record, including my IQ score. All the aunts and uncles, all the cousins—except for Julie, who looked unhappy—listened as if it were a matter of the gravest importance.

[I cannot emphasize enough the worshipful attitude of most of the Rabinowitzes toward material evidence of superiority, whether it was IQ tests, victories at games, degrees from Ivy League colleges, awards from professional organizations, or their favorite standard—money. Besides the fact that they were culturally inclined to this focus—the double whammy of living in America and their origins as poor immigrants—I believe Papa Sam's traumatic business failures during the Depression and their lowly status as not only Jews, but Russian and Polish Jews, infused these symbols of security and recognition with a powerful narcotic of affirmation that they became hopelessly addicted to. In a sense, just as the Latins in my family worshipped an illusion of social redemption which was to recede as they approached it, the Jews pursued symbols of success instead of real achievement, and were ultimately to feel hollow. Their own judgments and likes or dislikes were irrelevant: if the world didn't give them an award for it, then it wasn't worth doing. In one way, the Rabinowitz children were spoiled; in another, their childhood had a Dickensian gloom of joylessness.]

I was worried by Bernie's bragging. The eyes of my family—those wide-apart, slightly startled and clever Rabinowitz eyes—all tracked me. I was especially bothered by the amazed, almost appalled look on the faces of Aaron and Helen, Uncle Bernie's son and daughter. They had come home from college for this occasion. Unbeknownst to me they were having difficult times academically—which meant they were having an altogether miserable time since it was the current all-important symbol in their lives. Every compliment Bernie spoke about me was a blow to them. I sensed that much at least. I looked away from their hurt and envy to concentrate on Julie. Her beauty and genuine friendliness was attractive anyway, but it was her precocious sexual maturity that had a special significance for me. And her frown of disapproval about Bernie's talk was intriguing.

After telling the room what my teachers reported about me, Bernie hit them with my IQ. (It was said and experienced as a coup de grâce.) He went on to describe the chess match at his club. He told how I had fallen behind, how the Retail King goaded me and how he had encouraged me to "Never give up!"

At this point, Julie commented, quietly but distinctly enough to be heard, "That's disgusting."

"Julie, don't interrupt," Uncle Harry said automatically, without bothering to turn his head in her direction, as if this were an injunction he had to make often.

Julie's mother, Aunt Ceil, looked puzzled. She was much less intelligent than her husband and daughter; or at least claimed ignorance so they frequently needed to explain things to her. Julie and Harry behaved as if the need to correct Ceil was an annoyance, but it supported Uncle Harry's fragile self-esteem (he suffered greatly from living in the chill of his brother's gigantic shadow) and also nurtured Julie's genuine self-confidence. "What do you mean, dear?" Ceil asked, loudly, so that Uncle Bernie paused. "Rafael wasn't being disgusting."

"Not *him*." Julie shut her eyes, drew her legs together, coming to attention and inhaling. This pushed her breasts out against her angora sweater. I watched them.

[Strangely, perhaps hilariously, I must attempt to explain my interest in her breasts. I had been prematurely sexualized by my mother. The ways in which that made me different from other nine-year-olds requires careful consideration. After all, it is difficult enough to make correct distinctions between normal childhood sexuality and adult sexuality. Consider the mess geniuses such as Freud and other psychological theorists made of infantile sexuality, a concept they were brilliant enough to discover and human enough to equate with adult passion, especially as regards volition. That error led Freud to overrate it, Jung to dismiss it . . . This gets into a technical argument of little real use. But if a clear explanation eluded two generations of brilliant scientists, what hope do I have of elucidating the difference between normal childhood sexuality and that of an incest victim? Only this, that I have the benefit of their brilliance and error and, of course, the advantage that I experienced it myself. At nine I knew there was adult arousal, adult orgasm and understood erections in a pragmatic postpubescent way. I had been erect on at least three occasions because of the touch of another person, an important difference from the normal childhood experience of accidental or self-stimulated genital excitement. By logical extension that meant I had a tactile understanding of sex (the most profound understanding one can have) as well as the non-reproductive interest adults have in the human body. A normal nine-year-old boy (I mean, of course, a non-sexualized nine-year-old) might have factual awareness, might understand that Julie's breasts were a symbol of her adulthood and wish to see them, but he would not be genitally aroused by them in the adult way. To be even more precise about the distinction, a normal boy would not think that he *ought* to be aroused, would not aspire to be aroused. I did. I looked and thought, or rather willed myself to feel that I should like those breasts. At night in bed, when I was most lonely, missing the fantasy of my courageous and beautiful parents, I had begun to masturbate. Again, not in the adult sense, not because I was, to put it crudely, horny. I masturbated because I knew I could, as a matter of mechanical fact, not as part of normal child-like self-stimulation, which is for the pleasant sensation itself, unaccompanied by fantasy or an attempt to reach orgasm. No, my self-touching was that of an odd little man, wishing to heighten the experience using memories of my taboo experiences with my mother and hoping to achieve a climax as she had. Why this ambition? A blossom of reasons: to imitate the behavior of an adult male: to be desirable to my mother: to win back the love and comfort I had lost. My behavior wasn't really mature sexuality, with the desire to touch others and be touched by them, and it wasn't child-like self-pleasuring. I had been spoiled, unable to be a man or a boy and yet longing to be both. Thus, a twelve-year-old girl with the secondary characteristics of a woman seemed a perfect love object. Alas, I have succumbed to jargon.]

I looked at Julie's precocious breasts, her full lips, her long black hair (pulled back that day), her intelligent eyes, and felt I loved her, that I wanted to marry her. What she said that afternoon about Uncle Bernie's bragging made me love her more.

"I mean it's unfair of Uncle Bernie to tell everyone what Rafael's IQ is." She pronounced it RAY-FEEL, but my love for her continued to grow unchecked. "And I think it's disgusting to make him prove he's smart by beating another boy at chess."

"Julie," Uncle Harry said in the same critical tone he had used earlier, only it was more serious this time. This time he turned away from his brother and faced her, to emphasize his disapproval. "That's a very rude thing to say to your uncle. I want you to apologize."

Julie blushed. "I won't apologize," she said and clenched her fists, more to steel herself than to threaten. "He should apologize to Rafael."

"Julie!" Uncle Harry shifted forward to the edge of his seat—he was on one of the couches opposite Bernie's position in a wing chair—and wagged a finger at her. He *was* threatening.

"Take it easy, Harry," his sister Sadie said in a mild, humorous tone. "She's a woman now so you won't have any of your sisters on your side."

This comment broke the tension, causing general hilarity among the adults and teenage cousins. I didn't laugh, but I understood at least part of Sadie's remark. The other prepubescent children grinned reflexively at the grown-up amusement; they were puzzled, however, and searched their parents' faces for more information.

Julie's blush, needless to say, deepened. Her fists opened, however, and she didn't drop her eyes. "I think I'm right," she said with an effort, yet still loudly and clearly enough to be heard through the laughter.

Harry had his way out. It did involve humiliating his daughter, however. "Well, if she's got The Curse I can forget about an apology." This provoked bigger laughs from the adult males. There were looks of embarrassment on most of the aunts, including Julie's mother. Bernie's wife, Aunt Charlotte, appeared disgusted and Aunt Sadie frowned. The teenagers were deeply embarrassed. The kids were baffled. (I knew that meant Julie was menstruating. My mother made a sarcastic remark about The Curse as an introduction to her scientific explanation of the soggy red mass I found unflushed one morning. So I was right to love Julie: she was a little woman to my little man.)

Julie sagged. This time, she certainly looked as if she might cry.

"I don't think I understand, dear," Uncle Bernie's cello cut off all the uncivilized ruckus. He was given immediate silence to play solo. And I understood why he had such command. It wasn't merely his power and wealth. He made music while the rest of us made noise. I believed he represented what was wrong with the world but I was enthralled by the graceful sound of his evil. His tone to Julie was gentle; in charge, yet unhurried and tender. "What's wrong with my enjoying that Rafe won?"

"That's not what I said!" Julie was exasperated, embarrassed, and defeated. She looked at me for the first time. "I'm sorry . . ." she stammered to me. "I'm glad you're so smart and you won." She looked back at Uncle. I wanted to fling myself at her feet and promise to die for her. "I just meant you shouldn't talk about him to all of us like that—even if it is all good things. It's like he's your pet. And you shouldn't make him perform for your friends. He shouldn't have to win some dumb chess game to prove he's smart."

"Of course Rafe's not a pet." Uncle nodded slowly in my direction with regal grace and smiled broadly. "I'm proud of him. He's my nephew and when my relations do something I'm proud of, I want to tell the world." It may have been projection, but I swore I saw Aaron and Helen stiffen. Bernie had said nothing about his children throughout the afternoon games and birthday dinner. In fact, I don't think he addressed a single comment to them. He uttered a perfunctory thank-you on opening their store-bought gifts whereas he made a fuss about the poem I wrote to him, a quite dishonest—I thought at the time—verse of gratitude for his rescue of me. "You miss the point about the chess game," my uncle continued his exquisite melody. "Rafe did win. He didn't have to. But he did. He's not just smart, he's got the will to use his brains."

I felt the heat of their feelings and was warmed. Their love, their envy, their admiration, their pity—especially Julie's—was palpable, a nourishment.

[Let me be clear: I played my role enthusiastically. I was nine and ought not to be blamed, but I'm sure there are those who will blame me anyway, although they might express their disapproval politely. Not having sympathy for me. Amazement at my behavior. Not understanding how anyone could live that way. Sympathy, empathy, an understanding heart—they are talents, or at least faculties, that have to be developed, and regrettably their training is in short supply. I was not my real self to my mother's family: I lied implicitly and explicitly to them, although they meant me no real harm. Indeed, by their lights, they offered only kindness and acceptance. If you cannot see this situation as tragic, and instead must find someone to blame, you have several candidates and certainly I should be considered the prime one. But I must risk your intolerance by not understanding the thoroughness of my acceptance of Uncle Bernie's favoritism or the pleasure I took in triumphing over my cousins. Indeed, I was proud of the cleverness of the false self I created and the lies I told. To conceal this aspect would—as is so often the case in autobiography—sentimentalize my state of mind and eliminate the ambivalence and complexity which makes the human character worth studying in the first place. I needed Uncle's praise. His admiration was not as satisfying as living with my parents and possessing their love, but it was the best substitute available. I must accept blame for that fault, if you wish to label it as a flaw. I must accept ownership of a need to be the special heir of a powerful male. It is natural and it is also me.]

I lived in terror of losing my new crown as Prince Rafael. I told few outright lies and I told fewer truths. No feeling was revealed or given a voice without first undergoing a meticulous examination by the Stalinist censor and Jewish coach in residence in my head. I was undercover. I still had no Walther PPK, yet I was a master spy stalked by jeopardy. I was a Martian in residence on Earth, wearing a superbly crafted false skin of obedience and innocence to cover the otherworldly horror and beauty of my real self. I had my father's letter (I changed its hiding place often to avoid discovery) to read in the locked bathroom, or when I was supposed to be sleeping. After finishing a re-reading, I often held my little penis and manfully tried to stroke it to summon a passion as yet unborn. In the morning I had no reluctance donning my disguise. Would these people have loved and admired the real Rafe? No. I was not wrong about this assumption: if discovered, that child would have been cured or destroyed. He had to be kept hidden in his cramped cellar, quaking at the sounds of the policeman's tread.

I did not step forward and announce to everyone that I still loved my father and mother, that I had worked so hard to win the chess game in order to keep my uncle happy with me, that although I smiled when Bernie said I was going to begin Hebrew school to prepare for my Bar Mitzvah, I didn't believe in God and certainly not in the notion that I was Jewish, fully Jewish. Instead, I interrupted the scolded silence of the Rabinowitzes—shamed by hearing Bernie say I had the will to use my brains (with its implication that they did not)—and I asked Julie in a solemn voice, "Do you play chess?"

She looked confused.

Danny said, "Girls don't like to play chess."

Julie said, "That's ridiculous. I just don't know how."

"I can teach you," I said, moving toward the hall. "Come with me."

"Some other time, Rafe. We have to get going," Uncle Harry said and groaned as he rose from his chair. Inspired, there was a general commotion of goodbyes. They were relieved to go. They worshipped Uncle, but there were no comfortable benches in his temple.

I seized this moment of general noise and movement to slip up to Julie. I got on my toes to bring my mouth near her ear, exposed by the backward sweep of her hairdo. I admired its small perfect form and whispered to it, "I love you." She turned toward me in surprise, opening her lips. Yet before she could speak, I quickly, more like a stab than a caress, kissed her cheek and hurried away, frightened.

Heart pounding, I hid in the pantry and ignored the faint calls for me to come out to say goodbye. I had allowed Julie (and whoever else might have seen) a peek at my real feelings. I was in a panic, afraid I had lost control. I stayed hidden behind stacked cases of soda, particularly because I could distinguish Julie's voice above the others, mispronouncing my name as she wished me well.

Eileen had the night off. Once the guests were out the front door, Uncle Bernie—not Aunt Charlotte—called out that it was time for me to go to bed.

I emerged from my hiding place. "*You're* putting me to bed?" I asked as I approached Bernie in the kitchen.

"Think I don't know how? I put your mother and her brothers and sisters to bed a thousand times. Mama and Papa Sam used to work late at the store. At your age I was in charge of getting everybody to eat dinner, clean up, do their homework, and get into bed."

"Really?" We were walking down the hallway of Papa Sam's old wing, toward my bedroom.

Bernie laughed, a deep chord of pleasure. "Can't picture it, huh? You bet I did. Mama and Papa had to work to all hours at night. So I was the Little Father of the family."

I took his hand, his monkey's paw, strong, thick and warm, the knuckles decorated by fine black hairs. "I'm sorry, Uncle," I said and meant it.

We had reached my room. The chess set he had given me was on my bed, the pieces set up to move 14 of José Raúl Capablanca's first win of the World Championship Match against Steinitz. In the box of chess books Uncle had given me there was a collection of Capablanca's best games. He was a Cuban prodigy, a world-class competitor while a mere child, a champion as a teenager, and one of the greatest players of all time as an adult. I was infatuated with his games, identifying, or wishing to identify, with a Latin genius, and, of course, genuinely moved by Capablanca's purity and grace as a tactician. He was the Mozart of the game, a beautiful killer. Uncle looked at the pieces, frozen in the combat of giants, as if their presence were an affront. I assumed the mess bothered him. I let go of his hand and said hurriedly, "I'll clean it up."

"Sorry for what?" his voice asked after me as I swept away Capablanca's army. "You said you were sorry. Sorry for what?"

I had to think. I had forgotten what we were talking about. Remembering, I explained, "I'm sorry you had to take care of everybody when you were so little." I finished putting the chess set away. I turned back to Uncle. His round infant's head was cocked, curious and somewhat timid.

"I didn't mind taking care of them," he said. "I'll tell you something." Bernie sat in the child-size folding chair at the pine desk near the window. It had a view of the tennis court. Beyond there was a slice of the circular driveway. The headlights of one of our relative's cars bounced as it swung toward the main road. Uncle looked huge in the small seat. I sat on my bed, attentive. "I'm still taking care of them. I'm still tucking them in and checking their homework." There was a note of discovery in his voice. He raised his eyebrows and grinned with regret.

"I'm sorry," I said again. I was sincere, although not honest. I felt sorry for him. What else did he know but control? He was obliged to be in charge from when he was my age. I knew how hard that was: I remembered the loneliness and fear of being on my own for just two nights and days. I admired my uncle, despite the dubious morality of his success. I understood that the survival of his family had depended on his ability to harness capitalism's power.

He woke up from his contemplation. "Why are you sorry? I liked being in charge."

"I'm sorry 'cause you didn't have a choice," I said.

He bowed at that, as if I had produced an idol he was obliged to worship. He twisted his wedding ring again and again, eyes fixed on its gold.
"Are you happy here?" he asked and looked up at me.

I was afraid of his question. Was it a prelude to bad news? I didn't believe for one moment that I could allow myself to express any ambivalence. "It's great here!" I said with a piercing note of enthusiasm worthy
of the Broadway stage.

Bernie straightened. His worried grin opened to a smile.

"Thank you so much, Uncle," said Little Orphan Rafe. I rushed toward him, partly to hide my face from the pressure of his gaze, as well as
to let go of the real gratitude I didn't want to feel. What an alloy of manipulation and reality I was. (At the time, I believed I was a total liar.) I
hugged him with abandon, pushing my face into his blue silk tie and
Turnbull & Asser white shirt.

"Oh, that's okay, boy," his cello rumbled with regret. He squeezed me
tight. "You're such a polite and good boy. You don't have to thank me. I
didn't mean that." Gently, he urged me off from the finery of his clothes.
I was crying. From stress more than anything else: the dread that yet another horror was about to happen. "You're welcome to stay here no matter what, until Ruthie—until your Mom gets well—or even longer if
she likes. Maybe she'll come and live here too. But is there anything
wrong? Anything you want to be different?"

I moved away from Uncle with my face averted. I controlled the tears,
relieved there was no bad news. The emotional release and his kind reaction encouraged me, but only some. To repeat: I couldn't be sure that
I could afford to admit to a single genuine desire.

"You can tell me," he played low. "I won't get angry."

"Can I see my Mom?" I asked fast, as if the speed would somehow
make the request less of a risk. It had been more than a month. I wondered sometimes if she was still alive. They talked about her as if she
were, but that hardly reassured me. I knew that grown-ups lied, especially about important things.

"Well, she's at the hospital and I don't think they allow children
to—"

"Okay, forget it," I said fast, hurrying to reel in my request. I yanked
hard, hoping a quick retraction might also remove the memory of its existence. I knew he wasn't telling the truth. There was no obstacle capitalism could put in place that my uncle couldn't have removed for his
convenience.

"You miss her," he said as if this were a surprise. Was he surprised that he couldn't completely replace her for me? Or was he surprised that *he* didn't miss her? I think his lack of feeling for her, and the enjoyment of raising her child, was a mystery to his conscious mind. Although only nine years old, thanks to a boy's understanding of competition, more intimate and honest than any adult's, I understood there was some pleasure for my uncle in my mother's psychotic breakdown: the pleasure of winning, a clear confirmation of his superiority. Of all the siblings only Ruth had spurned his help and now she had to accept it, to submit her most precious possession to his control.

"Not too much," I said and almost believed the lie.

"What about your father? Do you want to see him?"

I was on full alert now. In the primary imagery of the paranoid and apocalyptic sixties, my bombers flew to their fail-safe positions and prepared for nuclear conflict. "No," I said.

"Why not?"

Why not? My God, I hadn't thought up a why not. I used the child's best defense. "I dunno," I mumbled. "I'm tired," I said.

"Think about it. You can go to sleep in a minute. Don't you want to see your father?"

I shrugged again and fell onto my bed. There was a unquiet silence, the false stillness of an ambush. From my sideways view of Uncle he remained in a fixed position on the child's chair, elbows resting on his legs, his Buddha head in his hands, contemplating me. I wasn't going to stop his interrogation that easily. "Am I going to visit Grandma and Grandpa this summer?" I asked in an innocent tone.

I was a good tactician. Bernie's focus was disrupted by my introduction of Jacinta and Pepín. He sat up and released me from his stare. "Your father's parents," he said and paused at the fact, as if it had a significance he understood only then.

"I always visit them in the summer." Whenever I re-read my father's letter, I wondered if something that he alluded to—a secret method for my mother to get a message to him—might be known to Jacinta and Pepín. But I didn't have the nerve to ask Bernie to allow me to phone them. Besides, I was discouraged by the fact that they hadn't called or written me.

"I thought you wanted to go to summer camp," Uncle said. We both knew that was an evasion. He was embarrassed by it himself. He stood up, went over to the window and pulled the cream-colored drapes closed.

"Does camp go the whole summer?" I prodded.

"Well, we'll figure this all out. Hey, it's very late. Hurry up and get into your pajamas."

I rushed to do so. I picked out light blue cotton Brooks Brothers pajamas. Of course, the store label had resonance for me, sending out a strong vibration of both my parents. Holding the fabric, I could hear the voices in lively argument—funny, passionate, and clearly audible above the hubbub of their communist friends. I remembered the surf of New York City's traffic and I felt their breath on my cheeks as they dispensed good-night kisses.

While I stepped into the bottoms, Aunt Charlotte walked in. I hurried to cover up. It seemed to me she looked at my penis with an almost scientific dispassion, but I'm confident this is a notion of my premature sexualization. It's fair to say that I had little more than the status of a servant in her eyes, only I was extra trouble since I took up more time and energy than the lazy cook or incompetent maid. I don't think she really noticed my nakedness. But she did have a male member in mind.

"It's late," she said to her husband in a scolding and suggestive tone. "I'm going to bed now. Aren't you coming up?"

"Just want to tuck Rafe in," Uncle answered in a sheepish, unmusical voice. I was surprised by the meek tone with which he answered his wife. I had little experience of their relationship. He rarely talked to Aunt Charlotte when I was around, mostly because they weren't often together, usually only on state occasions such as that day and thus when they had their guests to entertain. I knew she wanted him to join her upstairs for the pleasure a man could give a woman. I understood in a way that normal children couldn't have. His abashed response interested me. Was there something frightening about having sex with her? I looked at her, considering this side of their relationship. Charlotte's hair was in a Jackie Kennedy puff, dyed a severe, almost platinum blonde. Her full bosom was more of a formidable shelf than the warm small pillows of my mother or Eileen's lively freckled pair. And certainly she had nothing of the mystery and thrill I associated with the birth of Julie's passionate and idealistic breasts. I wished I could see them all bare to the waist, nipples revealed, instead of mere glimpses of white flesh flowing into intervening bras. I wished they were all on a couch together with their tops off and I could go from one to another, resting my head on each, sailing on Aunt Charlotte's, asleep on my mother's, laughing on Eileen's, and growing up on Julie's.

"Well, I'm going upstairs," Aunt Charlotte said. "I don't know how long I can keep my eyes open so don't take forever."

No doubt she believed I had no idea what all that meant. I hurried into bed while Uncle turned out the overhead light and desk lamp. I hugged my knees to my chest. I felt safe, but lonely.

Uncle's perfumed face closed in on mine. I don't remember which cologne he used that day. He changed brands often. He had worked in the fish market at age twelve, in the predawn before school, and had been teased about the smell by other boys. (This was another sad story of his childhood that he told proudly as a happy and formative time which had not hurt him, but helped make him great. Underneath the braggadocio, however, it was obvious he felt otherwise. He worked at the Fulton Market for only three months and yet the stink of that humiliation still clung to him in his twenty-four-room Great Neck mansion.) He hovered above me, smelling tart, the starched cuff and gold arrow-shaped link scraping my chin. His hairy fingers rested on the pillow. "You really miss your Mom?" he whispered into my ear.

That sent a jolt through my heart. I shut my eyes at the pain. "Yes," I whispered and held my breath at the chance I took.

"You really want to see her?"

"Yes," I leaked the word and shut the valve fast, afraid of the deluge behind it.

"But if you had to choose—" he hummed in my ear, the bow slipping and buzzing its note, "who do you want to live with, me or your parents?"

I hugged my knees, turned my face toward the pillow, away from his arrow cuff link and pungent face. "I want to stay with you, Uncle," I said and shivered with such violence that my teeth clicked together.

He kissed my temple and left. I waited until I felt sure he wouldn't return. Then I told myself to let go and cry. But there were no tears. I lay awake until Eileen came in from her night off. She was humming a tune. I knew she had been out on a date with a carpenter from the Old Country who had just emigrated and found a lot of work in the area. They were good times for New York; houses were going up everywhere on Long Island. I got a glimpse of Eileen tiptoeing across the hallway in her bra and panties as she went to fetch a clean nightgown from an ironed pile of laundry left by the maid outside her door. I pushed my hurt aside and instead held the fleeting image of her pink skin, mottled and bright, fixed in its place. I listened to her sing

"Danny Boy" while she brushed her hair in the bathroom. She sang low so as not to wake me. Her voice was sweet, free of the darkness and intensity of my kin. I heard no sadness or loss in the lyrics. I fell asleep without tears.

CHAPTER SIX

Misdiagnosis

AUNT SADIE WAS NERVOUS. SHE SWUNG MY HAND BACK AND FORTH TO soothe me, but her palm was gooey with perspiration. I was nervous also. I tapped my brown loafer on the marble floor, unable to stand still. We were in a large reception hall of the Hillside Psychiatric Hospital, a private facility set on four acres in Great Neck, waiting for Uncle Bernie to return from his conference with my mother's psychiatrist. We hoped Uncle would come back with permission for me to see her.

The central hall was part of Hillside's grand main structure, a stone and marble mansion built by one of the Roaring Twenties stock manipulators. His ruin in the crash and the forced sale of his possessions at depressed prices led to Hillside's creation by Dr. Frederick Gulden. Gulden was an early refugee from Nazism, trained by Freud himself, who had earned the good will of a wealthy widow for the "cure," or improvement anyway, of her manic-depressive son. In the late forties, Dr. Gulden added a three-story concrete dormitory for patients and the mansion itself was converted into offices and consulting rooms. The reception hall's high domed ceiling and sweeping marble staircase was an oddly imposing entrance for a sanitarium. Nor did the mahogany reception desk and its sour-looking occupant, Bill Reedy, make the place more inviting. Reedy drank heavily every night, nursing his hangover while on duty, staring at prospective patients and their nervous families through blood-shot eyes. He looked enraged that anyone had dared to enter his domain.

I was intimidated by Reedy's face: it started my foot going again. That disturbed Aunt Sadie. "Don't tap your foot, honey," she whispered and its echo scurried across the marble floor up to Reedy's florid cheeks and squinting eyes. His frown intensified, as if focusing to identify me as a miscreant. That set off another fusillade of foot tapping, completing the vicious circle.

Uncle Bernie was conferring with Dr. Halston, who ran Hillside in the 1960s for the semi-retired Dr. Gulden and, given Uncle's stature, had personal charge of my mother's case. When Bernie returned with him, they led us into a reception room in the dormitory wing. Its walls were painted green down to the level of the mopboard, then white down to the linoleum floor. The room where I saw my mother was furnished like a doctor's reception area; a couch, a love seat, a coffee table, a lamp, a magazine stand, and museum posters of masterpieces on the wall.

Ruth sat on the couch, shoulders slumped, eyes fixed on a copy of *Time* that someone had left open on the coffee table. Her hands were limp at her sides, palms up. She was very thin and her face seemed devoid of blood. I almost screamed—I thought she was dead.

Aunt Sadie sensed my panic. Her grip tightened and she pulled me close. My mother didn't look up.

"Your son is here," Dr. Halston said. He had thinning blond hair combed straight back and, as long as I knew him, wore glasses whose thick black frames looked more like goggles for a World War II pilot than aids for weak vision. He was a compact muscled man with a military posture, but his voice was thin and rather high-pitched. There was little natural warmth in it to begin with and Freudian training washed out any other coloration. "Ruth. Look." Halston waved Aunt Sadie to bring me forward. "Your boy is here to see you."

As soon as I realized she wasn't dead, I recovered my nerve. I broke off from Sadie, rushed to the couch and tried to hug my mother. I hadn't been given any instructions or advice by Halston about how to behave or what to expect. (I cannot fathom why not; I am amazed that no one discussed her condition with me in advance. Perhaps my memory is faulty.) Ruth didn't move. I pressed against her awkwardly, trying to fit into her limp body. Once I had wished she would never touch me again; now I longed for the energy and passion of her abuse. I felt her love for me had died.

"Mom," I said into her ear, leaning my cheek against hers, my arms attempting an embrace. "I'm here, Mom." I held a rag doll. I smelled her. Someone had perfumed her with an unfamiliar scent. She was dressed in a demure white blouse and a long blue skirt. The clothes were unlike her usual style, which was both more dramatic and always sexy. Hillside was really an institution for the wealthy, or more often, the mentally ill relatives of the rich. Except on the rare occasion that a patient became violent and required restraint (before the widespread use of antipsychotic drugs), Hillsiders were encouraged to dress neatly in their regular clothes; even catatonic patients were carefully groomed. Obviously someone had made up Ruth for the occasion. I was put out by her rouge, her eyeliner and lipstick. All were applied by a stranger. The incorrectly drawn lines made this Ruth seem more like an lifeless imitation, an approximate mannequin of my mother.

I wanted to cry but I was worried the visit would end if I showed I was upset. Dr. Halston urged me off Ruth, saying, "She needs time to get used to you being here." To hide my feelings, as I slid away to sit beside my mother, I pushed my forehead against the outside of her shoulder. She didn't react, hands at her side, palms up, face immobile, eyes blank and fixed on *Time* magazine. It was awful, worse than any state I had yet seen her in, worse than her rages, worse than her brutalized body on the car, worse than her seductions. She wasn't human.

Uncle came forward. His cello didn't resonate with its usual confident sound. "Ruthie," it quavered. "Rafe is fine, as you can see. We all want you to get better. Everything is taken care of. I don't want you to worry. When you're feeling better, you can come live with me, and raise Rafe, and . . ." I heard a tear in his powerful voice, a note of boyish awe and distress. He trailed off. "And . . . uh . . . everything will be okay. That's all. Don't worry."

I peeked out at Ruth's profile. I felt that Uncle's unusual display of tenderness would move her. No. She looked right through him.

Sadie covered her mouth, quelling a sob. She turned away. Bernie backed off, appalled. "I thought with Rafe here . . ."

Halston took my uncle by the elbow and moved him toward the door. He mumbled as they retreated, "No, she's totally schizo. Living in a fantasy world. I doubt she knows you're here."

Aunt Sadie choked out a phrase, "Don't talk about it."

I assume Sadie meant because of my presence, since Bernie's reaction was to glance in my direction. He turned, and nudged Halston to turn away, giving us their backs while they talked in whispers. Aunt Sadie joined them, forming a huddle at the far end of the room.

It was a short time, perhaps ten seconds, while Sadie, Bernie, and Halston weren't looking my way. I continued to kneel on the couch, angled toward my mother, my nose flattened against her shoulder. Ruth's eyes suddenly flashed with intelligence and mockery; big and green, they moved in their sockets while her head remained still. She whispered rapidly, lips hardly moving: "Rafe. Don't react. Just listen. Everything they say is a lie. I'm playing possum. I'll come get you soon as I can. Keep my secret or they'll put you in here. Be brave."

"Mom . . ." I started to answer, but I was stopped when Ruth's eyes glazed over and died. I glanced at the door to see Halston peer in our direction. Because of their thick black frames, his glasses were so obstructive that I couldn't tell whom he was scrutinizing, me or my mother. After a brief survey, Halston returned to the huddle.

Immediately Ruth's eyes came to life. Her lips moved into a smile. "Fool," she whispered.

"Mom," I said into her ear. "You're not crazy?"

Her profile crinkled with delight. "No. Read *Hamlet*."

"What . . . ?" I leaned closer. Her eyes dulled. Presumably Halston or Bernie or Sadie were checking on us.

Ruth resumed her lifeless pose, but she did whisper with unmoving lips: "*Hamlet* by Shakespeare. 'I am but mad north-north-west. When the wind is southerly, I know a hawk from a handsaw.' "

"Rafe, honey," Aunt Sadie called. "Come on. Kiss your Mom goodbye. You'll see her soon."

"What!" I shouted, startled. Ruth instantly returned to her impression of catatonic depression. (A very good impression if my memory is accurate; good, but no mimicry should fool a careful—or, at least undogmatic—doctor's examination.)

"We have to go, honey," Sadie said. She came near and beckoned me off the couch with an offer of her worried hand. I made sure to kiss my mother goodbye since the real her was present, entombed in her imitation of a corpse.

After I got up, Sadie bent down and kissed her little sister on top of her head, pressing her lips into my mother's thick mass of black hair. Sadie almost broke down again. Her plump torso heaved and she gasped out, "Get better, Ruthie. I miss you."

I wish I could report that my mother's eyes flickered, that she gave a signal she had heard her sister's loving if stupid plea for a happy ending, something that wouldn't have risked exposure of her performance and yet could have eased Sadie's pain. [I learned later how rigid, how tyrannical paranoia can be, especially when it is fueled by traumatic and therefore confirming events. My mother could no more feel pity for Sadie or trust her love than she could decide to discard her delusional and grandiose fantasies because they were interfering with her ability to be a good mother. There is no prison guard more alert or more tireless than mental illness. If Ruth could have trusted Sadie, then she could have trusted anyone; if she could have broken the wall of her terrible secrets just once then it would have crumbled altogether. There is no such thing as being a part-time paranoid psychotic.]

I glanced back as Sadie led me out. The mannequin of my mother was still propped up on the couch, dead. While we walked to my uncle's limousine, I marveled—silently, of course—at how she could possibly keep it up; hour after hour, pretending not to hear what was said to her, pretending to have no needs or desires.

"Is she like that all the time?" I asked Uncle Bernie, breaking the heavy silence of our ride home.

Aunt Sadie covered her face, overwhelmed by my pathetic question. Her reaction surprised me. We had no common ground: I was awed by my mother's strength of will; Sadie thought I was in agony about Ruth's condition, suffering from that vision of her as a zombie.

Bernie squinted at the view out his window. "No, not all the time."

A long silence.

"It's like she's dreaming," Aunt Sadie said, uncovering. She showed me a tired, but brave smile. "She's awake but she's dreaming. She wakes up sometimes, asks for things she likes. And she asks about you. She's not in pain. That's what the doctor said, right Bernie?"

"Yes," Uncle hissed. The farther we got from the sanitarium, the angrier he seemed.

He hated my mother, I knew that. They hated each other. I had to remind myself over and over: my uncle was bad. No, not bad. My mother herself had made the distinction to me: he was a good man who believed in a bad system.

There was another long silence. I shut my eyes somewhere in the middle of it and pretended to sleep. My aunt brushed the top of my head after a while and mumbled, "Poor baby."

"Sleeping?" Uncle asked. Sadie indicated yes. "What a mother," he mumbled with surprising bitterness, as if he were the son who had suffered.

"When will they start the treatments?" Sadie said.

"Tomorrow." Bernie's music was a single note, low and angry. "They'll do a series of ten and see if there's improvement."

"They put her out, right?"

"Of course! This is one of the most expensive and advanced psychiatric hospitals in the country."

"I know. It's wonderful of you, Bernie—"

"I'm not looking for thanks, that's not what I mean. I mean they know what they're doing. They use anesthesia and the voltage is set lower . . . Anyway, she won't know a thing about it. He said it lifts them out of the severe depression so they can begin treatment. You can't deal with her the way she is now. How can Dr. Halston talk to her? She's unreachable."

"I pray it works, that's all."

"Look. Anything is better than how she is now. It's a living death. It's worse than death."

"Shh!" Sadie was in pain. "Don't say that."

"It's the truth, God damn it."

"No, it's not. There's always hope."

I did not understand the implications of their conversation. Since I intend this to be read by a lay audience I should state what is obvious to any professional: although electroshock therapy is advocated today as an effective symptomatic treatment to major depression and is in use on roughly twenty percent of its sufferers, nevertheless, no one, including its admirers, considers it to be appropriate in a case of paranoid psychosis or posttraumatic stress, the two indicated diagnoses of my mother's condition. [Readers of my book *The Soft-Headed Animal* know that I do not believe in the use of the electroshock under any circumstances, including major depression. Evidence that prolonged use of electroshock therapy causes permanent brain damage is plentiful and there is no scientific proof that it cures depression itself. However, as stated above, even ECT's advocates would not recommend its use on a patient with my mother's problems.]

My mother received the wrong treatment. Nine-year-old Rafe did not know that. He did not know that keeping his mother's secret was doing her harm. Nor is the mature Rafe confident that had I been less skillful at deception, had I been found out and forced to confess that my mother wasn't really withdrawn—that she spoke to me and said she was deliberately fooling her doctors—I am not confident that I would have been believed. I hope I am not overstating Dr. Halston's error. All doctors make honest mistakes, especially when a clever patient is deliberately deceptive. But I am sure that, having made his diagnosis, Dr. Halston would not have been quick to overrule himself because of the account of a child, a child who could easily have made it up out of his own fantasies. Moreover, I understood my mother's motive and I respected it. What is madness to a normal adult made sense to me as a traumatized child: my mother, acting out of her paranoia, meant to be loving by her injunction that I should keep silent and not identify myself with her and her "cause." That would only have landed me in the care of the same monsters who tormented her. It is hard to understand, but Ruth's actions, which seem heartless and unconscionable to a normal person, were, by her lights, the actions of a loving mother.

I found *Hamlet* in one of the red leather-bound volumes in Uncle Bernie's study. I had permission to take any of those books. I was a precocious reader and I enjoyed being one. My father encouraged and praised such behavior and Uncle Bernie was in awe of it. The desire to please my absent father and to dazzle my prideful uncle got me to open the classics, but the power of their narratives kept me going. (With apologies to Alice Miller, I'm not sure anyone would develop a taste for culture without what she characterizes as abusive parental behavior, namely the narcissistic parent who demands precocity as a precondition for love. She's right, it isn't a recipe for happiness; but without it, Mozart wouldn't have existed.) I had already read *Plutarch's Lives* and a volume of *The Decline and Fall of the Roman Empire* out of Uncle's library. I had avoided Shakespeare because verse, much less verse in the form of dialogue, was discouraging. That same afternoon, after my tennis lesson, dressed in sweaty shorts, I pulled the second of the two-volume set of Shakespeare down from its high shelf and propped the book on my naked thighs. I remember the leather sticking to my skin. It took a while but I found the speech Ruth had quoted. Along the way there were other lines that lured me into reading scenes out of order. (To this day I have never read a Shakespeare play from beginning to end, but always out of sequence, as if I were assembling a jigsaw puzzle.) I was struck by lines that still resonate with meaning for me. "There is nothing either good or bad, but thinking makes it so" might well be on every psychiatrist's wall, for whether it is good philosophy or no, it is a necessary premise of the therapeutic process.

I loved the play. How could I not? Indeed, it is an indication of my mother's intelligence that she knew provoking me to read it would continue and extend her influence despite being held prisoner in the sanitarium. Think of it from her paranoid point of view: Hamlet has been separated from his noble father—a warrior king—by an evil and powerful uncle who has robbed Hamlet of his mother's love, his father's life, and his own claim to the throne of Denmark. There is, additionally, especially when read during the Freudian literary atmosphere of the early sixties, the incestuousness of Hamlet's relationship to his mother combined with a political rebel's philosophy, born of alienation. Hamlet is keenly aware of the world's hypocrisies and corruption: he is the disenfranchised child of a social system in the hands of the cowardly and murderous uncle. And this analogous predicament is delivered with poetic genius, its despair and rage sung so beautifully that the most painful moments also inspire delight in the sheer elegance of Hamlet's mind. Indeed, I found the Prince's situation—including his death—enviable. What to the normal adult mind is a tragedy seemed almost a triumph to nine-year-old Rafe.

My love affair with *Hamlet* caused trouble for me with Uncle Bernie's son, Aaron. It happened during a family brunch held shortly after his graduation from college, about a month after my visit to the sanitarium. Sadie's and Harry's clans were all there. It was a bon voyage meal: Aaron would be living on a kibbutz for the summer. After he returned, it would be decided whether he would go for his MBA, as his father wished, or try his hand as a painter, as he wanted. (I doubt my uncle believed there was anything to settle. But Aunt Charlotte, who was on the board of two museums, who frequented art galleries and bought Impressionist paintings, was a wavering ally for her son's artistic ambition.) His sister, Helen, was upstairs, supposedly suffering from a stomach virus, one of the convenient illnesses she contracted to avoid family occasions. My near calamity developed when Uncle bragged one time too many about me, in particular when he bragged about my reading *Hamlet*. He knew I had because the same day I visited my mother at Hillside, I asked permission to take the two-volume Shakespeare set into my room. I made the request both to read *Hamlet* and to make the point that I was doing so. (My pleasure in the play was real; so was my vanity.) So far, Aaron had suffered silently through itemizations of my brilliance on his visits home. He had already been tortured last night with my various school accomplishments. When

Uncle remarked over brunch that I knew *Hamlet* so well I could quote long passages from memory, Aaron gave up his stoicism.

"So what?" Aaron snorted. "He's nine."

"That's what makes it remarkable!" Uncle dropped his forkful of Nova, en route to a bagel. The heavy silver tines struck the equally heavy silver serving dish and resulted in a vibrating chord that harmonized with his remark.

"Enough!" Aunt Charlotte shouted. "We all admire Rafael, but enough is enough!" She pushed a stiff hair-sprayed lock off her brow. Its unloosed presence on her forehead was a novelty, caused by her exceptionally vehement movement. She managed her emotions carefully: that outburst was unmanaged and unique.

Bernie ignored her, nevertheless. He pressed Aaron. "How can you say he's nine as though that makes it nothing?"

"I mean . . ." Aaron was understandably aggrieved. His eyes stayed down, staring at the linen and his Limoges plate. His tone, although whiny, was not loud. "All I mean is—what difference does it make if he memorizes it? He can't understand it. He's memorizing the way a monkey memorizes."

This time Julie, my old defender, didn't speak up. She sighed loudly, a habit she has to this day when confronted with a situation that she wishes were different but that she has given up trying to change. At the time I gave her no credit; I concluded she was reacting with a girl's cowardice and hypocrisy. (My new understanding of male-female relations came from Hamlet's scenes with Ophelia. I had gloomily ignored Julie during brunch, ready to send her packing to a nunnery—that seemed an especially harsh punishment for a Jewish girl—if she dared to bring up the subject of my earlier rash declaration of love.) Despite my newfound contempt for the ways of women ("You jig, you amble and you lisp. You nickname God's creatures and make your wantonness your ignorance."), I spoke up for myself mostly to impress Julie. "I know what it means!" I shrieked in outrage.

"Oh yeah, right," Aaron said.

"Ask me any line in the play!"

"All right, all right," Uncle said. Other adults were groaning or mumbling to Aaron or to each other. They were sick and tired of this punishing dance Bernie made me and his children perform. I thought their disgust and unhappiness was directed solely at me. I believed they envied me. I didn't understand that besides Aaron, whose envy was merely a reflex triggered by his father, the others mostly felt pity for me—I was a sad little boy whose mother was crazy and whose father was worse, a Communist.

But I thought I was the noble Dane. I got to my feet, towering over the table at my height of four feet eleven inches, and brandished an elaborate silver spoon. "Go ahead. Ask me. What do you want to know? You want to know what quietus means? You want to know what bodkin means? Or fardels? Do you know what it means when Hamlet says to Horatio, 'If he but blanch, I'll tent him to the quick'?"

Someone, I think it was Uncle Harry, laughed. I must have made quite a sight. Some of my relatives were staring at me, open-mouthed. I didn't look at Julie, the real object of the performance, but I was sure she must be impressed. I stayed on Aaron, who was not shocked or amused. He was humiliated. His cheeks were red and his eyes were downcast.

"Well, wiseguy," Uncle Bernie asked him. "You started it. Do you know what it means?"

I was huffing from the exertion of my outrage, but I maintained my pose of challenge and contempt.

Aaron raised his eyes to me. There was hate in his look; the cornered kind, the hatred of a wounded animal for its tormentor. "No. But I know what 'the incestuous pleasure of his bed' means. Do you?"

It was an accident, of course. Aaron was attacking my presumed ignorance of sex. However, I had looked up incest in the dictionary, along with all those other words, and I understood very well what it meant. Indeed, I didn't have knowledge; I had experience without knowledge. For a ghastly moment I thought Aaron wasn't merely challenging my vocabulary, I thought he was exposing my secret. It took no more than a second for me to realize he couldn't be. Then my vanity was tormented. It longed for me to shout out that I not only knew what was meant by "the incestuous pleasure of his bed," I had lived it—though not as a pleasure. I was a merciless competitor in those days. I didn't shy from delivering the final killing stroke and that certainly would have been a coup de grâce. Don't misunderstand. I didn't come close to a confession about the incest. But I was transfixed by the prospect, at how it would be a perfect victory. I suppose I could have said I knew what incest meant; that wouldn't have been considered suspicious. And yet I felt merely saying the word was an admission I understood its meaning in an immoral way.

I didn't have to solve my dilemma. No one gave me a chance to answer. Aaron's vocabulary comprehension challenge was considered inappropriate by the adults. While I stared at him, stuck with my wheels spinning, he was rebuked. He lost even his mother's support; she was particularly outraged and ordered him out of the room. Aaron stormed off and I was brought a hot chocolate as either a compensation or a sedative. I drank this in silence, temporarily afraid of cultural arguments. They were more dangerous than their surface made them seem. I peeked out at Julie from time to time. She looked unhappy, but beautiful. Her long hair, black, shiny and very straight, trailed down the shape her new breasts made against her white angora sweater. I told myself she was sad because she had lost my love, in the same way that I thought Ophelia was tormented by Hamlet's abrupt coldness.

"My lord, I have remembrances of yours that I have longéd long to redeliver."

"No, not I. I never gave you aught."

"My honored lord, you know right well you did; / And, with them, words of so sweet breath composed / As made the things more rich: their perfume lost, / Take these again; for to the noble mind / Rich gifts wax poor when givers prove unkind."

I thought our situations weren't so different than the noble Dane and the fair Ophelia. Her father was a Polonius to Bernie's Claudius. I was in a fight to the death with the usurpers and couldn't risk exposing my cause to her for fear she would betray me. I had to pretend hostility and, like the Prince, I felt a generic disappointment in her sex. She was weak, after all. "Frailty, thy name is woman." And my brave mother was weak. Her weakness was manifested differently than that of Hamlet's mother, but at the source, Ruth was just as weak and just as useless.

When the brunch ended, Julie got up and moved behind my chair. I ignored her. She tapped my shoulder. "You said you were going to teach me chess." She spoke softly.

"Aren't you going home?" I said in my new guise as the ungracious Hamlet.

"No, Dad and Bernie have work to do. You're stuck with us all afternoon. Come on, teach me how to play." She took my hand and urged me out of the chair. We went to my wing of the mansion the quick way, through the kitchen and the maid's quarters.

Entering my room, Julie halted, put her hands on her hips, and swiveled her torso to survey it. There was a maternal attitude in this pose. I had a flash of insight: she was being my big sister, a sort of halfway mother. She didn't love me the way my grandiose imagination wished. I hadn't discouraged her with my new gruff tone. There was no romantic interest to discourage because she saw me as a little boy, not a tragic prince.

"This is very cute," she said, moving toward my desk and inspecting the books and papers on it. She lifted a story I had written for English class. "You did this? It's so long." She flipped the pages and came to the illustration at the back. I had scrawled line sketches of my characters in black; the only other color, a trail of blood leading to the scene of a killing, was crimson.

"Oh," Julie commented in dismay about my gruesome drawing. The corpse was female and the flow of blood trailed more from her groin than her heart, although in my story she had been accidentally stabbed through the bosom because she intervened between two men dueling over her. The assignment was to tell a story that would illustrate the theme of medieval chivalry. I had gotten an A minus, with a long comment that although my story was well-written and had something to do with chivalry, it wasn't really to the point. And the drawing was scary rather than ennobling, my teacher had complained.

"Read it," I said in a gloomy voice. Perhaps its violence would teach her not to play at being my mother.

"Okay," she said and sat at the desk.

She was very beautiful. Her skin was brilliantly white and her cheeks were red with good health. She was on the swimming team at her school; the daily workouts lent her an energetic and luminous appearance. Her neck was a column framed by long black hair that was also luminous. She glowed from her new maturity, her nascent womanhood. Looking at her, entranced by her reposed and yet robust beauty, feeling that she didn't see me as a lover—as a man who would satisfy her—but merely as a boy whom she ought to soothe and encourage, I got my first truly spontaneous erection. It is difficult for me to know, despite years of analysis, whether my feelings for Julie would have occurred anyway without my premature sexualization and my abandonment by Ruth and Francisco. But what is the point of such speculation? Those events *are* me, as much a part of me as my face, as much of a mask or an honest countenance as I make of them.

"It's very sad," Julie said, lowering the pages of my story. She frowned and her tone was stern. She appeared not moved, but disapproving.

"It's supposed to be sad," I said petulantly.

She softened. "You have a great imagination." She put the story back on the desk and turned to me purposefully. "Are you happy living here?"

Was Polonius behind the arras eavesdropping? I wondered. "Oh yeah! It's great here. Uncle Bernie's great to me. He gives me everything I want."

"He's very generous. But there are no kids living here. Aaron and Helen are all grown up. I heard you didn't want to live with Aunt Sadie, but maybe you want to live with us. We're only fifteen minutes away. You could still see Uncle Bernie. We come here practically every other weekend. And you would be close to your Mom."

I was mesmerized by the prospect of living in daily proximity to Julie, within hearing of her gentle voice, within range of her warm brown eyes, within reach of her angora sweaters and what gave them shape.

"You know Bill can't be bothered by me, but he'd love to have a kid brother." Bill, her sixteen-year-old brother, was present for only the must-attend family functions: Passover, Thanksgiving, Uncle's birthday. He was a moody adolescent, in rebellion against his coarse businessman father. He grew his hair long, he played bass guitar in a rock band; I was told he asked to join the Freedom Rides. I don't think I'd ever heard him speak more than a mumbled monosyllable. He didn't seem companionable.

Not certain whether to refuse or accept, I looked toward the window. A taxi entered our driveway, heading for the front door. There was a single passenger, a woman who appeared, in the flash I got as it went by, somewhat like my mother.

"Think about it," Julie said. "I'll go with you to talk to Uncle Bernie about it. He won't mind. I mean, he'll miss you, but he'd understand that it's better for you to be with other kids."

The doorbell rang. The mansion was so large there were two extensions for its bell. One was at the head of my hallway, near the kitchen so that the gong sounded loud to us.

"There's somebody here!" I said, thrilled, and ran off, to get to the door first. I saw a woman's figure through the side panel of glass. My heart raced as I pulled on the handle.

I got it open and there was my mother, an unexpected and, for a moment, unmitigated joy. Her head was covered by a scarf (she had been shaved near the temples for the electroshock therapy), there were black half-moons under her eyes that turned them stark and vacant, and she clutched a small overnight bag to her stomach, as though protecting it

from a thief. I was so happy I couldn't speak. I ran to hug her. I pressed
into the bag rather than Ruth.

"Hello, Rafe," she said in a high singsong. She held on to the suitcase
with one hand and hugged me into the luggage with the other.

I didn't answer or question why she had given up her pretense. I
pressed my chest into the overnighter and buried my face into her neck.
I was blind to the crowd that gathered to confront her; I listened while
she greeted her family over my head.

"Hello, Julie. You look so pretty. Is everybody here? What's the occasion?" Ruth's words implied she felt at ease, but she spoke haltingly and
at least an octave above her usual range. She sounded weak.

Julie didn't respond.

"Ruth," Aunt Sadie said. "Does Dr. Halston know you're here?"

"Hello, Sadie. Hello Bernie. Charlotte, you look gorgeous. As usual.
All of you look so handsome and beautiful. I came to see Rafe. He's got-
ten tall, hasn't he? He's almost up to my chin. Come on, let me see you,
Rafe."

She pulled me off her. I looked into her big haunted eyes. There was
no glint of green, no mischief, no sexiness. Only hunted desperation.
"There . . . Don't cry." She smeared tears off my cheek with a cold hand.
I didn't realize I was crying. "I came to visit for a little while. That's all
right, isn't it Bernie? You won't object to that." Her voice squeaked with
false lightheartedness. It was grating and worried me. Where was she?
Where was my mother? Each time I saw her she was refashioned into a
grotesque version of one of her extreme moods. (Indeed, I was witnessing, and had been witnessing for a year, the steady disintegration of her
personality, accelerated by stress and her improper treatment.) "You have
to let me see my boy once in a while, don't you? That's just common decency. Even under capitalism they have rules about that." Now there was
a hard, furious undertone. "Even sharecroppers are allowed to see their
sons."

Bernie mumbled that of course she was welcome. Sadie led us into my
bedroom. Sadie was the only one who came along and she appeared to be
nervous, wary of my mother. I guess, because of the spitting incident at
the U.N., they thought of her as violent. Or perhaps it was that Ruth
used to throw things when she fought with them as a child. She was the
youngest of a large family and no doubt she felt frustrated at her relative
smallness and consequent inability to impress them. I had heard stories
of her rages: once, she hit Harry with an ashtray; another time she had

poured syrup over Bernie's head. Since she had done violent things when they thought of her as normal, it was natural to be fearful of her in this unbalanced condition.

My mother didn't enjoy seeing my room or my schoolwork or spending time with Sadie and me. She looked at everything I showed her as if it were a potentially infectious object. She handled my story, for example, the same one Julie read, with the tips of her fingers and dropped it almost immediately back onto the desk.

"Sadie, could you get me something to drink?"

Sadie hesitated. "I don't know what they've got. Let's go in the kitchen and—"

"They have everything here," my mother interrupted. She didn't sound sarcastic, she said it gloomily. "Right, Rafe?"

"They don't have Coke," I said. "They have Pepsi."

"I'll have a Pepsi. Could you get it for me, Sadielah? Please, big sister?" She pretended to be little. She put her hands up in front of her chest, cocked her head, and pursed her lips. It wasn't good mimicry. There was too much mockery in it; whether of her own helplessness or of Sadie's attitude, wasn't clear.

It irritated Sadie. She stood up straight and said sternly, "Ruth, don't do anything foolish. You're out. That's the important thing. If things continue to improve you'll . . ." Sadie looked at me and stopped talking.

"Get visiting privileges?" Ruth spoke very softly, without threat, and yet she was ominous.

Sadie frowned. "I'll get the Pepsi. I'll be right back," she said and that did sound like a threat.

My mother watched her go and then turned to me, speaking hurriedly. "I can't fight his lawyers. I'll lose everything. And they'll keep on trying to get in. You know? They'll keep trying to get inside." She pointed to her right ear in a violent stabbing motion.

Of course, I didn't know what she was talking about. I knew it had something to do with me. "You're not staying?" I asked, although I knew the answer.

"He won't let me. I'm not well enough," she said and suddenly demolished her humorless whisper and grim expression with loud laughter and a display of teeth. But it wasn't a musical sound and her smile wasn't cheerful. Rage and fear were what they suggested, not good humor. She made a sudden grab for my arm and pulled me close.

I was scared by her grabbing me that way. In the joy of seeing her, I

had forgotten about her nighttime embraces. The aggressive move reminded me of what else the active Ruth was liable to do.

[This splitting off of my incestuous mother from the mother I needed
is a necessary creation of an incest victim's survival mechanism. The incestuous parent becomes a separate person with a separate set of memories for which there are a separate set of responses. Hence, in reaction to
severe abuse at an early age, there is also the creation of multiple identities for the victim, with different memories and different feelings.]

"Mom!" I begged. I was horrified, not only by the idea of her being
sexual, but of doing it in Uncle's house with everyone nearby. I assumed,
with the classic victim's psychology, that I would be blamed and punished if we were found out.

But Ruth was merely pulling me close to whisper. To whisper in the
hunted voice of her paranoia: "Give me the message your father gave you
for me. Quick, she's coming."

Rattled, I shook my head no, unable to articulate.

"Don't you have a message?"

I shook my head no. I was confused and scared. Did she mean the letter? No, she meant a new message.

Ruth squeezed my arm. It hurt. "Tell me the truth." I shook my head
again and tears formed. She seemed angry at me. I felt I had failed: that
I was supposed to have gotten a message from my father or done something that would have made me available to receive one.

I tried to pull away.

"Don't lie, Rafe! Tell me!" She shouted. The words swirled at me out
of her blackened eyes, eyes that had seen something horrible. And they
accused me. "You don't expect me to believe he hasn't sent you anything!"

"Ruth!" Bernie was there. He yanked me out of her clutches and sent
me spinning. I must have gone into shock because I have no recollection
of the next half hour. I know the arm my mother had taken hold of was
bleeding because later on I remember sitting in the kitchen while Eileen
stained the scratches from Ruth's jagged fingernails with iodine. I do recall seeing my mother fall over backwards a moment after Bernie pulled
me away from her. It may be that she recoiled on her own. It may be that
he hit her. Also, I remember, or think I remember, what he said after she
fell. It sounds implausible unless one has thoughtfully analyzed the conflict in my uncle between his need to be victorious in all situations and

his equally strong need to be beloved in all situations. He pulled me off, and, as she lay on the carpet, he said, "I love you, Ruthie."

I never saw my mother again. She wasn't permitted to visit me when she was released full-time from Hillside. Dr. Halston believed that the shock therapy had cured her depression and that long-term analysis would eventually bring her to normality. She was told that if she worked with him productively she would be able to see me and finally live with me again. Uncle set her up in an apartment near Hillside with a paid companion and she had five sessions a week with Dr. Halston. He believed she was doing well at the time the Cuban Missile Crisis began. Even that, although it distressed everyone, didn't seem to agitate Ruth.

She sneaked off on the day of Kennedy's apparent triumph, when Khrushchev agreed to withdraw the nuclear devices from Cuba. She set up a sign in the windy U.N. Plaza. It read: THIS IS THE WAY THE WORLD WILL END. She poured gasoline over her head while a confused knot of people watched and then she lit a match.

She died without regaining consciousness three days later. I was told she had been killed in a car accident. I didn't go to the funeral because I became violently ill, vomiting uncontrollably for hours. A doctor injected me with what I presume was a sedative. I was kept in bed for two days. Uncle Bernie slept on a cot in my room the night of my mother's funeral. Years later Aunt Charlotte told me he had never done that for his son Aaron or his daughter Helen. She thought it proved his love. I think it proved he felt responsible.

CHAPTER SEVEN

Hamlet's Ghost

THE WEEK BEFORE CHRISTMAS A BOX SENT BY JACINTA AND PEPÍN ARRIVED on a UPS truck. It was their yearly Christmas package, jammed with a dozen gifts for me. Each was wrapped in red paper decorated by many Santas and sleighs, and each was tied with festive red bows and each was identified by a green card on which my grandmother had written in a large oval cursive: *Feliz Navidad,* followed by the person to whom she had apportioned the gift-giving. Five were ascribed to her and to Pepín. One apiece were credited to Uncle Pancho and a cousin my age. Those gifts were traditional, the usual amount that Francisco would hide in the back of his bedroom closet until the night before Christmas. They would be put under our tree after I fell asleep alongside his and my mother's gift. What was new were the five additional presents allocated to my father.

Uncle Bernie handled the problem of these gifts clumsily. The day they arrived he left instructions for them to be put in my room without ceremony. I found them when I came home from school and opened them with Eileen, my caretaker. She was offended by Uncle's treatment of the Christmas presents. She expressed that disapproval loudly to me and not at all to her employer.

"You're half-Christian. He can't hide from that. He should put a tree out for you and you should go to Sunday school. Don't tell him I said so.

It's not my place, but you've got people who believe in Jesus, whatever may be wrong with your father. And they mean you to know about Christmas."

Judging from the gifts, Grandma Jacinta's true intention was to keep me warm—she had sent three sets of pajamas. Living in Florida she must have had an exaggerated notion of New York's winter. There were also two sweaters, a package of underpants and another of socks. The remaining five presents were small toys: two Matchbox trucks, a set of dominos, a yo-yo, and a book about dinosaurs.

I thought they were pathetic. Cheap and too babyish for me—heartbreakingly inadequate when compared to even a casual purchase Uncle Bernie might make on his way home from the office. They made me angry. After Eileen and I opened them she left the room to put the discarded wrapping paper in the garbage. I threw the Matchbox cars at my Lego storage chest so hard that I dented one of their doors. I crushed the yo-yo with the heel of my brown loafer and I scattered the dominos all over the room by flinging the box. The top came off in mid-flight and the white ivory rectangles spun out. I spent the rest of my rage trying to rip the dinosaur book in half. I was only a little ways through the tyrannosaur's head when Eileen reappeared.

"My God!" she gasped at the wreckage I had made of the Catholic presents. She grabbed the book away and let out a torrent of words about poor children who needed things if I didn't want them and my not forgetting that it was the thought that counted and many other clichés. I didn't listen. I sagged onto the bed and tried to hear in my head my father talking on the Miami radio station. I could. Francisco still reverberated in the old radio console's speaker, the music of his voice lightened by a sexy melody that was quite different from Uncle's somber cello. I was discouraged by both male examples: how could I match their vigor, confidence and commitment to principle? And why were the women so weak and foolish, stuck in the literal world, believing it mattered whether I was grateful for toys, believing it mattered whether my father had sent a message while he was so busy fighting for the revolution?

Eileen's monologue came to an end with a dramatic exit, accompanied by this closing line: "And that's all I can say as a God-fearing Catholic!" She came back in a minute wearing her winter coat and carrying mine. "Come on," she said, shaking my jacket at me as if taunting a bull. "We're going to church."

"I don't want to."

"Your grandparents want you to."

"Uncle won't like it."

Eileen nodded, moving her red mass of hair with emphatic agreement. "That's the truth. If he finds out I'll lose my job."

This threat made the excursion attractive. I liked secrets between a man and woman: they betokened love.

Eileen owned a beat-up Plymouth, possibly the same make and model Grandpa Pepín drove. His was kept in immaculate condition, despite the role he played as chauffeur for an extended family that included many young grandnieces and grandnephews. By contrast, Eileen was single. Her unsteady romance with the Irish immigrant carpenter was often rocked by violent changes of mood about his drinking, flirtations with other girls and reluctance to marry. She slept at Uncle Bernie's six nights a week, spending her night off with an aunt. Thus her car was rarely used. And yet its interior resembled that of a suburban mother of five— litter covered most of the floor and every inch of the back seat.

We drove off to church without leaving a note for Bernie or Charlotte. Both were still in the city. Eileen was confident we'd be back before they arrived. It was a Friday afternoon in December, freezing and gray. There was no snow on the ground, but the black road was streaked white by frost. We were only a short distance out of Uncle's driveway before we had to stop at a light. A car pulled up beside us and a tanned handsome man beamed across Eileen at me. It was my father.

The sight was electrifying. It felt as if his smile surged through my chest. I called out joyfully: "Daddy!"

Eileen was confused at first. She stared at me as if I had lost my mind. Francisco honked to get her attention. She shifted her stunned look to him while he got out of his car and came around to my side. I rolled the window down, using both hands to do it faster. I don't know why I didn't simply open the door. Dad did. Because of my fierce grip on the window handle I fell out. My father lifted me up into his arms. I had forgotten how tall he was. I was five feet myself, only seven inches shorter than my powerful uncle. Francisco, although leaner and much less threatening than Bernie in his manner, was a comparative giant at six feet three. His hug lifted me off the ground effortlessly. All that grace and strength was thrilling. And no one, no one on earth has ever said Rafael so musically. He pronounced it several times while squeezing me tight. He rolled the "R" and separated the "fie" and "el" long enough so that it sounded like thc drumroll for the main attraction, the summoning of a magical being, at once heroic and mysterious. If only I could be the Rafael my father called for. I felt no regret that I wasn't, simply fascination with his desire. I listened for myself in Francisco's song of my name, ready to accept the role if I could find the necessary talent.

Eileen's half-a-year-long disapproval of my father was defeated in seconds by his charm. "What a beautiful accent," he said when she demanded to know who he was, although I had made that apparent. "I'm Rafael's father," he said. "Are you from Dublin?"

Soon he had Eileen blushing as he admired her fair complexion and red hair. He praised Guinness and Irish sweaters, gave credit to the wet climate for her beautiful skin and to Irish poets for her musical voice. As is true of any charming person, his flattery was so bold she had to conclude that either he was sincere or the most monstrous liar on earth. I could see from thc shimmer in her light blue eyes that she had decided my father was as innocent as a newborn. "Latin men, you know," my father said, "go wild for redheads. Just ask Desi Arnaz. I was feeling sorry for Rafe. Now I see he's been having the time of his life."

He told her, not me, that he had come over from Cuba to get me. We were going to Europe, he said, Spain first and then maybe Paris. I revealed no excitement, although my heart beat fast. I felt it going madly underneath my winter coat, wool sweater and white school shirt.

"Spain?" said Eileen. "With that fascist general?" I don't likc to makc myself out to be a snob (or perhaps a sexist), but I was surprised that Eileen was sufficiently quick-witted to know it was surprising that my father was willing to have anything to do with Franco's Spain.

"Ah." My father was appreciative. At this point we were talking in the frigid air by the side of the road. Francisco had pulled his car over to the shoulder; Eileen had left hers blocking the way. Occasionally cars went around, passengers and drivers peering at us curiously. "You know international politics. But why I am surprised? The Irish are not only the most literate people on earth, they're the most political. I'm sure there's a Provo in your kin."

"No sir," Eileen blushed again. "Thank goodness," she mumbled.

"Well, it's a terrible thing to admit, but Spain is more friendly to Cuba right now than we are and things there are loosening up. Everyone is optimistic that when Franco dies . . . When he dies—" Francisco crossed his fingers on both hands and begged the sky for a long moment before returning his attention to us. "Then maybe Fidel will have an ally besides Russia." Francisco put his arm around my head—I was right at the level of his shoulder—and squeezed. "I thought we'd go back to the home country and look for our people in Galicia. They must be there, you know. I'm sure you've got dozens of cousins just waiting to meet their American counterpart. And besides, you're at the age that James said should be every boy's first view of the Continent. Although I don't think he had fascist Spain in mind."

Francisco seemed relaxed and extremely happy. His deep tan certainly made us look pale and drab. He talked and talked—a free-ranging banter about Sean O'Casey, the cold, my height, Eileen's red hair—until I was shivering. "Drive him back to the house," my father said. "I'll follow you."

Eileen was silent for the ride until we pulled into the driveway. She said, "He's a charming man," in a serious tone as if she had discovered something very important and confusing.

My father parked opposite the front door and greeted us as we got out of Eileen's Plymouth with, "I don't see any cars. I take it Bernie's not home yet. Well, Rafael and I have a plane to catch at Idlewild, so could you help me get him packed?"

"Packed?" Eileen said. "You're taking him away now?"

"It's madness, isn't it? I flew in, bought Rafael's ticket, rented the car and drove here. We have to be on a plane in a few hours." Francisco moved closer to her and reached for her right hand. She gave it to him as if it were the most natural thing in the world. He squeezed it fervently while he made his plea, although he sounded casual. "I heard the news just three days ago. All this time I thought—" He let go of Eileen's hand to tousle my hair. "I didn't know anything about what's been going on. I have to have my son with me. He's my good luck." He gathered me to him again and squeezed my head with his powerful arm. "And my future. You understand. I couldn't wait another week, or another day and yet I have to be in Spain tomorrow. I have a very important, really crucial dinner with a Spanish publisher in Madrid tomorrow night. Rafael and I are on a nine-thirty-five flight. Someone's going to meet us at Idlewild at seven who's done me a great favor and gotten a passport for Rafe fast. There's no time. We should be there early since I can't afford to miss him. We don't have to pack a lot. I'll buy Rafe any other clothes he needs over there."

Looking back on it I have to admire the presumption of my father's request. He was asking Eileen not only to make no fuss about ending her employment, but to help him pack up her income and send it off as quickly as possible.

He won half the battle. She took us in, showed Francisco where my clothes were and even found us an overnight bag. (My father hadn't thought to bring one. "Men," Eileen commented with a satisfied smile.) Then she disappeared. During her absence, while casually picking out clothes, my father continued his gay inventory of Europe, of how we would see bullfights, Flamenco dancers, the armor of Granada, the Ramblas of Barcelona—a complete tour of the country where Hemingway and Orwell had found both bravery and cowardice, enchantment and disillusion. I didn't know what he was talking about; I strained to understand. But that was home to me: walking the narrow ledge of precocity to get a view of my Daddy's passions. My beautiful father was back and I was ready to follow him anywhere. He made no mention of the revolution or my mother—to maintain security, I was sure. We were, after all, still in the enemy's hands.

Eileen returned with a grim and wary expression. We were almost done packing. She stood in the doorway and looked dismayed by the full overnight bag. "Um, I was just speaking with Mr. Rabinowitz—"

"Is he here?" my father seemed alarmed. I worried at that—was he frightened? No, I decided, he was merely startled.

"He's still in town, but he'll hurry over in his car. He said you're to wait—he'll arrange for transportation to the airport so you won't miss your plane. He's definite about it. Doesn't want Rafael to go without him having a chance to say goodbye—and he wants to talk to you right away. He's on the line. There's a telephone in his study. I'll take you there."

My father smiled. He was relaxed and confident again. "Oh, I don't think so. There isn't enough time. I can't take a chance." He turned back to the overnight bag, pressed in one more sweater and zipped it up. "Say goodbye to your beautiful nanny, Rafe. We're off to our homeland."

"Oh, he's waiting on the phone. You have to at least talk to Mr. Rabinowitz."

My father said nothing to that. He picked up the bag and gestured for me to take his hand. I did. We moved to the door. Eileen stepped in our way. She was very nervous. I don't know if she was actually trembling, but she could have been.

"I can't let you go without talking to him," she said, voice low, eyes on the floor.

"He's just a bully," my father said. "He won't hold you responsible."
He pushed me forward around her.

She gave way, at least physically. She called to my father as we entered
the hall. "You have to talk to him. He took care of your son! You owe
him a few words for that alone."

My father's hand tightened on mine. His cheeks sucked in—that was
his private look of anger, a look I had never seen him show to a stranger.
Indeed, by the time he turned back to Eileen it was gone. But there was
rage, operatic and inspiring, in his voice: "If Bernie gave me every penny
he has, he would still owe me. Took care of Rafael!" Francisco gestured
to the heavens with his right hand to show the preposterousness of this
claim and moved away from Eileen, apparently ready for us to leave, only
he paused again to add this final thought: "You tell your boss to steer
clear of me. If I get my hands on him I'll kill him."

He *was* brave, after all. I knew it. Hadn't he stood beside Fidel while
the most powerful nation on earth blockaded and invaded poor Cuba?
No one else—except for my weak mother—would have had the courage
to defy Bernie.

Despite the blast of his threat to Eileen, my father continued to huff
and puff with anger after we drove off. I watched his lips move: tiny
eruptions of the furious interior monologue.

Let me hear you, I wished silently. Let me know your thoughts. But I
didn't have the courage to ask. Besides, I knew the gist of his mute
tirade. He was indicting Bernie: damning him for being a capitalist, for
taking me away from my mother and for being friends with a president
who had tried to destroy Fidel.

"I'm sorry," my father said on the Cross Island Parkway. We had been
on it for a while and these were his first words to me since we drove away
from my uncle's. I had given up on his talking to me by then and was
startled by the sudden and unasked for apology.

"What?" I said, confused.

He glanced my way. His eyes glowed: the tanned face made their
whites bright and lightened the brown of his pupils to a shimmering
amber. He had lost weight, I noticed from this view of his profile. The
tan disguised his gaunt condition. Francisco's cheerful cheeks were gone.
I didn't like this look. I associated weight loss with the last few visits I
had with my mother. Each time I saw her she had shrunk, each time a
little bit more diminished by her illness, the institutionalization and the
electroshock.

"Don't be sorry," I said and felt confused and sad. I wanted to cry, but I wasn't aware of why. I thought I ought to feel glad: I had been rescued.

"I know your uncle was good to you. Or tried to be. I promised myself I wouldn't talk like that in front of you. But she provoked me." He glanced at me again. "My God, you've grown! I'm lucky to have a son who's so handsome and so smart." Francisco returned his attention to the road, putting on his signal, moving into another lane and accelerating to pass. He talked to the world that rushed up to our windshield. "I have nothing to worry about. The future holds no terrors for me." My father glanced at me again and winked. "Not when I've got you to take care of me in my old age. I've got nothing to worry about."

At Idlewild Francisco was nervous. He leaned against the car rental counter sideways and kept an eye on the doors behind us. Once that paperwork was finished he rushed us to another building away from the terminal. It was a warehouse of some kind and we entered a small waiting room, bare of furniture. A sleepy clerk manned the only counter. Above it was a sign that said something about picking up international packages. The people who appeared to get slips of paper from the clerk seemed to be truckers or delivery men. Our wait felt interminable. I whined about being tired, thirsty, hungry and so on. Eventually my complaints wakened the attention of the clerk. "There's a coffee shop over there," he volunteered. "You can get him a doughnut or something."

"I'm waiting for someone," my father answered. "I can't afford to miss him."

"Oh yeah . . . ?" The clerk was interested. "Bringing a package?"

"No, we just agreed to meet here."

"No kidding. Funny place to meet." He peered at my father, was puzzled by his frank and friendly face, and lowered his eyes. "None of my business," he added.

"Let me go get a doughnut," I said.

"No. It'll just be a little bit longer."

"You keep saying that! Let me go get a doughnut."

"No."

"I'll be okay."

Francisco moved to the window to evaluate the journey. It was roughly a block to the coffee shop. I would have to cross one airport intersection. But there was a light and the only traffic seemed to be slow-moving buses and vans. Otherwise it was easy—a straight line.

"Okay." Francisco gave me a five-dollar bill. "Get yourself a chocolate doughnut and a soda. Also get me a black coffee and two packets of sugar. Although it won't be the honest sugar of Havana," he added with a feeble smile. Earlier he had tried to distract me from my fatigue and hunger with stories about Cuba. I had expected to hear thrilling accounts of fighting with Fidel's revolutionary army against the invaders; instead I heard about sitting on porches and drinking espresso and of cutting sugarcane in the field with happy peasants who were being taught how to read. To me his stories were a letdown. His time in Cuba either sounded too similar to being with our relatives in Tampa or it sounded like a fairy tale about a place where the good king is beloved by all the people for his generosity. I knew my reaction would reveal my embarrassing political ignorance and naïveté—the thoughts of a bourgeois American boy—so I suppressed them. Francisco told many details about harvesting the beautiful sugarcane, including how if you peeled it and chewed the softer interior, a moist liquid was released that tasted sweet. "When I visited Havana at about your age, I used to chew it. The candy bar of the poor, Cousin Pancho called it. And the kids in Cuba still do. I saw them when I volunteered to help in the fields. I saw a gang of kids ask one of the cutters and they shared it on their way home."

"Give you cavities," I said with solemn disapproval.

"No, no. It's not like processed sugar. The sugar of the sugarcane is pure. Doesn't bother your teeth or make you fat."

"Really?" I asked and was again assured of the cane's innocence. It really was a fairy tale kingdom, I decided. The sugar didn't even rot your teeth.

Crossing the intersection was a breeze and I was glad—unaccountably glad—to be alone. My father's unending talk about Havana, about my height, the relentless self-consciousness of being with him was exhausting. I bought myself a thick chocolate doughnut and was quite happy with its unnatural sweetness.

My father enjoyed his coffee, too. "Ah," he smacked as he finished it. "Not your grandmother's coffee. But I feel refreshed. You were right. We needed something." He squinted at the gray airport roads. "He's late," he commented anxiously. "We have plenty of time," he added, but sounded unconvinced.

I fell asleep leaning against the wall. The weight on my eyes felt especially heavy, so heavy I couldn't open them when I heard a voice penetrate my dreams, a voice I thought I had forgotten, and that I wasn't happy to hear. It was the man I discovered in our old Washington Heights hallway, the Asturian who had brought my father's letter to my mother. He was grinning and telling me that message again, or trying to, only his mouth was full of gooey, oozing sugarcane. I struggled to open my eyes.

I woke up to see him, the real Asturian, standing beside my father (actually dwarfed by my father) and studying my face doubtfully. He wore a brand-new blue pin-striped suit, with a white shirt and a blue tie. He was little and looked littler in this outfit, a man stuck into a box of fabric with a hole for his head. I noticed and remembered because Francisco made a fuss about it.

"Pablo!" Francisco smacked the Asturian on the shoulder with his hand and let it linger while his fingers squeezed with affection. "You're dressed like the chairman of the board of ITT," he continued. "I don't know whether to shoot you or ask for a job."

Pablo ducked his head and smiled sheepishly, both pleased and embarrassed. He answered in Spanish and I understood that he said something about looking respectable for the authorities. He specified which authority but I didn't know that word. It must have had to do with getting a passport for me since that's what he produced from his pocket, a pale green object, somewhat larger than a wallet, with the word PASSPORT in embossed gold letters and below it, also embossed in gold, the bald eagle, head turned ominously sideways to fix us with one eye, clutching arrows in its left talon and an olive branch in its right one. E PLURIBUS UNUM was written on a ribbon streaming from its mouth, and beneath the fearsome bird, *United States of America* was impressed in gold script.

"*Mira,*" Pablo said, opening it.

I scurried over to see what he showed my father. It was page four, mostly blank except for this on top—

THIS PASSPORT IS NOT VALID FOR TRAVEL TO
OR IN COMMUNIST CONTROLLED PORTIONS OF
CHINA
KOREA
VIET-NAM
OR TO OR IN
ALBANIA
CUBA
A PERSON WHO TRAVELS TO OR IN THE

LISTED COUNTRIES OR AREAS MAY BE LIABLE FOR
PROSECUTION UNDER SECTION 1185, TITLE 8 U.S.
CODE, AND SECTION 1544, TITLE 18, U.S. CODE.

"What does that mean?" I asked.

"Shh," my father said and clumsily pulled both me and Pablo away
from the package counter. From the moment Pablo joined us, we had the
clerk's full attention. He leaned forward to get a look at the object that
so interested us; he could easily see it was a passport.

I thought my father was inept at how he reacted to the clerk's scrutiny.
He backed us out of the anteroom and onto the airport road. We left
without watching where we were going. A taxi honked at us. We had to
scurry away as it passed, missing us by inches. I looked down at my feet
to make sure they weren't squashed. During my nap, the sunny winter
day had become a raw, foggy night. A heavy mist oozed moisture, a fine
drizzle. We were quickly covered by a sheen of water. We hustled under
a covered sidewalk leading to the terminal. I looked back. The clerk
stared after us, not amused at our comic departure.

"That was dumb," I said to my father. "Now he's watching us. You
should have acted like it wasn't anything special."

Pablo laughed. He had a row of tiny bottom teeth; two were black.
"Sam Spade," he said and rumpled my hair. His fingers smelled of tobacco.

"Nevertheless, Rafael is right." My father straightened and appeared
loftily unconcerned. "Let's walk casually into the terminal."

There were molded plastic seats in the Trans World Airlines terminal.
I had never seen that kind before and I was amused that their slippery
surface caused me to slide right off. I had to make an effort not to fall to
the floor.

Pablo took out a *Daily News*. He spread it open in front of him, the
passport concealed inside, so that to an observer he and my father appeared to be studying a news item together. I couldn't see that well from
my angle, but I could tell they were looking at a small black and white
photograph stapled inside the passport. It was of a boy, a boy who had
dark hair like mine and a nose like mine and high cheekbones with deep-
set wide-apart eyes that also resembled the general look of my face. But
my prospective doppelgänger had spread his mouth into a smile for the
photographer, a broad goofy smile that revealed a missing front tooth. A
tooth that I certainly still had in my head. "*Coño,*" my father said as he
looked at me and then returned to the photograph.

"Let me see," I said, trying to climb onto my father. I was too big for his lap. I leaned across his body and rustled the *Daily News*. "Is that supposed to be me?" I asked, I guess too loudly, because Francisco shushed me and Pablo groaned.

"Now *you* are not careful," he said.

"Well, I have all my teeth," I whispered with so much intensity that my father shushed me again. "And he has too much hair."

"Your hair could have been . . ." Pablo used the fingers of his right hand to imitate a scissor cutting. Half the *Daily News* began to unfurl and he grabbed for it.

"Oh, right," I said. And then I cried out with inspiration: "And I'll keep my mouth closed!"

They shushed me. My father seemed quite angry this time. "How many times do I have to tell you? Don't shout."

"Sorry." I slunk back onto my seat. "But he doesn't look like me," I said, having had a closer inspection. The resemblance was superficial. His face was narrower than mine, his eyes were almost in shadow they were so far back, and his nose was fatter, more squashed.

"Listen." My father took hold of my bicep. His fingers were long and strong; they seemed to wrap around my skinny arm twice over. "This is very important. We had to use another boy to get the passport. I didn't have time to get you to take the picture. There's nothing seriously wrong about what we're doing, but you can't talk about it. They won't look at it carefully. Just keep your mouth closed so they can't see your teeth. Okay?"

"Okay. I said that first." I pulled my arm free. It felt numb.

"And don't talk about it to anyone. Okay?"

"Okay."

I was miserable. My legs ached, my eyes burned. Was I sick? There was an uncomfortable heat snaking throughout my body and pulsing in my head.

We approached the ticket counter. My father held out the passports, ready to hand them over to the clerk.

You're with Daddy, I said in my head, and you're happy.

Francisco gave the ticket agent my passport. He opened it.

You're with Daddy, I repeated in my head. And you're happy, I insisted, more intensely to myself, the prayer reverberating in my aching skull. I hoped this would not only get us past the ticket agent but also cure my illness.

To my horror, the agent didn't merely glance at my passport. He kept it open and started writing something on my ticket. Later I discovered he was copying my passport number onto the stub.

But I panicked while the copying went on. You're with Daddy and you're happy, I screamed to my throbbing temples. We got through without incident and started the long walk to the gate. You're with Daddy and you're happy, I said, softer to my hurting head.

"They'll look at it again there," Pablo said. "Just a glance before you go in."

"It's okay," Francisco said to me. "They didn't notice. Like I told you."

Our successful fraud didn't relieve my symptoms. Instead, nausea accumulated with the other pains. You're with Daddy, I whispered to myself, and you're safe.

Francisco's anxieties seemed to have abated. As we walked, he talked eagerly of seeing Spain again, of the poets and actors and radicals he was going to look up, of the hellos and love he would carry to them on behalf of Pablo. Pablo interrupted to call my father's attention to my condition. We had reached the waiting area at the gate; it was already crowded with fellow passengers and their well-wishers.

"What's wrong?" Francisco put a hand on my forehead. "Are you sick?"

"I feel crummy," I said.

"You don't have a fever," he commented. "You're probably hungry and tired."

"I don't wanna eat," I said. I had a horror of vomiting. I associated it with the day of my mother's funeral when I stayed home, throwing up almost continuously for hours.

"You can rest on the plane." He swung my hand up and down. My arm wobbled as if it were boneless. "Be cheerful. Even if it kills you. That's the only lesson about life I can teach you: life is too sad not to laugh at it." He turned to Pablo and half-mockingly, half-seriously began to sing: *"Adios, muchacho! Compañero de mi vida!"* He let go of my exhausted hand and embraced Pablo. This was still the early sixties in America: two men embracing earned us many stares. I was embarrassed by the looks from our fellow passengers. My father seemed to think we were safe. But Uncle was still out there, convinced I wanted him to rescue me, sure that I didn't want to be with my own father. I had told him so, hadn't I?

I was going to be sick. I couldn't bear the sensation of food rising. I sunk to my knees, put my hands on the cold floor and squeezed my body tight, flexing every muscle to keep the airport doughnut and the school lunch of macaroni and cheese and my breakfast of Cheerios down, safe within me, because I couldn't let it out, couldn't let them see the gunk inside.

"Rafael!" my father said, horrified. He pulled me up effortlessly. "What's the matter with you!" There was more annoyance than concern in his voice.

"*Pobrecito,*" Pablo said.

"You need to sleep," my father said, softer now. He hugged me tight; tight enough that I didn't have to make any effort to stand on my own. I breathed the slightly stale odor of his Old Spice cologne, combined with a fresher whiff of his real smell. Oddly, it cured me of my queasiness. I breathed in his heat and his animal nerves. He was a big, hot strong man. Of course he could prevent Bernie from taking me. I was safe, after all.

CHAPTER EIGHT

Sibling Rivalry

CARMELITA WAS WAITING FOR US AS WE EMERGED FROM THE ANXIETY OF clearing customs in Madrid. This time, when my phony passport was presented to the Spanish official, I was too scared to pray in my head for happiness. But the official's comparison of the photograph against me was perfunctory. He chatted with my father about why we were in *España:* were we looking up relatives? In this confrontation my father seemed brilliant to me. He relaxed on his heels, smiled, and told the story of my grandfather's emigration from Galicia to Tampa; he even began to recount the quaint anecdote of how Pepín romanced Jacinta by making up for her slow rolling of the cigars with his own superhuman speed. The customs man was charmed, but a supervisor (I think; or perhaps a stern colleague) looked cross and that spurred the agent to interrupt Francisco, stamp my passport without a glance and use a nub of white chalk to check off each of our bags, although there had been no investigation of their contents.

I was surprised by the lax security of this running dog of fascism. On the tedious flight Francisco had told me his version of the Spanish Civil War. It amazed me that we—and especially that I, a half-Jewish boy—were en route to a nation ruled by a man whose staunchest and most crucial ally had been Hitler.

"Did they exterminate Jews?" I asked.

He laughed. "Why am I laughing?" he caught himself. "There was the Spanish Inquisition, after all." And he explained about Spain's peculiar Jewish history, of the almost total annihilation of the literate, prosperous, and talented Spanish Jews, accomplished for the most part by murder and exile but also by massive conversion, the hiding of thousands behind new names and the adoption of Catholicism. My father told me—accurately, by the way—of the Spanish families who, to this day, turn their paintings of the saints to the wall at sundown on Fridays and then light candles, but don't know why. "You don't have to worry about anti-Semitism today," he concluded as we began our airplane meal.

But with his coffee and my scoop of ice cream, he changed his mind. "Maybe, just to be careful, you shouldn't mention to anyone that you're half-Jewish."

After that talk I had expected more vigilance from the guardians of the fascist Spain than we experienced at customs.

So had my father, evidently. "We made it," he whispered with a smirk of triumph as we walked, officially sanctioned, under a sign that welcomed us to Madrid in Spanish, English and German. I thought—we're safe, it's over, everything's okay—while barely noticing that there was a young Negro woman, tall and thin, except for large breasts and a pronounced potbelly, clapping and calling to us. Carmelita had broad lips painted vermilion and huge brown eyes whose whites brimmed with happiness at the sight of my father. She stopped her applause, came toward Francisco with measured speed and single-minded purpose, her skinny arms casting for him, gathering him with the blind confident greed of an octopus; a beautiful, exotic and apparently harmless octopus, but nevertheless a creature whose reach seemed boundless and whose grip looked unbreakable.

All eyes were on them. As I was to discover shortly, any black-skinned woman, much less one as exquisite as Carmelita, would have attracted stares in Spain during the sixties. I had a specifically American racist response to her: as a right-thinking red-diaper baby I saw her as Negro, noble and oppressed, and therefore probably a cleaning woman or a singer, since those were the only activities permitted by American culture and economics. I was amazed, therefore, when Carmelita spoke. She had a rich voice, deep and amused, which certainly would have made for a good chanteuse, but what stunned me was that she talked in Spanish, in the cackling, speedy Cuban of my Tampa relatives.

"*Y tú eres Rafael?*" she yammered at me with a broad smile of brilliant teeth. She had a remarkable mouth, huge and almost always parted, flashing her pink tongue and cheerful smile. Not liking her was impossible. *"Es muy guapo, verdad?"* she said to Francisco and then commented to me, *"Como tu padre."* These compliments on my looks—any likening of my appearance to my father's had to be praise—increased my confusion. Why wasn't she speaking in English, in the sassy trill of my former classmates from P.S. 173, or the slow Southern drawl of the Great Neck serving women? Obviously she had learned Spanish from my father, but why was she using it on me?

"I don't speak Spanish," I said.

"But you understand a lot," my father said. "And you're at the perfect age to learn. At this age your brain is like a sponge. In two weeks you'll be talking like a Castilian."

"No lo hablas?" Carmelita stroked my face lovingly. *"Qué lindo,"* she said, another compliment that I took as a way of praising Francisco. Not that I minded. I liked her a lot. Of course I was an easy mark: she was a woman and a woman's presence reassured me. A loving glance, a kind word, and any woman owned my soul.

My father, who had still made no reference to my mother or her death, didn't explain Carmelita either except to say, "Carmelita is Cuban. She knows some English, but refuses to speak it." The language of the enemy, I assumed, and felt ashamed that it was all I spoke. So there were Negro Cubans. [In case my ignorance surprises readers who may assume that my Tampa relatives were of mixed race and had dark complexions, I should explain that although a branch of my family is of mixed race, the relatives I had met—and whom I mistakenly thought of as wholly representative of the Cuban population—were of Mediterranean origin. One particular branch, the Pardos, are especially fair, with red hair and freckled skin. Of course to a true believer in Aryanism my white skin wouldn't truly distinguish me or my people from an African-American. Years ago, at the suggestion of my training analyst, I did as complete a trace as I could of both lines of my ancestors—Latin and Jewish—and discovered relatives of all races within four generations. I have an African great-great-uncle and a great-great-grandmother who was Chinese. Nevertheless, to my white-skinned American eyes Carmelita was distinctly a Negro, just as to my own eyes I was distinctly a Jewish-Spanish boy. I should also point out, although it is a tiresome cliché no one believes in anymore, that ultimately we all have the same parents. Race is one of the mind's most convincing and deadly illusions. As Freud might have written: racism is frequently the excuse for our savage behavior, but rarely its cause.]

We took a cab through the surprisingly New York–like Madrid streets. My father chattered to Carmelita in Spanish, telling the story— I could gather from the occasional word I understood—of our surreptitious departure from the United States. I watched my new world out the cab's window. The gray modern buildings whose coldness disgusted my father ("fascist architecture," he called it) reassured me. However, the sight of one of the *Guardia Civil* patrolmen was unsettling. I interrupted my father's account to Carmelita to ask about him, expecting to be told he was an elite soldier, a unique man, perhaps an executioner. Before he answered, my father pointedly glanced at the cabbie to remind me of his presence. The driver did seem interested in us, for obvious reasons—not only the racial mixture but now the mixture of tongues. Francisco explained with studied indifference, "He's one of the *Guardia Civil*. They're a kind of police. In fact, they *are* the police."

That fearsome man was merely a policeman! I suppressed my amazement, and my fear, because of the driver. I wanted to suggest we leave this country immediately. I would have much preferred to be in Cuba, fearing the arrival of hostile forces, than to scurry between the legs of the *Guardia Civil*. And my father, as I observed while we were driven to the hotel, was apparently right. The *Guardia Civil* were not only the regular cops, they were plentiful. I saw more than twenty on our drive. We'd have to be constantly on the alert. And they were scary, the scariest sight on the streets, in fact the only scary sight on those peaceful Madrid streets. Their tailored uniforms and patent leather boots were set off by a dramatic cape and a strange three-cornered hat: a combination of streamlined Nazi terror and the romance of medieval chivalry.

Carmelita had rented two rooms in a modest pension. She left us to get some food. We took the tiny, manually operated lift to the third floor. Francisco let me hold the lever with him; I was thrilled that we stopped the car almost flush with the landing on our first try. My father led the way to a single room with a washbasin and no toilet. It was charming but had the narrowness of a closet, hardly relieved by its one window. Next door was a room only a bit larger, sufficient to squeeze in a double bed. He said that was for him and Carmelita. "You get your very own room. You can pretend you're a grown-up, staying on your own in Madrid, Spain's capital, one of the world's great capitals. Of course I'm right on the other side of that wall, but you can pretend that tomorrow morning you'll get up, buy a ticket to the bullfights—"

"Can we go to a bullfight?" I asked.

"Well, it's winter. They don't fight in Madrid in the winter."

"Oh shit."

"Rafael!" Francisco scolded my language, but with a tolerant smile. "We'll have to go south to Cádiz to see a bullfight. You really want to see a bullfight?"

"Yes!" I insisted, more with annoyance than enthusiasm.

"Aren't you scared of—?"

"No! When can we go to Cá—" I hesitated.

"Cádiz. If you want to sound like a true *madrileño,* say it like this— KA-DEE-TH." He pronounced it with the aristocratic Castilian lisp.

"KA-DEE-TH," I said, so well that my father applauded. "When can we go there? Is it warm there?" It was cold in Madrid, a much bitterer cold than New York's.

"I don't know. I have no idea where we will go tomorrow. First I have to have dinner tonight with my Spanish publisher. I should say, the man who I *hope* will be my Spanish publisher."

"Tonight?" It was past eight in the evening. Carmelita had gone to buy sandwiches. I assumed they were for all of us and we would then go to bed.

"Oh, Spaniards think eating dinner at ten o'clock is early. In fact, we're not supposed to meet until eleven. You'll be asleep—"

"I'm not tired!" I probably shrieked this. Certainly my father reacted as if I were in the grip of a panic. He hugged me, awkwardly pushing my head into his chest and thumping me on the back. That made a hollow sound. No surprise there—I felt as if there was nothing inside me. Being in a foreign country with Carmelita and a father I had known only as a mythic figure for over a year, seemed to have taken the me out of me. Everything flowed out. I couldn't properly process the new sights. I stared at the bed, the sink, the window—banal and familiar objects—as if in this setting, with these people, they were fundamentally altered. Everything was strange, including me.

I did enjoy my father's comfort and was encouraged to make an effort. "Where's the toilet?" I asked after a while in his arms. I knew I couldn't stop him from leaving me; my worry was that he wouldn't come back. I believed I had to master my fear so that returning to me would be a pleasant prospect. I certainly didn't take for granted that the mere fact of my existence was a sufficient incentive.

"In the hall!" he said as if that were the most brilliant fact he had yet encountered in life.

"In the hall?" I said with as heavy and dubious tone as a nine-year-old can muster.

He took me into the corridor where, at the end farthest from our rooms, there was a bathroom for the floor. This facility was no larger than what we had in Washington Heights, yet my father presented the rather ordinary fixtures as if they were spectacular. Did he really think they were special or was that for my benefit? I believe, in his enthusiasm, in his mania (he had triumphed over Bernie and international borders; he was about to make a book deal), he actually thought that the normal-sized porcelain tub was "big enough to be a swimming pool," that the chain flush box toilet was "elegant," that the scented soap not only cleaned but "deodorized," and that the dulled mirror over the sink was "made out of a special glass to give ladies a more youthful look." My father wasn't a fool; but out of hope, he was often foolish.

Anyway, I didn't care how grand the hall bathroom was; I wanted privacy. Once my father confirmed that any guest might and would use it, I decided not to go to the toilet until we moved to a real hotel. I asked when that would be.

"What do you mean?" my father laughed. "Don't you think this is a real hotel?"

"You know . . ." I trailed off.

"I guess living with your uncle has spoiled you for anything but the Carlyle."

"No it hasn't!" Francisco had spoken in a neutral tone; but I heard a damning judgment underneath and wished I could retrieve my complaint.

"It's not your fault. It's what you're used to."

"No, I'm not. I don't even know what the Carlyle is."

Francisco must have been dismayed—he didn't laugh. "The Carlyle is a hotel for rich people in New York. You know, this is really a perfectly charming place. Your uncle's standard of living is—well, way beyond most Americans, let alone what people are used to in Europe. Even in the best hotel in Spain, although the bathroom would be in your room, it wouldn't be any better than this one."

Of course, if the bathroom were in my room, especially because it would have at least doubled its size, that would have made quite a dif-ference. "Oh, it's great," I said.

"Okay," Francisco said. But I had hurt his feelings. We walked back to my little room. My father said he was going to unpack and he left me alone.

I sat on my bed. The springs creaked with age. I looked at the close-by wall opposite and felt abandoned. Outside I heard an ominous clack-ing on the pavement; I thought it was the tread of an enormous horse. I went to the window and peered through a gap in the wooden venetian blinds.

They were the footsteps of a *Guardia Civil*. He was dreadful. He was overweight, but that made him no less scary. In the uniform, moving in-exorably under his cape and patent leather hat, like a sort of man-eating turtle, he was as terrible as any of his leaner and more fit brothers. I watched him go up the street, a slow patrol that I found as fascinating and as awful as King Kong's destructive progress through a peaceful city and I imagined what it would be like to sleep there, alone, listening to the footsteps of the fat *Guardia Civil*.

"Dad!" I called. I was too scared to move. I shouted again. "Daddy!"

Francisco appeared with his shirt off and a clean one in his hands. "What is it?" He looked scared too.

"Is Carmelita going to stay here?"

"That's what you were shouting about? You gave me a heart attack."

"I'm sorry."

He sighed and put on the shirt, buttoning it. "Yes. She's going to be with us from now on. But we'll talk about that in the morning."

"No. I mean, is she going out with you?"

"Of course not. You think I would leave you alone in the hotel? Is that the kind of father you think I am?"

I was ashamed. After all, he had never left me, he had been driven out of the country by death threats, and stayed away to fight against imperi-alism. "No," I mumbled.

"You know," he said in a soft voice, "I took a chance coming to the States to get you. I could have been arrested and had my passport taken away. But I didn't care because I wanted you with me."

Think of what he had risked to come get me, I scolded myself. I was very ashamed. I lowered my eyes to the tails of his laundered white Brooks Brothers shirt. Maybe I didn't deserve such a good Daddy.

"I kept it, Daddy. And I never told."

"What?" He moved to me and lifted my chin. "I can't understand you. What did you say?"

I was crying as I talked and the tears garbled what I said. "I have your secret letter. I know it was supposed to be destroyed but I kept it. Mommy was angry, I think." Once I started crying it was hard to stop, although I no longer felt bad. I sobbed, became aware of my father's mounting upset as he nervously tried to soothe me and tell him what was wrong, all the while feeling better beneath the tears.

[Note the cyclical testing of whether the father truly cares, characteristic of a battered child. Although no violence is present here, the emotional blows are similar. There is need for attention at any cost, even if it is painful.]

Carmelita returned while I struggled to stop weeping. She spoke softly to my father, shut the door and unloaded my sandwich from a red mesh shopping tote. She spread the wrapping paper on the tiny, almost doll-sized night table, and put my food on it while I calmed down. She watched us and rubbed her stomach gently with her right hand. I looked at her round contented face. She smiled at me lovingly.

"Now, what were you trying to say about a secret?" my father asked.

I took out my Indian wallet and gave him his letter.

To my surprise, when he unfolded the yellow paper's deep creases and read the first few lines of his handwriting, he frowned from lack of recognition. That lasted for only a moment before the shock and horror at what he was reading came into his bright eyes. He broke off to stare at me as if I were something he was afraid of.

I was surprised at that reaction; and yet I wasn't.

[My unconscious knew exactly what was going on. What marvels we are: seeing when we are blind and blinded when we see.]

I stammered fearfully. "I never told, Daddy! I was a good Communist. I never told."

Carmelita said, *"Comunista?"* She was baffled and looked to my father for an explanation.

I ran to Francisco and pushed my way into him, past the letter. I called to his astonished, paralyzed face. "I kept the secret, Daddy. I was good."

He pulled my head to him. "I'm sorry, Rafe." The tone of his apology wasn't to a child. The use of my more American-sounding diminutive is an indication of the closed gap between our ages. He was a huge man hugging a nine-year-old but his tone was man to man. "I've failed you. I don't know how you can forgive me."

"I love you, Daddy," I wept into his starched shirt, ruining it for his important dinner.

"I can't . . . Not now." He moved me off him and spoke in a rapid Spanish, way too fast for me to comprehend, to Carmelita. In moments, I found myself in her arms, pressed against her hot and swollen chest, smelling garlic that somehow clung to the rough fabric of her blouse.

Francisco left. He came back in about half an hour. By then Carmelita had coaxed me to eat my sandwich. She spoke to me in Spanish about everything, with a cheerful and welcoming smile, but without any helpful dumbshow gestures.

"Feeling better?" my father asked and didn't wait for an answer. He had finished dressing in a charcoal gray pin-striped Brooks Brothers suit. Carmelita exclaimed over him. He smiled and accepted the touch of her admiration—she stroked his hair and straightened his tie—while saying to me, "We'll talk about that letter tomorrow. We've got a lot to discuss. That was a scary time and I shouldn't've written the things I did. You don't have to worry about any of that. Okay?"

"It's not a secret?"

"It's better, in this country and in the United States, not to talk about being a Communist. And you should know that I'm not a member of the Communist Party. I haven't been for seven years. Nor was your mother."

"No?" I felt relief. I wanted to clap; but I knew that wouldn't have been right either.

"I support Fidel."

"Un fidelista!" Carmelita said as if she were announcing the arrival of a circus.

Francisco smiled at her and continued to me, "I support Fidel. But you don't have to keep that a secret. Not even here. Okay? We'll talk about it all tomorrow."

"Okay, Daddy."

"You'll be all right with Carmelita. Go to sleep and we'll talk about everything in the morning."

"Would you ask her to stay here until I fall asleep?"

"Sure." Francisco spoke to her in Spanish. She nodded as if that were a matter of course. My father reached for my nose and squeezed it between his index and middle fingers. The pinch hurt: it cleared my sinuses and made my eyes tear.

"You're a good boy," he said. "Wish me luck."

"Good luck, Daddy," I said and meant it. I didn't really understand how supporting Fidel was different from being a Communist. And I didn't know why you could talk about it in a Nazi-like country. And I was afraid to think about Carmelita's status (although, of course, my unconscious understood perfectly) but I was thrilled not to be a Communist. It was like having an abscessed tooth pulled—the pulsing infection drained quickly and the aching pain disappeared.

Later, I found the letter, the misunderstood document of my secret mission that I had hidden for so long, underneath my narrow bed when I pulled off the bedspread. Apparently, my father had dropped it during my fit of tears and it had floated underneath. Carmelita was out of the room doing something. I hadn't understood what she said before she went; she returned right away with a chair and a book for her to read while I went to sleep. I thought about giving the letter to her for my father, but decided I would do that myself when we had our discussion in the morning—the explanation of all the things that had happened and were to happen. I returned the letter to my Indian wallet and put that under the pension's uncomfortably flat pillow.

Carmelita read; I watched her. She noticed me after a while, lowered her book, and began to sing. It wasn't a lullaby and it wasn't a folk song. The tune was cheerful and the lyrics said something about mangos and boats. She laughed when she got to the end. *"Entiendes?"* she asked. I shook my head no. She came over and kissed me on the forehead. Her lips left a wet impression and I smelled garlic.

When I opened my eyes sometime later I realized I had fallen asleep and she was gone.

The room lamp was off but a harsh serrated light came through the wooden venetian blinds. I heard the unmistakable and dreadful footfall of a *Guardia Civil* on patrol. I began to feel anxious about him and then I laughed, reassured, as I remembered that I wasn't a Communist anymore. In a moment, I was fast asleep.

The next morning, a bleary-eyed Francisco took me out onto the gray, frigid Madrid streets. We walked for several blocks until we found a kind of storefront deli. There were countermen, but no Nova or bagels; instead they offered omelets or small baked breads. My father ordered an espresso and one of the miniature loaves with butter. I took mine with marmalade and also ordered a hot chocolate that was so sweet and thick I thought I was getting away with murder. My father saw the look in my eyes as I took my first few sips and laughed. "They make it rich, *verdad*?" He had been talking Spanish all night and kept slipping into it. Even his English was infected—he had an accent until his second espresso was downed.

"It's great," I told him. I was feeling good. Not the hyped and ardent sensation of rescue but a secure ease that I hadn't known since the night of the rape.

[Of course, no incident, no matter how terrible, can determine the whole of a person's emotional character; I don't mean to imply that. But a trauma can—as I am convinced it did in my mother's case—propel a neurotic into psychosis, complicate a simple flu into a body-wide infection that triggers other failures which mask and confuse both symptom and cause so that the original personality seems almost to have been a lie. To be sure, all of young Rafael's feelings and actions had a foundation in his character that preceded witnessing the rape of his mother and the humiliation of his father; and those inherent qualities helped determine how he would react. But to go to the other extreme, and make the real world a ghostly vision of the mind that has no life or substance of its own, is just as naive as believing we are merely innocent victims of society. I had been on a roller-coaster ride since the rape and, for the first time, I was sure my rollicking compartment had come to a stop. Indeed, I believe I could have been healed at that point. Had my father been a true parent—rather than a guilt-ridden child himself—he could have interceded here with a period of calm, restitution, and analysis. The traumatic memories were not deeply buried then; a competent therapist could have done me a great deal of good. This need for timely care may seem so obvious as not to require my raising it again and again, but the most casual observation of our shelters, foster care system, and the policies of our divorce courts shows it isn't understood well enough. And I have not brought up how we deal with adolescent crime.]

"How was your dinner?" I asked while my stomach twisted at the richness of the chocolate. (I kept on drinking it, though.) On the plane my father told me enough about his coming meeting with the Spanish publisher for me to understand that it was important to him both financially and for his well-being. Although sleepy, Francisco's manner retained the disguise of his charm, a charm I knew he would maintain in the face of disaster—*especially* in the face of disaster.

"Mmmm," my father sipped his espresso. "What a fantastic man. So sophisticated and intelligent. Well," my father fell silent, or rather reentered the talk of the previous night's dinner. His eyes twinkled at some comment that he had made; his thick eyebrows lifted with surprise at what his companion had answered. He came out of the reverie to me and smiled. "It was a real boost for me, a real lift to be with someone who appreciates my work. He kept saying over and over—it was embarrassing—what a good writer I am, that I'm an original, first-rate journalist. He understands the way I write. You see, I have this conviction that journalism, like fiction, has a narrative line." My father looked at me and seemed to remember who he was talking to. "You know, it tells a story. And this man, this important editor, he completely gets that, understands my approach. Given the right subject, he thinks I could establish myself as the leading expert on Latin America. Unfortunately, he doesn't think, since Franco"—my father lowered his voice—"is still in power, that he can publish a book sympathetic to Cuba."

"Oh," I said in a sad tone. I understood immediately, with a child's clear view of results rather than style, that all the flattery in the world wasn't going to pay our bills.

"You're like your mother," my father said. He hooked my nose with two fingers, pinching my nostrils together. "You don't care about the talk, you want to see the cash. But there was money in it. Even more money than what I proposed. Or there might be. He had a terrific idea for a book that he wants me to write. And I want to talk to you about it because it means we'd have to stay in Spain for at least six months, maybe a year."

My father ordered a third espresso. He asked if I wanted another hot chocolate. I was stuffed and my stomach ached. Thanks to jet lag, anxiety and an overdose of cocoa bean I was soon to have the runs. Before my bowels went into spasm Francisco told me of the Spanish editor's proposed book project. *A Spanish-American Comes Home* was the suggested title. "I'll think of something better," Francisco told me. Sweat had broken out on his forehead from the three espressos. It was cold outside, so cold that the windows were fogged in the center and, like my father, sweating at the edges. We were the only customers left in the place; everyone else had gone off to their jobs. "That's my editor's title. He's not a writer." The untitled book would be an account of my father and me traveling through the country of our heritage. The editor thought I was a delightful element; a charming appeal to women readers, who, my father assured me, were a huge majority of book buyers. The book would not only be graced by my father's unique point of view as a Spanish-speaking second-generation American discovering his heritage but there was also the storytelling delight of our encounter with relatives who my father was convinced still lived in Galicia. There would be plentiful and fascinating material in this meeting between modern-day Spaniards and their American cousins. The editor had already spoken with a literary agent in the United States who believed if my father wrote a brief outline she could sell this idea to an American publisher immediately and a similar conversation had taken place with an English agent about U.K. rights. My father's amber eyes, the deep-set, warm eyes of the Nerudas, glittered at the prospect of publication in three countries simultaneously; they shone, and yet shifted nervously with worry. "That would create quite a stir," he said, finishing off his espresso. I noticed the grooved center of his tongue was streaked yellow by caffeine. "I could also sell off chapters to magazines as we go along to finance the book." Francisco leaned toward me, hunched over the table and whispered, "But here's the bad part. Here's what you're not going to like."

My heart pounded, revved up in an instant to an anxious pace. What was it? What was the next calamity going to be?

"You can't go to school for the next year." Francisco smiled, pleased by his joke. "I'm sorry. No matter how much you argue with me, you can't go to school for the next year. You get to play hooky for the entire sixth grade."

"Yay!" I said and bumped the table with my knees. I didn't really know if I was glad not to go to school; but I was glad he had been kidding.

"No. I'm sorry. I won't change my mind. You have to stay out of school and eat chocolates and go to bullfights. Seriously, we'll be traveling too much for you to go to school. I can't promise you a completely free ride. If we stay anywhere long enough, I might arrange to hire a tutor."

"You mean, we're going to have servants?" I knew of tutoring only from Dickens novels.

"No," Francisco laughed. "My God, no. Although it's so cheap here, who knows? Maybe we could afford a servant or two." Francisco winked. "Unfortunately, it's against my political principles. But who knows what we can afford *en España?* If I could sell one chapter of the book to *The New Yorker*—well, that's absurd, they'll never publish me. But, say *Esquire,* or *Playboy,* or *Gentleman's Quarterly*. From the sale of one piece we could live for six months. Even the miserable *New York Times Magazine* that pays so little, even an assignment from them would pay for two months." Francisco surveyed the store, emptied not only of customers but its rapid countermen. There had been four or five of them. Now only one man stood sleepily by a soup pot, his ladle scraping the sides while he stirred. My father looked in his direction and pronounced, "The Almighty Dollar. The sun never sets on her." With that, presumably reminded of the check, Father got up to pay.

I stopped him with a question, a question that he had conveniently not raised or answered. "What about Carmelita? Is she going to be with us?"

Francisco returned to his chair. Its feet squealed on the tile floor. Maybe because of the talk about tutors that noise reminded me of the Great Neck elementary school's cafeteria. Was I glad not to be going there, where, for all my alienation from the other kids, I was a star? I didn't approve of Uncle Bernie and I had no fun when I was with him. With Bernie there was none of the thrill and laughter of the joyride my father made of life but there was something I could not identify, did not understand, something I both missed and resented. Francisco, still sweating from the espresso, looked at me with wavering, almost pleading eyes. Their insecure light confused me: why was he frightened of me? He had looked scared of me when I showed him his own letter the night before. How could that be? How could my big-voiced, articulate and handsome father fear me?

"Yes," he answered like a guilty suspect to my question about whether Carmelita was going to live with us. He grabbed the sides of his armless chair and nodded at me as if it were my turn to talk.

"Are you getting married?" I asked.

Francisco nodded. He swallowed. "We are married," he said softly. "I don't really believe in marriage. But Carmelita and I filled out a form in Havana—that's all you have to do there, declare yourself to be married—because she wanted it. I didn't. I never wanted to get married again. But she's a good woman and she loves you. She's not your mother. She's certainly not the woman your mother was. I loved your mother very very much," he insisted as if I had contradicted him. He looked away and added, "There will never be another woman like her for me." He cleared his throat again and said with a tone of finality, "Carmelita can't replace her."

I am convinced this extraordinary speech is an accurate memory of mine. To analyze it as a professional would require at least fifty pages of turgid abstractions. Let me shorten it for the general reader by saying that, as a way of explaining a second marriage to a child, it is a disaster.

[Besides, little needs to be added to what I have already written on romanticism in the narcissistic personality. *The Hard-Heartedness of*

Sentimental People, I confess, was largely inspired by my efforts to understand, rather than resent, Francisco Neruda.]

Perhaps my reaction to Francisco's explanation will seem more mystifying than my father's speech. I said, "How can she love me? She doesn't know me."

For a second Francisco stared without comprehension. Then he laughed. "You're a Gallego, all right." He smiled, got up and pulled me from my chair. He hugged me tight, pounded my back, and said in a booming, confident voice. "I better keep my eye on you. After all, Franco is a Gallego too." He laughed at what I assume was my shocked face and said, "I'm joking. But I have no worries with a son like you. You're strong enough for both of us."

"You didn't answer me," I said, after he paid the check and told me to button up before we returned to Madrid's cold.

"About what?" he said. He looked tired. Once the animation of discussing the new book idea dissipated, his cheeks became slack with exhaustion, his eyes dulled by sorrow.

"How could Carmelita love me when she doesn't even know me?"

He pushed me—not hard, but with detectable mean-spiritedness—toward the door. "That's enough teasing, Rafe. You know what I meant."

Within a moment he regretted that he had exposed himself and me to an unpleasant Francisco. We took no more than two steps away from the coffee shop and my father reignited his social personality. He draped an arm around my head in the frigid air, hunched down to keep his mouth nearer to my ears, and tried to sell me on his new wife. "Did I tell you what Carmelita did in Cuba? She's an Olympic swimmer. I mean, she was on the team, but she won't be going now, even though she was considered the best one, the one who had a real chance to win a medal for Cuba."

"Really?" I was excited and amazed. A woman athlete for a stepmother.

"Yes. She was a champion swimmer."

"Why isn't she going to the Olympics?"

"Um . . ." My father appeared distracted. He looked at something across the avenue. I followed his glance. There was a church of modern design, not very large, on the corner opposite. Along a windowless side, neatly painted by hand in black paint were these words: JOSE ANTONIO PRESENTE! Beside them was a cross and the years of José Antonio's birth and death.

"Why isn't she going to the Olympics, Dad?" I asked again.

"Uh, to be with us." He had come to a complete halt to look at the graffiti.

"What does that mean?" I asked about the writing after a few moments of silence.

"I don't understand it. José Antonio was the founder of the Falange."

"No," I complained. "What does *presente* mean?"

"It means José Antonio is present. He is here." Francisco removed a brown bound notebook the size of his palm from his coat and a black fountain pen. "He was the head of the *Guardia Civil* and the Falange, the fascist party." He flicked his pen in the air. "If I get a contract for this book I'll have to buy myself a Mont Blanc."

"Are you writing that down for your book?"

"Yes. I don't take notes, especially not while interviewing people. And I never, *never* use a tape recorder. But I wanted to write down the exact address since that's a detail I'd like to get right." It turned out later that this graffiti was hardly unique and wasn't really graffiti since it was officially sanctioned, rather than some sort of extreme-right-wing protest against Franco, a split in the ruling class, which is what my father thought he had detected. The handwritten sign distracted me from learning more about Carmelita's reason for giving up the gold to be with my father. Although I wouldn't have needed more of an explanation anyway: who wouldn't give up their own concerns for my wonderful father?

The book contracts were negotiated. The Spanish, American and English publishing houses didn't offer nearly what he expected for the book. But living in Spain was cheaper than he had estimated and the advances would be enough for us to live rather well for six months. We traveled to Galicia next, to Santiago de Compostela. It was very cold and we learned that the little town where my father believed our relatives lived was reachable only by a dirt road that was impassable to cars until after the mud season in March. Since we had no way of knowing when, if ever, our cousins might come into town in their horse-drawn cart (all the farmers used them) there was little point in hanging about. (Of course they had no phone, nor did the village nearest to them.) We moved on to the southeast coast, to the warm winter beaches that were already popular with German and English tourists in those days and today are mobbed by them.

We rented a two-bedroom apartment in the first of two high-rise hotels that had been built on the beach at Alicante. It wasn't that different in look or feel from a place we had once stayed in outside Tampa. The difference was the people, in particular the habitués at the bar downstairs. I became a regular there while my father took one- and two-day trips to various cities researching his book. (Very little of these excursions can be found in his memoir, *Land of Guns and Sighs*.) Carmelita wasn't much of a playmate. She didn't seem able to get enough rest; no matter how early to bed and how late to rise, she took a long nap every afternoon. I wandered the beach until five, playing with the German and English kids who came and went every few days, and then I stopped in at the bar for a Coke and a small bowl of green olives stuffed with pimentos. The young bartender, a handsome eighteen-year-old named Gabriel, or Gabby as the English called him, pretended I was a real drinker. He set me up with a flourish and joked if I ordered a second Coke that I might not be able to make it upstairs safely. He refilled my bowl of olives without charging me—that was crucial to my being able to afford a second Coke. Gabby was popular with all the tourists, especially with one middle-aged woman, the widow of an American businessman who had worked in Spain their entire married life and thus his death left her without a home, literal or figurative, in the United States. I realize today she was an alcoholic who spent her afternoons and evenings gradually getting drunker while she flirted safely with the dark-skinned, sleek-haired muscular Gabriel. She portrayed herself as a beauty whose sensibilities were too delicate for the corrupt world. She claimed her hope was that a wealthy tourist would fall in love with her and provide another ready-made life, but she made little or no effort to meet one. I don't remember her name. She was Southern and talked in her lovely drawl with me and Gabriel about the adulterous love affairs she had during her husband's business trips. "I was neglected," she would declaim defensively. "I was terribly, terribly neglected." Her dyed blonde hair draped down the exposed front of her generous bosom, a chasm that Gabby often took a lingering look into as he wiped the counter. I was frequently pressed against it when I said something precocious. Gabby flashed his bright teeth and told her she was still the most beautiful woman on the beach and that every man wanted her. Sometimes his flattery would move her to tears. She and Gabby performed this second-rate Tennessee Williams one-acter each afternoon, except that Gabby's secret life wasn't that he was gay—it was that he wanted to be a bullfighter. He confessed his ambition to me on a rare day when our Southern belle was absent. I had already cultivated the therapist's attitude of uncritical listening: I was privy to the longings of many of the adults at that bar during those months. Gabriel's in particular impressed me because I was also tempted by bullfighting as a calling.

By then I had seen a bullfight with my father on a trip to Sevilla and become a fan of El Cordobés, the most controversial of the fighters. He outraged purists not only with his long hair but more gravely by his flouting of the formal conventions of the ring. He invented such stunts—in fact I saw him do this one—as kissing the bull on the snout after a particularly brilliant series of passes left the animal dazed and confused. If his bull was especially unaggressive, El Cordobés would taunt him into a rage by hitting him on the nose with the sword or mooning him. Outside the ring, he was known for his love of rock and roll and American movies. Women loved his lean body and Beatles haircut, and he was insanely brave—even his detractors acknowledged that he was exceptionally brave. El Cordobés was sparing in his use of the banderilleros and the picador. The banderilleros were the men (this part of the fight looked very unfair to me) who used brightly colored sticks with sharp hooks to stick into the upper back of the bull and the picador was a tormentor on a horse who drove a stabbing instrument on a long pike between the animal's shoulders. These wounds force the bull's head lower, dropping his dangerous horns and exposing the vulnerable area for the matador's killing blow. A cowardly fighter would overuse them, virtually rendering the bull both defenseless and incapable of offense.

My father and I were lucky enough to see El Cordobés for our first fight and he was brilliant. He killed two fierce and gorgeous animals. (I can still see the brilliant trickle of blood drip down the bull's black fur, oozing from the gold handle of El Cordobés's sword.) His bulls were of the aggressive Miura breed and yet El Cordobés waved off the picador, so they weren't crippled. He did kiss his second bull on the nose but I didn't agree with the old men around us (they were probably in their forties and fifties) that El Cordobés's style was rude and demeaning to the animal. He seemed to love the bulls and I thought his execution of them was exquisite. His lean body vaulted above the horns and split their deadly points as he buried his sword to the hilt, killing the bull in an instant. They died a beautiful death, a death as magical as it's shown in art, but in reality isn't. [Bullfights are barbaric, savage, pretentious and thrilling—and, of course, provide a nearly perfect mass release for the Spanish id. Taking the violence of my childhood into account, especially the loss I had suffered without appropriate acknowledgment, my attraction to this spectacle seems inevitable. To symbolically control and triumph over death secreted a wish for the reclamation of my mother's life underneath the more obvious fantasy inherent for all males in bullfighting.]

Over my Cokes and olives, I quizzed Gabby about his training. He explained that since he couldn't afford to go to a proper *novillero* school (*novillero* meaning a novice bullfighter) he and some others would slip into the slaughterhouse pens at night and take their chances with both the animals and the night watchmen. I pleaded with him to bring me along. At first he didn't believe I was serious; then he became alarmed and made me promise I would say nothing to my father. Finally, tired of my nagging, he offered a compromise. He said he would take me one Sunday afternoon to a pasture about forty-five minutes inland where a friendly farmer used to allow him to play with the baby bulls whose horns were merely nubs. He said I could ask my father if that was okay (most Spanish boys ventured that far into the fantasy of bullfighting) but when I did ask Francisco, although he smiled proudly, he said, "Absolutely not."

"Why not?"

"If you want to do something athletic, let Carmelita teach you how to swim."

"I know how to swim."

"But she can teach you to be an Olympic swimmer." Over my protests, he walked into the kitchen to find Carmelita. She was preparing a fish soup for dinner. She stopped chopping up the vegetables when he told her his notion and answered in an irritated tone. That was when the evidence became too obvious for me to deny it. I had learned a lot of Spanish in the previous two months so I understood her reply and by now the obvious visual clue of her belly had become more pronounced— a round jutting shape that couldn't be mistaken for fat. She complained she didn't have a suit that would fit her with the baby. I knew I wasn't the baby she referred to. Besides, to illustrate, she pulled her loose dress taut around the basketball in her stomach. She talked about the baby ruining her stroke so she couldn't show me the correct moves and what my unconscious had known for weeks vaulted to the foreground. My mouth dried up. I interrupted their discussion of buying her a new bathing suit and said in parched English to my father: "She's having a baby."

He glanced at me and smiled. "Isn't that great? You're going to have a baby brother."

I couldn't answer. My mouth was too dry.

"Or maybe a sister," he added. There was no wariness or self-consciousness in his voice. He was unaware that this news might trouble or displease me. If that seems astonishing, my father being a sophisticated intellectual, all I can say is that I agree; it is astonishing, but entirely consistent with his narcissistic and sentimental personality.

"I can't swim like this," Carmelita insisted. Tears came into her eyes. Again, I understood a lot in a flash: why she slept so much and seemed so unhappy. She was distressed by the malformation of her athlete's body.

"You can stand on the shore and instruct him," my father said.

"No." She was firm. "You are his father. You teach him." She walked out. A moment later, the door to their bedroom slammed.

Francisco turned to me. "Women," he said in Spanish, accompanied by a look of rueful exasperation, a man-to-man look of our shared burden. "I'd better calm her down," he added in English.

They were in the bedroom, with the door shut, long enough for me to examine thoroughly the unwieldy box of this information: all its edges were razor-sharp; I saw no way to embrace the contents without wounding myself fatally. To my mind I had one asset in my father's eyes and that was my status as his only son. Countless times Francisco had thrown his powerful arm around my head and squeezed while saying, "You are my only son, the last of the Nerudas. Someday the world will say, 'Look at this man, the grandson of a Gallego peasant, who is so brilliant and handsome. How did he come so far?' And I'll answer, 'That's my son, my only child, my heir.'" From my point of view I had so little left: no mother, no home, no friends, no family other than this man and his unique relationship to me and now even that was lost forever.

I left the apartment and went to find Gabby. He wasn't behind the bar. But my Tennessee Williams heroine was on a stool beside a new boozy middle-age flirtation, this one an American who, surprisingly, seemed to be attracted by her garrulous self-aggrandizing style. In fact, he was so responsive, she was glad to see me. (The prospect of a successful consummation of a flirtation obviously appalled her.) She introduced me. His name was Tommy, an odd diminutive for a man who looked like a retired football player: six feet tall, thick-necked, face blotched by liquor, his crew cut almost entirely gray.

"Hey kid," he said. "You sound like an American. Ever been there?"

I explained the apparent contradiction of my name and my fluency in English.

Her strategy worked. Tommy removed the hand he had put on her shoulder and asked me how I came to be in Spain. I answered briefly, said

I was traveling with my father. I asked the Tennessee Williams heroine where Gabby was. She told me he'd gone to the kitchen.

I was welcome in there and I excused myself, ignoring Tommy's call for me to stay. I found Gabby being chewed out by one of the waiters. The harangue stopped at my appearance. The waiter asked if I needed anything.

"I want a Coke," I said and Gabby was released from the dressing down to attend to me.

Gabby called the waiter a cunt under his breath as we walked out the back way to get a case of Coke. That was why he had gone into the kitchen in the first place, he said. Once outside, on the gravel of the service entrance to the kitchen, I told him my father had given me permission to fight the baby bulls.

"Good," he said. "We can go tomorrow. We have to leave early. Be ready by seven."

That was good news because Carmelita and Francisco never woke before nine.

We returned to the bar. Gabby, the Tennessee Williams heroine, Tommy and I made a talkative foursome. Tommy seemed fascinated by us. He asked lots of questions and listened with enthusiasm to our life stories. He especially liked the fact that Gabby was going to teach me to be a bullfighter.

When the light faded, I said I had to go upstairs for dinner. Tommy said, "Hey, you like comics?"

Of course I did. I hadn't been able to read any of my favorites for two months.

"Come with me to my car for a second," he said.

"Another man's going to leave me flat, darling," our Tennessee Williams star said to Gabby.

"I'll be back, babe," Tommy said. He lurched forward and caught her unprepared to dodge a loud wet smack on the lips.

Only when, in the fading light, I was in the passenger seat of Tommy's car, greedily holding the six brand-new comic books, did I feel odd about being with him. He put his hand on my neck and rubbed it. "You're a good-looking kid," he said. "How old are you?"

I was alarmed. Only vaguely, of course, and I thought I was being silly and cowardly, but his manner was sufficiently worrisome for me to toss the comic books into his lap. "I have to go home."

Tommy shoved them back. "Hey, don't be like that. I gave 'em to you.

Take 'em. I got more in my apartment. You can come up tomorrow and take what you like." He put a hand high up on my left thigh and squeezed. "After you fight the bulls."

I cursed myself for having told him about my plans with Gabby. If I insulted him, he might tell on me. "Okay . . ."

"I'm in Three-A. Come tomorrow after lunch. Right?" He patted my thigh gently, interpolating each tap with quick strokes toward my groin.

I opened the car door, carrying the comics in my free hand. "Okay."

"Good boy," he slapped my behind as I got out. I raced into the building. I was overwhelmed with guilt by the time I reached the door. I was a fugitive again, a boy of secrets and rebellion. What should I do with the comic books? If I had to explain them to my father, then he might, in his infuriating gregarious way, befriend Tommy and learn about my plan. I put the comics under our doormat, intending to retrieve them after they fell asleep.

Carmelita and Francisco were in a good mood. She seemed especially affectionate toward me, stroking my hair after she served me a bowl of soup. My father told me they had decided to leave Alicante at the end of the month rather than stay for four months as originally planned. We would go to Barcelona. A really cosmopolitan city, my father added enthusiastically. "You're not making much use of the beach, anyway, right? And we can find you an American school in Barcelona."

"You said I didn't have to go to school."

"There'll be other American kids there. God knows what they'll be like. They'll be the children of corporate executives. But they're kids, after all. You'll like them and they'll love you." He said to Carmelita in Spanish, "Rafael is always the most popular kid in his class."

"No I'm not," I said bitterly.

"Yes you are."

"No I'm not!" Tears came with the anger.

My father shouted, "Goddamnit!" He stood up, his soup spoon still in his hand. "I can't say anything right!" He looked at the spoon as if it were the cause. He threw it at the sink. It clattered into the well and slid up, bouncing off the wall, and landed on the stove with a bang. "I can't satisfy everybody!" He shouted at Carmelita in Spanish, "I told you!" And he walked out. In a moment we heard the front door slam.

She hadn't looked up from her bowl during the explosion. She calmly took anther sip. My tears and rage had scurried into a cubby in my soul and I doubt I could have found its opening with a team of searchers.

What a bad boy I was! I counted my sins and my secrets and my bad feelings. No wonder I would no longer be my father's only child—I didn't deserve that honor.

The dreadful silence that followed my father's exit lasted too long. I wanted to fetch my father's spoon from the stove, but I was scared to break the tableau. Finally, Carmelita looked up at me. Her round face seemed serene. She said softly, "You shouldn't be rude to your father. Especially when he compliments you."

She was right, I believed, and yet I hated her for saying it. And, yes, I hated her for carrying the usurper in her belly. I didn't deserve to be the only son, but if not for her, I would be anyway.

While Carmelita washed the dishes, I reclaimed the comics from the doormat, went to my room, locked myself in, and started to read. I was halfway through my favorite, an X-Men Special Edition introducing a new character, when my door shook so hard the floor vibrated. My father's voice boomed, "Rafael. Open this door."

I shoved the comics under my bed and hurried.

Francisco was so friendly and charming in his manner that you could forget at times how big he was. He filled my doorway, all six foot three of him, trim, but still two hundred pounds, his smooth tanned skin not at that moment a pleasant contrast to his white teeth, but dark and menacing. His warm light brown eyes were cold with rage. He stared down at me and said nothing.

I have tried to portray how scary he looked, yet I wasn't intimidated. I was a foot shorter and a hundred pounds lighter, but in me there was a full-sized rage. "What do you want?" I asked rudely. "I'm busy."

He slapped me with his open palm. My head jerked to the side and snapped back to confront him. My legs trembled, my heart pounded, but my face seemed to have disconnected from those cowards, and remained still: eyes fixed on him, unflinching and tearless.

"You disobeyed me," he said.

I said nothing.

He flinched, rubbing his eyes with the hand he used to hit me. He uncovered to add, "Gabby told me what you're planning. Do you know how humiliating it is to tell a stranger that your son is a liar?"

"No," I said.

Francisco breathed in through his nose, snorting. His lips parted, showing teeth, and he raised his hand again.

I turned aside as if already struck. I watched the threatening hand out of the corner of my eye. It stayed aloft for a moment and then dropped to my shoulder. He pushed me. Like a frustrated kid in the schoolyard, my father shoved me as if testing whether I was willing to fight him. I was staggered but didn't fall. I certainly didn't shove him back.

"You're riding for a fall, young man," he said. His tone and manner were so unlike him that he seemed almost comical. He reached for the handle of my door. "You're staying in this room until you've had a chance to think about what you've done." He closed it halfway and added, "Think long and hard." He slammed it shut.

I pretended to be asleep when he looked in on me a few hours later. I read all the comics twice. I cried for a while, not satisfyingly. Finally, after locking my door, I kicked off the sheets and allowed the ocean breeze to tickle my hairless penis as I pumped, remembering those dark embraces with my mother. This time, perhaps because of the fresh wafting air, perhaps because, although I was merely ten years old, puberty had finally begun, the familiar pleasant sensation was more intense, almost painful. I teased that new sensation, re-creating the motion that localized it and then something terrible and wonderful happened: a spasm from knees to my chest and with it, a single drop of almost totally clear liquid hit my belly. I was confused and scared until I recognized the famous seed I had read about in the book on sex my mother had given to me years ago when everything was normal and safe.

So, I thought, trying to calm down from my initial horror: I am a man, after all.

CHAPTER NINE

The Murder of the Self

I WASN'T RELEASED FROM MY ROOM UNTIL NOON. CARMELITA BROUGHT my breakfast in, but she called me out for lunch. My father was at the table. His smile, his animated eyebrows, his musical voice continued to be absent. He showed no teeth, his brows were a line and he spoke in the drone of a bureaucrat. It wasn't really frightening; the imitation of sternness was just that—inauthentic and comic.

"Rafe," he said, "I have tried to understand why you would disobey a direct order from me. I can't think of a single instance of your being deprived or forbidden anything you want. And the first time I say no, you disobey me. I'm afraid that's exactly the problem—it was the first time I said no. You're spoiled. You're spoiled and you're ungrateful. Do you have any conception of how many children would like to change places with you?" He let that hang for a moment and then, with atypical clumsiness, answered his own rhetorical question: "Millions. The answer is that millions of children would give their right arm to have your privileges." (The truth of my father's estimate seems to me a damning indictment of the condition of children. It burns in my consciousness, a constant nag. And it is still true, that for the Rafaels of today, no matter how great their pain, in the eyes of the world it isn't pain at all.)

I believed at that moment, as a ten-year-old, two things: my father was right to be disappointed in me; and that if he knew my true self he would despise me. I had to find a place in this world, choose between my good father and my evil uncle. I chose my uncle because it seemed inevitable that only in his dark realm would I find admiration and love.

I lied energetically to my father. I told him I knew I was bad and spoiled and that I was glad to be sent to school in Barcelona. Francisco was startled by the apparent totality of his victory. I understood I was confirming his belief that I needed discipline, but that didn't matter since I was going to do everything in my power to escape my father, to be free of his impossible goodness. I would somehow get word to my uncle and thrive in the truer uncertainty of living as his ward.

Chastened, I was permitted to go out. I bumped into Gabby as I lingered near the office eyeing the public phone, heart pounding, mind racing, trying to think how I could call Uncle. Gabby scolded me, gently, for having lied. "Your father is very angry," he said. He saw that I was upset and added, "But he'll get over it. Want a Coke?" he asked brightly.

I declined. I had one avenue, perhaps, of escape. It wouldn't be through good-hearted Gabby; he belonged to my father's world. It was Tommy. He was a bad man, even if my suspicions were exaggerated. He drank too much, he admired a "foolish, decadent woman," as my father once called the Tennessee Williams heroine, and he owned comic books—"worthless trash" in Francisco's eyes. He wanted my company and that was wrong, no matter how far he intended to take it, and I could use that.

I was terrified, of course. Don't be fooled by the cold-blooded manipulativeness I had to affect to carry off my desperate act. All the fanciful ideas of neurotic, traumatized Rafe were an elaborate camouflage for the simple, although apparently paradoxical truth—I was fighting for survival. I climbed the stairs to be alone with a man I believed was a child molester so that he could help me become the ward of an evil man. In order to feel worthwhile, I had to live among people who were worse than me.

Tommy wore a bathing suit and nothing else. He reeked of cologne.

"Hey," Tommy said, startled. "You alone?" he asked nervously, although the answer was obvious.

He pulled me in roughly and shut the door fast. I saw all that pink flesh, soft belly overhanging the elastic band of his suit, droopy breasts, smelled his perfume and knew my suspicion was correct. He pushed me into his living room. The sun filled the room.

"Look who showed up," Tommy said to someone. I saw a figure in a chair, shadowed by the day's brilliance behind him. He was skinny and dressed in a seersucker suit.

I was convinced that Tommy had lured me here for this man. I was sure they would do something dirty to me and then kill me, perhaps because the killing was part of their pleasure.

"What's your name?" the thin man asked.

I was ready to accept my fate. A slow death as the disappointing son seemed worse than this quick one.

"Come on, kid. We know, anyway," Tommy said. He put his thick hand on my neck and pushed me forward.

The thin man stood up. "Well . . . ?"

"I'm Rafael Neruda," I said.

"Do you know a Bernard Rabinowitz?" the thin man asked. His tone was as formal and dry as Perry Mason's on TV.

I didn't answer at first, amazed that in this death there was resurrection.

"He's my uncle," I said. "Is he here?"

"He's on his way. He wants to see you. Find out how you're—"

"Can I go home with him?" I interrupted.

The thin man moved closer, appearing out of the sun as he blocked it. His nose was long and thin. He had pale blue eyes.

"How the hell do you like that?" Tommy said and grunted.

"You want to go back to the United States and live with your uncle?" Perry Mason asked.

"Yes."

"Don't you want to live with your father?"

"No."

"He mean to you, kid?" Tommy asked, massaging my neck.

"I'll ask the questions," the thin man said sharply.

"Okay, okay," Tommy said and backed away from me.

"My father *is* mean to me," I said.

The thin man turned his head to one side. He brought a long elegant hand to his ear and pulled on the lobe thoughtfully. "Call the Madrid office," he said to Tommy. "Tell them to have Mr. Rabinowitz phone here as soon as he lands."

"Maybe we should take—" Tommy began.

"Do it," the thin man said in a soft voice but with such conviction it had the effect of a barked command. Tommy left the room.

"How did your father get you out of the country?" he asked me.

"We took a plane from New York."

"No, that isn't what I meant." He reached into his jacket pocket and produced one of those light green passports with the gold embossed letters and the terrible eagle. "Did he have one of these for you?"

"Yes."

He was disappointed. "I see . . ."

"But it was fake," I pleaded. "A man brought it to him. It isn't my picture inside."

The thin man smiled without showing teeth. "Whose picture is it?"

"I don't know. Some other boy's."

The thin man put his passport away. Tommy entered and reported, "He's coming though customs right now. He'll call in a few minutes."

"There won't be any difficulties," the thin man said and he smiled again without showing a single tooth.

Two months later, in the chambers of a judge on Long Island, I was seated across from a small man in his sixties who had a bad cold. Beside him sat a black woman typing on a stenographic machine. As the judge asked me each of his questions, he blew his nose, so that I had to wait before answering if I wanted him to hear me. I gave the answers I was instructed to by my uncle's lawyer. I said my father was a Communist employed by Fidel Castro. I said he had taken me out of the United States against my will using a fake passport. The judge showed me the fake passport and asked if that was it. I said yes. When asked, I said I wanted to live with my uncle and that I was frightened even to see my father, much less visit him. I had had to say the same things to a Spanish official in Madrid. Other than those two nauseating confrontations, my return as a ward of my uncle was undramatic. I never saw my father. Later, I learned he had been put under arrest until we were back in the States. That was a matter of several days. In exchange for not contesting Bernie's custody, no charges in Spain or the United States were brought for his use of a fake passport.

The events of my life were at last tranquil. I worked hard to please my uncle. I tried to become a winner at all things, from academics to athletics. My pursuit ran all day and night, from early practice for the basketball team to college-level courses for advanced students offered by a community college. I gathered A's, chess tournament awards, swimming meet medals, praise from my teachers and offered the harvest to my beaming uncle with the innocent air of a maiden, revealing no personal motive for the bounty but to confirm the power of his fertile soil. By the time I was sixteen I had no conscious memory of the choice I had made in Spain. I believed simply that I had been raised by a madwoman and a Communist coward. I thought of myself—with the preposterous arrogance of the young—as a genius.

Uncle casually referred to me as a genius, in the way someone might comment that a teenager was tall or could run fast. His son, meanwhile, defied all his values, disappearing into the burgeoning counterculture of the sixties, abandoning contact altogether after Bernie cut off his trust fund allowance. His daughter married a vice-president in Bernie's company, moved to a grand house nearby and had three miscarriages. With each failure, her weight shrank and her drinking became more noticeable. Bernie spent little time with his wife—he had a mistress in the city I discovered later—and not much with me either except on the high holidays when he ignored his immediate family to talk to me about my future.

He decided I ought to be a scientist. "You're too smart to be wasted on business," he told me in his study, by the pool, or late at night in my room. Always the same words: "You're too smart to be wasted on business. Of course you could turn my millions into billions but that would be a disgrace. With my resources you could cure cancer." He confided to me, on my fifteenth birthday, that he had disinherited his son, taken care of his daughter through stock options for his son-in-law and that I would receive at least fifty percent of the bulk of his estate if he died before his wife, and all of it if she predeceased him. "But she'll bury me is my guess," he added in a neutral tone. "You take those millions and do something that the world will remember forever." He paused and looked thoughtful. His eyes glistened. I wondered if the shimmering was incipient tears. He stood up and said casually, "Just remember to mention my name at the Nobel ceremony."

"Thank you, Uncle."

He came over, ran his thick warm hand across the wispy hairs of my baby beard and whispered, "You're a good son," hurrying out before I could answer.

I thought myself so clever and deceiving. I didn't like him. I was grateful and moved that he had thrown over his son for me and I thought him bad and weak for doing so. Such ambivalence, this dual judgment of every situation, was my continual state.

Of course the unstable chemistry of my personality finally ignited. The match was my beautiful, good-hearted cousin Julie. My sexuality had been so compromised that for years she had been the focus of my fantasies. It is glaringly obvious, at this distance, why I would be attracted to a female family member who believed in equal rights for blacks and for an end to the Vietnam War, a passionate Jewish woman who felt protective toward me, who always looked past my precocious intelligence to the hidden lonely boy. I didn't have that insight into my libido: I was mesmerized by the movement of her white breasts under her black leotards and the fall of her shimmering black hair down her firm back.

In 1968 Julie was a senior at Columbia University. She had joined SDS (Students for a Democratic Society), a left-wing organization which was, that very year, beginning its transformation from a non-violent anti–Vietnam War organization into what would eventually become the ill-fated terrorist splinter group, the Weather Underground. As late as 1968, Julie's family and Bernie didn't appreciate—nor did the rest of America—how serious those young demonstrators were about changing the basic structures of American life: eliminating institutionalized racism, capitalism and imperialism. Julie was still regarded by her family as a bright, good girl whose participation in peace marches, lack of makeup and torn jeans were merely symptoms of a harmless phase, the young adult equivalent of an adolescent girl's fascination with horses.

[That analysis is not entirely wrong. The faith that society can be altered may flourish in middle and old age, but is far more likely to bloom in people with little experience; and the bravado required to take arms against the world's greatest military power is easiest to find in the invulnerable delusions of youth. We are animals, although we expend so much effort convincing ourselves we aren't, and the chemistry of explosive growth in adolescence, full maturity in the twenties and the rapidly accelerating decay of middle and old age are powerful tides that push and pull our supposedly objective brains from idealism to pessimism. Nevertheless, some revolutions succeed and others fail.]

That same year, my sixteenth, Uncle put me up for participation in a program at Columbia University created to nurture precocious math students. Dr. Raymond Jericho, a professor at Columbia, taking note of the historical fact that all great theoretical mathematicians had begun their breakthrough work while still adolescents and completed it by their early twenties, amassed a small fortune in grants to gather bright kids from the area, aiming to discover another Isaac Newton. We met on Friday nights and all day Saturdays at the university, so our regular schooling wouldn't be disrupted. The *Times* did a piece about us on the first day we met, dubbing it the "genius program." Even then the publicity struck me as a sign that Dr. Jericho didn't have his priorities straight. I got into hot water with him immediately, because I told the *Times* reporter, when asked what my specialty was, that I was working on an equation for time travel. "Really?" the reporter began to scribble and moved toward me. "He's kidding," Dr. Jericho said and punished me by forbidding me to work with Yo-Yo Suki (who later did important work in chaos theory) on cracking the Beroni paradox.

"It's too hard," Jericho told us.

"But you said we're geniuses," Yo-Yo said with his now famous deadpan. In those days, it baffled everyone.

"You two shouldn't be paired," Jericho said. "I've studied your files and you're too alike."

Yo-Yo, a very short, plump and pale Japanese boy with thick glasses, looked up at me—a six-foot-tall Jewish-Spanish kid, and in the best shape of my life thanks to swimming and tennis. Yo-Yo finished his survey and said, "Congratulations Dr. Jericho, you've just rewritten genetics as we know it."

We *were* an odd group of teenagers. That remark caused the room to laugh as hard as if we had been watching the Three Stooges and Mo had been decked with a two-by-four.

Our meetings began in January. By February, I was disheartened. It was the first chink in the armor of my image as the brightest student in America—an image that I believed was crucial to maintain my uncle's love and to secure his money. Of course (and this made it worse) the flaw was visible at that time only to me. We were divided in groups of four and asked to solve mathematical mysteries. My partners weren't the most brilliant (indeed, none of them distinguished themselves later in life, as did Yo-Yo and another boy, Stephan Gorecki) but it became apparent to me that although my partners were average for the group, they were much faster than I, both in calculation and in grasping theory. After four sessions, I had nothing to contribute to the group meetings, and it took hours upon hours of hard work between sessions for me to do the relatively routine homework on transitional proofs, proofs that had been discovered centuries ago. I knew I was seriously out of my depth when a student named Jerry Timmerman tossed an equation I had worked on for thirty hours back at me, commenting, "This is junk. If you're not going to really work hard you shouldn't be here. What did you do? Scribble this on the subway?"

My only pleasure in this genius training derived from the fact that Julie's apartment—which she shared with two other seniors—was a block away and she had offered to put me up on Friday nights. My uncle agreed to that, probably because it left him free to be alone with his mistress in his Manhattan pied-à-terre. After the battering Friday evening sessions, I staggered, defeated and frightened, down the long hill on 116th Street to be greeted by these women, bra-less under their peasant blouses, sometimes padding naked to the bathroom late at night or early in the morning, passing my bed on the living room couch, the flash of their bleached breasts and shadowed vaginas all the more exciting because of their sleepy and unselfconscious presentation. The gap in age— I was sixteen, the women were twenty-one—was apparently enormous to them. At least, that was my interpretation of why they thought nothing of having breakfast beside me in panties, reaching for the orange juice so that their T-shirts billowed out to reveal a dark aureole or a pink one or other fascinating details: a beauty mark on the soft underside, unshaven armpits, nipples hard as rubber one week, soft and quizzical the next. On my fourth visit, Julie noticed me stare at her roommate Kathy's dark mound, puffy and dark through her white panties. When Kathy left the room, I—erect and breathing hard—finally looked away to find Julie studying me. I had a terrible moment. I was sure, now that she knew I wasn't a sexless innocent, she would deny me the pleasure of these overnights.

"She's beautiful, isn't she?" Julie commented.

"Who?" I answered brilliantly. I draped my right arm across my lap in case the shape of my ardent penis was discernible.

"You don't have to be embarrassed," Julie said casually. She stood up to return the milk or the coffee—who was paying attention to that?— and showed her own tight buttocks in red panties, not covered by the gray men's tee she wore to bed. Julie's breasts were the largest, pushing against the material; her nipples always seemed about to punch through. They greeted me as she turned back to add, "The body is beautiful, you know man?" imitating a flower child, only I didn't know what she was mimicking.

[Feminist psychologists have rescued us from grave flaws in theory caused by male assumptions but one of *their* blind spots is a failure to understand—rather, empathize—with the quite extraordinary difference between the power of visual stimulus for the male, especially the adolescent and young adult male, as measured against female response. Every study conducted, no matter what the prejudice of its authors, has shown that, although women *may* be stimulated by pornography—especially if it is sensually and beautifully rendered—young men *always* are, even by a brief, cursory and crude exposure to nudity. Men are highly excited under all conditions, whether in considerable pain, whether their mood is depressed or elevated, whether their expectation is that actual sex is possible, probable or impossible and no matter whether the tantalizing form belongs to someone they know, don't know, love, hate or fear. The only exceptions are catatonics or other males in extreme states of psychosis. Feminist dismay at this fact of nature too frequently turns to disgust, disguised as thought, or to outright denial. Some have gone as far as to maintain that male response to visual stimuli is a product of socialization, of women being viewed as property. Anyone who has been an eighteen-year-old man knows that conclusion is worse than a flawed perception, it's dangerous ignorance. Men joke about the decline of sexual response after thirty, but the truth is that for most, it's a relief. Nature has loosened her enthralling grip just enough to allow at least a semblance of dignified thoughtfulness when presented with the supposedly abstract beauty of the human body.]

Sandy, the third roommate, appeared from the shower, hair wet, a big blue towel wrapped around her torso, and launched without preamble into an attack on Columbia University's plan to convert nearby buildings they owned into a gym and also faculty and student housing, in the process evicting poor, mostly black families. Her lecture was pornographic to me, although her square chunky body wasn't that appealing. Despite the fact that more of her was covered than Kathy and Julie, the simple knowledge that there was nothing on under the terry cloth, that if the tucked-in corner beneath her left arm should slide out I would be two feet from a totally naked woman, forced me to put both arms in my lap. Once again, Julie noticed the glaze in my eyes. She smiled knowingly at me while Sandy went through arguments that linked academic elitism to racism and then to genocide, until (as is always possible when talking abstractions) Columbia's desire to compete more effectively with their bête noire (Harvard) by keeping admission standards high and luring top-notch professors and students with offers of elegant apartments and new athletic facilities had been transformed into the moral equivalent of slavery and genocide. To my surprise, Sandy addressed most of her diatribe at me, laboriously explaining her terminology, obviously assuming these ideas would be shocking and difficult for me to follow. In fact, thanks to my boyhood, I understood Sandy very well. "We send their kids to die in Vietnam and destroy their communities at home," Sandy concluded.

Julie brought Sandy coffee and said, "It's so depressing."

"How do the kids in your school feel about the war?" Sandy asked when I did nothing but stare at her, arms still folded over my lap. She adjusted the top of her towel—it was coming undone slowly, a fraught and suspenseful visual.

"They don't like it," I said.

"Are they organized?"

Kathy, now dressed in jeans and a peasant blouse, reappeared. She carried a plastic bag with marijuana and cigarette papers. I knew she was about to roll a joint; I had once seen it done in the bathroom at school. Julie glanced at me a little nervously. "I don't think he knows what you mean by organize," Kathy said to Sandy. She noticed Julie's discomfort about the drug. "Oh," she said, "I forgot."

"You're against the war, right?" Sandy said.

"It's okay," I said to Kathy. "I don't care if you roll a joint." I knew the talk, but they were only words to me. The cool kids at Great Neck High who smoked grass lived side by side with me, so I could see them, but, socially, they were behind an impenetrable glass wall. I belonged to two cliques the hipsters held in contempt: the nerds and the jocks.

Kathy smiled with relief. "Your cousin told us not to corrupt you, but I forgot."

"You've smoked?" Julie asked, with some anxiety, which made no sense to me.

I nodded, unable to speak the lie. I felt the same about this as if she had asked if I were a virgin. It was unmanly to admit my lack of experience.

"Do you see how unfair it is that we're sending only the lumpen whites and blacks to fight in Vietnam?" Sandy said.

"Well, but . . ." I began, forgetting I didn't want to engage with her.

"But what? It's not unfair?"

"If you're against the war, how would it make things better if they sent all kinds to fight?"

"Because that would stop it. If middle-class white boys were dying over there, everybody would be screaming for it to be over."

Kathy and Julie and Sandy looked at me, enjoying (in a friendly way) the beautiful spectacle of what they assumed was a naive boy being illuminated by this insight—or radicalized, to use their jargon. It was awkward for me. I felt I was deeply in love with all three of them, although I thought Sandy was rather stupid and ugly, and that Kathy was a ditz. I admired their idealism and self-confidence and yet I thought they were doomed to fail. Also, I was very vain of my intelligence—which was getting punishing blows in the "genius program." All in all, I couldn't stop myself from dropping my guise of disinterest and ignorance of politics to show off. "But all wars are fought by the poor," I said. "Forty million died in World War II, most of them working-class, and that didn't end until we had dropped two A-bombs on civilians and pulverized all of Germany's major cities."

"That's different—" Sandy began.

"War," I talked over her, "is the logical end product of a competitive society. Capitalism is the most competitive of all systems and the United States is the purest capitalist nation in history. Without war, the United States would collapse."

"Exactly—" Sandy revved up.

"And so," I continued, "the government will sacrifice anything, all of us if they have to, to win. Faced with a choice between losing American control of foreign markets and suppressing American citizens, the U.S. will prefer to kill us. From their point of view, they have no choice. To win in Vietnam, LBJ would let his own children die. That's the logic of his situation."

"Wow," Kathy said and lit a joint. The loose end of paper burned in an instant, sending a long gray ash floating down onto the arms covering my lap.

"Right on," Sandy said.

"Oh God, Rafe," Julie said, not a rebuke, but in pain at my scenario.

"Why are you going to this elitist math program?" Sandy said. She sat down on a chair next to me. The towel split open across her left thigh up to her waist and I saw, shadowed by the terry cloth umbrella above her groin, a small, thick bush of black hair. I jerked my head up sharply and looked into Sandy's earnest, absolutely asexual glare of interest. "I mean, since you understand this pig system," Sandy added, "why be part of it?"

"Give him a break, Sandy," Julie said.

Kathy finally let out a small wisp of the smoke from her first toke and said in a choked voice, "Because he *is* a genius."

Her remark was almost as thrilling as Sandy's opened towel. By then, I had absorbed the fact that I wasn't a genius (at least I had enjoyed five

years of believing my uncle's delusion) and knew my fellow students
were aware of this dangerous truth. Maybe I could continue to fool people in areas other than mathematics: less objective disciplines, such as
world politics. You could say 2 plus 2 equals 5 in politics and be considered brilliant, rather than someone who can't add. Soon my uncle
would learn from Dr. Jericho that I wasn't a prize pupil. I had to compensate somehow.

"I know he's a genius," Sandy said.

Boy, this is easy, I thought and glanced at the widening canyon of her
towel. I could now see all of her most private region, including the re-
sumption of white skin above. What was in that forest? my whole body
wanted to know. I knew how to touch it, I knew what it meant to Sandy,
but what would it mean to me? Something extraordinary, I was sure, a
place where lies and secrets had no more use, where the truth was no
longer a danger.

"But you have a responsibility to use your big brain," Sandy went on,
"to help people. We're organizing branches of SDS in all the high schools
and you should be in the vanguard in your school. You could really educate others."

They all pitched into this topic, discussing among themselves
whether I should radicalize my high school peers or the geniuses at
Columbia. "Why not both?" Sandy said. But she agreed with Kathy and
Julie that, if I could get the prodigies to denounce Columbia's gym construction, it would really help the cause. And cost me an inheritance of
between two and three hundred million dollars, I thought.

"They wouldn't do it," I told the women. Each of them had a toke of
the joint by now and Sandy, who, unfortunately, had rearranged her
towel so my view was ruined, turned her hand toward me—the gesture
of Michelangelo's God offering life to Adam—only she was offering my
first taste of an illicit drug.

Julie looked worried, but said nothing. I took it. My fingers were
too close to the ember and I yelped, dropping the joint into Sandy's
lap.

Sandy retrieved it quickly and did something so seductive, and yet
with a bland matter-of-fact expression, that I was confused. She held the
joint to my lips, offering it like food to a baby, staring into my eyes as I
sucked in the smoke. It hit my lungs as fire. I choked, smoke poured
from my mouth and nose, my eyes watered, and my pride was shattered.
Sandy stood beside me—I had risen from the force of my lung's rebel-

lion—and patted my back. I felt her small breast against my right arm. Julie brought me a glass of water. I drank it sheepishly. But the beautiful trio didn't seem to think I was ridiculous.

"You didn't get any," Sandy said, offering the joint again.

"No," Julie said.

"Let me," I said, sharply. I surprised myself with the anger in my tone.

"Okay," Julie backed off.

This time, taking the joint, I was careful to grip it away from the ember. I sucked cautiously. They watched solemnly, as if we were participating in a sacred ritual. I held the little I inhaled for a while. I passed the stick to Kathy and opened my mouth. Nothing appeared to come out.

Kathy smoked, passed it to Sandy, who performed a trick—letting out a cloud from her mouth and reinhaling it through her nostrils. She handed the joint to Julie. She surprised me—I guess I still thought of her as basically my cousin, the conventional middle-class Long Island Jewish girl—by taking a long pull and absorbing the fire effortlessly. She looked at me. It was my turn. "You shouldn't have any more," Julie said. "You've got class in an hour."

"Jesus, don't mother him," Sandy said.

"Sandy," Julie complained. "He's a kid. We don't have the right to make decisions for him."

"Self-determination," Kathy said earnestly, choking out the words.

I laughed. "Like Vietnam," I said and giggled.

Kathy unaccountably laughed hard. Sandy's eyes glistened. "He's already high."

"I am?" I asked.

"I'd better give you some coffee," Julie said.

"Why don't you bring the whole group of geniuses here later?" Sandy said.

"We'll turn them all on and invent a way to feed the whole world," Kathy said. "That would be cool," she added. "A radical brain trust."

"There is a way to feed the whole world," Sandy said. "It's called socialism."

"They won't," I said.

"Of course it would," Sandy insisted. "If the whole world shared resources—"

"No, no!" Before realizing what I was doing, I grabbed Sandy's bare shoulder and squeezed affectionately. "I mean the geniuses won't come here and save the world. They wouldn't cross the street to save the world," I added. I enjoyed the surprisingly soft feel of Sandy's skin. She had such a tough body and angry face that I expected a harder shell.

Kathy guffawed. Sandy searched my eyes thoughtfully. I put the tip of my index finger on the point of her shoulder and slowly traced a line to her neck. Sandy turned her head and watched; so did Julie and Kathy. My fascination was complete: I felt as if I were scooping Sandy's silken skin onto my finger, skimming off a drop of her to keep for myself. I came to and jerked my finger back. It happened in less than a second, but I was exposed in that moment, more so than Sandy would have been if her towel dropped.

"Sorry," I said, abashed.

"What the hell for?" Sandy walked away. "Felt good," she commented and left the kitchen, saying, "I'm late for the strike meeting." She moved in a graceless waddle that I forgave her for instantly. I decided there was strength and honesty in her wide, flat-footed steps.

At that day's group, I was so high from my two tokes that my team's work, instead of being merely somewhat incomprehensible, was sheer gibberish. My inability to keep up with them showed me how little they relied on me under normal circumstances: no one complained about my silence and inactivity. In fact, they seemed to work faster. Without any help from me, they untied a knot that had frustrated us for two weeks. They whooped with joy and called Dr. Jericho to show off. He glanced at me (I discovered later my eyes were bloodshot) while they babbled to him. He congratulated them and pointedly asked to see me after the session.

I waited in my chair until all the geniuses were gone. Jericho turned a seat backwards, draped his arms on top of its backrest, and put his chin on his hands.

"How are you doing, Rafael?" he asked, pronouncing my name my least favorite way—RAY-FEE-EL.

"Okay."

"You don't seem happy."

"Happy?" I grunted.

"Is it the group?"

"I'm happy." The buzz was gone and my back ached. I was scared by this interrogation. What did he know? Had he talked to the other kids? Or to my uncle?

"Come on. Talk to me. I have eyes. I can see you're not relating to the others. Is it the work in particular? Is it working in a group? Would you rather go off on your own?"

"No," I said quickly. That would be a disaster; I'd have nowhere to hide. "I just—you know, I'm sluggish today. I haven't been doing my best work," I said, gathering belief in this lie. "I just haven't been contributing and I'm embarrassed. But that happens with me, you know? Goes in cycles. I can't do anything for weeks and suddenly I'm inspired."

"Really?" He was interested. "So you're used to having fallow periods."

"I have to get frustrated, you know?" Maybe this was true, I hoped. Maybe I'm a temperamental genius.

"I'll back off." He held up the palm of his hand. "I'm sorry. Don't want to interfere with the process. There's no rush. We're not on a timetable here." He stood up. "Just come up with something brilliant by May," he joked.

I went home resolved to become brilliant again. My self-deception didn't last long. I tried to work on the next step in our group's equation that night. I couldn't; I had fantasies about my beloved trio—kissing Julie, who became Kathy's breasts, and finally Sandy's tempting forest. Relieving myself of sexual tension through self-abuse (which describes perfectly my attitude to self-love) didn't improve my mental acuity. All week I was in a daze at school. I had been thrown out of gear. I noticed that my classes were not really demanding. I merely had to pay attention, discover my teachers' pet prejudices in history or literature or science, and mirror them back, memorizing what they thought important and remembering long enough to pass that month's test. Nothing truly difficult was demanded of us; no innovation, no inspiration, and certainly no genius. I was bright, of course. But so were many others who weren't getting my grades. The difference was that I was trying so hard. I wasn't dissipating my energy by charting the treacherous waters of adolescent courtship or rebelling against my parents (in fact, my academic single-mindedness *was* a rebellion against my dead mother and my exiled father). I was a fraud, I concluded. An above-average student and athlete running on high, easily outclassed when put up against real talent. Of course, I was precocious in general: my life experiences had been extraordinary and so I appeared wise. But, in the privacy of my head, I knew better. My wisdom was a combination of mimicry and an unpleasant awareness of how easily I could manipulate grown-ups through subtle forms of flattery. Thanks to my writer-father and the dreadful events of my childhood, I had read adult books. Long after Francisco's banishment my taste in novels continued to be overly mature. I enjoyed Dickens, Dostoevsky, Flaubert, Tolstoy, Dreiser and the rest of the sad and powerful opus of world literary distress, not because I was smart, as others assumed, but because they helped me understand the turbulent world that had churned my life into an odd, confusing arrangement. As a by-product, I could behave beyond my years in social situations. The terrible thing, I realized gradually over that week, was that I didn't know myself. In a very real sense to me, I didn't exist at all. I was a creation of the needs and fantasies of my various caretakers.

During homeroom that sad week, I made a list of all the things I did: tennis, swimming, listening to classical music, chess, reading novels, math, science, history, writing, and so on. I stared at each one, vowing to put a check next to those activities I enjoyed doing for their own sake. Several times I checked one. I believe I did pick reading novels, science, and listening to music. (At least I should have.) But I erased them as I remembered how careful I was to let Uncle or my teachers know what books I read or what composers I liked. Everything was mixed with the vanity of a performance. What did I enjoy when there was no audience to applaud my taste?

I flipped over the sheet and angrily wrote the truth: masturbation, Oreo cookies, Coke, spare ribs, hot dogs with sauerkraut, naked women—and I stopped. I wrote: women. I wrote: breasts, vaginas, belly buttons, necks, eyes, earlobes, long hair, curly, black, blonde . . . I loved women. That was the answer. Appetite. Pleasures for my stomach and my penis. That's what I was: a creature of desires, unsophisticated and certainly devoid of genius.

I tore up the sheet of paper, tore it up into pieces so tiny no one could ever reconstruct it. I buried the mass in my desk and looked at the students in my homeroom, some of them presumably my friends. Everything they knew and believed about me, no matter whether they liked or hated me, was false. Each day they took attendance, I claimed to be present, but I wasn't really there—I was hardly in my own skin.

The world swayed. My skull cracked open. My mind seemed to be exiting my flesh, leaving this stranger to find a home in another world, with different choices of bodies to inhabit. It was terrifying: I felt the core of my being try to escape from me. I shut my eyes, gritted my teeth, and whispered over and over: "You're real. You're real. You're real."

I was going mad. I knew it suddenly. I shut up and hugged myself, eyes still closed. Strange, I reflected, that I hadn't considered the likelihood before, given my mother. My uncle was the genius. My mother, my father and me, we were the bad seed the world thought we were, the envious weaklings of the earth who needed to be cared for by those who had genuine energy, conviction, and talent. The moral universe spun and spun in my head. I was so ill from the loss of self I couldn't get out of my chair when the bell rang.

I watched the others rise and leave. I wished I could cry out: "Please help me. I want to be me but I can't. I want to love you but I can't. I want to be loved but I don't know who I am."

"Forgot something?" my homeroom teacher asked.

"I'm sick," I said with perfect accuracy, for once.

Chapter Ten

Reality Testing

THE FOLLOWING MORNING I WAS TAKEN TO DR. HALSTON'S PRIVATE OF-
fice at Hillside Psychiatric Hospital. My uncle waited in the reception
area. I had hardly moved or talked since the bolt of terror in my homeroom. I offered no explanation, not to the school nurse, my aunt or uncle.
When asked, I would say in a whisper, "I don't feel well. I can't do anything right now." Bernie drove me to Long Island Jewish and they discovered nothing physically wrong. It was immediately clear to the school
nurse, my aunt and to the doctors—everyone except Bernie—that the
problem was in my head. He fought against this conclusion until nightfall. His initial reaction of denial was understandable. Abruptly, without
any apparent cause, his thoroughbred wouldn't run; he wanted to believe
the cause was a minor sprain, not the jockey and certainly not the demands of the race.

After the tests, I turned on the television in my room, lay on the bed
and watched numbly, not speaking or eating the food they brought in on
a tray. At some point I napped. I tried to keep my mind blank and my
body still. Thoughts could crack my skin and then I would leak out; I
felt movement might also do ghastly damage. When they forced me to
walk—from the examination table to the car, for example—that took
forever. I slid one foot forward, smiled mildly at my escorts so they
wouldn't be too annoyed as I paused, and after being sure nothing had

dropped from me or spilled out, then slid my lagging foot to join the other.

Uncle asked, "What's wrong?" over and over until he shouted at me, "Goddamn it, say something or I'll break your head!" His fists were clenched and his face flushed. He scared himself and walked out. I was frightened by his obvious lack of tolerance for my weakness, but to go back to performing for him was so much more dangerous and terrible, that his annoyance at my passivity couldn't shake me from it. He looked in during the evening several times after that outburst, glaring at me with rage, but said nothing, except on his last visit. "We'll see Dr. Halston tomorrow," he said. "He'll help you. Don't worry." The language was caring, his tone impatient.

So there I was, facing my mother's doctor. His thick black frames were the same he had worn seven years before, but his thinning blond hair was totally gone. Seeing him took me back to Ruth's insanity, and confirmed that I was doomed, like her.

"Tell me, Rafe— They call you Rafe?"

I nodded, very gingerly.

"Tell me, what were you doing when you were in class—was it a class?"

"Home—" I paused so my voice wouldn't shatter anything with too many syllables. "—room," I finished.

"Homeroom. That's not a class?"

I shook my head.

"Like a study hall?"

I nodded.

"Were you studying?"

"No," I said and a laugh came, unbidden, out of me. That was scary.

"It's okay to laugh," Halston said. "I'm not a teacher. This isn't the principal's office. You haven't done anything bad. You're not here to be punished."

I didn't believe him.

He waited for a response. When none came, he said, "I know you're very smart so I'm not going to pretend about what I'm doing. When someone has a mental illness—and maybe you do, I don't know—like any doctor, I have to take your temperature, a blood sample, a few X-rays. Only there's no way to do that when it comes to what goes on in our minds except by asking questions and the patient answering honestly."

I said nothing.

"I can't give you a medicine that will force you to be well. You have to want to be well. Do you want to be well?"

I nodded. I heard him but I tried not to use my intelligence at all. I stared at those thick glasses and wondered about them: were they plastic? They looked so strong I speculated they might be made of steel. But steel would be too heavy on his head. The weight might decapitate him.

"What you say here won't be repeated." He must have seen my look of contempt because he blanched. "You don't believe me?"

I didn't move at all.

Halston nodded at the closed door to his waiting room. "I promise you, on my oath as a doctor—and believe me, there's nothing I treasure more than that—no one, including your uncle, will ever hear a word of what you tell me."

I didn't wish to think it through. The words—money can buy anything—flashed in my head. I was obliged to answer: "I don't believe you." Challenging him was less scary than using my brain.

Halston didn't take offense, as I expected. He leaned back and ran a hand over his bald head. Must be nice, I thought, feeling a hard shell. "Is it because of me? Or would you not believe it about any doctor?"

"Nothing personal," I said. I chewed up the words by keeping my lips tight. That worked well for me. My skin didn't move as much and I could say more words with less effort. Unfortunately, I sounded like a cartoon character, or someone talking from inside a box.

"I see. Well, you must have some pretty terrible secrets."

"I'll say," I said in my new goofy voice and laughed again. Too loud. Have to watch the laughter.

"I envy you."

That surprised me.

"I don't envy your feeling bad. But my life hasn't been that interesting. Very little worth keeping secret." He clapped his hands and rubbed them together as if finished with a job. "Well. I guess we're stuck. I'm afraid that if you don't want to be treated that means you're sick and you'll have to stay here. I hoped we could talk and you could go home. You could come here a few times a week to talk about these secrets— which would stay secrets—and go on with the things in life you enjoy."

Oreos, masturbation, spare ribs.

"I'm always going to be honest with you," he said. "I don't want you to stay here. I don't believe you're really very sick. I don't think you belong in a psychiatric hospital. I'm sure you have worries and problems. We all do, especially when we're sixteen years old. But I think it's a tragedy you want to be treated like a hopeless mental case. Don't you?"

I shrugged. That wasn't something I dared think through.

"Do you want to stay here?"

"No."

"The only way to avoid it is to test me."

"Test?"

"Test whether you trust me to keep your secrets."

I nodded.

He waited a long time before saying anything more. The wait was painful. I saw my mother with her blackened eyes, wasted by her stay in the hospital.

At last he broke the silence. "What were you thinking in the homeroom before you felt like not doing anything but sitting quietly?"

Fear swelled in my throat, like food rising, but without nausea. It pressed up, untangling my tongue. "I was thinking," my cartoon character said in a fast mumble. It was Bugs Bunny talking, I realized. "I was thinking, Doc, that I'm not a genius."

"Ah!" Dr. Halston nodded vigorously. "You see, I knew we had something in common. I'm not a genius either."

I laughed, laughed very hard. I couldn't stop and then I was shaking and sobbing, sobbing so hard I was amazed. I didn't feel sad at all, and that was confusing. But, on the other hand, my personality didn't leak out with the tears.

Halston did nothing. He waited until it was over, then handed me a box of tissues. I blew my nose. I felt looser, less fragile. I put the wad of paper in an empty wastebasket. It was as heavy and as black as his glasses.

"Is not being a genius one of your secrets?" he asked when I returned to my chair.

"You bet, Doc."

"I'd prefer it if you didn't call me Doc."

"Sorry."

"But you can if you want. I'm not a parent or a principal. You don't have to obey me."

I didn't believe him so I said nothing. I had given up lying. It was the truth or silence.

"Is not being a genius a secret from everyone?"

"Yep."

"But especially from certain people?"

"Yep."

"Especially from your uncle?"

"Bingo."

"What would happen if he found out you aren't a genius?"

I thought that through. I had a lot of choices. I picked the one I believed would most impress him. "It would cost me two hundred million dollars."

"Well, that's a good reason to keep it secret."

"I'll say."

"Any other reason?"

"He wouldn't love me anymore."

Halston nodded. "Which reason is more important?"

"Important?"

"What are you more frightened of, losing his money or his love?"

I said nothing.

"Is that a secret too?"

"Everything is a secret."

"Well, I already know the big one, right?"

I said nothing.

"I see. I don't know the big secret. All right. But it's an important secret, right?"

I nodded.

"So, you've already decided to test me, why not make it a thorough test?"

"I want to go home," I said.

"We have another five minutes. That's what we're going to do, spend an hour talking every day, provided you continue to be willing to be well. You'll come here after school and you'll test me. You'll see whether, as you go back to living your life, anybody gets wind of your secrets from me. But you have to keep telling me or you won't be testing me and also you won't get well."

I nodded.

"So, for today, one last question. What bothers you more, losing your uncle's money or his love?"

"I don't know."

"Guess."

"Guess?"

"Take a guess. It's not a test. There's no right or wrong answer."

"Sure there is."

"Yes? What's the right answer?"

"His love."

"Then I would suppose your answer is the money."

I smiled. Halston smiled back. He glanced at the clock on his desk. "Okay. I'm going to let you go and call your uncle in here to tell him about your seeing me every afternoon. He'll ask me what's wrong and I'll tell him you had a panic attack, that as long as you and I can talk freely without him butting in, you'll be all right. He won't like that, but he'll accept it. Remember Rafe, what we say here belongs to us. I don't want you telling people my secrets either. Understood?"

I nodded. He stood up. I did too.

"I like you, Rafe," he said. "I'm going to enjoy our talks."

Uncle spent thirty minutes with him. A long, long time it seemed to me. Halston had probably cracked, giving in to whatever Bernie might demand. But the look on Uncle's face as he emerged was too confused and harassed for that to have happened. And he dropped the false tenderness, treating me with the real anger I knew he felt. "Come on," he said. "He says you can walk without help."

I tried skipping—not too obviously—to the car. Bugs Bunny's voice helped me talk; why not hop like him? Bernie glanced at my strange movements, but they were quick, so he didn't complain. In the car, Bernie grumbled, "He says you can go to school tomorrow."

I thought the doctor was crazy, but I said nothing.

"And then you'll go to him for an hour. We'll do that every day, except the weekends, until you're . . ." Bernie looked away. There was a long silence as we passed a shopping strip on Northern Boulevard. I forgot about Uncle and watched the world. I noticed things that I must have driven past hundreds of times without really looking. I spotted a Dairy Queen. I remembered how much I loved Brown Bonnets as a child—soft vanilla ice cream dipped in a hot chocolate sauce that instantly hardened into a molded shell. I wished I could have one now, but I would never dream of asking Uncle for something as pointless as ice cream.

"Dr. Halston wants me to call Dr. Jericho and withdraw you from the Columbia group. He says that's what you want." Uncle shifted, leaned toward me. At the heart of his powerful features were eyes that looked wounded and confused. "Is that right? You don't want to go anymore?"

I didn't answer. I wanted to go to Julie's. And it bothered me that Halston had specifically excluded the "genius program" activity. Wasn't that an indirect betrayal of the secret I had given him?

Bernie looked away. "If you didn't like Dr. Jericho and the others, why didn't you just tell me? I don't blame you. When I read the *Times* article I thought those kids sounded like creeps."

Another silence.

"We'll have to cancel your tennis lessons or move them to another time," he said.

"Cancel," I said.

"Oh, so you can talk." He leaned back and grumbled, "I hope this isn't a mistake." After another long silence, he sighed and said, "I don't want to spoil you like my kids."

I discovered something extraordinary the next day at school. I discovered that if I was silent through my classes, ate lunch alone, talked to no one during study hall or the movements from room to room, nobody minded. I found this so delightful I went to the bathroom to laugh about it in private. A couple of my teachers glanced in my direction when they asked their toughest questions and were puzzled not to see my hand up, but after a few such looks, they gave up. My friends—they were really jock teammates or nerd peers—spoke to me, asking whether I had been sick. I nodded, smiled, moved on, and no one remarked that I actually spent eight hours without saying a single word. It was hilarious to me. I hadn't been crazy to think I didn't exist. I really didn't.

I told Halston in a torrent of words. I detailed how I managed each encounter as a mute. In my excitement, I didn't notice that my Bugs Bunny voice was gone. He listened, chin propped on his right hand, smiling as if he also thoroughly enjoyed the joke. "And even with your sitting and doing nothing," he said, after my account was done, "nobody noticed you aren't a genius."

There was something nasty about that remark. I couldn't identify what. "Right," I said and retracted into my protective silence.

He waited patiently. When it was clear I would volunteer no more, he asked, "How did your uncle react to my conference with him?"

I shrugged. "He doesn't want me to be spoiled."

"What does that mean?"

"He doesn't want me to get lazy."

"What did you feel about that?"

I shrugged.

"Nothing? You didn't think anything? Or is that another secret?"

"No. I don't remember."

"Try."

I waited. All I remembered was the Dairy Queen. "I wanted some ice cream."

"Pardon me?"

"Ice cream. I wanted a Brown Bonnet at the Dairy Queen."

"Un huh. What made you think of ice cream?"

I thought he was being fairly stupid. This trying to keep me talking no matter how insipid the subject was silly. "I have no idea," I said.

"You sound angry."

"I'm not angry."

"When was the last time you had a . . ." he hesitated and gestured for me to help.

"A Brown Bonnet?" I said.

"Yes. When was the last time you had a Brown Bonnet?"

"You know," I said without thinking, "you're being pretty stupid." I don't recall if I brought my hand to my mouth, shocked at my rude if honest remark, but I certainly felt as if I should.

"Well, I warned you. I'm not a genius. But you don't have to be a genius to remember when was the last time you had a Brown—what was it? Derby?"

I laughed. He really was a stupid man. "Bonnet," I corrected him. "I used to have them when I was a kid. I guess the last time I had one was in Washington Heights."

"With your mother?"

In the middle distance, appearing at the edge of his mahogany desk, I saw it: that hot, nauseating day in Tampa, my arm in a cast, my father flirting with the Dairy Queen employee, and the slow-motion fall of my Brown Bonnet, smashing on bleached concrete.

"What are you thinking?" he asked, waking me from the trance of memory.

"I broke my arm." Halston nodded, almost as if he knew already. "I broke my arm in Tampa, visiting my grandparents. My father was away and when he came to get me at the hospital—" I caught myself. "Hospital? Was it a hospital?"

"Maybe it was a hospital. You were leaving a kind of hospital with your uncle. Perhaps that's why you remembered your father taking you from a hospital to buy you a Brown Hat."

I waved at the fog that had appeared, covering my vision of that day. I was forgetting something important. I tried to seize that image for examination, but it dissolved and I could remember nothing other than the chocolate shell shattering, ice cream oozing. I slapped my thigh. "I don't remember."

"It'll come," Halston said. "So. We have only a little more time and you haven't told me any secrets. What's the big one? Why don't we start at the top?"

By now I was aware that he hadn't been a fool to ask why I wanted a Brown Bonnet. I lurched from contempt for his intelligence to awe at his insight. He could not only read me when I lied, he could see things about me even *I* didn't know. That was unique in my experience; and my ignorance of myself was also a revelation.

"Well . . . ?" Halston asked. "Why don't we get the big secret out of the way?"

Maybe he could see through me, but maybe not. Maybe not to the darkest corner.

Halston smiled. "Doesn't have to be the big one. How about just any secret?"

"I jerk off," I said fast.

He nodded, bored. "Often?"

"At least once a day. Sometimes twice."

"Do you enjoy it?"

I laughed.

"Is that another stupid question?"

I thought about it. "No," I admitted.

"Well?"

"Usually. Sometimes, I don't know . . . I feel . . ."

"Dirty?"

"No. Bored."

Now he was interested. "You masturbate when you're bored or you're bored by masturbating?"

"Both," I said.

"Bored? Or lonely?"

"I'm never lonely."

"You're never lonely?"

"I like being alone."

"I see. When you masturbate, whom do you think about?"

I said nothing.

"Is that a secret?"

"I think about women."

"Women or girls?"

"Women."

"Women you know?"

"Uh huh." I was excited. This was like a hide-and-seek game. Only I wasn't sure if I was hiding from him or me. Whom did I *really* think about? The fantasies were a kaleidoscope of women, with only one pattern that was distressing—if my suspicion about the flash of that forbidden image was correct.

"Such as?"

I said nothing.

"Did I tell your secret to anyone?"

"No," I said. I had decided removing me from Dr. Jericho's program wasn't really a betrayal. I wanted to complain about it anyway, but I didn't, because I was also grateful.

"Is it your aunt? Do you think about her?"

I smiled, deeply amused by both the idea and the fact that Halston had made this guess.

"I see, I'm wrong again. Why don't you tell me? You know I'm not a genius. If we wait for me to guess right, it could take years."

"I think about my cousin sometimes."

"Your uncle's daughter?"

"No. My cousin Julie. She's my uncle's brother's daughter."

"Also a first cousin?"

"Yes."

"Is that a secret? That you have fantasies about her?"

"Sure."

"Okay. Our time's up. I'll see you tomorrow. If you remember anything about the ice cream, let me know then." He smiled. "That's your homework."

That night my uncle came home early for diner, a rare occurrence during the week. My aunt and I usually ate at different times, more to avoid each other than because of our schedules, so it was an exceptionally rare event for all three of us to eat together.

I was feeling pretty good after my day at school and my talk with Halston. I saw the beauty and logic of his plan. It took less effort lying when there was at least one person to tell the truth to. Besides, I wasn't really lying except by omission, thanks to the muteness. I also had an idea of what I could do to cure myself, thanks to what I thought was Halston's pointed questions about my sexual fantasies. I was a virgin— that was my problem. I loved women and had done nothing about it. That would make anyone nuts.

Claire, the middle-aged black woman who cooked and served me alone when there was no company, gave us a simple meal of lamb chops, asparagus, and mashed potatoes. When she left, Uncle asked, "How was school?"

"Okay," I said.

"I called Professor Jericho," Uncle said. "He said he was disappointed, but he understood."

"Who's that?" my aunt asked.

Uncle glanced at her disdainfully. "You know who he is."

"No, I don't." She lifted an asparagus to her lips and bit off its tip.

"You should."

There was a silence.

Aunt took another bite, chewed it thoughtfully, sipped from her gold-rimmed water glass. I thought she had dropped the subject when she asked, "So. Who is he?"

"God damn it," Uncle said softly.

"He's the head of the program at Columbia I've been going to," I said. That was so many words, spoken so normally, they both looked surprised.

"Thank you," she said. Aunt usually ignored me, but she was never mean when I did come into her vision. "Funny name for a professor. What does he teach?"

"You really don't remember," my uncle said. It wasn't a question. "My God, it was in the *New York Times*!" he said, as if that were something greater than reality itself.

"Oh, yes," Aunt smiled. "The genius program. You're not going any-more?" she asked me, pleased by this news, although I didn't feel her smugness was directed at me.

"Halston doesn't want him to go." That happened to be true, but as far as Uncle knew, he was lying—he had been told it was my choice. "His schedule is too tight."

"Rafael works hard," Aunt agreed.

"Can I still visit Cousin Julie?" I asked. Uncle frowned. "She's expect-ing me this weekend anyway."

"You've been staying with Julie?" Aunt asked.

"This is ridiculous!" Uncle turned from Aunt and pushed his plate from him, although he had eaten little. "What is the point of this game? You think hurting him," Uncle pointed to me with a sweeping gesture, the way a scantily clad model shows off a prize on a TV quiz show, "is a way to hurt me?"

"Well, isn't it?" Aunt asked. "I thought you loved Rafael. If I love someone, then when they're hurt, so am I."

What a day for revelations. Aunt wants to hurt me; and apparently she's been trying to do it all along. How did I miss that?

Uncle still had his arm extended toward me. He left it there and stared at his wife. "You admit it? You have the nerve to admit it." He got up now. His round face was ominous, his voice husky.

My aunt didn't seem frightened, although I was, for her. "Admit what? I'm not trying to hurt Rafael. That's something you made up. I was just saying that if someone hurts a person I love, then they're hurting me. You didn't seem to understand that basic fact of life."

As Dr. Halston might comment, it didn't take a genius to know she was talking about their disinherited son.

Bernie turned his back on the table, as if something had called to him. His face cleared of the threatening anger. He squinted into the darkened living room. I followed his eyes. The wall of leaded glass windows shimmered with dozens of small reddish circles, imitating their parent, the setting sun. He was looking for something else to do: prey to kill, a kingdom to conquer. I imagined that this was what sent him into the world to make millions; not the rigid logic of the materialism my parents believed ruled him, but his inability to win with the women in his life—my mother, his wife, perhaps even his mother, whom I never met. Women—they were the answer. Without their love, "chaos has come again."

"Rafe," he said softly. "Come with me."

I looked at my aunt. She was dressed in a black turtleneck, covering the wrinkles there that had been smoothed off her face by a surgeon. Her dyed blonde hair was combed up and back, stiffly puffed off her scalp by more than six inches, a passive and slightly bizarre leonine appearance, although it was presumably fashionable. I felt sorry for her. Her pretense of indifference to her husband's anger was unconvincing and pathetic.

Uncle patted the side of my shoulder, urging his reluctant thorough-bred to his feet. "We don't have a home here," he said with the smooth, resonant music of his cello.

Aunt raised her napkin to her lips and dabbed them. She ignored Bernie and looked boldly into my eyes. "God help you," she said softly.

"Come on," Uncle tugged at me. I got up. He said to her, "You're the one who needs to see a psychiatrist."

Embarrassed, I averted my eyes. Uncle turned me away and we walked out together. I heard Aunt laugh. A bitter sarcastic laugh, but full of real amusement nevertheless, not forced. "That's beautiful," she said to our backs, although not especially to us. She laughed again. Its mockery followed us through the house. I fancied I could still hear it long after we were shut up in Uncle's study.

He pointed for me to sit in one of his red leather chairs. He settled behind his desk and phoned someone. "Fred? Yeah it's me. I can't take it anymore," he said. "I want to do it now, no matter what it costs. Rafe is the only complication. I don't want to move him out of this school until the term ends. But he can't stay here in this—" he gathered energy to put his anger into it, "*freezer* with a witch. Yes," he glanced at me, "I think she has done harm. I don't see how it couldn't—" he looked away, "be very discouraging. It's as though he's invisible. God, what a bitch." He listened patiently to the man on the phone make a speech. I could hear the imploring tone of the voice on the other end but not the specific words. "I can't," Bernie finally answered. "I don't care if it costs me. Anyway, we'll see. We'll see if she really wants to roll in the mud. I can't wait to see how she feels being stripped in public. See how she likes having her heart cut open." He laughed crudely at something the other man said. "Yeah, right. If we can find it. Well, then her liver." He hung up eventually. I stopped listening; Uncle's talk was too ugly. He made other calls. I dozed off repeatedly, my head lolling forward and jerking me awake each time, only to go back to sleep and dream of Grandma Jacinta's *natillas*, her *plátanos maduros*, the hot sand of nearby Clearwater Beach and the endless Florida sky I watched while floating on my back in the Gulf's bathtub-warm water—blue burning into white at the horizon, majestic and empty.

I hadn't heard from the Tampa Nerudas since the catastrophic journey to Spain. After my testimony against my father, I made no attempt to communicate with them, nor, so far as I knew, had they. It might be that Uncle intercepted their attempts. It hurt that there were no more Christmas and birthday packages. But I couldn't blame them, considering what I had done to their son. I rubbed my face to wake up. Uncle finished yet another conversation. This last talk was with a female voice.

He told her he was leaving his wife that night. This meant the will would change totally to my favor. Someday the power of his money would be mine and I could afford to heal everybody's wounds. Even his son Aaron's, I told myself to assuage the guilt I felt at the wreck I had made of Bernie's home life. After compensating my father and helping the poor, I could return what was left to Aaron, restoring his birthright. I felt better about the whole situation until I remembered that if it weren't for me, healing Aaron wouldn't be necessary.

We spent the night at a motel in adjoining rooms. Bernie said he would rent a house in Great Neck until the end of the term and then we would move to the city and I would go to a private school next year. Before falling asleep, I asked again if I could spend Friday night at Julie's and he frowned again. He considered for a moment and decided to agree with an engaging smile. "Okay. But watch yourself. The women in our family are not to be trusted." He laughed as if this were a pleasant joke.

Over the next month, my life changed dramatically. Uncle rented a furnished three-bedroom apartment and hired an English couple, a butler and cook, to make sure someone was there on the many nights he never came home. A car took me to school, then to Halston's, and back to the temporary home with Richard and Kate, who served me as if I were an exiled and disaffected young lord, someone deserving of respect and pity. I visited Julie on Friday nights and Saturday mornings, joining Uncle and a woman friend for Saturday nights in Manhattan. The "friend" was Tracy, my uncle's mistress of many years, although they pretended to me to be recent platonic acquaintances. I told Halston many secrets; none were the big one. We reviewed what I remembered of the attack on my parents in Tampa. Halston didn't dig for too many details; I assumed that was because he had heard my mother's account when she was his patient. He also took me through my mother's abandonment of me during the Bay of Pigs invasion. Again, my recollections, at that point, were blocked, but Halston didn't have much interest in the details, anyway.

[I am trying to keep this free of later retrospective evaluations of Dr. Halston's technique because they would muddy a clear picture of the therapy as I experienced it then. At the time, the transference was excellent. Obviously, I had no distance on Dr. Halston's methods; therefore, to insert them into accounts of our sessions would distort reality. I am concerned, however, that professionals will need to know at this point that I wasn't blocked about the facts of what had happened in the past, not really, except for a few lurid details. I was blocked about what I felt and what the facts meant to the wider world. To use my favorite depiction of distorted thinking: I knew 2 plus 2 was the equation, I just didn't know that they would add up to 4—in my calculations, there was a different sum every day—and I had no conscious awareness that the answer of 4 was a taboo number.]

Halston focused on what I felt during the two days and nights my mother left me alone, especially my reaction to Uncle taking me to live with him after she was arrested. In general, contrary to what one might expect of a Freudian-based therapist, he concentrated on my contemporary relationship with Bernie. Indeed, it provided one of the rare occasions he seemed to argue with my perceptions.

"Uncle didn't rescue me," I said.

"No? You used the word rescue."

"Yes. But I asked him to. It wasn't his idea."

"He came and got you and took you in."

"Yes."

"Wasn't that rescuing you?"

"Yes, but . . ."

"But?"

"It wasn't his idea."

"I see. So it wasn't a rescue because you told him to."

"No, I don't mean that."

"What do you mean?"

"I mean I told him what he wanted to hear, so he would rescue me."

"What did he want to hear?"

"That he—" I paused. This was dangerously close to a final surrender. "That he . . . ?"

"That I loved him."

"And you don't love him?"

"No."

"Is that the big secret?"

"No," I said.

"But it's a secret?"

"Yes."

I enjoyed the talks, just as I enjoyed my silence at school, the falling away of my old friendships, and the new interest of the hipsters, as they noticed my hair growing longer and my withdrawal from participation in athletics. I shocked one of the school hippies when I approached him in the bathroom to ask if I could buy a nickel bag of grass. He watched, impressed, as I took a hit from a sample joint, released the smoke from my mouth and rebreathed it through my nostrils, à la Sandy. My credentials established, I was allowed to make the purchase. Thus supplied, I discovered a new joy, getting high alone at night and pleasuring myself in a luxuriant orgy, intensified by the heightened sensation and vivid fantasy the drug made possible.

Meanwhile, on Fridays and Saturdays I pursued my new goal, the shedding of my cumbersome, embarrassing, and—I was convinced—unhealthy virginity. The immediate obstacle, I believed, was a man, a member of Columbia's SDS steering committee with whom Julie was in love. At least that's how I interpreted their late-sixties style of dating: they slept together; he discussed everything with her; she adopted his ideas, sometimes with more passion than he felt; and they went together to most events, whether they were political meetings or the movies. They would have denied they were a couple, since they believed monogamous relationships were "bougie" (their slang for bourgeois), possession of a person being an extension of capitalist ideas; besides, Julie believed exclusive relationships were especially wrong for women, inevitably male chauvinist in practice, since inherent in the idea of ownership was the assumption of male control. This self-deception was accepted by their friends, thanks to their general political agenda. I need hardly explain why, despite my age and sexual inexperience, I was so much wiser about the depth and power of even a radical's need to love, be loved, and to possess his beloved with a monopolistic grip that would have impressed Andrew Carnegie.

In one way, Julie's lover encouraged my own hopes. Gus was a tall, skinny half-Jewish, half-Irish New Yorker raised by parents who had been members of the American Communist Party. Other than his reddish hair and freckled skin, he wasn't that different in physical appearance from me; and his social background was as close to mine as one could reasonably expect. I met him on the second Saturday I stayed with the women after my panic attack. Biting his nails, his legs bouncing restlessly, Gus questioned me about my politics, the kids at Great Neck High, and my reason for quitting the "genius program."

"Sandy," I said. She looked up from the picket sign she was creating with a black Magic Marker. A demonstration against the building of the gym was planned for later that day. "She radicalized me about it," I said, talking in their jargon. "I realized we were being exploited in an elitist way."

Sandy smiled. Her skin was too dark for a blush to be noticeable, but pleasure at my flattery was in her eyes.

Gus's mouth, which tended to hang open a little, like a friendly, over-heated hungry dog, drooped a bit lower and he nodded thoughtfully. "Right on, Sandy," he said and then resumed biting his nails. "You want to start a chapter of SDS at your school?" he asked as he chewed.

"I'm not a leader," I said.

"You shouldn't be," he said. He spat out a fragment of nail. "Leadership is dinosaur thinking. You should be in the vanguard of cre-ating a way for the other kids to educate themselves and create their own organization. That's why we don't believe in going into schools and set-ting up chapters ourselves. That's age chauvinism."

"Rafe would be a good choice," Julie said. She was in a black leotard and faded jeans. She looked extraordinary: at the peak of youth's bloom, her skin as luminous as porcelain, her black hair glinting, her big brown eyes full of passion and yet as innocent as a fawn's. To look at her for more than a few seconds was painful, although it was also a sublime pleasure. "He's political and a real teacher. And he wouldn't try to dominate them."

Gus nodded. "How can we help you do it?"

I said nothing. More secrets were piling up. The need to impress Julie and her friends, including her lover, was insistent, but I couldn't risk my uncle's wrath by openly embracing left-wing politics. And Halston? Dare I tell the doctor about my new secret life—or was it too close to my mother's madness? Halston might believe Ruth's ideology caused her lunacy.

"You know what?" Gus said. "Rafe should come to the demo today and to some meetings next week."

I marched beside Sandy that day. Julie and Gus walked ahead of us. I was apprehensive, expecting violence and then discovery by my uncle. But my first experience of political protest was like a stroll in the coun-try: getting high before we started, chanting together as we marched cheerfully in the sunny spring day, linking arms at the gym site to listen to a few speeches. Gus's was the best. His relaxed manner made him con-vincing. He talked to the crowd in the same tone and language he used in conversation—although it's true that his conversation was rather like someone giving a speech. Afterwards, we ate at the college hangout, the West End Bar. Whether it was the grass or the fresh air or my exaggerated feeling of having been brave, I was famished. I ate two hamburgers while around me there were more arguments between the tables as members of rival student groups took issue with Gus and the other SDS leaders, not about whether Columbia was wrong, but what exactly should be done about it.

It got to be time for me to head for my uncle's Manhattan apartment. I announced I had to return to the girls' place for my overnight bag.

"Overnight bag," someone repeated. "Far out," he added and laughed.

"I'll go with you," Sandy said.

"I'll take him—" Julie said.

"He can take my key and leave it there," Kathy said.

Sandy drained her coffee cup, stood up and said with a frown, "No, I gotta go, anyway. Come on." She left the bar quickly without me, as if I were an afterthought.

"Bye, honey," Julie said. She took my hand, pulled me to her and kissed me on the cheek. She had never called me honey before and the kiss, although chaste, was impressed firmly, with an affection that also seemed new.

Walking with Sandy, still thrilled by the lingering sensation of Julie's lips, I thought about why my cousin had become physical with me. It was because I marched in the demonstration, I decided, disappointed by that conclusion.

My gloomy turn of mind must have been obvious. "You okay?" Sandy asked while we were in the elevator going up.

The familiar construct of my relationship with Julie and her friends was depressing. I experienced this dismay (its cause so obvious from this distance) as an enervating achiness, like the onset of a flu, rather than as a realization that I had created yet another hall of distorting mirrors in which I would never find a true reflection or escape from my emotional maze.

[The dazzlingly rapid re-creation of self-defeating patterns in a neurotic is exactly what makes therapy so often frustrating for both doctor and patient. I have come, in a perverse way, to admire the resilience of mental illness. It is helpful for a therapist to bear in mind that neurotic behavior is actually a survival mechanism, however misguided. Its longevity is a sign of the patient's passion to live and in that paradox there is hope for a cure.]

Sandy put her hand on my arm and repeated, "You okay?"

The terror lived again. My skull was fragile, my skin vibrating: leaks were about to spring. Say what you're feeling, I urged myself, desperate to fend off madness. "I'm sad," I said.

Sandy nodded. She didn't ask why, to my surprise. She rubbed my arm and smiled encouragingly, but never said a word. The elevator doors opened. She marched out in her waddle walk, saying, "Come on." She opened the apartment door, tossed the keys into a bowl and kicked off her sandals. The soles of her feet were black. She extended her left hand, fingers asking for mine.

I looked at her, not understanding.

She wiggled her fingers again, eyes mischievous, and the request was clear.

She was strong and confident and I knew that she, unlike me, was real.

I gave her my hand.

She towed me through the hall into her room. Her platform bed was unmade, the yellow cotton blanket twisted at the foot, a pillow squashed against the wall. She kicked the door shut, pulled me to the bed and we sat, side by side on its edge. With a light touch, she stroked my left cheek once, ran her fingers through my hair, traveling to the back until she held my now very solid skull in her palm. She moved close to my lips and whispered, "You okay with this?"

My need was so heavy that I could hardly manage to do more than nod.

She kissed me. She pushed my lips apart with her tongue and explored my mouth restlessly; her hands were also restless—rubbing my back, kneading my neck, as if she wanted to mold me to her shape. I woke from passivity and pushed back into her mouth, for a moment tasting the eggs she had for brunch mix with my hamburgers, and then we were only a single human flavor. I touched her thin hair and dropped my hands to her back. It was soft, much softer than I expected from her vigorous body.

She broke from the kiss to unbutton my shirt. She undid each one with deliberate care, reverently. I kissed the top of her head once or twice as she descended and thought to myself: "Thank God. Thank God." When she reached my waist, she paused at the sight of the bulge in my jeans. She put a hand on it, raised her eyes and looked earnest. "Are you a virgin?" she asked.

I nodded.

This information seemed to galvanize her. She yanked my belt once, said, "Take 'em off," and stood up. She pulled her T-shirt over her head and into the air in a single motion. Without a pause, she had her jeans open. They dropped to the floor. She pushed them off the rest of the way with her feet. Fingers slid under her red panties and shoved. She stepped out of them and looked at me. I hadn't moved. The sight of her frank nakedness was mesmerizing. Her breasts were small, nipples dark and turned a little outwards, like poorly coordinated eyes.

"You're beautiful," I said.

She laughed. "Your turn," she said.

I didn't trust my trembling legs to stand. I tried to get my jeans and underpants off simultaneously while still on the bed. They got stuck on my thighs. I had never seen my penis in so ridiculous and desperate shape: levitating off me, flagging the world for attention. Sandy laughed again and pulled at the tangled mass of clothes. I flopped my legs up and down, like a baby being changed, as she negotiated them past my knees and ankles. She pushed my clothes onto the floor, then moved to lie beside me. We turned our bodies to each other. She kissed me briefly and looked at my erection. I followed her eyes. She lightly ran three fingertips up from its base to the head. It might as well have been an electric shock. My thighs and torso came off the mattress and I groaned.

"That feels good," she said, not a question.

I laughed.

She found my right hand and put it at the top of her bushy mound. She guided my finger to the moist split of her sex. "This is where it feels good to me," she said, holding my middle finger on the bump of her clitoris. "But not too hard," she said, moving it. "Like this—"

Without thinking, I flicked her hand away and straightened my fingers so they formed a smooth surface. Automatically, I gently rolled down and up, then side to side, massaging all of her sex with a subtle emphasis at the spot she thought so crucial. She looked surprised. I shut my eyes and remembered effortlessly: the gentle uneven pattern, down, up, around, side to side . . . The whole region loosened and opened as her warm body arched against me. Only this time, I was alive too, so thrilled by her belly's warm hug of my penis that I had to concentrate hard to replicate the complicated rhythm my mother had enjoyed.

I must seem stupid to the lay reader, or at least very confused, when I describe what happened next. Despite the surrender of Sandy's body, despite my own delicious excitement, a cold fact landed on my neck and froze my brain, severing it from the passion of my body. I understood, finally, with all the knowledge and emotional maturity truly necessary to comprehend the fact: *I had made love to my mother.*

By then, Sandy was no longer touching me to give me pleasure. She clutched me to her, grabbing an anchor as she surrendered to excitement. I increased the pace and penetration of my fingers as I remembered—and this was the most terrible, the most awful of revelations—what my mother had wanted me to do. Several times, on those illegal nights, she had squeezed her legs tight on my hand, urging me to press deeper. The demand had seemed angry and I had resisted, confused and, of course, unwilling. But I understood her request at last. I gave the answer she wanted to Sandy and finished my conversation with my mother as though it had been interrupted only yesterday, although she had been dead for six years and my part of our intimacy had been mute.

Sandy gasped, bucked, and moaned.

In a flash, as she climaxed, the mystery of my personality was solved, laid before me as clearly as in a scientific report: silent and manipulated, I had been my mother's passive lover, learning that I must please others or they wouldn't love me, and thereafter I re-created this dynamic with everyone else, massaging their pleasure centers so they would hold me close, mute and dishonest though I might be, because that was love to me.

The force of this revelation, one might suppose, ought to have paralyzed my passion and released rage at my maltreatment. I should have become impotent or violent. Instead, I let Sandy maneuver me on top, take hold of my penis and—a little puzzled by something, probably the fear in my eyes—guide me inside her.

And here was magic: horror was overwhelmed by joy. At last my longing had been embraced by someone other than me. My body was gleeful to find a luxurious home for its most deprived part. The psychological report in my head ignited. Its cold language burned off in a flare, forgotten. Insight and science no longer interested me. I became like any other person feeling utter pleasure, like anyone else enraptured by an embrace that, if it's a lie, is the most convincing ever devised.

CHAPTER ELEVEN

An Interpretation

BY MONDAY I WAS DESPERATE. WAITING FOR MY SESSION, THE DAY PASSED slowly. Losing my virginity hadn't chased away the cosmic terror always at my elbow, ready to suffocate me with panic. I composed a sentence that I repeated to myself when I felt it come too close—I am alone, a stranger on a rock spinning in a meaningless universe. Using those inadequate words to describe the awful sensation helped a little, but only as a stopgap until I could turn in all the secrets to my doctor.

"So," Halston said. "What's new?"

"I want to tell you the big one." There were all sorts of odd reactions throughout my body: ears ringing, stomach flopping, throat so tight the words had to be squeezed out.

Halston raised his brows, a vivid expression thanks to his bald head. "Why?"

"Why?" I was astonished.

"What's happened that makes you want to tell me?"

"I don't know." I was annoyed. "I just want to tell you."

"Okay."

"Don't you *want* me to tell you?"

"This is your time to talk about whatever you want."

I shut my eyes to dismiss the anger I felt at his game playing. When I opened them, Halston had propped his head on his chin and leaned sideways in his chair, an attitude that seemed to indicate only the mildest curiosity. "So. What's the big one?"

"I . . ." The speaking of it was harder than I expected. I mean physically hard. There were all sorts of explosions inside. I could have sworn I heard my heart pop and that my chest filled with blood. "I lied about my father."

"You lied about your father to whom?"

"To the judge, to the police. I didn't want to live with him anymore so I told lies." Now the discomfort left me, perspired away, although there was no sweat. I felt that kind of relief: cooling down to a pleasant exhaustion. "I said he was a Communist, that he treated me badly. Whatever Uncle's lawyers wanted."

"And they were all lies?"

"Well . . . Not the part about the passport."

"The passport?"

"He used a different kid's picture to make a passport to get me out of the country. It was against the law, but it wasn't . . ."

"Wasn't what?"

"Well, it wasn't really a crime. He didn't have time to get one for me and I knew all about it. I didn't mind."

"But he did do it?"

"Yes."

"And it is illegal?"

"Yeah."

"So, what did you lie about?"

"Well, I said he was a Communist and . . ."

"He wasn't a Communist?"

"No, not really. He *had* been, but . . ."

"He had been. How recently? I mean, from the time you said he was a Communist?"

"I don't know. A few years."

"I see."

Silence. Halston kept his casual pose.

"So you're saying I didn't lie?" I asked.

"I wasn't saying anything. I just asked."

"Oh come on!"

"Oh come on, what?"

"You're playing word games. I said those things to hurt him, to get away from him. I didn't really mean them. I said he was mean to me. He wasn't mean to me."

"I see. Then why did you say those things about him?"

"Because I was angry at him."

"About what?"

"About leaving my mother and me."

"Leaving your mother and you?"

"Yeah, after the attack. You know, he went to Cuba. And that's when she got sick. You know all about that."

"You keep saying I know all about that."

"That's the first time I've said it."

"You've said it before. Why do you think I know all about it?"

"Because my mother must have told you."

"Why don't we forget what I know from your mother? You said she got sick after he left?"

"Yeah, that's when she stopped talking, writing things down on paper—"

"She stopped talking?"

"Yeah."

"Why?"

"She said everything had to be kept—" I stopped before I said the next word—secret. The revelation felt like a slap. I looked at Halston.

He was still sideways in his chair, only mildly interested. "Yes . . . ?"

"I see. I was imitating what she did. But she didn't—I mean, when she started bothering me, she didn't stop moving." I laughed. "She kept painting the apartment."

"Bothering you?"

"Yeah, when she would, you know, in bed . . ." I gestured, inviting him to supply the proper term. I had no word for it. Incest was wrong, since that implied intercourse and activity on my part.

Halston frowned. He lifted his chin off his hand and straightened. "When she would do *what* in bed?"

"You know." I was ashamed. Besides, I thought, he knows; why did I have to spell it out?"

"I don't think you should assume I know anything. Why don't you tell me? If I know already, so what? I can stand hearing things twice."

My irritation at his playacting was strong. I looked away and talked to the floor, both to spare myself embarrassment and to hide my annoyance. "She didn't talk. She wrote things on paper, tore them up and flushed them down the toilet. And she kept painting—"

Halston interrupted, a very rare occurrence. Also, impatience crept into his usually neutral tone, "Yes, you said that before. But what did you mean, she *bothered* you?"

"I was getting to that!" I snapped at him. "She kept painting my room so I had to sleep with her."

"You *had* to sleep with her?"

"Well, I couldn't sleep in my room."

"So you had to share her bed?"

"Yeah."

Silence. Halston stared at me. He adjusted his glasses and nodded for me to continue.

"Well, I didn't understand what was going on, but, you know, she rubbed up against me and you know . . ." I trailed off.

"I don't," he said and continued to gaze at me with an intense, cold expression.

"Didn't she tell you?"

"Forget that I knew your mother."

I smirked. "That's a little hard."

"For the purpose of giving me information about her. I'm sure that's not too difficult. You said she rubbed up against you and . . ." He gestured for me to continue.

I looked away. "You know . . . She came."

"She came?"

"I don't know what to say!" I was infuriated by his coyness. What was the point of embarrassing me?

"You're saying that she rubbed up against you until she had an orgasm?"

"Right." I continued to avert my eyes. I was sad for her and angry that he had needlessly forced me to repeat her sin. "I mean, when I had sex with Sandy—"

"Pardon me?" Halston interrupted. His tone was full of feeling. He sounded outraged.

"I forgot to tell you. I mean, we didn't get to it." I looked at him boldly, proud of myself. "I lost my virginity on Saturday."

"Rafael," Halston leaned over his desk toward me. He usually called me Rafe. "What kind of game is this?"

"Game?" Now I felt I was in trouble. I hadn't been quick enough before, but my senses came alive to the fact that something was wrong.

"You come in here and say you're going to tell me your big secret and that turns out to be something everybody knows."

"What? What do you mean, everyone?"

"Anyone who knows your story. Your uncle has custody of you. Isn't it true that your entire family knows this story? Everyone you know is aware that you testified in court about the passport and your father's politics."

I was confused. For a moment, I couldn't see how he was wrong, although I was sure he was, and also I didn't understand why he was angry. "I guess."

"And then you casually drop these bombs. That your mother bothered you in bed and that you lost your virginity to your cousin. You say those things as if they aren't secrets."

"I didn't lose my virginity to Julie. I did it with Sandy. Her friend."

Halston waved his hand, dismissing the fact. "When did your mother bother you?"

"After my father left, before she—you know, before she went crazy and got arrested at the U.N." I understood now, understood the misunderstanding, and I was frightened. "She never told you?" I asked plaintively. Another blocked memory was unstuck for me: Ruth pretending to be catatonic and whispering to me that Halston was a fool. I was in danger. All my senses told me so: I wanted to run. But where?

"Forget about what you think your mother told me. Let's pretend I never met her. Tell me what you think she did in the bed with you?"

Think. He used the skeptical word think. "It was nothing."

"Nothing? You said before she had an orgasm."

"I don't know for sure. I was a kid."

"Why did you say she had an orgasm if you weren't sure?"

I was exposed. Part of me, the chess player in me, cursed my brain for having left myself so undefended. I couldn't contest him. We had come so far; and I thought we had made the journey together, abandoning the usual lies and tactics. I appealed to him to stop trying to defeat me. "Look, don't you understand why what I did to my father is a big secret? I've been living with my uncle because he thinks I hate my Dad and that I hate my mother, but I don't, I just wanted his money. I wanted to live well and I was angry at my Dad. He never did anything bad to me. It's a secret, a real secret. You can't tell anyone."

"Why? What would happen if everyone knew?"

"A son who lies about his father? Who lies to his uncle?"

"What lies?"

"That I want him to be my father. That I love him."

"You've told him that?"

I nodded. Surely he must see, he had to understand. How could he have listened to the story of my life and not comprehend what I had done?

"Did you tell your uncle what your mother did with you in bed?"

"No!" I was appalled.

"No? Not even that night when your mother was arrested and you wanted him to take you with him?"

"No."

"Wouldn't it have been another reason for him to pity you and rescue you?"

"It isn't a lie."

"I didn't say it was a lie."

"But you think I'm lying?"

"Why do you think I don't believe you?"

"I don't. I don't think anything. Look, all she did was hug me close and rock back and forth and she . . . I didn't really understand until I was with Sandy and I realized what Mom was doing."

"I see. So you realized only this Saturday what happened years before?"

"No. I just understood it better."

"If you didn't think what your mother did was so wrong, why didn't you tell me about it sooner?"

I held my head in both hands, rubbing my forehead, trying to reason it out. I wasn't used to talking about the past. Its pictures were clear in my mind. Without words, without their labels and their judgments, what had happened was simple. Only the words changed what they meant, that's the way it seemed to me: "There is nothing either good or bad, but thinking makes it so."

"I thought maybe my uncle found out, maybe he knew from you." That wasn't true. The instant I said it, I realized I never had such a thought. I simply didn't think much about whether anyone else knew. I didn't want to remember it had happened, and with my mother dead, to speak of it was merely cruel. Cruel and shameful.

"I see." Halston glanced at the clock, pulled his thick glasses off with his left hand and rubbed his eyes with the right. "Your father had left.

Your mother wasn't talking, writing things on paper and she painted your room."

He was believing me. I nodded eagerly and helped. "She never finished painting it. That's why I had to stay in her bed every night."

Halston put his glasses back on. "How many nights?"

"I don't know. A month. Two months. I can't remember."

"And every night she rubbed against you?"

"No, no. A few times." I remembered the first time, the gentle passage of air through my room. "Actually the first time was in my bed."

"She came into your bed. Your father was away—"

"It was the night he sent his letter. I think it was that night."

"What letter?"

"The letter explaining why he wasn't coming back to live with us."

"You slept in your mother's bed for a month or maybe two and a few times she rubbed up against you and made sounds?"

"She moaned. And moved around. You know, like she was excited."

"And you understood that she was having an orgasm?"

"I didn't know what an orgasm was. How could I understand?"

"Then how did you know she wasn't crying?"

"What are you saying!"

"Calm down. I'm only asking questions. Sit in your chair."

I hadn't realized I was out of it. I wasn't standing, actually. I was perched on the chair's edge. I sat back, stiff with anger. "What are you trying to tell me? That it didn't happen?"

"I'm not trying to tell you anything. I don't know what happened. Only you know. But you don't seem to be sure. You seem to have made up your mind on Saturday when you had sex with this other girl. I just want to help you to be sure. I think it's important for you to know what you feel and what you think happened."

I looked at the edge of his desk, at the carved mahogany lip and tried to project the past. What was there? A dark room, waking from sleep, her legs capturing me, rocking, low moans, her trembling. Were they sobs? Had I misunderstood?

"Let's go back to before your father wrote the letter. You saw your parents being attacked in Tampa. You saw something happen to your mother. What did you see?"

"I saw her naked. I saw a man—" I stopped. A man peed on my mother, that's what I remembered.

"You saw what? What was the man doing to her?"

"He was peeing."

"You saw pee come out onto your mother?"

I said nothing. The *Gusano* had an erection. He pointed his erection at my mother's face. No. On a city street? Out in the open? How could that be? I gave up, uneasy and angry. "What was he doing? You tell me."

"I don't know. You do. You were there."

"Of course you know. Mom must have told you."

"Your mother was ill. Very ill. You're not. It's possible, even probable, that you can remember better than she could. I know there's part of you that wants to be ill, but you're not. You can remember clearly and understand what you remember, especially if you don't think about how you wished things were, or what your uncle wishes happened, but what actually did happen."

"But I don't remember clearly. I was scared. He was doing something, maybe planning to rape her, maybe peeing, I don't know."

"I understand. But yet you're so sure your mother had an orgasm with you in bed?"

"I'm not sure."

"You're not sure?"

I wasn't. I looked down at my lap and wished I could see into myself and know the simple truth, no matter how ugly. "Why would I make it up?" I asked aloud.

"That's an interesting question," Halston said, his voice friendly again. He glanced at the clock. "Our time's almost up. Maybe you should think about that. Did you want your mother to have sex with you?"

I could hardly breathe. Had everything in my head been a lie? Were the secrets not secrets, the lies not lies, the truth a fantasy? Had I been hiding nothing?

"But if it isn't true, I'm crazy," I blurted out, not really talking to Halston.

"That's interesting. Why do you say that?"

"I'd have to be."

"Does it shock you to know that at one time or another, all boys fantasize about being their mother's lover?"

I shook my head no. Actually, it did. It shocked me, in this context, down to the bottom of my soul. I had vague knowledge, the conversational and literary awareness of Oedipus and of Freud using it to make a famous theory, but that went no further than a shadowy notion that sleeping with your mother leads to madness and that merely having the desire somehow caused emotional distress. What Halston was really referring to, infantile sexuality, was unknown to me.

"It doesn't shock you?" Halston repeated.

"You mean, they dream about it?"

"No. There's a period of time when all children wish to be their parent's lover."

I nodded wisely, although again I didn't really understand.

[I'm not a fan of ignorance and I don't approve of the general direction of modern education, toward specialized knowledge, and I dislike the silly love of professional jargon in psychology and psychiatry—indeed, writing this in laymen's language is an attempt to counteract that. However, all that said, I sometimes wish educated people knew a lot less about psychology and psychiatry, rather than the partial and distorted information they do possess. Too often, in our time, an educated person discussing human psychology resembles a five-year-old operating a Mack truck.]

"What I mean to say," Halston glanced again at his clock, "is that having sexual wishes and fantasies toward a parent is a universal experience during a certain time in childhood. But, of course, they aren't acceptable to us. Even as children, they are taboo. So people sometimes distort, or become confused, about events or feelings or even just wishes toward their parent. Our time is up," he said. He smiled awkwardly. "We'll talk about this tomorrow."

By now, of course, professionals can foresee the course of my therapy with Dr. Halston. He took me through the rape, my father's desertion, and my mother's incestuous behavior, and—without making any direct assertions, so that I felt the insights were mine—convinced me of several important conclusions about my past. First, that whatever the anti-Castro Cuban may or may not have been doing to my mother while my father was being beaten and humiliated, I saw it as a sexual attack because, out of terror, that was how my unconscious translated the reality, using my own taboo wishes as source material for worldly evil. I knocked down the Cuban with the gun, horrified by the sight of my id on top of my mother, castrating my father in the process (the image of his "decapitated head" in the hands of his attacker), and substituting for him as my mother's protector (with dangerous psychic consequences to myself). Hence, I felt that I had driven my father away from us (murdered him) and that I was obliged to take his place as my mother's lover, "forced," as it were, to fulfill the taboo Oedipal fantasy for which my mother, instead of me, was punished by madness and suicide. Of course, if Dr. Halston were presenting this interpretation, he would do so in much more learned—and coded—language, and without the details you have read of the actual events, many of them uncomfortably inconvenient to his analysis. Since Halston was in theory, if not in practice (he never put me on the couch and was only casually interested in my dreams), an unreformed Freudian, educated and trained in the 1930s and 40s, he is an easy target for criticism by a psychiatrist of my generation, but it is important to remember that, however misguided, he was applying his skill as he had been taught, and that he expected this understanding would help me. Even a great surgeon, holding a rusty penknife, can't perform a successful heart transplant.

Unfortunately, thanks to my natural affinity with psychoanalytic thinking, I soaked up Dr. Halston's analysis like a thirsty fanatic lost in the desert. What it meant to me emotionally was quite simple: I was an untamed beast whose life history was a fantasy. I had a new reason, a better reason, to keep my story secret. It was made up.

I resented my uncle more than ever. He had lured the loathsome creature in me out of its lair and gave it a club to kill my father. I said so to Halston. He, in turn, explained the concept of projection, and once again, there was no villain in the world but me. My ruthless uncle was just another dark face of Rafe's, another monster from my subconscious. I was the whole world: I had swallowed reality and everything was born from me: God and Satan, love and death, truth and lies.

It was hardly a surprise, then, that Sandy was infatuated with me. I seemed, even to myself, to have become quite irresistible, in a dreadful sort of way. She called me every night that week and, much to Julie's astonished and, I hoped, also jealous eyes, openly took me to bed with her the next Friday. That was how Sandy announced our affair to her roommates. The following morning we came to breakfast together, her arm draped around my bare shoulders—I was wearing only my underpants. I said in a friendly voice, "Hi Julie," to my cousin's grave expression.

Kathy, smoking a joint, hunched over the *New York Times,* looked up. "This is definitely heavy," she said in a mumble.

"Sandy," Julie said, nodding toward the hallway, "I have to talk to you."

"About me and Rafe?" Sandy said, letting go of me. She moved to the coffee pot. "You want some?" she asked me.

"Yep," I said and sat down. Kathy offered me the joint. I sucked in the harsh smoke and felt truly and beautifully evil. I had had intercourse three times that night, quadrupling my lifetime experience in a few hours. Sandy had taken me into her mouth, I had used my tongue the way I knew how to use my hand, I had rolled her nipples between my teeth, licked the soft tissue of her inner thighs and kissed the firm cheeks of her ass. I was brimming with self-hatred, but it was a supremely confident self-hatred. I may not be a genius, I thought, but I'm a genius at living.

Julie didn't answer Sandy. She stared at me—I grinned back—with a hopeless and rather sad expression. Sandy poured coffee for us, handing me a mug. She sat down, rubbed my shoulder lovingly for a moment before reaching for the milk carton. "Go ahead," she said, glancing at Julie.

Julie sighed. "I think we should talk about this alone."

"If it's about me and Rafe then he should be part of it," Sandy said.

"It's okay," I said.

"I don't think it's okay," Sandy said.

"I don't have a problem with what *Rafe* is doing," Julie said, surprising all of us with her angry, pointed tone.

"What does that mean?" Sandy asked, pushing her chair away from me to face Julie. The raspy sound it made on the floor lent an ominous sound to her question.

"Of course Rafe is going to like . . ." Julie shook her head, irritated and embarrassed. "I mean, I can't hold him responsible . . ." Again, she couldn't finish the thought.

"Responsible for what?" Sandy leaned forward, resting her elbows on her knees, coffee mug dangling between her legs. Her pose was like a construction worker's on a break.

"He's a *teenager!*" Julie said as if that settled everything.

"Not in bed," Sandy said and laughed with pleasure.

Kathy giggled, then lowered her eyes.

"It's not funny," Julie said.

"You wouldn't have a problem about this if I were a man," Sandy said.

"Of course I would. Everybody would. Especially you. You'd be screaming about what a pig you are."

Sandy shook her head, turned away from Julie, put her coffee cup on the table and said to Kathy, "I don't get it. I don't know what this is about."

"Look," Julie said. "I'm responsible for Rafe. He's sixteen years old. Look at him. He's dropped out of the math program, he's sitting in his shorts smoking a joint. This is crazy. This is just irresponsible. That's all.

You can tell yourself all kinds of stories, but what it amounts to—" Julie abruptly cut off her speech and slammed an open cabinet door shut. Its bang made us all jump. She shouted at Sandy, "God damn it! This isn't what we're fighting for!"

"You're not my baby-sitter," I said.

Julie, concentrating on her friend, glanced at me as if she had forgotten I was there. She was fully dressed, in the same leotard and jeans she wore to the demonstration the previous week. She looked more beautiful than ever, almost a different species than Sandy. Despite my odd state of mind, I understood that her concern for me was genuine—whether or not my hope that it was motivated by jealousy was right. It was obvious Julie cared about my welfare in a way Sandy did not, or ever would.

"I'm okay," I said to her in an intimate tone, wishing that the others weren't there. I felt, at that moment, that if we were alone, I would have had the strength to tell her the truth, that I loved her, had loved her since the day she had tried to defend me from my mother's scolding about the hunt for the *Afikomen,* that I knew she possessed something almost no one did: an unselfish heart. I could measure the breadth of its generosity against the narrowness of my own.

"I'm not angry at you, Rafe," she said softly.

"This is fucked up," Sandy said. She stood up and got between me and Julie. "Come on. Let's go for a walk and deal with this."

They left. Kathy passed me the joint. Looked down at her paper while I took a couple of hits. She raised her eyes when I passed it back and said, "The Vietcong are amazing, you know?"

I agreed.

I felt alone. Increasingly, as I absorbed Dr. Halston's interpretation, that was how I experienced life. Not the quaking terror of a self without boundaries, but claustrophobic behind the walls he had built. Since everything was really happening inside me, the real world had lost its frightening quality, its ability to trigger panic. That was good, but unfortunately, it had also lost its promise of redemption. By the time Julie and Sandy returned, I didn't care what they had said to each other, or felt impelled to act by the revelation that I was still deeply in love with Julie. One was unimportant, the other hopeless. I liked having sex with Sandy, and if Julie had managed to put a stop to it (she had failed) I would have been angry, but without much conviction, since other than the sex, I really didn't want to go on spending time with Sandy. When Sandy took me to her room after the walk, and somewhat gleefully told me of Julie's "bougie and fucked-up reaction to our liberated relationship," how she had "forced Julie to confront the contradictions inside her head," all I felt was despair that more people had become a victim of my evil machinations. Why were they all so helpless against me, whether they were dull or successful, Latin or Jew, adult or youth, Communist or capitalist? Was it a world of fools? Was that what my mother had really meant, that being crazy is knowing, really knowing, just how easily humanity can be manipulated and therefore, how hopeless it is to try and save them?

I believe it was then, or sometime during those weeks, that I first thought of adopting my mother's solution and killing myself. Her method didn't appeal to me. I learned of her self-immolation from Dr. Halston. I had known of the fact of her suicide for a few years, but not much about the details. He told them to me in a rather cold voice—her actions were, after all, something of a professional rebuke. He wanted to know why I asked, but I didn't tell him. I had no secrets from him and I was glad to have one. By then I had come to the conclusion that keeping secrets was part of my genetic makeup. The night I heard the full story of her suicide from Halston, I wondered why the images of Ruth, putting up her sign, pouring gasoline over her wild hair, staring at the crowds with her green eyes, and lighting a match, didn't move me, either to horror or pity. Because I didn't think she was wrong or foolish or mad to have done it, except for her choice of dying. Too painful, for one thing. And not damning enough. Her statement, THIS IS THE WAY THE WORLD WILL END, was too easy to dismiss.

I found a nearly full bottle of Seconal in my uncle's bathroom. There were more than enough to kill me. I stole it, convinced he would be less suspicious of it disappearing, given the confusion of three residences, the mansion, this temporary one, and his pied-à-terre in Manhattan, than if I merely took some of the pills. Besides, I wanted to be sure to die. I knew institutionalization would follow a failure and that was more horrible to me than life or death. I began writing my farewell statement. It would take a few days, since I planned a full confession as well as messages and apologies to Bernie, my father, Julie, my grandparents . . .

That caused me to wonder about Jacinta and Pepín, with a pang of loss. I was alone. Uncle, as usual, was in Manhattan, Richard and Kate had fed me and gone to bed, I had smoked a joint, written the first page of my suicide note, and there was nothing to stop me from picking up the phone, dialing long-distance information and calling them. Of course, my uncle would see it on the bill at the end of the month, but I would be dead by then.

I hesitated for an hour, crept down the hall to check that the servants were asleep, and then made my bold move, sneaking into Uncle's empty bedroom to use his phone. My heart was pounding. Why was I so nervous, I wondered, since I planned to end the world's ability to punish or reward me? I had to will myself through the enervating terror of dialing, my voice trembling as I asked the operator for the number. My fingers barely had the strength to write them down. I felt as if I were going to lose consciousness as I rotated the dial and waited through six long rings before I heard my grandfather's sleepy voice answer, in Spanish, *"Hola?"*

"Hello," I said in a croak.

"Jello," he said, alarmed now, waking up. "Who's calling?"

Hearing his old, sad voice, I was scared to talk to him. I cleared my throat of all the cowardly obstructions. "Is Jacinta there?" I asked, my intonations odd, either deeper or higher than normal, fluctuating wildly on the scale.

"What?"

"Is Jacinta Neruda there?" I asked in a grave voice.

There was silence. A long, strange silence. Finally, he said in a suspicious tone, "Who is this?" The words were separated. They reminded me of an actor I had seen playing Hamlet's Ghost. He spoke all his lines as slowly and morosely as a death march.

"Remember me," came into my head.

"I'm a friend." I could think of nothing better. I put my finger on one of the white buttons, ready to cut the line.

"A friend?"

"Yes. May I speak with her?"

Another strange silence. I had a wild thought: maybe he was tracing the call. That was so absurd I wondered if I were really a lunatic.

"I'm her husband," my grandfather said at last. "Do you know me?" he asked. He was up to something. He wasn't skilled enough to prevent me from hearing the calculation in each response and question, but I couldn't imagine what was the point of fencing with me. Why not just put her on? I didn't consider telling him my name. I was sure he would hang up on me. I should have called during the daytime. Probably he would have been out.

"No, sir. I only need a moment of her time. It's not an emergency. I have some information for her."

"You better tell it to me." He coughed. "I'm her husband. You can tell me."

"This is—uh," I was stuck. I couldn't believe he was being so difficult. "I can't."

"I'm sorry." He coughed again. "My wife . . ."

I put my finger on the button. I would call during the day tomorrow and get her.

". . . my wife," he continued softly, embarrassed, "passed away last year."

I cut the line. I held the dead receiver to my ear and pressed the button down firmly, as if erasing what he had said. But no matter how long I pressed, keeping the white button hidden in its black hole, she was still gone, gone without my noticing.

CHAPTER TWELVE

The Cure

ON APRIL 23RD, 1968, THREE MONTHS INTO MY THERAPY WITH DR. Halston, I had almost finished my suicide note. I was stuck on the last paragraph, my farewell to Julie. I wanted to apologize to her, reassure her that she had done all she could, and yet also prevent anyone from concluding my judgment of the world was wrong. I found the right words during lunch period and finished my written farewell. I would have my last session with Halston, my last meal alone, and take the pills after Richard and Kate were in bed. They would find me in the morning, certainly beyond any chance of rescue.

The car my uncle sent to take me to Dr. Halston was waiting at four. The driver was excited. He was listening to WINS, an all-news radio station, and immediately told me the news. Columbia radicals, black and white, had seized Hamilton Hall and were holding at least one administrator hostage, demanding the university sever all research and recruiting programs tied to the military and the Vietnam War and that plans for the infamous gym be canceled. There was, as always, a lot of confusion about who was doing what and an expectation of immediate violence. There were reports that some students were also being held hostage—totally false—and I used those rumors to get the driver to take me to Manhattan. He insisted he check with his dispatcher. I told him to explain that my cousin was probably caught in the middle of this situation and that my uncle would want me to come to the city and help him make sure our people were okay. The dispatcher, excited by the melodramatic picture I painted of a captured relative, agreed to the change in destination.

We reached Columbia around five. I had no plan. I was drawn to the site as if it held a promise of something great. I was rewarded. The staid building was alive. Students jammed the windows above colorful and outrageous banners they had draped over the grave stone facade. And facing them were not police, but more students, and adults too, a few arguing, but most encouraging them. I saw two middle-aged women put supplies into buckets that the radicals pulled up while the crowd cheered. The spectacle delighted me.

I spotted Sandy in a third-floor window. I called to her. She shouted back, "Join us!" The others with her at the window misunderstood slightly, thought she was referring to everyone, and took up her phrase, chanting to the crowd on the street, "Join us! Join us!"

I didn't move. Not frightened; thinking I didn't deserve to. From somewhere to my left came a negative answer. I looked that way. There was a trio who were obviously—given their white shirts, ties and blazers—from the "Majority Coalition," the conservative students. They shouted back, something about the right to go to class. They couldn't manage to make that thought into a chant; without rhythm and unity their words were lost on the air.

Sandy and her buddies answered: "Join us! Join us!"

Below her, on the second floor, a window was jammed with five blacks. They harmonized with another chant in between each "Join us!" I knew its correct spelling from the earlier demonstration. "No Gym Crow! No Gym Crow!"

All along the street the chants were taken up, drowning out the "Majority Coalition." Exhilarated, I crossed toward the rather forbidding pair of black students who seemed to be guarding the main doors to Hamilton Hall.

From above and behind, my approach was greeted with applause and cheers.

I noticed a pair of Columbia Security cops to my right. They stared at me as I passed. I reached the entrance. The taller of the blacks said to me, "Hey, brother," and opened the door to me. I felt a surge of relief, a feeling that, at last, I was home.

For about seven hours, life was vivid, fascinating, dangerous and fun. There were meetings, votes, discussions, tomfoolery on every floor, in every room. They aren't pertinent to my narrow, self-absorbed narrative except to say they delighted me, that all thoughts of self-destruction were forgotten.

Votes were taken on whether marijuana or liquor should be allowed. Both lost for obvious reasons of security and publicity. (However, I shared a joint with a black freshman, Billy MacFarland, in a broom closet—outlaws hiding from the outlaws.) Most of the discussions were preoccupied by the desire of the blacks to be alone in the occupation of Hamilton Hall. There were all sorts of abstract arguments brought to bear on this, but the most compelling, including for me, was the notion that they shouldn't seem to be acting under the leadership of white radicals, shouldn't allow the situation to appear as if they were merely followers. Of course, it hurt the feelings of the whites. (Especially mine; that transporting moment of being ushered in by a black who called me brother was spoiled.)

Around midnight, Sandy told me she was going to the apartment to get supplies. She kissed me, working her way to my ear, and whispered, "We don't have to rush back." I said no, mumbling I had promised somebody to help them watch the rear doors for a shift. That was an obvious lie, but Sandy didn't challenge it. She asked Julie to go with her instead. Probably that had some significance; I didn't think about it.

Half an hour later, I was on my haunches in a corner of the dean's office listening to the white and black leaders debate tactics when Gus called me to the phone. "It's Julie," he said, with a puzzled look. "She wants to talk to you."

"Listen, Rafe, we're at the apartment." Julie's voice made a nervous whoosh in my ear. She was rattled, although she tried to sound valiant. "There were detectives waiting for us when we got here—"

The phone was taken from her and I heard a smooth, almost amused, male voice say, "Rafael? My name is Gunther. Your uncle hired me. We've got your cousin and her friend here. They're fine. Nothing's going to happen to them. But they're gonna stay here with us until you come out. If you leave the building and the campus, you'll find your uncle in a car right across the street from the gate. Once you're with him, we'll let Julie and her girlfriend go. I'll put your cousin back on for a second."

Julie's trembling voice returned. "You have to come out, Rafe. You're a minor. They can use this against us."

Gus was next to me, smoking a cigar, wearing sunglasses, lounging in the dean's chair. "What's up, man?" he asked, seeing the stricken look on my face.

Someone turned up the volume on a transistor radio to hear a Stones song and I had to shout, "It's Julie. My uncle's outside. He's got detectives holding Julie!"

This public announcement brought the attention of the student leaders. Once they understood who my uncle was, they were furious. Gus took the phone. He told Julie to run from the detectives. She explained that wasn't possible. "We'll call back," he said.

"I'm going out," I announced. I couldn't allow my final day on earth to be another betrayal of people's dreams, no matter how hopeless.

Most of the radicals were against that, black and white. Some thought it was a distraction. They argued back and forth. The majority didn't believe my uncle would dare to continue to hold Julie and Sandy if they exposed him to the press.

"They'll say it's no different than what we're doing," I said and the whole room looked at me as if they had just noticed my existence. I had offered nothing to any of the discussions so far. I was happy to be a child among them, sharing their risks without fussing. I continued, "It's my decision. I don't want to fuck up what you're doing."

"That's cool," one the blacks said.

Gus called Julie to insist the detectives let them go before I walked out to Uncle. Predictably, they refused until I left the building. Julie told Gus not to worry, that they had no legal way of keeping her and Sandy and, without the threat of doing something about my "kidnapping," she would be fearless.

Billy MacFarland, whom I had known for only five hours, accompanied me down the stairs and hugged me before I went out. "Tell the truth about us," he said. He had confessed in the closet while we shared a joint, that he was sure this confrontation would end only with their deaths.

"Remember me," came into my head and, foolishly, but ardently, I said it to him.

On the street there were lots of people milling about, mostly supporters, and only one police car, although it was unmarked, parked behind my uncle's limousine. The door was opened by his driver and I ducked into its dark interior. The leather seat didn't give in to my body. I seemed to float on it.

"Don't lie," he said. "Did you go there to see if Julie was okay or join those hoodlums?"

"I went to join them," I said.

He shifted in the seat, turning all the way to face me. "Why?" he said.

"Why not?" I said.

He slapped me. The blow was unrestrained, with none of my father's embarrassment at losing control. My head hit the backrest and I let it remain there, sullenly. While the sting on my cheeks faded, I thought— nothing he does can hurt me anymore.

"Don't talk to me like that. I don't deserve that tone from you." The car was on the move, carrying me away from the island of revolt, back to Uncle's sleek city. "Do you know what Dr. Halston said to me?"

I shook my head, unconcerned. My secrets didn't have to be kept anymore.

"He said this was a good sign." Uncle made a noise. "The world's crazy."

"Did you let Julie and Sandy go?"

"That's none of your business. You're a child, do you understand? You're a minor. You're my ward. You don't have anything to say about where you go and what you do. They think they understand the world. What a joke. They're gonna get their heads broken and it'll do them good."

We were sweeping through Central Park, crossing to the East Side. I shifted to the door, pulled the handle, and it swung open. The black road moved like a swift river. I crouched on the car floor and hung my right foot out over its blurred surface. I shouted, "Let them go!"

"Sir," The driver called.

On my haunches, I shifted my left foot closer, inches from diving off. Uncle was still in his seat.

"Sir . . . ?" The driver slowed.

"Don't stop," Bernie said in a calm tone.

"Let them go!" I was screaming. I realized I sounded demented, although I felt fine. I felt good, in a way.

The river resumed being pavement when the limousine braked.

"Don't slow down," Bernie said to the driver in a casual tone.

The road became swirling black again. "I'll do it!" I screeched. I think I was crying.

Bernie leaned forward and shouted, "For what? For two stupid girls? You're worth a thousand of them." He was almost face-to-face with me. "I was ready to give you the world! The whole fucking world." In the odd light of the limousine, created by a band of floor bulbs and strobed by the rapid passing of the park's street lamps, Uncle's head was hideous and bloated, bigger than me, bigger than the car. "Everything else is just crap! There's you!" He poked me, hard, on my forehead. "And nothing else! Just you! Nothing else!"

I couldn't jump. I stayed halfway in, halfway out. Uncle settled back in his seat and looked out the window on his side. Eventually, we slowed down and stopped at a red light on the east side of the park.

The driver got out. He looked at me. "Could you put your foot inside, sir?" he asked.

I did.

"I'm locking the doors from the panel," the driver said to Uncle. "Let me know when you want me to give you control."

He shut my door.

I slumped onto the car floor, leaning against the seat. "I hate you," I said without much energy or conviction.

"Who cares," Uncle said with a similar lack of passion.

We stopped at his city apartment for twenty minutes. I was left in the locked car with the driver. Uncle went up, presumably to talk to Tracy, and returned with a suitcase. We drove to the Great Neck apartment in silence. It was almost three in the morning when we arrived.

"You'll stay here tomorrow," Uncle said, leading me to my room. "I'm going to see Halston in the morning. Obviously, he doesn't know what he's doing." Uncle looked at my bed thoughtfully. "I should have known. Years ago." Uncle left, saying, "Don't even think of sneaking out."

I opened the window. The air was mild, scented, alive. I tuned to WINS, the volume low, and listened to its hysterical, disapproving account of my friends in Hamilton Hall. There was no news. There would be soon, I knew, knew better than the grown-up world did. The whites would leave Hamilton and take over the other buildings, one by one, until the whole campus was shut down. I was sure, in my heart, they would be defeated, driven mad like my mother, cast out like my father, but I would not betray them. I would end my weakness, my greed, and my lying fantasies.

I took off my clothes and swallowed the whole bottle of pills. Across my body the spring air was delicious, a caress. The radio's voice was ugly and strained. I couldn't be a part of either the world's fragile beauty or its persistent terror. And so, Rafael Neruda, traitor and coward, was put to death.

CHAPTER THIRTEEN

Healing

AFTER MY STOMACH WAS PUMPED AT LONG ISLAND JEWISH, UNCLE arranged for me to be admitted to the Turson Child/Adolescent Psychiatric Hospital on Manhattan's Upper East Side to cover the ninety-day observation period required by law. A psychiatric resident, Dr. Susan Bracken, was assigned to my case. My life had been saved thanks to the conscientiousness of Uncle's butler, Richard. Alerted by my uncle that we were coming home in the middle of the night, he tried to wait up, only to doze off. Starting awake at four A.M. and finding that he had missed our entrance, Richard crept up to my door, heard the radio playing faintly and looked in to ask if I wanted something. He noticed the open window and my nakedness. Deciding I would catch a chill, he fetched a blanket and, while covering me, saw my note and the bottle of pills.

Susan Bracken is nearly six feet tall and has strong features as well as a deep voice, but she speaks mildly, probably an old habit from adolescent self-consciousness about her size. She came to interview me in my private room the following evening. She pulled the shades on my barred window, depriving me of a gloomy view of the East River shrouded by rain.

She startled me right away. "You really wanted to do away with yourself, didn't you?" she said, pulling a metal folding chair next to my bed.

My legs and arms were in restraints. My mouth was perpetually dry and my head throbbed. I watched her cross those long legs, her white doctor's smock swishing noisily. She glanced at the folder she had opened, propped by a knee. "You took so many Seconals that even getting to you so fast one of the emergency team was sure you'd be a vegetable." She smiled. "Actually, if my memory of the ER guys is right, they don't say vegetable, they say zucchini."

I didn't think her funny. I stared through the stabbing pain in my temples, wishing I could fire them out and disintegrate her.

"Lookit," she said. "I'm gonna lay my cards on the table. I know a lot about you already. I've got your—" she held up my farewell letter "—what do I call it? A suicide note? I mean, it's eight pages long. It's almost a short story." She lowered her flat wide brow, like an ape's I thought at the time, and studied my document. Thanks to her heavy forehead and deep-set eyes I couldn't see their color or expression.

"You're ugly," I said to her.

"The way I'm talking? Or the way I look?" She untangled her legs, leaving my folder on her thighs, and comically spread her arms as if displaying herself.

"Both." My voice, from disuse and the hangover, was a croak.

"Really? Everyone tells me I'm a," she put a sarcastic emphasis on the word, "*handsome* woman." She smiled at me. "I think I prefer being called ugly. Anyway, it's rather unusual for a suicide as determined as you to survive. I would say the chances you'll try it again are excellent. Oh, maybe not right away. You'll be too depressed for a while. Funny thing, but killing oneself seems to take a certain amount of effort. Real depression is just too overwhelming even to plan a suicide. Anyway, I've also, thanks to your uncle, got all of Dr. Halston's private notes. That's quite unusual as well, but I guess your uncle can make unusual things happen."

I nodded.

Susan shut my folder and dropped it to the floor. She put her elbows on her knees and leaned close. I got a clear look at her eyes. They were a muddy brown and too small for her big face. They were also, although she looked boldly at me, somehow shy. "Here's my problem. I have all this history about you and yet I haven't heard it from you. I don't really know if I should get your history again, assuming you'll talk to me, or whether I should violate my training and tell you that, unfortunately, I've already reached a conclusion about you, maybe even a wrong conclusion, and that I'm interested in your story, very interested, and I want to talk to you although I think I'm too prejudiced to work with you."

I groaned. "What are you talking about?" I croaked.

"You sound hoarse. Want something to drink?" I nodded. She poured a cup of water from supplies on the night table, put a straw in it and held it to my lips. When I was satisfied, she said, "I'll just say it. I think you like being a victim. I think you like feeling guilty. From reading your letter, it seems as though you, not your parents, not your uncle, not the world, but *you* are responsible for everything. I wouldn't be surprised if you told me you think you started the war."

Very quickly we were having a fight whose tone was an intimate argument between equals. Susan brought up the events in Tampa and Spain, insisting I was a child and had no responsibility for my actions, my inactions, my thoughts, or my desires. She didn't touch the subject of incest, one way or another, whether it was fantasy or truth. I objected, throwing at her Dr. Halston's (I thought they were mine) insights about my memories being projected fantasies from my id.

She finally cut me off. "What crap. Look. Did you get those Cubans to attack your mother?"

"No—"

"Did you make your father go to Cuba and desert her?"

"No—"

"Did you make your mother go crazy?"

"No—"

"What did you *do*, actually do, that was wrong?"

"I told you. I lied about my father."

"Oh yeah, right."

We had been talking forever it seemed to me. "Isn't our time up?" I asked. My head hurt worse than ever, arguing with my arms literally tied was intensely frustrating.

She laughed. "Listen, I'm so out of the textbooks, stuff like that is beside the point. I told you. I can't work with you. I've got all kinds of problems with your way of seeing things. Here's what I mean. You told Dr. Halston you lied about your father because you were angry that he had left you and your mother?"

I nodded.

"So why did you go away with him in the first place?"

I had no answer, but I was sure that was because I felt ill and tired.

"Were you happy to go with him to Spain?"

I nodded.

"How come?"

"I loved him!"

"But you were so angry at him you lied and made him an exile from his own country? So why did you go in the first place?"

"I was testing him. Or really, testing myself, seeing if I could suppress my murderous impulses toward him."

"You're saying it was an elaborate plan of a frustrated ten-year-old's ego? Not just a scared little boy who was glad to see and be with his Daddy?"

"Go away," I said.

"You see. You're losing this argument. That's another thing about you. You don't like to lose. You expect to win at everything. You think you can take care of everyone, fool everyone, and when you can't, you don't think you have a right to live. It makes me very angry." To my amazement, she actually shook her fist at me, then released her grip and ran the hand through her tangled, dull brown hair, the same muddy color of her eyes. One mass of it was left stranded in the air as though a breeze were blowing, although the room was hot, its air stale. "I can't treat you. Lookit, I know why you lied about your father. I'm supposed to lead you to it gradually, but you probably know that."

I nodded.

"You say in your letter after Halston began treatment you read many books on psychology?"

"I read some."

"Some. I bet you read plenty. So you know the technique?"

I nodded.

"You know why I think you did that?"

I shut my eyes.

"So you could win, so you could defeat Halston, even if winning meant beating yourself."

I opened my eyes. She was right. I hadn't liked being surprised about the Brown Bonnet. I smiled.

"But you're not so smart. You know why? Because nobody is. Not even Freud. You aren't smart enough to figure out why you testified against your father."

I felt odd. For the first time, a little scared. What was there to be scared of? I was dead, really. I was furious and unhappy to be alive, but what could scare me?

"Think about it. What changed from when you arrived in Spain to when you decided to leave? What was new? It's right here." She tapped the folder, still on the floor, with her foot. "It's not in your letter, it's in Halston's family history. Under the heading of siblings. It's important to know, as I'm sure you found out from your reading, it's important to know if a patient is an only child, and also what order."

I stopped thinking. I shut my eyes and saw nothing, no past, present or future. I prayed for her to leave.

"Do you have a half-brother or a half-sister?"

I opened my eyes. The room was glazed pink for a moment before clearing to its hospital fluorescence.

"You don't know and neither does Halston. Okay," she bent over, got the folder, and stood up, straightening her white smock. "I'm going. But ask yourself, who did you send into exile? Your father or that sibling?"

The horror for me, at this revelation, was that I had forgotten completely about Carmelita's pregnancy. Until Susan mentioned it, I would have said I was an only child. And, more shocking than that, I wanted to argue about it. I wanted to say: How do we know that child was ever born?

Susan moved toward the door and then, apparently irritated beyond all reason, turned back. "You blame yourself for all the world's problems. You make yourself into the greatest villain in the history of the world, full of terrible feelings and fantasies. But the one, perfectly natural, unpleasant feeling, your sibling rivalry, *that,* oh no, not that, that you don't remember, that you don't even notice." If someone had come in they might have assumed, from her passion and my passivity, that she was the patient and I the doctor. "You're not a terrible person, Rafe. You're not so great either. Here's the awful secret, the thing you've been keeping even from yourself: you're just like everybody else and there's no escape from that. Not even suicide." She waited for this to sink in and then she laughed. "I should be defrocked," she said and walked out.

I was ready for her when she appeared next, late the following morning, bringing my lunch.

"You're lying," I said, while she maneuvered the tray's legs so the boiled chicken, peas and mashed potatoes would levitate above my chest.

She untied my right hand and offered the spoon. I took it. "No kidding. What about?"

"You *do* think you can treat me. That's just a lame trick."

"No, you're wrong." She pushed the left side of her messy hair out and it stayed there again, signaling for something. A cab? A hairdresser? She was big and odd, like a clown. "I told them today to assign somebody else. You'll be seeing Dr. Blaustein this afternoon. He's very good."

"You're lying," I said, my mouth full of peas. One of them fell onto my neck.

"That's why I'm here. To tell you I'm out. Didn't want you to think it had anything to do with our talk yesterday. It's not your fault. You've read about countertransference, haven't you?"

I shook my head no. She explained it. That the doctor's personality and history could interact harmfully with the patient flabbergasted me. I ate less and less while she expounded on this theme.

"Well," she said, standing up. "I'll call the nurse and she'll clear your meal. You know," she moved to the other side of the bed and untied my other hand, "I don't think we need these restraints." She looked at me with an encouraging smile, her head hanging low between her broad shoulders. Her hunched posture was another habit born out of self-consciousness about her height.

"Do you think Halston did a bad job with me?"

"Horrendous," she said with utter conviction. I had no idea at the time how outrageous this statement was, a complete violation of ethics and sensible procedure. It was also, I believe, a brilliant stroke, the very quality that makes Susan a gifted therapist. "And, on top of that, since he had treated your mother, he should never have treated you. There's no excuse for it."

"Why? Because she killed herself?"

"No. Because he wasn't listening to *you*, only to you. He had heard another side. He had years of impressions and judgments about key events in your life that hadn't come from you. There was no way for him to give what you told him proper weight. He was prejudiced before you walked into his office. And there was the relationship to your uncle, to someone who had given him so much money. He couldn't be open to receive your signals without a lot of interference."

I must have fallen into a trance thinking hard back to every session, every exchange with Halston. I was startled when Susan said, "What are you thinking?"

She had sat down again, elbows on her knees, hair still askew, peering at me with her small, shy and yet intent eyes.

"I'm thinking something you won't like," I said.

"Big deal."

"Big deal?"

"Lookit. You gotta do me a favor." She straightened, locking her fingers together, and stretching her long skinny arms. "You gotta stop paying attention to what everybody else thinks." Done with her body-yawn, she sat up, head back, allowing herself to be tall. "You're carrying too big a load. To hell with what the rest of us think. So—what were *you* thinking?"

"I was thinking, if Halston was a bad doctor, why didn't I see it?"

Susan smiled. "Beautiful. He does a bad job and it's your fault. You know what that is? That's pride. Yeah, I know, you think it's modesty, you think it's being tough-minded, hard on yourself. It's grandiose. You were upset and confused. You were vulnerable. You didn't have a chance in hell with Halston. No one would." Susan shook her fist at me. "Don't you get it? You're a kid. You've been nothing but a kid your whole life. You haven't had a chance with any of these people, from your mother to your uncle. Yeah, yeah, I know. You're smart." She gestured to the dismal room, the barred window, my untied restraints. From the hall I heard the almost perpetual moan of a seventeen-year-old schizophrenic. "Look where it's got you."

I felt like crying. My head was still broken by the drugs and everything hurt, keenly, unrelentingly. "Please," I said.

Susan leaned forward and said softly, "What?"

"Please. I need you to be my . . ." I was about to sob so I stopped, shut my eyes, forced the emotion down, and sighed. When I opened them, Susan was rubbing her forehead. The violence of her motion left streaks on her flat brow. She was uneasy. "Please help me," I finished the thought.

Susan stared at me solemnly. I pleaded for rescue with my eyes. I was no longer sure what I had turned my back on. What had I wanted to die to avoid? There were double images for everything: my mother the lunatic, my mother the prophet; my uncle the barbaric king, my uncle the lonely patriarch; my father the revolutionary, my father the coward; my nation, the richest and most free, my nation, greedy and murderous. Was there really a different truth, a life I had lived and never known?

Susan looked down at the backs of her hands. Like the rest of her, they were long and bony. She turned them over, as if studying her palms. She had parted the index and middle fingers from the ring and pinky, making V's, the silly and mysterious Cohen sign. She closed and opened them like scissors and glanced at me.

She looked surprised. "Why are you smiling?" she asked.

"Do you know what my name means?" I said.

She looked confused.

"My name," I said. "It's a promise from God."

Postscript

DR. BRACKEN'S WORK WITH ME AS A PATIENT TOOK TWO YEARS. THE reader does not need to go through the laborious, frustrating and often confusing process of the reconstruction of the facts, feelings, fantasies and truth of my past that was Susan's difficult job, a job she did, I think it's fair to say, brilliantly. The narrative account you have read was what we discovered in our work. Susan used many unconventional techniques, including having me do research to confirm certain memories.

My uncle was patient and faithful to his guardianship of me. He paid for all that help. To be sure, he was often angry with me and for a time seemed to be permanently disappointed about my prospects. Susan got me back in school by the following term and, although I was not the compulsive student I had been, I did concentrate on the sciences. My uncle wasn't thrilled that I chose psychiatry as my discipline, but he understood, as I assume anyone would, why I felt obliged to devote myself to the imperfect science that, finally, in the hands of a talented practitioner, had saved me. Susan helped me understand the danger of my illusions. I chose psychology knowing I was not a genius and that I could not rescue the world, but I confess I embarked on my career with the hope that I might return, in a small way, the gift of peace and forgiveness granted to me by all the men and women who had dared to attempt an answer to these child-like questions: Who are we? Why do we do what we do? And—most naive and beautiful of all—can we change?

PART TWO

Gene Kenny:

A Case History

CHAPTER ONE

Countertransference

WITHIN MINUTES OF MY FIRST INTERVIEW WITH GENE KENNY, I KNEW I didn't like him. I was twenty-five. I had received my medical degree from Johns Hopkins, done my residency at Bellevue, and was completing my training under the supervision of Dr. Susan Bracken at her clinic in Greenwich Village. I had no hint that treating Gene would profoundly alter the course of my life, I had no inkling of the tragedy that would engulf him, but I knew I didn't want him for a patient.

Gene wasn't my first patient, not by a long shot. He was, however, among the very first I worked with under Susan's guidance. She had opened a community mental health clinic in a brownstone on Tenth Street, off Sixth Avenue. Uncle and Susan both considered me to be overqualified for this low-rent venue, but I wanted to learn from her and I liked the fact that the free or moderately priced therapy offered would attract a different class of patient. The well-heeled, articulate, attractive, mild neurotic that is typified in the public mind by Woody Allen movies, it seemed to me, had plenty of talent at their disposal.

In 1977, the year Gene Kenny began treatment, the clinic saw a wide variety of distress. Alcohol and drug addiction, wife and child abuse (and one case of husband abuse), a constellation of sexual disorders, crippling anxiety and chronic depression—all were plentiful, displayed by the diverse population of New York City, ranging from artists to Lower East

Side gang members. What our patients had in common, with one exception, was lack of money. (The exception, an elderly woman, featured miserliness among her many anal-retentive attributes.) Of course schizophrenics also showed up, and a few people with problems I discovered were purely physical, but whose symptoms were first apparent in behavior—brain tumors, thyroid problems, certain kinds of migraines and one man with a collapsed lung. (He assumed his agonizing pain was psychosomatic. Not surprisingly, later on he did become my patient.) We referred those cases to Bellevue Emergency, as well as the schizophrenics, although we did see a few of the latter as outpatients.

Gene was fifteen. He had a full head of thick black hair, pale unhealthy skin, pouting lips, a strong chin, dark eyes, and a long skinny nose set slightly off center, like one of those Picasso Cubist faces. He looked European, although I must confess I don't know what that means when, as a technical matter, everyone who isn't black or Asian looks European. I guess what I mean is that his features were clearly not mixed. He seemed to be the child of generations of breeding from a specific region—Eastern Europe to my eyes. I was surprised when he opened his mouth and spoke in a thoroughly American way.

"They told me I was supposed to sit here," he said from his slouched position in a chair. It was placed by the right wing of the desk. We were in one of two basement rooms for private sessions.

I had come from a group therapy session upstairs. It was eight o'clock, my last appointment of a twelve-hour day. I sat in the desk chair. "Hello, I'm Dr. Neruda."

"Yeah," he said. He averted his eyes with child-like shyness, a boy of eight, rather than the sullenness of an adolescent.

"You're Gene?"

He nodded. He rolled his full lips inward, between his teeth, and pushed them out, over and over, eyes intent on the surface of my desk. He appeared to be very nervous.

I had already read the preliminary interview, done by a New York University psychology graduate student interning for Susan. These were the facts: Gene was fifteen, an only child, in the ninth grade at the One Room School, a progressive private school in the Village, living with his parents on Lower Broadway. His father's occupation was listed as photographer, and his mother's as a copy editor working for a school textbook publisher. Since they qualified for free treatment, their income, at least on tax returns from the previous two years, was modest. (The private school was paid by his father's mother. This could mean their income didn't reflect their actual wealth; but Susan's policy was first to decide if the patient deserved treatment and worry about payment later. If we took on Gene and discovered his grandmother was a millionaire, we would hope to be paid eventually. Anyway, this was less of an issue for me than for the other two staff therapists. I didn't need a supplement to what Susan paid me.) At the bottom of the interview a paragraph stated he complained of sleeplessness, palpitations, loss of appetite, difficulty concentrating in school and that his mother had brought him in. She reported that Gene's school had suggested they seek help; the school's psychologist, a friend of Susan's, had recommended us as a low-cost option. To relax him, I began with questions we both knew the answers to.

"Did your mother bring you?"

He nodded. "She's waiting."

"How old are you?"

"Fifteen."

I went through a few more. Then, "So, what's going on, Gene? Why are you here?"

"Mommy brought me," he said.

I noted that he used a child's term for her. "You don't want to be here?"

He shrugged. His eyes roved the desk.

"Many people prefer to talk while lying on the couch. Would you like to lie on the couch?"

He frowned. His eyebrows were thick and jet black against the pallor of his skin. They were expressive and let me know he certainly did not want to. They crossed together in a frown, reared up in surprise, and then scanned the couch with an unmistakable look of fear and disgust.

I was about to tell him he could stay in the chair, when he said in a mumble, "Okay." He hurried to the couch, never looking in my direction. He sat on the edge, head hanging, and waited, as if ready to be punished.

This was the moment when I experienced a strong feeling of dislike for Gene. It shocked me. I had never felt anything like it as a doctor. Both at the hospital and at the clinic, I had hostile, repulsive, sometimes physically deformed patients; patients who were trying and upsetting because of both their behavior and their appearance; patients who were virtually autistic or psychotic. I treated one schizophrenic who moved his bowels while I took his blood pressure. Certainly I hadn't enjoyed many of those encounters but I never felt dislike, a complete lack of sympathy.

"You can take off your shoes," I said, following a routine.

He pushed off each of his Keds sneakers without untying them and flopped back. Only his torso, however. His legs draped over the side, feet skimming the parquet floor—another indication that he wasn't happy about lying down.

"Do you want to be on the couch?"

He shrugged. I saw, but pretended not to. "What did you say?"

"It's okay," he said, almost inaudibly.

"I'm glad we're doing what you want," I said and immediately regretted it. What in God's name did I mean by this taunting comment?

"What?" he mumbled.

"Nothing," I said, compounding my mistake. A therapist should be the last person on earth to maintain that something said casually has no meaning. Besides, he had probably heard me. His "What?" was a reaction to the oddness of my remark. My cover-up just made things worse. For a moment I considered ending the session and fetching someone else to see him. Unfortunately, Susan was the only other staff present at that hour and she was busy.

"You can put your feet up," I said.

He winced. His reaction was unmistakable: my suggestion caused him pain. Yet he promptly raised his feet to the couch. He submitted, but did not relax: keeping his knees bent, arms rigid, palms pressed onto the cushions, as if prepared to leap up.

I left my seat to move to the wing chair placed a little behind and to the side of the patient's head on the couch. That would keep me out of sight unless he twisted his head and gave me an angle to view his expressions. Although it may strike the reader as silly, this seating arrangement was a deliberate reform of the tradition, which is a chair placed directly behind the couch, to prevent both therapist and patient from any chance of seeing each other's face.

Gene heard my movement. Our floor had buckled from water damage over the winter and groaned at the slightest pressure. His head snapped to the side, his feet arched, and his right arm reached out as if to ward off an attack, like a newborn's startle reflex.

"I'm going to sit in this chair," I explained. Gene twisted to watch me. "If I stay behind my desk you'll have to shout."

He nodded. I settled into the wing chair. Gene remained in his pose. It was an uncomfortable position he couldn't maintain for long.

I decided to unveil the mystery of my suggesting the couch. That was one of Susan's lessons—don't build unnecessary walls between patient and doctor. "I prefer it when people are willing to lie on the couch," I said. "That way I can listen to you without having to think about my own face—whether I should smile or frown or look blank. That takes away from the time I should be spending listening to you. And you're free to let your thoughts wander. It frees both of us to concentrate on you and not on our manners. But if you don't feel comfortable we can work with you sitting up. I see several people who hate the idea of the couch and we've done fine."

For a moment he remained frozen in that awkward twist. Then he allowed his head to fall back and his arm returned to his side. His knees straightened a little.

"So you're staying on the couch?" I asked.

He shrugged. Shrugging while lying down is difficult but he could move his skinny shoulders as expressively as his eyebrows. I was trying to elicit something positive or negative from him, a clear statement of personal preference. His passive behavior and suppressed anger at his own obedience is a common pattern; I hoped to learn whether that was typical of all his relationships or a defense mounted for this situation.

"So, Gene, do you want to stay on the couch?"

"I guess." That was a barely audible murmur.

"Do you want to be here at all? Or is it entirely your mother's idea?"

Another silence. His fear of answering was palpable. "I don't know," he said at last. He seemed relieved to have come up with this temporizing response.

"Guess," I said.

"Guess?" he asked, his adolescent huskiness breaking up into a child's trill.

"Yeah. Take a guess. Do you want to be here?"

"I had to," he complained. "One Room told my Mom I had to."

"So it's not your mother's idea?"

He shrugged.

"And you don't want to be here?"

"I don't know."

I waited.

He waited. Then he complained, "How can I know until afterwards?"

"You can't know whether you want to be here until after you've come and gone?"

Again, Gene tried to twist to see me. He could only accomplish that by raising himself but he didn't feel that rebellious. He gave up, letting his head lie sideways, mouth in a pout.

"What do you mean?" he said, back to a mumble.

"You said you can't know whether you want to be here until afterwards." I paused. I was about to push this beyond my formal training. Susan wouldn't mind, but, strange as it might seem after her success with me, I wasn't comfortable with her bolder methods. "I don't believe you," I said mildly.

"It's true," he said sadly. "I don't know if I like something until . . ." He trailed off, sighed, and then added, "Sometimes for a long time."

I had my answer, in a way. He was passive about everything. Well, I thought, brushing aside my transitory dislike, this is an easy case. We'll identify his feelings and with that recognition a gradual confidence in expressing them and insisting on their acknowledgment will relieve his depression and anxiety.

"I think you're confusing two things," I said. "Not wanting to be here is a feeling; knowing whether you're right not to want to be here is a judgment."

Gene shut his eyes. He drew up his legs. Turned sideways on the couch, that put him in a fetal position. His left hand drew close to his chest. I peered at it and discovered what I expected to: his thumb was hidden inside his fist. He was fighting an urge to suck it.

"I want to know what you feel, Gene. I'm not worried about whether you're right or wrong to feel it. That's something you can decide, or maybe the world can decide. Personally, I don't think there is any right or wrong when it comes to feelings. Actions, yes. Not feelings. Our job is to help you know what you feel."

Gene opened his eyes. He brought the fist with the hidden thumb up to his chin. "I didn't want to come," he said, his voice trembling. He paused, hardly breathing. What did he expect from me? Shouting? Violence?

"So you don't want to be here?"

He nodded. His fist covered his mouth now, the entombed thumb centered on the lips. Was he pushing them in and out as before? That was a sucking motion. Freud would have his diagnosis by now. He'd grab a helmet and flashlight and move resolutely back into the cave of time to illuminate the story of Gene's breast-feeding—and, I knew uneasily, he might be right to go on that quest.

"Do you want to be on the couch?"

He shook his head, moaning a little. He had regressed dramatically and it happened again: I didn't like him. Why was he so undefended? I felt an urge to shout at him to sit up and act like a man. Fight me, I thought, staring at the ball he had made himself into.

"Then why are you lying on it?"

He shook his head and moaned again.

"Gene, I don't know what that sound you're making means."

He moaned some more, head still shaking no.

I lost it again. "If you don't talk to me, I'll have to end the session." There was sweat at my temples. I was literally hot from emotion. I was shamed by all these blunders, but I couldn't seem to stop making them.

His moaning ceased at my scolding, of course. He dropped his fist to his stomach and covered it with the other hand. His face looked sweet and innocent. "Sorry," he said in a low, contrite voice. Thanks to my mistake I had lost ground.

I should end the session, I thought. "If you——" I sighed, tried to settle down. "If you didn't want to get on the couch, why did you?"

"I thought you wouldn't like me," he answered clearly.

"Why do you care if I like you?"

His thick eyebrows did their dance, up in amazement, down in a frown. I suspected this was a mimicked expression. Mother? Father? Probably mother. He added a shrug and said, "You're the doctor."

"If I told you to jump off a building, or I wouldn't like you, would you do it?"

"Yes," he said immediately and rolled onto his back. He stretched out, growing before my eyes into adolescence. "I like being on the couch," he said. His innocent expression, the Picasso baby face, seemed to evaporate. His eyes narrowed; his full lips pouted.

"Is that how it works with everybody?"

"What?" he said—snapped it actually, in a loud irritated tone, very much the fifteen-year-old.

"Do you want everybody to like you?"

"Do I want everybody to like me?" he repeated musingly. "No," he said, finally. "But almost everybody."

"And would you jump off a building for almost everybody?"

"Yes," he said and smiled at the ceiling. It was a becoming smile, his wide mouth generously displaying an array of white teeth.

"Do you like being so accommodating?"

"What?"

"Do you like being someone who would jump off a building to get people to like you?"

"Yes," he said. He grinned. He was in full rebellion, goading me. The changes were rapid. He moved up and down the scale of maturity like a virtuoso playing the piano. There had to be more to his mystery than simple passive-aggression or an oral fixation. "What made the school think you should come here?"

"I don't know," he said.

"Come on, Gene," I snapped. What was that? I had once again lost control of the dialogue. "Is it your grades?" I added, trying to recover.

"We don't get grades."

The One Room School was a failed experiment from today's point of view in education, a sixties anomaly—open classrooms, no tests, teaching through projects rather than rote learning. I knew that and had my own opinion of their methods, but the therapist's view of the world isn't necessarily the patient's. I wanted Gene to describe his landscape. "What do you get?"

"Pass, fail. So I guess it's a grade. They say it isn't. You know . . ." He sighed.

I knew. To an adolescent, adults remain hypocrites no matter how hard they try not to be. "Are you failing your courses?"

He nodded. "I guess. We haven't gotten a report for the fall yet. I didn't finish two of my projects. That's how you pass. I was supposed to write a play for English and I messed up the biology field project. I'm bored, that's all. I could do them, but I don't have any energy."

He was too comfortable with this subject. "What does your father do?"

"What?" Startled, his right leg came up.

"What kind of work does your father do?"

"He's a . . ." Gene hesitated. "He's a photographer."

"For newspapers? For advertising?"

"No." That was said firmly. "He's an artist." Gene gave the word a slight English accent.

"Un huh." There was something here. I waited.

"That's not how he earns a living," Gene said.

The phrase sounded borrowed. Maybe this was his father talking. "Oh?" I said.

"He earns a living as a carpenter." Gene warmed to this subject. "Well, more than a carpenter. He designs what he builds."

"Yes?" I sounded interested, since he was. "What sorts of things? Cabinets?"

"All kinds of stuff. You know, like, people will want their kitchens built, you know loft people need their kitchens built, 'cause usually . . . because it was industrial space."

Another borrowed phrase. Nevertheless, for the first time Gene was talking effortlessly. I asked more questions and he was glad to give me details. I let him ramble and enjoy the memories. He used to be picked up from grade school on his father's lunch break, and he helped during the afternoons, measuring, hammering, sawing wood, cutting Formica, taking pleasure in being his Daddy's assistant. His mother's full-time work for a textbook publisher had meant his father often took care of Gene during the week, bringing him to class in the morning and covering the afternoons, until he was old enough to be on his own after school.

"When was that? When did you start coming home alone?"

"I don't know," he said impatiently. Gene didn't want to change the subject from descriptions of his father's jobs. "I didn't go home for a long time. I went to where Daddy was working, even when I was old enough to walk alone. I remember he had a job in Brooklyn—"

I interrupted. "But you don't go to his jobs now?"

"Well . . . no. Dad doesn't do that much design and building anymore."

"He's concentrating on his photography?"

"He has a show."

"A show?"

"An exhibition. In a very important gallery." Gene said the words— "very important"—as if they were themselves very important words. He seemed to stop breathing afterwards, lying still.

"Is this his first show?"

"No." Angry. "He has a lotta shows."

"A lot?"

Gene grunted. He didn't want to talk about this.

"How many?" I asked.

"Well . . . he had a show every week in The Garage."

"The garage?"

"Yeah, with his friends. After the *Times* came, then there were lots of other shows."

"Whose garage is it?"

"What?"

"You said—"

Gene cackled. He twisted his head. "Not a garage." He was amused and contemptuous. "*The* Garage. You know."

"I don't know anything about the art world. You'll have to explain."

He wasn't enthusiastic, but he certainly did explain, in a programmed formal tone. He impersonated his father to tell me at length about the dilapidated car repair shop on Houston Street that he and other artists of various kinds had taken over to exhibit their work—somewhat illegally, it seemed; in any case, there had been a squabble that ended with their being thrown out. Gene detoured into the internecine arguments among the sculptors, painters, photographers and the like, using a grown-up's language and affecting a cynical attitude. He went so far afield I had to interrupt to return to the main road. "You said something about a gallery?"

"Bullshot," Gene said.

I was taken aback. "Is that the name of the gallery?" I asked skeptically.

"Yeah," Gene said impatiently. "*The* Bullshot."

"I don't know anything about the art world. That's an important gallery?"

"The most prestigious gallery for new artists in New York," Gene said solemnly. Still Father talking. He paused. He added, remembering another of his father's comments, "And New York is the center of the art world."

"So this is a very important show for your father?"

"Yes," Gene said, sadly.

"Is there an opening night?"

"Yeah." Gene was impatient. "Is it time for me to go?"

Ah. The opening was a source of tension. "We have more time. And when is your father's opening?"

"What? Oh. No. The opening was two months ago."

I was surprised. It must have gone badly. "How did it go?"

Gene recited angrily: "It was a sellout. Dad got a rave in the *Times* and in the *Voice*. Now he's one of the most important photographers in the country." He crossed his arms over his chest and frowned at the ceiling.

He's jealous of his father's photography work, I thought, excited. Its success represents abandonment. [Obviously, there was also an Oedipal theme in Gene's reaction. And I was interested in the ego psychology involved: Gene identified with the carpenter-father; when he lost that role model, he regressed to childhood. However, in those days I was enthralled by Susan's psychological bias, the loss of object and its emotion of grief and abandonment, rather than the deeper drive to conquer the father, or that his father's transformation into an artistic success threatened Gene's ego. I believed then that the various schools of theory were contradictory choices, not colors of the palette. I was a long way from understanding how combining them can paint a three-dimensional portrait.]

For the first time, I felt in control. "Okay, Gene," I said. "Our time's almost up. I've enjoyed talking to you. I think it would be good if you could come here three times a week. How about Mondays, Wednesdays and Fridays? Would that work?"

There was a silence. The hidden thumb rose to his chin. "Three times a week?" he asked meekly.

"Is that a problem? You could come after school on your way home." My suggestion of a time was deliberate. I knew he missed the afternoons he used to spend with his father; the therapy's transference would be helped by associating it with them. If that seems like manipulation to non-professionals, I agree. It *is* manipulation, but not wrongheaded or malicious. For the therapy to work, we needed to replace the comfort and strength those childhood hours gave Gene. Indeed, the hope was that the therapy's afternoon care would be superior, a relationship Gene could eventually discard voluntarily, rather than something whose loss he resented and mourned, leaving him weak and helpless.

"I guess. For how long?"

"An hour."

"No . . ." The hidden thumb rose higher. "Uh . . . How long do I have to keep coming here?"

"That's something you'll decide with your therapist."

"You're not my . . ." he hesitated. "You're not going to be . . . it?"

I had made too many mistakes with him. I was glad to have had a little insight into his dysfunction but I couldn't recommend myself to be his doctor. In fact, I felt I had work to do with Susan about my inappropriate reaction to Gene. "Well, this was a preliminary interview. I'll discuss with Susan Bracken—she's my boss—who's best to see you. And you also get a vote. If you don't like the therapist we pick, you can tell us."

"Can't you?" Gene sounded frightened. His lips pushed in and out. "Can't you be it?"

"I might be able to." I knew I ought to ask him if he wanted me to be his therapist, but I didn't. My reluctance, it seemed to me, was another proof I shouldn't. "Why don't you put your sneakers on and get your mother? Come back and we'll all discuss it."

Gene obeyed silently. He moved slowly, as if his muscles were exhausted and sore. That, I had noticed, isn't unusual when a patient has had a productive session. It's hard work, exercising our heaviest emotions. At least I hadn't totally failed.

I was curious to meet Gene's mother, the forgotten object, as it were, of our session. I saw immediately that he had learned his meek mannerisms from her. Her head appeared at the edge of the plasterboard door— so flimsy a sound insulator we kept a white noise machine on all the time in what we laughingly called the waiting room, really a converted closet. They took their time before coming in; presumably Gene gave her a thorough report. Her hair was much curlier than Gene's and a different color, an unnatural reddish brown. Dyed to cover premature graying, I decided. They had the same big dark eyes. Hers were bright and eager to please. Her mouth was wide like Gene's, but the lips were thin. They shared the aquiline nose, although hers was perfectly centered.

"Hello?" her head said and then more of her appeared as I got up. They shuffled in together, Gene almost hiding behind her. She moved in sideways toward the couch, then sideways toward the desk, a silly maneuver of indirection. She was skinny, with a girlish figure, and her shoulders, like Gene's, were broad and bony. She hung her head between them, somewhat like the submissive approach of a friendly dog. "I'm Carol, Gene's mother," she said. Her voice was a pleasant surprise, deep, mellifluous, and confident.

"Nice to meet you," I said and shook her hand. It was limp and soft, begging to be taken care of. I let go quickly.

"Gene enjoyed talking to you, Doctor. We're both grateful you spent so much time with him."

I gestured for her to sit. "Gene, why don't you pull up that folding chair?" I sat down. Gene obeyed with excessive haste. Carol perched on the edge of her chair, eyebrows up, expectant. Her facial expressions were cartoonish, exaggerating the feeling she wanted to express; they left an impression of disingenuousness. This family just wasn't my cup of tea. I experienced a moment of inner despair, a weakness of mine that a good Self-Psychologist would have wanted to investigate, that I can best summarize as a feeling of fraudulence and hopelessness. I felt I had no business trying to be a healer, that I simply wasn't compassionate or smart enough for the job. I had been analyzed, however, and I knew what had triggered this feeling: first, that I hadn't immediately corrected the many mistakes I made in the session, and second, that I was in the process of lying—the truth was that Gene had already been assigned to me. Covering up mistakes and telling lies were bad for my Self. "I think Gene would benefit from coming here three times a week, say Mondays, Wednesdays and Fridays, probably after school if that fits into his schedule."

Carol nodded her agreement throughout my speech, well before I was done, bobbing her head like a doll with a spring for a neck. It was annoying, conveying a blind desire to please rather than genuine agreement. "Great, okay, that'll be fine," she said all at once when I paused.

"I'll discuss with Dr. Bracken who should be his therapist and then Gene could meet—" I stopped because Carol had her hand up, like a student eager to be called on.

"Gene told me he really wants you to be his doctor," she smiled at me regretfully, head cocked to one side, as if to say— What can you do? In fact, she was making a demand. Here was the source of his passive-aggression. "Of course it's not up to us. I explained that to Gene. After all we're not paying, and I'm sure you're very busy, but don't you think it's a good idea for him to have a doctor he likes?" Gene stared straight down at the floor, embarrassed. She grimaced helplessly as if she were also embarrassed.

"It's more than a good idea," I said. "It's necessary."

Carol nodded and smiled approvingly at me. She glanced at Gene. He still had his head down. "You see," she said to him. "I told you there was nothing to worry about."

"But Gene hasn't met any of the other therapists. He might like someone else even better."

Carol's eyebrows came down to frown, her wide mouth shrank into a pout. "He couldn't like anyone better than you," she said. "He was completely comfortable with you."

"It's not really my decision to make unilaterally. I have to discuss it with Dr. Bracken."

Carol's hand was up again. "Enough said," she said. "I'm sure it will work out." She leaned so far forward she seemed almost to be on my desk. "One other thing," she lowered her voice, although not enough for Gene to be excluded. "We haven't told Gene's father about this and I don't think it's a good idea to tell him about Gene coming three times a week. Not for a while. I only bring it up because if you send any mail or need to phone about Gene I'd like you to send it to my office or call me there, okay?" She put on her mask of a regretful smile again. Her hands went up and out to show her helplessness, her embarrassing, but inescapable need.

I smiled. A woman asking me to keep a secret. How was that for a change of pace? "In that case, I'm afraid Gene won't be able to come here." I felt as if I were mimicking her phony smile of regret, so I cleared my throat and tried to look solemn.

Her eyebrows were way up, her mouth was open. "Really?" she said with so much feeling and emphasis that it was comic.

"If Gene were an adult, it would be different. But he's a minor and it's the law that we must have parental consent to treat him. Of course no one outside of his father or you has to be told. And everything he says to me is confidential, including from you and his father. The only way I can make an exception is if there's a compelling reason to keep it from his father."

"There is." She was very earnest now, jaw set, eyebrows in a line, her voice grave. She didn't seem to have any neutral expressions; they were all violent. "He really really wouldn't approve. He doesn't believe in psychiatry."

"That's not enough for the law. There would have to be, at least from you, a statement that his father is abusing Gene or threatening him in some way. Is that the case?"

She shook her head vigorously. "No, no, but he wouldn't allow it. So Gene couldn't come anyway. So there's no point in telling him. Anyway, I'm his mother. You have my consent."

"I'm sorry. If you look at the form you were given—do you have it?"

"What?" She looked down at her purse. "Oh. Yes."

"Both parents have to sign. It's the law, as I said before, unless you're alleging abuse. You're not, correct?"

She had gone blank. She did have an expressionless expression. She didn't move or speak.

"If Mr. Kenny," I continued, "wishes to discuss Gene's treatment with Dr. Bracken, I'm sure she can allay his anxieties. Gene is unhappy and needs some help. It won't last forever, there's no charge, and there's no social stigma. Besides, outside of his immediate family, no one needs to know."

"Okay," she said abruptly. "I'll tell him and he'll sign the form. I'll take care of it." She was stern and displeased with me, her former pliancy and eagerness now as foreign to her facial terrain as water in a desert. "When should Gene come?"

"Well, how about Monday at four-thirty?"

"And you'll be his doctor?" Her question was almost a reprimand.

"As I said, I'll have to consult—"

"I'll call Dr. Bracken. She's the one to bother about all this. I shouldn't bother you." She stood and said, "Let's get out of Dr. Neruda's hair, Gene."

Gene got to his feet immediately. Carol moved back to him, put her hand on his shoulder and pushed him at me. "Goodbye and thank you, Dr. Neruda," she said to me in a loud slow beat, obviously prompting Gene to repeat the phrase.

"Thanks," Gene mumbled.

"Shake Dr. Neruda's hand," she prompted.

Head down, Gene offered a limp hand.

"Do you want to shake my hand?" I said. What was I doing?

Carol goggled at me. Gene looked up, directly into my eyes. That was a first. His were shining. He smiled with his version of his mother's wide mouth; broadly, but not a cartoon. "No," he said.

"Then let's skip it," I said. "See you on Monday."

Carol's shoulders went way up. "Okay," she said, and the shoulders dropped. "Thank you very very very much," she added in a breathless whoosh.

I bought a sandwich from an all-night deli on Sixth Avenue, came back to our stoop, and ate half while waiting for Susan to finish with her last patient before tossing it. I didn't have much of an appetite; anyway, the pastrami was dry and fatty. She came out a little after ten and glanced at me, surprised. "I thought you'd gone."

"I fucked up," I said.

She locked the door behind her and studied the dark building lovingly, the way a mother might regard her sleeping child. This look was the only pride I ever saw her take in her creation. (It *was* quite an achievement. People who normally wouldn't, received first-rate therapy for little or nothing; and she had raised the money to open another clinic in Brooklyn just that month.) When she turned back to me, she hurried down the steps, taking my arm. "I don't believe it," she said.

"I had my worst session ever."

"Tell me." I reported my reaction to Gene and his mother while we walked north on Fifth to Susan's loft on Sixteenth Street. I wasn't any-where near done by the time we reached her place. She invited me up. I declined, worried I'd disturb her husband, Harry. "He'll be asleep," she said. She was right. We sat at the butcher block table near the wall of windows at the front of her loft so our voices wouldn't disturb Harry— there was only a half wall to seal off the bedroom at the rear.

Susan listened patiently, making no comment during my account of the session. She surprised me with her first question. "Do you usually ask patients to move to the couch so fast?"

I thought about it. "No. Sometimes not for several sessions."

She nodded as if she had assumed that. "So?"

"I don't know. He was upset and uncomfortable physically. He really didn't want to look at me. I thought we'd never get going. He was so preoccupied about avoiding . . ." I trailed off. I knew she was asking for a deeper meaning, not this surface explanation.

"You were uncomfortable," she said at last.

"Yes. I was, right from the start."

"Why?"

I began to describe again those first moments, Gene's obedient man-ner and appearance, his oval face, the off-center nose, my musings, about his being Eastern European.

Susan cut me off. "Kenny? You said his name was Kenny?"

"Yeah."

"That sounds Irish. What's his mother's maiden name?"

I opened my briefcase and removed the preliminary interview taken by the NYU intern. "Shoen," I said with a laugh.

"Sure doesn't sound Eastern European," Susan said. "Who did he re-mind you of? Who do you know who's Eastern European?"

"Lots of people. My mother's family, all my friends from Washington Heights. You. Harry."

"And you," Susan said. "You're half—Eastern European."

Harry appeared at the opening in the half-wall. His hair stood up in the air. He was in underpants and a T-shirt torn at the left armpit.

"Hello, darling," Susan said.

Harry came over and kissed her sleepily. She slipped a finger into the tear to tickle him. He pulled away. "Not in front of the help," he said. He studied me and then put a hand on my shoulder. "What's wrong?" he said.

"Rafe had a session that worries him," Susan said.

"Oh yeah?" Harry was a psychiatric social worker who worked with prisoners and their families, fighting a desperate battle against recidi-vism and the legacy of criminal behavior to their children. He tried to smooth down his hair. "I hope you really fucked up," Harry said. "Sent the patient screaming to Bellevue."

"Doesn't sound serious at all," Susan said. "In fact I think the patient likes him."

Harry groaned. "Shit. I knew it. Want some coffee, Mr. Perfectionist?"

"Sure," I said. The kitchen was open to the breakfast area so he could talk with us while measuring the coffee and filling a kettle.

"I saw him as me," I said. "The pathetic me. The suicidal me."

"Maybe," Susan said. "Okay, so let's go over it. You think he doesn't want to move to the couch but he does it like a sullen little boy and you feel what?"

"I hated him."

Harry laughed. Susan was skeptical. "Hated him?"

"It revolted me. There was something about the way he reacted, as if I were going to do something bad to him and he just resigned himself to it."

"A perfect description of psychotherapy," Harry said.

"Do something bad?" Susan asked wonderingly.

"I remember thinking at one point that he was worried I would hit him."

"Possible abuse came up, didn't it?" Susan asked. "About the father. When the mother made that—"

"That came from me. I said the law wouldn't allow her to skip getting the father's permission unless she was alleging abuse."

"What?" Harry said. "Where did you get that gobbledy-gook?"

"The mother was trying to get Rafe to agree to keep the therapy secret from the boy's father," Susan explained.

"I needed to invoke the law or she would have kept after me forever."

"We do require the parents' permission," Susan said. "That was appropriate."

"A little hyperbolic," Harry said.

"I can't become part of whatever neurotic dynamic the mother has going with the father. And, besides, treating him in secret could easily become a legal issue," I said. "You can't treat minors without the knowledge of parents and I assume that means both parents."

"Absolutely," Harry said. "But it's medical ethics. Why drag in the law?"

"You didn't assert yourself," Susan said.

Harry turned off the whistling kettle and shook his fist at me with mock outrage. "Be more phallic. You're a goddamn M.D. You can sic the AMA on her."

I covered my face. Despair, fatigue, disappointment in myself, the feeling that everything I had learned and worked for had been wasted overwhelmed me—and the knowledge that these reactions were excessive only made them worse.

"Rafe." Susan said my name quietly, but it was a prompt. "Come on. Keep using your brain. Don't indulge."

These were key phrases from my therapy with her, Pavlovian in their effect. I uncovered, looked into her eyes and listed the reasons aloud. "I was angry at her, convinced I couldn't stand up to her, so I grabbed for you first as a defense."

"Help, Mommy," Harry said.

"Shh," Susan said.

"He's right. Then I reached for the law—"

"Help, Daddy," Harry said.

"And I was scared that if I was her only obstacle, she would talk me out of it *and*, typically irrational, I was scared if I stood my ground, she would use that as an excuse not to bring Gene in for therapy."

"But that's what you wanted, not to have him as a patient."

"Me. *I* didn't want to treat him. But I didn't want to give her a way out of giving him treatment."

"Sure is irrational," Harry said. He put a cup of coffee in front of me. "She brought him in. She wanted him to be treated—"

Susan cut him off. "You didn't believe her?"

"The school forced her to bring him in. No, I believe she wants her son to think of himself as sick. I don't believe she wants him well."

"Huh?" Harry said. "That's quite a leap."

"I know. I said I was out of control. Anyway, he needs treatment. I wasn't confident that refusing to keep the therapy secret from his father was correct."

"You were worried it was something you reached for to get out of being his doctor," Susan said.

"Right," I said. "So I wanted to leave the decision to you."

"Bullshit," Harry said mildly. "You were just being chicken."

"No," Susan said, equally mildly. "You let Felicia see you without telling her parents."

I nodded.

"Felicia?" Harry asked.

Susan explained to Harry while he brought her a cup of coffee. "Felicia came in eight months ago. All by herself. She's twelve. Her mother was a prostitute—"

"I remember," Harry interrupted. "Your miracle cure. Twelve-year-old heroin addict turned into a ballerina. My wife, unfortunately, is right.

You could have gotten into a shitload of trouble for seeing Felicia on the sly."

"That's the point. Why wasn't I willing to take a very modest chance for Gene? It was a disgusting impulse."

"No!" Susan slapped my hand, lightly, but it was still a slap. "Use your head. You were using it in the session. You're not now."

"I had a reason? A good reason?"

"Yes!"

I recalled the provocation: *Carol lowered her voice, but not enough for Gene to be excluded* . . .

"She was driving a wedge between Gene and his father," I announced brightly, like an obnoxious A student in class. "The loss of the father-object is his central issue. I want the father to know his son is sick and I don't want to strengthen the mother's grip of guilt and shame about his need."

Susan clapped. "And what's more—you're right. Don't you think, Harry?"

"Yeah, yeah. He was right in theory, but in practice he was a chicken."

"I was," I admitted happily. "But it wasn't just coming from my gook, I was still making a therapeutic choice."

"You should have taken the responsibility yourself," Harry said. "And not laid it on Susan or the fucking law."

"You're right. I had to be his father."

Susan nodded. "His loss is acute."

"Too acute given the slight provocation. That's why I suspected abuse. It wasn't just projection."

"How could it be projection?" Harry said. "Your father didn't abuse you."

Susan shook him off. "Shut up for a second, Harry."

"Be happy to," he said, sitting down.

"You have to be Gene's doctor. It's important for you and Gene."

"I can't do it," I said.

"What do you feel?"

"Scared."

"Of what?"

"Failing."

"Oh, heaven forbid," Harry said.

"You have a right to fail. Your mistakes were minor. The transference, especially for one session, was excellent. And you have real empathy for him. Your intense dislike is an inversion of empathy."

"He's a boring case," I said.

"What?" Harry said. "What the fuck does that mean?"

"I'm not even sure we should be treating him. He's having some anxiety attacks, fucking up in school a little, okay, but we've got much more serious cases waiting for help."

Harry gestured to Susan, like an emcee turning over the stage to a guest.

"You're contradicting yourself," she said. "You said before you believe he really needs treatment."

"I'm talking triage. We've turned away people on the verge of nervous breakdowns. And he's boring. Even a mediocre therapist could help him."

"Rafe!" Susan said, ringing Pavlov's bell.

"Yes?" I answered dutifully.

"Do you really think his problem is boring?"

It didn't take long to see through myself on that one. "No. Somehow he's too close to me, to my unresolved father issues. He's a simple case for anyone but me. You should be his doctor. *You* could help him."

"Not better than you can. And what's more," Susan put her long-fingered hand on my arm. Her grip was both insistent and reassuring. "He can help you."

CHAPTER TWO

Defending the Ego

I CANNOT RECONSTRUCT THE NEXT TWO MONTHS OF GENE'S THERAPY with the kind of exact details I've given of our first meeting. I took meticulous notes that night after discussing it with Susan and Harry, for one thing, and for another, my work with Gene proceeded typically for a while. Getting his history was an easy process. He was forthcoming. Even his denials and repressions were, from a therapist's point of view, straightforward.

At first, what attracted my attention was the unusual emphasis, for those days, on the father as a caregiver. Gene's mother was really the family's main financial support. Perhaps this was about to change thanks to his father's successful exhibition, but certainly during Gene's childhood she had the steady job; his father, at least in Gene's memory, was the comforter, the nursemaid and cook, the mother-object. Not that Carol reversed sexual or emotional roles with her husband or he with her: she was clearly feminine, he clearly masculine. Thus the Oedipal dynamic was in place: Gene vied all the more for his mother's attention because her work made it precious. However, he didn't have to strive hard. Once she came home, Gene's father abandoned the field to his son, vanishing into his darkroom. This led to an emotionally incestuous intimacy between Gene and his mother, hitting the Object Relations school's central button: improper separation from the mother. [I was already distrustful of diagnosis and treatment based on theoretical constructs. I had had success—admittedly little at that time—by keeping to the specifics of my patients' lives. For Gene, whether Freud or Horney or Sullivan or Erikson or Mahler would have been able to fit him neatly into their systems, the drama was the rivalry both mother and son felt with the father's photography. His problem, I believed, was that this drama was entirely performed in his unconscious, his role as thoroughly repressed as if he had been locked out of the theater before curtain.]

Gene drew this picture of his childhood: during the week he spent most of his free time with Daddy, on the carpentry jobs or in the park or at home; when he lost his father, it was not to the mother, but to photography. That distinction was clearly defined in Gene's mind from the beginning and continued to this day. He was allowed on the carpentry jobs before he could walk; as an adolescent, he was still forbidden from his father's darkroom. The reasons given masked the real meaning of the distinction for Gene, reasons he couldn't argue with, namely the dangerous chemicals, the lack of space, the fact that darkness had to be maintained. His father was unwilling to allow Gene to play with his expensive camera or his lenses and Gene didn't care for substitutes, such as a Polaroid they gave him for his sixth birthday. It was far easier to let him hammer a nail into a spare piece of wood than allow him to waste a roll of film. And, in my mind, there was also the possibility that Gene simply hadn't inherited a feeling for photography. This last consideration is heresy to most psychological theories. Gene's lack of interest in photography has to be emotional, a rejection based on psychodynamics, rather than a matter of personal taste. I was unwilling to make that assumption. After all, the untouchable cameras, the forbidden darkroom, the unsuccessful rivalry for his father's attention when it came to photography, could just as easily produce a profound affinity for it, rather than indifference. My instincts told me that Gene merely happened to prefer carpentry to photography. There are natural gaps between people: that a gulf isn't self-manufactured doesn't make it any less potent for the psyche. Indeed, it might be more painful to feel an incapacity for something that is so beloved by the beloved.

I didn't make an effort to uncover this conflict for weeks, allowing Gene to paint as complete a "neurotic" picture of his life as he liked. I began to probe only when he completed his distorted canvas. (His condition didn't seem urgent: after two sessions, Gene reported his anxiety attacks had diminished and he finished the English and science projects,

late, but soon enough to get "passes" from his teachers for the first term.)
It was a month into the therapy before I asked a provocative question. Did
Gene remember the first time he was forbidden to enter the darkroom?

There was the usual denial, typical not only of Gene, but most patients. He said he had no memory of the first time. Therapy's conjuring
trick—it never fails to amaze me—happened a session later. Gene came
in with a clear recollection from age four, not of his father barring the
darkroom's door, but his mother. Evidently he had wandered in and she
found him opening a toxic fluid. From then on she insisted his father
lock the darkroom at all times.

"Mom always worries about me being safe," he commented and continued with a long diversion about her overprotectiveness in general.
Gene portrayed her as a cartoon of fearful motherhood. But none of his
anecdotes showed her to be excessive or unusually nervous, except with
respect to the father's photographic equipment. I didn't confront this illusion right away. I disagreed with Susan's impatient methods, in spite
of their success with me. Gene wasn't a suicide lying in a ward. I agreed
with Freud: Gene needed to unearth his feelings with his own hands. I
asked repeatedly about these early memories: his mother's injunctions
against the darkroom; her shrieks if he touched one of his father's cameras; her insistence that Gene not accompany his father when he went out
to take photographs. I allowed Gene to walk past the truth blindly over
and over and instead explain Carol's guarding of his father's art as overprotectiveness of Gene. This was obviously false. She made no objections
to Gene using saws, hammers, drills and the like, all potentially dangerous. She allowed Gene to swim in rough surf when they visited friends
at the beach, to take the subway to school alone at age nine, and many
other minor freedoms that a neurotic mother would not permit—or a
normal but careful mother, for that matter. Gene, however, could recite
those contradictory facts and continue to insist his mother's sole concern
in making rules against entering the darkroom or touching the photographic equipment was to protect him.

"How about today?" I finally asked him. "Do you think your mother
is still worried you'll accidentally poison yourself?"

Gene was silent. He pushed his lips in and out—a persistent manifes-
tation of resistance.

I waited. I trusted that Gene's desire to please, or perhaps to get well,
would eventually overcome these quiet rebellions. He was silent for a
long time and then said, "What did you ask? I forgot."

I repeated the question exactly.

He snorted, "No." Then he mumbled, "Well . . . She's worried I'll mess something up and Dad'll get angry."

"What would happen if your father got angry?"

"What!" he said. Symptoms of alarm appeared: his right leg rose up, his head twisted to look in my direction, the expressive eyebrows lowered, his voice cracked. In our sessions so far, there had been no mention of anger from his father. I made a note of it, remembering Carol's fear of her husband's reaction to learning of the therapy. Until then I had assumed Carol barred Gene from contact with the photographer-husband out of rivalry, her own unresolved Oedipal conflict, since she wasn't permitted in the darkroom either, or invited on picture-taking walks. Why should Gene be allowed to share in what she was denied? Maybe that was wrong. Maybe she was afraid that if Gene entered the forbidden darkroom, the father would hurt Gene. It could be she was shielding Gene from encountering a man she genuinely feared, preserving the fiction of the benign carpenter working in the light of day and banishing the dangerous artist to his lair.

"What would happen if your father got angry at you?" I asked again.

Gene remained frozen in his startled pose, hardly breathing.

"What's your father's name?" I asked. My instinct was: let's make him a man. Let's bring him into the room as a person, not an archetype.

[I was green when I treated Gene, making mistakes left and right. The above, however, is a foreshadowing of my later methods. How can we ask a patient to look realistically at his own life if we only mirror the distorted images of his neurosis? Susan was right to abandon the dogma of uncritical listening, although I think she was sometimes too quick to intervene. There's a middle ground, a way of being neither a mirror nor a cop, but a signpost pointing to a new direction when the patient can see only the well-worn dead end.]

"Uh . . ." Gene's right leg dropped. "Um . . ." He let out an embarrassed laugh. "I can't think of anything but Daddy."

"You can't think of your father's name?" I said gently.

"It's crazy," Gene said, wonderingly, impressed.

I made a note of this, learning something for myself, as well as about him. It may seem trivial to the reader, but I was struck by how this simple technique helped make Gene aware of his own awe, the mythic quality of his father.

Gene slapped the couch and the name came out: "Don. His name is Don."

"People call him Don or Donny?"

"Donny?" Gene was amused. "No."

"Don," I said in a deep voice, giving the name grandeur and power. Gene laughed again. "Yeah, right."

"So what happens when Don gets angry?"

"Huh?" His leg went up again and he twisted his head. I waited. "Well, he gets angry," Gene said, annoyed.

"Does he yell?"

"Of course he yells." Then silence.

"Does he curse?"

"Curse?" I waited. "Yeah, he uses bad words."

Bad words, indeed. "What bad words?"

Gene snorted. "You know . . ." His legs moved up and down. He shifted his torso also, squirming. He wanted out of this: it was so much more comfortable in his fantasy of a mother protecting him from dangerous chemicals.

"Tell me anyway."

"He says—shit."

"That's it?"

"You know." Gene moaned. He turned toward the back of the couch, hiding.

"Does it embarrass you to repeat them?"

No answer. I waited. Gene talked to the cushions in a monotone, "He says, shit, fuck, motherfucker, asshole."

"To you?"

"Not often." Gene's voice was low. "He says it more to himself. 'I'm an asshole,' he says. 'That motherfucker wants me to fail.' Dad thinks his friends want him to fail. He always—"

"What does he say to *you* when he's angry at you?"

"Don't be stupid."

"How is that stupid?"

"No. He says to me, 'Don't be stupid.' " Gene didn't laugh at my mistake. Am I feeling stupid? I wondered. Pay closer attention, I wrote in my notes.

"Does he call you a motherfucker?" I asked. Talk about a loaded question, I thought to myself.

"No," Gene said. "He once called me a stupid shit."

"What about?"

"Huh?"

"When did he call you a stupid shit?"

"I don't remember when. I was a kid. I don't know how old."

The resistance was, for Gene, quite strong. "I mean, what provoked Don to call you a stupid shit?"

"Oh. I dropped a box of nails in an elevator." At last Gene shifted onto his back, no longer speaking to the cushions. "You know, an open one in a loft building. They all spilled down to the bottom." Gene wasn't happy about this memory, of course, but there didn't seem to be much tension. His legs had relaxed, his face was smooth. I noted that the incident recalled involved the good father, the loving carpenter.

[With some amusement, I see now, looking over my notes from that session, that I jotted down: "Good father—Jesus. Photographer—Satan?" Since Gene's father was raised Catholic and his mother Episcopalian, presumably I was considering the symbolic quality of the good father as carpenter. I hope professionals will forgive me for my disorganized and pretentious thinking—I was twenty-five after all.]

"Did Don get angry at you about handling his camera or being in his darkroom?"

"No way." Gene's defensive annoyance had returned. He brought up both legs and hugged his knees.

"Why not?"

Gene yawned. More tension. He let go of his legs and they flopped on the couch. "I never touched him."

"Him?"

"Them. I never touched them."

"You said, him."

"No, I didn't."

To this day the beauty of a Freudian slip never fails to amaze and delight. I feel it's his most elegant and profound observation. If that had been Freud's only accomplishment he would deserve to be honored. Gene never touched *him*, the photographer, the real father hidden in his darkroom.

"What do you think would have happened if you had touched Don's camera?"

"He would have told me to leave it alone."

"Leave it alone?"

"Not touch it." Gene was angry. His tone was grim, and he was fidgeting, rubbing his face, feet restless.

"Has your mother ever touched his camera?"

"No," Gene said.

"Never?"

Gene shook his head. "She's scared she'll break them."

"So he's never gotten angry at her either?"

"He gets angry at her. Just not about his stuff. We don't mess with it."

I was ready to wind this down. There was so much material here, including the phallic implications, it was pathetic and almost funny. Gene and his mother abandoned every night by Don, disappearing with his long lenses that they couldn't "touch" into a darkroom with toxic fluids, living in so much fear of his anger if they intruded that neither dared to test it. Besides, Gene had had enough of this troubling exploration. He was exhausted and still resisted mightily. He had done plenty of digging for one session. I tried what I thought—here with a beautifully unconscious move of my own—was a safe way out for both of us.

"How did Don react to your coming here?" I hadn't asked before. When Carol phoned to say her husband had signed the consent form, she commented, unasked, that Don still didn't believe in psychotherapy but was willing to allow it if the school thought it would help Gene. Since she wasn't my patient I didn't probe. At least, that's what I told myself.

On hearing the question, Gene froze, legs rigid, arms at his side, a frightened quiescence. "What?" His standard first defense, pretending not to have heard.

Instinctively, I sensed the truth. My intuition about the meaning of Gene's reaction was complete, fitting perfectly into the puzzle of his history and personality. I sensed that Carol had lied to me, never informed her husband, forged Don's signature, and made Gene a partner in the deception. My guess should have excited me. It didn't; I was dismayed. But how could I feel good? I ought to have, I *must* have known this might be a key question and yet I had asked, telling myself it was neutral, an exit, not an entrance. Could I drop it? Review both my stumbling on it and the likelihood of my intuition being correct? I checked the clock: five minutes to go. So what? I could run over—I had a half-hour gap anyway and I didn't believe in cutting off productive time. Out of fear, I was spinning my wheels, and that also bothered me. Gene lay still, hardly breathing, playing possum.

There was no way I could simply let it pass. "Your mother said Don wasn't going to approve of your coming here," I said. I didn't want to appear to be trapping him, although I might be. "How did he react?"

"I dunno," Gene said quickly and looked at his watch, something he never did.

"We have time," I said.

"Okay," he said.

"He didn't say anything to you about your being in therapy?"

"No," Gene said easily. He took a relaxed breath. "He's never said anything to me about it."

And I knew why. At least I felt sure; but of course I could be wrong. Anyway, to make the accusation was dangerous, whether I was correct or not.

"Does he ask you what we talk about?"

"No," Gene said, relaxed.

"So you've never discussed it?"

"Nope."

"How about your mother?"

"Oh yeah. She always asks what we talk about."

"Do you tell her?"

He nodded.

"You know you don't have to discuss our sessions with her if you don't want?"

"Yeah," he was sarcastic. "Thanks. I know."

I let him go. I had twenty-five minutes free. I had a problem; I was rattled. I wanted to run up one flight and interrupt Susan's group. Glancing at the master schedule, I noted she was working with family members of alcoholics and drug addicts, shocking them, no doubt, out of their illusions about themselves as victims, waving her gangly arms, her broad forehead wrinkling sternly. Later, she would support them, when they took their first frightened steps toward independence. I wondered what it was like for Harry when he made love to her, exciting that skinny contraption of energy and strength? I laughed, knowing this meant I was feeling truly needy and inadequate.

I called my cousin Julie at her office. She had been appointed as the artistic director of the West End Forum, one of the most prestigious off-Broadway theaters in New York. Her assistant put me through when I said it was urgent, although she was in a meeting.

"Rafe?" she asked.

"I love you," I said.

"What's wrong?" she said.

I laughed. "You should be the shrink. Are you free tonight?"

"First preview. Wanna come?"

"If I can talk to you at some point."

"Definitely. Although after the performance I may need you to treat the cast and playwright first."

"After I treat them, you'll close in one night."

"What's wrong?"

"I think I should go into plastic surgery."

"Oh, so you want to be in show business too."

"No, I just think I should only be treating the surface of things."

"What does Susan say?"

"I don't want to ask her."

"But I thought she's your teacher, your trainer, or whatever."

"I have to be more phallic. Time to grow up. So I want to ask your opinion. That's my version of maturity."

She laughed. "Boy, are you in trouble."

"Boy is right. I've got patients till nine."

"You can see the second act."

I don't remember the play. The second female lead came offstage screaming at the male lead after curtain, but Julie and the playwright seemed pleased with the performance. After they had a brief conference, I got Julie to myself for a late dinner in a Japanese restaurant next door to the theater.

I told her about Gene and my dilemma. "I'm convinced the mother never informed his father."

"You mean . . ." Julie had cut her shimmering black hair short, but she still reached for the missing mass from time to time, and ended up teasing the bristles at her temples. She did this for a moment before finishing, "You mean she forged his signature?"

"I guess. The important thing is that she's told Gene to keep it a secret from me."

"Wait a minute. I can't get over this. This woman is so scared of her husband, she forged his name—"

"That's not important—"

"What's she scared of? Does he hit her?"

"No. Much worse. He ignores her."

Julie frowned. I noticed for the first time—it was too dark in the theater—that her eyeliner was iridescent blue. She was dressed in a black silk man's shirt and tight black jeans. She had a man's haircut, lipstick very red—her appearance was eccentric. Was it some sort of dress code for theater people? Julie had worked as the artistic director of a regional theater in the Midwest while I did my residency. When she came to New York for this new job a year ago, she dressed like a hippie—worn jeans, workshirts, hair long, usually no makeup. I wondered (and noticed that I wondered) whether this new style was a lesbian costume. In the Village I had seen this look on lesbian couples; for that matter, her former hippie appearance also fit their dress code. The playwright was a lesbian. That was the subject of her play and she told me it was autobiographical. There had been a lot of physical affection between the artistic director and the author. I'm a sick person, I thought and fell further into despair.

"Hitting her would really be better?" Julie asked while I spiraled down.

"That's not my problem. Gene can't keep that secret from me. It's a terrible burden."

"So confront her."

"She shouldn't exist!" I cried out.

Julie laughed. "What does that mean?"

"She's not there. In therapy, the patient and me, that's the only reality. I can't go outside, step into his real life, without weakening the transference. If I call the mother, whether she denies it or not, I'm diminishing Gene, making him a child, a bystander, when I want to shore up his ego. Build it really. He doesn't have one. He's a creature of his parents."

Julie peeled off a pink sliver of ginger and chewed it thoughtfully. "Gotta tell you the truth, Rafe."

"No you don't."

"I don't understand a word you're saying. You're making me feel stupid. Why can't you just call the father to chat about the therapy? If he knows, the conversation will seem innocent. If he doesn't, you've exposed the situation without—"

"I'm the parent now," I interrupted.

Julie winced. "Don't be angry at me."

"I'm not. I'm angry at myself."

"What for? You haven't done anything."

"Look. I'm the parent now. Gene needs to deal with these things with me, reenact these dynamics with me so he can learn to master them. If Gene had decided to lie to his father, that wouldn't be a problem even if he were lying to me about it. That would become part of the process. But this is being done by an outsider. I know it, and—" I stopped. The answer was simple. It violated my book training, but Susan would approve. I resisted the temptation to phone her immediately to ask permission. No, I would just do it. Next session with Gene, first thing. If I was wrong, so be it.

Julie sipped green tea. She nodded at me over her cup to continue.

"I've got it," I said. "Thanks."

"What is it? What's the answer?"

"I'm going to ask you something. I don't want you to be angry at me. Just remember I'm upset."

"Ask me something? What is it?"

"Are you a lesbian?"

Julie put down her cup. She made a sound. Her big eyes opened. "Rafe," she said, as if calling for help.

I reached for the hand that had held the tea mug. It was warm and smooth. Her fingers grabbed me tight. "I'm in love with you," I told her.

"I love you too," she said.

"No," I said. "I mean I want to possess you."

She blanched. Her pupils dilated as she looked directly into my eyes. "But . . ."

"But?"

"We're . . ." She shrugged.

"Cousins."

"Isn't that . . . ?" she looked down.

"A taboo," I said. "Yes, maybe that's the reason I want you so much." Julie frowned at this unpleasant thought and I was encouraged. I pulled on her hand and she looked up, confused and excited. I was full of hope. "Or maybe," I said, taking the chance at last, "or maybe you're the only woman on earth for me."

CHAPTER THREE

Breakthrough

TWO DAYS LATER, WHEN GENE NEXT APPEARED IN MY OFFICE, I HAD reason to be thankful to him. Julie and I had become lovers and I was happy, happier than I had ever been. My life seemed complete or as complete as I had any right to expect. I was doing work I enjoyed and I was in love. Happiness, Freud said, is a childhood wish fulfilled: I had wished to be a healer and for Julie to love me. Perhaps both were mine.

I resisted the temptation to tell Susan of my dilemma with Gene and my intended solution. (I didn't immediately tell her about Julie, either.) I knew my frank declaration to Julie and my going it alone on Gene's therapy were related events and so I felt, in a magical way, that my success with Gene on this issue would affect my love life. I was quite nervous while Gene untied his Keds and lay back on the couch.

"Gene, before we start, there's something I want to talk about. We've never talked much about therapy, I mean its ground rules. This is your time. This is your place. And it's a safe place for you. I may push you to talk about things you'd rather not. It may seem, at times, as though I'm making you feel things you'd rather not. And I'm not perfect. I make mistakes, but no matter what is said here, it stays here. This is a safe place for you. I won't repeat things you say to anyone, especially not to your mother or your father. Because you're a minor your mother had to bring you here and I met with her, but with adults that doesn't happen.

Some adults see therapists for years and their friends and relatives don't even know they're in psychotherapy. Some therapists tell their patients not to discuss what goes on in sessions with anyone. I don't. That's your decision. I don't believe I should make that decision for you. Now I have a problem. It's a simple problem in one way. In another, it's not. My problem is, I don't believe your mother did what I asked her to that time we all met. I don't believe she told your father you were coming here. I don't believe she showed him the consent form or got him to sign." Gene's legs were up, of course, and his thick eyebrows were down. "Now that doesn't matter. I don't care. I'm satisfied that your father wouldn't object to your seeing me. I don't feel his consent is necessary and whether she lied or not won't change anything about your coming here. But— and it's a big but—I don't like that your mother has put you in the po- sition of lying to me. If *you* want to lie to me about something, that's okay."

Gene laughed, skeptically.

"I mean it. I don't think there's any reason for you to lie to me about anything. If you want to lie to me, that's between you and me and we can work it out. But keeping a secret for someone else is not okay. It's unfair to you."

"She doesn't mean to do anything bad," Gene said plaintively. "She was scared if Dad found out, I . . ." He trailed off. His legs slid down and he turned a little in my direction. His voice was soft and childish. "She was just trying to help me."

So my intuition was right. I was thrilled. I felt, irrationally, that I had a right to my work and my love, had been granted the title and deed to my own happiness. I suppressed my elation, of course. I was in mid- session, very much at the heart of Gene's problem. "What is she scared of, Gene?"

"That he'd get angry at me."

"Angry at you for seeing a therapist?"

"No. Yes. No. I mean, angry that I'm sick."

Thanks to this new confidence in me, we made rapid progress that week. Gene brought up memories of his father's intolerance of illness when he was a boy. The stories were typical of a neurotic's: the meaning for Gene was out of proportion to the facts.

Within a few sessions we arrived at the key memory: one afternoon Gene had a sore throat after school. He thought he was in kindergarten or first grade, his age roughly six or seven. His father had a big job on the Upper West Side, building shelves for a gallery owner—thus this carpentry job was more than a way of earning a living, it was a backdoor contact he hoped would help get him a show. Gene wanted to go home. Don wouldn't postpone returning with Gene to the job; he had promised the gallery owner to be finished by the weekend and it was Friday. He phoned Carol, but she insisted she couldn't get off early. Don coaxed Gene uptown, buying him a toy, dosing him with Bufferin, interrupting his work to buy him pizza and an orange soda. (I had to dig for these details from Gene; what he wanted to remember was his father's impatience and neglect.)

The most poignant aspect of the anecdote was its climax. By six o'clock, when the gallery owner came home, Gene felt feverish and nauseous. Afraid to interrupt his father, Gene had been suffering silently in a corner, choking on the sawdust, forlornly staring at an art book of Bosch's visions of hell. He watched his father greet the owner and nervously show off the nearly completed shelves. The man wasn't satisfied. There weren't enough tall deep shelves for the art books. Don tried to explain that he could easily remedy this insufficiency, but the gallery owner complained that the two extra days it would take meant he couldn't have a brunch on Sunday he had planned for a brilliant new painter visiting from Brazil. Don, in Gene's memory, was seen for the first time as weak: apologizing, fawning, insecure, no longer the masterful artisan, but a fearful sycophant. Don promised he would work all night to repair his error.

"What? The noise'll keep me awake."

"I'll work quietly," Don said and, in Gene's memory, bowed his head to whisper penitently, "I'm really sorry."

"I'm not paying for the extra time," the gallery owner said.

"Of course not. It's my fuck-up," Don said. "Look, my kid is sick. I had to take care of him. I got distracted."

The gallery owner turned to look at pale, meek, ill Gene. "If he's sick why is he here?"

Gene immediately threw up on the book of Bosch paintings. That image was keenly alive in his mind, vivid and horrible, of an alien orange substance erupting out of him. He recognized chunks of the slice of pizza. It soaked into the book's binding, oozing between the threads. His father yelled while the gallery owner shrieked that the book was ruined, the shelves were useless, his weekend a disaster. He bullied Don into carefully cleaning the Bosch book while insisting that Gene sit in the bathroom, alone, in case he had another accident. The gallery owner eventually threw Don and Gene out, refusing to allow Don to return and also refusing to pay him for the work.

That extended the horror of this incident. Carol wanted Don to demand payment, but he was too ashamed and furious. He wanted to forget it. Gene, it turned out, was seriously ill with scarlet fever. He ran a high temperature for two days. He lay in bed, listening in a delirium to bitter quarrels between Don and Carol. Why didn't Don demand justice from the mean gallery owner? Carol demanded. They had it out late Sunday night while they thought Gene was asleep. The argument ended with Don slapping Carol. She walked out and didn't return until the following evening. Gene, although he was very uncomfortable, was afraid to ask Don for any nursing while she was away and also afraid that his mother would never return. He suffered terribly and in isolation.

Getting to these facts and feelings took many sessions. How Gene perceived each character's motivation and demeanor was veiled and massively defended. Only through specific questioning could I get Gene to see that the image of his father's behavior he carried with him—uncaring and violent—didn't match what seemed to be his father's rather passive approach to his problems. Nor did the image he carried of his mother—caring and victimized—jibe with her passive and neglectful behavior. Odd though this may seem to a lay reader, we spent months—not exclusively, a little bit each session—reviewing each of his father's and mother's choices. Why, I asked, did Carol, who presumably had a somewhat flexible schedule, not leave work an hour or so early and help out Don? (She had on other occasions.) This was a question Gene had never asked himself. He didn't want to now, either. Why didn't his father get a sitter and take Gene home, rather than drag him to the job? Why did he use Gene as his alibi for his own mistake? And so on. I was a pest, crawling over every inch of the story, asking such things as, why did Don feed him pizza? (An odd food for a sick child, I commented.) I found fault with everything they did and was very critical of *both* his parents.

Gene was irritated—understandably—by this apparently absurd microscopic examination of their care. He believed I was wrong to attack his parents as parents: the incident proved gallery owners were wicked, that his father lost his strength when he tried to please people in the art world (this was not articulated, but clearly felt), that illness in general wasn't tolerated by his father, and that the slap proved Don had a violent temper which Carol and Gene had to avoid provoking at all costs.

Throughout, the common theme we discovered for the whole family was passivity and fear of anger. Gene, it turned out, had felt feverish before going to school and worse during the day, but hadn't told his parents or his teacher, afraid of annoying his teacher and interfering with his father's or mother's work. It was obvious to me Gene had been taught years earlier that he wasn't free to interrupt adult plans. Certainly he had been sold on the notion that there was nothing wrong with his mother and father placing his needs second to the authority figures in their lives, blaming each other or Gene, rather than confronting the true obstacle: their own fear and resentment of authority. Gene's cover-up of this neglect was greatest when it came to his mother. He was shocked when I commented that her walking out and not returning for twenty-four hours while Gene lay feverish wasn't caring.

"She was scared of Dad," he said. "He hit her."

For the one hundredth time, it seemed to me, I had to ask, "Did he punch her?"

"No, I mean—"

"What did he do, exactly?"

"I told you. He slapped her across the face."

"Was she hurt badly?"

"No—"

"Was she bleeding—?"

"I know what you're saying. Okay. But she was scared. She didn't know if he would stop. She told me she thought he was going to kill her."

"Okay. Your mother thought he was ready to kill her. And so she leaves a sick seven-year-old boy alone with this monster?"

I wasn't trying to impose any particular point of view on Gene. My example here may seem to be partisan, but in other conversations, I took his mother's side. What I was really trying to do was to get Gene to stop blindly accepting his parents' version of these events and discover what he felt. In some cases, perhaps I *was* trying to lead him to feelings he ought to have had—that's a difficult charge to defend against. I was not interested in the objective truth. Many people who are upset by psychotherapy assume its sole concern is to make mothers and fathers into villains. If Gene had been a different sort of neurotic, one who was in love with an image of himself as victim, I might have defended his parents' actions. The moralistic way of seeing life that pervades all religions and cultures makes some people ill, especially children. In the end, it doesn't matter whether Don or Carol or Gene is right or wrong about each of these actions (although how a seven-year-old with a fever could be wrong about anything is beyond me), what matters is that Gene was deeply affected by incidents such as the one described and yet he was a stranger to his feelings. He was as cut off from what each moment meant to him while it was happening as if he had never been present.

He had entombed himself in his mother's and father's experience of these events. He hid himself within his mother's opinion that Don was merely trying to be a good father and husband by taking Gene along on this important job rather than what Gene actually felt, that his father was passive and his mother neglectful. He convinced himself of Carol's opinion that his father had been a poor workman for the shelf error and a bad businessman by offering to repair it, when, at the time, Gene actually felt his father was dishonest and weak. We discovered, in the therapy, that Gene had silently counted the tall and deep shelves while the gallery owner raged about them, and found that his father had built the right number. He couldn't accept that his father agreed with a false criticism, so he covered up this unpleasant fact with his mother's distortion that Don *had* made a mistake, but should have demanded payment anyway.

To shore up all these facades, the teenage Gene was also convinced of Don's version, that his father was accurate in using Gene as an alibi; that Don made an error because he had to take care of a sick child. In fact, the seven-year-old Gene knew the job was done properly and felt that he had been a good little boy, trying hard not to bother his father. It may confuse or annoy some readers that Gene's judgments and feelings contradict and differ from how they might have felt or acted. (By the way, Rafael Neruda saw these actions and behaviors differently than seven-year-old Gene.) But that's the difference between reacting to someone in life and as a therapist. Even if one believes Gene could be wrong in his feelings (for example, that it was understandable for his illness to be treated so casually in relation to his parents' work), even so, before the mature Gene could come to that conclusion, he had to know what he felt as a seven-year-old. How can someone change their opinion if they don't know what it is? It's up to Gene to decide—if he needs to—whether his mother or his father was the better parent or whether their actions were good or bad. That comes later. My job was to present the evidence for the only participant who had no lawyer. My seven-year-old client's guilt or innocence, in the eyes of Catholicism or Communism or feminism or capitalism or est or the op-ed page of the *Times*, was irrelevant to me. My job was to bring that seven-year-old back to life, to introduce Gene to himself, and let him be his own juror.

Over the next year, we returned again and again to this story. It had many doors to the interior of Gene's heart. The vomiting, for example, was an entrance to the basement where Gene hid his anger. It was a fierce struggle getting down there. Gene denied the vomiting had any significance for a long time, insisting it was a coincidence, although it was immediately preceded by Don blaming Gene's illness for the shelf error.

Remember, we discovered that, in fact, there hadn't been a mistake. Gene confirmed this for both of us by checking his memory with Don the same day he informed his father that he was in therapy. Much to Gene's surprise (not to mine) Don didn't object to his seeing me, although he was dismissive of its being useful. Once over that, Gene told his father that he remembered counting the tall and deep shelves and found them to be correct. Don, Gene reported, was delighted. "You remember that?" he said with a smile and they had a rare relaxed afternoon together. Don even showed Gene some recent photos he had taken. Being reminded of the shelf fiasco—given his current success as a photographer—was pleasant for Don. The bullying gallery owner was now fawning toward the newly successful photographer. Indeed, Don confided to Gene, a friend recently told Don that the gallery owner bragged to him that his shelves had been built and designed by the "brilliant Don Kenny." Later that night, Don joked to Carol, with Gene present, that he should send the gallery owner a bill now. The adults laughed. This is, of course, the difference between adult and childhood experience. For them, it was a parody of their conflicts and neurosis; for Gene, it was the tragic original.

I knew Gene's therapy was almost done the day he finally relived what *he* felt, not what his parents had told him to feel, at the moment he threw up on Bosch's vision of hell. He had long since understood that he was desperate to believe his father's lie. Given a choice between Don as a disingenuous opportunist, willing to blame his child rather than confront the gallery owner, or as a decent man who couldn't juggle the dual responsibility of fatherhood and work, Gene much preferred the latter. Don's cover-up was that Gene was ill, so Gene performed on cue. What had remained hidden from Gene was the deeper feeling, what in jargon we would call the introjection of Gene's rage at the betrayal, the deep betrayal not only of himself by his father, but the much more terrible betrayal by Don of Gene's cherished image of his father. It is fair to say, in psychological terms, that Gene would rather die than see his father as he really was, a man who would neglect his child, abandon his dignity, and lie, in order to get his work exhibited. And so the real Gene did die. But the rage at the murder was there and it erupted out of him, pieces of himself spilling on the art. Erupted, but in the safe way—with the marvelous self-defeating logic of neurosis—in a way that could punish his father, the gallery owner, and the alibiing Gene. From then on Gene was to despise himself, the child who was a willing accomplice to the death of Don the self-assured carpenter and his beloved apprentice son.

Gene wept the day he relived the incident as himself. In great silent drops, he mourned. First he said, "I knew he didn't love me," in a dreadful tone of conviction and the tears rolled. "I knew that he didn't really care about anything but his pictures."

"And you threw up on a picture," I said, pedantically and with wrong-headed coolness, I'm sorry to report.

"Yeah . . ." There was a painful silence. "He didn't care about himself. He didn't even care about me."

Of course, this was not a moment of common sense or realism. I know it is the melodramatic emotions therapy evokes from apparently simple events that makes it so easy to dismiss. In life, some would slap Gene and tell him to grow up. Others would hug him and say, "Of course, your father loves you. He was just confused and scared. We all make mistakes . . ." and so on. Unfortunately, that isn't the way children experience life. It isn't really the way we feel inside, either, in the softest and most hidden part of ourselves. People often confuse not having visited that interior with its not existing.

It took another year, our third, before Gene was able to accept both what it had meant to him as a child and what it meant in the real world. He was, at last, able to see his father as a whole man, not as a pair of extreme choices. And he was also able to see that a quarrel between his parents wasn't somehow a by-product of his scarlet fever.

The last gain was useful. His parents split up during the third year of his therapy. It turned out that Don had been having an affair with one of the women painters in the Garage group for years. He broke it off and simultaneously left his wife. After several successful shows Don felt confident his career was launched successfully and he abruptly became unwilling to stay in a fractured marriage or continue a fractured love affair. Clearly, he was so driven by the outside world's view of him that once Don was an acknowledged success he felt entitled to seek romantic happiness as well.

Gene understood the divorce's cause and effect better than his parents. In fact, he had experienced their problems, covering up for them, years before they confronted them. (Actually, they never did confront the truth of their lives. Carol told herself the marriage was happy until Don became "swell-headed." Don told himself that Carol had convinced him he was a worthless and unlovable man; thanks to his success he discovered that he was fine, and concluded she was the sick one.) It was this aspect of Gene's neurosis, his willingness to be the fall guy for his parents' conflicts, that I came to like. I never liked the Gene who pulled with his mother against his father's ambitions, the Gene who vomited his rage on his father's art. He was too much like the young Rafe I still did not approve of. But this Gene, the child who understood his parents' need to pretend that their long dead marriage was still alive, that Gene I could feel sorry for. And I was proud of how patient and mature he was in dealing with the grandiose Don and his grief-stricken mother after the separation.

I have only covered a section of Gene's analysis and his life. Therapy's most encouraging and beautiful by-product, the flowering of personality once the bonds of illness are loosened, was quite vigorous and impressive when it came to Gene. The boy who had never shown a dedicated interest in anything—intensity for work and ambition being a betrayal of his mother and a frightening impersonation of the father who hurt him—quickly found an interest in electrical engineering and computers, then at the beginnings of the microchip revolution. Both mother and father were baffled by his scientific and mechanical interests. Carol was literary and Don visual. They were ignorant and hostile to technology's pragmatism.

Gene, by sixteen, worked hard in school for the first time. I suggested he try for a summer program at Johns Hopkins offered to bright high school students. (I had him tested and found out he had extraordinary math aptitude, something that had been hidden by his attendance at a progressive non-testing school.) He qualified easily. There he discovered his love of computers and his knack for understanding not only their abstract logic but their mechanism as well. One Room, to their credit, allowed him to concentrate on this new interest. Our therapy ended when

Gene graduated high school, got into his first choice, MIT, and left for Boston. There he hoped to learn how to build the machines that were already revolutionizing our world. The therapy was ready to terminate anyway. Gene had developed, emerging as a distinct and clear image from his parents' darkroom.

I asked him, just before he left for college, what he liked about computers.

"They do what you tell them."

"Not when I'm doing the telling," I said. I still can't fathom them.

Gene laughed. After a moment, he said, "And they don't tell lies . . ."

I closed the book on Gene. As I saw it then, not wrongly, only too correctly I'm afraid, Gene's mature fascination with the building of computers was an homage to the happy hours he spent with the hammers and saws of his childhood. He had returned to their pleasures, standing on adult legs as a builder, at last becoming the illusion he had loved, the carpenter-father who used his hands to make things. Only this carpenter was going to build machines that wouldn't tell lies. He had lived for so many years with only a vision of hell. Now he had a vision of heaven.

CHAPTER FOUR

The Widening Gyre

I CONSIDERED THE THERAPY A SUCCESS AND, TO BE HONEST, RARELY thought of Gene. What lingered was its personal meaning, in particular the trigger Gene provided for my love affair with Julie. Unfortunately, my happiness with Julie did not last.

I couldn't persuade her to marry me. For a long time, much longer than was fair to me, she pretended her career was the reason. After she drifted from off-Broadway theater into producing low-budget films, she announced she needed to relocate in L.A. to break into the mainstream movie business. When I offered to follow her out there, she confessed her true worry—that we had no future because of the potential for genetic trouble should we have children. That explained why she had always insisted on keeping our love affair a secret from the Rabinowitz family. I believed, and this fueled a bitter final quarrel, Julie's concern about having children masked a keener fear: that she couldn't bear the prospect of lifelong disapproval from her mother for making an unseemly marriage. Julie was outraged that I accused her of caring what her mother would think, but I'm sure readers can guess how convincing she sounded to a psychiatrist.

I was unwilling to continue the relationship as a haphazard liaison at a geographical remove—and a clandestine one to boot. Nor was she, really. A mere six months after taking a job in Los Angeles in 1984, she married a heart surgeon (significantly, I thought) and had two children within four years. In fact, her new baby's birth announcement, my second cousin Margaret, was in my briefcase the night I returned to the Ritz-Carlton Hotel in Boston and was given a message that Gene Kenny had phoned, leaving a number to reach him at the Sheraton in Cambridge. It was 1988, nine years since our last session.

I didn't return the call right away. I was tired. I had just completed my fourth day of testimony in the Grayson Day Care case, a widely reported and scandalous trial of the systematic sexual abuse of five children in Boston by a married couple running a small baby-sitting service out of their home. Two days of direct and two more of cross-examination were followed by a round of television interviews, climaxing with the oddness of appearing on *Nightline*. I felt debilitated. (It's strange to be interviewed by someone whose face you can't see. You sit in a room with a cameraman and a sound engineer, reacting to a voice in your ear, and yet you have to manage your face, because the audience has the illusion that you can see Ted Koppel. You can't. Koppel has a monitor, not his interviewees. I'm told Henry Kissinger gets one, but I'm not sure I believe it. This gives Koppel a considerable psychological edge—he can communicate with the audience through facial expressions without his subject knowing. Koppel sounded annoyed when I informed the audience that I couldn't see him. I've been on since then so I know he doesn't bear a grudge for my repeated attempts to undermine this broadcasting trick, but I still don't get a monitor.)

I was physically exhausted but mentally exhilarated. The Grayson case was my first taste of the media's infatuation with personalities. I hadn't built up any resistance to its evils. Until then, working out of small offices in White Plains, I and my colleagues, Diane Rosenberg and Ben Tomlinson, had labored in obscurity. We consulted on a few child abuse prosecutions and handled the caseload of the local Child Welfare office. Our work with the Grayson Day Care children focused on the most damaged boy, known in the press as "Timmy"—the name of one of his multiple personalities. As is typical of multiple personality disorder, "Timmy," and the other characters this traumatized six-year-old invented, was a defense against the repeated acts of sodomy and psychological terror committed by the Graysons. Our work with "Timmy" and the three other victims had been routine—we gathered facts, the details of the abuse. The children were still deeply disturbed; indeed, the ordeal of the trial had made "Timmy" worse in some ways.

I was called to testify on their behalf because of the defense's tactic—
the only one available to them after the children's accounts were un-
shaken by cross-examination—of suggesting the possibility that we
had put the allegations into the children's heads. The defense was quite
correct to go over this. Certainly bad technique might create fantasies
of abuse in children and lead to false accusations. Because we had been
scrupulous, videotaping all the interviews and avoiding leading questions, because the Grayson abuse seemed so lurid to an American public that was then relatively naive, and because the defense attorney
could make little headway attacking our methods, we attracted undue
attention and seemed to be a success story. I was conscious that we
merely performed competently and yet suddenly I was speaking for
abused children everywhere. I didn't deserve to be on all the networks
as an expert. I did my best to emphasize that I was merely one of hundreds working in the field, not special. Nevertheless, by the end of the
media's love affair that day, I began to feel I was—in the language of
my old neighborhood—hot shit. There was something real to be excited about, though. At least for one day, "Timmy" and the other children were believed.

I anchored Gene's message under the phone, thinking I would try him
in the morning, and then it rang. I had meant to ask the desk to hold my
calls, but I wanted to wait a while in case the assistant DA tried to reach
me. I might be needed for redirect. I didn't recognize the deep, mellifluous voice that said to my hello, with a hint of amusement, "Is this
Dr. Neruda?"

"Who's calling?" I was cautious. There had been many crank calls during the trial; two had been not only obscene but violent. The ghastly
threats they made were probably empty, but how could I be sure? I tried
to goad the second threatening caller into seeing me. He did keep talking for a while, although only to persist in describing a gruesome abuse
he planned for "Timmy." He wouldn't take my suggestion that we meet
seriously. I meant it. He needed help. His fantasies weren't harmless,
whether he acted on them or not.

"It's me." The pitch rose and I immediately recognized the voice.

Gene was tipsy. He told me he had been drinking all evening, cele-
brating triumph for him and the company he worked for, Flashworks.
They had presented their prototype of a new mainframe computer at the
International Computer Convention held in Boston the day before and
orders were pouring in. "We made the fastest machine in the world,"

Gene said. "And the friendliest," he added with a laugh. "They love us. We're gonna bury Big Blue."

"Big Blue?"

"IBM. Listen, I know you're busy, but could I come by for a drink? I saw you on *Nightline*. I mean, I only saw it. I didn't hear you. There was too much noise in the bar. But I read in the papers what you did. It's great."

"Thanks. I didn't do it alone, I—"

Gene wasn't listening. "Could I see you? Just for fifteen minutes. I know you're busy. But I read in the paper your office is in upstate New York—"

"Not very far upstate. White Plains."

"White Plains? That's enemy territory. Anyway, we live in Massachusetts and when we come into New York to visit Dad, we stay in the city, so this is my chance to see you."

"It's late for me to go out, Gene—"

"I'm not that far from you. Just one drink?"

"How about tomorrow? For breakfast."

"I'm leaving first thing. Only take up a half hour and then I'll get out of your hair."

This grown-up Gene—he was twenty-six now—certainly didn't sound or act passive. That was gratifying and his eagerness was touching. He was a success of mine. Why shouldn't I bask in a real therapeutic win, rather than the overblown praise of the trial?

We met in the lobby of the Ritz and went to their staid, virtually empty bar. Gene seemed a little taller, although he still had his mother's wiry body and smooth youthful skin. He was dressed younger than his age, in a rumpled blazer too short in the sleeves, chinos that were too long, spilling over his scuffed loafers, and a denim shirt with a casual red knit tie. If Gene claimed to be a freshman at Harvard he would be believed. His boyish appearance didn't give him the look of an IBM killer, but his was the world of computers, which I supposed was populated by youthful gunslingers.

He gushed about me for a little bit while we waited for his gin and tonic to arrive, saying he had followed my involvement with the Grayson case from the beginning, and that it didn't surprise him I had become a famous psychiatrist, although he was surprised (and disappointed, I wondered?) to find out that I treated children exclusively. He asked when I had left the Tenth Street clinic for White Plains and why I had chosen to focus on abused kids, but his interest in my replies was perfunctory. Soon he was telling me about himself, with considerable pride. He had joined Flashworks, then a fledgling company, immediately after graduating from MIT and was put on a team of engineers and hackers given the critical job of designing prototypes, racing against a rival group within the company as well as against the other two major computer manufacturers. Flash II, the machine so successfully debuted only the day before, represented two years of grueling work, and promised, Gene claimed, to make Flashworks the number one computer company in the world. "Can you believe it? I'm a success."

I said I could believe it and congratulated him. I noticed he was wearing a wedding ring. "You're married?" I asked.

"Oh yeah. Junior year at MIT. And I got a son!" He was on the edge of his chair, talking energetically, though slurring his words. His eyes retained his boyish timidity, a tendency to avoid mine, rarely glancing at me, and those were darting movements, as if to catch me unawares. "He's six." He squirmed in the Ritz's huge leather wing chair and pulled a wallet from his back pocket. It was falling apart, stuffed with bills and slips of paper. I looked at several photos of his boy, Peter, and his wife, Cathy. Peter's hair was curly blond, the curls from Gene, the color from the mother. He had an appealing face, also a mixture of his parents: Gene's big wondering eyes and expressive eyebrows; his mother's strong chin and tight mouth. Cathy's looks weren't a surprise. Other than the sandy blonde hair and pinched mouth, she had Carol Kenny's shape and attitude—wiry, head pushed forward, eager for approval, smiling too hard. Stop being a shrink, I told myself, and said, "What a beautiful family, Gene."

"They're great!" he said. "Thank God for my wife. She made me who I am." He glanced at me—the darting look of confirmation—and then away, reaching for his drink. "And you. I'd have no life at all if it weren't for you." He drained his glass, bouncing ice cubes against his teeth.

"*You* did it, Gene. You've made a success of your life. You know, that's the scam of psychiatry. The patient does all the work and we take all the credit."

Gene put his glass down. He cleared his throat and frowned. "I don't believe that," he said quickly and rushed on. "Cathy once asked me about you and I realized something terrible, really embarrassing." He checked on me fast and then focused on a hunting print behind my chair. "I never asked you anything about yourself. I just poured my heart out for three years and never found out anything about you."

"You were right. You instinctively understood that I was merely a symbol. You knew everything about me you had to know."

That earned me the longest look of our relationship: head cocked, his wide mouth twisted into a blend of curiosity and amusement. "What do you mean?"

"I was a stand-in for whomever you were working things out with. Sometimes I was your mother, sometimes I was your father, sometimes I was you, or parts of you anyway." I realized I had fallen into pomposity, used to lecturing from all the testifying and interviews. I waved my hand. "Don't worry about it. If you hadn't gone off to college we probably would have continued the therapy for a while—"

"Really?" Gene interrupted pointedly.

"Not for long. Not really to discover things, just a more gradual end to the therapy. If you had had separation problems in general, we certainly would have taken our time, but you were eager to get on with your life and that's healthy. Anyway, as part of that weaning, I guess you could have asked some things and realized I was just a person, someone quite different from the incarnations of the therapy. But I don't approve of therapists and patients becoming friends afterwards. I trained under my psychiatrist—you remember Susan Bracken?"

"Sure. She was your doctor? No kidding."

I nodded. "First she was my shrink, then she was my training analyst, finally my boss. We became good friends. But she'll always be something other than merely a person to me. In fact, I no longer work for her partly because I couldn't resist the urge to run to her for help with every patient. And, although I like to think I'm her friend, she'll always be more than just a friend to me." I looked at my watch. "I really have to get some sleep . . ."

"Sure." Gene waved to the one sleepy waiter left on duty. He asked for the check, which was instantly produced. Gene stopped me from reaching for it. "It's mine. This is the first time in my life I've got an expense account." He sent the waiter off with a hundred-dollar bill.

"How are your parents?"

"Dad's great. I mean, he's moody. You know, up and down about his career, but really he's having a good time. And Mom." He sighed. "Mom never really got over the divorce and then she got sick."

"Something serious?"

"Yeah. Ovarian cancer. She died just before Peter was born." Gene spoke with no affect, as the jargon goes. No sadness, no anger. Just the fact. I considered the timing. His mother had died three years after our last session, while his new wife was pregnant and he was graduating from college. The death of a parent is always stressful, naturally, and those circumstances would have made it much more so. To borrow a phrase from Gene's work, my professional systems came on line, a bit wearily, but instinctively.

"I'm sorry, Gene," I said with all the feeling I thought he should have. I didn't have to fake it; I felt true sympathy. His relationship with his mother had been difficult and, as far as I knew, unresolved. The timing of her death was cruel; not that death can be well-timed, but, given her emotionally incestuous relationship to Gene, somewhere it must have felt to him that she died because he had replaced her with another woman, another family. Had Gene really managed this without the need for help? If so, that was impressive and meant our work together had been much more successful than I had any right to expect.

[Cure is used too casually, to say the least, in my profession. Psychopharmacologists use it when an objective observer might say the patient has had his most severe symptoms overwhelmed by chemicals. Talking therapists use it when others might say that a particular issue has been resolved. In theory, a cure should mean that a patient has achieved a feeling of harmony—homeostasis—and has the strength to regain that balance on his own each time life deals one of its inevitable blows. In my experience the latter is the rarest of accomplishments. An event such as Carol Kenny's early death just as Gene was pouring the foundation for his own family, often sends a patient back to therapy, usually to repeat what was done before, but sometimes—this was Jung's main preoccupation—for the sake of consolidation and further growth. Some believe, in particular psychopharmacologists, that this apparent recidivism proves talking therapy doesn't work. That seems to me to underestimate life's difficult terrain. To scale one mountain doesn't mean a higher one won't require a guide or that previously acquired skills were useless.]

The waiter had returned. Gene occupied himself with taking his change and leaving a tip. He hadn't acknowledged my sympathy. He stood up, feet wavering from the alcohol.

"It must have been hard on you."

Gene pressed his lips in and nodded. "I thought about calling you."

"You could have. I hope I made it clear—"

"Oh yeah. I knew that." He was so unsteady on his legs that he reached for the wing chair with his left hand. "But what could you say? She didn't last long. They caught it late. Cathy got me through it. And then Pete was born. I was just sorry Mom never got to see him." He looked down and was a sad sight, in his prep school clothes, seemingly on the verge of tears. The frantic energy of the computer triumph was gone. "Well," he said with a sigh. "Time to go home."

I walked him downstairs to the lobby, pausing near the doors. I asked him if he wanted me to recommend therapists near his home.

"You got a network, huh?" Gene said with a laugh.

"I can ask around and—"

"Thanks," he lightly touched my shoulder and immediately let go. "Everything's okay now. Really. I gave you the wrong impression. If Flash II had been a bust, I would need help, but now I'll be fine." I got one of his sideways glances: his eyes were bloodshot and, to my mind, scared. The doorman asked if Gene wanted a cab. He said yes and offered me his hand. "Thank you for everything. That's what I wanted to say."

I shook his hand and said, "Wait." I removed a card from my wallet. "Here's where you can reach me. Call if you want me to recommend someone to see in your area. Or just to talk, of course."

Gene declined with a shake of his head, eyes down. "I'm okay." Then he accepted the card. "Okay. Thanks." He hurried out the revolving door, stumbling when he reached the curb. The doorman took his elbow for a moment. Gene looked back before entering the cab and waved, still, to my eyes, a little boy bravely going to school.

I knew it was only a matter of time before I would hear from him again. He called a few months later, in the spring. He said he was having trouble sleeping. "We worked like madmen on Flash II," he told me. "Eighteen, twenty hours a day. Sometimes I didn't sleep for two nights running. I guess I can't get back to norm, I can't unwind. Is there someone I can see who will give me some sleeping pills?"

Obtaining sleeping pills, unfortunately, is easy in America, the land of instant gratification, so I assumed this was a smoke screen. I wondered why Gene was embarrassed to admit he needed help. Did he feel he was letting me down? "Let me make some calls and get a few names for you. I want to make sure I can tell you something about them so you have a basis for making a choice."

"Well . . . it might only be for a session or two, you know. Don't go to too much trouble."

Yeah, why go to any trouble? It's only your mental health. I was annoyed. Passivity and the self-defeating fear of satisfying his needs—his symptoms were back, full-blown. Maybe Gene had been right to be afraid to ask me for help; my vanity didn't seem to be taking it well. "No trouble," I said. "You know, Gene, I don't really think merely taking some sleeping pills will help. You might need only a few sessions, but if this has been going on for months, there's more to it than getting a night's sleep."

"Oh," he said and was quiet.

"I'll get you some names and call you back."

Once again, I felt there was an odd connection between Gene and myself, and I was relieved I could pass him on to another therapist. The timing of his reappearance felt provocative. That very day Uncle Bernie was in the Tower at New York Hospital, about to undergo a gruesome radical treatment for advanced pancreatic cancer. His doctors planned to flood his body with a massive dose of chemotherapy, dangling him over the edge of death. His appendix and spleen were to be removed. His kidneys would be continuously filtered, a respirator would breathe for him, his blood would be changed many times over. For three days he would run a fever of one hundred and four. He would probably need to be packed in ice to keep it that low; any higher and there would be brain damage. And throughout this there would be excruciating pain, none of it able to be relieved with morphine; Uncle would have to endure unaided. Basically the idea was to kill all the stem cells, followed by a bone-marrow transplant from his daughter. If he survived, presumably the cancer would be permanently gone. The treatment was a roll of the dice. To me it sounded like the old joke: if the medicine didn't kill him, he would be cured. This procedure had been tried only six times. Four were a success—in the immediate sense, since the survivors had been in remission for merely a year. The two failures died within twenty-four hours. Of course the numbers were too small to be meaningful. The rationale for its horrific risk was that Bernie was doomed anyway.

Before leaving for the city, I had a free half hour to call a friend from Hopkins, Bill Roth, now at Cambridge Hospital. I assumed he could recommend psychiatrists near Gene in Massachusetts. I was in my office in White Plains, used as a base for our work with abused children. We were minutes from a state-run child welfare center where Diane, Ben and I were on the staff, our prime responsibility. The Grayson Case continued to keep at least two of us traveling to Boston, now for the sake of treating the children rather than satisfying the law. Thus, things were backed up at the welfare center and I was going to lose at least three more days because of Bernie.

"Is your ex-patient a serious fruitcake?" irreverent Bill asked. "Or just a whiner?"

"I think he could use some grief work, but I don't know for sure. I've been out of touch."

"Oh, you want a hugger. How about Toni? Remember her?" She was an excellent psychologist we knew at Hopkins. "She's somewhere in the Massachusetts burbs now. She could make anyone feel glad to be alive. Press against her melons and you could watch your house go down in flames without a peep."

"She only hugged you, not her patients. Also, my patient wants a psychiatrist to write prescriptions. He thinks he needs sleeping pills."

"And you approve?"

"I'm hoping the genius you recommend will see through my patient."

"I'm looking at the map. Toni can't be more than half an hour from this guy. Why don't you tell your patient that if Toni thinks he needs downers, you'll write the prescription?"

"I thought of that. But I assumed you'd call me a control freak."

"What's wrong with being a control freak?"

Toni was a good choice, in many ways a better choice for Gene than I was, certainly now that Gene was an adult. I tried her, but she was out. Getting to her and then to Gene would have to wait. It was time to drive into the city to gather with what was left of the Rabinowitzes at New York Hospital. More to the point for me, I needed to make what might be my farewell to Bernie.

When I got off the elevator on Bernie's floor, Aunt Sadie was there, leaning on a cane. She had broken her hip two years ago in Palm Beach, chasing after Daniel's firstborn near the pool. She walked without a limp, using the cane when she felt tired. She feared another fall; it offered security more than support. "Oh, Rafe," she said. "I was just going for coffee. They won't allow any food in there."

I hugged her. Her cane tapped against my side. She was clear-eyed when I first saw her. While we embraced, I felt her head tremble against my chest. Sure enough, as we broke the clinch, there were tears.

"I was afraid you wouldn't be here," she said.

"Of course I was coming."

"I thought you'd get stuck somewhere with your work."

"Sadie, what's wrong?"

Her old face was soft and benign: padded cheeks, eyes uncertain, mouth slack. Uncle Leo had died suddenly five years ago, a massive coronary. Her sons and grandchildren lived in Houston and Chicago. She saw them only a few times a year. And the hip, too, of course. She was sarcastic: "You're asking what's wrong?"

"I mean, is there something new?"

"*She's* here." Sadie said the pronoun with scorn. "She" was my uncle's second wife, Patricia, about twenty years his junior, a sharp-tongued real estate broker who sold Uncle his home in Palm Beach and then sold herself to him. The family, meaning Sadie and Bernie's daughter, believed Pat was more interested in Uncle's money than in him. They had been married for a decade, and happily so far as I knew.

"Well, she *is* his wife."

"Can't stand her. Not now," Sadie added, pulling away from me, brushing lint off her blue blouse.

"Don't you see her all the time in Florida?"

"Not if I can help it." Sadie narrowed her eyes. The look reminded me of my mother. "She's counting his money right now." But here was a difference between my mother and her sister. The stern, suspicious look evaporated and Sadie laughed at herself. "Don't listen to me. I'm crazy. Old and crazy. She deserves his money. She's been good to him." She moved to the elevator, focused on her cane, which she wielded more like a toy than an aid, jabbing the floor, using its handle to press the button. "He's my baby brother," she said, her throat clutching on the word baby.

I studied her face. It was placid. "He's a strong man," I said. "He could make it through this."

"Doctors are crazy. They like to torture you before you die. What do they care? It's all about money."

"You sound like a communist, Aunt."

"I didn't mean you, dear. You're a saint," she said with absolute seriousness.

I laughed and then sang softly, *"El veinticuatro de octubre, el día de San Rafael."*

Sadie smiled. "What's that?"

"The twenty-fourth of October is the day of Saint Rafael," I translated. "My saint's day. My grandmother Jacinta used to call me on the twenty-fourth and sing it."

"Was she religious?"

"No."

Sadie frowned. The elevator arrived. She entered. Behind her was a tired orderly in a dirty smock, a mop and bucket beside him. He leaned against the back, eyes closed, ignoring us. Sadie pressed a button, still frowning, preoccupied. "Your mother used to say she was a sweet lady." The doors closed on her.

I found Uncle in a huge corner room, commanding a sweeping view of the East River and Manhattan. His wife, Pat, was with him. She was tanned and fashionably skinny, dyed black hair brushed back flush to the scalp, and dressed with understated elegance: white blouse, black skirt, and a rope of simple but expensive pearls around her neck. She said, "Here he is," as I entered. She kissed the air near my cheek, a hand squeezing my forearm. "He's been driving me crazy waiting to see you." She went to the door. "I'll keep everybody out until you're done with Rafe." She left, shutting it behind her.

Although his face was still full, Uncle had already lost fifty pounds. His hair had receded halfway back and was all gray, but the skin had amazing youthfulness—few lines and the translucent glow of a newborn. He sat in a chair by the windows, wearing a long navy blue robe, a glass of water beside him. There were piles of legal documents on a table. He stood up and that's when the frailty of his torso became obvious. His head was too big for his skinny neck and wasted chest. I hugged him. He patted my back tentatively. "You look great," he said and pushed away. He seemed unsteady. I took his left hand and held it while he carefully settled back into the chair. My eyes fell on his knuckles. The tufts of hair were white now, still seemingly brushed into an elegant knot, but looking sparser because of their color. There were several liver spots, a big one under his thumb, another beneath his pinky. There was a persistent tremor in the wrist that vibrated to his fingers and kept them perpetually animated. He gestured for me to pull up a chair opposite him.

When I did, he handed me a letter. "Read it."

It was from Aaron, his son, now forty-six years old. They hadn't seen each other for twenty years. He wrote he had heard about Bernie's illness, that he was sorry and hoped he improved. He wanted his father to know that after many years of drug addiction, five years ago he had at last found help and kicked the habit. He had a job he enjoyed, was living in Iowa with a woman he loved and got to spend summers with his teenage son, Isaac, from a previous marriage. He didn't want anything from

Bernie, although he would like to come see him, but he hoped Bernie would pay for Isaac's college education, since he was a bright boy and deserved a future. Aaron doubted that his salary as a teaching assistant would be enough or was likely to change. "I'm not an ambitious man," he added. He was being frank, he wrote, because he knew Bernie didn't like people asking him for money and he thought if he were indirect that would only make the request more irritating. He wasn't asking anything for himself. He was sorry that he had been such a disappointment, that although he felt he had reasons for the hard times he'd gone through, he understood he was responsible for his estrangement from Bernie, his divorce, and his limited career prospects. Nevertheless, he didn't think it was fair for his son to be punished for his own fuck-ups. Believe it or not, the letter ended, "I love you."

I read the letter twice. I wasn't happy about it. I felt Aaron was unnecessarily guilty and brusque and pathetic. His current life wasn't that limited. He enjoyed teaching, was writing short stories, and had had three published. He loved his second wife very much. She was pregnant, a fact he omitted. And I felt he should have bragged more about Isaac, a delightful, intelligent young man. Bernie would have been proud, if the presentation had been more realistic, less manipulative, less ashamed. Obviously, I had been in touch with Aaron for many years, although Bernie didn't know. That had been Aaron's wish and I kept the secret. Secrets follow me everywhere, I thought. "Did you know about this?" Uncle asked.

"The letter? No."

"How about Aaron?"

"Yes."

Bernie took the letter. He shook his head at me, smiling wanly. "Why didn't you tell me?"

"It was none of your business."

Bernie grunted, amused. He put the letter on the pile of documents. "You helped him, right? That's how he got treatment."

"I gave him a phone number. That's all. *He* did it, Uncle. Don't turn it into that."

"So you want me to do what he asks?"

"Isaac's a bright boy. He should be able to go to college and not have to worry about tuition and living expenses and so on."

"What's he want to be? Aaron doesn't say."

"Musician. Plays the trumpet. Wants to go to Oberlin. He has a lot of talent."

"Another artist." Bernie gingerly lifted his glass of water to his lips and sipped. He smacked them afterwards, just a little, yet there was something infantile about it. "What a creative family I have. I'm so lucky."

"You are lucky."

"Oh? I spent my whole life, every fucking minute, doing things for my family. They're ungrateful and they're a mess. Can you explain that to me?"

I didn't answer.

"I bet you can. I bet you can explain so my hair would stand on end."

"You're angry at me?"

"You should have told me. Not telling me means you think I'm a child. Or a bully. Is Aaron my fault? Was that my fault, his blowing his mind on drugs, was that my fault?"

"I'm a head shrinker, Uncle. Not a rabbi. I'm not an expert in blame."

"A lot you know. Rabbis are experts at fund-raising. No," Uncle pushed Aaron's letter away. It fell off the pile on its end, like a car that had been pushed off a cliff. "Nobody's to blame for anything," he said bitterly.

"Why are you angry at me, Uncle?"

"You should be my doctor," he said casually. He looked at Manhattan. The sun was going down, casting a slanting light on the glass towers of Midtown. "I told you I wanted you to cure cancer." He smiled slyly. "I knew this day would come."

"I'm . . ." I was about to say, I'm sorry, but that was foolish and untrue. I had what many might feel is a harsh point of view toward this situation. Uncle was over eighty years old. The belief that facing death in old age should be to struggle wildly is too immature and unrealistic for me to accept. "Rage, rage against the dying of the light" is a failure to understand nature. Bernie was used to controlling events, but that had also done great harm to his relationships. I had hoped he would face his end with more grace. That was childish of me, as well. But, for better or worse, he had become my father and I wished he would set a better example for me. The last gift a parent can give is the lesson of how to die.

Bernie waited for me to elaborate. When I kept silent, he continued, "You didn't say on the phone what you think of this treatment."

"Treatment?"

"Yes, treatment. What is it, if it isn't a treatment?"

"There are other options. Options that would be less painful, less—"

"But I'd die. No question, they tell me."

I said nothing.

"I'm going to die anyway, that's what you think."

"You're forty years older than the other test cases. The only reason they approved you for this is because of your money."

"You think you're telling me something I don't know?"

"You might live for up to a year, relatively comfortably, with normal treatment."

"Relatively comfortably," he repeated and shook his head.

"There would be time to see Aaron, to meet your grandson, to say your goodbyes to everyone who's important to you."

"The people who are important to me are here."

"But no one says goodbye, right? That would be unsupportive."

Bernie smiled at me. He slapped my knee. "Only you. You're the only one who has the balls to tell me I can't make it."

"Maybe you can make it. But maybe it isn't worth it."

"To live another five, ten years?" He stared at me. I nodded. "That isn't worth it?" he asked, incredulous.

"Maybe not."

"You're crazy.'

"You don't know what crazy is, Uncle," I said.

We both laughed. Uncle took another sip of water. When he replaced the glass, he raised Aaron's letter from its wrecked position and restored it to the top of the pile. "Is this grandson of mine, this paragon Isaac, is he white?"

I was surprised. I thought for a moment. "You've checked up on him."

"That black wife of his—"

"Ex-wife."

Uncle waved his hand. "She the one who got him on drugs?"

"I don't know. I doubt it. She's the one who kicked him out. Made him face the addiction."

"Bernie Rabinowitz's one real grandson has rhythm," he said in a mocking tone; but it sounded hollow. His daughter, Helen, had never been able to conceive. Her two children were adopted.

"Look at your nephew," I said, pointing to me. "The Rabinowitzes are a regular United Nations."

Bernie smacked his lips. "I'm dry all the time. Get me some water, please. There's fancy water in that refrigerator."

The refrigerator was only one of a number of conveniences added to the room. Besides the table covered with papers, there was a stereo system, a Xerox machine, tape recorders for dictation and a huge device that I didn't know was a first-generation fax.

Pat looked in while I brought him a glass of Evian. "Helen and the kids are here."

"And the genius?"

"Helen said Jerry's still at the office. He'll be here soon."

"We'll be a little longer," Bernie said imperiously, his usual tone with Pat.

She rolled her eyes, but disappeared compliantly.

"She's the only one who takes and doesn't whine."

"How about me?"

"You criticize. That's worse than whining."

"Does Jerry whine?" I asked, referring to Helen's husband, now the president of Uncle's company.

"Jerry loses my money and blames everything and everyone but his stupid management." This was an old complaint. In the early seventies Uncle had retired from the day-to-day management of his company, turning it over to his son-in-law. To Bernie's amazement, Jerry sold off Home World, the discount electronics and appliance chain Bernie had bought and expanded in the sixties. With profits from the sale, Jerry invested heavily in Manhattan real estate. Not the low- to middle-income housing that had made Bernie rich in the forties and fifties, but elaborate office buildings and luxury apartment complexes. At first, Wall Street loved his maneuvers. In 1972, various improprieties came to light—four city inspectors eventually went to jail—and then the 1973 recession hit New York hard. By '74, the value of Uncle's company's stock dropped from twenty-three dollars a share to seventy-five cents, demolishing Bernie's and Jerry's paper worth from six hundred million dollars to less than thirty million. Uncle came out of retirement. In a series of dazzling moves, he rescued the situation. He called on his old friends, made sweetheart deals with banks, billed and cooed with the state and city government, and managed not only to keep Jerry out of prison, but out of the papers too. By 1980 Bernie had restored the stock to ten dollars a share. In an act of generosity and loyalty—it seemed to me—Bernie stepped aside for Jerry again. This second succession was going better. By

1988, the stock was up to twenty-five and Bernie had returned to the Forbes list of the one hundred richest Americans.

"I thought Jerry is doing great now," I said.

"Ronald Reagan did great," Bernie said. "Jerry went along for the ride." Bernie took another long drink of water. I was reminded of my mother; he didn't see the world very differently from her. He believed, as did she, that social tides bear individuals at their whim, that often successful businessmen are driftwood who imagine they are Olympic swimmers. Indeed, Bernie's edge had been the clear vision of his brand of Marxism: he didn't try to make waves, he rode them. As if he were thinking along those lines, he wiped his lips and said, "It's time to get out of real estate, especially in New York," he said. "He thinks Bush will keep things good. They're so greedy," Bernie said. "It isn't hard to make money. Buy low and sell high, that's what's hard. But these geniuses think the good times go on forever. I keep telling him, it's supply and demand. We've built and built and built. Prices have to come down. The Japs want our real estate, he says, that proves things are going up." Bernie grunted. "I'm supposed to take that seriously? I know this city." Bernie nodded at his view of Manhattan, certainly commanding and panoramic. His buildings were reduced in size, toys for the gigantic hands of his wealth and power. "Nobody makes things anymore. Maybe they will again, after the disaster, maybe . . ." He grunted. "It's gone. My father's world is gone."

"Have you been in the Korean grocery stores?"

"What?" Bernie looked at me sharply, squinting, as if I had brought him something to examine.

"They remind me of the old Jewish delis. Whole families work. The children. Everybody. Twenty-fours a day, seven days a week. The kids do their homework between making change."

"They're fools too," Bernie said. "My father was a good man, but he was a fool." He laughed suddenly. "Kids do their homework and make change. You approve?"

"I approve and I don't."

"What the fuck does that mean?"

"They include their children in their work, I like that. Apprenticeship has many benefits. Much less alienating than going to school well into adulthood for what amounts to learning a trade from a stranger. But they have no childhood and that's too hard. They may grow up to be hardworking, decent and successful, but their hearts will be empty. They'll never feel joy as adults because they have nothing in the bank to draw on."

Bernie stared at me, his head trembling slightly. His eyes were fierce, as challenging as ever. "It's better they grow up to be drug addicts like the blacks?"

"No. But there should be some other choice."

"Your trouble is, you think people can be happy."

"I think they should be given the chance."

"Enough. It isn't that I think you're wrong." Bernie glanced at his pile of papers, at Aaron's letter. "I *know* you're wrong," he said quietly. "Now listen," he leaned toward me, although he lowered his eyes. "If this goes badly for me, I've left enough for you to try to save the world." His head came up with a broad smile, dentures gleaming. His attitude was a confusing mix of humor and malice. "You want to help this grandson of mine, go ahead. They get nothing from me."

"What happens if you live?"

"Tough." Bernie took another sip. I said nothing. I didn't believe him. He put the glass down and said, "Go and get my adoring family."

This was goodbye. Too many others had gone without my acknowledgment. I took his trembling hand. He was surprised, but gripped me hard. My thumb brushed across the white knots of hair, the knuckles that had fascinated me so long ago. "I love you, Uncle. You saved my life."

Tears welled in his hard eyes. He shook his head as if denying it.

"No, I'm not pretending there weren't things you did wrong. And that I did wrong. I don't mean that. I mean, you did the best you could and it was more than enough. I'm grateful."

He covered my thumb with his other hand and squeezed, a tear falling. He shut his eyes, sighed, and said, "I'm proud of you." We sat there, holding hands, for a while. When he opened them again, his eyes were red. "Are you happy?"

I nodded. "Sometimes."

"Because of your work?"

I nodded. He sighed again. "You did a good thing with those Grayson kids in Boston. Is that what you'll do with my money? Help kids?"

"I'm going to try."

Bernie nodded. He let go of my hand, shut his eyes, and put his fingers to them, pressing as if he wanted to push them into his skull. "Okay," he sighed, straightened, and looked at me. His eyes were clearer, but still sad and guarded. "Okay," he repeated and added in a doomed voice: "I'm ready to see them."

Two days later, he was dead. As I feared, his last forty-eight hours were spent in an agonized delirium. From my internship, I was used to the wreck medicine can make of a human being and, with everyone's permission, I made sure that once Uncle was too far gone, there were no more resuscitations. By the time they let him go in peace, his heart had been restarted twice. At the finish, the bold thirteen-year-old who once led a band of Jewish kids in triumphant battle against the toughest of the Irish gangs weighed less than eighty pounds. It was an ugly death, unworthy of him.

I finally reached Toni the day of my uncle's funeral. She had two free hours a week and would be glad to see Gene. When I called Gene, he greeted my brief explanation of Toni with a doubtful, "Oh."

"You sound unhappy."

"I don't mean to be sexist, but . . ."

"You're uncomfortable with a woman therapist?"

"Well . . . You know, I've been sleeping pretty well since I called you. So maybe . . . Or is that—like when you're on your way to the dentist— the tooth stops hurting?"

"Could be. If you see her and don't like her, I'll be happy to get you the name of a male therapist."

"Okay," he said in a forlorn tone that meant it wasn't okay. I was too tired and sad to explore it further. I had a thought that deserved to be analyzed: this guy is bad luck for me. I was in distress, not only about Uncle's death and funeral. Ahead of me that day was the uncomfortable prospect of seeing Julie for the first time since her father's death. She was then unmarried and childless.

I didn't have long to wait. I saw her standing alone outside the temple in Great Neck, on the fringe of the parking lot, smoking a cigarette. Although Julie was, besides being the mother of two, a movie producer living in L.A., she allowed her hair to show gray. She was right to. The streaks of white threading her flowing black hair added to her elegance. She tossed the cigarette down and opened her arms to greet me. From my car as I pulled in, she had looked worried and upset. That surprised me. She never liked Uncle and the incident at Columbia banned him permanently from her heart. I was pleased that, as I walked toward her, her unhappy expression relaxed and she smiled.

"Oh, Rafe," she whispered in my ear while we hugged. "Is this what the future has in store for us? These fucking funerals?"

Embracing her called up sexual memories for me: resting my head on her belly; her behind bucking in my palms as she climaxed; toes stroking my pants under the table at a bizarre Seder at Aunt Sadie's. I was naughty about this embrace in our mourning clothes. I pressed against her and didn't let go until she pushed me off with enough emphasis so that her discomfort was clear.

"You look great," I said, my husky voice concealing nothing.

"I do not. I'm an old mother of two."

"Don't fish. You know you look great."

She smiled. "Okay. Thanks." She patted her stomach. "I worked hard, believe me. It's against the law to have a tummy in L.A." Without a break, her face crumpled into the worry I had seen from the car. "Mom's upset. She's really bad. Worse than even for Daddy." I nodded. Julie searched her black purse and came out with a cigarette.

"I thought you gave them up."

"Just while pregos. I don't smoke around the kids or Richard." That was her husband. "He'd kill me."

"You smoke secretly from your husband?"

"He knows. I just don't smoke in front of him. Are they all crazy?" she asked without a transition. "Was it the money? They—" she nodded at the temple. The lot was full. The service was due to begin in five minutes. I had arrived late. Traffic was worse than I expected—every route I tried was under construction. "They act like God has died."

"Maybe He has, for them. Remember, he pulled them out of poverty and he saved them again fifteen years ago."

"He's also fucked them up permanently." Julie blew out some smoke and then covered her mouth with her free hand. "I'm horrible."

"No, you're not. You're just stronger than they are."

Julie came to a rest. Her nervous movements were frozen, cigarette dangling, eyes on me. "What do you mean?"

"You refused to be dependent on him. And you made it. You made it on your own."

"How about you? You—"

"You know I never would have made it without Uncle's help."

"He also hurt you. Hurt you horribly."

"Yes. But he meant to do the opposite. And when it came right down to it, he did help me."

Julie let go of her cigarette, stamping it into the gravel. "Let's go in before I piss you off too."

It turned out she had had a fight with her mother. Ceil was angry that Julie had left her kids and husband behind in California. Julie was right. The surviving Rabinowitzes did seem to be a tribe who had lost not merely their chief, but their god. In particular, Aunts Ceil and Sadie were devastated. Uncle's daughter, Helen, was also stricken, although grief seemed to improve her character. Back at the house, she didn't drink at all, a remarkable difference, given that she was, in my judgment, an alcoholic. Helen tended to her aunts with grim concentration and told poignant stories about her father that surprised me; anecdotes of Bernie teaching her to ride a bike, dancing with her on her thirteenth birthday, all from before I lived with them, when, apparently, he spent more time with her and Aaron. Even Helen's husband, Jerry, who must have felt some relief to be finally rid of his boss, was quiet, modest, a little frightened. Aaron did not come, although I had tried to coax him. My cousins, Daniel and the others I had raced against for the *Afikomen,* were there, with spouses and children, some content, some a mess. All were awed, convinced a great man had died. Julie did not fit in with them, either intellectually or emotionally.

When the visitors thinned out, leaving the immediate family, Julie's quarrel with her mother started up again. Ceil complained that Julie coming alone to the funeral was disrespectful. I stepped between mother and daughter and took Julie outside, onto the sloping lawn. We walked toward the tennis court where I had had so many lessons, sweating to impress Bernie.

"Will you tell me what this is about?" Julie said. "My kids are three and seven months. I can't bring them to a funeral. And how is it disrespectful? To Bernie? To this bimbo wife of his? Mom hates her."

"Your mother wants her grandchildren here. She wants to feel life, that's all. To know that it goes on."

"That's why I want her to come back to L.A. with me and stay for a couple of months. I know she's lonely—"

"She wants you to honor the life she's led. That life is here. Here in gracious, sensitive, cultured Great Neck." Julie laughed at my mocking tone. "You don't have to. It's not your obligation to shore up her fantasy."

"You do. You play along. They were mean to you, they were so fucking mean to you, and they *still* don't appreciate you. They think you're some sort of failure. Jerry talks to you like you're a family retainer. But you take it all so patiently. You give and give and give to them and they don't notice. I don't know how you can stand it."

"I do?" I had learned long ago that a degree in psychology doesn't confer perfect self-knowledge—or perfect anything for that matter. We had reached the court. I found the switch for the lights and flipped it, curious if they were working. A white glow, not harsh, but brilliant nevertheless, flooded the area. Swarms of bugs appeared, gathering at the large rectangular bulbs. I wondered if the painted asphalt of the tennis court had been maintained. From outside, it was hidden by green bunting to camouflage the fence's interruption of the lawn. I opened the gate, to check on the condition of the surface. When Bernie bought the house from his first wife, Charlotte—she left the U.S. to marry a businessman who worked in South America—I assumed he intended to resume the old family gatherings, the huge Seders and birthdays. But there had been no family parties. Uncle used to resurface the court every five years. The gate creaked loudly, a bad omen. But the surface was smooth, the lines bright, the net tape shiny. It was a ghost to me, an apparition from my childhood.

Was Julie right? Did these people think I was a failure after all? Had they taken the fantasies of my childhood to heart and continued to think of me as Bernie's failed prodigy? And was I concealing something from them, accepting scorn while feeling superior? "I play along?" I asked Julie again. "I'm not aware of being phony. I feel sorry for most of them. For Aaron, certainly. And for Sadie. She's always been very close to her family. I think she took my mother's suicide harder than any of them and she loved Bernie, really loved him."

"Jesus." Julie slumped down onto the grass outside the gate. She reached for a cigarette. "You're making me feel like a shit."

I kept my eyes on the glowing, pristine court. "I'm in love with you," I said, too cowardly and too ashamed of giving in to this feeling to look at her. "It's been seven years. Supposed to go away. But I think of you every day and I realize today that I want you more than ever. I made a mistake. I should have taken you on any terms."

I didn't hear anything from her. I thought, in the distance, someone shouted joyfully from the house. That didn't make sense, a whoop of happiness from people in mourning.

Finally, I heard her lips make a noise as she took another puff. But she didn't speak.

"Maybe that's why I keep bringing up family obligations," I continued. "Just a sneaky way of complaining that you didn't . . ." I couldn't go on. I felt alone. I leaned against the fence and remembered a perfect shot I had once hit against someone, I wasn't sure who, a down-the-line backhand on the full run, a typical stroke for a professional, but the only one I ever hit, a taste of greatness. Pointless in my life, yet I could still see the ball spinning over the net for a winner as if it were yesterday, as if it were full of meaning. "I'm sorry," I said and turned to Julie.

She was huddled beside the open gate, head down. I knelt beside her. She looked up, face wet. She spoke passionately, but clearly. "That isn't fair. You ended it. I said we should just go on—"

"In secret? For our whole lives?" I argued, passionately, as if no time had passed.

She straightened and pushed me with one hand, like an annoyed kid. "You have no right to keep it alive now. I love Richard and I love my children. Don't make me feel guilty about that."

I took hold of her shoulders and moved her toward me intending to kiss her. "I wanted to force you to—" I stopped.

"Force me to what? Tell them?" She nodded at the house. The tears had abated. She wasn't in conflict. I was. These were settled matters for her. "How could we have made a family together in front of them? I have beautiful children. You don't know. You've ignored them."

"You know why."

"You'll do anything for them, for Aaron, for Helen, you'll gush over their kids and you won't even look at pictures of mine."

"You can't expect me to be glad that you're happily married."

"I *am* happily married."

I let go. The impulse to kiss was certainly gone.

"I know you don't want to believe that," Julie said. "But I am. I love Richard. I'm furious at you that you won't let go and see me for who I am. I'm a middle-aged woman with two kids and a husband. I was never as complicated as you wanted me to be. I loved you and I was willing to give up having a family to be with you. I couldn't do better than that." She sighed and covered her face. "I'm just as conventional as they are," she mumbled. "That's the truth."

She was right, not about the last remark, but about me. Losing the fantasy of Julie was as painful as actually losing her, maybe more so. Her hands came away. I stared and tried to see the real woman. Was she there, the girl who had fought my mother and my uncle on my behalf? The woman who had once brought me the grace of mature love? The tennis court's clarifying light left nothing for my imagination. She looked tired and her eyes were dead to the silent pleas in my own. She was a stranger and that meant in some way I was still a stranger to myself.

In the distance, a voice called, "Ray-feel!" A figure ran toward us from the house, a shape I didn't recognize.

Julie squeezed my arm. "Be happy, Rafe. You deserve it." She stood up. "Get away from us. We're not good for you."

"Ray-feel," the figure called. He was carrying two racquets and a can of balls. The dumpy shape reached the border of the court's lights. It was cousin Daniel, in his black trousers, his jacket and shirt off. He looked like a photograph of a turn-of-the-century boxer: bare-chested, big-bellied, in long dark pants. "Tennis, anyone?" he said and laughed.

"You drunk?" Julie said quietly.

I stood up.

"Come on," Daniel offered a racquet. "I bet I can still beat you."

"I'm sure you can," I said and walked Julie back to my dead uncle's house.

CHAPTER FIVE

The Rosenhan Warning

TONI REPORTED THAT GENE TALKED A BLUE STREAK IN THE FIRST SESSION, but said nothing. He was preoccupied by an offer from his boss, Theodore Copley, the leader of Flash II's creative team. Copley had confided in Gene that he was seriously considering a job at Flashworks's main rival, Minotaur. If he accepted, he wanted Gene to come with him. Gene believed the anxious contemplation of this decision—to leave the company where he had been successful and move his family against his wife's wishes to another state—explained his insomnia. Toni was unconvinced. I hadn't sent her any information on Gene or told her details of our work together. She asked for them now. I declined.

"Why? It would save time, no?"

"Remember Rosenhan?" Rosenhan was a psychology professor who sent a group of his graduate students into a psychiatric ward with instructions to fake schizophrenia. None were exposed by the experts, despite the fact that the impostors had been briefed only superficially about what to simulate. To prove his thesis beyond doubt, Rosenhan then presented a group of experienced psychiatrists with genuine schizophrenics, telling the doctors ahead of time that they were fakers. The doctors interviewed the real schizophrenics at length and agreed they were phonies. Rosenhan's chilling conclusion: the psychiatrist sees what he expects to see.

"I'm insulted," Toni complained. "And intimidated. I feel like I'm taking a quiz."

"No, no. I'm concerned that what I thought was a successful therapy with Gene was a failure and I don't want to prejudice you. I'm not sandbagging. I have more faith in your working with Gene than me."

"Rafe, that's a crock."

"No, I mean it. I'm not really good treating grown-ups. I'm mesmerized by the past. I get stuck in the archaeology. With children, I'm always in the here and now."

"Sounds like a rationalization."

"It's not." I thought back to the grown-up Gene, in his student clothes, his boyish manner. Was he a grown-up?

Toni interrupted my silence. "Anyway, I thought Gene was a kid when you saw him."

"Yeah, a teenager."

"So?" Toni sounded triumphant.

"So what?"

"You're telling me you don't think you're a good therapist for teenagers?"

"Toni, remember Bertha?" Bertha was a fifty-two-year-old black patient during my internship at Hopkins, a mute whom I and my colleagues diagnosed as schizophrenic. Toni discovered Bertha was from Haiti, did some research and eventually uncovered Bertha's conviction that she had been hexed by a neighbor who, like her, practiced an obscure religion, a kind of Santería, a mix of Catholicism and a Voodoo sect. Toni gathered a group of us in the cafeteria at midnight during a full moon, lit purple candles, and we performed a ceremony (our solemnity was aided by two bottles of cheap red wine) that involved borrowing a skull from the anatomy lab. One week later, a cheerful, confident Bertha was discharged. That was one of many instances of Toni's unusual ability to avoid the Rosenhan syndrome.

"I don't follow, Rafe. Bertha was basically a cultural problem. Nobody thought to talk to her in her own terms."

"And that includes me. I didn't mean Rosenhan was your problem. I'm not testing you. I'm testing my former treatment."

"Well . . . Okay. I still think you could save me time. Anyway, Gene is convinced his problems are all about work. Actually, I believe work is the one place he's comfortable."

She could be talking about me, I thought later. I hadn't taken a vacation in six years, I hadn't allowed a woman into my heart since Julie, my friendships were really all professional, my evenings devoted to writing a book about "Timmy" and the Grayson Day Care case. I decided it was time to take time. Besides, I had decided to use half of my ten-million-dollar inheritance from Uncle (obviously, I was not his sole heir) to construct a two-story building to house a clinic for the treatment of abused children and there wasn't any insight I could contribute to its design and construction.

I also arranged to pay for Isaac's college education. I told Aaron it was Bernie's wish—in a sense, that was the exact truth.

Aaron didn't believe me. "Yeah?" he said. "Show me where it says that in his will."

"There wasn't time to change his will," I said.

"Thank you, Rafe," Aaron said. "That's what I should be saying."

With that off my conscience, I tried again to reach my father in Havana, writing to the last address Grandpa Pepín had for him. (Naturally one of the by-products of Susan's therapy was that I reestablish contact with my father's people. Although this irritated Uncle Bernie, my suicide attempt had frightened him enough so that he tolerated it. I was eighteen when I stood on the old porch and made my apology and explanation to Grandpa Pepín of why I testified against his son. He nodded when I was finished and said, "I understand. You were brainwashed by the barbarians." Confused, I mumbled, "The barbarians?" Grandpa nodded in a direction over my left shoulder. I turned to look. Far in the distance, past the low roofs of what seemed to be miles and miles of modest homes, light in the windows of a new office building twinkled at me. I looked back at Pepín. "You mean the capitalists?" I asked. "I mean the barbarians," he said and never raised the subject of my treachery again.) This was my fourth attempt to resume contact with Francisco since I petitioned successfully to restore his American passport and again there was no response. For almost a decade he could have returned to the States. To my knowledge, he hadn't. Through a colleague, I was introduced to the Cuban attaché to the U.N. Other than confirming that my father was alive and well, residing where I had written him, all he could suggest was that I go to Havana to confront Francisco. Since my letters to Francisco were requests to come see him, and I now knew that he had definitely gotten them, I assumed such a visit would be unwelcome. Perhaps I was merely intimidated. From both Grandpa and the Cuban attaché (who claimed to know my father fairly well) I got the distinct impression that Francisco had money problems. I arranged for fifty thousand dollars—an American ransom, the Cuban attaché joked—to be deposited in a Canadian bank in his name. That was a legal and safe way to deal with both America's and Cuba's different brands of restrictions. The money wasn't refused—indeed, a bank official told me the account was immediately activated—yet no letter or phone call was forthcoming.

I had asked for forgiveness and received none. Maybe that was just. I didn't want to seek more punishment, despite my guilty feelings.

The spring and summer of 1988, I made an effort to relax and take care of myself, limiting my hours with the children to no more than eight a day, joining a health club (and using it), and, the most significant change, ignoring my reservations about becoming involved with a co-worker. During the Grayson Day Care case, Diane Rosenberg split up with a man she had been living with since college. We became close, apart from the intimacy of our work. I resisted, for more than a year, risking our friendship by introducing romance, not only because I was putting companionship in danger, I was also chancing the loss of an intelligent and dedicated colleague. I had no illusion that if we were to become estranged lovers we would be capable of returning to the harmony of our platonic relationship.

To be blunt, our first few attempts at sex were self-conscious and a little comic. If, as Freud observed, there are six people in every bedroom—the lovers and the ghosts of their parents—then the bedroom of two psychiatrists is as crowded with spirits as Halloween. I suggested a change of scene might relieve the awkwardness and we took our first vacation in years together. The two weeks in Paris were idyllic in every way. We shed more than our clothes. Assuming the naive skins of tourists, we discovered our bodies could dance in the dark without poltergeists mocking our rhythm.

Taking time away from my work seemed to improve my results. In July, "Timmy" made a series of dazzling breakthroughs—a rapid integration of his multiple personalities that began with a deeply moving and eerie scene in which the various selves were introduced to each other. Also, my book on incest was well received and debated in a healthy way, even by its critics. August brought the opening of the clinic, although some of the construction wasn't finished; the revelation to our friends that Diane and I had become an item was greeted with less surprise and disapproval than either of us had expected; and I worked hard to finish the book about the Grayson trial, inspired by "Timmy's" bravery facing his painful memories and what I had learned from his remarkable insights into the methods and motivations of his abusers.

The last week of August, Gene appeared. He had followed his mentor to Minotaur. Its research and development labs were in Tarrytown, thus Gene had moved his family to northern Westchester county. I hadn't heard from Toni since our Rosenhan conversation. Gene told me she hadn't been much use to him; he stopped seeing her after only three ses-sions. "It was a practical problem anyway. I had to make this decision and it was tough. I was scared to stay and scared to go." He wanted to see me professionally. He felt the new job—he was going to be project director for Minotaur's new machine—would put him under unbearable pres-sure. Unbearable was his word.

"I don't see adult patients anymore, Gene. I'm devoting all my time to the clinic. The few adults who come here will see other therapists. I specialize in working with children who have been severely abused. I'm not up to date treating adults."

"You mean they've made therapy new and improved?"

"There's always good work going on. It's no different than anything else. If you came to see me you'd have to play Candyland and draw pic-tures with Crayolas."

"Sounds okay to me. I'm pretty good at Candyland. I'm better at Monopoly."

I laughed. "You sound healthy to me, Gene. Are you sure you really feel the need for therapy? Feeling pressure at taking a new job is realis-tic, you know."

"Well . . . thanks. But . . ." He sighed. "Forget it."

"No. I don't want to forget it. Go on. But what?"

"I remember you saying I could always come and speak to you. For a tune-up, you called it."

"A tune-up?" That sounded like Rafe the cocksure therapist. As if I were a master mechanic and people were machines that could be regu-lated with precision. I had promised him I would always be there to lis-ten. He had trusted me with his tenderest feelings and now I was too busy?

I explained that I had moved from White Plains. The new clinic was in Riverdale. He said the drive was no problem and that his schedule was flexible, since he was a project director. He came at lunchtime, the hour I took off as part of relaxation from compulsive work. The construction of rooms for monitored interviews started at that hour, since we tried to keep the mornings quiet. The work crews were installing video cameras behind one-way mirrors—to lessen their obtrusiveness and improve the coverage for the sake of testimony. Our objective was to meet the re-quirements of the law without inhibiting the children. Every minute of contact had to be recorded or we could be accused of influencing the process and yet, particularly for early sessions, the obvious presence of cameras is distracting. We planned to show the children the equipment and the one-way mirror, then go into the regular rooms—they don't seem much different from a cheerful kindergarten—and forget their existence. (Although some therapists tape without telling the children, I felt that was unfair. Unfair and too similar to the kind of lying typical of abusive adults.) We were going to videotape whether or not the law was potentially involved. How could we know in advance, for one thing, and the tapes should provide a useful tool for therapists to review and evaluate.

Gene recognized the video cables on his way in. I explained over the noise of the drilling and apologized.

"Are we being recorded?" he asked. He was in jeans, a wrinkled white button-down shirt and Top-Siders. His black hair was long, one bang cutting off an eyebrow. The style seemed too youthful for an adult. His face had few lines. With a little hair dye he could pass for an eighteen-year-old. Maybe he wasn't clinging to youth emotionally; perhaps, chemically, he wasn't a man yet. How could I know? (Joseph Stein, with whom I had renewed our childhood friendship after a twenty-year hiatus, had become a world-renowned neurobiologist, devoting all his energies—as have dozens of other talented people—to discovering how the brain works. Although Joseph still had faith that one day science would be able to locate the precise mechanism the drives every action, thought and feeling of humans, he frankly admitted to me that, as of today, we know very little; each discovery leads to more questions.) Gene not only wanted to be a boy—so did his body. What, in the end, do we really understand about rates of aging? It so often seems that everything in human nature can end up being argued as to which is first, the chicken or the egg. I wanted to keep an open mind. After years of training and work I was less sure of all theories. And how confident could I be of technique? Gene and I didn't seem to have changed much. We were back where we started, asking the same questions.

"Recorded?" I stalled.

"I saw video cables and tape machines," Gene pointed outside.

"That's for the rooms where we work with children. Unfortunately, with kids, everything becomes a legal issue. We're required to report to the police any accusation, whether we believe it or not. I want to stop child abusers, of course, but the truth is, I care much more about helping the kids. There's part of me that wishes we were only asked to ease their pain, not help punish the guilty. The recording equipment isn't used with adults unless they are accused of hurting kids." Gene continued to look outside. After a silence, I added, "This is a safe place. What you say to me stays here."

"I remember you used to say that all the time. But it isn't true." Gene smiled in my direction, although his eyes avoided mine. I was pleased that he had chosen to contradict me. In reviewing notes from our earlier work together, I concluded his trouble expressing anger hadn't been worked through. I had been wrong not to encourage him to resist me actively.

"You don't feel this is a safe place?"

Gene's eyes were focused on my shoulder. They briefly scanned my face and settled on a point off to my left. He crossed his legs. "Oh, I guess it's safe. I didn't mean that. I meant it's not true that what I say here stays here." He paused and added softly, "I've read your books."

I had published only two that contained histories of my patients. Following tradition, I summarized, with the names altered and other details changed for further disguise. Nothing I had written was like this text. Certainly nothing was revealed about me, and little of the real dialogue. Even so, I had asked my patients' permission first. More to the point, I hadn't used Gene's case in any form. "I've never written about you, Gene."

Gene brushed his long bang off his brow and glanced at me. This time, as he smiled, some teeth showed. "The Vomiting Boy?"

"Ah," I said, understanding.

"You changed a lot, but that was me, right?"

"No," I said. "You're not the Vomiting Boy."

Gene looked directly at me. He swallowed. His Adam's apple seemed very prominent, more than I remembered. He uncrossed his legs. "Really?" he said, astonished; and a little sadly, I thought.

"It's discouraging," I said. "I had the same shock as a medical student. There are so many commonalities in human experiences. Vomiting is often a release of suppressed rage, especially in children. The Vomiting Boy was a different patient. I asked if he minded that I use his story and he agreed, provided I change facts that would identify him." I paused. Gene continued to stare at me with a mix of confusion and sadness. I added softly, "I would never have written about you without asking first. And of course you could say no."

"I never want you to write about me," he said. He pressed his knees together and crossed his arms. He looked at my chest.

"Fine." An observer might think he was in my office under duress. Of course, I hadn't asked to see him, I had discouraged him. This apparent contradiction didn't confuse me. For one thing, I believed he was disappointed that he wasn't the Vomiting Boy.

"There's stuff . . ." Gene looked out my window and fell silent. The venetian blinds were open. Vans, a Dumpster, and a wheel of electronic cables dominated the view.

"Do you want me to close the blinds?"

"What? Oh. No."

"There's stuff—you were saying."

"That's why I couldn't talk to Toni. You know. There's stuff I just can't have anyone else know." He smiled. "It's not kid's stuff anymore. Just the work things alone are big secrets. I don't even want them to know I'm seeing a shrink."

"No one has to know anything. I won't write anything about you or discuss your case with anyone. But, as I think I've said before, I'm not treating adult—"

"I can't," he cut me off. He shook his head well after saying the words, back and forth, again and again, denying it over and over.

"You can't what?"

"I can't see anyone else. I don't trust anyone else."

"And yet you thought I had betrayed you?"

"No." He frowned.

"No? You thought I had written—"

"Yes, yes you're right. Are you always right?" His tone was intensely annoyed. That was new to me.

"What do you think?" I asked.

"I think you're always right."

"Well," I said, smiling, "you're wrong."

Gene didn't get the joke. "I know. I always seem to be wrong."

"What are you always wrong about?"

"I'm always wrong with women. Does any man ever win a fight with a woman?"

"Yes."

"I don't think so."

"Whom have you been losing fights to?"

Gene shifted in his seat. It was a captain's chair, comfortable, but plain. My seat was an indulgence, a black leather Knoll Pollack swivel. Behind me were built-in book shelves, to Gene's right were built-in filing cabinets. The door was solid pine, the walls and ceiling soundproofed, as were all of the consulting rooms. I had grown weary of white noise machines. Gene looked at all these things, as well as the halogen standing lamp, the other armchair. "There's no couch," he said, looking out the window. A worker walked past with a take-out container of coffee, smoking a filterless cigarette.

I got up to shut the blinds. "No, there isn't," I agreed. "They're distracting me," I said about the workers as I rotated the venetians halfway, enough to block the view, yet allowing strips of sunlight to penetrate.

"You don't use the couch with kids, I guess."

"Sometimes. I don't plan to see children in this office. Maybe some of the adolescents. I warned you, I'm not set up for traditional long-term therapy. Do you want to lie down? There's—"

"No, it's okay," he said quickly.

I was amused by a recollection of our first conversation, the desires reversed about lying on couches, but the attitudes almost identical. "You're a man, now, so it's time to sit up," I said. My tone was unusually lighthearted. Why? Did I think he was taking himself too seriously? How would I know?

Gene nodded. He continued to look around; at my phone, a typewriter on a side table, photographs of my mother, my father, Uncle Bernie, Julie, Grandma Jacinta and Grandpa Pepín, framed diplomas and a drawing in charcoal by "Timmy." It was a representation of one of his dreams—a boy playing soccer on a frozen lake, standing atop blue water and kicking a gleaming white ball over a blood-red horizon.

"Why are you here, Gene? What's on your mind?"

"I still can't sleep."

"Trouble falling asleep or staying asleep?"

"Both."

"Have you had a checkup recently?"

"Yeah. I had to when I changed companies. For the insurance. I'm fine."

"What wakes you up?"

He was looking at "Timmy's" drawing, frowning at it.

"Dreams?" I asked.

"Yeah," he said.

"What dream wakes you up?"

"I don't know if it wakes me up."

"What dream do you remember best?"

"I've had this one many times." A saw revved up close by my window. Evidently they weren't as soundproofed as I hoped. Gene jerked to look in its direction, but he kept talking, "I'm in a gym. I *think*. It's a little like the gym at One Room. Big and empty, with windows at the top. It was in the basement so the windows were almost at the ceiling."

"Are you alone in the gym?"

"At first. It's very still and peaceful. I think somebody wants me to do something, but I don't know what."

"Does not knowing worry you?"

"I'm not worried at first. And then she appears."

The saw whined and shut off. Its silent aftermath added drama to my question: "Who is she?"

"I don't know," he was quick to say. He held his breath for a moment and added, "Just the sight of her scares me."

"What does she look like?"

"Sometimes she's blonde. Kind of, you know, sandy blonde hair like my wife. But she's not my wife. Sometimes she has black hair, but it's the same shape. You know, the same hairdo."

"Long hair?"

"No. More like a helmet. She's wearing a dress, a long print dress, but it has no top."

"So it's a skirt?"

"No. It isn't. I don't know how to explain, but it's a dress with the top off."

"So she's bare-breasted?"

"Yeah."

"What do they look like?"

"They're huge. I mean, you know, like *Playboy* centerfold breasts, only they're not pretty. The nipples are big and hard and very brown, sticking out at me."

I wrote down—nipples/penises. Gene noticed and frowned. Anyway, it was silly to take notes. I opened my drawer and put the yellow pad inside.

"Does it excite you?"

"No." The no was said defensively, fast and too loud.

I said nothing.

Gene glanced at me, brushed his bang, although it hadn't fallen back across his face. He took a breath and said, "She walks toward me and opens her mouth wide." He stared at nothing. The skin under his eyes was darkened by fatigue; and the eyes were bloodshot.

"Un huh. And does she say something?"

"I think she's going to."

"What do you think she's going to say?"

"What?"

"What do you think she's going to say?"

"She never says anything."

"I know."

"You do? How?"

"You would have said already. What do you think she's going to say?"

"Something nice. I don't know what."

"Something about her breasts?"

"Her breasts are gone now."

"Gone? Or she's clothed?"

"No. I don't notice them. She spits at me." Gene looked down at his lap. He fit the fingers of both hands together and twisted. "She doesn't say anything. I'm sure she's going to be nice, but she spits at me."

"What happens to the spit?"

Gene looked up. He cracked his knuckles so hard that the noise made me queasy. "What?"

I didn't say anything.

"Well, I don't know. I guess— No!" Gene sat up, fingers separating, eyes up toward the ceiling. "I scream— 'Go away!' " Gene blinked fast and said in a rush, "I don't wake up. I thought I woke up when I yell, 'Go away,' but actually the room disappears before the spit hits me. That's what happens. I couldn't remember why I didn't think the dream wakes me up. It's the second part that wakes me up. They're connected."

"I see. What's the second part?"

A pause. Gene interlocked his fingers again. I hoped he wouldn't crack them. "I'm at my terminal," he said finally, as if he were making a judgment.

"Your terminal?"

"Yeah, before the spit lands I'm at my terminal, going over the board design for the, well it should be Black Dragon, but it's not. I'm still working on Flash II. Black Dragon is the—"

"Don't explain now," I cut him off sharply. "You're at a terminal . . . ?"

"Yeah. Mine."

"And . . . ?" I was urgent.

He answered quickly, "The specs don't make any sense to me. They should. They're simple stuff. Just the memory chip locations and—well, it doesn't matter. I should be able to understand them, but I don't. And then I realize all I have to do is hit Escape— That's weird."

"What's weird?"

"Well, I use a mouse—you know, I mean, in reality. I don't hit keys when I'm touring the machine."

"Un huh. But in the dream you think about hitting Escape . . ."

"Escape. Pretty obvious, huh?"

"Maybe. Go on."

"Okay, so I realize if I hit Escape, the screen will clear and I'll understand everything, I'll understand the whole machine, in one clear image, you know, I'll have it all and we'll be golden."

"Do you hit Escape?"

"Yeah," he said sadly.

"What happens?"

"The garbage freezes on screen, the whole machine freezes. So I go crazy. Do something you're not supposed to. I make a terrible mistake." He stopped, panting breathlessly.

I waited. Gene rubbed his chin, then frowned. "What do you do?" I prompted.

"I turn it off. That would erase all the garbage—but it would also erase the answer."

"And then you wake up?"

"No. Not yet. I turn it off, but it doesn't go off. The screen clears, though."

"And that's what you wanted."

"Yeah—"

"You made a terrible mistake and got what you wanted."

"No."

"No?"

"No. A message comes up, like one of Skip's practical jokes."

"Who's Skip?"

"One of the hackers at Flash. He liked to play practical jokes. Bug your program so you think it's malfunctioning and, just when you think you've got it licked, he'd have a message come up in Calligraphy letters. Very elegant and obscene."

"What's the message in the dream?"

He said the words slowly, with portent and doom in his voice: "You are a son of a bitch." Gene nodded and spoke to himself, "They're connected. Not different dreams but the same."

"After you see the message, you wake up?"

Gene nodded. "They're connected," he said in a mumble. "I wonder how many times I've had this dream."

"Me too," I said.

Gene smiled. "Aren't you supposed to know?"

Again the hostility at my all-knowingness. I had failed him—that was the message. But he couldn't say it straight out and the judgment was uncertain or else why had he returned to see me? Unless he had come for a refund. "No," I said. "You know everything. There's only one expert on Gene Kenny and you're it.'

"Then I'm in deep shit." Gene sat forward, lowered his head and rubbed his cheeks, pulling the skin down so I saw more of his red, exhausted eyes.

"Are you under a lot of pressure now?"

"Yeah, that's why I took the job."

"You took the job to be under pressure?"

"No, no." He was impatient. "That's stupid," he said. He looked up abruptly, shocked at himself. "I'm sorry, I shouldn't have said that. I don't mean you're stupid. That's one of my problems. I keep snapping at people. Saying things I mean." He snorted. "I mean, saying things I *don't* mean." He banged the side of his head with his right palm. "I've gotta get some sleep." Now he looked at me, imploringly, a child asking for desert. "My wife thinks I should get some sleeping pills."

"Let's go through a typical day, Gene. Let's go through your schedule." I had to coax him into taking this inventory seriously. He repeatedly tried to summarize. His summaries, when we tracked each hour carefully, turned out to be wrong. He felt he was selfishly wasting time. In fact, Gene was busy at work (I couldn't judge then how productively) and always doing things for other people. His wife complained so often and repeatedly of how early their son, Peter, woke up that Gene took it upon himself to rise with him, usually about six A.M. Gene made breakfast for Peter, dressed him for school, packed his school bag, made his bed (although there was a cleaning woman who came two times a week), and brought a cup of coffee to his wife before leaving for his office at seven-thirty. There he worked without a break—often without lunch—until at least six in the evening. During crunch time he would work until midnight. That period would be coming up in a year or so on the new machine—Black Dragon was its in-house nickname. On Flash II, working right through until dawn was common. When he came home, he summarized that he did nothing but sit around like a zombie. Zombie was his word. In fact, he cleaned up the dinner dishes, gave Peter a bath and played a game with him, read him bedtime stories, and then returned to studying specs or other matters related to work.

"When do you make love?" I asked.

This question made him apprehensive. His legs crossed defensively; hands also covered the region. [Some therapists would have made much of the instant armoring of his genitals; but these movements are routine, exhibited by many people in an awkward interview. I note them and consider them significant only when I detect a distinctive pattern, such as Gene's unwillingness to look directly into people's eyes.] His face opened, eyes wide, the skin smoothing. He seemed more boyish and ashamed than usual. "Well, you know, it's hard. We can't do it until Peter falls asleep and my wife often falls asleep before he does or she gets too tired. Pete doesn't sleep much and he wakes up a lot. He comes into our bedroom around one or one-thirty almost every night."

"Every night?"

It turned out that Pete came into their bedroom perhaps twice a week. Gene said he lived in dread of Peter discovering them making love. Dread was his word.

"Doesn't your door lock?" I asked.

"Yeah . . ." Gene didn't seem to think that made much difference. "But he would hear," Gene finally said when I pressed him on this point.

"Do you think Pete knows that you and Cathy have sex?" I asked.

The question flabbergasted him. His mouth opened. He gestured to my shelves as if someone were standing behind me, also amazed. "I . . . I . . ." He made some sort of noise. "I don't think so. It never occurred to me—I mean, not while I was a child."

"What never occurred to you?"

"That my parents . . . You know, that they . . ." He seemed to blush. Or, at least, to be embarrassed.

"*You* walked in on your parents making love, Gene. Or at least, you walked in on your father kissing your mother's breasts."

"I did?" he said, astounded. His voice was full of wonder. His eyes trailed up to my ceiling, mouth open. "I did," he confirmed it. He looked at me suddenly, intent. "How did you know?"

"You told me." I waved a hand. "It's no trick, Gene. I reviewed my notes on our sessions. You told me years ago that in the old loft—remember there was no lock on your parents' door . . . ?"

"Yeah, it was a sliding door."

"Right. You had a bad dream, about a spider, and you went into your parents' room. It was very dark, but there was a shaft of light from the street lamps that fell across your parents' bed."

"Right," he was nodding, eyes unfocused, looking into the past. "Right. And I thought Dad was biting Mom."

"Do you remember what happened?"

"She saw me."

"That's what you told me."

"She saw me and I left."

"Is that all you remember?"

"Dad yelled at me?" he guessed.

I said nothing.

"That's wrong?" Gene asked plaintively.

[Of course there is no right or wrong. His current memory didn't jibe with what he told me before, but that didn't mean he was now wrong in the psychological sense. The memory is just as important in *how* it is wrongly remembered. For us, facts are not the truth—that's why we often find the law to be frustrating and unjust.]

"Gene, I've already run ten minutes past the hour and this is complicated, so—"

Gene got to his feet quickly, mumbling while I explained, "Oh, okay, I'm sorry."

"Don't be sorry," I said sharply.

He froze and stared at me. His thick eyebrows lifted, quizzical.

"*I'm* sorry," I said. "I'm frustrated I don't have more time. Gene, that's going to be a problem if you want to keep seeing me. My schedule is loaded and inflexible. In fact I only have my lunch hours free and I don't think it's a good idea for me to skip lunch that often. I really can't see you more than two times a week. I hope that's not too little."

"Yeah, I understand. It's the kids who really need help. You can't waste time listening to me whine."

"Gene, to be accurate, you haven't whined until now."

"Oh, I was just kidding."

"It sounded to me like a disguised complaint. It isn't that I think the children need me more, or that I value you less, it's just that I've promised my time to them already and I'm not a superman. I can't go without eating or without a break more than twice a week."

[The above is a violation of barriers. I was asking Gene to see me as an ordinary human being, which—according to the transference theory—is impossible and, more to the point, undesirable. I did it deliberately. I hadn't lost my temper. I had decided if I was going to work with him, a new approach was called for. I believed Gene was stuck, or rather, in love with being a boy, staying safe in his timidity and lack of demands. To once again accept a role as his substitute parent would be counterproductive, I believed, no matter how theoretically correct.]

"I'm sorry," Gene said.

"No, you're not," I said mildly. That took him aback. "How about Friday, same time?" Gene nodded slowly, still in shock at my blunt tone. "Do you know your way out?" He rose, groaning, as if his muscles were sore. By now the van from the South Bronx with my group of five foster care teenagers should have arrived. The courts had removed these adolescents from their homes into an almost equally bad system. They had horrendous problems: they were severely abused by their families and surrogates, their schools were inadequate and they lived in dangerous neighborhoods, surrounded by crack addicts. Their economic and emotional prospects were virtually terminal. Gene was right. I did disdain his middle-class complaints to some extent. And yet I understood that emotions don't exist in a relative universe: Gene's pain from the splinters in his toes might as well be shafts of steel in his heart. Pain is all-encompassing to us. No one can be proven to be better off than others; they can only feel better off. Pointing out to Gene that his life was comparatively easy would merely add guilt to his woes—that is religion's failure. And yet indulging his childishness would keep him forever seeing only the imagined monsters in the shadows and not the joyful daylight everywhere else—that is traditional therapy's failure.

Gene left. The receptionist buzzed me to say my group of teenagers were waiting in the Group A room. I opened my desk drawer and turned off the hidden tape recorder, ejecting an audio record of the session. I wrote Gene Kenny on the strip of paper attached to the cassette's spine with the date and the number "one," then put it into my briefcase for reviewing later during my late afternoon session on the health club's treadmill.

"Liar, liar, pants on fire," I said to myself before going to my real work.

CHAPTER SIX

Mighty Opposites

THREE MONTHS LATER I WAS ARGUING WITH MY OLD CHILDHOOD FRIEND
Joseph Stein about dreams. We were double-dating. I brought Diane.
Our relationship became so deep and satisfying since our summer trip
that, as winter approached, we found ourselves wondering why we
shouldn't marry or at least move in together. Joseph brought his steady
boyfriend, a young jazz musician named Harlan Daze, a stage alias. After
we saw a movie in the Village, had pizza nearby at John's, we walked the
ten blocks to Joseph's garden apartment for coffee.

In 1982, Joseph and I had renewed our friendship thanks to television. (We were chosen by a talk show host to represent opposing sides of
an argument raised in my book, *The Soft-Headed Animal*. I had criticized
the use of Ritalin and neuroleptic drugs on children; Joseph was there to
explain their effects and disagree with me. To the host's dismay, he
agreed that, in practice, they were overprescribed.) As a neurobiologist
engaged in basic research into the human brain—this is old news to anyone with a superficial interest in science—Joseph, in addition to his chair
at Columbia, was consultant to a major pharmaceutical firm on the development of neuroleptic drugs. His theoretical breakthroughs led to
practical experimentation and yielded tangible results. Prozac, a very
specific serotonin enhancer reputed to have milder side effects than drugs
then in use, had debuted earlier in the year. It rapidly became the most

widely prescribed antidepressant in the United States. Joseph was far from being the only person responsible for Prozac's development but he was acknowledged as a necessary component of its creation.

"Dreams are nonsense," Joseph said, not for the first time that evening or in the second incarnation of our friendship for that matter. We disagreed so completely on the causes of human behavior that we had a pact to avoid the subject as much as possible. Unfortunately, it was a treaty that Joseph was frequently guilty of violating.

Harlan lifted a cup of espresso off an elegant Chinese lacquer tray and handed it to me. Harlan would not have seemed gay to someone with a stereotyped notion of homosexuals—specifically, Joseph's mother. She was widowed now and still lived in Washington Heights, one of the many reasons Joseph, although his lab and teaching duties were at Columbia, lived way downtown, putting a distance of one hundred and seventy blocks between them. Joseph told me he lived in terror of accidentally running into his mother while with a boyfriend. Harlan, ten years Joseph's junior, hardly seemed, with long blond hair tied in a ponytail, black jeans torn at the knees and a white T-shirt, like a colleague or a graduate student. Still, Joseph's mother would never have suspected him of being gay. His tall lean frame was always hunched; he moved like a prowling panther. A cigarette (that Joseph complained loudly of) seemed to hang perpetually from his lips, and his voice was as deep and rarely used as a cowboy's. I liked him for at least two reasons. First, he made Joseph happy. And second, I enjoyed that Harlan often pricked my old friend's arrogance and pomposity, both of which were rapidly inflating that year thanks to his success. "Maybe *your* dreams are nonsense," Harlan said in a mumble and smiled at Diane.

She had been uncomfortable so far that evening, silent before the movie and all through dinner afterwards. I assumed this was because the previous three times she had met Joseph, she didn't like him. She said she felt she didn't exist for him. "I don't mean sexually," she added. "I mean he acts like I'm not there at all." I understood. To Joseph, all women were his suffocating, perpetually cleaning and cooking mother, especially a strong-willed Jewish woman like Diane. He was as sexist as Pat Buchanan, quite different from the cliché of the homosexual who is especially sympathetic and understanding of the plight of women. I wondered how he treated his women graduate students and associates; or how many he took on, for that matter. And I also contemplated the irony of a mother whose grip was so tight on a famous scientist's life that he chose lovers who would be invisible to her.

"You've read Allan Hobson's paper?" Joseph said to me, ignoring Harlan.

I nodded. "It's sophistry."

"Did you study the data?" Joseph emptied his cup of espresso in a single gulp. He dismissed me with a wave of his hand. "I bet you skipped the numbers, right? Psychiatrists," Joseph added, addressing this comment to Diane, much to my and her surprise. "They're pseudoscientists. I bet he didn't even understand Hobson's argument." Diane stared at him blankly. "Hello?" Joseph said to her.

"I'm a psychiatrist and I—" she began. Diane is a short, thin energetic woman, her black curly hair as fiercely complicated and indomitable as her personality. She has a pert nose, pale skin covered with freckles and bright brown eyes that are unfortunately dulled somewhat by eyeglasses. (She refuses to wear contacts.) Her alert, friendly manner and smallness lend her an uncanny youthfulness—at thirty-four she was still carded by bartenders—and also a benign quality to her anger. Her tone was furious and irritated, but I could see Joseph was unaware of danger. I knew she was about to fire off an angry and much deserved reproach that I also knew Joseph was ill equipped to handle without firing back, so I interrupted. In a war between Diane and Joseph surely I would be the casualty.

"All Hobson's data shows is *how* dreams are created by the brain," I said over Diane.

"Oh you missed the point! I knew it!" Joseph leaned forward and dropped his cup and saucer before they were level with his oak coffee table. The cup clattered and slid off, tipping over.

"Jesus," Harlan mumbled. He righted the cup and waved a scolding finger at Joseph. "And this is the good china."

"No I didn't," I answered and heard anger in my voice. "Because science can identify how we mechanically produce dreams doesn't speak to whether they are meaningful or generated by emotional conflict. It's a false argument."

"Oh, I see." Joseph appeared quite amused. "So you're telling me that Prozac's success doesn't prove we've identified what causes depression."

This was his real point in fussing over the meaning of dreams. Prozac had received final approval from the FDA only four months before, and Joseph was very proud of the remarkable hoopla with which it had been covered by the general press. I had said nothing to him about it, except for routine congratulations. Apparently he felt he had decisively proved me wrong in our long-standing argument over whether drugs or talking therapy were more effective and wanted to hear me cry uncle.

I considered letting his breach of our treaty pass, but I couldn't. "Yes, that's exactly what I'm telling you. No amount of successful drug manipulation of mood proves that depression or dreams or anything else isn't generated by conflict and feeling. Masking symptoms isn't the same as a cure."

"I don't believe this." Joseph slapped both hands on his thighs and twisted away from me. Again he addressed Diane. "He actually said it. I can't believe it."

Diane crossed her legs, adopting an atypical supercilious attitude that, frankly, she couldn't quite pull off. "What can't you believe? Please tell us. I'm dying to know," she said and smirked at him.

Joseph ignored her sarcasm. He stood up. "Let's drop it," he said and then immediately continued, "You won't admit that we've done it. We've cured depression, we've cured anxiety, fuck—we've cured neurosis! We've proven that it has nothing to do with whether Mama wiped your ass for you or made you do it yourself. It's just a goddamn chemical imbalance. How can you, a trained scientist, argue that depression is caused by anything but a bad brain recipe if we can wipe it out with a pill?"

"I can argue it very easily," I said calmly. My momentary anger had passed.

"How!" Joseph shrieked at me, not very differently from when we were ten years old.

"Let's drop it, Joseph."

"Oh, you want to drop it. Because you're losing."

"Cool it," Harlan said and lit a cigarette.

"Stop smoking," Joseph snapped.

"You wanted to drop it a moment ago," I said.

"*I* don't want to drop it." Joseph pleaded to the others. "Everybody take note. I don't want to drop it."

"Okay, you don't want to," I said. "I do."

"I don't want you to drop it, Rafe," Diane said. That was uncharacteristic: she would normally argue her point of view herself. And her tone, even when addressing me, was cool and contemptuous.

"See? You lose," Joseph said. "We're not dropping it."

I looked at Diane. I couldn't read her. Did she feel it was my job to take him down a peg—or was she testing my willingness to fight? Either way, this was unlike her typically bold and straightforward manner. "All right," I said and returned my attention to Joseph. "What was—oh yes, how can I argue that depression is caused by anything except a chemical imbalance when you can relieve it with a drug? Am I to understand, Joseph, that since scientists can impregnate a woman with frozen sperm you have concluded that what makes babies is a syringe?"

Harlan laughed. Joseph dismissed me with both hands. He was a small man, no more than five three. Small and unathletic, yet the old man's clothes he wore as a boy were long gone. He dressed in Armani suits for evening wear, Banana Republic clothes for casual wear, and jogging suits for a night like the one we had just spent. He was in a red and white one now, on his feet, twirling away from me in disgust. "That's bullshit." He turned to face me. "That's beneath you, Rafe. I'm sorry to hear you resort to that bullshit."

"I'm sorry, too. I don't want to resort to bullshit. What's wrong with my point?"

Joseph stared, as if searching for signs of sarcasm. He couldn't find any, since there were none. He sighed. "Artificial insemination proves that a sperm and an egg make a baby, not love."

Silence greeted this remark. Not a respectful silence, recognizing logic triumphant. I think we felt dismay at what this implied for humanity's future.

"So your point," I said, after the room's gloom persisted long enough for Joseph to check each of our expressions, settle back in his chair, pick up his espresso cup, note that it was empty and replace it on the coffee table. "So your point is that since Prozac can relieve depression's symptoms—"

"Not its symptoms!" Joseph's tone was so sharp that Harlan jerked his head away and pretended to clean out his ear. Diane smiled at him. Joseph ignored his pantomime. "Don't diminish it by saying symptoms. What is depression if not a collection of symptoms?"

"Exactly," I said. "What is depression? That's the question you haven't answered, any more than artificial insemination answers the question of what is life. A patient goes to a doctor and complains that he can't sleep, he has no appetite, he has trouble concentrating, he feels his life is joyless, and that there's no hope for any of these things to change. The doctor says he's suffering from depression. He prescribes your drug and some of those things are changed. He eats more, sleeps more. His doctor praises him, his family praises him—"

"That's not all—"

"Let me finish. The patient goes off the drug. And he can't sleep again, he can't eat, he has trouble concentrating—"

"So?" Joseph appealed to Diane. Evidently he had given up on me. "You put him back on the drug. How is that different from a recurrence of any illness? A person is infected, you give him an antibiotic. That doesn't mean he can't infect again."

Diane looked to me, mouth set, arms crossed, like a professor waiting for an answer. I could understand why she might, sensitive to my friendship with Joseph, refrain from answering him herself, but why look at me so crossly? I hoped the annoyance was meant for Joseph. Harlan also looked at me expectantly. They appeared to be demanding that I refute my friend. I wasn't sure that I wanted to refute him: I wanted to know if he was right or wrong and I doubted debate offered certainty.

My tone was an appeal, not argument: "Tell me, Joseph, how is it different from the person who feels awkward at a party, getting drunk every time he goes to one? Or a ghetto kid—who is right to feel his life has few prospects—buying crack to feel a surge of bliss? Have you cured depression, Joseph, or simply created socially acceptable addicts? Maybe you've helped the depression. Or maybe you've invented your own illness, and used that to overwhelm depression."

"Oh, come on," Joseph said. "Are you telling me antidepressants are completely useless in your work? That you would rather have people sink lower and lower—"

"I see you still haven't read my book, Joseph." He didn't respond. Harlan smiled to himself. Getting no admission or denial, I continued, "Yes. At best drugs are useless. At worst they add a new problem. I never use them."

"Because you're biased," Joseph said conclusively, as if making a private judgment, not scolding me.

"Because they're dangerous." I insisted. "Are you denying that tricyclics are addictive? Are you denying that neuroleptics cause tardive dyskinesia?"

"In *some* patients!" Joseph complained. "That's why I didn't finish reading your book. You throw out everything because some of the drugs aren't perfect. Is the couch perfect?"

"No. In fact the couch is slow and hard work. Hard for the doctor, hard for the patient, hard for their families, hard for everyone. Not drugs. They're easy. Drugs make patients easy to deal with. Easier for doctors and hospitals and their families. But what they don't do is cure depression or schizophrenia. And what's more, Joseph, and you know this is true, long term those drugs diminish personality—"

Joseph was on his feet. "I knew it. You haven't read the research on Prozac." He finally married his actions to his clothes and went jogging, out of the living room and down the hall to his study.

Harlan leaned forward, shook the espresso pot, and asked Diane if she wanted more.

"Not if you have to make it," she said.

"I don't mind," Harlan said. "I'm depressed. I got nothing better to do." He stood up, carrying the empty pot. "I like the idea of Joey inventing his own disease."

Joseph appeared with reading material for me. One was a dissertation in manuscript. There were two issues of the *New England Journal of Medicine*, and finally a popular paperback by a psychopharmacologist. "She's a dope," Joseph said as he handed over this book, "but read her case histories in the last chapter for the descriptive data on Prozac's effects. You haven't read it, right?"

"Right," I said. "Remember, Joseph, I would never use drugs on children—"

"I know, I know," he handed me the rest of the pile. "These reports indicate that Prozac is different from any other antidepressant. It's only been in use a year—"

"I know that, Joseph."

"—and I want you to look at the rat studies on kindling."

"Kindling?"

"You don't know about kindling?"

"No," I admitted.

"That's irresponsible," Joseph squeaked.

Harlan groaned.

Joseph's voice stayed high. "I'm sorry. But it is. I know you don't believe in psychopharmacology," he appealed to me, "but that doesn't mean you should ignore neurobiology. Freud wouldn't." Diane mumbled something. I couldn't hear what because Joseph continued, "The kindling research has a bearing on your abused kids. They prove that emotional trauma can change brain chemistry."

"They *prove* it?" I asked.

"In my opinion that's the only reasonable conclusion you can draw from the kindling studies. Stress and trauma start a vicious cycle in the brain. And I believe the inescapable conclusion is that it means it can only be healed with drugs."

"Give me a break," Diane said. Joseph ignored her.

I glanced at the *New England Journal of Medicine* article. "Prozac and the New Self," it was called. I said, "Point taken. I haven't done enough reading to debate it with you." I looked at my old friend and let him win. "Okay, Joseph, I'll do my homework."

CHAPTER SEVEN

A Crisis of Faith

I SHOULDN'T BELABOR THE OBVIOUS TO PROFESSIONALS. WITHIN A FEW years, Joseph's claims for Prozac were widely hailed in the media. Nowadays, it is an almost accepted fact that Prozac produces profound character changes in many patients, particularly mild depressives, people with low self-esteem, or emotional sensitivity, namely the sort of neurotic who had been considered psychoanalysis's exclusive province. Namely patients like Gene Kenny. Prozac's supporters claim that their patients aren't merely relieved of the immediate physical effects of emotional pain; their experience of everyday rejection, loss, conflict, guilt and so on is altered, both in how they feel and react.

So why not prescribe Prozac for Gene? Readers of my book *The Soft-Headed Animal* know there is no proof, as Joseph Stein himself admits, that *any* psychological condition, ranging from schizophrenia to mild mood disorders, is organic. Shocking though it may seem to a lay audience inundated by half-truths and wild claims from psychobiologists, geneticists, and drug companies, there is no scientific proof that what we call mental illness exists. When autopsied, the brains of suicides, schizophrenics, manic-depressives, indeed the whole range of psychiatric disorders, show no measurable difference from the brains of people we label as mentally well. Only *if* (and this *if* is crucial) the "mentally ill" were subject to shock therapy, neuroleptics or sedatives do their brains show damage. Few things in psychiatry are as clear as this evidence: mental ill-ness—insofar as one can consider it organic—doesn't exist and the fash-ionable physical and chemical treatments, if used for long, may cause brain damage, irreversible damage that truly *is* a mental illness.

This confusion between the fact that drugs can change how people act and feel, and whether this constitutes a cure of their psychological crises, runs through every level of our society. Prozac, as an example, is sup-posed to "treat" depression by raising the amount of serotonin in the brain. And yet no scientist can show that depressed patients have lower levels of serotonin than people who are considered normal. (Some psy-chobiologists, to make their flawed logic consistent, respond to this fact by suggesting the entire population take Prozac.) When Prozac *artifi-cially* raises serotonin, a minority of patients report they have more en-ergy and accept defeat and frustration with less sadness. What its advocates leave out is that snorting cocaine can be shown to have the same effect, just as smoking cigarettes can be shown to improve concen-tration, and that alcohol can relieve anxiety. The difference—and it has a profound effect on the results of clinical trials of psychiatric drugs—is that when people medicate themselves with illegal narcotics, cigarettes, or alcohol, they don't have a psychiatrist telling them they are ill when sober and cured when drugged. None of the material Joseph gave me clarified the murky logic of psychopharmacology. Insight alone doesn't always cure. Drugs don't cure. Not if the goal is an independent being, a person who is free from both a therapist and a pill. We like to call our profession a science, our patients sick, and our treatments medicine, but the psychiatrist, whether armed with a drug or a couch, is treating a per-ception of illness with only the prejudiced testimonies of its victim and an intolerant society to confirm his success. In that context, broad claims of success must always be regarded skeptically. Then and today, I could find no proof that medicating Gene Kenny would have been anything more than surrender to the modern culture of instant gratification.

Nevertheless, our New York coffee table scientific argument had sev-eral important consequences for me. What I did not, and could not have realized at the time, was the consequence it would have for Gene Kenny. That night his case seemed to be the least likely to be affected by the question Joseph and I debated. What was significant appeared to be en-tirely personal. Diane maintained an angry silence during the cab ride to her apartment. I had Joseph's recommended reading in my lap. I tried to begin a few conversations. She answered in monosyllables, including when I apologized on Joseph's behalf for treating her as if she weren't a psychiatrist. "I'm just a stupid cunt to him," she insisted. When we ar-rived at her door, she said, "Maybe you should go to your place tonight."

"Okay," I said, fighting the shrink's impulse to talk this out immediately. She believed in that principle as fervently as I and must have had a good reason to delay.

Her tension at rejecting me relaxed. She kissed me affectionately and whispered, "I'm sorry. I'm just very tired."

Not much of an excuse for a trained analyst. I played along. "Sure. Call you tomorrow."

I wanted to study the articles anyway. I had an intuitive feeling that there was something valuable in Joseph's dogma. And there was. I stayed up late reading, especially fascinated by the kindling studies on rats that suggest stress and rejection create biochemical changes which may then go on to have a life of their own. Of course they don't really answer the age-old cause-and-effect argument, but they do call into question whether talking therapies alone can succeed in undoing the damage. They also, by the way, imply that early treatment is vital, very encouraging for someone who, like me, treats abused children and sometimes despairs of preventing long-term difficulties. I had lured "Timmy" out of his multiple personality defense against his abusers, but how could I feel secure that he wouldn't suffer again later, in much the same way that Gene had reappeared with his old problems in a new guise?

By morning, I knew I had to investigate the kindling research. I called Joseph at eight o'clock. He promised to send unpublished material on a variety of neurological studies. Joseph was gracious and not smug about my apparent surrender to his point of view. (I didn't tell him that I was unimpressed by the Prozac data.) Diane phoned soon after I hung up.

"I'm sorry," she said in a sleepy voice. Her register is naturally low and husky. The morning gave her an even lower octave. It was sexy.

"Nothing to be sorry for," I said.

"Did you sleep well?" she asked.

I told her, probably with a little manic excitement, that I had been up most of the night reading and I felt exhilarated.

"You don't mean you agree with him?" she asked.

I tried to explain that I didn't think agreement or disagreement with Joseph was the point. I know I concluded with pomposity. "What's important is the truth," I said.

Diane grunted. "Well, I certainly wouldn't want to stand in the way of the truth."

I was irritated. Diane is an excellent practical therapist: no one could be more dedicated and few of greater help to their patients than she. On the theoretical level, however, she lacks curiosity or broad-mindedness. Her bias is for what has evolved out of Freudian-based talking therapy, what I practiced in my first go-round with Gene, namely the therapist replacing bad parenting with good parenting, providing some insight and a lot of warmth and encouragement. In graduate school, once Diane had her "faith"—as is all too often the case with psychologists—she read opposing philosophies or techniques only to refute them.

"Somewhere out there is an answer, you know," I said grumpily. "And if it can be found a lot of people's lives will be better."

She didn't reply at first. I heard her bed sheets rustle. I could imagine her shifting to sit up, raising her navy blue blanket to cover her breasts. "She's lovely," Aunt Sadie commented to me after I introduced Diane. "She looks like your grandmother when she was young." Sadie meant my mother's mother. I was amused—and sufficiently appalled—to check an old black and white photo of Nana to reassure myself that the similarities were superficial. That Diane was a product of a long line of strong Jewish women was undeniable, however, and in that sense my feelings for her *were* incestuous. "I love that you're tall," she whispered one morning, legs drawn up, curled into a ball, cuddling against me as I stretched out to the limits of her bed. Had my mother once said the same words to Francisco? I pictured Diane: warm and trusting in my arms. Be careful, I thought, you don't want to become a stranger to her intimacies. She sighed. "Look, Rafe, who are you kidding? You'll be the last shrink on earth to say to your patients, 'Take two Prozac and call me in the morning.'"

"Of course."

There was another silence. She sipped something, probably coffee from the big white cup she had bought in Paris on our trip, to remind her of our room service breakfasts, especially their delicious, strong coffee.

"Can I say something?" she asked.

"Sure."

"Your friend Joseph is jealous of you."

I laughed—couldn't stop myself in time.

"I'm serious," she complained. "He's not only jealous of you. He's in love with you."

I glanced at the clock. Although it was Saturday, we had a series of sessions scheduled, beginning in an hour and a half, with three children housed in temporary shelters. The family and juvenile courts had appointed us to evaluate them. The weekend, unfortunately, was the only time Diane and I could fit them in. One was severely battered by a stepfather; another, a seven-year-old girl who had been raped and sodomized by her thirteen-year-old uncle; and the last was the abusive adolescent uncle, Albert, himself a victim in early childhood of his mother's sadistic and incestuous behavior. (She would force Albert to perform cunnilingus and, after orgasm, burn him with cigarettes or whip him with an electric cord. Being subjected as a child to a combination of sex and violence, by the way, seems to be the background profile of serial killers. With Albert, especially, the implications of the kindling studies might be particularly meaningful.) Surely Diane understood that too much was at stake for me to care if Joseph's motives were impure. Albert, the nascent serial killer, had been put on Ritalin for attention deficit disorder by the state hospital. The psychiatrist who ordered the medication had decided that a thirteen-year-old African-American, living in the South Bronx, who had never known a father, whose mother was a crack addict, who, from the age of five, had been used for sex and physically tortured by his mother, was suffering from a chemical imbalance rather than from his life. Ritalin is a much less specific drug than Prozac or other drugs Joseph was then developing. He had conceded publicly (as have most scientists) that, whatever Ritalin's benefits to caretakers as a sedative for disruptive children, it is dangerous, both addictive and likely to cause brain damage if prescribed for long. Sure, it quiets upset children—it would quiet any child. Ritalin's widespread use for the so-called illness of attention deficit disorder, or the even more specious "illness," learning disorder, was my main concern in writing *The Soft-Headed Animal*, the book Joseph had never finished. My duty with this thirteen-year-old rapist—besides the legal question of his state of mind when he sodomized his niece—was to evaluate his care. Joseph's arguments were not academic—to us or to our patients. He conceded that Ritalin was a poor choice; his point was that the severe trauma experienced by children altered their brain chemistry irrevocably and, no matter how skeptical I was, I couldn't prove him wrong simply because no drug exists that truly helps.

"Diane, we have to address these ideas. I can't go before the judge and say, well, I don't approve of drugs, and leave it at that. I don't really care what Joseph feels about me—or to be more precise, why he bothers to proselytize. If you're suggesting he feels a thwarted desire for me and that he expresses it through competition—"

"Well, as usual, you've put it much better than I could. That's exactly what I think he's about."

"I understand. But so what? None of us can bear too close an examination of our motives. If I rejected this data out of homophobia or professional pride, I would hardly have improved matters."

"How about rejecting it because it's wrong?"

"I don't know if it's wrong. That's why I have to study it."

"What's new about any of it? They've been making these claims—"

"What's new to me is some proof that perceptible chemical changes occur after trauma. It still means the change is caused by emotion and conflict."

"Then it can be changed by talking through the conflict."

"Maybe. But maybe not if the trauma is severe enough. It doesn't prove drugs are the answer. But—" I hesitated to say we, since I didn't want to imply disapproval of Diane, "I really should know about it. Frankly, I'm ashamed to admit, out of my own prejudices, I ignored some of this research. In fact, some of these studies that suggest trauma can cause ongoing neurological damage were published while I was still in medical school. *I'm* guilty of being too close-minded." I felt I now had to include Diane or I might seem condescending. I added, "You and I have a duty to investigate anything that might help. We're doctors. We're not supposed to toe a party line."

"Look— You're not understanding me— I don't— This is a mistake—" Diane blurted each of these phrases rapidly, cutting them off and then resuming with an exasperated tone. The sheets and blankets whooshed. It sounded as if she had gotten out of bed. She had a wireless phone and liked to roam while talking. I was reminded of the day a year ago when she called to ask if I would entertain her while she mopped the kitchen floor. I was charmed. That was when I knew we were more than friendly colleagues. Just as, although I was irritated by her defensiveness about how Joseph treated me, I knew her protectiveness was love. Its recipe, after all, has a few ingredients that are best stirred beyond recognition.

"What's a mistake?" I asked. We were late and needed to cut this conversation short, but I didn't want to seem to be running from it.

"You're too conscientious," she said in a decisive tone. "That's all."

"Can a doctor really be *too* conscientious?"

"The world's gonna break your heart, Rafe, if you care that much about everybody and everything. Joseph's not a friend to you. He wants to brag to the world that he's taught Rafael Neruda how to treat his patients."

"Now you're being neurotic," I said. And immediately regretted it.

There was a heavy silence. I heard her breathing and that was heavy also, labored and dangerous.

"Sorry," I said quickly. "I mean, Joseph isn't like that and anyway he can't take credit for my work. We're not really in the same field. No one would believe him, for one thing."

"Okay. Let's drop it." Her tone was irritated and irritating. "We have to get going."

"Look, maybe Joseph's research can help improve my treatment. Why is that something to be afraid of?"

"You're not understanding what I'm saying. Is that deliberate? Do you really not understand?"

"I really don't."

"Okay." She sighed. "Let me try to say it again. You've cured dozens and dozens of kids—there are plenty of people out there, like Felicia, like 'Timmy,' who owe their lives to you, and Joseph talks to you like you're incompetent. And he treats me like I'm a waitress. I can't take it. And I don't think you should take it. I think it's neurotic!"

"Diane, I discovered a long time ago that no blessing is unmixed. Joseph has a brilliant mind and for him to use it well he needs the illusion that his is the most brilliant mind in the world. That need is nothing to envy, because it's doomed to be unsatisfied. I value his friendship. I know, and I know it for sure, that if I really needed Joseph, he would do everything to help me. But when we play games—and that's what an argument is to Joseph, a game—he has to win, or at least seem to win. That's what he needs from me."

"So you're enabling him?"

"Diane." I couldn't fight my irritation. "I'd really prefer it if we didn't use jargon."

"What you mean is, if *I* didn't use jargon."

"No. Jargon is jargon no matter who's using it."

"Look, Rafe, honey, all I'm saying is if a patient talked like you are—"

"Diane, we've got to get going. I'll pick you up and we'll finish this on the way. Okay?"

"I'm done. I've said what I have to say." Her tone was clipped.

"You sound furious."

"I'm not. I'll be waiting downstairs."

At first I didn't feel my reaction. I left calmly, happy to be in my car driving on the empty Saturday morning streets. A few blocks from Diane's apartment, however, my heart raced as I rehearsed replies, some angry, some earnest. But when I turned onto her street, I laughed. It was funny. We were having a fight, a married fight.

I stopped laughing.

We were having a fight over our identities, testing the limits of each other's private selves. Just how deep did I want Diane to plant her flags in my life's terrain? She didn't know about Joseph's rescuing me from the streets of Washington Heights. She didn't know that he had spent his childhood in isolation, that he had no clue how to conduct a friendship. She didn't know that Joseph himself belied his conviction that all of human character is merely a matter of how the chemistry was mixed at the instant of insemination. Joseph's ideas were driven by the emotional need to prove his parents had no damaging effect on him. How could he blame them for anything after what they had suffered in Germany?

Diane knew none of this and, to be fair to her, how could she comprehend my behavior without the information? (I also wondered why I hadn't told her. Did I resent that I owed Joseph anything? Did I want to maintain an illusion for Diane's benefit that all the giving was on my side?) The most tangled knot for me was the self-consciousness of any exchange with her. I was sure Diane wouldn't agree that, in spite of Joseph's emotional need to believe environment had no impact on people, his ideas might still have a great deal of objective truth. Once I told Diane his history, she would probably feel affection for him and she would forever dismiss him intellectually. This weakness, a reductive view of human beings reinforced by her training, a need to feel in secret command of why people behaved as they do as a prerequisite for tolerance, was the dark side of her initial interest in psychology.

In the same vein, I believed she dismissed my fear of falling victim to what Joseph suffered from—seeing only those facts that confirm a comforting theory of life—as nothing more than a by-product of the traumas of my childhood. She knew of the passionate ideologies of my childhood and its results: my mother's suicide, my estrangement from my father, Uncle's alienation from everyone he loved, my nervous breakdown, my own attempt at self-murder. But those bald facts weren't really all of it. Not even my mother's incest (a secret from all but Susan Bracken and Diane), not even that would fully explain my attitude. The lurid events are too overpowering in themselves; in their glare, the effects on the real person cannot be seen. She would have to hear as complete an account as this to understand. And would she hear it? Or would she hear it as a psychologist? I didn't want to be Diane's patient.

Or did I? Did I need *her* as a woman or as a therapist? Did I want to be loved or understood? Were both possible? With Julie that was never a question. She was a part of my life despite her ignorance of all its facts. She understood without telling. She loved without questions and answers.

Of course I could push our relationship through this impasse. A single anecdote about Joseph's mother would melt Diane's objections to him; a recounting of how he saved me from my mother's abandonment would silence and embarrass her. She would tolerate my investigation into his research as some sort of repayment and leave me alone. But that was a trick really, a manipulation. Did I want a relationship that I was managing?

These questions played in the background while Diane got in the car, kissed me with an open lingering mouth, settled in the seat and energetically reviewed aloud her notes from our first interview with the children we were about to see. Apparently the subject of Joseph was closed. Just as well, I thought. The mid-November day was cool, but a pale sun struggled to make us comfortable and implied that day might be our last chance to enjoy being outdoors before winter settled in. Entering the clinic, I longed to escape the office. Diane did too. She whispered, "I wish we were in Paris."

The last of our interviews, Albert, our abused and abusive thirteen-year-old, arrived late, just before lunch. With him, atypically, were two men. One waited outside with Al while the other came in to speak to us privately. He identified himself as a paratherapist—a term new to me that I assumed meant he was a glorified attendant. He explained Al had attacked another boy at the Yonkers shelter that morning. Al broke the boy's arm and threatened to gouge out his eyes with a spoon he had filed down. They decided to bring him to our session anyway, although he was going to be shipped back to Metropolitan State Hospital and would lose his privilege of coming to see me for the other two scheduled sessions. I would have to see him in Met State's adolescent lockup ward in the future. (That meant a barred room reeking of garbage from Dumpsters behind a side door.) The paratherapist, a bald man, asked if he should stay in the room for our session. Diane was upset by the news of Albert's violence. I said she should call a cab and go home. She protested weakly; I insisted. She had confessed during our drive up in the car that Al's brutalizing of his niece (Diane's patient) prejudiced her against him. The news of this attack on another child would only intensify her dislike. After she left, I told the attendant I could handle Albert alone.

The bald paratherapist looked me up and down. There was something funny about being evaluated in this way. I was more than a foot taller and eighty pounds heavier than Al.

"Okay, I guess it'll be safe. But don't turn your back on him. All right? Technically we shouldn't've brought him here, but they said you would insist and we can't take him to Met State until three for some crazy reason."

Al shuffled in, ignoring the chairs, and sat on the floor, his back against the wall. There was a welt above and around his right eye. His skin was a deep dusky black. Al's face was elegant, a high forehead and strong chin, eyes dark and brilliant. He was a handsome boy with no adolescent awkwardness. I asked if he wanted something to drink. He said he'd like a Coke. I offered ice water. With Ritalin in his system he could do without adding caffeine. I noticed his mouth was slightly swollen. After I gave him the water I asked about his bruises and he said, sullenly, nodding at the door to the waiting room. "They did it."

"Not the boy whose arm you broke?"

"He didn't lay a fucking finger on me. They punched me. They enjoyed it too. You know, the bald guy's a fag. He wants my sweet ass."

For the next half hour Al told me how he would have enjoyed scooping out his victim's eyes, or better still, cutting off the bald man's balls.

He told me he was sorry Diane wasn't there. He liked looking at her tits; he wished he could bite off her nipples. He wondered if cutting off a nipple would cause a lot of blood to flow. Those were some of his milder remarks. In my previous interview with him he had been sluggish and quiet, the docile manner of a drugged kid, not this, the "monster" that was supposedly caused by a poor brain recipe. Was he off the Ritalin? Not according to his chart. Had he been dumping it? Supposedly his caretakers were too smart for that: the boys were watched while they drank their medication.

I listened patiently to his horrible threats for ten minutes and then commented, "I'm disappointed in these fantasies."

"Yeah? I'm sorry. I'm real sorry."

"What about me? Don't you want to do something terrible to me?"

"Yeah? You want me to? You want me to fuck your ass?"

My fatigue caught up with me, amplified by despair at Albert's situation. I had been up most of the night reading. If the kindling studies on rats (and Albert seemed very much like a rat at the moment) were applicable to people, then when his mother used him sexually and tortured him physically his brain chemistry was altered (presumably to compensate for the extraordinary stress) and that change was ongoing, serotonin or dopamine or lord knows what flooding him in excessive or insufficient quantities, fighting off rage, despair, and loss from a past that no matter how distant or well understood, continued to hurt him without a break or diminishment. But if true, why couldn't it be measured against a so-called normal brain? And yet it might be true anyway. Could I fight its control with mere words?

"No, you probably want to fill my hole," Albert was saying. "You want to suck my cock?" Albert stood up quickly. I didn't move: I wasn't frightened of him. He wasn't threatening me, anyway. He pulled off his shirt. His chest was a boy's—flat, ribs showing. A line of four scars began above his right nipple and to the right of his navel: circular puffs of twisted bleached skin where his mother had pressed out her cigarettes. He tried to cup the dark nipple beneath the first scar, but it was too flat for the gesture to work. "You want to suck my tit?"

Of course my colleagues love to prescribe drugs for patients like Albert, I thought. Perhaps it was the right road, maybe Prozac was the leading edge of some bright future where psychiatrists can heal with the ease of GPs curing ear infections, but that wasn't why my colleagues were so eager to abandon psychotherapy for pharmacology. It was despair at the hopelessness of human relations, of our ability to heal each other with love and understanding.

"Albert," I said, "I want to take you off Ritalin."

a rebound effect, that his brain was accustomed to the doses of Ritalin and now demanded more and more. His physical movements were jerky, foreshadowing the damage neuroleptics and Ritalin can create, namely tardive disorder. [Neuroleptics cause tardive dyskinesia—loss of muscular control resulting in painful disfiguring spasms—in at least twenty percent of patients who take them for longer than a year. I had seen research that showed Ritalin, not a neuroleptic, can have the same effect and much quicker on children. Hence my alarm.]

While I tried to take Albert's pulse, the attendants pushed me aside. I hadn't heard them enter. The bald one put his knee on Albert's chest. The other grabbed his feet, staring at his genitals, mouth open with disgust.

"Did he hurt you?" the bald one shouted.

"He never touched me," I said. "Get off him. You're making it hard for him to breathe."

Albert reached—ineffectually, like a drunk grabbing for support—for the bald man's shoulder. In response, the paratherapist put his other knee on Albert's stomach and slapped his face.

I shoved the bald man. He was perched awkwardly and toppled easily. "Get off!" I shouted. "I said he can't breathe!"

"Hey!" His companion complained.

The bald man glared at me, but didn't make a move.

I told them to call an ambulance to take him to Columbia Presbyterian. I checked Al and was sure that he had a concussion. He slipped in and out of consciousness, losing it at one point for over a minute, his respiration so feeble that I began mouth-to-mouth and was prepared to do a tracheotomy. He roused enough from the CPR. I made sure his air passages were unblocked, that he was warm, and I quizzed the attendants about his medications. They claimed to know nothing. I didn't believe them. I suspected they had raised his dose of Ritalin. I went along in the ambulance to the hospital. I called ahead to a friend in residence there who met us at the emergency room.

What followed was hours of bureaucratic hassles. X-rays confirmed Al had a concussion. The shelter insisted Al should be transferred to Metropolitan State. I wanted him kept overnight at Columbia until I could get the results of blood tests.

Until then, I had had good relations with the head of the Yonkers shelter, Becky Thornton. Not this time. She was outraged by my interference and stonewalled my questions about Albert's assault on the boy as well as what drugs he had been given. She threatened to get a warrant and have Albert transferred by the police.

"You don't want to do that," I told her. "You don't want me to go to court to vacate the warrant and demand an investigation. You don't want people to ask how Albert got ahold of a weapon—"

"It was a spoon!"

"—or how well the children were being supervised or to have me testify to the brutal treatment I witnessed by your employee."

"Tom and Bill were trying to protect you. That's all."

"Tom and Bill could have accidentally killed Albert."

"That's an outrageous charge."

"No it isn't. Something was affecting Al's respiratory system and once he concussed he was in real danger of total failure. That would have been a disaster for your shelter and for my clinic. I don't plan to expose their negligence. But if you interfere with Albert's care, I will. At this point, I have no confidence in your people."

"Look, I admit we can't handle him. That's why we want to transfer him to the Met State. We took him to your clinic as scheduled only because I knew you'd throw a fit—"

"Throw a fit? When have I ever thrown a fit?"

"Excuse me. I knew you would *complain* if we transferred him without your seeing him. It was out of respect."

"It wasn't out of respect. The court ordered those visits. You had to bring him. Do yourself and me and Al a favor. Leave him at Columbia overnight."

"And what if he attacks somebody there?"

"He has a concussion."

"That's not a guarantee."

"I'll take full responsibility for him. If something happens, it's on my head."

"I need that in writing."

Her two attendants, Tom and Bill, were still at Columbia. I wrote a note to satisfy her and gave it to them.

To be safe I would spend the night at his bedside. Albert was certainly capable, psychologically, of attacking someone, or escaping, or committing suicide. I could order them to put him in restraints or heavily sedate him, but that was exactly how people like Al, who have no one to sacrifice themselves for their benefit, are treated by our system. Drugs are used in place of contact; indifferent or hostile attendants instead of care. He had been bounced from psychiatric jail to shelters to foster care since he was rescued from his mother—Al's rape of his niece was what called the police's attention to his own abuse. I believed this new attack was another call for rescue. Something had happened; maybe it was the medication. Didn't matter. I had to show him that someone was willing to deal with him as a person. Otherwise, certainly he would be lost. Lost as a human being; not as a menace. Eventually, the system would let him out and he could well become the world's notion of an unfathomable monster—a vicious serial killer.

I called Diane and explained. She listened to the full account, not commenting until I was finished. "I fucked up, honey," she said. "I was a wimp and I dumped it on you. I'm sorry. I'll come right over."

I insisted she rest and perhaps join me in the morning. I told her not to blame herself for her antipathy to Albert. And we discussed the beginnings of a plan.

When our talk was over, I walked down the hall to Al's room. He was tied to the bed. I wouldn't have the test results until morning. He was awake. His right foot was shaking, the leg's quadricep bulging and releasing rapidly. He stared at me. I untied the straps and massaged his leg. The spasms were ferocious and completely local. The rest of his body was enervated and motionless.

"Is it hurting you? The spasms?"

He shook his head. "I don't feel pain, you know," he said.

I couldn't help the muscle—its demonic animation seemed to mock me. I covered him with another blanket and asked if he wanted to eat.

He shook his head.

I rang for the nurse and told her to bring soup.

When it arrived, he said, "Don't want it."

I spooned up some and held it near, but not at, his lips. He stared at me. "What?" he asked.

"I think you should reconsider."

He turned his head away, then quickly back to swallow the soup, as if tricking me. I measured another spoonful and waited. He looked at me this time without any hostility. "I ain't gonna change," he said.

"That's what everybody else thinks," I said.

"Except you?"

"Me? I don't know. I don't have an opinion. Whether you change or not I'm still here to help."

He took the spoonful, swallowed and then said mildly, "I tried to fuck him."

"The boy whose arm you broke?"

"Yeah."

"You tried to rape him?"

"No. He wanted me to fuck him. He's gay."

"He's gay? They told me he was ten years old."

"So what?"

"At ten I don't believe people are gay or straight."

"That's bullshit. Everybody knows people are born gay."

I offered another spoonful of soup. Al said, "I can feed myself."
I gave him the bowl. He ignored the spoon and took a long drink.
"Are you gay?" I asked.
"I'm nothing. I can't fuck."
"That's why you broke his arm?"
"That gets me hard."
"And then you can fuck?"
"Yeah." He smiled at me. "Fuck them over. Then I can fuck."
"I see."
"Now your johnson is happy."
"I don't know what you mean."
"That makes *you* hard. You got a jones for knowing shitty stuff."
"I'll listen if that's what you mean."
"I can tell you lots of nightmares. None of that Freddy the Thirteenth shit. Real nightmares. That what you want?"
"Yes," I agreed. "You tell me all the shitty stuff."

CHAPTER EIGHT

The Wishing Well

TWO DAYS LATER, WITH LESS THAN TWO HOURS OF SLEEP UNDER MY BELT, I was startled by Gene's appearance at lunchtime for his session. I had forgotten our appointment. Diane, Ben, and our recently added therapist, Rand Carlton, were on their way out of my office after a staff meeting. Diane and I had told the others of our idea that we add a ten-room dormitory to the clinic, hire a few non-professionals we knew who had experience with abused children, and house those, like Albert, who were truly at risk in the welfare system. They were enthusiastic. Diane, still feeling guilty, told Rand and Ben that she had lost her nerve on Saturday and deserted me. I said her reaction was understandable, that Albert's mental condition was frightening and now we knew why. The tests showed he had toxic levels of Ritalin in his system, prescribed by the Metropolitan State's casual psychopharmacologist, who had spent less than ten minutes talking to Albert. I consulted Joseph as soon as I had the results. To his credit, he admitted that probably a rebound effect was in play; the medicine, instead of curing Albert's alleged hyperactivity, was now its cause.

"Shrinks," Joseph said. "They love to prescribe. Didn't he know raising the dose—?"

"—He doesn't see a human being when he looks at Albert," I said. "He sees a repulsive frightening black boy."

Joseph advised me on weaning Albert off Ritalin to minimize what was sure to be a severe withdrawal. When Joseph suggested I try another drug to ease his suffering, I said quickly and loudly, "No!"

"Okay," Joseph said. "But you won't dismiss Prozac because of this?"

"They're not using it on kids, are they?" I asked.

"Well . . . I don't know. Maybe." He sighed. "Probably."

"Listen to me, Joseph. I'll keep an open mind and study your miracle. But do yourself a favor, try to issue some guidelines."

"We do. Rafe, nothing can be done about sloppy doctors."

"Joe, that's not really an answer. The truth is, you don't know exactly what you're doing."

"We know enough."

"Do you know what serotinin does?"

"Well, the monkey studies—"

"Do you know *exactly* what it does?"

"No. Not exactly, Rafe. We don't really understand the brain."

"So why fuck with it, Joe?"

"But Rafe. Be realistic. If we don't try the drugs on people how do we know if they work? There's no progress without risk."

"I'll keep an open mind, if you do a good job of monitoring how Prozac is being used."

Joseph laughed. "Deal," he said. He laughed again. "As if I really can."

Our lawyer, Brian Stoppard, obtained an order from a friendly judge on Sunday to keep Al at Columbia Presbyterian under our supervision. I stayed by his bedside until Monday morning. By then, though still on a low dose of Ritalin, the flu-like symptoms of withdrawal had begun. He moaned while asleep and his sleep was more akin to a delirium: sweat soaking the sheets, legs twitching or bicycling in the air. A nurse's reaction to his condition illustrates the difficulty with patients like Albert. She saw him, asleep, legs rotating in the air, and said, "He's a real psycho, huh?"

I hired Tania Gold, a sixty-year-old woman with many years of foster care experience, to relieve Diane and me on Monday and went to the clinic.

If I had remembered my appointment with Gene I would have canceled. I was exhausted, anxious, enraged and confused. I knew the drugs in use were no good. But the kindling studies rattled me. What if emotional trauma caused unseen brain damage that no amount of talk could cure? Then my cause was hopeless *and* there were no medicines to help.

I could believe Joseph on a theoretical level; not in practice. The only solution I could see was to care for these children more thoroughly, minute
by minute. Seeing them two or three times a week was a farce. They
needed more than insight; they needed consistent care and attention,
consistent limits and consistent rewards; they needed, more than anything, patience and, if not love, then commitment. Yet there were ob-
stacles and risks in that plan. Brian had listened to my legal requests
patiently. He said, because of the criminal charges against Albert, his release to us would be tough; the other children were easy, especially with
the plan for a new wing. He commented, "That's going to cost a fortune.
Is it covered by Medicaid?"

"No. Locking them up and drugging them is, because supposedly
that's real medicine."

"I see. How about foster care? You would get government money—"

"—Don't want to muddy the waters. We're their doctors, not hired
caretakers. I'm sure we can get some foundation grants, but it won't
cover half the expense."

Brian lowered his voice. "Rafe. I have a question. Can you afford all
this?" he asked.

Indeed. Good question. I would be spending the balance of my inheritance, a sum I had promised Bernie's money manager I would preserve
at all costs so it could provide an income for the rest of my life. Once that
capital was gone, to earn a living I would need my work to become profitable. Treating these kids didn't look like a gold mine.

Those were my thoughts when Gene entered; he apologized for being
early (only by two minutes, in fact) and shifted in the chair opposite. I
stared at him, surprised by his existence. Monday at noon, our regular
time for three months—and yet I had forgotten.

Gene looked at me. I hadn't shaved or showered. He furrowed his
thick eyebrows at my seediness, then glanced away shyly. "I had the
dream again," he said. "Only this time you were in it."

Gene went through the familiar dream: he is alone in the gym of One
Room as a bare-breasted woman approaches with threatening nipples; he
thinks she will say something nice; instead, she spits at him; he shouts
for her to go away and his wish is granted; only she doesn't go; Gene
does, into his computer lab to sit at a terminal that has the answer to his
whole problem. But it won't yield the truth. Gene is forced to risk losing everything by hitting Escape, and yet that doesn't work. He must
destroy it all by turning off the truth teller. However, it doesn't turn off.

Instead, at last, comes the terrible message: "You are a son of a bitch." Here, as a new twist, I entered the dream. Gene admitted the dream Neruda was also his father, a shifting image hardly bothering to maintain what he considered to be its obvious symbolism. The Neruda/Don figure said, "You're a good woman."

"I think you said, 'woman,' " Gene added. "Maybe it was 'daughter.' I can't decide."

"Decide?"

"Remember. Actually, I'm pretty sure it was 'daughter.' 'You are a good daughter.' " Gene was silent for a moment. When he spoke it was in a loud voice, a touch too loud for my tired ears: "So? You think I'm homosexual? Or, I mean, *I* think you think I'm homosexual?"

I laughed. Rather, a snort of amusement escaped, derisive and arrogant. Gene was ashamed; he lowered his eyes. "I'm sorry," I apologized without an explanation. "You keep asking me to interpret this dream. Is that what I should do? Tell you flat out what I think it's about?"

"You can? I mean—it means something?"

"I don't consider myself a brilliant dream interpreter. I'm getting a message from it. But I think you're trying to send a message to yourself, not to me."

Gene's eyes were fixed on my chest. He glanced up at me to say eagerly, "What is it?" and immediately lowered his eyes to my torso.

"You were secretly glad your mother died. She wasn't providing mother's milk with her swollen nipples, only frightening anger, so you wished her away, you made her into a terminal and escaped to the answer of your computer. At first I thought the message on the screen—You are a son of a bitch—was your judgment of yourself for this wish. But actually I think it's a judgment of your mother—buried anger at her surfacing. Take the message literally: you are a son of a bitch. The computer, of course, is your machine and it always tells you the truth. My guess is that this new comment from me or your father—we are probably strong images of yourself—is a longing to be recognized as a good child in spite of your anger at your mother and your wish that she die."

Gene had forgotten his fear of looking into my eyes. He stared. His prominent Adam's apple moved up and down.

"Of course there are other messages and emotions in the dream," I continued. "The woman who seems to be both your mother and your wife—the woman in the gym?" Gene, still dumbstruck, nodded. "With her swollen maternal nipples, who you think is going to say something nice, but instead spits? That's a complicated one. She's a phallic woman—her nipples, her spit, which is an ejaculation of rage. My guess is that she is also your father—or *you* trying to be manly. I know it sounds odd but compression is common in dreams. The woman figure is rage. Your mother's rage, your father's rage and your rage at Gene the needy son. But I'm convinced when you shout, Go away, and she disappears into a terminal—the first of your puns—or rather, when you disappear from One Room to making computers—which represents your rejection of both your mother and father—I'm convinced that's you sending her off to death. Gratefully." I yawned. I was tired, true, yet I knew the yawn was also tension at what I was doing, abandoning the technique of my youth, risking an open confrontation with Gene's psyche. "And you've continued the androgyny theme with a father figure— me or your father—telling you that you're a good woman or a good daughter. Of course, this is all part of a theme in your life—so maybe I'm imposing it on your dream symbols. You aren't very phallic and you're afraid of women. You're especially afraid of expressing anger at them or being phallic with them. One thing is perfectly clear. The punning message is precise: 'As a son of a bitch, you are a good daughter.' "

"My God," Gene said in a husky whisper.

I waited.

"My God," he said again, still whispering. "My God, you're smart."

"Not me, Gene. You. You're the gifted punster. You're the one with the insight. Years ago, I missed all this. Your deep sexual frustration and fear, the emotional confusion about gender, I dismissed all that because I didn't want to seem to be criticizing who was earning money in your parents' household. I was so politically correct that I overlooked the emotional confusion of your relationship to your parents. I had no insight, Gene. It's all you. 'As a son of a bitch, you are a good daughter.' Your castrating mother wants you to be a weak man. The dream is your creation, your judgment, your desires, and your joke. It's quite witty."

"I can't hear what you're saying." Gene bent forward, hands rubbing his thighs. He shook his head in despair. I peered over the desk. His knees bounced up and down. "I hear the words. But I don't—I can't understand them."

"You're scared."

"Everything you said was right." Both hands went to his forehead and pushed up his thick hair. "But I can't remember a word you said." He jerked his legs together and apart, over and over, fingers massaging his temples. I was impressed by the suddenness and intensity of his anxiety.

"Okay, Gene. I'll go through it step by step. You don't have to remember anything. Forget everything I've said and I'll go over it again."

"You must hate me," he mumbled.

"Why?" I couldn't help expressing astonishment. "Why would I hate you?"

"I wanted my mother to die?" Tears welled in his eyes; his mouth drooped stupidly.

"No," I said firmly.

"No?" The hands dropped. The legs ceased. Relief was coming.

"You were glad she died."

I might as well have kicked him in the stomach. He doubled over, lips pushing in, and he groaned.

"She was furious at you, she was spitting at you, and you wished she would go away. And she did. Like magic. Actually, you're very guilty about it. You think you killed her and you're punishing yourself for it. That's why you can't concentrate at work and you can't sleep. You've murdered sleep and your machine is frozen. The only escape is to admit you're a son of a bitch. And you hope I'll tell you that you were a good daughter."

"I'm doing okay at work," Gene said with so serious and gloomy an expression it was comical.

"That's what you say to me. That's not what your dream is telling you."

"We'll get Black Dragon done no more than two months over schedule. Maybe three. But I can debug the machine faster than anybody in the world. That's why Stick brought me over." Stick was the nickname for Gene's boss, Theodore Copley. "But I think I'm concentrating okay. I just need to sleep." Gene slid forward to the edge of his chair and held a hand out to me, pleading. "That's why I can't let them know I'm in therapy. If Stick thinks I'm a burnout, he'll dump me. These are bad times for computers. I don't know . . . I mean, I moved the whole family down here and she said it was dangerous."

"Cathy or your mother?"

"Cathy. My mother was dead."

"Gene, you're running from what we're talking about. Your problem isn't the deadline or the shakeout in the computer business. Your problem is, you think you killed your mother because you were glad she died.

Not *you*, the wide-awake Gene. Your unconscious does. It's confused about your anger at her and what happened. But you didn't kill her. Cancer killed her. And you aren't the good daughter of a son of a bitch, no matter how hard you try to be. Being afraid of Cathy and not having sex with her isn't going to stop her from rejecting you or dying. You have to listen to yourself. You're afraid and guilty about things that don't exist and never happened. Your mother felt abandoned—" I shut up because Gene was crying.

He cried silently, face scrunched up, cheeks red, like a kid bawling; but he was a man, so the effect was grotesque. "I loved my mother," he stammered and sobbed out loud at last.

"Of course you loved your mother. In fact, you *still* love her."

Again, abruptly, his aspect changed. The sobbing ended. He peered at me through wet eyes, with hope.

"This isn't about whether you're a good person, Gene. Forget goodness. You did nothing to your mother. No matter what your secret thoughts or feelings, you did everything a good son should do. It's because you loved her, because you wanted her love so much, that you were glad she died. She had become a vengeful woman to you and that was too painful so you wished she would go away and then fate took her away. But you are not the center of the universe: you did not kill her."

Gene took a long, deep breath. "But what you're saying—"

"Who's saying it, Gene?" I interrupted. "Who's doing the dreaming?"

"Okay. So, then, I wanted her to die—"

"You wanted her to stop hating you. You wished the rageful, disappointed mother would go away. But you didn't want the real woman to die. In fact, you're so scared of losing her again that you won't confront Cathy about the fact that you don't have sex, that you think she doesn't love you."

Gene pouted. He was quiet. He settled back in the chair, hopelessly, shoulders slumped. "We have sex."

"How often?"

He answered reluctantly, "Not very often."

"Do you think Cathy loves you?"

"No."

"Do you think she wants to make love with you?"

"No."

"I don't know, Gene. I'll be honest. Maybe Cathy doesn't love you. Maybe she doesn't want to have sex with you. I don't know. I don't know because you don't ask her to love you. You're too scared of killing her if she becomes an angry, rejecting woman. You're scared to be a man because you're supposed to be a good daughter."

I waited. Gene's fingers were locked together, hands resting in his lap, his tearful face solemn, eyes on me. He was as attentive and uncomfortable as a scolded child. He nodded after a while.

"How are your ears?" I asked with no mockery.

"I hear you," he said.

"Okay. But so far I—Rafael—I haven't said a word. That was you talking to yourself. Now I'm going to speak." I opened my desk drawer and took out twenty-four tapes. "This is the audio record of our sessions. I lied to you. I'm not smart enough to remember everything you say or how you say it, so I use the tapes to review every word. In your case, I've listened to them several times."

I waited for a reaction. He didn't speak or break his penitent pose.

"Here's more from me, your therapist. You have me appear at the end of the dream to fulfill a wish. It's a wish you have about coming here. You have me say, 'You are a good daughter.' That's what you want from me. You don't want me to help Gene Kenny the man. You want me to certify the crippling image of your childhood. You want me to sustain your unhappiness. I don't want to do that. I won't collaborate with your parents', your wife's, and even your desire that you be a good daughter. You're not a daughter. And, more to the point, you're not good. You are the man who wants to build machines that tell the truth, you want a woman who is passionate and wants to make love to you, you want to be free of guilt and timidity and that man is suffering. I'll help him but I won't help that other weakling."

I pushed the tapes at him.

"Take them if you disagree. Remember, in the end, this is merely one opinion. I admit I could be wrong, but unfortunately I'm stuck with my beliefs. I'm not your father, I'm not God, I may not even be a competent psychiatrist."

Gene's eyes went to the tapes. And stayed on them.

"But if you want to continue, I need them. You're a very clever man, even when you don't want to be, and I need all the help I can get."

I waited. He took his time deciding. When he left, the tapes were still on my desk.

CHAPTER NINE

Detoxification

I HAVE REVIEWED MY DECISION TO CONFRONT GENE MANY TIMES. I WAS physically and mentally exhausted that day. My empathy for him, thanks to my distress over the fate of Albert and other abused children, was at an all-time low. And yet I still find many objective reasons for my open declaration of war on Gene's character. I can't say that the attack, although my motives were compromised, was poor technique.

For three months I had listened to a passive, unhappy life: a man who hadn't had regular sex with his wife since the birth of their son; a man working overtime for a boss who was seductive in his verbal flattery, but unrewarding financially; a man who, when he managed to sip joy, immediately poisoned it with his dismal self-valuation.

Gene had been instrumental in the creation of a machine—Flash II—with worldwide sales of eight hundred million dollars; he received a Christmas bonus of fifteen hundred and didn't complain, although the fact roiled. When Stick Copley lured Gene to move to Minotaur he was promised a six-figure salary. After Gene accepted the new job, resigned from Flashworks, and bid on a house in Westchester, Copley informed him that for the first two years his salary would be merely fifty thousand, promising, without offering a contractual guarantee, to double Gene's income when Black Dragon was finished successfully. This time (unlike the bonus incident) Cathy made life so uncomfortable for Gene that he did protest to Stick. Copley soothed the Kennys with an offer of a no-interest loan from Minotaur to buy their Westchester ranch house. Gene did not perceive that this perk was, in a sense, as dangerous as a coal miner buying groceries on credit at the company store. I goaded him into checking the promissory note; sure enough, the no-interest loan could be called if he left Minotaur or was fired. Of course, Gene hadn't bothered to have the agreement looked at by an attorney because Stick advised him not to, saying Gene would save a small fortune in legal fees. To be blunt, my patient was a sap: more eunuch than husband; more slave than employee.

The one light of his life—his six-year-old boy, Pete—was nevertheless a guilt-ridden and debilitating relationship. At least it wasn't one-sided. Pete adored Gene. And why not? He was a generous gift giver; he was a consistent and reasonable disciplinarian; he provided unconditional love. Gene felt guilty that he had spent many evenings at the office while on deadline for Flash II, thus he volunteered to be the night nurse when Pete responded to the move from Massachusetts to Westchester with a series of ear infections and attacks of strep. At his new job, Gene was often distracted, worrying over Pete's desires, his feelings, his struggles at school; Gene was as preoccupied by pleasing his son as a prince court-ing a beautiful maiden. Gene bought Pete favorite desserts on the way home; he dreamed up and programmed games on their home computer to help Pete make friends. Gene attended all school events, despite Stick Copley's thinly disguised contempt for the absences that resulted. Gene worked through lunch and on weekends to be let out to hear Pete play four notes on a recorder in his school assembly. Did he resent his son's neediness? No. Did he feel his boss was unfair? No. Did he dispute Cathy's repeated intimations that Pete's illnesses (she assumed they were psychosomatic, although I didn't) were really Gene's fault, since he had forced them to move? No. Gene did not defend himself when he shouldn't, as most do; and he did not defend himself when he should, as all must.

How did he describe himself? "I'm a lousy father. I'm not helping on Black Dragon. I'm a lousy lover. I'm selfish. I'm lazy. I'm inconsiderate."

After I confronted him about his dream, I made a rule for our future sessions that turned Freudian-based psychology on its head. I refused to discuss past events. By the past, I mean his mother and father. We stayed with his contemporary relationships, only going as far back as his courtship and marriage to Cathy. This raised, with an intensity that was remarkable compared to our previous work together, the subject of Gene's sexual life.

"I was a virgin when I met Cathy," Gene said.

"No you weren't," I replied with my new attitude: direct, almost impatient.

"Well . . ." Gene's problem of eye contact became hilariously exaggerated whenever sex came up. Typically, he looked at a point near my body or at least in my general direction. Now he turned to the venetian blinds. But he couldn't face them either. Gene lowered his head to stare at the gray industrial carpet. "Practically."

"You slept with your girlfriend in high school."

"Only twice."

"Still, Gene. There's no such thing as being practically a virgin. What are you saying? That other than your first two times, the only woman you've made love to is Cathy?"

He was thoroughly embarrassed. And humiliated. He grunted, covered his eyes with a hand. Usually, I would work to deal with that emotion first. But, and I'm sorry if this makes the lay reader dislike me, I persisted heartlessly: "Is that correct, Gene? Or have you slept with anyone else?"

"I can't . . ." Hand still over his eyes, he shook his head.

"Sure you can," I said.

Long silence. The hand dropped. In a low, shamed voice, he said, "Remember when I saw you in Boston?"

"Of course."

Gene looked up boldly—right at the venetian blinds. "I went to a prostitute."

I didn't react to what he thought was significant. "And that's it?" I asked. "Your high school girlfriend twice. Cathy, I don't know how many times. Not very often from your hints. And one visit to a prostitute."

Gene's mouth pursed angrily. He breathed through his nose. He sat still, fuming.

"I bet you've counted them up, Gene. Have you? Do you know how many times in your life you've had sex?"

A wonderful thing happened. Gene rotated his head—only his head—to look right at me. He delivered his line with a sarcastic smile, "Counting masturbation?"

He was fighting me. The flag of his manhood might be tattered and absurd, even to him, but he had raised it anyway.

"No," I said. "Not counting masturbation."

"Yes."

"Yes, you have counted?"

"Yes. How did you know?"

"You have a mathematical mind, Gene. Do you have an exact number, or an estimate?"

"A very close estimate."

"I'd love to hear how you made it."

"Well, we need to establish criteria," Gene said. "Are we talking about intercourse?"

"Intercourse?"

"Yeah." Gene was having fun now. He shifted his body to face me, leaned forward, head up, eyes shining. "Do I leave out blowjobs?"

"The prostitute was a blowjob?" His face fell. I cursed myself silently. That was a mistake. I meant to goad him a little: to rouse his pride, not rout it. I did my best to recover. "Yes, all sexual encounters meet the criteria. Mutual masturbation, oral sex, anything that involves someone else and results in a climax."

Gene's stricken look was erased. But the gleam didn't return to his eyes. "A climax for one or both parties?"

"Just you. Only you count as far as I'm concerned."

"You're a sexist, Dr. Neruda," Gene said. He was valiant, after all, striding on the deck of his new boat, brandishing a sword at the guns of my battleship.

"That's right," I said. "When it comes to you I'm a sexist. So how did you arrive at your number?"

"Well, the first three months we did it every day. And I remember doing it twice a day at least three times. So that's ninety-three."

"And the two times in high school."

"Right. Ninety-five."

"Why don't we call it a hundred?" I proposed.

Gene's energy ebbed. He didn't really want to continue. He dropped eye contact. "Well . . . That's not . . ."

"Okay. Ninety-five," I said. "Go on," I prodded.

He sighed. "I have to guess for the next year."

"You mean, until Cathy got pregnant with Pete?"

"Right. Best I could do was a steady decline. You know? Four times a week for a month, then three, then two, then once a week for the rest of

the year." He brushed his thick eyebrows with the thumb and ring finger of his right hand; his dark eyes stared moodily into space.

"So, that's what? Sixteen the first month?"

"It's a total of sixty-two until she's pregnant." Gene's voice descended
and his body sagged in the chair.

"What's the total?"

"One hundred and fifty-seven by my senior year at college." His enervated tone had no humor, or hope.

"And then?"

Gene rubbed his eyebrows faster, lowering his chin, until his eyes and
mouth were shielded by the palm of his hand. He sighed again.

"And then? Pete is six and a half, right, so that's—"

He cut me off, testily. "Maybe once a month. That's a little optimistic,
but we did have one week in Florida . . ." he trailed off.

"So that's twelve times six and a half—"

"No." Gene's hand dropped. He sat up, turning to the venetian blinds.
"I'm lying. Maybe once every two months. Maybe." His chin tightened
as if to keep his mouth from trembling. "Thirty-nine. Six and a half
years. Maybe thirty-nine. Probably more like thirty-five."

"What's the total?"

"One hundred and ninety-six."

A grim silence followed. I was keenly aware of the absurdity of our ac-
counting, nevertheless his despair crept into me, distorting the objective
silliness of our research. "Wait a minute," I said. "Aren't we forgetting
the nine months she was pregnant?"

Gene shook his head. "No," he said, in more of a groan than speech.
"We didn't do it while she was pregnant."

"Not once?"

"No. Not after we knew for sure."

"Why?"

"She didn't—I mean, she let me once, but . . . She hated it, so . . . I
mean she was pregnant. I didn't want to force her to have sex with me."

"As opposed to now?"

Gene glanced at me; then away, mumbling, "What?"

"You force her to have sex now?"

"Practically." He grunted.

"Do you really mean—force?"

"No, I don't force her, of course not." Extreme irritation. "I whine. I complain. Day after day I bring it up until it gets too embarrassing and she has to let me. It takes about two weeks."

"She never initiates sex?"

To admit this was too shameful for words. He nodded slightly, shifted further from me, eyes drifting to the carpet.

"Have you ever stopped asking for sex and waited—"

Again he cut me off impatiently, as if I were slow-witted. "Yeah! I tried that. I stopped asking. Five weeks later, I started begging again."

"What do you mean, begging?"

Dragging the ashamed, muddy river of their intimate relations to find the body of reality took five sessions. Typically, his summary was a distortion. He didn't beg or whine; he nagged, throwing numbers at her. "It's been a week, honey," was the sweet nothing he whispered in her ear. Catching her undressing for bed, emerging from a bath, bent over the stove, Gene would hug her awkwardly, probably groping a little (although I couldn't get him to admit that) and ask for sex regardless of the situation's romantic deficiency or impracticality.

It was clear, even from Gene's presumably prejudiced testimony, that Cathy felt her life consisted of dreary work done in isolation. True, she didn't have a job, Pete was in school every day until three, Gene helped with the boy's care, and the cleaning woman came twice a week to do the heavy work; but that left five days of making beds, scraping dried jam from the floor, gathering the endless toys Gene bought and Pete scattered; and the shopping, cooking, making play dates, picking up and dropping off, went on without a break. To add to her woes, she was a stranger to the neighborhood. The mothers of Pete's new schoolmates had a six-year head start sharing the trials and hilarity of raising their kids. They were friendly to Cathy on the surface, not truly intimate. From her point of view—Gene himself saw this—his work gave him an absorbing task and instant comrades. She could fit in neither with the mothers who worked nor the mothers who stayed home: the first group had no time for her, and she felt condescended to; the second had their schedules and friendships formed long before she arrived.

In their family life she craved privacy. Gene's arrival home was the signal for her to disappear. Rarely did they do things as a threesome. Gene played with Pete on the computer or in the yard. Cathy went off by herself—to read on the bed, or take a bath, or go shopping—anything to be away from what must have seemed like a prison to her.

Gene did not describe Cathy's life in exactly these terms, yet he came close to them. He was far from being unsympathetic to her. The reverse was true: he felt guilty. What he did not see (and I was sure must be the case) was that when Cathy rejected him sexually, she was probably rejecting what he had come to represent in her life: a series of dreary, lonely and unsatisfying tasks that were reincarnated each day.

Why didn't she work?

With the repetition typical of therapy (retracing old ground with firmer and firmer steps) three more months' worth of sessions were required to push through the vines of Gene's guilt and confusion, hurt and anger, until Cathy's passive self-defeating attitude and behavior were clearly revealed. She had failed to graduate college because of the unplanned pregnancy. She had intended to go on to medical school. The options available to her—secretarial, finishing her education, clerking in a store—she thought demeaning or too difficult to accomplish, considering where they lived and Pete's schedule. Besides, she didn't know if she wanted to become a doctor anymore. She felt too old to start now and yet she wasn't interested in anything else. Just as her lack of friends in their new location was a false complaint (Cathy had been the same depressed, passionless wife back in Massachusetts), so was the complaint of not having a vocation. She made no serious attempt to discover or pursue one. I knew what Gene believed she really felt. It was time to probe this wound.

"You don't think she loves you?"

Gene nodded. He believed she blamed him for the unplanned pregnancy, blamed him for her choice not to abort, blamed him that her college fantasy of womanhood and marriage was a poor match with the reality. In short, her spoiled life was his fault.

During lulls, for six sessions in a row, I asked, "You don't think Cathy loves you?"

"I don't care if she loves me," Gene said on my sixth try, and with that answer pushed us onto a new path.

"You don't!" I was glad at this novelty. I exaggerated my shock.

"No."

"Oh come on. You're telling me you don't care if your wife loves you?"

"No."

"You've said many times that it hurts you."

"I was lying."

"You don't care at all?"

"No," Gene insisted, petulant and stubborn. Since I changed my method, he often chose to resist me in the style of an adolescent. I was pleased by his pugnacious attitude—we were moving out of childhood at last.

"Hard to believe, Gene."

"I really don't."

I waited.

"You know why?" he continued after a silence. "Because I don't believe people love each other for a lifetime. That's just bullshit. Everybody knows it's bullshit. That isn't what scares me."

"Okay. What scares you?"

"I don't think she loves Pete."

He wanted to turn back to the safe trampled ground. We needed another push—our last breakthrough was four months old. "Now that *is* bullshit," I said.

Gene seemed delighted. He said nothing, and grinned at me.

"Gene, you've done a very good job of trying to convince me you're the better parent, and that's okay. It's natural that parents compete about who's better to the kids, but this is a low blow. Of course she loves Pete."

Gene continued to grin. There was malice in it, too. I was thrilled. He was silent for a while, the smile twisting into a frown. When he responded at last, it was a blunt challenge: "How do you know?"

"How do I know?"

"You've never met Cathy or Pete."

"That's right. All I know is what you've told me."

"You're on her side," Gene said. He looked right at me, pointing a finger. "You don't believe a mother could not love her child. That's your problem. That's why you can't help me. You think it's always the father's fault. Well, if it weren't for me, Pete would be a very fucked-up kid. He'd have no friends, he'd be too shy to talk in class and his teachers wouldn't know how smart he is."

"Is Pete smart?" I asked, curious.

My question left him open-mouthed. He had his trunks on, fists up, feet dancing, jabbing me with lefts and rights while I was chatting at a tea party. "You know he's smart."

"I do? You've never said."

"Of course I've told you he's smart."

"No you haven't. I assume Pete is smart. But you've never mentioned it." His hands were down. "Cathy's a good mother," I punched.

He stared at me, dazed.

"Or I should say, she's a good enough mother. And you're a good enough father."

"Good enough?" Gene said. "What does that mean?" He was disappointed by the grade I had given him as a father.

"A good enough parent is a term a psychologist invented to deal with the fact that even though all parents make mistakes and expose children to their neurosis most of them do little real harm. To raise a healthy child, it isn't necessary to be cheery and always loving or always consistent. You just have to be good enough. Both of you are good enough. And Pete is doing fine."

"How do you know?" Gene demanded. "How do you know we're not beating the shit out of him? How do you know what we really do?"

"Okay," I said. "Either you're good enough parents or you're an exceptional liar. Not only inventive, but you have great endurance."

Gene sulked. I waited. Gene turned away from me.

I said, "Why does it annoy you I think Cathy loves Pete?"

"It doesn't. I just don't agree. I live with her. I see her with Pete. You don't."

"Okay. If I'm so wrong, why does it annoy you?"

"Because you're my doctor. You should be on my side. And you're not. You think mothers are always right."

[This may seem to be an extraordinary statement. If anything, I had erred on the side of defending Gene against his mother and wife. His complaint is really against his own rationalizations for Carol and Cathy; projecting them onto me permits him to fight them. Since I had abandoned transference, I wasn't pleased.]

"That's bullshit, Gene," I said.

His eyes returned to me—to study the stranger I had become.

"I think Cathy is blaming you for the choices she made about her life. I think she's being unfair and unloving to you and you know that's what I think. But I'm not going to let you escape from confronting her about what really bothers you with a fantasy."

"What fantasy?"

"You're angry at her that she doesn't love you and you're too scared to say so, but it doesn't scare you to say it using Pete as a stand-in for yourself. That's not fair to your son. And it's not fair to Cathy."

"You're saying it's easier for me to say she's a lousy mother than she's . . ." he trailed off.

"An emasculating, guilt-inducing, passive wife," I finished for him matter-of-factly.

For a moment, he was quiet. Then Gene laughed. Loud and thoroughly. He broke off to ask, almost coughing, "What did you say?"

"An emasculating, guilt-inducing, passive wife. She made choices. She decided to have Pete, marry you and drop out of college. She regrets them. But they were her choices. You didn't bully her—"

Gene raised a hand to stop me. "I'm not innocent," he said.

"Oh?"

"I—I mean, I immediately offered to marry her and I talked about how much I wanted a kid—"

I cut him off, shouting: "I'm sick and tired of you always being on the side of mothers! You never think it's their fault. It's always the father who's the bad guy."

Gene grinned. "Okay, okay." He nodded. "I get it."

"Let's cut the crap, Gene. She wants to blame you. You don't want to be blamed. Tell her to change her life. Have a little guts, will you? We've analyzed you to death. You know why you're scared to confront her. Your mother and father never confronted each other about their problems and when they did their marriage ended bitterly."

Gene concentrated on this observation, staring at it so deeply he fell in and lost himself. "Maybe if they had talked when they were young . . . Maybe they would have stayed—"

"No," I interrupted.

"What?"

"Stop looking for guarantees. There aren't any. If you drop your solicitous husband act and be yourself with Cathy, maybe she'll leave you. I don't know. You're a coward, Gene. It's as simple as that. Other people are just as scared, just as confused, just as vulnerable. You're not more sensitive than anyone else. You're a coward."

"I'm not—" Gene shifted his eyes away from the windows to look in a direction he always avoided: the door. "I mean, there's no—" He stopped.

"What!" I shouted.

"I'm not gonna take this."

"Then don't."

He stared at me, opened his lips, shut them. He took a long breath through his nostrils and stood up. I worried he would lose his nerve. At last, in response to a mysterious inner cue, he turned on his heels and walked out.

*   *   *

Two days later, Diane and I appeared in Juvenile Court to plead that our temporary custody of Albert (which had been in effect for nearly six months since his release from the hospital) continue in place of his sentence for three years in juvenile prison for raping and sodomizing his niece. It was May 2, 1989. We were petitioning Judge Martina Torres, who had found him guilty a week earlier. The timing was right because the new wing to house him and others was finished. During his trial—which coincided with construction of the dorms—he and three other boys had been sleeping on cots in Room A; two counselors stayed in Room B to supervise and care for the boys on evenings and weekends.

Albert, no longer on any drug, stood between Diane and me in Judge Torres's chambers. He was nervous, shifting back and forth on his feet, head moving side to side. When I gave him what I hoped was an encouraging look, I was startled by his eyes. They were full of feeling. Anger, helplessness, and despair swirled in a storm of pain too turbulent for encouragement to becalm. How could the judge look at those eyes and not pity him? But we didn't rely solely on the law's keen vision into Albert's emotions. Instead, Albert had been dressed for respectability in a blue blazer, white shirt, chinos, loafers, and a cheerful yellow tie that Diane had picked out for him.

Her show of support was important since she had treated his victim, his niece. Shawna was now living with a Quaker couple in Pennsylvania who planned to adopt her. She had adjusted well to her new circumstances. The immediate symptoms of her suffering—she had been neglected by her mother and beaten by her mother's boyfriend for years before Albert's assault—were relieved. Her reading and writing had improved dramatically; she made friends easily, slept and ate well. Nine months ago, before Diane's therapy, those basics were almost impossible for Shawna. Indeed, at the time, a social worker and a psychologist appointed by the court to evaluate Shawna had labeled her as "learning disabled" and "preschizophrenic."

[The latter is a new vogue term. It's gibberish. Everyone who is not schizophrenic is preschizophrenic. The psychologist brilliant enough to predict schizophrenia is yet to be born.]

A few months before this hearing, Albert wrote his niece a letter apologizing for the rape. Shawna replied in a big hand, full of lovely circles.

She wrote on lined yellow note paper: "Jesus loves you, Al. And I love you." Both letters were in the brief submitted to Judge Torres.

We watched her study them or at least appear to; she had had two weeks to review all the documents. Also in attendance were our and Albert's lawyer, Brian Stoppard, and an assistant district attorney, Richard Bartell.

"Are you sorry for what you did to Shawna?" Torres asked, dropping Albert's apology on her desk.

"Yeah," Al said, wildly searching Torres, then me, and finally Diane. Diane touched the sleeve of his blazer.

"What are you sorry about?"

"What?" Albert said, startled.

"What is it about what you did to Shawna that you regret?"

Albert looked to me, bewildered. "Tell her the truth, Al," I said. Diane frowned at me, puzzled. Although she saw Albert every day, she hadn't been working with him and we tried to avoid, in the interests of romance, bedroom work chatter.

"I'm sorry that—" Al glanced at me again. I nodded. He continued to Judge Torres, "I'm sorry I uglified sex for her. It's a beautiful thing. I was wrong to do it ugly."

Diane took off her eyeglasses and wiped them with a piece of tissue from her pocket—that meant she was nervous. The judge frowned at me. As for the assistant DA, Bartell, until then he had taken as neutral a tone as possible for a prosecutor, not withdrawing the State's request that Albert should be locked up, yet not making the case with much passion. He lowered his eyes at Al's comment. I bet he was thinking he'd better get tougher. He could see the headline: THEY LET HIM FREE TO RAPE AGAIN.

Albert, unaware his comment was worrisome, snapped his fingers softly, a tic when anxious. That, along with poor grades, restless shifting of feet and colorful speech, had earned him the diagnosis of attention deficit disorder.

I said to him quietly, "Al, I know you're nervous—I think we're all nervous, but snapping your fingers is probably making everybody more nervous."

"Oh." Al grabbed his right hand with his left, as if his will alone couldn't control it. "Sorry," he added to the judge. "Just a habit," he said. He glanced at me and I nodded to encourage him to expand on his explanation. I had told him many times that he lived in a world with a sensitivity to the actions of young black males which, no matter how unfair or fair, shouldn't be underestimated. I told him not to modify his behavior. Instead, he should talk more about his desires and fears, making clear what he was feeling, to become, as much as possible, an individual human being in the eyes of the prejudiced. "I'm scared," he said to Torres. "That's why I do that. I'm real scared right now."

I wondered if Torres knew how hard it was for Albert to make that admission—an admission of weakness that could get him killed in the projects.

The judge nodded. "I understand. There's nothing to be scared of—"

"Forgive me, Judge," said Brian Stoppard, the only one who seemed calm, "but there is a lot at stake here for Albert. His fear, as Dr. Neruda would say, is realistic."

I appreciated Brian's comment. I don't think Torres did. Needling a judge might seem stupid, but Brian had succeeded for us in every case, using a demanding, sometimes condescending attitude.

"Of course this is a serious situation," Torres said to Brian testily. "Thank you for reminding me." She softened to speak to Albert. Perhaps that was the point of Brian's tactic: to make himself, the white middle-aged man, appear more aggressive than his client. "Albert, I want to do what's best not only for society but for you as well. The law understands that you're still a minor, a child. Punishment isn't all we're interested in. We want to help you change. Could you explain to me a little more what you mean when you say you regret making sex ugly? Does that mean you wish you had had sex with Shawna instead of raping her?"

"Judge—" Brian started.

She shut him off. "Don't interrupt, Counselor." She looked at Albert.

He rubbed his hands together hard enough that we could all hear the friction on his skin. He turned to me, eyes pleading.

"Keep telling the truth, Al," I said.

He answered her question, but addressed me, "You know things like that were done to me too. Now I see sex as ugly. The ugliest ugly. I did that to her. I don't know. Maybe it always be ugly to me. Didn't want to do that. That stay with you always. Didn't want to do that shit to Shawna. She's real pretty and that fucked it for her. That's the worse thing I did."

Diane had not only relaxed—there were tears forming. Bartell stared at Albert, amazed. The judge put a hand to her chin and appeared very wise. "I think I understand. Now tell me, Albert, do you understand that it's wrong to have sexual relations of any kind with a child?"

Albert's mouth hung open. His hands continued rubbing. I could see that he didn't understand what the judge was worried about.

"Judge," I said, "may I ask your question in a slightly different way to Albert?"

"Yeah!" Albert said loudly, relieved.

A laugh escaped from Bartell. Immediately, he shut it off.

Albert's handsome face became a mask of disdain. I understood that in fact he was embarrassed and frightened, but his strong features and dark skin would appear scary to a stranger, especially a white stranger. "Shit," he mumbled.

"What did you say, Albert?" the judge asked.

"Sorry," he said. "Didn't mean to talk out of turn."

Torres nodded for me to proceed.

I asked, "Albert, would you like to have sex with Shawna?"

Albert frowned. He snapped his fingers three times quickly, as if summoning a waiter. "That what she mean?"

"The judge would like to know if you want to have sex with children."

"That what she think of me?" he asked, not demanded.

"No, Albert," Torres said. "I don't know. I'm asking."

"Don't she know?" Albert continued talking to me as if we were alone in the room. I'm sure that rudeness seemed arrogant. I knew it to be fear.

"You should tell the judge everything. That's the only way you can be sure she knows what she needs to know. You can't count on us."

Albert faced Torres like a soldier reporting. "I can't do it, you know? I can't have sex. They say my . . ." he gestured, shyly, at his crotch, "they say it's fine. But not in my head, you know? It's uglified. Rafe—I mean, the doctor—he thinks it will change. But I don't know. I can't fuck anybody." Al realized the word he had used and quickly added, "Sorry, I don't mean to disrespect you. That's just the word, you know. I'm sorry."

Embarrassed, Bartell averted his face from Albert to stare at Torres's shelves. He had read my report so I assume his reaction was to the spectacle of Albert's admission of impotence, not to the fact.

Torres, however, reacted well. She was matter-of-fact. "Albert, I see now how I misunderstood you. I don't think I asked you the right question. Let's say Dr. Neruda is right. I'm sure we all have confidence he is, and your problem eventually goes away and you can have sex whenever and with whomever you wish. Okay? Can we suppose that?"

"Yes, ma'am," Albert said.

"Would you then try to have sex with a child?"

"Course not." Albert was insulted. I knew because he sucked in his left cheek as if to bite it. "I thought I said that."

Torres looked down at the papers on her desk. She spoke with a lowered head. "Dr. Neruda, at your clinic there is no security, correct? Any of the young men could simply walk out?"

"Yes."

"Your Honor," Stoppard began, "they are supervised at all times—"

"I know, Counselor. I meant, specifically, that they are not locked in at night or during the day for that matter. Their presence and time is accounted for, but they're on their honor in terms of leaving the grounds, is that correct?"

I answered, "They are not permitted to leave the grounds without us and they are supervised, but there is no physical barrier to escape. Of course, Albert has lived within those rules for the past six months."

"There was a seven-month gap between Albert's attack on Shawna and the child at the shelter. What makes you confident that Albert will continue to be responsible?"

"I've worked with Albert five days a week and sometimes on weekends for six months. That is the equivalent of years of therapy for most people. I believe I know him well, perhaps better than anyone but Albert himself. His desire to live a productive self-sufficient life, a life where he can be a useful member of our world, is very strong. In fact, I believe his violence against Shawna was a perverted expression of a desire to be helped out of the hopelessness and violence of his family. I don't think Albert will run from his friendships and his work at our clinic because it's a safe place for him. As you know, he and the other boys are tutored daily. They have the opportunity to make friends in the local basketball and soccer leagues. He has a life with us that he would miss. That's the best barrier against violence and escape anyone can create."

Judge Torres opened a folder and gestured at a paper. "I have an amicus brief filed by the Yonkers Adolescent Center and Metropolitan State. They both endorse your therapy, Doctor, and recommend Albert stay at your clinic. But they also decline to agree with your statement that Albert isn't dangerous to himself or others. Met State goes so far as to recommend that you install security measures. I'm sure you understand, Doctor, that my concern for Albert's well-being must be secondary to the well-being of society. Besides what you have already said, what further assurance can you give me that Albert won't do harm to others?"

"I can't think of anything, Your Honor, except that I am putting my clinic, both its federal and state funding, as well as my own money, at risk. If Albert runs away or is violent then our work and my reputation will be severely damaged. May I also comment that, in my opinion, the reservations expressed by Yonkers and Met State are a statement for their self-protection, rather than a prediction of Albert's behavior."

Torres smiled shyly. "I'm afraid, Doctor, that as a jurist I can't read beneath the lines as you do in your profession. I must take them, as I take you, at face value."

"I understand," I smiled back. "As I say, I'm prepared to stake my reputation and the survival of our clinic on Albert. That's as much confidence as I've got in me."

Torres said, "And that's as much confidence as the law has a right to expect." She opened her hands in a gesture to Albert. "It's up to you. You have a chance to make a good life for yourself, Albert."

CHAPTER TEN

Change

A WEEK PASSED WITHOUT GENE APPEARING. FINALLY HE LEFT A MESSAGE saying he would come in at his regular time the next day and I should call back if there was a problem. I cleared the hour—Diane and I had planned to have lunch—but didn't respond, curious to see if he needed reassurance to show up.

He didn't. He entered with a determined air, a new attitude, striding to his chair, sitting upright, eyes unflinching. "You're right," he said. He waved a hand. "I thought about it for days and days. I practically crashed my car into a tree going back to the office—you know, the day I walked out. By the way," he said, glancing away briefly, then forcing his eyes to me, "I'm not paying for the two sessions I missed. You threw me out. I mean, that's what seems fair. I know I left, but you pushed me out."

Gee, that meant I would be out one hundred dollars. "I agree," I said solemnly. "Does this mean we're resuming therapy?"

"If you're willing," Gene said. "You're right. I'm weak. I'm scared. I'm chicken. I'm going to start behaving differently, but I could use a friend—" He stopped. "But you're not a friend, are you?"

"I feel friendly toward you. Friendship is different than being a doctor and a patient, though."

"I need your help," Gene said boldly, not sounding as if he needed anyone. "Is that bad? Is that part of what's wrong with me?"

"In a way."

"So I shouldn't be here?"

"If you are going to make a serious effort to change your life, it's reasonable to want an ally. I'm happy to be in my comfortable boat rowing along while you swim to a new land, Gene. I won't get wet. I won't drown. I don't think you'll drown either. What I don't want is to stand beside you on the shore wondering if the water's safe. It isn't safe. And I can't do the swimming for you."

Gene became thoughtful and silent for a while. He crossed his legs, rubbed his chin, and then commented, "I think I should ask for a raise."

"So do I."

"Stick has invited me to his house. I mean Pete and Cathy too. For a barbecue. Black Dragon has a green light. We have to have a prototype in a year. I know what that means. In a month, he'll cut the deadline to six months. I'm going to be working like a dog. And I'm the project director. He can't trust me with the company's biggest new product and pay me fifty thousand."

"Sounds right."

Without any transition, Gene said in a rush of words, "I've been going to prostitutes."

I waited for him to elaborate. He shrugged and seemed to wait for me. "This past week?" I asked tentatively, "Or . . . ?"

"No, for the whole time I've been seeing you. I'm up to about once a week now. I've been seeing this one—uh, she's a blonde—her name, well, she says her name is Tawny. That's not her real name."

"Doesn't sound it."

"I've lied to you about it."

"Okay."

"Ever since that time in Boston, I've been going to whores. And I never told you."

"Gene, that's your privilege. You want to lie to me, you're going to succeed."

"You're not angry?"

"Not about your going to prostitutes."

"But you are angry?"

"I'm annoyed you didn't tell me, because that meant you wasted some of your time here, and that means you wasted some of mine as well."

"I'm sorry."

"Okay. Do you want to talk about it now?"

He did, in a detailed narrative, with relief and some enthusiasm in his voice. While still living in Massachusetts, he noticed ads in a giveaway paper at the mall's drugstore. He called one, telling himself he was curious if it was real, incredulous that an illegal activity could be solicited openly. He hung up on hearing a woman's voice ask if she could help. That fascinated him, the way the prostitute answered. "Hello? Can I help you?" He phoned four more times, he estimated, cutting the line on her greeting. Eventually he answered, asking for details. She described her body in numbers, said what she would do (some of her offerings were in code words he didn't understand) and named her price. Her blunt manner wasn't a turn-off; it was his own reaction that appalled him: he was eager to try her. The only thing about the whore's sales pitch that daunted him was the cost—one hundred and twenty-five dollars for an hour. There were a few weeks of temptation before he tried one and there was another month or two, when he moved to Westchester, before he found another giveaway paper, made calls, and settled on seeing "Tawny" regularly. I asked if he was concerned about AIDS. "Oh no. They're clean and also they make you use a condom. Even when they give you head."

I offered no comment or judgment. He seemed to be deliberately draining sex of passion as well as emotion. Also, there was anger in his actions. That was immediately clear, at least to me, when I asked Gene to describe how it became a regular habit.

"I didn't go a lot at first. But since I started seeing you last summer, and especially since we talked about how little sex . . ." He interrupted himself with an irritated outburst, "I'm sick of begging my wife. Instead of begging I just go and get what I want."

"And you like blowjobs."

That was hard for him. He swallowed and answered grimly, "Yeah, I like blowjobs. I guess that makes me a creep."

"A creep? I think it makes you a normal, ordinary man."

"Why am I going more and more since I started seeing you? You're supposed to make me better. I'm getting worse."

"Well, for one thing, you didn't talk about it. You didn't deal with it here."

"That's true."

"And there's also the possibility that you're doing what you want, that you don't want to have sex with Cathy, that you like having an accommodating partner with no emotional complications."

Gene stared at me angrily, but what he said was, "No, I don't. I feel bad about it. I feel like a loser. If I'm doing what I want, why does it make me feel bad?"

"If you're not doing what you want, why are you doing it?"

"Because I'm a loser."

"Maybe that's what you want. To feel pleasure and then feel like a loser afterwards."

[I did not offer a full analysis of the visits to prostitutes. I did not tell him outright, nor lead him to what I suspected, namely that this was another avoidance of expressing anger, secretly punishing his wife without risk of counterattack or rejection. There was also the rebellion and anger at me, for making him face his sexual deprivation. Each time we met and he didn't tell me that a twenty-two-year-old girl had been bobbing her head on his erection the day before, he no doubt felt a secret victory over me, that I was not all-knowing, that he was not merely the mild-mannered Gene Kenny, but a competent man who knew how to get what he wanted when he wanted. Why didn't I probe this area? It's a paradox of therapy. I didn't because Gene wanted me to for the wrong reason: to punish him for his anger and his self-gratification. I chose to expose the cause: his need for pleasure; and the neurosis: his fear of seeking it openly.]

Our talks stayed on the surface, a cool, somewhat superficial review of his behavior, rather than searching for underlying conflict or motive. We had moved from character analysis to reports of action and effect. In a sense, the therapy was over. He wanted me to coach him, to cheer him on, to be an eavesdropper as he wrestled with the self he had known all his life, in particular the inclination to thwart his own desires. If Gene asked me to supply a judgment, such as going to whores is bad, I declined. When he said he wanted to wait until Black Dragon was under way before asking Stick for a raise, so that he would have more leverage, I said, "I don't think he can replace you anytime." Rather than explore the rationalization, the power of his fantasy of punishment by Stick if he made any demand, or its origin in his relationship with his parents, I emphasized the here and now. The notion was simple: force Gene to act more confident than he felt, hoping that behavior would tow feeling.

[How is this different from behavior modification? First, because of the years of analysis that preceded it. Second, I never dictated any action, I merely cut the ropes of fear.]

Gene's prediction about Stick moving up the schedule for Black Dragon was accurate. At the barbecue, Stick asked Gene to help him with the cooking. While assembling trays of chopped meats and chicken, Stick admitted he had lied in his estimate to the marketing and sales VPs, as well as to the Dragon Team, so that when they needed more money than was budgeted, as he knew they would, he could offer a quicker finish as the inducement. And Stick confessed to a darker motive. Another group, led by Copley's main rival at Minotaur, was at work on a machine slated to be their next new product. Were Black Dragon to be ready as soon as January 1990, it would knock out his rival's machine. If Stick's accelerated schedule became known at this stage, his rival and the marketers in the company—the men Copley hoped might one day name him CEO—would disapprove: Minotaur couldn't sell both machines simultaneously.

Excited and flattered that Copley confided in him, Gene overlooked the manipulation and deception involved, satisfied to be an intimate. And, thrilled to be at a gathering with no one else at his level (the other guests included only Minotaur management) Gene became convinced if Dragon worked Stick would promote him. On top of all these delights was a bonus. Gene met Stick's twenty-six-year-old daughter for the first time. He brought her into his account of the splendid afternoon repeatedly: "Then Halley said something great. I can't remember exactly how she put it, but . . ." he went on to paraphrase her observation. They were cynical, one a smart crack about her father being so ruthless he used to cheat while playing Candyland with her. "She's really beautiful," Gene told me. "I mean, she's *incredibly* beautiful. And so fucking smart. I couldn't believe how smart she was." His open enthusiasm was unusual; as an isolated interest, I paid it little attention. She was the daughter of a man he more or less worshipped, for one thing. And he was switched on sexually in general, full of anger at his rejecting wife, made more confident by the illusion of successful sex "Tawny" provided, as well as by the glamour and excitement of the event itself. He was giddy—Gene even spoke admiringly of Stick's barbecue sauce.

"What about the raise?" I asked.

He went deaf, a familiar defense. "What?"

I repeated the question. Again, he said, "What?"

"You said you were going to ask Copley for a raise," I elaborated to improve his hearing. "Did you bring that up?"

"It was a party," Gene protested.

"Sounded like you had a long business talk in private while making burgers in the kitchen. You could have brought it up then."

Gene scowled, raised his right hand to his thick eyebrow, and stroked it thoughtfully. "Cathy told me not to."

"She was in the kitchen?"

"No," he almost groaned the word. "Before we went. I told her what you said I should do and—"

"Hold it. I didn't tell you to ask for a raise. *You* told me you wanted to ask for a raise."

"You know I could buy a book for this kind of stuff. *What You Want and How to Get It.*"

I laughed, delighted. "You're right. Assertiveness training. We can go on *Donahue* together. Gene, I'll be the first to admit that we're no longer doing traditional therapy. Anytime you want to stop is fine. Anyway, I'm surprised at Cathy. I thought she feels Stick is taking advantage of you."

"Yeah, but, after all, I've worked for Stick for seven years and this was the first time he had us to his house. She thought it was rude to ask him for money the very first time he had us over. I mean, she didn't know he was going to have a private talk . . . you know, and I had promised her I wouldn't bring it up so . . ."

"Did you want to bring it up?"

"Yeah I did."

"But you didn't because you had promised Cathy not to?"

"Okay, I'm a schmuck. I have to have Mommy's permission."

"See? That's why we're not doing traditional therapy anymore. You already know the answers. You know you need Mommy's permission and I'm sure you remember that Don didn't ask the gallery owner to pay him for the shelves."

Gene smiled. "I wish I could throw up on an art book right now," he said. He conceded he ought to discuss his salary with Stick. In fact, I wasn't especially concerned about his work relationships. Stick had trusted Gene to be Black Dragon's project director and Gene seemed to have little trouble with the men under him. Perhaps his experiences as an unfairly treated employee taught him to manage subordinates well. More likely, the comfort of having authority allowed him to assert himself, and his gentle nature inspired others to be independent and creative. Gene often praised the kid hackers under him, commenting that they had all the ideas, he merely got out of their way and occasionally checked their homework. "I'm like a kindergarten teacher with a classful of geniuses. I just make sure they don't eat the crayons." His desire to wait until Stick admitted the importance of Black Dragon—as he had at the barbecue—before asking for a raise seemed to me to make good sense. That he didn't seize his first opportunity was no crime.

The regular visits to "Tawny" were another matter. They worried me. Not out of prudery. Gene's marriage needed more intimacy, especially romantic intimacy, not less. And his fear of acting manly was hardly improved by choosing what is, in effect, an infantile sexual relationship. Gene's description of the visits to "Tawny" could be seen as regression: the male is stripped, excited, soothed, and sometimes bathed by an au pair, supplying attention in place of the preoccupied mother. Gene obviously thought he had solved his problem with Cathy. She didn't want sex so he would get it for a fee elsewhere. He continued to see passion as one-sided (that Cathy might want sex was never considered) and satisfaction as unemotional—it didn't matter that "Tawny" couldn't care less about Gene, just getting her one hundred and twenty-five dollars.

[I could have corrupted Gene's enjoyment of "Tawny" by informing him that clinical studies of prostitutes reveal the overwhelming majority were molested as children, usually by a male relative, and that their true sexual orientation is lesbian or at least their sensual side is so blocked by rage and self-hatred they don't enjoy physical passion. He probably wouldn't have believed me—I'm sure "Tawny's" performance of liking Gene was excellent. And such a revelation would have been a sneaky attack on Gene. I was more interested in revealing his behavior than destroying the illusion of hers.]

Gene did ask Copley for his raise that very afternoon. I heard the story three days later. To Gene's surprise, Stick agreed without an argument that he deserved a salary of one hundred thousand. There was no anger, no mockery, no emotional rejection at all. "You're the best man I've got," Stick said. Days later, Gene still flushed with pleasure as he repeated the compliments. "I just don't have it in the budget," Stick went on. "I'd have to tell them about our secret plans to explain why you deserve it. They think you've got a year to bring Dragon in. But in six months, after it's done, I'm going to propose you become project coordinator for the entire company and then we're talking a lot more than 100K. Maybe even a quarter million plus stock options." Stick went on to elaborate his vision of their future: once Dragon was a hit, he would become CEO, Gene the VP of R&D, and together they would expand the company's product line.

"That's gonna mean getting more people, more bright people," Gene said.

"That's why I need you, Gene. Nobody is better at picking talent and getting it to work than you. Those kids out there would throw themselves on a burning circuit for you." Repeating Copley's praise, Gene was thrilled all over again. He let the flattering words reverberate and then caught my eye. "He actually said that," he added.

"I'm sure," I said. "And I'm sure it's true." I waited.

Gene took a long satisfied breath, smiled at me, and seemed to have nothing further to say.

"So you didn't get the raise?" I finally had to ask.

"He can't now. You see that, don't you? I mean, you understand?"

"I understand what he said."

"Oh!" Gene sat up, reminded. "And he also promised a big bonus, a real bonus, if Dragon makes it. He said something about my getting a piece of its net profit." Gene shook his head at the thought, awed by the size of this promise. "I mean," he mumbled, "that would be millions."

"What did Cathy say?"

"I didn't tell Cathy. I told Tawny," Gene laughed at himself. "Probably shouldn't have. She might raise her rates. Got me a bonus, though. She did—" he stopped himself, glancing at me self-consciously, and continued in a louder tone as if to drown out the previous phrase. "Anyway, when I got home, I told Cathy we had to have sex more often. And she said I was right! I couldn't believe it. She actually apologized—"

"Wait a minute. Slow down." Gene adopted his typical pose of the attentive schoolboy: hands in lap, eyes downcast, waiting patiently for the lecture. I almost laughed. His reaction, I must admit, made sense. I *had* sounded like a scold. I hesitated before continuing. What should I do? The slow way would help him only after the events were long past. Hadn't I decided to experiment, to abandon established method? Wasn't this direct approach my Prozac, my magic pill of self-confidence and clarity? "First, even though it's just a detail and you didn't mean to tell me—what did Tawny do after you told her you might become a millionaire?"

Gene nodded, a mute concession that he had tried to cover up. "Okay," he sighed, his lips pursing before he elaborated further. When he did, he gave the words as much dignity and solemnity as possible. "This time she didn't use a condom when she gave me . . ." he gestured to his groin and then shrugged.

I was amused. Copley intoxicated Gene with fables of the future and escaped without spending a nickel. Gene repeated them to a prostitute and got better, if possibly more dangerous, service. Gene, emboldened by his new phallic stature (although at least one was a phantom), demanded that his wife pay more attention to his needs and she agreed. It was as if I were viewing some sort of ego-feeding chain. I had to hand it to Stick—he was a great salesman.

"What did Cathy say when you—well, what did you say to her exactly?"

"After Pete was in bed I brought her a cup of coffee in the living room and said I had to talk to her. No whining. I just said, very calmly, that I was unhappy she didn't ever want to make love to me, that she only did it when I asked her to, and then only after I asked a lot. I told her I wanted that to change or I would have to assume she doesn't want to be married to me."

"Did you tell her about asking for the raise?"

"No, I didn't want to confuse things."

"How about the next day or the day after that? This was three days ago, right?"

"Well, after I made my speech, I left the room. We didn't talk in the morning and when I came home Pete was there. After I put him in bed, I went right to my desk and worked. Cathy came in eventually, and she was crying. Or she had been. She apologized, said she knew she was being mean to me. She said when she heard Stick talking at the barbecue to the others about how hard I had worked on Flash II, how I had saved their ass on the debugging with the whole future of the company on the line if I didn't get it done right, she realized how much pressure I had been under and she felt bad. She said that she knew there was something wrong with her, that she was too tired all the time and she was going to change. So then we made love . . ."

"You made love that night?"

"Yeah," Gene said. He had been quite serious. Now he grinned. "This asking for what I want works. I'm telling you, you should write a book and we'll go on *Donahue*."

Maybe Stick should write the book, I thought to myself. Certainly he should be the one to promote it on *Donahue*. "And after making love?"

"I fell asleep. Last night I had to work late at the office. We really haven't had a chance—" he cut himself off. "Anyway, I don't have to tell her. She was really impressed by Stick. She hadn't spent much time with him before the barbecue. She told me she was wrong to have fought me about moving here. She said he's going places and I was right to follow him. Look, he's confided in me. If he asked them to give me a raise, not just a raise, but to double my salary, it would blow the plan. That's not in my best interest."

"How about a gesture of good faith?" I asked.

"What?" Gene frowned.

"Well, surely he could budget you a fifteen percent raise without having to justify it by admitting to the pushed-up schedule for Dragon? And fifteen percent would do you some good. That would be seventy-five hundred extra. Cathy might be able to get a little more help, especially if you're going to be on a sixteen-hour-a-day work schedule for the next six months. It might free her up to return to school or something else that interests her. Now that she's more aware of her own unhappiness, she might be willing to improve her life."

For a while, Gene sat still, staring blindly at my book shelves. He slid the fingers of both hands together and I tensed, anticipating the crack of his knuckles. He slid them in and out several times, finally locked them, and twisted his hands outward; as usual, the popping noise of bone against cartilage made me feel queasy.

"You know, that's going to be a problem," he said.

"What?"

"I'm not going to be able to come here as . . . Well, maybe I could get here once a week."

"How about asking for a fifteen percent raise, Gene?"

"What's the point?" He sounded aggrieved. "It's only six months and then I'll be golden."

"The worst that can happen is he'll say no. Praise is exciting, Gene. It feeds the ego. But the body will starve all the same."

Gene sucked in his cheeks, held his breath for a moment, then exhaled explosively. "You're right," followed this wind. "Okay. I'll ask."

"As for the sessions, I don't know what we can do. You can talk to me by phone if that makes it easier—"

"No!" Gene objected with a touch of horror.

I raised my brows.

"I can't risk them overhearing at work."

"I could try to find time in the evening—"

"No, I'll be working nights. I just—I don't know. I may have to stop coming."

I was suspicious. To be sure, Gene had, at long last, confronted his wife with his true feelings and he had asked Stick for his due, but what I saw happening would allow both breakthroughs to be resealed. He was unlikely to improve on the intimacy of his marriage during the relentless work schedule ahead. His demand of passion from Cathy was a neurotic's: I want you to love me now, only I'm not going to be around. True, he had made a request of Copley. What he got were future payoffs, while Stick got what he wanted from his project director right away. Even if Copley came up with a fifteen percent or a ten percent raise, Gene's true situation wouldn't have changed much. Not that I thought Stick's promises were lies. Why should I doubt them? If Black Dragon catapulted him to CEO of Minotaur, why wouldn't he promote Gene, a loyal and successful player on his team? That was no favor; that was, as my uncle would say, good business.

Our time was up and Gene seemed in no mood to be decisive about our schedule. He said we could meet again this week and probably next as well. I promised to look at my hours and find alternatives.

I went home eager to tell Diane about the session. She enjoyed hearing the details of my work with Gene because he was an anomaly in my practice, a break, for both of us, from the harsh stories of the children.

I'm ashamed to admit that I mocked Gene and his woes. Diane had moved into my apartment two months before and I found her in the tub, covered with bubble bath, her young face, eyeglasses off, child-like as it floated, bodiless, on a sea of white foam. "I want sex and I want you to want sex or I'm leaving you," I said as I entered.

Diane lowered her mouth to blow a puff of bubbles in my direction. "Okay, big boy, come and get me."

"Oh *I* wasn't talking. That was my patient talking to his wife."

"No kidding!" Diane sat up all the way. I watched the foam slowly

Albert let go of his breast. "Maybe you want to suck my cock." He jerked the belt of his jeans and quickly unzipped, pulling both dungarees and underpants down to his thighs.

The reality of the damage his mother had done to his penis—it had been described in his medical file and by Albert verbally—was much more horrible to see than I had imagined. I pressed the edge of my fingernails into my palms to help control my features. It was crucial not to react with either horror or pity. I asked, "When did he see you?"

"You want to suck it?"

"When did the boy you attacked see you naked? Today? Or did it happen a while ago?"

Albert rotated his hips, gyrating like a stripper. He grabbed his wounded penis. "I could make it into a pussy. They can do that. They make a hole in you and push it in. They make a clit outta this"—he squeezed the scarred head to almost nothing—"so you still get off."

"Did he see you in the shower? The bathroom? Where?"

"What the fuck you talking about?"

"You've taken off your clothes to show me what your mother did. I understand. But I need to know exactly what happened with the other boy, Albert—"

He let go of his penis and stopped gyrating. He frowned and interrupted. "Don't call me Albert. Okay, fuck face? That's not my fucking name."

"What should I call you?"

"Zebra. You like that? Call me Zebra."

"Is that what he called you?"

"He didn't call me nothing. You ain't so smart. You think you know everything, but you don't know shit. You think you making us better? You think Shawna's better?" That was the niece he had sodomized. "She's sucking off all the boys. She's seven and she gives better head than your wife."

"Did she suck off the boy whose arm you broke?"

Albert smiled. He turned around and showed off his buttocks. The burn on his right cheek had the shape of its cause, an iron's triangle. "Kiss my ass." He was facing the wall. He lowered his head and rushed at it. His skull whacked hard against the plasterboard. The impact pushed him back a step or two. He paused and then repeated the action. His legs wobbled this time. He staggered. I was up from my chair now. He gathered himself, slammed into the wall again, and collapsed.

I hurried over and rolled him on his back. Blood flowed from his left eyebrow. His eyes were unfocused. He probably had at least a mild concussion. I was worried about what was in his system. One possibility was evaporate to reveal her neck and the rise of her breasts. "Tell me every-thing!"

After my report, we made love, sliding on the porcelain to the sizzle of popping bubbles. Our mood was silly and full of confidence. "Call me Tawny," Diane whispered as she pulled me in.

Chapter Eleven

Debugging

STICK FOUND MONEY IN THE BUDGET TO GIVE GENE A FIVE PERCENT RAISE, and the intramural race between machines went on. Since Gene couldn't fit our sessions into his intensive schedule, we talked on the phone for a half hour once a week, Wednesdays at twelve o'clock. He called from a quiet booth at an International House of Pancakes five minutes from Minotaur; if he were spotted it would seem that he had taken a break from a quick lunch to call home. Cathy hired a woman to pick up Pete after school, do light cleaning and some shopping. She enrolled in SUNY at Purchase to get her Bachelor of Science degree, postponing until graduation the issue of whether she would pursue medicine.

Two months into this schedule, Gene missed a phone appointment. He called the following morning to explain that a crisis had developed suddenly. His voice was hoarse, exhausted; he sounded harassed. He said he was working round the clock and wasn't sure if he could promise to be available on Wednesdays.

"Do you want to skip it for a while, Gene? You don't have to break it to me gently. I can take it, you know."

He sighed loudly. "Yeah, I got nothing to talk about except the machine. When it's done, we can go back to our regular schedule. I'll need it. I've forgotten what people are like, much less how to talk to them."

I did hear from Gene once more before the machine was finished, in

August of 1989. Assuming I understood his explanation correctly, the late delivery of a key component for Black Dragon had delayed the prototype as well as the debugging process. The latter, in the case of a new machine, is a rechecking of the parts or wiring of the hardware to find what's causing the prototype to fail. Debugging was Gene's primary responsibility. He described the work as long, dull and meticulous. Although it requires few advanced computer skills, this purely practical task is, in a sense, more crucial than the imaginative brilliance of original design. The idea might be flawless, but how could you know until you had reviewed every minute connection, every tiny component?

Gene added, as an afterthought, that the rival machine was dead; indeed, Stick's rival had been fired. "You don't sound happy," I commented.

"Well, it's all fine provided I can debug Black Dragon so the damn thing works." There was fear in his tone, real fear, not simply tension. I understood his investment in this work much more—hearing that quavering, scared sound—than from all our nostalgic conversations about the pressure and triumph of building Flash II. The machine was his real life: he gave all his passion to it, and loved his creation with an unguarded and reckless heart.

I was impressed, a little concerned, but not alarmed. I expected him to succeed, and if not, I felt confident I could help him adjust. Besides, soon I had my own crisis at work, as threatening and profound as any I had faced, a challenge that led me to doubt the value of my work with children and whether my creation, the clinic, had a right to exist.

The beginning was innocent enough. A colleague at Webster University, Phil Samuel, asked us to supply him with tapes of our first few interviews with young children (six and under) who were victims of sexual and physical abuse. He promised merely to view them for his own guidance, make no copies, and return them promptly. Why? I asked, reluctant to release these sensitive videos. Samuel had recently finished a clinical study, which he offered to send me before its publication, that showed young children are extremely susceptible to suggestion. Indeed, they proved to be vulnerable to an interrogation so gentle and unobtrusive that it hardly qualifies as suggestion. The study's design was admirable. Two graduate students conducted private interviews with eight children. They were asked a series of questions about routine experiences, such as, "Have you been to the beach?" Among the banalities was a ringer. "Were you ever bitten by a mouse?" was asked in a neutral tone. At first, all the children said no. The interviewers didn't react, didn't re-

peat the query, and didn't follow up. A week later, the same questions
were asked of the same children. This time, half changed their answer,
agreeing they had been bitten by a mouse. The follow-ups were neutral
and bland. "Where were you when you were bitten?" "Did you have to
go to a doctor?" Within three sessions, all had said yes and added a host
of imaginative details. I was skeptical of his results—until I read the
study and watched his videos.

I brought them to Diane. She brushed them off without looking.
"This is the same old crap in a new disguise: Children can't be believed.
It's the witch hunt defense."

I insisted she watch the videos on a Sunday. We sat together as child
after child, without any intimidation or insistence on the part of the ques-
tioner, invented complicated stories of events that never happened. One
boy's fabrication was particularly vivid. He said he had gone into the cellar with his older brother, they had fought over an action figure until his
brother pushed him into a pile of old clothes. Hidden in the pile was a
mouse who bit his right index finger. He was taken to the hospital, ban-
daged, given an injection and sent home. His father put out traps, the
mouse was killed, buried in the backyard and, in a final twist of justice,
his brother was punished for shoving him. After the fantasy was in full
bloom, the boy's father was instructed to tell him that, as far as he knew,
there had never been a mouse, a visit to the hospital and so on. The boy
freely admitted the story was just pretend. The father told him that was
okay, no one would mind, and he could tell the truth in the future.

At the next interview, the graduate student informed the boy he knew
his father had talked to him, knew the events were false and that he could
say so without fear of a scolding. The boy refused to recant. He insisted
vehemently that every detail was true and proceeded to embellish further. In Samuel's opinion, the more this boy was doubted, the deeper the
imagined event was pushed across the border into reality. Fantasy had become traumatic memory.

"So? It's just one kid," Diane said.

I showed her the written data. All the children eventually provided
descriptions of a biting mouse that never happened and, when challenged, were loath to abandon them. Yes, they were young enough to be
genuinely confused about the difference between fantasy and reality; nevertheless, they qualified for testimony in court. (The significance of their
ages in terms of giving evidence is far from academic. In the courts, children six and under had been considered to be the most reliable witnesses

of abuse, presumably because they were too ignorant of sex to make it up. I had sworn that was my expert opinion to more than a dozen juries, without allowing for a smidgen of doubt.)

While she read on, I left to make coffee. When I returned, Diane had rewound the tape to watch key moments again and again, looking, I knew, for some mistake in the tone of the question asked at the first interviews: "Were you ever bitten by a mouse?" The question was asked as casually as possible. And the first response was equally casual—a simple no. The next week, sometimes a hesitation, sometimes an assent; yet by the third week, all nodded their cute little heads to say solemnly in a wounded tone, "Yes."

I wondered if somewhere Freud was laughing.

Diane finally shut off the machine. She pushed the documents away with her foot—they were scattered across our coffee table—pulled off her glasses, leaned back, and shut her eyes. "In the end," she said, her voice deeper than usual, "it's just a story about a mouse." She remained stretched out, hands behind her head, eyes closed as if she were going to sleep. Her composed freckled face looked as cute and innocent as a fantasizing child.

I waited for her to elaborate. She seemed to be falling asleep. The subject was closed. I laughed scornfully. "That's it? That's what you got out of it?"

Her eyes, only her eyes, opened. "You know what I mean."

"I don't."

She unlocked her hands, dropped her feet from the coffee table, sat up and argued, "There's a big difference between a kid accusing a mythical mouse of biting him and accusing a real person, especially a relative, of playing with her vagina."

"I agree. But why don't they give up the fantasy when they're told everybody knows it's untrue and that doesn't matter?"

"Come on!" Diane shook her head at me. She stood up and then seemed to realize she had nowhere to go.

"Come on, what?"

"That's ego, that's formation of identity. They know the lie has no consequence. What's going to happen—the mouse will be punished unfairly? They're defending their pride, not the lie."

Diane's point was a good one. That's exactly why they wanted our tapes: the mouse study's implications were limited. I believed Phil Samuel had no ax to grind in the increasingly bitter debate within and without psychology over the accusations of children, from their reliability to whether the process of questioning and cross-examination is as harmful a trauma as the event under investigation.

[Of course, adults long to convince themselves that the accusations of children are unreliable. In crimes between adults, victims can always be suspected—again, wrongly—of somehow being a party to their suffering. A mugging caused not by the mugger but by the victim unwisely wandering into a dangerous neighborhood; a rape caused by a woman's provocative dress, rather than by the rapist, and so on. This is all part of the natural desire to deny random danger and viciousness in life. How much better to think of the world as an obstacle course that can be negotiated skillfully to a happy ending. At least children are presumed, albeit somewhat superficially, to be innocent. Other than Freud and child abusers, few articulate that children wish for sex with adults, and Freud wrote of fantasy, not actual collaboration. Inevitably, all parents hurt their children, most trivially, nothing like real abuse; and yet even that trivial guilt haunts us and we wish for an exorcism. Our route to maturity, without therapy, requires we believe our hurt didn't happen or that we can safely ignore the pain as exaggerated. I don't resent the unwillingness to believe; for some, it's a useful defense. I'm angrier at those therapists who—either through sloppiness or ambition—do incompetent work and confirm the widespread impression that children routinely make up stories of physical and sexual abuse.]

I called Phil the next day to learn more about the hypothesis of his new study. He said he wanted to test if children who had no experience of sexual abuse would fabricate such stories as easily as a biting mouse. He said we were regarded as the most thorough and impartial interrogators (we videotaped all sessions, used dolls rather than words to pinpoint exactly how the kids were touched) and he wanted to imitate our technique. I asked him to describe the new research. Eight children were to undergo a routine examination by a pediatrician that would be secretly taped. The doctor would do a few innocuous and pointless things—listen to their bellies with a paper cup to his ear, tickle them lightly under one arm with a feather—not skin to skin, clothes always on—and count the toes with a tongue depressor. At no point would their genitalia be exposed or touched. We might consider these actions to be a silly bedside manner and perhaps sexually symbolic, but no reasonable person could consider them to be molestation and they are far less physical and stimulating than ordinary parental embraces or sibling rough-housing. A week later, copying our procedure and technique, using dolls and questions that are stripped of direct sexual refcrcnccs, the children would be asked about the examination as if an accusation had been brought against the pediatrician. Samuel wanted to see our tapes of real victims of abuse to train his graduate students for that phase of his study.

Diane objected vehemently in general and she was certainly opposed to my sending tapes of the Peterson case, the one most suitable for Phil. Henry Peterson had accused his wife's father of sexually molesting his granddaughters, ages six and four, while they were in his care. At the time of the alleged abuse, Henry and his wife were in the midst of a bitter divorce; he had had to relocate out of state and she often traveled on business, so the Peterson girls were basically being raised by the maternal grandparents. Henry Peterson's lawyer, leery of many recent failed child abuse charges, had asked us to question the girls. Diane handled them exclusively. She uncovered a systematic, progressive molestation by the grandfather. He fingered their vaginal lips during baths, rubbed up against them in their beds at night, and eventually, as the girls put it, "Grandpa peed on my tummy." The girls said when they complained to Grandma, she spanked them with wooden spoons so hard that they bled. Since no penetration was alleged and the beatings were claimed to have taken place months before (the girls moved out when their mother changed jobs and no longer had to travel) there was no physical evidence to confirm or contradict the testimony Diane had elicited. The psychological condition of the Peterson girls was alarming, however. They had severe night terrors, had completely regressed in their toilet training, were fearful of their grandparents and would shriek if any man, including their father, tried to touch them. For us, that is emotional corroboration. I had no doubt that the stories were essentially true, if not absolutely accurate in every detail.

I wanted to include Diane's interrogation of the Peterson girls precisely because, unlike patients such as Albert, there was no corroborating physical evidence and their ages were in Samuel's target. Most of our patients were older than his cutoff of six. (The age limit isn't arbitrary, it's developmental. The study sought to examine the ease with which a child might blur fantasy into reality. After six years of age, a child bears a greater resemblance to an adult liar. Phil Samuel was testing the reliability of young children to testify at all, not their willingness to lie. He believed that the inventive boy in the mouse study didn't understand the distinction [for adults] between the "game" of being asked questions by a clinician and official testimony. In many cases, a child his age would not be required to appear in open court. A deposition under circumstances similar to the clinical interview is sufficient, and a private retraction, such as the admission to his father that the story was pretend, is regarded as denial typical of abuse victims.)

Diane objected that the case against the grandparents was not a criminal procedure—Henry Peterson had merely asked the court to forbid them visitation rights and, with the agreement of the District Attorney's office, wished to spare the entire family any attempt at punishment. Her complaint didn't seem relevant to me. Samuel had agreed that he would merely view them to imitate our questions and use of dolls. I didn't see any harm.

We argued this to a draw in the morning, went off to our separate appointments for the day, agreeing we would settle it at home in the evening. My schedule that day was an unusually happy one for me. Albert had been accepted into Dorrit House, a boarding school in North Carolina founded by the posthumous donation of a wealthy tobacco baron for boys from disadvantaged backgrounds. In view of Albert's excellent behavior and academic progress in the nine months since Torres had allowed his sentence to be served at our clinic, as well as the six months before the sentence (a total of fifteen months of therapy and exemplary conduct), Judge Torres agreed to extend the strictures of his parole so that Albert could to go boarding school.

Albert packed the night before and said goodbye to the staff and his roommates at a small party. I drove him to the halfway house in Brooklyn where his mother was a resident. This was to be their first meeting since both their arrests two years ago. After their goodbye, I was to take Albert into Manhattan to meet a van that would transport him and six others to Dorrit House.

The women's shelter in Brooklyn was a converted rooming house. We were led to a garden in the back. Albert stepped onto a brick patio with two wood picnic tables and green metal folding chairs. Albert and I had to duck to clear the sliding door. His mother, Clara, was at the far end, on a grassy elevation, waiting under a tall maple with her arms crossed. It was late August, a hot, humid day. The leafy tree looked damp, exhausted and sooty. Clara watched her son approach as if he were a stranger. She was in a red blouse sufficiently unbuttoned to show her impressive cleavage and the beginnings of a black bra. Her flat belly and long legs were emphasized by tight white shorts; I noticed later they had impressed lines on her upper thighs.

I was shocked by her youthfulness. She was fifteen when Albert was born; that meant she still wasn't thirty years old. I knew that as fact. Seeing with my own eyes her smooth creamy brown skin, her girlish figure, and the dignity of her high cheekbones and long nose, did not match an expectation of meeting a mother, much less the most monstrously abusive mother in my experience, and as bad as any in the literature for that matter.

I was also taken aback that they had allowed Clara to dress this way to meet Albert. Involuntarily, I looked to our escort for an answer. She was a young and beautiful African-American woman, but she was wearing a dowdy blue dress that dropped to her sandaled feet. I had no idea what authority she had, and I realized my questioning look to her was absurd. Obviously, someone felt it was up to Clara how to present herself to Albert and up to him how to react. All in all, I had to agree. If she persisted in sexualizing her relationship with him, then he should know it.

Albert went no farther than the brick sitting area. "Hi," he said shyly and lowered his head when his mother didn't answer, uncross her arms, or move in any way. She seemed to stare through us; not angrily, in a trance.

"I'll be right inside," our escort said. "You want to join me?" she asked me in a low tone.

I shook my head. Albert had asked me to stay with him the whole time. He was afraid of Clara; and was afraid of himself. He had vivid fantasies of cutting her open, her stomach in particular; sometimes he longed to strangle her while she begged to be forgiven. Often, while in the midst of a pleasant and innocuous activity, he could feel the grip of her hand as she kept his head between her legs, pushing his lips to her sex; sometimes, the recollection was so vivid Albert jerked his shoulders to free himself from her insistent fingers. The memories were clearer and more immediate with each passing day. Recently, his ability to masturbate had returned and, although that was relief in one way, sexual feeling also brought with it images of torment and vengeance. I had worked with him to keep it specific to Clara, not to fight the memories or fantasies about her, not to generalize them in an effort to forgive her. "*She* did it," I said more than once. "Not anybody, not any woman. *This* woman. Remember it was her face, her body, not anyone else's." Of course, when I gave him that advice, I had no way of understanding just how vital and beautiful was the person who tortured him.

"Let's sit down," I said after some time passed and Clara remained in a sentinel's pose. I pulled one of the green chairs away from the bench and sat. Albert copied me, moving his seat as close to mine as possible.

I wondered how I would feel if, after my therapy with Susan, I had the chance to see and talk with my mother. Clara unfolded her arms. She moved at us with a slow, long-limbed walk, eyes on the flower beds she passed. Her attitude was so casual it seemed insulting. I reminded myself that Albert was facing a very different woman than my mother, that his scars were not only deeper, his injuries more severe, but they were also visible forever, wounds anyone who tried to cherish him would see and touch in the very act of love. The closer she got, the angrier I felt. My body tensed as if I were threatened—or perhaps, more accurately, as if I were restraining myself from attacking her.

"Hey Al," she said with a little wave of her fingers, not raising her hand. She sat on the step up from the bricks to the grass, legs together, knees reaching her chin. She smiled at him regretfully. "You look good."

I watched him react, mostly to take my eyes off the unfathomable mystery of her appearance, a pretty young woman who seemed to know nothing about life, who appeared untouched. Albert is darker than his mother; he shares her dignified features, however. His wide eyes showed a lot of white as he took her in. He didn't say anything.

She nodded as if he had spoken, and as if she agreed with his comment. "You going to school?"

Albert nodded. Barely.

"Where's it at?"

"North Carolina," Albert mumbled.

"Your Grandma's from North Carolina," she said, looking up at a passing jet. She watched it trail off. "I think," she added, returning her eyes to Albert.

"I hate you," he said, gulping on the last word as if he were choking with tears. His eyes were clear, however, head stiff on his long neck.

Clara seemed not to have heard. She looked him up and down, checking his outfit. The survey was leisurely. Abruptly, her eyes came to me. She said, fast, like an ambush, "You gotta be here?"

I didn't answer, startled by the suddenness.

"They say you gotta be here, that it? I can't be alone with my boy?" Clara nodded at the house behind us. "She's there. You gotta be *here*?"

I turned to see. Our escort stood just inside the glass door, watching.

"She won't let me do nothing to him," Clara was saying as I shifted back to face her. "I make a move—I kiss him, I try to shake his fucking hand, she'll talk me to death. Shit, I'd rather die than have her talk at me. I ain't gonna touch him."

Albert said gruffly, "You heard me? I hate you."

Clara dropped her head, arms drooping, a puppet whose master had let go. She hung there, lifeless. From the street, summer sounds washed over the garden wall. A water pistol fight, the ping of a basketball dribbled fast on pavement, a radio playing rap music. A man shouted, "Hey Tony! Hey Tony! You fuck face. We have to go." The music shut off. A girl screamed with glee. The basketball rattled on something metallic. Clara came to life. She sat up, stretched, elongating her skinny arms and neck. Under her arms, there were faint white circles, maybe from a deodorant. She slid off the steps onto her knees.

"You're my baby," she whispered passionately, arms forward now, fingers calling to Albert. "You always gonna be my sweet baby."

Involuntarily, I pushed my chair back. I thought I heard the glass doors open, but our escort didn't appear. Albert, on the other hand, hadn't moved. His dignified face was set, cheeks puffed, eyes in a rageful stare.

Clara gushed on, low and intense, like a lover. "I know I hurt you, baby, but that was crack, that was the life, that was all the shit happening to me. I love you, baby. That wasn't me hurt you. I'm your Mama, baby." She moved herself: eyes brimmed with tears. I noticed her wide full lips, painted vermilion—they were luscious and innocent.

"Who you think you talking to?" Albert said. The words were tough; the sound he made wasn't.

"I'm talking to my son. You always gonna be my son—"

"You talking trash for the Man?" Albert nodded at me. They both glanced my way, but only briefly. They locked eyes again. "You won't fool him," Al continued. "You'll fool me sooner than you fool him. And that's hopeless, 'cause you ain't never gonna get a lie past me."

Clara's wide mouth was open, hands extended, fingers calling for him to come to her, tears streaming, "I'm not saying I did nothing. I'm not lying about it. I know what I did. Everybody knows what I did. There's nothing for me to get out of lying." Clara seemed to notice she was on her knees and that appeared to surprise her. She reached back to the step, and pulled herself on it. She gave us her profile as she confessed, "I know I'm bad. I know there's no excuse—"

"You're making excuses, that's all you're doing," Albert said, again talking tough, but his voice cracked on the last word.

"I'm just saying I love you, that's all."

"You're saying it wasn't you."

"Not the real me," Clara insisted. "I didn't touch you before I smoked." She looked past him to me and said, "Explain it to him. I'm not saying I didn't do it. I'm not saying it ain't my fault. I'm saying I love him and I wish to God it never happened." She had moved herself again, fresh tears running over the dried tracks.

"You say it was the drug," I commented.

"You know it makes you crazy," she argued with me. "You telling me crack don't fuck you up? That what you tell him? I'm the same person now? I ain't the same. That's a lie too. If you be telling him that, it's a lie."

"No!" Albert bellowed. Clara winced. I heard a footstep behind me that I assumed came from the escort. The bass of Albert's shout reverberated until there was complete silence, except the basketball, whining as it struck the concrete in a pounding rhythm. Only when his yell died away did he continue, in a deep tone of conviction, "You trying to say it was somebody else. That's all you trying to say. You trying to take away the only thing I got left. People feel sorry for me and they want to help me. That's the one fucking thing you gave me and now, you greedy bitch, you want that too." Albert stood up. He was already turning away, obviously scared he was about to lose control. He tossed back at her, "I hope you die." He walked past me, bumping my chair.

I got up to follow him. As I reached the escort, standing in the patio doorway, I turned back for another look at Clara. Albert's mother sat up straight on the step, eyes dead, her stained face tranquil. She stared at me as if we had never met.

I got home late. The van leaving for Dorrit House had been delayed. In fact, that was good luck. Obviously, Albert was very troubled by the encounter and, I felt, in grave danger. I had been lax in leaving so little time between these two momentous events in his life. I had misgivings when the shelter gave us Albert's departure day as his only opportunity to visit Clara; but he insisted he wanted to see her before leaving New York and I decided I couldn't object to that.

We talked in a coffee shop across the street from where the van was parked. Its driver was checking under the hood for the source of the engine's cough. Albert sat opposite me, ignoring his slice of cherry pie and glass of milk. He breathed shallowly, his shoulders were hunched, his arms half-raised, like a boxer in a fighting crouch. His barely suppressed rage was electric: the waiter didn't linger on Albert's side of the table. I noticed when he returned to the cash register, he kept an eye on us. I tried to get Albert to express himself directly. When that failed, I asked him to describe how he would like to kill his mother.

Most people, I suppose, would react with at least a show of disgust or horror at my question. Albert and I were old hands at these nightmare conversations. "I don't want to," he mumbled in his tight-lipped rage.

"Tell me how you're thinking of killing her. Strangling?"

"Talking ain't gonna stop me. You kidding yourself. I'm fucking kidding *myself*. I'm glad I'm going away. When I blow, I don't want it to fuck you and my buddies."

"I'm not trying to talk you out of killing, Albert. I know I can't stop you with talk. I want you to tell me what you're thinking so you'll feel better."

"You're full of shit."

"Are you gonna rape her first? Or just choke her?'

"Just let me go, Rafe. I'm gone, man. I'm really gone." Tears appeared, although he still had a warrior's pose.

"Choking her would stop the lying."

"I don't wanna choke her!" he shouted, much too loudly. I sensed the quiet gather around us. I didn't look, fearing eye contact with the waiter would imply I needed help.

I spoke low. "What then? A gun?"

"I'm gonna put Zebra down her throat. Okay? I'll stuff her ugly face. I'll choke her with my come."

"You can't kill her with sperm."

"No, I can't," he smiled. "You're right. That's just to warm up. I'll cut her belly open and take out her stomach. She'll be alive. That's how the Japs kill. They hand you your guts so's you can watch yourself die."

"Do you know why you'd like to kill her that way?"

"Oh fuck, man. It don't matter. I'm still gonna do it no matter what the fuck it a symbol of."

"You're going to make her pregnant. Make her heal your penis with her mouth, fill her with your sperm, make a new you in her belly and open her womb to bring him out alive. You're going to be reborn out of the monster and that will kill it."

Albert stared for a moment and then he shook his head sadly, pitying me. "Man, that is the dumbest shit you ever said. I mean, you've said some dumb shit, but that's the master dumbness."

"She won't die in the real world, Albert. She can only die in your head. That's where she lives. That's her home. That's where she gets her mail, that's where she cooks her meals and that's where she hurts you."

"Then I'll cut my brain out."

"With drugs? Like she did?"

"She smart. She ain't hurting. She got them turned around, living in that nice house, showing her stuff. She probably fucking all of 'em. She probably fucking that dyke who opened the door like she was a fucking African princess. Staring at me like it's me who did it to her. Women, man. They fucking hate us. Clara, she ain't a monster. She just did what they all want—cut our fucking dicks off."

He finally took a stab at his cherry pie, consuming almost a third of it in a single gulp. The danger hadn't passed, yet it lessened with each angry word. As long as he gave the twisting rage a voice, he wouldn't need to hurt somebody—at least not that day. For Albert, I'm afraid, most people would think all his victories to be no better than King Pyrrhus's.

It was late when I came home to find Diane in one of my sweatshirts (it reached to her bare knees) waving a pot holder at me with a smile. "I made dinner, can you believe it? A real dinner." Her smile disappeared. "What's wrong?"

I told her the story, sitting sadly on one of the two tall stools at our kitchen counter, too exhausted to take off my jacket, soaked through from my travels through the hot day.

"Sounds like he'll be okay," she said. She touched my hand, gently stroking it. "You did great work."

I had reported with little emotion, my voice fading from hoarseness. I felt that I wanted to cry and my legs hurt, aching as if I had run a marathon.

Diane came around and hugged me from behind. She kissed my neck and whispered in my ear. "It must have been hard on you, very hard."

"I'm scared," I said and I was crying.

Diane maneuvered to hug me face-to-face. I felt ready to let go of all the tears I had ever wanted to release, when she said, "Oh baby."

That reminded me of Clara and poisoned the endearment. My tears stopped. And I wondered, since I could be given pause by so slight a contact with Clara, how would Albert ever trust love?

"I love you," Diane was saying and I listened to her, just her, a woman

I could trust. She led me to the couch, urging me out of my damp blazer, and rested my head on her lap.

"I'm tired," I admitted, as if she had asked a question.

"Take a nap, my sweet man. Close your eyes."

"I want us to get married," I said and the tears were back. I sobbed into my sweatshirt, smelling bubble bath. "I want us to make a new baby," I said in a dopey child's voice.

Diane didn't ask what I meant by new baby. Probably she understood. Anyway, she answered in a confident voice, "We'll get married and make beautiful babies and be happy forever and ever."

I shut my eyes, felt the aches burn hotter and hotter. Soon I was asleep, dreaming of dark highways jammed with stalled vans, blocking the road. Men shouted at each other in Spanish, accusing and helpless. The women laughed, showing their breasts. And children, faces pressed against the windows, waved to me to go past them, onto the empty road ahead.

CHAPTER TWELVE

Happiness

ALBERT PHONED EVERY FRIDAY AFTERNOON, THE TIME DORRIT HOUSE SET aside for the boys to make a fifteen-minute call home. Within a few weeks, he sounded fine. He was enthusiastic about the sports program; he had made the freshman football squad and it surprised him that the courses weren't daunting. "Guess I didn't trust the tutors," he said, meaning the people we hired to bring the four boys at our clinic up to speed academically. He was also pleased that his schoolmates respected each other's privacy about their pasts. He could not avoid the common shower room; but no one joked or was revolted by his scarred body. The quarterback of his squad, a half-Chicano, half-Cherokee from the Midwest, looked at them openly and said, "You've been there, huh?"

Albert didn't know what he meant, but he said, "Yeah, I been there."

After that, they were friends. Albert was the coach's favorite running back on the freshman squad, and had been promised he would make varsity next year.

"Shit, you make the football team and they respect you," Albert said. "I gotta tell you, I love it. I put on the pads, hit everything in sight and you know what? I don't feel pain. I smash into guys, they roll on the ground yelling, but it's like nothing to me. And I'm beautiful in that uniform. You should see me, man. I look like a fucking god. You should see."

I promised I would.

"This is sublimation, right?" Diane said when I told her. "Not repression?"

"I think it's happiness for him, anyway."

"I hate football," she mumbled. "Couldn't he have joined the theater program?"

"Oh yeah. That would cheer him up. He could do Greek tragedy."

"Give me a break. I'm just saying, Al's really a very sweet boy."

"But it's not a sweet world," I said. I must have looked grim. Diane reached across—she was driving us from the clinic to meet Joseph and Harlan at a restaurant—and tweaked my nose. I jerked away, laughing.

"It's not a sweet world," she repeated in a mock-petulant tone.

"Well, it's not," I complained, still laughing.

"Thanks for the news flash."

"I love you," I said.

She smiled. "Oh!" she checked the rearview mirror, switched lanes to exit the West Side Highway at Seventy-ninth, and said, "I spoke to Jonas Friedman about your friend at Webster."

"Phil Samuel?"

"Yeah. Jonas says it's not true he's impartial. He's done some work for the defense in that, uh, Seattle case—the MacPherson Day Care?"

"He couldn't have. He's refused to testify about the mouse results for anybody."

"That's right, Jonas said he won't testify. But he does consult for them. He drills the lawyers in how to take psychologists apart on the stand."

I had stalled Phil about sending tapes of Diane's interviews of the Peterson case. He knew about them because I let slip we had interviews of children in the target age group before talking with Diane and then had to backtrack when I decided to respect her reservations. Instead, I sent along our guidelines for a course Ben Tomlinson teaches at John Jay University to police psychologists, detailing how to use dolls and minimize prompting, especially the silent encouragement of body language and vocal cues. Samuel called the day before, asking for the Peterson tapes again. I said I needed to discuss it with the therapist involved, then promptly, and conveniently, forgot to ask Diane.

Asking her now was unlikely to meet with a favorable reception. We were stopped at the light on Seventy-ninth. I didn't say anything until it had turned green and we were crossing Riverside, heading east.

"I don't believe it," I said.

"Jonas wouldn't make it up."

"The person who told Jonas might be mistaken."

"Samuel told Jonas himself!" Diane smiled. She was pleased, I suspected, because, in her mind, this relegated the mouse study to the enemy camp. "He bragged about it at a conference," Diane continued. "He told Jonas he knew the MacPherson case was crap and he wanted to help the defense."

"I'll call Phil tomorrow and ask."

"Why bother? If I were you, I wouldn't have anything to do with him."

"Because I want to know for myself." I took a breath before taking this leap, "And because I still want to send him the Peterson tapes."

Surprised, Diane turned to stare at me. She forgot she was driving, I guess, because she went through a red light; immediately there were screeching brakes, horns honking. She stopped short and we were stuck in the middle of the intersection, surrounded by bumpers and furious drivers. It took a minute to untangle the mess. No one had collided with us. We ignored the various raised middle fingers and shouting faces. Diane turned onto West End and pulled over next to a hydrant. She was breathing fast, frightened by the near collisions.

"You okay?" I asked.

She put a hand on her chest and took a deep breath. "You're not serious," she said after a while.

"Serious?"

"About sending the tapes?"

"I'll talk to Phil. If it's true that he's taking sides now, I won't send them, but if not, then I want him to have the Peterson tapes. I reviewed them—"

"You reviewed them!" Diane said, shocked.

"Yes. I looked at them and your technique was flawless. I'm proud of it, and if he's going to imitate anyone's procedures, I'd like it to be yours."

"My God," she whispered. Diane shook her head, removed her glasses, shut her eyes, rubbed them with her fingers, and finally put the wire-rimmed frames back on. She looked at me as if she might have something new to see. When it was still me, she shrugged her shoulders and sighed.

"What?" I asked.

"I can't get over how naive you are. It's—well, there's something charming about it. I guess it's part of why I love you, but, at the same time, I'm appalled. And a little scared."

"Scared of what?"

"I think it's dangerous to our work."

"Do you want me to drive?" I asked.

"Excuse me?"

"Well, if we're going to meet Joe and Harlan for dinner at seven, we'd better get moving. It could take half an hour to find a parking spot."

"We'll park in a lot. Okay?" Her irritation was escalating to anger.

"Okay." She sighed again, again shrugged her shoulders, and again shook her head in disapproval. I waited a moment, trying to sort out my feelings. Finally I said, "I don't think I'm naive. And, to be honest with you, I'd rather you didn't mix praise with insults."

"Huh?" Diane shifted to face me. "What does that mean?"

"Don't tell me I'm appallingly naive and that's part of my charm, but it's dangerous. If you're going to attack, at least have the guts to attack openly."

"You think I'm attacking you?" She was open-mouthed with shock. "What I just said, you consider an *attack*?"

"I apologize. My mistake. But you called me naive about a professional matter and that is, at the very least, a disparaging remark."

"Okay. I'm sorry. You're not naive. But I think you're crossing a line. You're definitely not respecting me as a professional."

"How?"

"It's my work. I don't want you to send tapes of my work to be used in any research."

"Even if that research is impartial?"

"I don't believe there's any way you can know that. And even if you find out he's open-minded right now, I don't believe there's any way you can predict how Samuel will eventually use those tapes. He might not be impartial six months from now. And also," she raised a finger to indicate this last item was crucial, "I don't believe any study of the fantasizing of normal children says a thing about the veracity of abused children. You know perfectly well we don't investigate charges of abuse without some sort of corroboration, either physical or emotional. We'd have ruled out all those kids in the mouse study after observing that their behavior was otherwise normal. And you also know—" she pointed at me as if I were a misbehaving toddler, "you, of all people, know that abused children fantasize in the opposite direction, not imagining worse abuse, but imagining love."

I looked at her scolding finger and waited until she noticed and lowered it. "Diane," I said quietly, "if you review what you just said carefully, I really believe you'll see a contradiction. If healthy children are shown to fantasize abuse easily then any accusation is suspect. The distinction you just drew actually makes Phil's study more urgent, not less so. Also, if he can prove that children easily fantasize non-sexual events, but can't so easily fantasize sexual abuse, then he'll strengthen the credibility of abused kids when they testify. You're also ignoring the fact that he will go forward with the pediatrician study whether we cooperate or not. Pretending he doesn't exist won't make him go away."

"You're not listening to me!"

During my long speech I allowed my eyes to drift away from her, watching the evening bustle of pedestrians on West End: going home with briefcases or groceries; children in disheveled school clothes, lugging backpacks; exhausted joggers returning from the park; the homeless standing at each corner, cups out, like toll booths. When I looked back to Diane at the noise of her distress, I was surprised to see just how upset she was. She scrunched up her freckled nose, lifting her glasses above the eyebrows, squinting at me, her mouth in a grimace of pain.

"What's wrong?" I said, meaning the pain.

"You're not listening to *me*," she pointed at her chest. "You're acting as if I'm some kind of employee, like I'm your graduate student. That's my work, goddammit! You have no right to make decisions about it. You have no right to give it away without my consent."

I hadn't looked at it in this light. Mostly because I didn't think of the tapes as belonging to either of us; rather, they belonged to the clinic, to our work; they should serve our colleagues, to help them help the children.

While I absorbed the difference in our perceptions, Diane faced forward and added to the windshield, "And I'm pissed off that you looked at them without asking me. It's like you opened my mail or something. Or read my diary. No," she looked at me again. "It's like you checked up on me. 'I'm very proud of your work,' " she quoted my compliment as if it were an insult. "Like you're my teacher giving me a grade."

"Okay," I said, more to myself than her. "Okay, I understand now. We're really not getting each other. I'm sorry that's the impression I gave you. Believe me, it's the opposite. At first I assumed you'd have no objection. When I found out you did, I held them back. And if you don't want me to send them, I won't. I don't think it's your work, however, any more than the tapes of Albert are my work. Our tapes belong to all of us and they belong to our profession."

"That's naive, Rafe," Diane said in a new tone. Solemn and blunt without an edge of hysteria and wounded feeling. "I know you're not naive, but to expect people not to feel proprietary and protective of their work is naive. I'm willing to believe you would react differently if *I* gave away your tapes, but then you're exceptional. Most people would feel what I'm feeling."

"Okay," I said. "All I want to say right now, what's really important right now, is for you to understand that I have nothing but the greatest respect for you and the work you've done and that I will never release your work, or even my work for that matter, without your blessing."

Diane smiled. "Now you're going too far." She leaned over and kissed me. "You can do what you like with your work." She settled back, obviously relieved, pleased with me. "But I don't think you should give anything to that snake. He's a liar and you can't trust him."

"I'm going to talk to him," I said. "Now, we'd better get going. We're late."

We arrived at a quarter after seven, fifteen minutes late. Joseph and Harlan weren't there, although they had picked the place—a chic, expensive and loud restaurant called Café Luxembourg. By then Diane and I had made up. I still didn't know what I should do about Phil. I was disturbed by the gossip Diane had told me and I was considering whether I ought to go to Webster University and talk to him face-to-face. If he had drifted into the child-can't-be-believed camp, then I wanted to remonstrate: the mouse scenario was significant, but inconclusive; should he proceed to the pediatrician test prejudging it, that could pollute the results, just as a therapist's prejudices might elicit false stories. At the same time, although I had resolved the misunderstanding between Diane and me, I was disturbed by an aspect of her behavior that I hadn't yet challenged, mostly because I didn't have the facts to do so. Since refusing to deal in any way with Samuel, she had been on the phone to others checking up on him. I worried this indicated that she had drifted into the child-must-be-believed camp. All accusations of child abuse can't be true, any more than the reverse. Part of our work, unfortunately, was mixed up with the law's tedious need to pretend there are immutable facts and just punishments. Diane, it seemed to me, was too defensive. No technique is perfect. As a scientist, her first reaction should have been more curiosity about Phil's work and less energy for debasing him.

At seven forty-five, Diane and I were still waiting at the bar when Harlan rushed in, pushing roughly through the crush of people between us. But upon arrival he stared as if we were a disappointment. "He's not here," he said, not a question.

"Joseph?" Diane asked.

"Shit," Harlan said. He had cut off his ponytail since we'd last seen him, and cut off most of his blond hair as well, so that it seemed to be a flat top, although it was too long to qualify in some places, and the sides were slicked down, not shortened. He wore his usual tight black jeans with no belt, a black silk shirt buttoned to the collar with no tie, and old-fashioned black high-top Converse sneakers—at least they had laces. He hadn't shaved in several days, but I could tell he wasn't starting a beard. His light blue eyes were so young and troubled they undercut the tough style of his outfit and grooming.

"What's wrong?" I asked.

"I don't know where he is," Harlan said, not angry, with resignation.

"You had a fight?" Diane asked.

Harlan looked around. "Is there a phone?" He made a move to push back toward the maître d'.

I grabbed his arm. "What's happened, Harlan? Tell me."

"I don't know." He lowered his head as if shamed.

"You mean, you're not supposed to say?"

"I don't know!" he complained. "I gotta go. Gotta find him." He pulled away, or tried to.

I held on to his arm. "Harlan, you know Joseph and I are old friends."

"I'm sorry. Go ahead and have dinner. If I find him, we'll—"

"Harlan, tell me what's going on. I want to help."

A woman beside us at the bar was listening. In those cramped quarters, she had little choice except to pretend deafness. Harlan glanced at her. Diane suggested we step outside.

The street was lively. We walked toward West End, into a warm September breeze blowing from the river. The strip of sky visible between its tall apartment buildings showed a brilliant sunset, the variety of color enhanced by the haze of pollution hanging over Jersey. Harlan told the story in a jumble, making it more complicated and longer than its simple facts. In June, he and Joseph had agreed to be tested for AIDS. Both had practiced safe sex for years, but they knew they were vulnerable anyway, given the long incubation period. Harlan kept his promise and his result was negative. Joseph, however, canceled his appointment and postponed several more. Harlan was amazed that a scientist could be so superstitious about knowledge when it came to his own body. "It's not like the test is gonna give you AIDS," Harlan argued. Finally, Harlan presented Joe with an unspecified ultimatum that succeeded. Joe had gone for the test three days ago. He was supposed to get the results that morning; he promised to call Harlan at home as soon as he heard. He hadn't phoned. When Harlan tried to reach him, he discovered Joseph had canceled a lecture, failed to show at his office at Columbia, and hadn't appeared in his lab all afternoon. He was supposed to come home to change to meet us for dinner and Joseph had failed to do that as well. Harlan took for granted that Joseph had been told he was HIV positive. That wasn't his immediate concern. He was scared Joseph had killed himself. He said they knew two men who committed suicide within a short time of hearing the news; Joseph, contrary to Harlan and their gay friends, had approved of their action, at least in casual conversation. "It's not suicide," Harlan remembered Joseph saying. "It's just a very effective painkiller."

That sounded like my mad, rational friend.

I asked about the hours of each canceled event and when his office or lab would be empty. Once it was clear that Joseph couldn't be alone in either place until now, I suggested Harlan call the office and lab again. He reached an answering machine at the office; no answer at the lab. He said a machine usually picked up at the lab.

"Can we get in?"

"Not if the door's locked."

"No, I mean the building."

"The guard knows me."

I said we should go there. Neither Harlan nor Diane questioned my choice. I told Diane she could go home. She said, "Are you crazy?"

She drove us to Columbia. Not to the scene of the demonstrations of the sixties (I was reminded of them anyway) but to an old building on Amsterdam and 118th. The floors aboveground were faculty housing, a normal apartment building. Through a side entrance, manned by a sleepy guard behind a folding bridge table, we took an elevator to three subterranean levels where there were laboratories and also, Harlan explained, the university's furniture storage.

The elevator was wide, an open cage, and moved slowly to gain power for hauling. We passed two landings lit by yellowing fluorescent bulbs.

"This is spooky," Diane said.

"I always say to Joey," Harlan commented in a wistful tone, as if he were talking about the very distant past, "this is where they keep Kennedy's brain."

I smiled. Diane said, "I feel dumb. What do you mean?"

The elevator shuddered as it stopped. "It's missing," Harlan said grimly.

I pulled the elevator gate open. "We'll find Joe and Kennedy's brain."

Harlan nodded, trying to smile. He moved on, turning to the right. The hall was gloomy, although wide. He passed two dented gray metal doors, stopping at the third.

I touched his shoulder as he reached for the knob. "Wait," I said. Maneuvering around Harlan, I put my ear to the door. I heard something, too faint a noise to identify.

"Somebody's in there," I whispered. "Would you pretend not to be here?"

"What?" Harlan was outraged.

"I think it's possible he'll answer if only *I* call out, as if I'm alone."

Harlan looked at Diane. She nodded encouragingly. He looked back at me. "That sucks," he said.

"Because I'm less important to him, I'm easier to face."

He shrugged. "Okay."

I knocked. Not loudly or insistently. Casual. I waited. No response from inside. "Joseph," I called out, loud, but only to be heard. "It's Rafe. I took a wild guess you'd be here."

I thought I heard a cough. Then nothing.

"Come on, Joe, it's spooky out here. You know me, I'm not gonna bug you. Just want to talk."

Nothing.

Harlan whispered, "Maybe the guard has a key."

I heard something shatter. Glass, I thought. Harlan reached for the knob. I caught his hand and shouted, "Joe! It's Rafe. I'm alone. Don't leave me out here. It's too fucking scary." I motioned for Harlan and Diane to move away. Diane urged Harlan down the hall and he allowed himself to be towed away.

I knocked again. "Come on, Joe, or I'm gonna get really scared."

Without a warning sound of feet or a lock turning, the door opened. Joseph faced me, bare-chested under a partially unzipped black nylon warm-up jacket. He stared at me through smudged eyeglasses as if I were an intrusive door-to-door salesman. "How did you get here?"

"Harlan brought me."

Alarm. The door began to close. "He's here?"

"No." I stepped in, forcing Joe to move back. "Just me." I shut the door without locking it. I blinked at the bright, expensively furnished place, as different from the gloomy hall as possible. It consisted of two large rooms, the first an office, jammed with desks, computers, printers, file cabinets and, I noticed, an elaborate stereo system. Everything was well-ordered, the kind of neatness I associated with Joseph's mother's housekeeping. The partition to the other room was mostly glass, as was the door. There light also flooded a big room, dominated by row after row of chemistry tables, covered by microscopes and big machines I couldn't recognize, as well as racks of beakers. In the lab, things were jammed together and, although it might be as organized as the first room, my eye couldn't tell if that were so—it appeared as a jumble of in-comprehensible technology.

"I don't have to explain?" Joe said quietly.

"It's definite?" I asked.

"Oh, he'll do another, just for form's sake. They're pretty sloppy some-times, but," Joe grinned, "what would you think if I told you I expected a different result? Denial, denial, denial." The grin disappeared. "You want to see something funny?" Joe opened a filing cabinet, flipped con-fidently through it, came out with a folder, and removed a letter. He gave it to me.

I sat on a desk and read. The letter was from a prominent AIDS re-searcher, apparently also an acquaintance, upbraiding Joseph for ignoring AIDS in his work. He pleaded with him at least to help raise money, if not devote himself to the search for a cure. The letter wasn't formal: he accused Joseph of being a self-hating gay man, frightened of exposure if he associ-ated himself with AIDS; he begged Joseph to accept his identity and be-come an inspiring scientific gay leader. I checked the date: two years ago.

"Such bullshit," Joseph said when I finished. "I was scared, that's all. Like a superstitious Jew from the shtetel. Close your eyes and it'll go away."

"I thought you didn't want to come out because of your mother."

"That's everybody's excuse." I gave him the letter back. He made sure it lay flat in the folder. He returned the document to its rightful place solemnly, pushing the cabinet shut slowly. "He wouldn't respect that. And, tell you the truth, even if Mom died I don't think I'd," he added mockingly, " 'come out.' " He pushed the cabinet flush with a bang of emphasis. "Why the fuck should I have to announce my sexuality? Do you have to announce you're heterosexual? Do you come with any warn-ing labels? Do you tell your patients your mother committed suicide?" I must have shown a pained reaction. He put his small hands out, saying, "I'm sorry. There's no comparison." Joseph lowered his head. I noticed his baldness had progressed a lot, leaving him little more than a laurel. He raised his head abruptly and squealed, "I just don't care about viruses! They're not interesting. Not compared to the brain." He wandered away from me, pleading to his file, "I wanted to find out how *we* work, all of us, how we're different from the animals, not how a fucking disease works. Who wants to study the Nazis when you can study Einstein?" Joseph walked into the second room and talked to the lab. "What kind of scientist drops everything because something is killing the people he wants to fuck?" He passed down a row of tables, turned and sat at a corner. My vision was partially blocked by a row of big white machines. I heard something crunch and wondered if he were eating potato chips.

I followed him in, stopping a few feet from his seat. The area around him was covered with glass shards, apparently from broken beakers. There was a tart odor I worried about, being ignorant. Had he allowed something toxic free?

"Why am I gay?" Joseph asked me with the innocence of a child.

I smiled.

"No, I'm serious. What's the current psychobabble? You know where we're at—is the hypothalamus smaller, is it bigger, is it pink? Are we genetically encoded? Can we find the address? I never really gave a shit. Small potatoes. If I found the answer to how this works," he jabbed at his head, "then we know everything." He reached into one of the white machines and came out with a beaker, holding it gingerly by its curved lips. He let go. It smashed on the floor. I winced, afraid of flying glass. "I'm not gonna know now, even if it's possible to know. Maybe it's not for us to see. Maybe the brain is the face of God. So, tell me, please tell me, why am I a faggot?"

"Are you destroying important work?" I asked.

"Of course not. This is childish," he gestured to the circle of broken glass. "There are records of everything. It can all be done again. I'm being a great big baby." He lifted another beaker and released. After the crash, he insisted, "Tell me. You've always been real polite about it. Why do I like men? 'Cause Mom is so anal? 'Cause Dad used to kiss me on the lips? 'Cause she used a rectal thermometer until I was thirteen?"

I laughed. "Well, they're more accurate, aren't they?"

"I really don't want to die," Joseph said, eyes filling suddenly. "You know, I thought I was gonna be the exception."

"Harlan said you were both careful."

"No, not the exception to AIDS. I thought I was going to be the first person to live forever." He reached under his glasses to wipe away tears, although none had fallen.

"Joe, just so that I'm sure of what's going on, you don't have full-blown AIDS, do you?"

"Ain't I lucky?"

"You could live for a very long time. They might find a maintenance cure, like insulin. Supposedly—"

Joseph pushed the white machine off the table. I think it sparked when it hit. Many beakers fell and the noise was terrific. A small cloud of smoke rose and dissipated quickly.

"Denial, denial, denial!" Joseph shouted. Screamed actually, out of control.

I let the noise settle. When Joe was finished yelling, he became transfixed by something behind me. I glanced back. Harlan stood at the entrance to the lab. Diane lingered in the office. The lovers looked deeply at each other: Harlan's light blue eyes sweet and pleading; Joseph's small and dark behind his dirty glasses; they seemed cold and unsympathetic. Did he blame Harlan? How could he? Was he angry that Harlan had tested negative? Was the rage general and merely being displayed? After a long moment of this mute exchange, Joseph returned to me and asked, "Come on. Enough politeness. Tell me why. For once, I won't give you an argument."

I stood up. "I'll let you two—"

"No!" Joseph banged the table with his fist. It made no sound and must have hurt. "Tell me. I really want to hear." His eyes had welled up again. "Come on, Rafe. It's a simple question. I'm gonna die 'cause I like it up the ass. I deserve some kind of answer, don't I?"

"There are a lot of different ideas—"

"I want *your* answer. Don't bullshit me. I don't give a fuck about other people's theories." Joseph lowered his head again, as if he were praying to Mecca. "Please," he whispered. "Say something I can think about. Something I can believe. Something I can make fun of." He seemed to be crying, although when he raised his head, no tears had dropped from his full eyes. "Give me something to think about, Rafe."

"I think it's very specific, Joe. I don't believe in general theories." Harlan had gradually moved closer, only a foot or so behind me. I turned to go; allow him to take my place.

"Well, you know a lot about my fucking specifics," Joe said. "Don't turn away from me." I faced him, side by side with Harlan. "So why me?" Joe insisted. "I never wanted women. Not once. I was born this way. I don't remember ever having a choice. That's the way it feels for me. But you think that's crap, right? It's 'cause Mom didn't let me sit on the furniture, 'cause she wouldn't let me have sleepovers with my buddies, 'cause she wouldn't leave me alone, not for one fucking minute." He really began crying now, head forward, propped up by his fingers, speaking to the hard surface of the lab table. Harlan pushed past me and bent over Joe, rubbing his back and shoulders tenderly, kissing his neck, his cheek, his temple.

I turned to go.

"No!" Joe shouted. Looking back, I saw Harlan had stepped away, off to the left. My friend was on his feet, yelling at me. "Come on! Give me something."

Harlan, Diane and Joseph were positioned on three sides of me, a triangle that felt like an ambush. I couldn't hold down my sadness at my friend's condition much longer. I knew right away what his death would mean to me. He was the last connection to my childhood, the last person who knew me when I felt normal: the son of loving, energetic parents, part of a world that made sense.

"Remember *Portnoy's Complaint?*" I said and giggled nervously. I had lost control.

Joseph lifted his glasses to wipe his wet face. "What?" he mumbled.

"Remember how much you liked it? You said it was your autobiography."

Joe's mouth hung open stupidly as he nodded.

"Philip Roth fucks women. He *loves* fucking women. Maybe he's really gay and you're really heterosexual. It doesn't matter, Joseph. Theory is garbage. Ideas are white noise." I smiled and opened my hands to the triangle of questions, gesturing to each, showing them that's all I had to offer. They didn't seem satisfied. I let my arms go wide and then slapped my chest hard with my palms, shouting, "We live here! Here! In our bodies."

Harlan returned to Joseph's side, putting an arm around his small lover's shoulders. They looked at me as if I were a performer and they hadn't made up their minds if they were enjoying the show.

"You're not dying because you're gay. And I won't tell you why you're gay. I know, but I'm not gonna tell you. Why not? Because you're happy about it. You've always been happy about it. We're not supposed to look at happiness, Joseph. It's the face of God."

He said something. So did Diane. I don't remember what. I think I ended up crying more than Joseph, I'm not sure. I do remember that he teased me about it.

CHAPTER THIRTEEN

Adjustment

PHIL SAMUEL CAME TO NEW YORK ON OTHER BUSINESS. HE SUGGESTED we meet for breakfast in Greenwich Village at Elephant & Castle, a restaurant whose clientele, wobbly wood tables, piped-in classical music, and menu of spinach omelets, croissants, and espresso provides the sort of atmosphere a tourist would expect from the neighborhood's bohemian reputation. Actually, it's a dowdy relic of the sixties, a haven for the now decidedly bourgeois population of aging gays, radicals and artists who live in the expensive town houses nearby. Phil beamed at our surroundings. He was dressed in a white Brooks Brothers button-down shirt, a single-breasted blue blazer that was an inch too short in the sleeves and beige corduroys smoothed at the knees.

After we ordered, he said, "I love New York. My wife and I came here for breakfast on our honeymoon." He leaned forward to ask in a whisper about our waitress, "Is that a woman?" Her skinny body was covered in black, her head shaved to the nubs of a crew cut, and a diamond was embedded in her right nostril.

"Yes," I said.

"Lesbian?" he asked, eyes restless, scanning the patrons.

"Maybe," I said. "But not necessarily. Fifteen years from now she could be living in Scarsdale raising three kids."

He laughed heartily.

"Although," I added, "even raising kids in Scarsdale, she might still be a lesbian."

"Right!" he said and laughed again. Our waitress reappeared. She plunked our coffees down with a sullen attitude, as if we were her boring male relatives and Mom had nagged her into helping out. "Thank you," he said, trying to be friendly.

"Un huh," she said and wandered off.

"Don't the kids at Webster dress like that?" I asked.

"Not that far-out."

"Far-out," I said.

"Groovy," he said and laughed again.

I asked after his family. Listening to him talk cheerfully about how he strained his back roller-blading with his seven-year-old daughter, or describe rising at dawn to take his nine-year-old son for hockey practice, I both envied him and felt I couldn't understand him. This was a contented man, rounded so as not to bruise on the world's sharp corners. What made him want to be a psychologist, albeit a researcher, specializing in child abuse? Was Diane right not to trust this kind of removed scientist, living in suburban academia? Was this man driven to find proof that children were unreliable witnesses to abuse because, for him, the thought of adults savagely tormenting children was unthinkable, as difficult to imagine as the gender of our waitress? And what did it say about me that a paradigm of normality seemed as odd—and as unlikely—as a little green man from Mars?

I asked whether he had helped the defense in the MacPherson case, as Diane's friend Jonas claimed.

"They saw the mouse study and asked me to testify. Tell you the truth, the case is so bad, I almost did. But I couldn't do it in good conscience. The mouse study doesn't prove anything about testimony of sexual abuse. Who told you they contacted me?"

"You did. You told Jonas, and he told a colleague who told me."

"No kidding. I was only teasing Jonas. I wanted to get under his skin. He attacked the mouse study at the San Francisco conference. Don't tell me he took me seriously."

"Apparently." Gossip among professionals is always suspect and I decided not to press this point. Anyway, I hadn't trusted Diane's information.

"I was stunned by the results," he said when I brought up my reaction to the mouse study and the question at hand—whether I would give him the videotape of Diane's work with the Peterson girls. I told him no on the phone; I reassured Diane that my purpose in seeing Phil was to sound him out. She hadn't convinced me that her work with the Peterson girls was her private property and should be withheld from science at her whim. I agreed to see Phil to give him a chance to convince me of his objectivity (relatively speaking, of course); then I could give him the video with a clear conscience, although I would be risking a bitter quarrel with Diane. That was the dare. Could I oppose her when I knew disobedience might destroy our relationship, a relationship I valued more and more every day? The old Rafe (or should I say the young Rafe?) had been roused from his long sleep and now he whispered that the way out was to be secretive, to slip the tape to Phil without telling Diane, and accomplish both objectives, the testing of our methods and the preservation of my love.

"You expected the kids not to make up stories?" I asked.

"No. Kids are always making up stuff. I expected them to be sloppy. You know, not consistent from one account to another. Fantasy becoming reality, or really memory—that I didn't expect."

"Maybe they're just being stubborn."

Phil frowned and shook his head. "With all us grown-ups telling them it's okay to admit they made it up? No punishment, no questions asked? What's to be stubborn about?"

"Perhaps they're being stubborn about their pride in themselves, in the integrity of their identities. I think children care much more about their dignity than truthfulness. Truth doesn't count for much in their world. In their world, the hypocrites are in charge."

"What?" Phil had taken a bite of his croissant. Flakes lingered on his lips. He wiped his mouth with a napkin, swallowed and said, "You're not going in for that."

"Going in for what?"

"You know, that old sixties nonsense—the world's corrupt so no one can make rules. Parents have to set limits. These kids come from good homes. Consistent parenting. Reasons always given. They aren't being raised by hypocrites."

"Really? Then they're truly exceptional. Hypocrisy is the logic of parenthood."

"Come on. What the hell does that mean? That's an irresponsible statement."

"Phil, it's merely an observation. Adults tell what we call white lies or break trivial rules at least several times a day in front of their children. The phone rings. Don't say I'm here, you shout to your spouse. You order them not to cross against a red light, but you do it when you're in a hurry. They overhear you complain bitterly about your in-laws and you don't let them show even a flicker of irritation at Thanksgiving. You complain your boss is an idiot, but they can't say a word against their teachers—"

Phil cut me off. "That's a ridiculous comparison. The lie about the mouse is elaborate and has no value. Children understand the difference between lies of convenience and make-believe."

"I wasn't making a comparison, Phil. I was merely saying that truthfulness is not highly valued by children. And there *is* a motive for the mouse lie. They're preserving their right to be believed, a very important thing to establish once a child is going to school and has a life outside the home. Very few parents react to controversies over fact between their child and the outside world with complete faith in their child's version. And yet children want their parents, of all people, to have blind faith in their veracity. Admit you lied about the mouse and you might not be believed ever again."

Phil frowned, pushed his plate away—there was only a hard nub of croissant left—wiped his mouth, took a sip of coffee, and stared down at the table. He was thinking it over—a hopeful sign. "I don't know . . . I'm not sure I buy it. Anyway, it's not subject to proof. It's in the realm of speculation and I don't—I've never had much faith in pure theory."

"It's no more of a theory, Phil, than your study's conclusion."

He sat up straight and stared at the top of my head. "Our conclusion is based on the data."

"No, there's a leap of faith, namely that children don't know the difference between fantasy and reality, that it isn't a willful lie. And you're not consistent, Phil. A moment ago you said children know the difference between lies of convenience and make-believe. Your mouse study created an unrealistic situation: there was no penalty for telling a lie. Phil, how many adults do you think would tell the truth if there was no consequence to being caught? Why do we have perjury laws? When you first brought the kids in to be asked questions, were they impressed with the need to be honest? Were they sworn in? No, a friendly stranger was playing a game, the kind of conversational inquisition that children experience every day, that they frequently spice up with their fluid imagination. Then, they're doubted. Suddenly the rules have changed. Accuracy and truth are paramount."

"But that's the point. That's how we interrogate children about child abuse. We don't bring them to a police station or make them swear on a Bible."

"Sure, but we don't say we're merely asking some questions to while away an afternoon. Disturbed kids are brought in to see doctors to help make them better: it's not a casual situation from the start. And we don't ask questions casually, giving no more weight to whether an adult played with their genitals than to whether they've ever been to a baseball game. Children are not that insensitive to their surroundings. They know saying their father sodomized them is of a different order of importance than whether they accuse a make-believe mouse of biting them."

"That's exactly why we're doing the pediatrician study. That's exactly why I need to copy you technique. I need to test the real situation."

Now he got me thinking. I looked into his eyes, earnestly searching mine, and felt convinced of his sincerity.

He pressed me. "Look, I haven't come to any conclusions. It's easy for a kid to make up a story about a mouse. They've got all the information they need for the invention. I don't see how a kid who's never been molested could know how to make it up. But we need to do a study to confirm that, or the mouse results will seem to prove kids aren't reliable."

"No one's reliable, Phil. That's the point. Anyone, at any age, can tell a willful lie."

"*Too* unreliable. I think you're splitting hairs, I really do. Anyway, if we follow your clinic's technique you should have nothing to be afraid of."

I stared at the empty chair beside me. On it, inside a manila envelope, was a duplicate of the tape he wanted. I hadn't brought it prepared to be convinced. At least, I told myself that. I tasted the old fear and weakness in my belly, the suspicious lonely adolescent revisited: unsure of anyone's version of the truth, frightened to pick a side, wanting to know and yet scared of the answer.

I made him repeat his promises. He would view the tape twice that evening, make thorough notes of Diane's technique, and drop it off at my apartment on his way out of town the following morning. No one would know. It would be our secret.

But deceiving Diane was worrisome; and of course, as the cliché tells us, it is a tangled web. I was caught in it immediately, on my way into the clinic. Diane followed me into my office to ask how the breakfast had gone and I had to make up a different ending to the meeting. Even so, the partial truth I told—that I was convinced of Phil's sincerity—provoked a reproof. "He's bullshitting you," she said. "He says he's objective and when his study is done, he'll point to his skewed results as the reason he's changed his mind."

"I don't believe that," I said and yet her conviction left me in doubt. Underneath, despite layers of education, training, and the scars of experience, was I too trusting: a simpleminded child in a world of devious adults?

Anyway, it was done. The video was returned as promised with thanks and a note that he was impressed by the technique.

In the months that followed things went well at the clinic; the severe cases we took into round-the-clock care made excellent progress. We were losing money, but not so much that I couldn't make up for the deficit. I signed a contract to write a book about our in-residence therapy of disturbed children that would cover the losses for two years. Reports from and about Albert were encouraging. His grades were good—B's—and he had made many friends at Dorrit House. Diane's involvement in the Peterson case finished with a settlement that forbade visitation to the grandparents and included their paying for ongoing therapy for the girls. (Because they had moved, Diane was not going to be their therapist.) The grandfather refused treatment for himself, in spite of the fact that if he had agreed there was a promise that the visitation ban might be lifted.

In February of 1990, after a five-month silence, Gene called. He was ebullient. Black Dragon was finished. He and Halley—he had to remind me she was Stick's daughter—were presenting it at the Annual Computer Convention in a few days. Could he come see me before he left?

I offered the end of that day, six o'clock. He arrived fifteen minutes late—an unprecedented event. I was about to leave, convinced his tardiness meant an emergency cancellation.

"Wow, you've sure made a lot of changes," he commented. He could have been speaking about himself. He was dressed differently, in pleated rust corduroys with wide wales and cuffs, a black turtleneck, and an expensive-looking jacket, also black, yet decorated with subtle flecks of white. His shoes were fashionable too, black oxfords with orange stitching and thick soles. Though each item, taken separately, was eclectic, the whole came together and made Gene appear at once an academic and a retired millionaire. His hair style had also changed—the thick locks were trimmed and moussed straight back, showing off his high forehead, surprisingly small delicate ears and lending an impression of forcefulness that was helped by the direct look in his eyes. He hadn't entirely overcome his tendency to avoid contact, but his glances were surveys, rather than shy downward demurrals. "Looks like you're running a hotel."

"We house some patients here now and we keep staff overnight as well—hence the dorm."

"Oh . . ." he nodded and continued to look boldly at his surroundings, including me, although he didn't linger. His legs were active, bouncing up and down; his fingers were restless also, intertwining, cracking, then drumming on his knees.

"You're late, Gene."

"I know, I'm sorry. But there was some last-minute stuff at the office and I rushed over, thinking I could just make it. When I realized I was going to be late, I thought about calling from the car, but I didn't have your number and I couldn't remember it. Isn't that weird? That means something, right?"

"You've never been late before, Gene."

"And that means something too, right?"

"Probably."

"Yeah, it definitely means something, because in the past I would have been so worried about getting here on time, I would have left ridiculously early and they wouldn't have found me with their so-called emergency."

"It wasn't an emergency?"

"Well, now that I'm a VP in charge of R&D . . ." Gene smiled and spread his arms, asking for applause.

"Congratulations."

"They need me round the clock. You know how it is. *You* run a big organization."

"Is that why you have a car phone now?"

"You don't miss a trick. I've got a cellular and a beeper. Don't ask me why I need both. Well, to save on the batteries. Anyway, since I've lost so much time, I'd better get right to the point. I think I'm in love."

He was moving so fast I wanted to laugh. I was tempted to ask if he was on amphetamines. That sarcastic thought provoked a real suspicion. "Are you taking Prozac?" I asked.

"What?" Gene shook his head as if waking himself. "What did you say?"

"Are you taking Prozac?"

"No. I mean, I don't think I am. Isn't Prozac some kind of psychiatric drug?" I nodded. "God, that is a strange thing for you to say. No, I'm in love, that's what I'm on. Or don't you believe in love?"

"I think it was you who said you don't believe in love."

"Did I? Well, that's because I didn't know what love is. Man, it's great. It's the best."

"You're having an affair with Halley?"

"No. I mean, not yet— Hey, you knew." Gene pointed at me, like an athlete signaling to a teammate that he had scored a big basket. I can't begin to express my surprise at this gesture: in the context of his hampered body language during our sessions over a thirteen-year span, the movement was a rude obscenity. "I've talked to you about her?" he asked.

"Not really. But when you called, you went out of your way to say she's going to the convention and then you come in saying you're in love. Even Dr. Watson could figure that out."

"Jesus. Yeah, I'm worried it's too obvious. Cathy is definitely suspicious."

"Suspicious of what?"

"Of me and Halley."

"I thought you said you weren't having an affair."

"I kissed her," he said in a rush, an embarrassed confession; and yet with a sly, proud grin.

"You kissed her. And what did she do?" I gestured for him to elaborate.

"Well, she didn't slap me." He breathed in deeply and held it.

"Did you expect her to?"

He frowned at me. Finally he released the air. "No. I don't know. I was scared to touch her. I'd been thinking about doing it for weeks. I was watching her lips while she talked about the convention . . . They're big, you know, especially when she puts on a lot of lipstick. I wasn't even sure if I thought they were beautiful. But I couldn't keep my eyes off them. And I lost track of what she was saying. She stopped talking. She looked at me with a smile, as if she knew what I was thinking, and said, 'Hello? Are you there?' And I didn't care about anything. Not Cathy, or little Pete. Or even me. I don't even remember deciding to kiss her. Suddenly, I was just doing it. Right there in the new conference room. Right next to a wall of glass. Anyone in the parking lot could have seen us. I didn't even think about that."

He was entranced by the memory. I waited while he replayed the kiss, sighing softly, crossing his legs, briefly touching his lips as if hers were still lingering. "She kissed me back," he said at last. "You know, she responded. Her mouth opened—" he caught himself and laughed. "I really opened wide. It was like being in high school—you know, French kissing."

"Sounds like fun."

"It was. It was great." He looked at me, straight out, unafraid and defenseless, a curious child. "Am I terrible?"

"For enjoying a kiss?"

"Come on. You know where this is going. Isn't adultery a mortal sin?"

"I'm sorry, Gene. I'm not a priest."

"What happens if I fall in love?"

"You said you are in love."

"I'm infatuated. What happens if we do it and she still wants me?"

"I don't know. I'm not a soothsayer either. Anyway, isn't that the wrong question? What happens if you do it and you still want her?"

"I don't think I'll stop at anything. I don't think even Petey would stop me."

"What has Pete got to do with it?"

"Huh? Come on, aren't you carrying this shrink act too far? Pete's got everything to do with why I'm married."

"Not Cathy?"

"I'm not still married because of my great marriage, that's for sure."

"You'd leave if it weren't for Pete?"

"You know that."

But I didn't. I knew nothing of the kind. "Gene, what are we doing?"

His legs were stilled. His newly confident eyes lowered. "What?"

"Are we resuming therapy? Are you planning to come here regularly?"

"Can't I?" he asked with the old, familiar plaintiveness.

"Do you want to?"

"I'm in a crisis."

"Does that mean you want to?"

"I should, shouldn't I?"

"Do you want to?"

"Yes!" His irritation slipped out, and his eyes dropped to the floor.

"Your schedule allows it?"

"Well, Dragon's done and . . ." He stopped and drifted off into deep thought.

I waited and had my own reverie. I didn't want to resume our sessions. Gene didn't need my service. Sure, he could use a good therapist—or even a mediocre one—to sort out his marriage conflicts; so could Cathy, for that matter. But this person sitting opposite was a well man in relative terms. To be blunt: I hadn't become a psychiatrist to treat husbands who longed for sex with younger, more beautiful women than their wives, who stayed in marriages believing it was for the sake of their children. These might be unattractive, reprehensible feelings, but they don't qualify as mental illness. And be honest, I argued to myself, you don't want him as a patient. You didn't miss these sessions.

"I'm scared," Gene said softly. He lifted himself, straightening in the chair, and lifted his eyes as well, to look at me sadly.

"Of what?" I asked, also softly.

"I feel like I'm out of control."

"You are."

His mouth opened, ready to answer, and then shut.

"You've fought all your life to control yourself. To control your anger, to control your natural desire to be recognized for your work, to be satisfied romantically, to be loved and appreciated. You controlled yourself as a child because your parents wouldn't let you *be* uncontrolled. You controlled yourself as a husband because you were frightened Cathy wouldn't love you if you were sexual. You controlled yourself with Stick because you were afraid he wouldn't accept you as ambitious. You're letting go of all that control. You've been gradually letting go for a couple of years, and now you're almost free."

"So why am I scared?"

"It's called neurosis. It's an irrational fear, but of course it isn't irrational to you. You were more frightened of what would happen if you announced your desires to people, than of not getting what you want. It doesn't make common sense, since you have nothing to lose by asking for what you want if the alternative is not to ask at all. The worst that can happen by asking is that someone will say no. But it made sense to you because it isn't the no that you're afraid of."

Gene smiled to himself. He asked in a low voice, "What am I afraid of?"

"You're afraid of yourself. Of how you'll feel when you ask and are told no. You're afraid of your anger and your sadness at rejection. And you're also afraid of how you'll feel if you ask and are told yes. By not trying, you're able never to fail. You asked Stick for more responsibility and he's given it to you. What if you fail? By not asking you were avoiding test-ing yourself. It made you miserable, but it kept you safe. By not asking Cathy to love you, you were lonely, but at least you didn't risk hearing she doesn't. By not making yourself available to other women you pro-tected yourself from falling in love. There's a logic to neurosis and it's been your friend since you were a child, since that day you threw up on the gallery owner's book, and probably long before that, when you found your parents making love."

"What do you mean?"

"Remember? When you walked in on them making love?"

"Of course I remember. But what do you mean about—? I *mean*," he laughed, "what did it mean to me?"

"They were embarrassed and upset—"

Gene interrupted. "Dad yelled, right?"

"That's what you told me."

"And Mom scolded me the next morning. Told me never to come in without knocking."

"And why did you go to their room?"

"I needed something, right? Medicine? Wasn't I sick?"

"That's not what you told me years ago."

"What did I say?"

"You had a dream about a spider. You woke up. You were alone. It was dark." I waited.

"I was scared," he said.

"You didn't say you were scared. Maybe you were. But you said you were lonely and you wanted company."

Tears formed. He swallowed, squeezed his eyes shut and rubbed them with the tips of his fingers to conceal his emotion. When he uncovered, he nodded and looked grim, but composed. "That's right."

"You felt alone," I said. "And after they kicked you out, you felt their love for you was a sham, that nobody needed you, that the world was having a party, a secret passionate celebration, to which you were not in-vited."

"It can't be that simple," Gene said.

How curious and yet proud is the human animal: looking for answers that, when found, are a disappointment. "I don't think it's simple, Gene. It's quite complicated. I don't mean that if all that had ever happened to you was one incident of interrupting your parents making love, you would be the same person. I don't even mean that everyone would have reacted the way you did. You have a natural timidity, a gentleness that is easily shocked and offended. It's made you a good father and a loyal employee. It made you a loving son, a very loving son to parents who, frankly, weren't all that loving to you. And it wasn't just those two incidents. There were hundreds of them, reinforcing each other. We've just isolated the archetypes, symbols of your life experience. And they didn't really stop you. Here you are, working to change. You've been brave. Much braver than people who have no trouble shouting for what they want, who can hardly keep still for one second if they aren't satisfied."

Gene put a hand on his moussed hair. He touched the smooth surface, combing back what was already combed. The gesture, a new one, gave an impression of self-containment, of calmness. When it was completed, he said quietly, "Thank you."

"So," I smiled at him. "What are we doing, Gene? Are we resuming therapy?"

"I want to stop." He said this easily and simply and then seemed to hold his breath with dread anticipation, as if the ceiling might collapse on him. I nodded and waited. He exhaled. "But I'm scared to." He cleared his throat. "You tell me. Do I need this?"

"People always need to talk honestly with someone about their life. Before this hiatus that's how you used our sessions. Frankly, I can't spare the time for that. I'm under a lot of pressure at the clinic and I'm working on a new book. I care about you, Gene, and I want things to go well for you. I'd like you to resolve the problems in your marriage, one way or the other. I hope you'll continue to insist on what's due you at work and keep on challenging yourself. But you're acting on those desires. If anything goes wrong, if you need to talk about something in particular, I'm here, any hour of the day or night. I believe we should have a few more sessions, just to wind down. If you'd like to continue seeing someone regularly I can recommend—"

"No," he interrupted, gently but firmly. "You're right. It's time to grow up. I should be out there on my own." We agreed to have three more sessions and then terminate.

I saw him next after the Computer Show. Black Dragon was well-received. Orders were not what they had hoped; but they weren't for their rivals either. The recession was hitting computers hard. The machine was a technical triumph, however, and that was to Gene's credit. He and Halley made love every night during the trip. Gene said it was the most passionate and exciting sex of his life. He found her fascinating and spent most of the session telling me stories about her life: her brief career in Hollywood trying to be an actress got some attention but he mostly talked about a trauma that particularly fascinated Gene—the death of her younger brother five years ago in a skiing accident. He knew about it vaguely because Stick took a week's leave for the funeral, although Copley had never discussed the tragedy with Gene. He was moved by her love for her brother and her grief. She told Gene he was the only person she had been able to talk to about her brother's death. She praised him for his empathy and said he was the first man who truly understood her. She openly admitted she wanted him to leave his wife and marry her. Halley said she was so in love that she would accept him on any terms, but she hoped for a full commitment.

He went home confidently, albeit with a grim determination, prepared to confront Cathy with the truth. He didn't go through with it, however. He claimed he was thwarted by the surprising warmth of her welcome home. She didn't greet him with her typical petulance. She hugged him tight and kissed him passionately while Pete tugged at them, until they all toppled to the floor. Gene's little boy crawled over him while Cathy snuggled both of them. She had cooked an elaborate dinner, complete with fresh flowers and candles for the table; Petey had built a Lego model of Black Dragon. Gene was pleased and embarrassed by his predicament. Of course, he expressed the appropriate emotions: guilt that Halley loved him; shame that he was betraying Cathy; fear that he was hurting Pete. But it wasn't hard to crack the thin shell of these civilized formalities and get to the yolk of his true reaction: glee that there were two women who wanted him; relief that he was, after all, a desirable and successful man.

"What do I do?" he asked me.

"I don't know, Gene. I know you don't believe me, but I'm really not a priest. It's up to you to decide what's right and what's wrong. I'm sure you remember what you thought about your father when you found out he had been having an affair all those years."

"Yeah," he agreed, for the first time keen guilt worrying his cheerful face. "He just made it worse."

"But you're not your father, right?"

"Right."

"What's right and what's wrong is up to you, Gene. My hope is that you will act on *your* feelings, not what you imagine someone else wants you to do."

[I assume some of my lay readers may be shocked by my casual reaction to Gene's affair. I'm aware from television talk shows and popular psychology books that in the United States confusion has arisen between what is mental health and what is moral behavior. There is also a humorless lack of awareness of moral relativism. In France, if Gene made Halley his mistress, he would not be frowned on by society unless he was so cruel as to rub it in Cathy's face. In the U.S., the deception itself is often regarded as tantamount to illness and he would be considered noble if he walked in the door, told Cathy he had fallen in love with another woman and wanted a divorce. I'm sorry that so many popular psychologists encourage confusion about the role of therapy: a judgment of Gene's affair, except insofar as the situation was generated by years of emotional and sexual passivity, is a matter for social mores or religious convictions. As I've noted before, my job was to introduce Gene to his real self, not to shape that self to suit my notion of good behavior. I assume there are some professionals reading this who would interpret Gene presenting a crisis in his marriage two sessions prior to termination as a way of prolonging therapy—in short, a cry for more help. I admit I believed then that there was an element in his behavior of creating material for me, providing an event he could claim was overwhelming and therefore justify a continuing dependence on our sessions. Indeed, this is part of the reason I reacted casually. It was time for Gene to deal with his life without a pretense that he wasn't fit for the job. The transference had reappeared: I was the last barrier he couldn't climb comfortably, the last excuse not to act on his feelings. Bear in mind, if Gene got himself into real trouble, I knew he could, and moreover, *would* come to me. Should he divorce Cathy and need support, I would supply it or find it, but I wasn't going to hold my breath waiting for that drama. To put this as simply as possible: I did not consider his adultery to be an illness that I could treat.]

On March 15th, 1990, I began our last session by offering Gene the taped record of our work together. At first, he seemed embarrassed. He grinned, touched the hard shell of his moussed hair, and said, "What am I gonna do with them?"

"Whatever you like. I told you I needed them for our work but that's over and—"

He raised his hand from feeling his smooth hair, like a student asking for the teacher's attention and interrupted, "What happens if I need to come back?"

"I'll keep them if you want. They'll be safe. I just thought it was right to offer them."

"No, you keep them. It's too final if I take them."

He talked about the situation with Halley. She was traveling a lot, trying to sell the company's products, not the relatively popular Black Dragon, but their less successful line of personal computers. Her frequent absences relieved his feeling of urgency about his marriage and the affair. Besides, Halley had kept her word: she continued to see him when in town without pressuring him to leave Cathy. Of course, this had a perverse effect on Gene, worrying him that perhaps Halley didn't love him as much as she claimed. I must admit I was skeptical about the authenticity of her feelings. Why had she taken a job with the company her father was running, especially since she didn't seem to have any background or interest in computers? Why, if she was as beautiful and intelligent as Gene described her, was she involved with a married man who, to be blunt, didn't seem sufficiently dynamic to inspire an illicit love? I guess I assumed from the slight facts that she was a female version of the old Gene—that she got herself into situations and relationships which were guaranteed to thwart her desires, probably because she didn't want to face other, deeper needs. And she obviously had some version of an Electra complex, working for her Daddy, involved with his number one man. Probably, given Gene's status as a kind of adopted son of Copley's, there was an element of making love to a stand-in for her dead brother. And, perhaps unfairly, I assumed she was much less fascinating a woman than Gene believed her to be. Her true motivations were beside the point, however. What seemed utterly clear—and a little unpleasant—was that, for the first time in his life, Gene was in control of the people around him. Stick was under pressure at the company, in danger of being fired by the board for dipping sales, indebted to Gene for their only successful product and dependent on his management to bring in a new line for next year. Now that her husband needed her less desperately, Cathy had become a loving wife. Gene commented on this irony: "It's weird, you know? It's kind of sick. Now that I'm getting laid a lot, she wants sex. And it's getting better. Not as good as with Halley, but better. I love her less," he said, "and she seems to love me more." He noticed Freudian oddities, observing that the names of the two women in his life were strangely similar: Cathy and Halley. "Sometimes I have to think twice before I say them, it's so easy to make a mistake," he told me and cackled, not truly mean-spirited, more a childish delight at his surfeit of pleasures. He was like the youngest sibling after the older ones have moved out—amazed and thrilled that he no longer has to worry about his big brothers and sisters gobbling up all the dessert before he gets his share. He looked at the choice in his life—to stay married or go off with Halley—nervously, of course; but also with excitement; that at last he was the playwright of his own drama. Whatever misgivings I may have felt about my help in freeing Gene's id were calmed by my knowledge that in the end I was confident he was a caring man who would do his best for all of them.

"I'm probably gonna call you tomorrow," Gene said. "I'm probably gonna be back here in a week."

"I don't think so," I said.

"But just in case I pull this off, I want to thank you for—" he interrupted himself to say, "You know I spoke to Dad the other day."

"How is he?"

"Complaining, as always. His career's not going well. But, anyway, he asked me how I was doing and I told him, I really told him. Everything. You know."

"Halley also?"

"Yep. And he actually lectured me about how important it was to try to keep my family together. Can you believe it?"

"Yes," I said. "I remember how long he tried to."

"I guess that's right. Anyway, he said, even though he had a hard time living with Mom, that the years we were together, you know, when I was a kid, that, in the end, it was the happiest time of his life." Gene swallowed, moved. When he could speak easily, he added, "He told me when he has another show, he's going to put a picture of me and Mom in it, a picture he took when I was a child." Tears appeared in Gene's solemn eyes, the same worried and yet trusting eyes that had looked at me furtively thirteen years before, pleading for rescue. "He said I was a good son and that he was proud of me. He said he knew I would do the right thing."

"I agree with him," I said.

Gene sighed. "Anyway, I didn't mean to say that to compliment myself."

"You're sure about that?" I asked with a smile.

"Really," he smiled back. "I meant to say that I would never been able to talk to him about all this if it weren't for you. I would never have been able to get through Black Dragon, or have had the nerve to come on to Halley. Even if that was wrong, it made me happy. It's thanks to you."

"Well, you're welcome. But you—"

He interrupted. "I know. I did it. Still. Thanks."

He stood up, dressed that day in fashionable black shoes, faded blue-jeans, a black polo shirt, and a light gray sport jacket, his hair slicked back, his eyes, at our parting, at last direct and unafraid. He put out his hand and said, "I hope this is goodbye, Dr. Neruda."

As I shook it, I have to admit a surge of vanity: I was proud of what I had wrought.

Chapter Fourteen

Closure

Joseph Stein died a year after my last session with Gene. He survived less than two years since testing positive, a mere fourteen months following the first symptoms of full-blown AIDS. To the horror of his colleagues and friends, he made no attempt to stave off the disease, refusing not only standard therapies but those in the experimental stage that, in his privileged position, he could have had access to. He dropped out of sight after the onset, severing contact with everyone, including his lover, Harlan. No one knew that he took a long tour of Asia and Europe. Later we found out that during his travels he twice fell ill with pneumonia and tried to avoid hospitalization. The second time, the delay in getting treatment killed him: the infection was too far gone and complications led to heart failure. He died, of all places, in Poland. His behavior was pointed, clearly suicidal. He knew better than anyone that with proper preventative care he might have lived for many years. I learned of his death from his mother. She nursed him for the final three days of his life. At last her nightmare came true: she returned to the scene of the Holocaust, to the sick bed of a son who was vulnerable to every germ.

Surely Joseph meant something by these actions. Whether they were a rebuke or a homage to his parents, I don't know. Whether his purposeful trip to Poland while dying—he collapsed at the Warsaw airport—was part of a delusion or merely curiosity about the scene of his parents' drama, again I don't know. Mrs. Stein didn't volunteer if she knew and I felt asking whether he explained himself to her was inappropriate. Besides, she might be ignorant of his reasons. Until he called to say he was dying in a hospital in Warsaw, she hadn't heard from him in a year. She told me when she arrived the next day at his bedside, he was incoherent most of the time. She reported that in one of his lucid moments he said there was something in his will for me, and I had better do what he asked or he would never let me win at chess. "What does that mean?" she asked.

"He always beat me," I said. "He was always smarter than me and he liked to remind me of it."

"I'm sorry," she said. Her calmness, now widowed and without her child, intimidated me. She was tiny. Her pale skin hardly obscured the veins and bones of her hands. Her chin quivered all the time and her eyes were as lifeless as a doll's. Yet speaking of her son, her voice was strong, apparently untroubled. "He was crazy. Didn't know what he was saying. He was very fond of you. He probably thought it was a funny joke. He liked making people laugh," she said, a quality of Joseph's that I must have missed.

I understood when the will was read. Other than a trust fund for Mrs. Stein, he left his money to Harlan. Joseph's cold behavior to his lover, breaking off their relationship and making contact impossible, only intensified Harlan's grief. He said, "Fuck you," when we heard the clause leaving the money to him, but he broke down on his way out, sagging into the arms of a mutual friend to sob. Mrs. Stein watched them comfort each other impassively. She seemed all the more isolated because she hadn't met most of Joseph's intimates until his memorial service. I felt useless to her and angry at Joseph. I was angry at him for many things, in particular his legacy to me. His message referred to the fact that he left me his papers, all his research on the brain, in the hope, he wrote, that I would use my skill to explain his theories to the general public. Was that nastiness? Egomania?

To my surprise, Diane took his side. "I think you're wrong," she said to my speculation. We were walking home from the lawyer's office in Midtown to our apartment on the West Side. It was an early spring day. Although cool, the sun was out. Central Park was crowded with people wearing as few clothes as they could bear. "He left things to only three people—his mother, Harlan and you. The three people he loved most."

"Or resented the most."

"Come on, Rafe. And he left you his work, the thing he valued most.

He's trusted you with it, even though he knows you don't agree with him. That's quite a compliment."

"I don't know. Maybe it just amuses him to think of me saddled with the job of disseminating ideas I don't agree with."

"I'm sorry, but I don't think that highly of Joseph. I shouldn't speak ill of the dead, but he was too much of an egomaniac to risk throwing away his life's work just to tease you. He trusted you. He knew you'll do him justice."

"Fuck you, Joseph," I said. But I began reading and making notes on his papers the following weekend.

Two weeks later I took on a collaborator for the job, Amy Glickstein, a brilliant young neurobiologist who shares Joseph's faith in biochemical determinism. I asked for her help after an incident of great significance in my personal life that changed my attitude as to whether I was fit for the job of exclusively representing a point of view other than my own. My father returned to the United States. I learned this in a straightforward way, but it was still a shock. On a Thursday afternoon, I picked up the phone at the clinic and a reedy male voice asked in Spanish if I was Rafael Neruda. When I said yes, the caller continued in rapid Spanish that I couldn't follow. I interrupted, asking if he could speak English.

"Not good English. I am Francisco Neruda," he announced.

I stared into space for what felt like a long time, but was probably only a moment. I said without thinking, "No, you're not."

"Yes. That's my name. But they call me Cuco. I am your half-brother?"

Then I understood. Embarrassed, I said, "Of course, of course." And I added, foolishly, "Nice to meet you." I continued to fumble. "I mean, talk to you. We never met, so . . ." At last, I stopped the silliness. "*Perdóname.* I didn't know your name. In fact, I don't really know anything about you. I'm sorry, but no one told me. Are you Carmelita's son? Born in, let's see——?"

He interrupted. "That is correct. I'm twenty-eight years. No one informed you of anything?"

"Informed me about you?"

"No. Excuse me. I'm not clear. My father—excuse me—our father, he thought . . . He asked me to call."

"Is he here? Are you here? Are you calling from the States?"

He told me they were in Tampa. Grandpa Pepín was having trouble with his mind, he said, and they had come to take care of him. I spoke to Pepín every other month and he seemed to be in excellent physical health, except for arthritis in his knees that especially annoyed him because he could no longer garden. He was ninety-two years old, living alone in the same house whose porch and lawn were the scene of my World Series injury. He didn't like to travel and, for reasons the reader well understands, I didn't care to visit Tampa. I hadn't seen him in six years. Listening to my half-brother's brief explanation, I felt so many different pangs of guilt that I almost laughed. No matter how many psychological textbooks I might consult, here was one situation where I was the bad guy, pure and simple. Three male relatives were down there whom I had neglected or betrayed or pretended didn't exist. Once I accepted the fact that I was hopelessly and forever in the wrong, I relaxed. Self-justification may do wonders for the ego, but it's exhausting and probably bad for the hairline as well. "How can I help?" I asked. "Do you need the names of doctors?"

"No, thank you. *Abuelo* has a doctor. Dr. García."

"Yes, I know," I said, a little peeved. After all, when Pepín outlived two generations' worth of Latin doctors, I had helped find younger men such as García, each time warning the new doctor to conceal the fact that his parents were anti-Castro refugees from Cuba. Grandpa didn't trust non-Hispanics or anti-Communists to treat him—the truth is, he wasn't that happy about putting his health in the care of people a third his age no matter what their ethnicity or politics. Although I had seen Pepín only five times since I was a child, I liked to think I had done my best to stay in touch and help. But who was I kidding? I wasn't close to him. Pepín had never told me about my half-brother or my father's whereabouts, claiming he didn't know, when obviously he did. "Tell me, what's wrong exactly? You said he's having trouble with his mind?"

"He can't help himself. He needs someone to cook and clean."

"But there's a woman who comes," I began, again referring to something I had arranged. There was no shaking off my guilty desire to prove I had made some attempt to be good. I was ashamed that Grandpa Pepín had lapsed into senility and I hadn't noticed from our phone conversations.

"Yes? A woman comes?" My brother seemed surprised.

I heard someone in the background call out, "Cuco?"

"A moment, please," he said. He talked to the voice in Spanish.

I held my breath. I became conscious of my heart beating. I swallowed the welling in my throat. I was sure the voice I heard answer faintly was my father's.

My brother resumed speaking to me. "Understand," he said, meaning,

I think, not that I should understand, but that he understood. "*Abuelo* needs help twenty-four hours. He's," he lowered his voice as if trying not to be overhead, "forgetting. He doesn't always know you. Excuse me. I don't mean you. I mean any person."

"I understand. Are you looking for a full-time nurse or a home? What kind of care are you—"

"Excuse me," Cuco interrupted. He spoke to the voice in the background. Again, I remained still, straining to hear. There was a distant groan of irritation. Cuco said, "Wait."

Immediately, a deep resonant voice took over the line. A voice I had known all my life.

"Rafe, it's me." The strength and self-assurance was unmistakable, and also unchanged, as though not a day had passed. "Your grandfather insisted I inform you. We have to find him a nursing home. Goddammit," he mumbled, not to me, presumably about the situation. "He wants you here," he resumed in a commanding voice. "Come or not as you like. I don't give a fuck," he added casually, without the malice his curse implied. "I promised him I would call. I've kept my promise." I heard the hollow noise of the receiver clatter home to its cradle and the connection died.

I felt for a while that I, not Ma Bell, had been silenced. Mine did last longer. The phone rang—actually it doesn't ring, it coos like an electronic bird. I answered mechanically and made up some excuse, saying I had to call back, instead of finding out what was wanted. I recovered from the shock by thinking about how to go. Straight to the airport? Not bother to pack, just get on the first plane? Should I tell Diane and let her come along? Would she insist? Should I go at all? I have to admit I was tempted to ignore them. If I pretended they were phantoms perhaps I would be guilty of nothing. I knew myself too well to do that; this was one of the times in my life when I wished I had never read a psychology book.

And yet I did behave as if I had never been analyzed or was capable of self-analysis. I called Julie. I had to look up her office number and it turned out to be wrong anyway. The person who answered told me her new one. I got through the area code and the exchange before stopping. What in God's name could Julie say that would help?

At least I had come out of my paralysis. I phoned several airlines and booked two tickets on a flight in four hours. That should be enough time to go home, pack, and get to the airport. I went down the hall to catch Diane as one of her sessions ended. First, I told her I had to find a nursing home for Grandpa. She asked how long I thought I would be gone. Then I said that my father was down there. She walked to the receptionist and asked her to cancel our appointments for Friday. I guess I was testing her. She passed.

On the flight I told her stories of Tampa. What she knew of my childhood was really the big picture, the lurid highlights, but it wasn't those things that lived in my head. I ended up talking mostly about Grandmother Jacinta's indulgences of me: making grilled cheese sandwiches at ten o'clock at night, storing up *natillas* in the refrigerator, watching me through the screen door while I played on the street, calling out that I should come in for lemonade. I could feel the cool hand of her palm on my forehead as I sat at her yellow Formica table and gulped the drink. I was moved by the memories. Diane held my hand. I stayed quiet after that, surprised by the spreading lights of Tampa at night. I didn't remember the city being so big. I mentioned that to Diane. She surprised me by saying that she'd read in the *Times* it was one of the fastest growing cities in America. The airport was certainly large, as if they expected millions to arrive. In fact it was eerily deserted.

When I gave the address to the cab driver, he picked up a book of city street maps, looked in an index, then flipped to a brightly colored page. He said, "What was that address?"

I told him again. "Sixteen fifty-three St. Claire Street."

"You sure you got the right address?"

"Yes," I said.

"That's not a hotel. There are no hotels there."

"No. We're staying in a house."

He looked in the rearview mirror at me. "You been there before?"

"What's the problem?" Diane asked me.

"It's the right address," I said to him and continued to Diane in a normal tone, so the driver could hear, "Since the area is mostly black he's assuming I've got the wrong address. It used to be a very poor, but respectable Latin working-class neighborhood. Now it's crack heaven. And worse," I added, "the spics have moved out and the niggers have moved in."

The driver pulled away from the curb, but he glanced at me in the mirror, checking whether I was being sarcastic. I showed nothing. "Is it safe for your grandfather to live there?" Diane asked.

"He's lived there for seventy years. I couldn't get him to move."

"That's a shame," the driver said. "So Grandpa's stuck with the house. Probably can't sell it."

"Probably not," I agreed.

"You never said anything about that," Diane commented. It sounded like a complaint to me. "Weren't you worried about an old man living in a neighborhood like that?"

"Who me? You know I never worry about anything." She didn't laugh. "He told me once he would rather be dead than move. I thought that closed the subject."

She peered at me, squinting at the flashing lights of passing cars, saying nothing, waiting as if my answer wasn't satisfactory.

"His politics," I said softly. "Remember their politics? 'Rise with your class,' " I quoted, " 'not out of it.' He would never move."

She looked away, at the window on her side. "I guess it's hard to leave a place you've lived in your whole life," she commented. I was annoyed. That was a shrink talking: arguing with my understanding of my world.

"His closest friend left about twenty-five years ago," I said, "when the first blacks moved to St. Claire Street. So did all the cousins of my generation. They moved to nice middle-class neighborhoods. If he'd gone with them he'd have familiar people and things around him. It's not so clear that staying was timidity on his part. When his block was integrated, the black families who moved in were respectable working-class people. Grandpa was the first Latin to knock on their doors and invite them over. He's still good friends with the family next door. In fact, they keep an eye on him. They're not any happier than he is about what crack has done to the neighborhood. I know it's hard for those of us who live in New York to remember, Diane, but there *are* people who act out of principle, rather than neurosis."

Diane put her hand on my leg and rubbed. "Take it easy," she said in a whisper.

"Okay," I said. "I'm sorry."

We both watched the streets as we neared Pepín's house. Whores patrolled the avenue where I had once stopped at the Dairy Queen for a Brown Bonnet. There was a racial joke somewhere in there—Brown Bonnets of some kind were still for sale. On my grandfather's street most of the houses and tiny lawns were well-kept. But there were bars on the windows and no one on the porches. On a humid spring night they used to be full of people gossiping and arguing politics, calling across to each other, their kids strolling to a now abandoned store on the corner for candy. Our driver was nervous when he had to stop at the light on Nebraska to make the turn onto St. Claire. Eyes checking and rechecking his side and rearview mirrors, he crept forward gradually so he was virtually through before it went green. I gave him a big tip. Some cabbies would have refused to take us.

We carried our overnight bags to the dark porch. A gate covered the door. To ring the bell you had to reach through its bars; Grandpa's sounded a plaintive pair of notes, a corny ding-dong. From the avenue a block away I heard a series of popping sounds, like distant firecrackers.

"What's that?" Diane asked.

"Who is it?" called a thin voice that had told me on the phone he was my brother.

"It's Rafael," I said, rolling the R and lingering on the L. Diane glanced at me.

Inside, another voice spoke inaudibly. A light came on in the front room. There was a sliding noise and an eye peered through a circular peephole. "That's him," I heard my father say and the eye disappeared. After that came another pause, then some fumbling with locks. At last the door opened.

Cuco filled the entrance, dressed in a white T-shirt and what looked like new blue-jeans. He was at least three inches taller than me, six seven or six eight, his eyes the warm brown of my father's. Otherwise, the family resemblance was not obvious. His skin was coffee-colored, his hair kinky, and his features were rounder, less defined than my father's. His chin, for example, barely existed. And although he was far from fat, he had inherited Carmelita's big bones and square shape: he did not have the wide shoulders and narrow hips of the Gallego that my father used to brag about. In fact, he looked as if he would be an excellent outside linebacker, a big man whose long legs and thick body could make him both quick and punishing. I thought of Albert, graduating high school that spring. He was being heavily recruited by top colleges as just that—a premier defensive player, the next Lawrence Taylor, his hyperbolic coach liked to say. Cuco's voice, however, was far from suggesting brute force: high, thin, and gentle. "Rafael?" he said and smiled sweetly, his broad cheeks opening to show little teeth set in a crooked jumble, like a Mediterranean hillside town. "Come in," he urged, easily lifting our bags with one hand, as if they were empty.

"Were those gunshots?" Diane asked him as she entered.

"I think so," he said with a sad shake of his head as he shut the door behind us. "All night, there are crazy noises."

"I'm Diane Rosenberg," she said and offered a hand that looked preposterously small. The two of them made a hilarious sight; Diane is a foot and a half shorter than Cuco.

I looked around. The furniture was unchanged from thirty years ago, except that the couch had been re-covered. Everything looked neat and tidy, but if Grandmother Jacinta had seen it she would have fainted. The rug wasn't shampooed, the credenza's surface wasn't polished, and the drapes needed washing. Behind Cuco was the door to the bedroom where I had napped after returning with my arm in a cast. It was dark. I maneuvered to see the dining room and beyond to the kitchen. There was a light on in the kitchen, but no one in evidence. "*Abuelo* is asleep," Cuco said, gesturing to the front bedroom.

"Is my—" I changed my mind about how to put it. "Is Francisco here?"

Cuco looked toward the kitchen, then back at me. His pleasant face now seemed pained. "Yes. He said if you need a bed, take that room." Cuco indicated the doorway off the dining room, where my parents used to sleep when they visited.

I gestured to the kitchen. "I'm going to say hello." I asked Diane, "You'll be okay?"

Cuco took Diane's elbow with a huge hand and gently urged her toward the couch. "We'll talk and become friends," he said.

Diane beamed at him. "It's not fair."

"Not fair?" Cuco was puzzled.

She sat on the couch. "Your family. God made all the Nerudas too big."

I walked through the dark dining room toward the kitchen. The house had seemed small to me even as a boy. To my adult eyes, it was so shrunken from the memories of childhood that I felt as if I were dreaming. I was a giant now beside these tokens of the past. At least, I was physically. Stepping into the kitchen I could swear my legs buckled. I paused to look at them, surprised I hadn't collapsed. The linoleum was the same black and white squares. Out of the corner of my eyes, I saw the yellow Formica table with its aluminum legs. I looked up at the sink to see if my grandmother was cleaning a plate I had dirtied from a late-night snack. There were bars on the window she used to look out while preparing meals, but, of course, no Jacinta. I inhaled for courage and turned to survey the table. My father wasn't there.

I heard a step behind me. I jumped. At least it felt as if my heart did. I turned to face the small television room where they kept the fold-out couch that had been my bed as a child. My father stood astride the door sill. His hair was all white, thinner of course and receding, completely exposing his high forehead. His thick eyebrows were still mostly black. He stood straight, just as I remembered him, his chest out, proudly. He had no paunch, although his face was full. He was very tan. I was impressed by his handsome, dignified, and commanding appearance. That had not been an illusion created by my childhood, after all. My father was no fantasy.

"Hi Dad," I said, and now I had shrunk to the size of a boy. The sound of my voice was foreign to me: unsure, sweet and scared.

He said nothing. He watched me as if he were seeing something that didn't require a reaction, as if I were an image, not a living thing.

"You look great," I said. I seemed to have no defenses, no ability to plan what came out of my mouth. "I'm really glad to see you." I studied him again, amazed that this vigorous figure was seventy-four years old. Perhaps because of the stories of Cuba's economic woes, or more likely some sort of guilty projection, or worse, a deeper wish from buried rage, I expected the years to have treated him harshly, to find a withered broken man.

"I'm not glad to see you," he said in that extraordinary voice, so convinced of its correctness, so musical and dramatic—the kind of voice that sells us cars, beckons us to fly the friendly skies, and reads us the news headlines. "I hoped you wouldn't come." He glanced down pensively. When he looked up again, he nodded toward the dining room. "You brought someone? Your wife?"

"No. We're not married. But she's a friend. I mean, we're very close . . ." I stammered like an embarrassed teenager.

"You mean you're fucking her," he said and chuckled. He caught himself doing it, glanced at me and then away, frowning. "We're going to look at two nursing homes tomorrow and pick one. Then I want you to return to New York. For my father's sake, I'll act courteous in his presence. Otherwise, don't speak to me." He stepped into the television room, and seemed to remember something. "Unless," he added, beginning to swing the door at me, "you don't mind being ignored." His timing was perfect, shutting it in my face with his last word.

When I returned to the living room, Cuco interrupted whatever he was saying to Diane to ask, "You are done talking so fast?"

"I said hello." Diane twisted to look at me. I added, "Maybe we'd better find a hotel."

"No, no," Cuco said. "There are no hotels. And we have a date."

"A date?" Diane asked.

"At a home for seniors. Eight o'clock. That's early, yes?"

"Yes," I agreed.

"It's better you stay here." He smiled at me, showing his jumbled teeth. Cuco added, nodding in the direction of the kitchen, "He's hard-headed."

I was amused. Hard-headed was a favorite comment of my grandmother's, what she used to say when caving in to a demand she didn't approve of—my third Coca-Cola of the day, allowing me to swim less than an hour following a meal; or, permitting a more dangerous act, letting my hair dry in the air after a shower, rather than insisting she towel it. "You're so hard-headed," she would say and pretend to rap me on the skull with her knuckles. Once, she got into a fierce squabble with my father and I was thrilled when she said it about him too. "We're both hard-headed," I called out cheerfully. Francisco and Jacinta stopped their fight. They looked at me, puzzled for a moment, and then their grim faces broke into smiles. "He's proud of it," Grandma said, and laughed so deeply, she held her belly. Francisco took my head in his arms and squeezed out the world. When he released me, although my ears were ringing, I could hear him say, "He's right. Hard-headed people get things done."

What have we gotten done, Father?

"How about you, Cuco?" I asked. "Are you hard-headed too?"

"Me?" He touched his chest with the palm of his hand, astonished. "No." He smiled at Diane. "I'm soft-headed," he said and laughed pleasantly.

I sat opposite them, in the armchair where my father used to hold court on cool nights, explaining the world to his family. "Tell me about yourself, Cuco. Do you mind? We're brothers and I don't know anything about you."

"No?" He shook his head as if this were a sad and astonishing fact. "You said. On the phone. That you were not told about me."

"It's my fault, too," I said. "I could have asked."

"Yes?" He seemed skeptical.

"Do you live in Havana?"

The answer was, some of the time. He was a coach for the Cuban Olympic baseball team. He had been a player—a first baseman, he said.

But he'd hurt his back a year ago. He stood up to illustrate the problem. I was surprised when he got into a left-hander's batting stance.

"You're a southpaw?" I said, pleased and proud, for some odd reason. We had no lefties in the family: the novelty somehow made me feel he really *was* my brother. I could almost hear myself boring someone sometime in the future with ancedotes of Cuco's left-handed feats.

"I throw right," he said.

"No kidding. Did you always bat left-handed?"

"No," he said, eager to explain, breaking out of his batting stance into the pose of a frozen runner. "You know it's faster to first base if you're a lefty." He pointed to the bedroom. "And there's the hole at first and second when there is, you know . . . ?"

"A runner on first," I finished for him.

"You know baseball!" he said and actually clapped.

Diane laughed. "Rafe's a big baseball fan."

That was something of an exaggeration, but it was the one sport I kept track of, and I even attended a couple of games each season. I asked, "You played first base for the Cuban team?"

"For the national team. You're a fan, but you don't know me?" He wasn't petulant, merely curious.

"They don't cover Cuban baseball here," I explained.

"We know all your players." He nodded to himself. "They censor news about us, that's what they say. Many of our boys are as good as the major leaguers. Linares is better than most of your players."

"We know your players are good," I assured him. "They tell us that much."

"It's a pity they can't come here and play for our teams," Diane said.

"Yes?" Cuco asked, again with that mild tone of surprise. "Why?" he added.

"Why?" Diane repeated. "Well, you know, so they could be in the big games." She knew she had gotten herself into an awkward spot. She pressed on anyway, "So they could become famous and play in the World Series."

"It would be good for a Cuban team to play in your so-called World Series, but not so good for the Cuban players to become toys for the owners."

Diane didn't blink. She insisted, "The players here have a lot of power, almost as much as the owners."

"No," Cuco said, confidently.

"Yes." Diane was just as confident about the life of a professional ballplayer, and, I suspect, just as ignorant. "Anyway," she added. "It's wrong that you can't play here. It's a shame when people aren't free to do their work wherever they want."

"Yes, you're right," Cuco said. Diane cocked her head at him, surprised. I wasn't.

"You agree?"

"Yes, of course."

"But you can't say that in Cuba," she commented, not provocatively, with sympathy.

Cuco sat down sideways on the couch, angled to her, his massive legs as big as a coffee table. "Why not?" he asked.

I laughed. Diane and Cuco looked at me. "The embargo, Diane. We're the ones who stopped American baseball teams from having spring training games in Cuba. We're the ones who first made it illegal for a Cuban citizen to play professionally in the United States."

"But," Diane stopped herself. She glanced at Cuco and then shrugged. "Forget it."

"But what?" I asked. "It's okay," I assured her.

"But Castro wouldn't allow it anyway."

"Fidel has asked for it!" Cuco gestured to the ceiling, his reedy voice squeaking, strained by passion. "He has called for a stop to the embargo since 1961. He has—" Cuco shut up, to stare at something behind me.

I looked. My grandfather had emerged from his bedroom, wrestling with a red pajama top. He had no bottoms on. His face, chest and legs had the leathered brown of people who are always in the sun, in contrast to his waist, where a bleached triangle was spoiled only by the prunish darkness of his genitals. "*Coño,*" he mumbled sleepily. The pajama shirt was on backwards, his right arm through the left sleeve, the other empty. He jerked his shoulders back and forth; each time the empty sleeve whipped around, slapping him in the face, like a misbehaving tail.

"*Abuelo!*" Embarrassed for Pepín, Cuco rushed into the bedroom and came out with his pajama bottoms. He didn't notice they were wet at the groin.

Grandpa pushed them away, saying in Spanish they were no good. Cuco returned to the bedroom. I helped Grandpa with the top. "It's on backwards," I explained, as I eased it off.

"Rafael?" he asked.

I slipped the top onto his arms and began to button it in front. "Yes, it's me," I said. I smelled the faint odor of urine.

"You just got here?"

His body was almost hairless from head to toe, except for his groin. Even there, the hairs were all gray and the hair tended to fade away. Pepín was six feet tall and wiry—the outlines of muscle and bone were visible, as if his skin were a size too small. "Yes, Diane and I just got here," I said, shielding his nakedness from her as I indicated her presence.

"Your girlfriend?" he asked, peering around me.

"Diane. I told you about her, remember?"

Pepín squinted at her.

"Hello," she called.

Cuco emerged, carrying bright yellow pajamas in his arms. Pepín ignored him in favor of properly greeting Diane. He stepped around me and walked over to the couch, extending his hand and politely bending over so she could easily reach it. He remembered his Spanish manners, but forgot, however, that he was naked from the waist down. "Hello," he said. "I'm Rafael's grandfather." The offered hand was in line with, and no more than a foot from, his privates.

"*Abuelo!*" Cuco complained, bounding over. His huge body made the floorboards quake. He unfurled the yellow bottoms, holding them against Pepín's stomach. The yellow top fell.

Meanwhile, Diane gamely took Pepín's hand and shook it. "Nice to meet you."

Pepín finished the greeting and turned on Cuco. "What's the matter with you, *chico*?" he asked. "Did you ask if they want coffee?" he demanded, wandering in the direction of the kitchen.

Cuco danced beside Grandpa as he moved, keeping him covered. He nodded at the old man's waist and said in an intense whisper, "*Mira!*"

Pepín looked down. He frowned at the confusing sight. He was draped by the yellow bottoms and wearing the red top. He felt the yellow fabric, pressing it against his thighs. He reached around and touched his naked buttocks. "What did you do?" he asked Cuco in Spanish.

"They're not on you," Cuco answered in Spanish. "You came out with nothing on."

"But why are they yellow?" Grandpa said.

"The red ones are wet."

Grandpa thought hard. He touched the red top I had put on him. "This isn't wet."

"It's okay," Diane said, guessing incorrectly about what they were debating. "I'm a doctor."

"You're a doctor?" Grandpa asked her in Spanish.

She repeated, uncertainly, "Yes, I'm a doctor. So don't worry."

Pepín looked at me and said in English, "You said she was your girlfriend." His face changed: chin pushing up pugnaciously, eyes narrowing. He walked over to accuse me in English, "You trying to fool me?" He had exposed himself with this maneuver. Startled, Cuco wasn't quick to cover him. "You bring doctors and say they're girlfriends." He must have felt the air on him. He looked down as Cuco came over, waving the yellow bottoms like a bullfighter. Pepín saw his nakedness. "My God," he exclaimed in Spanish. "They've stolen my pajamas!"

Eventually, Cuco and I convinced Grandpa that Diane was both my lover and a doctor and that we were not interested in acquiring his pajamas. Once fully dressed, resplendent in yellow, Pepín again introduced himself to Diane. "I'm Rafael's grandfather," he told her solemnly. This time he took her hand and kissed it. "I'm sorry. I get confused when I wake up." He rubbed her hand for a moment. "Cuco," he said, "did you make them *café*?"

"It's too late," Diane said. "I'm fine."

"I asked you before," Pepín remembered. He turned and shuffled toward his bedroom pensively.

"Good night, Grandpa," I said and kissed him on the forehead.

At my touch he looked at me, the rims of his eyes white, the centers dull. "Good night," he mumbled. "Must be going senile," he added and tried to laugh it off, although he waited for me to comment.

"No, you're not," I mumbled and then regretted it, since I didn't know if he was aware of the nursing home plan or what he might have to be persuaded of to agree to go.

I had trouble falling asleep. Cuco was right. There were crazy sounds. Sirens every half hour, and those popping noises, so many I concluded they couldn't be gunfire. At one point, from the street facing the backyard, I heard several people running hard until there was a loud clattering noise, as if a row of aluminum garbage cans were rolling on concrete; that was followed by a profound silence. By then I was wide awake. Diane, to my surprise and annoyance, had fallen asleep quickly and remained out, undisturbed. Probably I couldn't have slept no matter how tranquil the night. After the crashing of metal, I listened to what should have been the soothing rustle of palm trees brushing against the porch. Instead they reminded me of lying on my mother's belly after the attack, her heat healing my bruises, peering up before I dozed off, to watch in the half-light the wild restless motion of her eyes as they checked the door, the windows, or sometimes stared ahead, at a terror I understood, but couldn't see.

Finally, I must have fallen soundly asleep since I woke up alone, roused by loud and cheerful talk from the kitchen. That was not so different from waking as a child to the lively background noise of Grandma feeding my parents while Pepín interrogated my father about Cuba. The Florida sun striped the room through the bars and venetian blinds, one set horizontal, the other vertical, making a shifting graph paper of the bedsheets. I listened. To my surprise, the friendly conversation was between Diane and my father. This got me out of bed quickly. On my feet, I staggered for a moment, dizzy with fatigue. I heard Diane laugh and say, "Oh, but you have to finish your book. It would be fascinating for Americans to read what it's really like." I was excited. I dressed quickly in the jeans and polo shirt I had stuffed into the overnight bag. I heard my father answer, "You're an easy audience. You're already in love with a Neruda. God help you," he added. The buoyant happiness I felt was like a miracle cure. Was it possible? Could it be that this was all I needed, that years of recrimination and loneliness were going to be washed away in a single scrubbing?

I went to the kitchen, stopping in the doorway. Diane was saying, in answer to an offer from my father, "I would love to visit Cuba. Shouldn't we, Rafe?" she asked me. Her casual tone was effortless.

"Yes, we should." My father was in a chair next to Diane. In front of him was a cereal bowl with a puddle of milk and a few drowned Cheerios. Behind him stood Pepín, his hands resting on my father's shoulders. Grandpa's face was impassive, a distant look in his eyes. He was dressed in clean linen black pants and an ironed white shirt without a tie, although it was buttoned to the collar. He was clean shaven. Here and there, on his chin, under his nose, by his left temple, were dots of dried blood where he'd nicked himself. Diane wore white shorts and an oversize blue cotton top that would gradually slide off her left shoulder until, when it was bare, she'd pull it up and the erosion began again. Her plate was covered with toast crumbs. The room was already hot from the morning sun and pungent with the smell of brewed coffee.

"*Quieres café con leche?*" Cuco asked from the stove. He shook a tall tin pot at me.

"Yes, thank you," I said.

Cuco put the espresso maker on top of a low flame. He poured milk into a saucepan and lit another burner to heat it.

"The coffee is incredibly good," Diane said.

"Cuban coffee puts hair on your teeth," my father answered.

"Good morning," I said in his and my grandfather's direction.

Neither answered. Francisco raised a coffee mug to his lips and sipped. Pepín looked through me.

Diane filled the silence before it widened too much. "So what's our schedule?"

"We have to leave in fifteen or twenty minutes," Francisco said. He stood up carefully, taking his father's hands off him and holding one of them to maneuver him gently out of the way. "Speaking of hair I'd better brush mine. And comb my teeth too. We don't want these gringos to think we're white trash," he said to Pepín. He seemed to notice something. "Don't button this," he said, unfastening Grandpa's collar. "You're not wearing a tie."

"I'm cold," Grandpa said in Spanish and redid the button.

"You're cold!" Francisco answered him in Spanish. "Man, it's already seventy. And the sky's clear. By noon, it's going to be eighty, eighty-five." He reached for Pepín's collar.

Grandpa slapped at his son's hands. "It's air-conditioned in those places," he said.

Francisco gave up good-naturedly, patting Pepín on the side of his shoulder. "How do you know, old man?"

"Those crackers air-condition everything."

"And they're right. I'm sick of the tropics. You can't think in the heat." He said to Diane in English, "It's too hot down here, that's what we're saying. The brain doesn't work."

"Oh, I love it," Diane said. "I'm sick of it being winter."

"Winters in New York," Francisco declaimed, looking up, arms spreading, like a hero in a Broadway musical about to transpose into song. "Beautiful women in long coats." He smiled at her as if she were one of them. "And that air! There's nothing like taking a deep breath on Fifth Avenue on a cold February night. Clears all the junk out of your head."

"You've been away a long time," Diane said. "Now the air is polluted."

"It was always polluted. Wonderfully full of pollution." Diane laughed. "Really," he assured her. "There are ideas in that air. It even makes the stupid people think. They don't think great thoughts, but at least they think. Down here, and in Cuba, when it gets too hot, everybody sits around stupefied, sweating their brains out. You can't have a serious conversation in Havana until the sun sets. And in Tampa! It's too humid. Even at night, it's impossible."

"Don't say that to her!" Pepín slapped Francisco's back, but feebly, hand trembling. "This is a good place to live. Of course she likes our weather. Nobody wants to be cold."

"Don't get agitated," Francisco said in Spanish. "I'm not serious."

"You sound serious," Pepín complained. His mouth quivered as if he were going to cry. He switched to English and insisted to Diane, "Many people like to visit Tampa. They put up a new building almost every day. And we may get a baseball team," he added to Cuco. "People love to come here," he said to me.

"Of course," I said. "Diane and I will come every winter to escape the cold."

This earned me a stare from my father, the first look that acknowledged I was in the room.

"That's right," Pepín said. His trembling hands went to his already buttoned collar, ready to button it again. "You can come for *Noche Buena* and stay through New Year's. Make a good vacation." He looked down, confused that he couldn't button the collar. "Ah," he said and added in Spanish: "It's buttoned."

"Absolutely," I said. "That's what we'll do."

"Great," my father said as he moved to leave the room. "Why don't you make your reservations now?"

Diane reached for him. "Wait."

Francisco paused at the doorway.

"Is it all right if I dress this casually?'"

Francisco stepped to her, bent over, and kissed her on the forehead. "You're lovely. Don't worry, they won't mistake *you* for a peasant. They'll know they're dealing with a superior person." He moved off, out of the room, saying, "But us Latinos, we'd better put on the dog."

Cuco poured the heated milk and espresso in a large mug for me. Pepín continued to stand in the middle of the room and look at nothing, his hands worried and worrying at his clothes, touching his cuffs, pulling at the ironed crease of his pants, feeling his collar. At one point he undid his belt buckle, stared at the separated pieces, then refastened them. He smiled afterwards and commented in Spanish, "It's hot, no?"

By then Cuco had left to dress and Diane and I were talking in whispers. We had tried to engage Grandpa in conversation, but he seemed not to hear our questions, and that was the first time he had spoken on his own. "Do you want to open your collar?" I asked.

"My collar?" A hand went to his throat. His fingers pressed all around the top button and he frowned.

I stood up. "Should I undo it?"

"No, no," he backed away, turning toward the barred window, a hand guarding his throat. "No," he said once more, softer, sadly.

I sat down. Diane held my hand. "Your father's very charming," she said.

"I told you."

"And he's very handsome."

"I can't believe he's seventy-four."

She squeezed my hand. "You look like him, you know. Very much like him."

"That must stick in his craw."

"No . . ." Diane was disappointed. "He must like it."

"Makes it harder to deny me." Pepín tapped me on the shoulder. "Yes, Grandpa?"

He spoke in English. "This is no problem. Don't worry about it. It will be no problem."

"I won't," I said. He patted my shoulder and winked. "What shouldn't I worry about?"

"Today! Don't you remember the appointment?"

"Oh, yes. I'm not worried," I assured him.

"Good. Because there's nothing to worry about."

Cuco appeared, dressed in what appeared to be brand-new chinos and a white dress shirt, also with no tie. "We must go. Papá's bringing the car out of the garage."

That was the first time I heard Cuco refer to my father as Papá, his natural address for Francisco. I envied him and had to push down a swell of resentment. Perhaps that was why, when we went outside to find Francisco behind the wheel of Pepín's white Buick, I walked to the driver's window and leaned in to ask him, "Do you have a valid license to drive in America?"

Francisco stared ahead as if he weren't going to answer. Cuco opened the rear door for my grandfather and Diane. There was some conversation amongst them about where Diane should sit. I maintained my position, leaning in, less than a foot from Francisco's face. My father turned his head to me after a moment. I felt a jolt in my chest as his warm brown eyes looked deep into mine. They seemed the absolute master of what they surveyed. "No, Officer," he said with a mocking lilt. "As a matter of fact my license has expired."

"Then I'd better drive," I said.

Francisco looked forward again. Diane and Grandpa had gotten into the back, Diane in the middle, Grandpa on the right, with space on the left, presumably for me. Cuco opened the passenger door. "Sit in the back," Francisco said to him in Spanish and slid over to the passenger side.

So I drove. My father directed me in a cold authoritarian voice, as if he were training a dog. I obeyed like a star pupil.

After we left the first home, Grandpa said over and over in a faint voice that the place was nice. We rejected it, however, for being little more than a dreary boarding house run by a thin man with an unctuous manner. The manager followed us all the way to the car, saying he hated to rush us, since he thought Mr. Neruda was a gentleman and also obviously very intelligent. "He would be an asset," he said, a curious choice of word I thought. "But," the manager added ruefully, "I have one vacant bed and it'll go quickly." I got a smile out of my father by whispering as I pulled away from the curb, "Uriah Heep."

Francisco forgot to maintain his unresponsiveness. "Yes, he's probably stealing their Social Security checks and feeding them gruel."

"Right," I said. "Or taking the checks and burying his clients in the backyard so he can save on the gruel."

"Shhh," Diane said and caught my eye in the rearview mirror. She glanced at my grandfather, who, indeed, appeared to understand enough of our sarcasm to be alarmed.

Francisco told me the next address and what my first turn would be. In the back seat, Cuco and Diane explained to Grandpa why Uriah Heep's Retirement Home wasn't right for him. Perhaps because this gave us a moment of privacy, my father volunteered to speak to me, albeit in a low voice. "You read Dickens?"

"Because of you," I answered. "You practically forced me to read *Oliver Twist* when I was eight. And in Spain you used to read *Great Expectations* to me before bedtime."

Francisco nodded and mumbled, "You remember."

"Of course," I said. "As a matter of fact, when they're old enough, I encourage my young patients to read him. From their point of view, Dickens doesn't seem all that out of date."

"He was a genius," my father said, sadly, as if this were a fact lost to the world.

The second appointment was at a larger facility, a hundred beds. The rooms were double occupancy. At Uriah's establishment Grandpa would have been squeezed in with five other men. Here, although the rooms were institutional, like a hospital's, at least they were bright, clean and a reasonable size, allowing for a few personal possessions. Again, Grandfather announced it was nice over and over as we toured. I was puzzled by his anxiousness to agree to become a resident of either place. I expected his senility to take a different form: fear and resistance to change. I understood when I took his arm as we walked down a flight of stairs to see the Activities Room. I whispered to him, "You really like it here?"

"Yes, it's nice," he said for what seemed like the twentieth time. "For a few weeks, it's okay," he added in Spanish.

"A few weeks?" I asked. "What do you mean?"

"It's nice," he said in English. "Until my mind clears," he said in Spanish; then back to English, "It's nice."

The bigger, more modern nursing home divided us. Diane and Cuco were in favor of it. Most of the residents were Latin, the staff seemed competent and not harassed. There were things to do besides watch television with Uriah Heep. And it was near old Ybor City, where my grandfather had once rolled cigars. In fact, we drove to Ybor City proper to eat my grandfather's favorite lunch, Cuban sandwiches at the Tropicana. Francisco and I didn't demur from Cuco's and Diane's positive comments about the nursing home, but we didn't concede the decision was made either. Not that I felt my agreement was a factor for Francisco. As for Grandpa, the question was settled. "Let's go back and tell them I'll come in tomorrow," he said, seeming much livelier as he bit into a flattened hero loaf, mustard oozing from its edge onto his fingers.

Francisco wiped his father's fingers with a napkin. "Tomorrow? What are you talking about? They don't have room until next month and there's papers, lots of papers to sign. All those Medicare and Medicaid forms, right?" he smiled at Diane. She had questioned the administrator about insurance procotols, the liquidation of Grandfather's assets, and so on, inadvertently showing off her expertise in dealing with bureaucracy. She handled all the paperwork for our clinic. She had impressed my father. "And we have to sell your house," he added to Grandpa.

"Sell my house?" Grandpa took another bite speaking as he chewed, flakes of bread falling onto his chin. "You can't sell my house. It's for you. You and Cuco. You're going to live there."

"Until you're settled, yes. But we have to go back to," he lowered his voice to add, "Havana." There had been a warning from Grandpa before we entered the restaurant that all the waiters were Cuban exiles. "Maybe they'll ask for Cuco's autograph," Francisco had said breezily then, but he seemed wary now, checking the room after he said Havana, as if it might cause an eruption.

When the check came, I took it. My father grabbed the slip of paper out of my hand, saying, "No," firmly, again the dog trainer.

"Is there a phone here?" Diane asked. "We should get our messages," she added to me.

"Yes," I agreed. "Grandpa, is there a phone here?"

"What?" He had been silent since Francisco told him they were going to sell the house on St. Claire Street.

"Where is the phone, Grandpa?"

He looked at me with old eyes, dead at their centers. "I don't know," he said with profound regret.

"If I remember," Francisco said, "there's a pay phone near the bathrooms. I'll show you."

"You first," I said to Diane. She and my father stood up. Francisco pointed the way for her and continued on to the cash register. He handed over the check and money while saying something to the man behind the register. He laughed at my father's remark and immediately they were in a friendly conversation. I felt someone watching me as I watched Francisco. I turned to find Cuco staring at me.

"He can talk to anyone," I said.

"Yes," Cuco didn't seem any happier about that than I. "Sometimes I think the less he likes you, the more he's your friend."

I smiled at Cuco's insight. "Yes," I said.

"But it is not true," Cuco said. "It appears that way because he's harder on us, the people he loves."

"Thank you," I said.

"Thank you?" Cuco turned up a palm to indicate his confusion.

"For including me in the people he loves."

"But of course he loves you."

In Spanish, Pepín said, "It's hot in here, no?"

"Do you want me to unbutton—?" I began and then waved my hand, giving up.

Cuco ignored Grandpa's interruption. He continued to look at me intently.

"He doesn't," I said. My chin quivered.

"Yes," Cuco insisted. "He told me about you. So did my mother and . . ." he nodded at Pepín.

"How is your mother?"

"I don't speak to her."

"You don't speak to her?"

"You don't know?" Cuco frowned. He looked at the remains of our lunch, moving one of the bread crumbs with a thick index finger into a puddle of water. It floated a little and then he crushed it. "She defected," he said, obviously ashamed. "At the last Pan-American Games, she disappeared. We heard she was in Miami." He sighed and returned his gaze to me. "They don't tell you about me, but they tell me about you. He tells me," he nodded toward Francisco, counting his change, still talking in great good humor with one of what he calls "the *Gusanos*," the worms who deserted Cuba in her hour of need. "He says you are a great man in this country."

"He doesn't mean that as a compliment."

"Yes. He does. He says you are a great doctor. He says you work for the poor. He says you could be wealthy and treat only the privileged classes, but you fight for the black children. That is what he says of you."

I couldn't answer right away. I found myself watching Francisco. Another man had come up to the register and now there was a three-way conversation going. I didn't look at Cuco when I said, "I betrayed him."

"*Yo sé,*" Cuco whispered. "My mother told me what you did. She didn't forgive you." He grunted bitterly, presumably at this irony, and then continued, "But he does. He says you don't want to be a Neruda, but you have no choice. You can't escape your blood."

"What?" I couldn't help myself from chuckling at Francisco's melodramatic narcissistic fantasy. I forgot about studying him, and instead looked at my brother. I put a hand on his bicep. I was startled by the size and strength of his muscle.

"He says, you *are* a Neruda." Cuco was grave. And his eyes were sad. "That is a compliment."

I understood the sadness. I kept my hand on his powerful arm. "So are you," I said.

It was Cuco's turn to watch Francisco talking. We could hear the music of our father's voice, not the individual notes. Eyes on Francisco,

Cuco asked, softly, "You think I am?" And then asked me again, this time with his wounded eyes.

"Oh yes." I nodded. "We're both Nerudas."

When Diane returned she said, "Sally's got messages for you." Francisco had finished talking with his new pals and was headed our way.

"Anything urgent?"

"They're *your* messages," Diane said with mock primness. "I told Sally you'll call back."

I went to the pay phone. My messages weren't urgent, but one alarmed me anyway. Phil Samuel had called to ask if I wanted a copy of his new study. He could fax it or mail it. If the latter, he wanted to know whether he ought to send it to my home address.

"That's weird," Sally commented.

"Did he leave his number?"

"Yeah. Do you have a pen?"

I copied the number down on an old American Express receipt I found in my wallet. The phone was next to the two restroom doors. I looked back and saw Diane waiting for me. I decided to call Phil later.

Grandpa was already in the back seat of the car, head resting on Cuco's shoulder, asleep. Francisco stood on the curb. The sun blinded me as I got near, gleaming off the chrome trim of Pepín's Buick. While I blinked at him, Francisco said, "Unless you have an objection, I'll arrange for my father to go in next month. He seems to like it."

"You're staying until he's settled?"

"Yes, of course," Francisco said haughtily.

"Remember," Diane said, "if you transfer all his assets to you, then Medicaid picks up the bills. Otherwise they'll clean him out first."

Francisco squinted at the shimmering windows of the restaurant. "I don't know . . ."

Diane touched his arm. "I'll get the name of someone down here who can advise you how to handle it. There's no reason for his life savings to be wasted. You and Cuco should have it, that's what your father would want."

"There's no legal danger," I said.

"What?" Francisco's tone was sharp, ready to discipline. "Who said I was worried about trouble with the law?"

"You didn't, I just—" I began.

He cut me off. "Do you have reservations for a flight tonight?"

"We're going back tonight?" Diane asked me.

"I haven't had a chance to make reservations," I said to my father.

"We should stay until tomorrow," Diane said.

For the first time he was cold to her. "No," he said, opening the rear passenger door, "you're leaving tonight."

We rode in silence. Grandpa didn't wake up when we stopped in his driveway. Cuco called his name several times, but not until he gently eased the old head off his shoulder, did Pepín's eyes open. "Are we here?" he said in Spanish. He peered at the overgrown azalea bushes he used to trim every weekend. "But this is my house," he continued.

"Yes, we're home," Cuco said.

Pepín asked plaintively, "Aren't we going to the old people's home?"

I stayed behind the wheel, silent, unable to move. Francisco didn't reply or shift his eyes from staring ahead at his father's porch. While they helped him out of the car, Cuco and Diane explained to Pepín that we had already been to the nursing homes. Pepín remembered as they shut the rear door. "They were nice," I heard him say as it slammed. We were alone in the car, becoming uncomfortably hot the instant its air-conditioning was off.

"Life is hateful," my father said with quiet conviction, seemingly to himself. I heard him pull on the door handle and quickly, faster than I could think to stop myself, I touched his arm.

"Wait," I said. Out of the corner of my eye I watched him let go of the handle. I removed my hand. I didn't have the courage to look at him. Nor did he want to see me. We faced forward, watching Cuco and Diane guide Pepín up the steps. Diane glanced back at one point, noted us, and moved on. Cuco also gave us a hard look while he held the door for them to enter, and again as he shut it behind him.

"Well?" my father demanded. "In a few minutes, we'll suffocate in here."

"Do you want me to turn the air on?"

"No. Just say what you have to say."

"I was a very disturbed child," I said, letting go of the wheel, my hands feeling the sloping dash. The vinyl was warm to the touch and the sun bleached my hands.

"There's no reason to go over all that," my father said impatiently, but without rancor. "You're sorry. I know. You wrote that in your letters. Of course you're sorry. I believe you. Is that it?" He shifted closer to the door, ready to leave.

"I was ten years old, Dad. My mother had committed—"

He cut me off quickly, fearfully I felt, but also in a declaiming voice, as if he were making a speech. "This is a new thing that's happened here. I was amazed when I picked up *Newsweek* at the airport. And I found some of this nonsense in the *Nation* magazine. I mean, it's everywhere, even the *New York Review of Books*. And television, too. All those silly chat shows. Not chat, I don't mean chat—"

"Talk shows."

"That's right. They call them talk shows. God. It's hilarious, their idea of talk. I mean, it just saturates the culture."

"I don't know what you're talking about," I said. I rested my forehead against the steering wheel, neck exposed, and indeed, felt ready for decapitation.

"You *don't?*" He was so emphatic I had the illusion I felt his breath on my cheek. "You really don't? Well, it makes sense. If you live surrounded by it, and it's part of your work too, of course, so . . . Well, we're all creatures of our time and place. I suppose I can't blame you for falling for it."

"Please," I begged the odometer. "Just say what you mean."

"I *mean* this nonsense that no one is responsible for their actions. Everything is excusable because of its supposed root cause. It's as if we were to decide Hitler had a perfect right to murder twelve million people in the camps because, after all, he was traumatized as a boy. Probably it was a Communist who rejected him when he applied to be an architect. Or was it a Jew? Anyway, that was abuse, wasn't it? Or perhaps his father spanked him when he got poor grades and it was a Jew who gave him the F, so naturally he had to kill six million of them. You know, I can't forgive the WASPs for what they did to Latin America, or their terrible arrogance about making money, as if it were a sacred act, a duty performed for God, but there was one thing you can give those Episcopalians, when they fucked up they believed it was their fault, not their toilet training."

I turned to look at him, my head still resting on the wheel. My skin squeaked against the fake leather. Francisco's face was flushed, eyes alive, staring through the window but not seeing what was there, a look of abstraction I remembered from my childhood. He wasn't in Tampa with me. He was debating somewhere else, to a grander audience. "You were the one who taught me that the simpleminded morality of society isn't the truth."

"What?" He looked at me, annoyed. I had called him down from the thrilling heights.

"You were the one who taught me that property is theft, that ignorance isn't stupidity, that slavery didn't end with the Civil War, that—"

"Look." Francisco waved a finger at me. He probably wished he had a rolled newspaper. "Of course. Of course. Everybody knows that. Only a cretin, a reactionary cretin, believes laws are the natural order, instead of rules made by the winner. But let's say it happens one day. I mean, it's laughable to say right now, but let's say one day the earth is one government, a perfect communist world, with an abundance of goods, power completely decentralized, everything shared, everything democratic. There will still be thieves. There will still be criminals. I don't know. Maybe it's only ten percent of the population, maybe it's five, maybe it's twenty. Doesn't matter. There will always be criminals. All of them," he nodded toward Nebraska Avenue, empty now in the midday sun, but the night inhabitants were easy to recall, the whores and drug dealers and addicts—"all of those godforsaken people aren't criminals. Some of them are without hope, without any reason to care. But some of them are bad, that's all, pure and simple. And the same is true for the ruling classes. Many of them do what they do because they think it's right. Some of them are scum who love to rule others. What people do, in the end, in their personal lives, is their responsibility. Understanding history doesn't mean individuals aren't to blame. It's an incredible phenomenon what's happening here. I don't understand it. Politically, I mean."

"Sure you do," I mumbled. Sighing, I raised my head from the wheel, trying to straighten out. I was going to have to move on, get reservations, fly to New York, forget last night and today, call Phil Samuel, finish the book on Joseph's work, get married, have children, age and die . . . I needed to sit up straight, look forward, and drive on, without clemency or pardon. "Of course Americans don't want to accept responsibility for anything. We can't, or we won't, solve our problems on a social scale. It's easier to go to a shrink than to rebuild our infrastructure."

"So that's what you think." Francisco shifted in his seat. Sweat rolled down the sides of his temples.

"Do you want me to turn on the air?"

"Let's open the windows."

We rolled them down. Francisco breathed in Tampa's warm pollution and sneezed. A finger under his nose he asked, "Then how can you be a psychiatrist?"

"I don't treat those people, I treat . . ." I sighed. My father's point of view, his impatience with child abuse, wasn't as unusual as he liked to believe. People just don't know. They hadn't sat with me for all those hours, not with criminals trying to get a lighter sentence, not with celebrities looking for a hook to their autobiographies, but with the broken bodies and the lonely eyes of the abandoned. I sighed again and found my father regarding me with genuine curiosity, waiting for me to answer, perhaps for the first time in thirty years, actually prepared to listen. "I can't make racism go away, Dad. I can't convince my fellow citizens that owning a Mercedes isn't as satisfying as having a just world. But I can pull a few of their discards out of the sewer and try to wash them clean."

Francisco smiled with his lips closed, a gentle smile of regret and, I fancied, a smile of forgiveness. "You can't change the world a person at a time."

"I don't think I can change the world, Dad."

He turned away, looking at his childhood home. "What you mean is: the world can't be changed. That's what you think Cuba proves. That's what you think this"—he gestured to the barred houses and the baking, empty streets—"this so-called triumph of capitalism proves. But you're wrong." He rolled up his window and opened the door. He put one foot out, then twisted his torso back in my direction, showing his handsome face, convinced of his command of me. "I'm seventy-four years old and I can assure you, the world can be changed. It *has* been changed. It's been changed for the worse."

CHAPTER FIFTEEN

Catastrophic Failure

"I DON'T THINK YOU'RE GOING TO FIND THE PEDIATRICIAN STUDY TO BE good news," Phil told me when I reached him at home on Sunday. Diane was out, having brunch with an old friend. I sat on the couch, morosely watching the weekly television news roundup shows, listening to reporters and columnists pretend they were historians or psychics, making sweeping judgments about the importance of yesterday's presidential news conference or equally confident predictions about the year ahead. (When the Berlin Wall came down none of them had been able to imagine a single brick would be chipped merely a few weeks before the event. Watching Tom & Jerry cartoons would have told me more about our political future.)

"Why is that?" I asked Phil, my finger on the remote's mute button, wondering why Sam Donaldson didn't spend more money on his toupee. At least, I hoped it was a toupee.

"Well, the best thing is for you to read it and you should look at one of the videos. I'll send a video too, okay?"

"Sure. But give me the short version. What did you find?"

In the background I heard a little boy ask, "Dad! Come on! You said you were going to play."

"Just a minute." Although Phil's words were harassed, his tone was friendly. "I'm talking to somebody for a minute, that's all. Then we'll finish the game. Now go outside and wait for me, okay?" He lowered his voice to explain to me, "I'm being shot with laser guns."

"Hope it doesn't hurt," I said. Sam Donaldson had given way to a young woman in a string bikini, her buttocks undulating as she carried two six packs of beer across a pink beach heading for turquoise water. A young man who would not need Sam's toupee for quite a while joined her and, in an unlikely action, seemed more interested in holding the beer than her.

"That's the great thing about laser guns," Phil said. "They make a lot of noise, but when they blow a hole in you, there's no blood."

"We must issue them to all the armies of the world."

"Listen, Rafe," he said, "this study is going to rock you. I'm sure you'll be tempted to reject it out of hand, that's why I hope you'll look at the video. We used your techniques. You'll see that. But it made no difference. Almost half the kids made up stuff about what the doctor did to them. Incredible stuff—sticking stethoscopes in their vaginas, ramming their anus with tongue depressors. One boy said the doctor swallowed his penis and wouldn't give it back until he touched the doctor's penis. Well, you'll see. They had no trouble fantasizing without verbal cues. In terms of proving that children under six are reliable witnesses, it's a disaster. I'm delivering the paper at the Arizona Children's Forum in two weeks. I'm sorry, but I've got to recommend that psychologists refuse to assist child abuse prosecutions when the alleged victims are this young. God only knows how many innocent people we've ruined."

I turned off the TV. "Phil," I heard myself chuckle. In fact, my mouth was dry and my vision compressed, so that my lap and the carpet under my bare feet seemed to be all that was left of the universe. My voice, however, was as smug and self-assured as Sam Donaldson's. "You're being a little melodramatic, aren't you?"

"Look at the study, Rafe. I'm not saying when there's physical proof we should ignore the children's claims. Obviously, if there's evidence of an STD or bruises, that's a different story. But even then, you can't put a kid under six on the stand and have any confidence that the details will be accurate. And if there's no physical corroboration, forget it. They just don't know the seriousness of what they're saying. They make it up out of the garbage that's in all of us about sexuality and they have no clue—how could they?—that it's going to destroy people."

"Do you make reference to me in the study?"

"Of course not. And not to your techniques, but Rafe, come on, people in the profession will know these are your guidelines, this is your procedure at the clinic."

"But you tested other techniques, also, right?"

A pause. Far, far in the background, I heard the whoop of children chasing each other and faint sounds of toy sirens.

"Phil?" I called.

"Rafe, your techniques are the purest, the least polluted by adult prompting. No verbal cues, all dolls, no pressure, everything videotaped. There was no reason to use other techniques. If yours don't work, the others would only be worse."

It was some time before I got up from the couch. I took a shower and I shaved, although earlier I had planned to indulge and leave the stubble until Monday. I went back and forth on the question of whether to broach the subject with Diane. I could tell her about Phil's call without confessing the mistake of my broken promise. But I had to admit to myself that giving Phil the tape of her sessions with the Peterson girls was an error, at least in tactics, if not principle. Now, when I read his study, if I found it to be flawed, and wished to attack the findings, Phil's reply would be more persuasive, and devastating to me personally, should he choose to reveal the origin of the techniques he tested. And I had no doubt he would betray me and reveal his source. He could do so and believe himself to be not only honorable, but noble, a scientist saving the innocent from persecution.

On Monday I followed my routine. I concluded there was no point in taking action or speculating until I had seen the data. Phil's packet arrived by Federal Express on Tuesday. I read most of his paper during my lunch hour, enough to know the extent of the damage. I decided then that further delay in telling Diane was unconscionable; besides, the objective situation was urgent. At two o'clock, fifteen minutes before I was due to lead a group session, just as I packed Phil's study and video in my bag to show Diane at home, Sally buzzed me to say that Gene Kenny was on the line.

Don't answer it, a primitive voice warned. I knew then that I was in bad shape mentally. An unhappy, dangerous Rafe had been given a voice again: "He's bad news," it said. "And you're not fit to treat anybody."

I picked up. "Gene?"

"Oh hi," he sounded relieved. "I'm sorry to call."

"Why?"

"I mean, I know you're busy. I just—I'm a little upset, that's all. And I didn't know who else to talk to."

"What's wrong?"

"I don't know where to start." I explained I had only fifteen minutes, but I could see him tomorrow morning. (Was I reaching for distractions? I wondered and then cursed Phil. What had he done to me? Was I going to doubt my every move? That isn't fair, I decided. Phil didn't invent my insecurities.)

"No, I can't tomorrow. Maybe next week. I just need to talk for a few minutes, that's all." And he did, saying he left Cathy some six or seven months before; two weeks ago they completed negotiations and signed a divorce agreement. He ended the marriage because he wanted to be with Halley all the time. It was terrible to do this to Pete, but living with a woman he didn't love was making him a bad Daddy too, he felt. He was distracted with his son, quick to anger, and eager to avoid being at home. By divorcing Cathy at least he would get to spend quality time with Pete—quality time was Gene's phrase. In fact, a number of artificial phrases had crept into his speech. I associated them with marketing. He said at one point, "And I needed to get my energy focused on the future, not a dead-end relationship. I need to create opportunities and maximize my potential," explaining why he also believed that living with Cathy was holding him back at work.

"But the real reason is that you wanted to be with Halley, is that right?"

"Yes," Gene said solemnly. And a natural tone returned. The harried executive was replaced by a vulnerable man. "I love her. I've never felt like this about anybody. I get sick to my stomach thinking about losing her."

"Why do you worry about losing her?"

"I *am* losing her," he said and his voice broke.

He reported they had been virtually living together for a couple of months, not openly because of the ongoing divorce talks, but they were free to do so now, even to plan marriage, which is what he wanted. Halley was resisting, however. She felt they shouldn't rush into marriage, that Gene couldn't be sure he wanted to make that commitment right after his divorce, and that probably moving in was premature. After all, she pointed out, they were together almost every night anyway. "Let's keep things the way they are for a while," she said.

"That's sounds reasonable," I commented.

"She's letting me down easy," Gene said, desperate and convinced.

"She's not breaking up with you. She's not refusing to see you."

"She doesn't have to. She's going to be away anyway. We've bought a French company—I mean, Stick, you know, he's CEO now, and the majority owner. He was part of a leveraged buyout of Minotaur and then we took over—well, I'm sure you read about it."

I told him I hadn't and that it didn't matter for the moment. I asked him how long Halley was going to be traveling.

"I don't know, I don't know," Gene mumbled. "I mean she's supposed to help set up this liaison office in Paris. She'll be going back and forth and there's talk about maybe, I mean now that the Soviet Union is open to us, that maybe she'll take some trips there—"

Sally buzzed me. My group was ready. I urged Gene to make an appointment. He said he wasn't sure about his schedule. He would call tomorrow. "Just tell me, what do you think? Am I exaggerating?"

"Maybe you're scaring her. She might be right. Perhaps you're so eager to get married because you're anxious about the divorce from Cathy becoming final. But let's meet," I urged him. "I'm more interested in why you feel so strongly about Halley—"

"I love her! I can't live without her," Gene said with such conviction I was startled. It was rare, surprisingly rare, to hear. Of course my patients were adolescents and children, nevertheless I had treated adults at Susan's clinic and I worked with parents or other caretakers. I was nonplussed. I wanted to say, "But that's absurd." Instead, I mumbled, "I see." After we hung up, I caught myself wondering: how do you know it's absurd?

[My vanity doesn't wish to leave the reader with an impression of intellectual naïveté. Naturally, as a professional, I would hear any patient's assertion that he or she can't live without someone not as an expression of true love, but some other disturbance. I confess this random thought, or feeling rather, to show the depth of my confusion at the time.]

Our conversation influenced me. I decided to make a clean breast to Diane. That was a struggle. Diane and I were supposed to go out to dinner with friends. I canceled the date. She found out before I had a chance to inform her. She confronted me in the clinic's parking lot when we met to drive home together.

"Lilly told me you canceled tonight. Something about an emergency."

"Did I say emergency?" I managed to summon a smile. "I guess I am panicked." I lifted my briefcase and said, "I've got Phil Samuels's new study."

Diane frowned. "Fuck him," she said. Her pert nose wrinkled. "It's so bad we can't eat dinner?" I noticed the few hours we spent out in the sun down in Tampa had already manufactured many new freckles. It wasn't anatomically possible for her to appear threatening. I knew I was in trouble with her, and that did frighten me, but I couldn't be scared of her.

"It's so bad we may have to give up breakfast too. Anyway, this isn't the place to talk about it." I got into the car. She stayed outside, still frowning. Her short bobbed black hair trembled faintly as she tilted her head. Her right index finger made a circle around her temple, and then she pointed at me. One of our teenage patients, who was playing basketball on the half court adjoining the lot, saw her do it. He let the ball dribble away while he laughed uproariously, clapping slowly as he doubled over. Diane blew him a kiss and got in.

"So what does this motherfucker's brilliant new study say?" she asked in a mock English accent, as if she were a duchess.

"I'd rather talk about this at home," I said.

"No chance, bub. You canceled dinner, so number one, you're cooking and number two, you're explaining yourself right away."

I tried a distraction. "You're in a good mood."

It worked. "I had a great day," Diane told me and went on to explain that she'd had a breakthrough with a seven-year-old girl who, a year ago, had been found by the police locked in a closet, her legs scalded by immersion in a tub full of hot water. She talked enthusiastically about her patient's progress for a while. Diane was saying, "She actually made a joke about her burns," when she caught herself and figured it out. "Wait a minute. Nice try. Tell me about Phil. Or at least give me the study to read."

"Now?" I asked, merging onto the Henry Hudson Parkway.

"Cut it out," she said as sternly as she could. "Quit stalling."

"Remember the construct? Kids six and under were brought in for a routine physical examination by a pediatrician. Everything is video-taped, of course. The doctor does a few unorthodox things: listens to their feet with a stethoscope, puts a paper cup on their stomach. Clothes are never removed. Then they were interviewed by therapists, as if there had been a charge of sexual molestation. Almost half the kids made up outrageous things about what the pediatrician did. Vaginal penetration, anal penetration, foundling of the genitals, the works."

"In how many interrogations?"

"Most of the kids who made up stuff did it by the second session."

There was a silence. I didn't look over at her. It was a lovely end to a mild spring day. To our left, the West Side of New York stood guard over the broad river on our right. The brown, silver, and white buildings were aged by grime and neglect; yet they were standing, to my eyes, as timeless as the flat shimmering water.

When Diane spoke, her light tone had darkened. "What aren't you telling me about this, Rafe?"

I waited. I swung around one of the highway's sharp curves, made narrower by a lane closed thanks to perpetual construction. Litter flew up from the car in front of me and slapped the side window. We were near our exit, near our home. I was apprehensive as I let the secret out, but I have to admit to a little excitement also, a feeling that at last I would learn something I might otherwise never have known for sure about our relationship. "Remember when Phil came to town almost a year ago?"

"Un huh," Diane said with such emphasis that I was convinced she had already guessed what I was going to say.

"I gave him the tapes of your sessions with the Peterson girls. He copied our technique."

"Jesus," she said quietly, but distinctly, making two widely separated syllables of His name.

"I haven't looked at the video," I continued. "I don't know how carefully—"

"It doesn't matter—" she began.

I talked over her, "And he doesn't identify the source of the technique."

"Oh, swell! Isn't that just grand? What a wonderful generous guy."

There was a long silence. I kept my eyes on the road. Perhaps a minute or two passed while I exited the highway, turning onto Riverside. Our garage was only a block away. I had to stop at a light. Then I looked at her. I was surprised, very surprised, and, at last, frightened by what I saw.

Diane's youthful face was turned to me. There were her girlish freckles, without frowns or wrinkles. Her features were calm and settled. But behind the round wire-rimmed glasses, her eyes were full of tears.

Our argument—the first of many, but in a real sense, the only important one—lasted until dawn and ended with her packing a bag to move out. First we watched the tape. Diane read the study, I re-read it, we watched the tape again. Since she subsequently attacked the finding in many public forums, her reaction is no secret. She believed Phil's study was corrupted by the pediatrician doing unorthodox, albeit harmless, things in the examinations. She complained—irrelevantly, I thought—that routine examinations are never conducted without a parent being present. And she asserted his graduate students merely imitated our techniques without any imagination, using the dolls right away despite the absence of preliminary indications of abuse.

"It's bullshit," she said to me at three o'clock in the morning. "You know it's bullshit. We would've stopped the interviews after the first round of questions. I would never have gone to dolls, not without some symptoms of emotional upset. It's just got nothing to do with the real world. He set out to prove kids are unreliable because that's what he wants to believe."

By then, I believed more talk was hopeless, but I spoke anyway. "We can't guarantee the performance of all therapists. You might not have fallen into this trap. But there are lots of mediocre or poorly trained professionals—"

"How do you know that? And what does it mean, anyway? Of course incompetent people can fuck up any procedure. Jesus Christ, a surgeon can kill somebody doing an appendectomy. What the fuck does that prove?"

Our disagreement boiled down to this: Diane believed our work was under siege by a culture unwilling to take responsibility for its neglect; that even if a small number of child abuse accusations by young children were wrongful, that was far preferable to returning to the old days when incest, beatings, and killings went on without any attempt to halt them, or treatment being available to abandoned children who have no resources. I replied that I had no intention of giving up our work with children we knew were abused, but to participate in interrogations that would be used in custody battles or criminal procedures, unless there was physical corroboration of abuse, was immoral. "I can't be party to something that might put innocent people in jail or cost them their jobs or make them pariahs to their families and their communities," I said.

"But that's totally impractical," Diane said, apparently still unable to absorb the fact that I was more than merely rattled by Phil's study. "Under the law, we *have* to report all accusations to the police. We'd have to close the clinic. Beside, we'd lose our grants. And even if we can some-how hobble along without funding, we'll have to turn away half our prospective patients without bothering to diagnose them. What about them? What about the kids who will slip through and end up crippled or worse? We can only be responsible for what we do. And I'm *sure* we haven't hurt any innocent people."

"How can you be sure?" I asked her. I was sitting on our bed with my legs crossed under me. She had just taken a bath, in a vain attempt to calm down, and looked tiny in a big white terry cloth robe and some-what blind too, since her glasses were off. The robe opened slightly as she paced, arguing. I could see her white thighs and the shadow of her sex. I felt regret, but no remorse. I was tired; not because it was past three in the morning; I was tired of uncertainty.

"I'm sure!" She walked up to me. She was small, but from my posi-tion on the mattress she looked big. "Are you telling me, are you really saying to *me*, that you're not sure? Do you think there's any chance Grandpa Peterson was innocent?"

This was our real fight. I bowed my head and said it. "Yes."

"No," she said, pleading really. "You're not serious."

"Yes. I think this means there was a chance we were wrong. I'm not blaming you . . ."

"Of course you are!" She pushed her hair up on both sides, forming a curly pile on top. Her neck was white and her ears small, perfectly formed. "I can't believe it. Fuck you, Rafe." There were no tears now. She glared at me while holding her head. She cocked it at me. "Why?" she asked and let go of her hair. She looked utterly bewildered, shrinking in the robe. "Why do you want to destroy us?"

No logic can answer such a question. For Diane, there was no signifi-cant distinction between this intellectual disagreement and the harmony of our relations. I had apologized over and over for lying to her about the tape, but, in the end, that wasn't what had hurt her. I was betraying her beliefs, her work, and worst of all, I had betrayed something she felt she had earned many times over: my faith in her.

"Don't you see what these bastards are doing?" she yelled after I didn't respond. "They don't give a fuck about this so-called truth you're always talking about! He's just trying to make a name for himself."

"His motives don't matter," I mumbled.

"What kind of shrink are you? 'His motives don't matter!'" she mocked me. "And your motives don't matter either, huh? You're punishing yourself, that's what this is all about. You're letting your father beat you up."

"That's specious," I said with utter contempt.

"That's specious?" Diane arched her back and squinted at the ceiling. She was breathing hard, as if running to catch up to the meaning of our fight. "You're right," she said softly in a panted whisper. "I'm just a second-rate shrink. You must be so tired of living with an inferior mind." With her eyes still raised, she opened her robe. Her skin was pink from the bath, her nipples dark and hard, the black hairs of her pubis matted and damp. "This is what I'm good for." She lowered her eyes to me. The grief I saw in the car was now rage. "You're right. I wasn't thinking." She came over to the bed and grabbed my hair. She pulled my head to her fragrant belly and pushed it down to her sex. "You want to be your Daddy, don't you? I'm supposed to die for your fucking principles." She lifted my head and came close to my face, her mouth opening. I thought for a moment she was going to spit. "You're right. I'm so stupid. I keep letting you get away with being the bad bad boy with his bad bad secrets. Well no more, Doctor. From now on, I'm gonna be the Mommy you deserve." She released her grip. "You're gonna feel sorry about me too. Very sorry."

From there, if possible, things got uglier. Despite my desire to make this a full account of the complicated interrelationship between my life and my treatment of Gene Kenny, I don't feel I need to go step by step through the degeneration of the longest sustained love affair of my life. The position I took was straightforward: the clinic would no longer participate in investigations or I could no longer work at the clinic. Nor would I help to rebut Phil's study until I had a response I believed in; Diane's criticisms were unconvincing or beside the point.

Yes, I agreed with her that Phil's study was part of a deep need in America to deny the dysfunction and abuse inherent in our society, a culture that permits, in some ways encourages, the systematic destruction of family life among the poor, especially poor urban minorities. From the popularity of biochemical determinism to the widespread use of Ritalin (ninety percent of its prescriptions written for black male children), from the disproportionate attention paid by the media to legal maneuvers that use child abuse as a means of getting profitable clients off to the cynicism about taxation for social services, all symbolized to me, as they did to Diane, that middle-class America wants to believe it is entitled to live only for its own satisfactions, that altruism is not only useless, but actually immoral. She was right about the motivation for Phil's study and the use it would be put to. But, for me, as it had been my whole life, ideology is not an answer to an issue of fact. If our techniques were flawed, nothing could justify continuing their use.

I don't mean to disparage the good intentions in Diane's position. Her defense of her own beliefs, her willingness to blind herself to the possibility of error, may well be the only way to function effectively in our society. My problem was that I wasn't sure I wanted to function effectively anymore. Out of respect for her sincerity, I put up no resistance to her demand that I turn over management and all the assets of the clinic to her. My lawyer howled at my sudden impoverishment—the buildings and grounds were worth millions and they were all I had left of my inheritance. I knew, however, that Diane had no intention of cashing in: she was going to continue the fight and I felt, right or wrong, she deserved to be armed.

As to her perception of my motive, I have no satisfactory answer. Perhaps I was beating myself up, or acting out my parents' drama, or one of the other psychological dysfunctions she taunted me with that night. Perhaps ideas had nothing to do with my leaving the clinic and ending our relationship. I am certainly aware of the basis for such a conclusion. I was not convinced.

In the tumultuous weeks of bitter argument that followed, I lost track of Gene. He called twice. I missed the first and forgot to return it. The second time he reached me.

"She's dumped me," he said with hardly any introduction. His voice was enervated. "She says there's no one else, but I don't believe it. She's fucking some guy in Paris. But that's the least of my worries."

It was late April by then. In deference to Diane, I said publicly that I was taking a sabbatical, rather than talk about my real situation: not only did I wish to sever my connection to the clinic, as the new boss, Diane didn't want me to continue in any capacity. I repeatedly refused to respond in the press to Phil's study. Diane, cleverly I thought, went on the offensive right away, denouncing Samuel for using our technique improperly. In so doing she neutralized his ability to make an impression with the revelation that the techniques he tested were ours. In fact, the study wasn't causing as much of a fuss as I had feared. Diane's side of the argument was as well-organized and funded as

Phil's. They called each other frauds and scoundrels in polite scientific terms and the predictable groups chose up sides. Whatever the outcome, this fight was going to be long and bloody. Diane was barely speaking to me by this time. She told me in our last extended conversation that she couldn't stand my holier-than-thou attitude; that I was worse than Phil: at least he had the courage to fight for what he believed. I was cleaning out my desk the day I spoke to Gene, preparing to leave the next morning for the Prager Institute in Baltimore. They had offered a year's grant for me to do any work I chose. At first, I planned to edit Amy Glickstein's first four chapters on Joseph's work, as well as check the final galleys for my book on our in-house therapy for the severely abused.

"What's the most of your worries?" I asked Gene. I happened to have my address book in my hand. I flipped to find the number of a therapist near Gene. He obviously needed attention.

"Cathy's moving out of New York. She's going to live with her mother in Arizona."

"Can she do that?"

"I never thought—fuck." Gene sighed. "Oh God, fuck me."

"What is it, Gene? Can't you stop her legally?"

"I was too impatient about the divorce. My lawyer told me to fight for some kind of clause, but Halley convinced— oh fuck, I can't even think about what an asshole I was. Cathy says Pete can visit me in the summer." He coughed. He sounded congested.

"Why does she want to move? Is it money?"

"No, no," Gene was weary of the subject. "Money won't keep her here. She says Petey's not doing well in school and her mother will help and anyway, she wants to go back to medical school."

"Maybe she'll give you custody."

"Are you kidding? She's punishing me. She's furious at me for Halley."

"What does your lawyer say?"

"He says if she goes, we can sue, but, you know, that doesn't mean we'll win and, in the meantime, I've lost him. I've lost everything."

"Well, not everything."

"Yes, everything." Gene sounded very faint all of a sudden. He said something too low for me to hear.

"What?" I asked.

This time the answer came loud. "I was fired."

"You were fired?"

"God," he said, more to himself.

"When, Gene? When did this happen?"

"Yesterday."

"By Stick?"

"Yeah. He fucking fired me. Can you believe it?" He breathed heavily into the phone. "I can't leave New York now. Not to go to Arizona, anyway. I've got to get a job fast. I'm sure I can. I mean, even though the business is in the toilet. No matter what Stick says, my reputation is great. I've already got one lead and I'm sure I could get something over at Apple."

"When did you and Halley break up?"

"It's not connected. She didn't dump me because he was going to fire me. She hates him. I mean, she's obsessed with him, but she still hates him."

"When did you break up?"

"Two weeks ago." That would have been around the time of the call I had missed. "Jesus, I wish you hadn't asked me that," he said in a sad whisper.

"Why?"

Gene sighed. "Why do you always have to think the worst of people?"

"That's my job, I guess. Gene, I'm leaving tomorrow for a long time. Maybe a year. But there's a terrific guy whom you should see—"

"Stop that!" Gene shouted. I looked at the phone I was so astonished. When I returned it to my ear he was saying, "If you don't want to see me, fine. You want me to hang up, I'll hang up."

"I don't want you to hang up. But I can't—" I gave up. "Look, let me give you the number where I'll be, okay?"

"Okay. Hold on. Okay, shoot." I told him the number. He repeated it back to me and said, "I'm fucked. I can't believe how fucked I am. I mean, what else can happen? Is a building gonna fall on me?"

"I think you should see Cathy."

"What?"

"Go and talk to her. Don't use lawyers for this. Explain to her how much it means to you to be able to see Pete. Explain that, at least until your job situation is settled, you need everything else to stay the same."

"I can't tell her I've lost my job. You have no idea how vindictive she is. I don't know what she might do with that information. Maybe she could get full custody and keep me away forever. You don't understand."

"I'm sure she's angry at you. But you're still Pete's father. It's worth a conversation. If you don't think you should tell her about the job, okay. But talk to her. At least tell her about you and Halley breaking up."

"Huh. That's a thought." He breathed heavily for a moment. Then he coughed again. "Maybe. Maybe I could make it seem like I broke up with her and . . . I don't know. Maybe. I'll try. I'll call her. You're gonna be at this new number tomorrow?"

"Yes. Call me anytime, Gene. Okay? And I'll call you in a few days if I don't hear from you."

He made sure I had his current number. He sounded a little calmer. At least, he said, "Thanks, I feel better."

An hour later, when I left the office, Sally asked me to step into Group Room B to check whether I wanted some files she had put aside. She opened the door for me and I saw a computer-generated banner; COME BACK SOON! before I heard the chorus of, "Surprise!"

All the kids I had treated were present, along with our full staff of therapists and resident counselors, including Diane. I think the biggest surprise was Albert, huge now, soon to be a freshman at Notre Dame, holding a champagne bottle in the air, threatening to douse me with its contents.

"I haven't won anything!" I complained, shielding myself.

The Prager Institute provided a secluded cabin for me to use as a study. The next day I was there, organizing Joseph's papers. I certainly didn't feel I had won anything at all. I started to work on Amy's chapters right away, but it proceeded slowly and painfully.

Gene never phoned. I tried him three days later and got a machine, leaving a message. Two weeks passed before I got the call. A high-pitched voice with a Queens accent introduced himself as Detective O'Boyle from the Westchester County Police. "Do you have a patient named Gene Kenny?" he asked me.

"What's this about, Detective?"

"Well, I can't tell you what this is about, unless you tell me you got a patient named Gene Kenny."

"I'm not treating him right now, but yes, he's a patient."

"Twenty-nine years old? Black hair, brown eyes. Married to Cathy Shoen. Nine-year-old boy named Peter. Worked at Minotaur Computers?"

By now I was alarmed. I straightened in my chair, found a yellow pad, and wrote on it, "May 12, 1991. 11:37 A.M." I thought to myself, No, it can't be. I said to the detective, "Yes, that's him. What's wrong?"

"Mr. Kenny committed suicide last night. He left a note addressed to you."

I shut my eyes. Some plant or weed growing around the cabin irritated them and kept my nose running. I had taken an antihistamine but my eyes were burning anyway. Again, I thought, No, it can't be. Then I opened my eyes.

I don't remember in which order O'Boyle recounted the facts, but I remember the facts. Gene went to his wife's house late the previous evening. Pete was asleep. They had a quarrel. At some point Gene hit Cathy. He didn't stop hitting her until she was dead. He woke up Pete around one o'clock. Concealing from the boy what had occurred, Gene walked his son to a neighbor's house. He told them Cathy was ill and he was taking her to the hospital. He asked if they would bring Pete to school in the morning. They were suspicious, but they were also sleepy and they agreed. Gene returned to Cathy's house, wrote two notes, one to me, another for the police. He turned on Cathy's car, closed the garage door, and waited in the front seat to die.

I asked O'Boyle if he would read Gene's note to me. He said he wanted to. He hoped I could explain it.

" 'I'm sorry, Rafe,' " O'Boyle recited. " 'I tried to convince her, but she just wanted to hurt me. Anyway, she was right to want to hurt me. Would you do me a favor? I don't know if you can keep Cathy's mother's hands off Pete. I'm sure my father will do nothing. But could you try to help Petey? Only you can help him. None of this is your fault. You did everything you could. You cured me. I'm not a neurotic anymore. It's just that I can't bear the normal misery of life.' "

O'Boyle asked if I could explain the last two lines. I had trouble talking at first. I cleared my throat several times before I could manage to say, "I guess he must have read Freud at some point. It's a paraphrase of something Freud wrote about the goal of therapy."

"Oh yeah?" Considering the subject of our conversation, the detective seemed remarkably at ease with me. "What's that? What did Freud write?"

" 'The goal of therapy is to replace the neurotic's unrealistic misery with the normal misery of life.' "

"No kidding," the detective commented. He read aloud the last few sentences of Gene's note one more time. " 'You cured me,' " he quoted

Gene in a mumble. "'I'm not a neurotic anymore. It's just that I can't bear the normal misery of life.'" O'Boyle raised his voice. "I still don't get it. Can you explain it to me, Doc?"

I didn't try.

Postscript

I WENT TO NEW YORK THE NEXT DAY. THE FIRST PERSON I SAW AFTER Gene's death was Susan Bracken, but an account of that meeting, as well as her surprising judgment of my work with Gene, belongs to the next section. I found out there would be no public funeral, no public memorial, no event that would mark Gene's passing. That was understandable. He had murdered his ex-wife and committed suicide. One could hardly expect a big family funeral. Gene seemed, from our therapy, to have no close friends; other than the Copleys, the intimacies he formed at work didn't penetrate his personal life. Halley and Stick wouldn't and didn't feel obliged. That left Don Kenny.

Detective O'Boyle told me Gene's father had arranged for the body to be picked up that afternoon to be cremated the next day. Perhaps Don planned to have someone say a few words; perhaps his friends would accompany him in his hour of grief and that would be Gene's memorial. I still don't know. I checked on Pete's whereabouts right away. Sure enough, Cathy's mother had come and would take him to Arizona.

After talking with Susan at her clinic in Greenwich Village, I walked down to the Bullshot gallery. I knew from my conversations with Gene that they represented Don's photography exclusively. The gallery is typical of SoHo, on the ground floor of a cast iron building. The ceilings are high, the walls white, the space wide and deep, its openness interrupted only by the supporting columns, which are sometimes painted white to fade away into the background or a bold color to make them stand out. Here they were done in black, which seemed to accomplish neither. A half wall divided Bullshot into two rooms. The front was devoted to a new photographer whose work seemed to be blowups of microscopic things, although I didn't stop to find out.

In back there was a retrospective of Don's work. 'The Garage Years," they called it. Thanks to Gene, I understood the reference. This was the first time I had seen the pictures that figured in my early sessions with Gene. They were straightforward portraits of people, traditional to my eyes. That surprised me. It's true they were not formal poses, the setting was always outside, and there was invariably an object at the center which provided drama or at least a comment on the person. The truth is, I didn't linger to appreciate them. I spotted what I hoped to find right away and moved to it.

The photograph was large, perhaps two by four feet. Black and white, of course, processed into a sheen that reminded me of old Hollywood movies. At its center is the white stone head of a lion. I've never bothered to check, but I assume it's one of the lions outside the Forty-second Street Library. A young, not beautiful, but apparently contented Carol Kenny leans against the side of the lion's head. Standing on the statue's base and partially in her arms is Gene, no more than five or six years old. Carol has a grip on his little wrist, feeding his clenched hand into the open jaws of the roaring lion, positioning it between the sharp canines. This dominates the center of the photo, and naturally your eyes drift to the boy's face to see his reaction.

He's not looking at his threatened hand, but at his young mother's face. His hair is wild and thick. His big eyes shine and his skin is smooth. All that is to be expected. But his expression is remarkable. And that's the surprise. There's no mock fear, and certainly no real fear. His mouth is wide open, showing the different-sized teeth of a growing child. And he's laughing. He's laughing with all his heart. He is full of trust and joy.

I decided then, that at least for me, the passing of this soul would not go unnoticed.

PART THREE

Evil:

Diagnosis and Cure

CHAPTER ONE

Case Review

"HOW MANY PATIENTS HAVE *YOU* KILLED?" I ASKED SUSAN. WE WERE walking through the Farmers' Market in Union Square, carrying take-out cappuccinos we bought at Dean & Deluca's on University Place. Flanking us were stalls of fresh fruit, vegetables, and home-baked pies, tended by men and women who didn't look like farmers. The goods are grown and baked upstate and sold three times a week in this open-air market, handwritten signs proclaiming their organic and healthful origins. New Yorkers are eager buyers. Susan and I were obliged to progress in baby steps because of the tightly packed crowd.

"Stop that," she said, whacking me on the shoulder. She diverted to the right to examine a row of apple bins. She backed off quickly, mumbling, "No, not Harry's favorite." She was fifty-three years old. Because she allowed her hair to be completely gray, demurely pulled back into a bun, she appeared older. Otherwise, she was hardly changed: tall, hunched over, all bones and limbs. Her flat forehead had a few more lines, but her muddy eyes remained friendly and always curious. Harry and Susan still lived in their loft on Sixteenth Street. Her clinics continued to operate in the Village and Brooklyn. "Let's go into the park," she said.

"Yes, ma'am."

We crossed between the stalls to reach Union Square Park. It was

lunchtime and there too were mobs of people: students and office workers eating sandwiches off paper bags spread on their laps, aiming hot
dogs at their mouths, or catching the tips of pizzas between their front
teeth. One couple necked passionately, their feet ringed by pigeons
searching for crumbs. "You didn't kill anybody," she said. She perched on
an empty stretch of wall dividing the park from the market. She opened
her container of cappuccino and licked the foam on the underside of the
lid. Her long legs kicked slowly back and forth, a grungy pair of New
Balance sneakers brushing the pavement.

I stayed on my feet facing her and raised a lumpy manila envelope in
my right hand. "I have tapes of all my sessions with Gene."

"You do?"

"I mean, for the adult period. Not from your clinic."

"You taped every word?" I nodded. Susan sighed. "Yet another reason
to hate technology. So now you're going to torture yourself listening to
them?"

"Actually I was hoping to torture you."

"Forget it."

"You know, Susan, in your old age you're developing a Yiddish accent."

"A little hostile today, are we? Well, you're right. Half the time I feel
like I'm running a very cranky temple." She sipped her cappuccino and
laughed. "Did you ever read Freud's letter to . . . I forget who. Anyway,
he was very excited that Jung had become a disciple. You know, this was
long before the Great Betrayal. He was so excited because Jung was a
nice Christian boy. We need Christian practitioners, he wrote. Sigie was
worried everybody would think psychoanalysis was just a Jewish thing."

"Maybe that's what killed Gene. I fed him chicken soup when what
he needed was a martini."

"I'm not worried," Susan said. "If you can make jokes, I'm not worried."

She changed the subject, asking after Diane. She knew the cover story
of my sabbatical from the clinic, not the truth. I told her everything. She
wasn't pleased. "What do you want? Someone to punish you?"

"Are you my friend, Susan?"

"Of course. I love you."

"Then don't be clever with me. You trained me. I want you to review
the case and give me an opinion."

For the first time she looked at the bulky envelope. "You'd better take me to the Wiz." She nodded at the discount electronics store facing the west side of the park. Red signs pasted inside its windows proclaimed a sale. Susan shrugged. "My tape player is broken."

We walked to the Wiz and were forced to pick out a boom box; they had nothing smaller. She gave the salesman her Visa card. He went off to get the purchase approved. She asked me what Gene wrote in his suicide note. I told her the gist of it. She said, "Are you going to do something about his boy?"

"Not right away."

"No?" Her skeptical tone implied disapproval.

"I'm not treating anyone until you review his case."

"All done," the Wiz salesman interrupted, returning with her credit card. He also handed her a yellow receipt. "You give this at the front and they'll give you the boom box." He offered her a pink copy. "This is your receipt."

"To the front?" Susan was confused. "Who's at the front?"

The salesman leaned over to show her. Beside the scanners at the door to discourage shoplifters was a huge black man in an Oakland Raiders cap. "That man. You give him this," the clerk touched the yellow slip, "and he'll give you the radio." He tapped the pink slip. "You keep this."

Susan pointed to the radio out on the counter. "Why can't you just give me this one?"

"This is a display model. He's got to—" the salesman gave up, exasperated. "Just go! Give him the yellow. He'll give you a radio same as this, but brand-new. In the wrapping and everything. It'll be perfect."

"Why don't you have the brand-new ones out here?"

"These are only for display. We keep the stock in the basement.. It comes up there and he gives it to you."

Susan turned to me. "Do you understand this system?"

"Perfectly," I said. "It's part of the inventory control. More shelf space, fewer goods to shoplift and it's tougher for the employees to steal. My uncle claimed he invented it when he owned Home World."

I had piqued the salesman's curiosity. "Your uncle ran Home World?"

"Yes."

He leaned on the counter, gestured to me to come closer, and asked in a low voice, "What happened to them?"

"His son-in-law sold it and then, I don't know, they expanded and suddenly went bankrupt, right?"

The salesman shook his head and looked troubled. "It's a jungle, I tell you. Cut-throat business. They were big," he said, leaning back, his eyes scanning the Wiz's formidable space.

"Let me ask you something," Susan said to the salesman.

"Don't start." He put up a warning hand. "Give him the yellow. They bring it up from the basement and you got your radio. In the wrapping. Brand-new."

"No, no," Susan said. "That's not my question."

"What? What's your question?"

She pointed to the distant pickup counter and the man in the Raiders cap. "What's his name?"

"His name? You want to know his name?"

"Yes, what's his name?"

"Anthony. His name is Anthony."

"Okay," Susan said pleasantly, wandering off. "Come on, Rafe. Let's see if Anthony does what he says."

He did. Susan insisted I walk her back to her office, unpack the boom box, plug it in, load tape number one and test that it worked. When I heard Gene's voice say, "Are we being recorded?" I shut my eyes.

At least, that immediately intrigued Susan. She listened to me evade Gene's question, and asked, "You didn't tell him?"

I hit the Stop button. I gave her a list of the key sessions. Brief notes explained their subject matter. The heart of those sessions the reader already knows. I told Susan it would probably be sufficient for her to listen to just those tapes.

She squinted at my list. "Ten," she said and pouted. "Even that's ten hours. I don't know when I have the time. Could take me a week."

"Take two weeks. Take twenty. I'm doing nothing until I have your opinion."

"And this nothing you'll be doing, where will you be doing it?" I told her I planned to return to the Prager Institute and wait. She invited me to stay at their loft. "You could help me here at the clinic. You'll be doing me a big favor. I'm short-handed. Billy's got the flu. You could fill in for him. He's family therapy. Mostly kids. So you're perfect."

"Nice try," I said. I went downtown to Don Kenny's show in SoHo, saw the photograph of Gene and his mother with the lion, and returned to Baltimore.

I didn't do nothing. Since I had listened to nearly twenty hours of the tapes before taking them to New York, I prepared additional notes for my case review with Susan. And I tracked the movements of Pete Kenny and Mrs. Shoen, Cathy's mother. After three days in New York, she took him to her home in Phoenix.

I made a series of calls. By a stroke of luck, I found a child psychologist in Phoenix, David Cox, who consulted in the local public school system. I knew Cox from a conference in Boston years ago and felt confident enough to phone him and explain my situation. I told him I assumed Mrs. Shoen would put Pete in school in the fall and wondered if he could check on the boy.

Cox went me one better. He called back on Friday, having spoken with Mrs. Shoen. Cox phoned her out of the blue, saying he had heard gossip about the tragedy and offered a sympathetic ear. Mrs. Shoen was relieved to discuss her situation. Pete still didn't know the truth; he was told his parents died in an accident. Perhaps that is the truth, I thought. Mrs. Shoen made an appointment to come in next week and Cox assumed he would eventually get to see Pete.

"Let me know if I can be of any use," I said.

"I could use some background on the father."

"Sure. But for now, you should just deal with Pete, don't you think?" Cox tried again to find out more than the sketchy details I had already surrendered, but I stalled him. "As far as I know, the boy didn't have emotional problems."

Cox was silent for a moment. When he spoke, his tone was polite. Too polite. "Well, besides the murder-suicide, there was the divorce."

"I mean, of course, prior to those events. Gene wasn't seeing me during the divorce or after it."

"Of course there was some history to the divorce," he commented, again with excessive politeness.

"Call me after you see Pete and we'll talk," I said.

Susan phoned Saturday afternoon. She had only taken four days. "Well," she said, "I'm almost done. Why don't you come here tomorrow?"

"When?"

"Twelve? For brunch. We'll let Harry sleep late and have Nova and bagels."

I knew better than to ask for a preliminary judgment. I fancied I heard in her tired voice the sadness she would feel at having to tell me I had failed. The confirmation seemed inevitable. Five days of a queasy stomach and five nights of restless and abbreviated sleep had already convinced me. Sunday, although I hadn't managed to doze off until after midnight,

I woke up at four-thirty exhausted, a typical symptom of depression. I decided to drive to New York immediately.

After parking the car, I walked the quiet Sabbath streets for two hours to get some exercise, found a coffee shop one block from Susan's, pushed down my irrational feelings, and reviewed my notes with a cold, if bleary, eye. I felt ready by the time I buzzed the intercom to her loft.

Harry opened the elevator door—it leads right into their living room. "I'm going, I'm going," he said. He was in green nylon gym shorts with PAL embroidered on the side. His gray T-shirt had a hole the size of a quarter over his stomach. There was a volleyball under his arm. He entered the elevator as I exited. As he passed, he patted my shoulder affectionately. "Hope you're here when I get back."

I stood alone in the gloom of their living room. The loft's windows are at the front and back, leaving the middle untouched by natural light. Susan appeared from the kitchen area carrying a platter with bagels to the table.

"Sit," she said as she went by.

The table was drenched by the sun. Gleams came off the silverware. My eyes watered and I longed for sleep. From my position in the shadows, a brilliant Susan poured glowing orange juice into a shimmering glass. She was a vision of goodness. A goofy goodness, however. Her hair, freed from its bun, spread out stiffly and unevenly. Her denim shorts appeared to be fashioned by her own hand, loose threads trailing down her legs. The white men's dress shirt she wore must have been Harry's; the sleeves were two inches too short, her thin neck was lost in the wide collar, and there was at least a foot of air between the material and her body. Still, she was an unearthly white, like the Good Witch of the *Wizard of Oz*, and the sight paralyzed me.

Noticing that I was stuck, she urged, "Come on." I didn't move. She put the juice down. "You did right by him, Rafe. I'm sorry. I know you hoped I would tell you that you did a lousy job, but you were good enough."

"Good enough," I repeated.

"Come and eat. Yes, good enough. At times, much better than good. Occasionally you were too casual. But you did a fine job. You have nothing to be ashamed of."

I trudged to the table and sat.

"You look terrible," she said, cutting a onion bagel and handing it to me. It was hot. The cream cheese would melt, I thought, unhappily.

"I'm not sleeping well," I said.

Susan slabbed a lot of cream cheese on a poppy seed bagel for herself. "I buy this low-fat cream cheese for Harry, so I have to eat twice as much. I hope that makes sense to you. Harry says it doesn't."

"It makes sense," I said.

She speared slivers of pale red Nova with a fork and carefully arranged them around the hole of her bagel. She glanced at me. "You're not eating either? No sleep, no food and what else are you not doing? Oh, that's right, no human contact. Just living like a monk going over your papers."

"What was my biggest mistake?"

"I'm not sure you made any mistakes." Susan opened her mouth wide and took a ferocious bite.

"Come on. Everybody makes mistakes."

"Why nothing about the prostitute?" she asked through the mouthful. She swallowed, gulped a third of her orange juice, and asked, "Why didn't you challenge that?"

I opened my briefcase and took out my notebook.

"*Oy,*" Susan said. She put a hand on the cover to stop me from flipping it open. "No. Just talk. In fact, that reminds me. What was this with the taping? With *your* memory? Felicia still calls you Mr. Memory. What for? Didn't you learn anything from Watergate?"

"I like to think Nixon has more to hide than I do," I said. "I guess I was wrong."

"Why the taping?" she insisted.

"The technology was there for legal reasons having to do with the kids. Parents often consult in that room and—" I reached for my orange juice, thought about taking a sip, and didn't. "The technology was there. I suppose I could have . . . I didn't like him!" The truth came out suddenly and surprised both of us. I think. "I never liked him. You remember what you're interested in. I was worried I wouldn't be able to concentrate on the banalities of his life. All I ever expected to hear—all I did hear, really—were the classic complaints of an excessively conventional middle-class man. A thoroughly civilized, timid, unimaginative loser." I was almost shouting.

Susan took another bite. This one was smaller. She chewed thoughtfully. Sweat broke out from under my arms and at my temples. I couldn't remember perspiring for the past week, although it had been humid in

Baltimore. I drank my juice and waited for her. After she swallowed, she said, "You're very angry at him. He really let you down."

"Pathetic. Puerile. Egotistical. Savage." These were all judgments of my anger at Gene, not disagreement with Susan. The reverse, in fact.

"Welcome to the human race," Susan said.

For two hours, she walked me through my reactions to Gene, emphasizing not my therapeutic maneuvers, but the events in my life that coincided with their implementation. We found, as the case history reveals, that often I reacted to him as an analogy to what was happening to me elsewhere. For example, the decision to confront Gene openly with the psychic material of his dream as I, for Albert's sake, chose to convert the clinic into full-time care.

"So I was wrong to interpret the dream so bluntly," I said at the conclusion of her review.

"No, I don't think you were wrong. Maybe you were a little harsh." She changed her tack. "It was quite a brilliant interpretation."

"Thank you."

"You're welcome. But I don't think you appreciate how brilliant."

"What do you mean?"

"You uncovered all this rage at women, at his mother, which is what he turned his wife into, as you told him. When his mother rejected him—"

"He rejected her. By marrying Cathy."

"She felt abandoned. But Gene felt she rejected him. That was your insight. You said it yourself to him. She became a vengeful woman because she felt abandoned first by her husband and then her son. And how did he react? He wished her into the terminal. He wished her to die."

My hands were trembling. I had drunk a lot of coffee since waking at four-thirty and that was part of the reason. Only part. Susan covered my shaking fingers with her hand and stroked soothingly. "You need some sleep. Some real sleep."

"I should have known, that's what you're telling me. I should have known Gene might kill his wife."

"No! He never battered her. How could you make that leap?" Susan slapped my hand. "You've got to stop trying to be the bad guy. You can't get rid of all the evil in the world by swallowing it yourself."

"All the evil in the world?" I repeated. "What kind of shit is that?"

Susan asked gently, "Don't you believe in evil?"

"In what sense? As the missing mass of the universe? You're not telling me Gene was evil?"

"Of course not."

"Then what? When Gene killed his wife it was just an evil cloud that happened to rain on him? Evil is a judgment, Susan. To us, Hitler is evil. To a member of the Nazi party, he is good. You like cream cheese. Some people like butter."

"You wanted butter on your bagel?" she asked, amazed.

"No! Of course not."

"I didn't think so. Look, I'm not going to argue philosophy with you, Rafe. I'll get a headache. There was no way you could know he might one day make that wish to be rid of a vengeful woman into a reality. Everything was going wrong with his life. He'd been fired, he'd lost the woman he loved, his wife probably really gave it to him. What did he have left but his son? Oh, that's a question. What's your opinion of that relationship?"

"With Pete?" I drank more juice before answering. "Gene hoped to repair the traumas of his childhood by how he raised Petey. Don Kenny was emotionally distant from Gene. Physically close when he was young, which Gene repeated with Pete, by the way, and then Don was totally self-concerned once his career took off. In the end, it was the Jungian nightmare. Gradually Gene repeated his father's pattern. Gene's performance as the dutiful husband and attentive father was self-conscious. He really wanted to be a killer in the computer business and to have sexual adventures. When he first came to me he was living this lie, trying to make it up to himself for his father's betrayal. I concentrated on letting him discover what he really wanted. Then it was up to him. He chose promotion and Halley over his wife and son. Is that evil?"

"It's selfish."

"Is that evil?"

"It ain't good."

I laughed. "And I was supposed to let him go on with his illusions? He was miserable. His wife was miserable. They weren't having sex, they were hardly talking. Was that . . . ?" I stopped.

"What?"

"I'm a fool. At least they were alive. I seem to have lost all common sense. Of course they were better off."

"All right!" Susan dropped her knife onto her plate. It clattered angrily. "That's enough. I'll tell you my opinion. I know you won't like it.

I know you'll reject it, but this is the simple truth: Gene was weak. He came to you, over and over, no matter how many times you tried to discourage him, and he asked you: help me be strong, help me be a man. Each time you did, he got scared. And finally, you left him no choice. Nowhere to hide. That's what you did with the dream and later, with the prostitute, right?"

"The prostitute was a distraction."

"Yes, I would—most therapists—would have spent a year, maybe two just on that diversion. He asked you to do the impossible and you did it. *That* was your mistake." Susan leaned back with triumph.

"Doing my job was a mistake?" I asked, incredulous.

"No! *He* was the mistake. You cured his neurosis against his will. He didn't want to be cured. He wanted to be comforted. He wanted you to fail and he wanted to blame you and go on living miserably, but you were too clever. You fixed something he didn't want fixed."

"Then I did kill him."

The elevator landed on their floor. Its locks tumbled.

"He was a schmuck, Rafe! Sooner or later he would have killed himself. He needed backbone, not insight. He was like the princess and the pea."

The door opened. A volleyball rolled out, dribbling softly across the dark living room.

"Harry?" Susan called. She got to her feet, anxious. "Is it your back, Harry?" She whispered to herself, "He's too old for this nonsense." She moved toward the open door. As she neared it, Harry leapt out, pretending to be a ballerina, his thin arms aloft, dancing on the tiptoes of his dirty sneakers, his ample belly trembling underneath a T-shirt darkened by perspiration.

"I'm beautiful," he sang tunelessly. He stopped and looked at me. "Am I a role model? No, I'm just the greatest volleyball player in North America. Parents are role models."

Susan shut the door with a bang. *"Meshuga,"* she said, tried to frown, but it expanded to a smile. Harry attempted another pirouette, stumbling into the couch; she laughed with delight.

Harry gathered himself and strode over to her. He pecked her on the lips. "And here is my groupie, willing to perform whatever sexual service I want."

Susan backed away from him. "Take a shower. Then I'll be your groupie."

"The hell with that. I'm eating." Harry walked to the table, grabbing a bagel and a knife before he settled in a chair. "Well, what's the verdict?" he asked me, still standing.

"You're telling me she didn't tell you?" I said.

"I'm telling you she didn't tell me," he answered. He sat at last, reached for the cream cheese and paused, outraged. "You ate all the cream cheese," he accused Susan.

"There's plenty."

He showed me the container. Three-quarters was gone. "This is enough for . . . what? Half a bagel?"

"I got another," Susan said, disappearing into the kitchen.

Harry fixed his bagel and whispered, "She told me you did good work."

"That's not what she just told me," I said, as Susan returned with another box of low-fat cream cheese.

"What did you tell him?" Harry said. He grabbed the container away from her. "This is mine. You've had enough."

"Maybe Rafe wants more."

"What did you tell him?" Harry insisted.

"I told him he went too fast." Susan sat, brushing her wild hair back. "That's the only mistake I can see," she said to me. "Maybe if you were fooled a little, and it all went slower, maybe he wouldn't have been so shocked to discover he was living in a real world, with real troubles, and real pain."

"You're right. I rushed. I was competing with Joseph. I had Prozac envy."

"Prozac envy," Harry said and chuckled. He had made himself a towering bagel, using up all that remained of the Nova. "Well, we all make mistakes. Right?" Harry took a bite. His cheeks puffed. Susan and I watched his mouth work. He looked at me, eyebrows up, asking me to agree. He shifted his eyes to Susan and then frowned. He swallowed. "I mean," he had to pause to swallow again. "We can't succeed with every patient."

"You don't understand," I explained. "It's not that I couldn't succeed with this patient. A year ago, I told him he was fine. I said, 'You're cured. Go and live your life.' Well his life ended pretty quickly. Obviously, I made a mistake."

"You didn't make a mistake!" Susan shouted.

Harry dropped his bagel. "What *is* your problem? What is so terrible about making mistakes?"

"He didn't," Susan pulled her wild hair back and pushed her face at me until she was only inches away, her eyes lit by the sun, intent and earnest. "You mustn't fall for that. This was not your failure. It was Gene's."

"You're just softening it," I mumbled.

"When did I ever soften things for you! Listen to me. Of course you weren't perfect. Nobody's perfect. But for every time you rushed or missed something, there are a dozen times you got it just right. That wasn't the problem. Gene was the problem. He was weak. Right from the beginning and all the way through—he was always weak. Nothing terrible ever happened to him. He walked in on his parents screwing. His father was an opportunist. His mother was a silly passive woman. So what? Think of your kid patients. Think of what they survived. Think of you." Susan touched my arm. She whispered, "Everybody isn't created equal, no matter what the Constitution says."

"Excuse me," Harry said.

I was staring into the comfort of her forgiving eyes, wanting never to look away.

But Susan looked away. She cleared her throat. "What is it, Harry?"

"Rafe," he said. "Can I ask you a question?" I gave him my attention. "Do you always take it this hard when you lose a patient?"

Susan stared at the table.

I smiled at him. "Yes," I said. "I guess it's narcissistic. I apologize."

"I got somebody going down the drain on me once a month." He shrugged. "I guess this guy was special."

"No," I said.

"No?" He was amazed. "Jesus, what happens to you when it's someone you really care about?"

"Harry, go take a shower," Susan said.

"What?" Harry sniffed his armpits. "You can smell me all the way over there?"

I mumbled, "Leave him alone."

Susan banged the table with the end of her knife to emphasize each word: "I won't let you add this to your list of sins."

"I'm not saying he sinned!" Harry complained. "I was just saying sometimes you do your best and it's not good enough. You know, like a team foul. The therapy didn't work, but no one's to blame. That's happened to you before, right? I mean this isn't the first time a patient went bozo on you, right? All I wanted to know—" Harry stopped talking. I was watching him so I didn't see the face Susan made that shut him up. "Why are you looking at me like that?" he asked her.

Susan waved the knife at him. Its blade was coated white from the cream cheese. "He's never lost a patient," Susan said. "This is the first time for him. Okay? Now go take a shower. Everybody loves you, Harry, and you don't stink, but go take a shower anyway. Rafe and I have some more things to discuss, then we'll all go for a walk on this beautiful day."

Harry stood up. He looked out his tall window for a moment. He turned and walked past me a step or two. "How long you been practicing? Fifteen years?" I nodded. I felt his hand on my shoulder. "Never?" he asked.

"Susan's exaggerating," I said. "My patients kill themselves regularly. It's just that usually I don't tell them they're cured."

He patted my shoulder twice and left. Susan waited until she heard the bathroom door close. She looked out the window. "This is ridiculous, you coming to me. I'm not qualified to judge your work, to answer these doubts. I know I'm right, don't get me wrong, but you've always made too much of me."

"You saved my life—"

"No—"

"—How can I make too much of that?"

"I'm competent. That's all. You don't have a realistic memory of our work together. You did most of it. You'd come in with a memory or a dream and, halfway through the session, you'd analyze it while I was still busy copying down what you said. You healed yourself with that meticulous brain of yours. And with your vision, your terrible, clear vision that won't let anyone off the hook, especially not you. That's the only character problem you've got left from the bad old days. You won't give yourself a break."

"You won't tell me I failed because you're scared of what I'll do if I come to that conclusion. But you're wrong, Susan. I can accept that I screwed up. I won't freak."

"No?" She stood up and began to cover things—the orange juice container, the cream cheese—while scolding me. "You threw away your life's work at the clinic because of some crazy research that made you think maybe, just maybe, you *might* make a mistake. And not just *you*. You were worried maybe one of your colleagues would make a mistake."

Everything was covered now. She picked up the knife and licked off the white residue of cream cheese. "It's clear as day to me that Gene was responsible for what happened to him. But I can't convince you because deep down you know I'm not your equal. And you're right. What you need is to go back to your real work with children. Every day you don't work with them is a loss to the world. That's your failure, Rafe. Not this—you should forgive me—this poor schmuck who destroyed himself and his family."

"Susan, you reviewed my treatment of Gene just now and showed me that I made shifts in my approach to him because of events in my life. My technique was—"

"Oh come on! We're human beings, Rafe. You know that. Of course that's what happened. Good or bad, that happens with all therapists. It's a relationship, after all."

"Will you admit that it was at least partly my fault?"

"No." She tucked the orange juice carton under her arm and loaded her hands with the empty bagel platter and the cream cheese. "It was Gene's fault. You asked for my opinion. I admit I'm just an ordinary run-of-the-mill therapist but I'm telling you no one I know, no one I've ever met, could have done a better job." With her hands full, she nodded at the rest of the brunch's debris. "Help me clean up this mess." The Good Witch wandered away from the sunlight. As she retreated into the dark, she called back, "Make yourself useful."

CHAPTER TWO

Judgment Day

I DISTINCTLY REMEMBER WHEN MY PLAN FIRST TOOK SHAPE. I WAS OUTSIDE my studio on the institute's grounds, sitting in a lawn chair I had borrowed from the main house, positioned under a leafy maple for shade from the intense June sun. On my lap was a notebook in which I was trying to begin a standard case history of my work with Gene. I had recorded my successes; why leave out the failures? Contrary to what Susan said, there had been others, although none so shocking and unexpected as Gene. I decided to write a book of my mistakes, beginning with his case.

I intended to start with an account of my last few sessions with Gene. I was about to introduce Halley and Stick when I realized that, although I had been told over and over of Halley's beauty and Stick's charisma, I had no idea what they looked like. For a moment I was convinced Gene had told me she was a blonde, but I became unsure. I would have to listen to the tapes again, a dismaying prospect. Well, it doesn't matter, I concluded, and then it hit me.

It doesn't matter? Surely it mattered to Gene and he was my subject. And Stick's living presence also mattered, the timbre of his voice and the look in his eye when he fired Gene. Would I wish someone to tell my story, of my terror in Tampa, or my collapse in Great Neck, without knowing the sound of Bernie's cello or at least taking a look at a picture of my skinny green-eyed mother and her tall Latin husband?

The hand poised to write halted. A breeze lifted the heavy arms of the maple. I shut my eyes as the moving air washed over me. I knew nothing about Gene's life. I thought of myself as the greatest expert in the world on the subject, yet I had neither seen nor heard nor touched any of its crucial elements. When I opened my eyes, I closed the notebook.

About an hour later I walked into Prager's research library to ask what kind of computer they used to store their database. I was disappointed, keenly disappointed, to hear it wasn't Black Dragon or anything made by Minotaur Computers. I wanted to see one of the machines Gene helped build.

I phoned their corporate headquarters in Westchester. I intended to ask the operator to give me their sales department but an operator didn't answer. At least not a live operator. There was an automated system. I was instructed, if I had a touch-tone phone, to press the pound key (I had no idea whether the pound key was the asterisk or the number sign) followed by the extension I wanted, or to press other numbers to reach various departments. If I did nothing, I was told an operator would be on to help me. One of the alternatives was to press five and the pound key to reach their executive offices. I guessed (wrongly) that the pound key was the asterisk.

"Good morning, Minotaur," a female voice said almost immediately.

"Theodore Copley please."

"His extension is eleven. Please make a note of it. I'll transfer you."

What was I going to say? I wondered. That was a novelty. Unplanned speech isn't something psychiatrists engage in with a stranger. Of course, he wasn't really a stranger.

"Mr. Copley's office."

"Is Mr. Copley there?"

"Mr. Copley's out of town. May I take a message?"

"No, that's all right," I said, abruptly feeling stupid. "Is he in New York?" came out of me, without thinking.

"Until Wednesday he's in the city. But he'll be picking up his messages."

"At the convention?" I continued with my blind guessing.

"Convention? No," she enunciated slowly, becoming suspicious. "Can I take a message, sir?"

"No, I'll call back. Thank you."

I sat at my desk, my hand still on the cradled receiver, feeling foolish. I realized the first issue was whether they knew my name, or indeed, of my existence. Gene told me he wanted to keep it a secret from Stick that he was seeing a psychiatrist, but Cathy knew, and presumably he also told Halley. I couldn't remember a specific reference to a discussion of his therapy with Halley and, upon reflection, that was odd. There's usually quite a strong reaction from a patient's partner about his or her psychotherapy. (Cathy, for example, frequently complained I was causing trouble in their marriage. She was perfectly right, of course.) At the very least there's an overpowering curiosity; more typically resentment and criticism of the doctor; and sometimes competition that takes the form of the partner beginning his or her own therapy. Gene was besotted with Halley. He must have confessed everything about his life to her. She, I guessed, would have eventually informed Stick. If not before Gene's suicide, certainly after.

I called the Minotaur automated system again, waited through all the announcements, and finally got an operator.

"Good morning, Minotaur," said the same voice that had told me to make a note of Stick's extension.

"Halley Copley, please."

"Extension five-three. Please make a note of it. I'll transfer you."

"Ms. Copley's office," said a male voice after several rings.

"I have an urgent fax for Ms. Copley. Is she in Paris or—?"

"She's here."

"Thanks. I'll fax it right away." I hung up before he could become inconveniently helpful.

I packed an overnight bag. I could drive there before the end of the workday. I took only clothes. I couldn't remember, not even when Diane and I vacationed, a time that I was without at least a notebook. There was something invigorating about the improvisation and leanness of going to see her immediately.

Minotaur wasn't hard to find. It dominates a flat stretch of land roughly a quarter mile from the Tarrytown exit on the Saw Mill, bordered on one side by a pond, by woods on the other. There are two long massive beige structures that house the labs. In the center is a four-story office building, mostly glass. The testicles are bigger than the phallus, I thought, as I turned into the two-lane driveway. Actually, at the entrance the two lanes widen to four, each gated, for entering and exiting on either side of a security booth. The outer lanes are automated, allowing employees to swipe an ID card through a machine that opens the barrier. The interior lanes, for visitors, require you to stop and confront the guard.

The guard was a skinny young man, no more than twenty-one, with brilliant red hair. He wore a pale blue uniform, including a hat, although it was hot. The hat was too big for him, covering most of his forehead. "Hi," I addressed him in an official, harassed tone. "I don't have an appointment. I'm here to see Halley Copley. Her extension is five-three. My name is Neruda."

He reached for a phone and repeated, "Mr. Neruda?"

"Hold it for a sec. She doesn't know my name. Say that I'm here to talk to her about Gene Kenny's suicide."

He stared at me for a moment. "Excuse me?"

"Eugene Kenny. He worked here. He committed suicide four weeks ago. Did you know Mr. Kenny?"

"Me?" he asked nervously.

"He worked here, right?"

"I don't know." He gestured to the automated gate. "If they work here, they just go right through."

"So you never had any contact with him." I stared at his photo-badge to read his name. "Is that right, Patrick?"

"No, sir. I mean, yes sir."

"Do you know anyone who did? I want to talk to anyone who knew him."

"No, sir. But personnel or maybe Ms. Copley could help with that."

"All right, son. Go ahead and tell Ms. Copley I'm here."

He turned away from me to whisper into his telephone. I don't know if he told Halley's male secretary that I was a detective, but that's what he assumed. He met me in the main lobby. He was as tall as I, and as thin and young as the guard, but his hair was brown. He stood in front of a white Formica reception desk, manned by a pretty black woman wearing a phone headset. "Detective?" he said, approaching with his hand extended as I came in through a smoked glass door. "I'm Jeff Lasker, Ms. Copley's assistant."

"Detective?" I repeated with a smile. I shook his hand. "No. I'm Dr. Neruda. I'm a psychiatrist. I guess this *is* a kind of detective work. Forensic psychiatry. But I'm not working for the police. At least not at the moment." I didn't hope to accomplish anything through these mildly deceptive tactics except to hurry up the process of seeing Halley.

Perhaps I hoped to catch her without a chance to prepare herself. I wanted as spontaneous a reaction as possible.

"So you're not here at the request of the police?" He wasn't bristling, merely confused.

"I've spoken to Detective O'Boyle and he asked for my help with something about Gene, but no. I just want to have a talk with Ms. Copley for my own sake. This isn't official. Is she available?"

"Do you have any identification? I'm sorry, but we have to check." He didn't sound sorry.

"No problem," I said. I showed him both my driver's license and my AMA card.

He was more interested in my medical identification. He gave it a long look and then offered me a becoming smile. "She's on an overseas phone call right now, but she should be available in ten minutes. Why don't you sign in here?" He pointed to a book on the receptionist's desk. "And I'll take you to the conference room. She'll be with you soon."

The conference room was banal. A long rectangular black table, black leather swivel chairs, two water pitchers. The only unusual item was an impressively sleek computer set apart at a workstation in the corner. Nevertheless, seeing the nondescript room gave me the sort of chill one might feel in the presence of a great landmark. I looked out the smoked glass windows and confirmed that they faced the parking lot. This was the scene of Gene and Halley's first kiss.

I didn't care about anything. Not Cathy, or little Pete. Or even me.

I settled in one of the swivel chairs, but soon I was on my feet. My eagerness to see her was disturbing, but I couldn't dampen it. I paced until I thought to check whether the computer was Gene's machine. The label read H-1000. I was ignorant of that model. It could still be Gene's handiwork. I hadn't seen him for his last year at Minotaur, a period in which he was supposedly in charge of all design. Perhaps this was his last creation.

Stop romanticizing, I warned myself, and moved to the window to stare at the dull view of parked cars, giving my back to the door.

When it opened I didn't turn. I saw enough of a reflection in the dark glass to know a woman had entered. She lingered just inside the conference room, her hand still on the doorknob. I waited.

"Dr. Neruda?" she finally spoke. Her voice was deep, perhaps somewhat hoarse, but I doubted her sultry tone was caused by a cold in the throat. Gene said everything about her was sexy.

I turned for my first look. She was shorter than I expected. Gene's awed passion for her had inflated her height in my imagination. In fact, she was petite, five four, certainly less than a hundred pounds, small hands and feet. She wore a bulky black jacket over a white blouse buttoned to her neck, but there was enough of a rise against those layers to let you know her breasts were probably not petite. Her nose and brow were delicate. I was also surprised by her coloring. I had pictured her as blonde and fair. In fact, her long straight hair was raven black and her skin, unblemished and smooth, appeared almost tanned. Her full lips were painted bright red, her eyes were dark circles, set a little too close together, and they glistened, watching me somberly. The overall effect was like a doll: pretty, small, passive, and lovable.

"Halley Copley?" She nodded, still not fully in the room. I walked to her, my hand out. "Nice to meet you." Her head tilted back, eyes forced to rise to maintain contact with mine as I came near. They didn't waver. It was an unafraid gaze, yet not bold. She gave me her hand. It was as small as a child's. The tips of her fingers were cool. Her handshake was quick and firm. She let go and gestured to the table. "Have a seat, Doctor."

"We could go somewhere else," I said.

She was en route to the head of the table. She pulled the chair out, asking, "Excuse me?"

"If being here is uncomfortable for you," I said softly, the way one might speak to a grieving widow. "We could go to your office or we could take a walk."

My unexpected remark interrupted her intention to sit down. She released the chair and looked back at me over her shoulder, long shimmering black hair draping her jacket. This gave me her profile, a single eye staring with what seemed to be a flash of anger. Makeup can cover a great deal, but I was sure at that moment it was not covering grief. "What?" she said and gave up on sitting. She faced me.

"I thought you might prefer to talk somewhere else," I said.

"Doctor—" she tossed her head slightly, as if her hair were in her eyes, although it wasn't. "Are you a doctor?"

"Yes, I'm a psychiatrist."

"Excuse me, but I don't know who you are." She laughed. Not really a laugh; she released a burst of air, a kind of snort of feeling. I can't describe it easily. Although the noise seemed a mixture of several emotions—scorn, astonishment, amusement, resignation—they weren't truncated. Each of these feelings was somehow fully expressed, their contradictions resolved, confusion expelled. She took a deep breath and looked away as if, with that said, I and the mystery of me, no longer interested her.

"I'm sorry. Let me explain."

She nodded, but her eyes didn't acknowledge me. With her hands on the back of the chair she stood in perfect tranquility, waiting without anticipation.

"I treated Gene Kenny for many years. He first came to me as a teenager. And I saw him again for a few years just before you both met. Unfortunately, he stopped seeing me during the past year, and I'm . . ." I paused, thinking how to be honest without revealing too much. I didn't want to pollute what she might say about Gene.

"You're guilty," she finished for me in a private tone, as if she were alone in the room.

She's managing me, I noticed. Listening carefully and reacting self-consciously. "Well, I'm certainly concerned. Gene didn't seem to me to be suicidal—"

She made another sound, a different chord of feeling—disgust, sadness, amusement, and a hint of relaxation. She touched the back of the chair, lightly pushing it toward the table. "You were sure wrong about that." She walked in my direction, but there was no eye contact; she was moving to the door. "I don't want to talk about it," she said without strain, the words neither a rejection or a rebuke, merely a fact. Her small left hand reached for the doorknob. I noticed she wore a big old-fashioned men's watch, square-shaped, divided into two small clocks set to different times. She opened the door, ignoring me. "I'm leaving," she said as she passed through to the hall.

"Why?" I called in a very loud voice. I hoped to stop her determined progress with a provocation.

"I don't want to talk about Gene with you," she answered back, not slowing or stopping. There was another expulsion of feeling—this time astonishment, regret, and irritation mixing with triumph—as she turned the corner and disappeared into the main lobby.

I stood alone in the room for a minute or two. Reviewing the encounter, she did seem, in fact, to be grieving. Gene told me she had been heartsick at the death of her brother. She claimed not to have unburdened herself until she met Gene, who listened sympathetically. Even if that was a flattering exaggeration, it still meant she was reluctant to express loss. Also, she immediately assumed I felt guilty, an obvious projection. Nevertheless, my instinct told me otherwise. Anger at me was perfectly natural, perhaps justified. But the utter lack of curiosity, the quickness to avoid even the pleasure of attacking me, was too cool and rational for a head clouded by sorrow.

A guard appeared. This one was bald and overweight. He told me it was time to go and gestured toward the lobby. I was amused. I must have smiled, because he frowned and said harshly, "Come on," as if I had shown resistance.

The redheaded guard raised the gate for me before I reached his booth, hurrying my exit. He glared at me as I drove past. It was too late to return to Baltimore. I took the Saw Mill to the city and considered during the drive whether my desire to break through this wall Halley had thrown up was anything more than stubbornness. What right did I have to intrude on her or her father? None, of course. Once I reached the Fourteenth Street turnoff from the West Side Highway, I had to admit there was nothing but willfulness behind my decision to go on.

I asked Susan and Harry to put me up for the night. I lied to her, saying I was in town to get some of my files from the clinic. I was sorry to give her a glimmer of hope that Diane and I were reconciling. I realized, while we opened her couch into a bed, that I was reincarnated as the boy Rafe: alone, keeper of secrets, on a mission whose goal I could not quite define. From a clinical point of view, I would have had trouble arguing with a professional judgment that I was displaying symptoms of a nervous breakdown.

In the morning I phoned my lawyer, Brian Stoppard, the high-priced talent I had inherited from Uncle Bernie. He knew I could no longer pay him four hundred an hour, but that hadn't stopped him from taking my calls.

"Do you know anything about a man named Theodore Copley?" I asked.

"Copley. Sounds familiar. I can't place him. Who is he?"

"He's the—I *think* he's the CEO of a small- or medium-sized computer company called Minotaur."

Brian let out a Bronx cheer. "Not small, Rafe. Now I remember him. Minotaur used to be medium-sized, but he just bought out Haipan's American division and he took over some Frog company too. He's backed by somebody you know—Edgar Levin, Irving's son."

I was thrilled. Irving Levin was a crony of my uncle's, a real estate baron nearly as rich as Bernie in the sixties. He had two sons. Edgar expanded his father's holdings and now owned varied chunks of the city, from cable television to a slice of the Mets. Alex, the younger son, went west to Hollywood and produced several hits. He and Julie were friends and colleagues, or at least they were five years ago, the last time I spoke to her. So I had at least two avenues of approach.

Stoppard continued talking while I celebrated privately. "In fact, one of our partners, Molly Gray, handled Edgar's investment in Minotaur. And you probably know Molly's husband. Stefan Weinstein? He's a shrink too."

"Of course. Brilliant man. But I've never met him."

"He's brilliant even when you meet him. Talk with Molly. She probably knows more about Cowley's financing than he does."

"Copley," I corrected him.

"Cowley, Copley, what's the difference? All those high WASPs are the same. Give them a sailboat and a gin and tonic and they think they've seen God."

"You're a racist, Brian."

"WASPs aren't a race, they're a club. I should know. I'm a member now. What's up? I hope you're raising money to open a new clinic. Do you want me to get Molly on the line?"

"No thanks. I assume Edgar will know my name—"

"Are you kidding? He still talks about how you psyched him out in some golf tournament—"

"Junior tennis. He remembers? That was twenty-five years ago."

"Yeah, well, it was probably the last time he lost anything to anybody. Except for him, everybody in New York is losing their shirt. Communism is collapsing and they're taking us down with them. Even your cousin is in trouble. Of course, we should all have his troubles. Poor guy might actually have to live on ten million a year—"

"Enough, Brian. I'm sorry your life is so difficult."

"Yeah, look who I'm complaining to. St. Francis himself."

"*Vaya con Dios*, Brian."

"Bye, Rafe. Let me know if you want to talk to Molly. Jesus," he said with a despairing sigh to someone in the background as he hung up, "he told me to go with God." Perhaps everyone is having a breakdown, I thought.

I called Levin & Levin's corporate headquarters in Manhattan. It took quite a few transfers to reach Edgar's secretary. Her tone in reaction to my request to speak to him implied I was irrational. "He's not available," she said. "What's this in reference to?" she asked with a remarkably undisguised note of contempt.

"It's a personal call. I knew him as a teenager."

"I see," she said with amusement, as if identifying me as a harmless lunatic. "I'll tell Mr. Levin you called."

"Don't you want my number?"

"Sure," she said breezily and I knew she didn't believe there would be a return call. She might not bother to relay my message.

"What's your name?" I asked.

She didn't skip a beat at my non sequitur. "Ms. Dean."

"All right, Ms. Dean. I have an urgent favor to ask of Edgar. It's merely that he introduce me to someone. I think he'll be angry if he finds out you were slow to let him know I phoned. My name is Dr. Rafael Neruda. I need to talk to him today. Will you be speaking to him within the hour?"

Her tone changed, but she wasn't rattled. "I can't give out any information about Mr. Levin's schedule. Those are his instructions. If you leave a number where you can be reached, he'll call you back."

"I can't." I was at Susan's, but I didn't want to wait around. "I'll call back in an hour. Please give him the message as soon as possible." I hung up without the courtesy of a goodbye. Had my uncle behaved like these modern millionaires, erecting so many barriers to talking with them? Had they truly become the Marxist nightmare: unapproachable royalty?

An hour later, Ms. Dean's tone changed. "Oh, yes, Dr. Neruda. Please hold on. He's in his car. I'll transfer you."

There were two rapid beeps. "Rafe?" Edgar called to me from the distant end of a windy tunnel.

"Hello, Eddie. Are you really in a car?"

"Ridiculous, isn't it? They haven't perfected them—" his voice disappeared completely for a few words "—a time saver. How are you? Are you in New York? I'm busy today and tonight, but are you free tomorrow for a gala dinner? I'm hosting a benefit for the ballet."

"I don't think so, Eddie."

"Edgar. People call me Edgar now." I think he laughed, but he was drowned for a moment by a whoosh. "Hello?" he called, surfacing.

"Edgar, I'm calling to ask a favor. I need an introduction to Theodore Copley."

"Stick Copley? What sort of introduction?"

"An employee of his, or an ex-employee, was a patient. He committed suicide four weeks ago."

"Hold on, Rafe. Don't go away." The two rapid beeps were repeated. Ms. Dean's distinct voice returned to the line. "Dr. Neruda? Mr. Levin asked if you could call back in five minutes. Although what would be best is if he could call you back."

"I'm at a public phone."

"I see. Could you possibly call Mr. Levin from a residence or an office? We're having some trouble with the connection and that would work better. Sorry." I was two blocks from Susan's and I still had her key. I agreed.

At the loft, I called Ms. Dean again. This time, when she transferred me, there was no preliminary beep. Also, Edgar had come out of the wind. "Hello, Rafe. That's better, isn't it?"

"Where are you now?"

"In my office. I don't know why the cells were so bad today. Maybe because you were calling from a public phone. How come, Rafe? What were you doing out on the street?"

I paused to think it through.

"Are you there, Rafe?" Edgar prompted me out of my reverie.

"Why didn't you want to continue the conversation from your car? I'm ignorant about modern technology."

Edgar chuckled.

"Okay, Rafe. I should've known you'd see through me. Car phones are really radio signals. Anyone with a scanner can listen in. And public phones are easy to pick up too, although I don't suppose someone's following you with a telescope mike. I know it sounds silly, but there are people so eager to make a killing on Wall Street they eavesdrop for info on a tender offer, the next quarterly report . . ." He made a noise. "Anything. Anything they could make a dollar on."

"And your wanting to make this a private conversation had something to do with my mentioning Stick Copley's name?"

Edgar chuckled again, although this was more of a grunt. "Yes, wise guy, of course. I'm in business with Stick. I'm what my Pop used to call a silent partner in Minotaur, and you said something about an employee committing suicide. You know Gore Vidal's definition of a paranoid?"

"No," I said.

"Someone who is in possession of all the facts."

"Let me relieve your anxiety. My patient's suicide doesn't have any bearing on Minotaur's business. At least that's not why I want to talk with Copley. I'm curious about what my patient was like during the past year. We were out of touch."

"Tell me something, Rafe. You wouldn't, by any chance, happen to be writing a book?"

I hesitated.

Edgar continued in a relaxed tone that managed somehow to communicate ominousness. "You see, I'm ignorant about modern psychiatry. Haven't been to a shrink in ten years. I don't know if you fellows are in the habit of washing your dirty linen in public."

"Are you being combative out of habit, Eddie, or do you really not want to help me?"

He grunted. "You know, I think I like being called Eddie. But I can't indulge it. Eddie Levin sounds like a counterman at the Second Avenue Deli."

"I'm sorry. Do you really not want to help me, Edgar?"

"I just don't want to piss off my partner. You say this guy worked for Stick and he committed suicide? Doesn't sound like a model employee. What was his story?"

"Edgar, everything I know about my patient is confidential. I'm not a gossip."

"*That's* what I wanted to hear." Edgar's smooth tone shifted. He was ready to help, so he immediately sounded less friendly. "Okay. How do you want this done?"

In fact, there was a Minotaur board meeting scheduled to begin at eleven and run through lunch at a private room in the St. Regis Hotel. It was arranged I would meet Copley there after they adjourned. (All this was a fortuitous consequence of my knowing Edgar; as a major investor in Minotaur, he was of course on the board.) Following Ms. Dean's instructions, I arrived at the St. Regis by two-thirty and identified myself at the desk. I was passed on to the concierge, who summoned a bellhop, and said he would take me to Mr. Copley. We went up to the sixteenth floor, passed a hallway with two rows of serving carts littered by empty trays, into a large ballroom naked except for a piano covered by a sheet, and then through a door the bellhop unlocked.

I passed into a medium-sized room that appeared to be a 19th century library. The bellhop held the door for me and left, shutting it behind him. Every inch of wall space was covered by built-in mahogany shelves filled with green or red leather-bound books. In a leather wing chair at the far end of the room sat Theodore Copley. Beside him, on a low wood coffee table with brass fittings, was a silver tray with a black Wedgwood coffee pot and two matching cups and saucers. He stood to greet me. His appearance, having seen his daughter, was a surprise. His hair was much lighter than hers, almost blond, moussed straight back off a small forehead. And he was big, nearly six feet and broad-shouldered. His cheeks had the haggard look of a dedicated exerciser. His skin was fair. Deep lines ran across his forehead, radiated from the corners of his eyes and trailed down his starved profile. Only his eyes were dark, like his daughter's, sharing her solemnity and brilliance. His double-breasted suit had the natural fit of hand-tailoring and the dense look of fine cloth.

He was cordial, offering a strong hand that waited for mine to let go, and gestured to the coffee. I declined. "We had a big lunch," Copley said. He puffed out his cheeks to indicate he was stuffed. He was all muscle and bone and I doubted he had really eaten a lot. When he inflated his cheeks they were so elastic he reminded me of Louis Armstrong playing the trumpet. I wondered if he had once been fat. He reached for the Wedgwood cup. "We had steak. I haven't eaten red meat in years and I don't think I will ever again. Leaves me feeling groggy."

"Thank you for seeing me on short notice."

"Well, I was pretty curious when Edgar said you were Gene's psychiatrist. I didn't know he was seeing anyone."

I was convinced that was a lie. His eyes shifted away from me as he said it, although they hadn't wavered until then, not when he sat or reached for the coffee. Also, he crossed his legs and put his hands together, both gestures of self-protection.

"I saw your daughter yesterday. Or I tried to."

He raised his brow as if that were news, but he didn't say it was, and his eyes stayed on me, a faint smile on his closed lips.

"I thought maybe Gene told her he had been in therapy and she told you."

He shook his head. He glanced down, lifted the sharp crease in his charcoal gray pants and said, "She wouldn't tell me something like that." He uncrossed his legs, leaned forward and refilled his cup. "They had a love affair," he said and his eyes were on me, unexpectedly, since he was pouring. He didn't miss the target and he knew, without looking, when he needed to stop. "Daughters don't gossip about their love lives with their Daddies." He put the pot down and leaned back with his filled cup.

He shrugged. "At least mine doesn't." He sipped. "How can I help you, Doctor?"

"Well, obviously, I failed with Gene. I feel responsible—" I smiled and paused. I had caught him by surprise, evidently. His cup was in midair, stopped en route back to the saucer on the table. He studied me with absolute concentration. He appeared to be physically frozen, as if his brain was so busy thinking it couldn't bother with anything else. "I *am* responsible, I should say. I treated Gene, off and on, over a fifteen-year span and he destroyed himself. Basically, I want to check over the crash site. Figure out what I did wrong. I know it's unorthodox and an intrusion, an unfair intrusion on you and your daughter, but you were both important to Gene and knew him well. I hoped you might help me figure out where I went wrong."

He remained stuck for another moment. Then he released a gust of air through his wide thin lips. Not his daughter's complicated expression of noise; his was closer to a horse's neigh and communicated a single clear message: scornful dismissal. "I'm sorry," he shook his head, no longer frozen in position. The cup went back to the saucer. He sat straight in the chair, a hand skimming over his tie, flattening it against his white shirt. "I apologize. It's none of my business."

"What's none of your business?"

"How you evaluate yourself. I have about a half an hour before my next meeting, but I'll be glad to answer your questions about Gene. Edgar told me of your fine reputation. In fact, I think I recognize you. He said you've been on television a fair amount. I watch way too much television. Very bad habit."

"Thank you. I appreciate your help. But please, go back a moment and tell me what you were thinking when you said it was none of your business how I evaluate myself."

"Well, I don't know very much about psychiatry. I took Psych 101 like everyone else, but I don't see how you can be blamed for Gene's suicide. I mean, in the end, *we*," using his index finger, he poked himself on the lapel of his suit, "each of us are responsible for our own will to live. I don't see how you can give that will to someone. In fact, if anything, *I'm* probably more responsible for Gene's suicide than you." Copley turned away, showing me his profile. His chin lifted and he studied one of the rows of leather-bound books. He brought a hand to his eyebrows, rubbed them thoughtfully, and dropped it to join his other hand. He locked the fingers together and—to my horror—cracked his knuckles. It was exactly the gesture Gene had adopted in the latter years of his therapy. An imitated mannerism, just as he had once imitated his mother, mimicking someone he perceived as powerful. And the hair, the moussed hair, I realized—that too Gene had copied. Copley, meanwhile, spoke to the leather-bound books. "I mean unintentionally, of course. I fired him because he . . ." he slid his fingers together again and I winced ahead of the sound. This time, when he flexed, none came. ". . . Well, he burned out. He flamed out and he got real arrogant too. Demanded promotions and raises even though he lost control of production. *I* pushed him over the edge when I fired him." Copley calmly moved off the books, his gaze returning to me. He brought a hand to his moussed hair, to smooth what was already flattened. "I'm sorry Gene killed himself. But I don't regret firing him. I would do it again. You can't save a drowning man if he's in so great a panic he'll take you with him."

I didn't say anything, returning his stare. I considered carefully, and as literally as possible for a psychiatrist, the merit of his remarkably frank speech. Stick must have interpreted my silence as confusion (perhaps it was) or as offended sensibility. He shrugged. Another wan smile played on his lips. "I'm sorry to sound ruthless," he continued. "I was a certified lifeguard as a teenager and I remember the instructor's little rhyme about what to do if a big man, a grown man, is drowning. 'Throw,'" he tossed an imaginary sphere onto the library's Keshan rug, "'Don't go.'" He wagged a scolding finger. "I'm sure you could talk to everyone who knew Gene, find out everything there is to find out, and, in the end, the answer lies in whatever happens at the mysterious moment when life is created. Something was left out when they assembled Gene. There was a bug in the programming."

After I thanked Copley and left, I told myself to give up. And yet I wandered from the St. Regis into a bookstore, the old Scribner's on Fifth Avenue, now swallowed by a national chain. I asked if they had anything on lifesaving.

"You mean CPR?" the clerk asked.

"I mean being a lifeguard," I said.

We climbed narrow stairs to a small balcony at the front where they kept sports books. Nothing. Check at the library, the clerk suggested.

Feeling more and more amused by my foolish pedantry, I found a phone booth and called the YMCA near the clinic in Riverdale where we took our resident patients for swimming lessons. (Inner-city kids—

Albert, for example—often don't know how.) I asked for Jim Gagliardi, one of the instructors.

"What's up, Rafe?" Jim's voice echoed in the tiled acoustics of the indoor pool.

"If I say to you, 'Throw—Don't go,' does that remind you of something?"

"You've got it wrong."

"I do?"

"Yeah, you mean for lifeguard training? It's, 'Reach or Throw—Don't go.'"

"I left out Reach."

"Yeah," Jim said with a laugh. "Hope nobody drowned."

CHAPTER THREE

First Interview

COPLEY DIDN'T LIKE IT MUCH. HIS TONE WAS GRUFF WHEN I REACHED HIM at his office in Tarrytown the following day. But he agreed to persuade Halley to see me again.

"I can't promise you she'll be happy about it," he said. I noted, however, that he was sure she would do it. We arranged I should call her in an hour.

I got through right away. Jeff, her secretary, said with pleasant efficiency, "Good morning, Dr. Neruda. Please hold for Ms. Copley."

"Hello." She was on immediately, hurrying to deal with me. "I don't have any time this week. How about lunch next Tuesday?" I was impressed by the neutrality of her tone. As if relations between us were a perfect blank.

I wanted to know how much pressure they were feeling to accede to Edgar's request to be helpful. "I'm only in New York until Friday," I said. "Are you free in the evening? We could have dinner."

"Dinner," she repeated dully. I was sure she wished she could complain about my impertinence. "I'll be at Edgar's benefit tonight. Are you going?"

I was amused by this probe. "He invited me, but I don't have a tux."

"That's not much of an excuse. Edgar could get one for you."

"Probably. But we wouldn't have much time to talk. Besides, your date would be annoyed."

"Daddy is my date. He wouldn't care. And we could go for coffee afterwards." She was almost flirtatious.

"No, I'm really too shy and awkward at big events. How about tomorrow night?"

Her tone shifted, slipping from playful to cool without a lurch. "I'll have to let you know in the morning. I'm not sure if I'm free."

"When should I call you tomorrow?"

"Why don't you give me your number and I'll call you?"

"I'll be in and out. Best thing is for me to call you."

She sighed, exasperated. "All right. Call at eleven. Bye," she hung up without waiting for my farewell.

The next morning Jeff had instructions for me. "Dr. Neruda, Ms. Copley asked if you could meet her at seven outside her gym. She *loves* her workouts." The lilt of his mocking aside suggested he might be gay; and its informality was the first sign something had changed since yesterday. "Then you'll have dinner. Her gym is on the Upper West Side."

"In the city?"

"Yes, we're both reverse commuters." Jeff's friendliness was becoming fulsome. "Do you have a favorite restaurant?"

"No, I'll leave that to you. Why don't you pick a place?"

"Oh, I think *she'll* do the picking," he commented.

I arrived at her gym forty-five minutes early. The Workout occupies two floors of a five-story office building; tall windows on three sides aren't dressed, exposing its huffing and puffing clients to Broadway. I didn't wait on the street. I entered, said I was interested in becoming a member, and asked for a tour. I listened patiently to my guide's enthusiastic talk about The Workout's personal trainers, no-nonsense atmosphere ("This isn't a singles club"), and up-to-date equipment that wouldn't leave you permanently crippled as other health clubs were liable to. I asked to see these modern marvels. We passed many complicated machines before coming upon Halley at the treadmill. She was listening to a bright yellow Walkman's earphones, her dark eyes fixed on the scurrying pedestrians below her.

"Oh, there's someone I know," I said to my guide, leaving him, and moving beside Halley.

She wore white shorts and a gray T-shirt. Its sleeves were rolled up, exposing her shoulders. I have always found the crook of a woman's shoulder and the curve that begins the shape of her breast particularly alluring. Hers was completely exposed, olive skin glistening with perspiration. Most of the side of her bra was also visible. I stepped directly in front of her. A dark wedge of sweat bled between her breasts. As I suspected on our first meeting, beneath her business jacket she had concealed an impressive display.

When she recognized me, I waved. She blinked. For a moment, she couldn't decide whether to allow this interruption. I smiled and crossed my arms, signaling I had no intention of going. She pressed a button on the treadmill. Its motor shifted, and her pace slowed. She removed the earphones with both hands. I enjoyed that sight: her arms raised, holding the black arch aloft as if it were an electronic halo.

"You're early," she said, neither playful nor annoyed. Her deep voice wasn't struggling hard for air.

I turned toward my puzzled guide. "Thank you. I'll stop by the front desk on the way out."

"Sure," he said. "We have a twenty percent discount this month," he added as he left.

"I told him I was interested in becoming a member."

"But you don't live in New York," she said. She put the black halo around her neck.

I smiled. "That's true."

She didn't return my smile. Her black eyes evaluated me for a moment. Her full lips opened as if to speak. Instead, she released one of her complicated exhalations of feelings and checked her dual-time-zone watch. "I need another ten minutes on this and a half hour to get dressed." She hit a button on the machine, quickened her pace, and replaced the earphones. She stared through me while she ran, as if I were one of the pedestrians below.

I couldn't hold that indifferent gaze. I lowered my eyes and noticed her fine legs. Often being short costs elegance. Not for Halley. And she was very fit. There was virtually no jiggle to her shapely thighs. Gene had praised this body to the skies and that was no delusion.

"I'll wait outside," I said, although I knew she couldn't hear me. Walking away, I felt compelled to look back. I did so at the head of the stairs. From that angle, the tall windows were made opaque by the reflection of the ceiling's light. For her as well: she watched her towering image run at Broadway. I looked at the gleaming glass facing me. I saw a frail picture of myself in retreat.

She took longer than promised, appearing at seven-fifteen. Her hair was damp, combed back and gathered into a ponytail. She wore white jeans and a thin black cotton sweater; her small feet were bare inside black penny loafers. The eyeliner of her work makeup endured; otherwise, her face was unadorned, lips pale, forehead shiny. The message was clear: this is not a date. "There's a pretty good Japanese restaurant three blocks from here," she said. "Nothing fancy. After last night, I feel like something light."

"Good idea." We began the walk. "I'm sorry to be so nosy, but—"

"You're thorough and conscientious," Halley finished my sentence. "I searched for you in Nexis."

"Nexis?"

She paused. This forced me to stop and look her way. Without makeup or the armor of formal clothing, she was as small and sweet as a little girl. A little girl with large breasts. "You don't know what Nexis is?"

"No."

"It's a database library you can search and retrieve with a modem and computer." She resumed walking. I followed suit. "It's got every word in newspapers and magazines going back to the sixties. I read a profile of you in *Vanity Fair*. Are you doing a book about Gene?"

"I'm considering it."

"He told me he was seeing a famous psychiatrist, but he never told me your name."

We had to stop at the corner for the light. I watched her impassive profile. "Did you love him?"

The light turned green. She stepped off the curb. "No," she said softly and crossed the street.

I was left behind, struck dumb on the corner. I had to trot to catch up. Before I could ask her another question, she said, "You're a child psychiatrist."

I nodded.

"How come you were treating Gene?"

"I saw a few adult patients," I lied.

"Here we are," she said, gesturing to an open door and passing through a beaded curtain. She couldn't have known the magic of her choice. I noted the theater a few doors away. It was the same place. I had eaten in this modest Japanese restaurant. Almost fifteen years before, Julie and I had gone there for a late dinner. It was the day I discovered

Gene's mother had lied to me and the night I worked up the courage to tell Julie she was the love of my life. I was embarrassed by the reflection that, in trendy New York, this restaurant had done a better job of maintaining relationships than I.

Halley concentrated on the menu, not speaking until she had decided. When she closed it firmly, she found that I was staring at her. What she saw in my eyes was undiluted admiration for her beauty and honesty. Hers was blank and indifferent. "Why didn't you take better care of him?" She asked this question with no hint of the anger and bitterness it implied.

"I took the best care of him I know how."

"Are you going to be honest in your book?"

"Yes. You know, Gene told me you said you *were* in love with him."

"Right," she nodded, as if that required no elaboration.

"So you lied?"

"I always say that when a man says he loves me. Either I tell him I love him or I stop seeing him. I wanted to keep seeing Gene."

"Why do you tell men you love them if you don't?"

"I don't believe in love. I think when people say they're in love, they're making it up. You know, convincing themselves. Just because I can't fool myself is no reason to be mean to the other person. I act like I'm in love. I do the same things people who think they're in love do, so it's not really a lie. Anyway, it's no more of a lie than when they say it to me." She nodded at a hovering waiter. "Are you ready to order?"

She asked for green tea, miso soup, and two pieces of crab sushi, not enough to make a meal. "That's all?" I asked.

"I only eat what I really love. Just a little of what I really love is plenty."

"So you *do* love something," I said. I ordered the deluxe sushi platter, which I knew would be enough food for two people. "I eat a lot of what I love," I told her as the waiter departed.

"Are you flirting with me?" she asked in a grave and earnest tone.

"Yes," I said, smiling as engagingly as I know how.

She nodded, relaxed back against her chair. "And it doesn't bother you that I didn't love Gene?"

"I guess I don't approve. Why didn't you tell him what you just told me? That you can't love anyone, but you were willing to behave as if you loved him?"

Halley sounded one of her complicated notes of feeling. I couldn't begin to separate the mixture. "He wouldn't have understood," she commented. "He was a baby about things like that."

"Things like what?"

"You know, men and women." Her green tea had arrived. She sipped it. "And sex," she added, after swallowing.

"Why bother with a baby?"

"I liked that he was innocent. He was the first man I was with who was less experienced than me. It was almost like being with a virgin." She stared into the middle distance. Her close-set eyes nearly crossed. She smiled at the memory. "He was sweet." She came out of it and reached for her tea. "For a while."

"Until he left Cathy you mean?"

"I told him not to leave her. That was a mistake." She sipped her tea and returned the mug to the table with a frown. "I didn't say that, you know."

"You didn't tell him it was a mistake?"

"No, that's not what I mean." She leaned forward and touched the back of my right hand lightly with her index finger. The brief contact was insanely thrilling: she sent a shock through me that wasn't caused by static electricity. "You asked me why I didn't tell Gene I *can't* love. I didn't say I can't. I said I don't believe in love."

"I don't see the difference, Halley."

"I'm sure that when I do believe in love, I'll have no trouble being in love."

I laughed. "And they say psychiatrists like to split hairs."

"I'm not splitting hairs. I don't believe in God either, but that doesn't mean I can't."

"You're just not persuaded yet?"

"Right." The waiter arrived with miso soup for both of us. She gave her food absolute attention. She scooped a spoonful, regarded it, spread her full lips, and poured some gently into her mouth. She tasted that small amount slowly and thoughtfully, as if this was the first time. "Mmmm," she said aloud and added a sigh of comfort.

"So you don't think I took good care of Gene?" I asked.

"You were his shrink and he committed suicide," she said softly. She shrugged, as if she regretted having to point this out, but had no choice.

"I agree with you."

"You do?" She was gentle. "You think it was your fault?"

I nodded. "Your father doesn't agree. He told me no one can give someone else the will to live."

She was preoccupied with another lingering taste of soup. When she had thoroughly enjoyed it, she said, "The only reason he doesn't blame you is because he doesn't believe in psychiatry. He thinks it's fake anyway."

I laughed. "I see. So by you I'm a failure, and by him I'm a fraud." I laughed again.

She seemed rattled by my amusement. She put her spoon back in the soup bowl. "You were lying."

"What?" I picked up my bowl and drank half the hot soup. I was perspiring anyway from our walk in the humid streets and I decided it would be good to be soaked through.

Halley reached back and pulled off the elastic tie of her ponytail. Her hair had dried. With a toss, she restored the elegant shape of our first meeting. "You didn't mean it when you said was it your fault." She turned to check herself in the mirror on the far right wall. Briefly, she touched her face, like a primitive verifying that the reflection was actually her. She looked back at me and said matter-of-factly, "If you're going to be sneaky then I won't talk with you. I don't care what Edgar or Daddy want."

"You don't understand," I pleaded. I slumped in the chair. My chin wobbled with emotion. "I was laughing because I was relieved. Everybody keeps telling me it isn't my fault and I'm not a fraud and I don't believe them. I was relieved. Relieved to finally meet people who know the truth and don't mind giving it to me straight."

Halley's pupils opened wide as I confessed. She rested her elbows on the table, leaning toward me. Her small hands came together, forming a hollow pyramid. "Can you really accept that you've made a mistake just like that?"

"Just like what?"

"Well . . ." She dropped her hands. She smiled. I realized I had never seen her smile before. The tempting lips opened, her mouth spread generously, and she showed a row of perfect teeth. "I admire that. I really admire someone who can take responsibility for screwing up without making excuses."

"I bet your father's like that," I said.

She nodded. A fond look came over her, softening the brilliance of her smile. The affection was unselfconscious. She noticed that I noticed and the smile disappeared. She lowered her eyes. "I don't want any more soup," she said. "Could you tell him to clear it? I have to go to the bathroom."

When she came back, she was made up, lips a deep purple, high cheeks emphasized, the shine on her intelligent forehead gone. "I made myself pretty for you," she said calmly. "I wasn't being very nice. I'm sorry. I should've known better when Edgar told me about you. And from that profile I read. You're not a sleazy guy who wants to do a number on us."

"You were right to be cautious."

"Edgar says you have an amazing past, but he wouldn't tell me what."

"That's because he doesn't really know."

"What do you mean?"

"When I was living with my uncle in Great Neck people knew something scandalous had happened that got me into his custody, but they only heard rumors. Uncle was careful to keep the truth secret."

Halley unwrapped and separated her chopsticks. She aimed them at the two pieces of crab sushi that had replaced the soup. They were laid before her on a black lacquer dish curved like a small boat. "He said you had psychological problems as a teenager."

"I killed myself," I said.

She meant to pick up one of the sushi. Instead, she withdrew the chopsticks. "You killed yourself," she repeated, provoked, but confused.

"I died. I wanted to and I did."

"You mean . . ." She leaned back, rested the chopsticks on the black lacquer dish. Her pupils were wide again. Her breasts rose and fell faster with excitement. "You mean you tried to commit suicide?"

"I *did* commit suicide. I was rescued by accident. I destroyed myself. Not physically. I killed my *self*. I had to build a new me."

"And there's . . ." her deep voice ran dry. She cleared her throat. She licked her lips. Her eyes were moist. I assumed I would move her, and I had. Recovering, she continued, "There's really nothing left of the old you?"

"He's dead." I picked up a shrimp sushi and swallowed the long piece in a gulp.

"That's impossible." She began a laugh; it evolved into one of her expressive noises. "I mean, as a shrink, don't you think it's impossible?"

"You've done it too." I took another sushi—I didn't know what it was—and swallowed it whole. Her pretty face didn't move. She watched me.

"What are you talking about?" she asked finally.

"When did you tell Gene that you didn't love him?"

"I don't like this conversation," she commented. It *was* a comment, spoken casually, as if to a third party, requesting that the subject be changed.

"Were you surprised that he left Cathy for you?"

Halley picked up her chopsticks and captured one of the pink squares. She bit off about half and chewed thoughtfully. She appeared to taste every nuance. She shut her eyes with a private look of pleasure. The slow undulating motion of her lips was obscene and titillating. She opened her eyes as she swallowed. "I want to make a trade."

"Okay. What's the trade?"

"You tell me why you killed yourself and I'll tell you about Gene."

For me, this was the moment of decision. Perhaps to the reader I may appear to have already surrendered to the novelty of this situation, but in my mind, I hadn't yet crossed the line from a curious psychiatrist to the role I came to play, until I had to choose whether to satisfy Halley's appetite. To think clearly, I disengaged from her steady gaze. A view of Broadway was available through the window. Instead, I shut my eyes to look at my past. I felt the warmth of Florida and heard the regret in Julie's voice on my uncle's lawn. Striped by New York's amber lights, I watched the gentle motion of my mother in a half-painted room. *Use your peasant brain,* a man quoted my father. "You can live with me," little Joe Stein said, sorry for my tears. Before I knew it, I was looking at Halley again, and I had decided.

"Do you know what Rafael means in Hebrew?" I asked her.

She sat up straight, a little startled. "In Hebrew? No. I'm not Jewish."

"Of course you're not." I laughed. "Silly of me. I am. I'm only half-Jewish. And I'm half-Catholic."

I gave her a précis of the extravagant events of my childhood and adolescence. I lingered only on the details of the most secret fact, taking special care to make my mother's incestuous behavior clear. For a half hour, she listened raptly, her shining black eyes concentrated on me, including when she consumed her other piece of sushi. After I finished, she asked, "And what does Rafael mean in Hebrew? You never said."

Her eyes strayed to my half-full deluxe platter. I picked up a piece from my surfeit and offered it. She gestured to her plate, accepting my gift, but not allowing me to feed it directly to her beautiful mouth. I surrendered the food to her dish. "It's a promise from God," I explained. "It means: He Will Heal."

She nodded and armed herself with the chopsticks. She ate my offering in her deliberate manner. When it was thoroughly enjoyed, she asked with a playful smile, "Do you think you can heal me?"

"You haven't kept your half of the bargain. Were you surprised when Gene left Cathy for you?"

"He didn't leave her for me."

"That's what I used to think."

"So you *are* blaming me."

"No. It isn't your fault you're intoxicating. But you could have warned him. You could have said, when he announced he was leaving Cathy, 'I don't love you.'"

"I did." She shrugged. "I told him there was no reason to leave her, that I would go on seeing him anyway. I didn't care that he was married."

"You preferred it, right?"

"Yes." She raised her arms, stretching and yawning indolently. "It's stuffy in here. Let's walk."

I rose, gesturing to the waiter. "No more? All done?" he asked.

"Just the check, please." While he totaled it up, Halley said, "I'll wait for you outside." I watched her go. The waiter handed me the check. As I counted money from my wallet, I commented, "You sure are successful."

"Yes," the waiter said. "Very good business."

"I ate here a long time ago. I was surprised you were still in business."

He took my money and frowned. "No. Must be different place. We open only two year."

Watch yourself, I thought, as I joined Halley outside. The air was still and humid on Broadway. There was a strong smell of rotting food. "Walk me home?" she asked, turning uptown.

"Sure."

Without self-consciousness, she put her arm through mine. "Your story is incredible. I don't mean incredible. I mean amazing. You must be a very strong person."

"I'm so strong I can even carry your gym bag." It dangled from her other arm and seemed to me to spoil her graceful walk.

"How sweet," she said, passing the bag to me. I slung it over my free arm. She walked slowly, enjoying each step.

Released by a light, a trio of cabs rushed past. They created a breeze of carbon monoxide and I remembered Gene. "Gene told me about that conversation."

"What conversation?"

"The one you were referring to. When you told him you didn't mind if he stayed with Cathy. That you would keep on seeing him."

"So you know I didn't want Gene to leave her."

"He didn't tell me that. He told me you said you *were* in love with him. According to him, you said you were so in love you would take him on any terms."

She stopped walking. We weren't at a corner. Her arm remained through mine, although she turned toward me. "When did I say that?"

"A couple of years ago."

"Oh," she said, apparently relieved, head tilted. "I don't remember. I thought you meant when he left Cathy for real, not when he was just talking about it."

She resumed our parade. We passed a homeless man sprawled on top of an IRT subway grating. "How does that happen to somebody?" she asked in the lilting tone of a hurt and bewildered child.

"I don't know anything about him," I said.

"I bet you can explain. Edgar said you've done a lot of work with disadvantaged people."

"I won't be distracted," I said. "I know you think I'm going to judge you for how you behaved with Gene, but I'm not. Gene was willful about his illusions. He might have made it all up, and even if he didn't, that doesn't mean you're responsible for what happened."

"Okay," she said softly. "Ask away."

"What I'd like to know is whether there was ever a time you might have agreed to live with him, to be married to him, to—well, take on the pretense of loving him full-time?"

We had reached Seventy-sixth Street. "This way," she said, steering us toward Central Park. She paused at a newspaper kiosk and bought tomorrow's *Times*. She took my arm again and continued our walk silently. By the time we crossed Columbus Avenue I was about to repeat my question. The moment I made a noise, she cut me off, "No. I never fantasized about being with him. I was sad, very sad, because my brother had died. Gene was a comfort. You know. And he was safe. I thought he was safe. I never believed him. Not for a second. I never thought he was going to leave her. She was a terrible bitch, but men stay with women like that. They have affairs, sad affairs, but they stay." We were half a block from

Central Park. A cooler, cleaner breeze came from its tall darkened trees. She let go of my arm to brush a wave of her hair from her face. She took a deep breath, held it, and spoke as she exhaled, "Anyway, I approved of him leaving her. I thought it would be good for him. I thought he was just using me as an excuse. And I read somewhere that men never stay with the women they leave their wives for. That's true, isn't it?"

"Nothing is true for everybody."

"This is me," she said, stopping under an awning to a typical white-brick postwar high rise set between two brownstones. "Do you really believe we're all so special?"

"Yes."

"Guess you've never looked at market research."

"That wouldn't change my mind," I said. I offered her the gym bag. She didn't take it. "Want to come up?"

"Were you seeing other men the whole time you were involved with Gene?"

She laughed, a pleasant laugh, not mocking or offended. "You think I'm a tramp."

"No, I think you're extraordinary. I think Gene was ordinary and he wasn't up to you. That's not your fault. I'm testing his version of reality. He thought you were all his until about a year ago. He told me you met someone else in Paris on a business trip."

She frowned. "In Paris?" She nodded. "Oh, right. That was when I realized I had to start letting him down easy. So he thought . . ." She stared at the sidewalk, nodding to herself.

"Halley, all I really want is a simple answer. Was there ever a time you were Gene's?"

She lifted her right foot and touched a crack in the pavement with the toe of her shoe. Still looking down, she asked, "Does the doctor want to know? Or Rafe the man?"

I moved close, putting the bag into her arms, leaning against it. I whispered these words, "Were you ever really his woman?"

She looked up at me. Her lips were close to mine. I felt her warm breath as she said, "No."

"I have one more question."

"You sure you don't want to come up for coffee? Brandy, maybe? I think I've got some."

"When your father phones later, what will you tell him? Or are you supposed to call him?"

Her face changed. The smile was wiped away, the seductive sparkle in her eyes dimmed out. That didn't surprise me. Her recovery was a surprise. She blinked once. And then she was confident again, eyes frank and unafraid. "I'll tell him he has nothing to worry about." She stepped back, swinging the gym bag playfully. "Is that okay?"

"Perfect," I said, turning and walking away.

CHAPTER FOUR

Fieldwork

I DECIDED TO DRIVE TO TARRYTOWN THE NEXT MORNING, ARRIVING UN-expectedly at Minotaur. The guard in the Plexiglas sentry box was new to me. I had to work hard to get him to call Copley's secretary, explain I was there unannounced, and ask if I could come in anyway.

Once in the central glass building, I was kept waiting for an hour in the same conference room where I first met Halley. Eventually, a middle-aged woman with a helmet of silver gray hair and a substantial stomach appeared. She told me she was Laura, Mr. Copley's assistant, and I should follow her. We took a mirrored elevator to the top floor, the fourth. Up there, the floors were black marble. (I was informed later that, since the engineers regularly came from the labs in the adjoining buildings to meet with executives in the business offices, carpeting was avoided because static electricity can harm computer circuits. The engineers themselves thought that the fear of carpeting was silly, since static electricity can be discharged by touching any piece of metal.) Laura led me past medium-sized offices. One of them was Halley's. Jeff looked up from his desk and called out, a little too loudly to be natural, "Hello, Dr. Neruda."

Laura didn't stop. I called back a hello, my feet sliding on the marble floor as I tried to catch up to her. We turned at the corner directly into

Copley's outer office, Laura's lair. She gestured to a black leather couch and sat at her desk.

She glanced at her phone, told me he was on a call and would see me shortly. Did I want coffee or something else to drink? I declined all hospitality. The waiting didn't bother me. Not since the summer I graduated high school had I been in my current situation. I had all the time in the world.

At long last, Laura said, "He's free. You can go in." How she knew for sure was mysterious: her phone hadn't beeped or rung.

The mahogany-colored door sealing Copley off from his assistant was roughly eight feet high and at least four feet wide, almost a moving wall. Its handle was a thick brushed-steel bar, about a foot long. The gigantic door created an illusion: my brain assumed that opening it would require a strong effort, so I stumbled when only a slight push was required. Rattled, I didn't close it behind me, moving straight at Copley. He rose from behind a country French table, bleached white and marked by long use, that he used as a desk. No files or papers were in evidence. A black computer terminal was rigged on a black stand to one side of his antique desk. He greeted me as he did at the hotel, courteous, not friendly. There was the same firm handshake that waited for me to let go first. "Excuse me," he commented and looked over my shoulder as he made a maneuver with one of his feet.

I heard a whoosh and turned to see the massive door shut by itself. I looked back and noticed his right foot lift off a button almost flush with the floor. "Cool, right?" he mumbled, gesturing for me to sit in a square black leather armchair positioned opposite his tall-backed swivel chair, also black leather, of course. "Did I forget we have an appointment?" he asked.

"No. I'm only in town until the weekend and I had a thought. I was hoping you would be kind enough to see me today so I could ask if it was all right. Only take a minute."

"Great. Shoot." His lined starved face was still while he waited for me to talk. I was reminded of Mount Rushmore.

"My little talk with Halley was very helpful. It's obvious that Gene was fooling himself about their relationship. So now I suspect everything he told me. Clearly, I took in his version of events too uncritically. I wanted to check on his claims that he was very important here."

"He was. He was vice-president in charge of product development, the heart and soul of the company. That was his job for the last year, year and a half. And before that he was project director of Black Dragon, our biggest success so far." Copley pointed to the terminal beside his country French table.

"Is that Black Dragon?" I asked eagerly.

"Not really. That's just a terminal connected to Black Dragon. It's a midsize mainframe—" He interrupted himself, leaned his head against the tall chair, and asked, "Do you know much about computers?"

"No. Nothing. That's one reason I came. I couldn't understand half the things Gene was telling me when he discussed his job."

"Isn't that a problem?"

"A problem?"

"I mean, treating someone whose work you don't understand?"

"Obviously. Look at the result." I laughed bitterly.

A faint beep came off the rectangular black phone on his desk. He looked at it without making a move to answer. He appeared to be reading something. From my position, I noticed a raised ledge at the top of the phone; on it was a liquid crystal display, but I couldn't see if anything was written there. "Excuse me," he said. "I need to take this call. Only be a second." He lifted the receiver and said, *"Bonjour, Didier. Ça va?"* He chuckled. *"Oui."* He listened somberly for several seconds. "Okay," he said. "We'll give them a week. Gotta go. You'll be at home later? *Au revoir.*" He hung up. His fingers intertwined. He looked thoughtful. I expected him to crack his knuckles. Instead, he said, "I only have time for another question or two. Where were we?"

"You were explaining," I said, pointing to the black terminal beside him, "that really isn't Black Dragon."

"Right. This is just a station to access it. The mainframe is down the hall."

"Gene designed Black Dragon, right?"

"Well, he supervised its design and the production of the prototype. Actually, a brilliant kid I hired, Andy Chen, really designed its guts."

"Oh, sure. Gene talked about someone named Andy. I don't think he ever mentioned his last name. Said he was a genius."

"He is. Excuse me, Dr. Neruda. But I don't really know what we're accomplishing. Gene probably exaggerated his importance a little. We all do that, don't we? But he was very important here. And he was a valuable employee, until the last year, year and a half, when he just burned out. To be honest, that's a hazard of our business. Building computers is a young man's game. The competition is ferocious. Every year MIT and

Stanford graduate a new crop of geniuses. Every four months somebody invents a new chip. Practically every day there's new and hungrier software. To survive in this business, someone in Gene's position has to get out of the trenches and make the transition to management. I gave him that opportunity by promoting him to vice-president. He couldn't hack it. He wasn't leadership material. He hit the wall hard. Some people bounce off and sink peacefully to a lower place. Some people pick themselves up and, I don't know, buy themselves a cabin in Vermont or a hammock in Tahiti and enjoy the rest of their lives. Gene imploded."

"Gene worked very hard and long hours—"

"All the engineers do," Stick interrupted, impatient.

"Maybe that's why they burn out."

"Maybe. But there's no other way to get it done. Work a forty-hour week and you fall two years behind. Ask IBM." He sat forward, as if about to rise. "Sorry, but I really have to . . ."

I interrupted him. "Just one more favor. May I speak with Andy Chen? If I remember right, he worked closely with Gene."

Copley snorted and shook his head. "Dr. Neruda, I really can't have you wandering the halls."

"It's almost lunchtime. If he's free, I could buy him . . ."

Copley cut me off, "I doubt Andy eats lunch. He's project director and he's got a brutal deadline."

"This is my last request. My final imposition. I'm grateful for your patience. You've been very helpful, just as Edgar said you would be. Talking to Andy Chen would wrap it up."

His reaction to my cornering him was interesting. He smiled. Just as Halley had seemed pleased when I guessed correctly that she and Stick were going to consult later about our dinner, he took defeat (albeit a minor one) not only with surprising grace, but with amusement. The lines of his gaunt face multiplied as his smile widened and he did something that was just lovely. He winked at me. "Okay, Doc, you win. Would you wait outside while I check with Andy? Believe it or not, I can't order him to have lunch with you today. He has a crazy idea his job is to build machines for me, not have lunch with VIPs." He pressed the button on his black floor. I heard the whoosh of the door opening for me to leave.

Rejoining Laura in her office, I got a good look at her phone as she asked me, "Would you like something to drink while he talks to Andy?" Copley hadn't said a word to her, but I understood the mystery of their clairvoyance by now. In addition to the LCD display, there was a small keyboard to type messages to send to the other phone. I said no thanks to the drink and complimented her, using Copley's nickname. "Stick told me you were the best assistant in the world and now I know your secret. It's that amazing phone."

Her tone was skeptical, "*He* said I was the best?" But she flushed with pleasure. I nodded. She touched her phone. "Well, you're right, this is my secret. It's great, isn't it?"

"Yeah. Stick said you can tell him who's on and he can tell you what to say while he keeps talking to someone else."

She glanced at the massive door, although it was shut, before saying softly, "Exactly. It does a lot of amazing things. You know, someone here invented it, but we decided not to market it ourselves."

"Oh. So it's available to the public?"

"Not really." Again, she glanced at the door and spoke in a half-whisper, "They made a stupid, simple version. This is our prototype, the only one in existence. I'm terrified it's going to break."

"But you've got two buildings full of repairmen."

"The man who designed it doesn't work here anymore. And with these nutty guys, you give them something to fix and who knows? It could come back as a blender." Her magic phone chirped. She answered. She said, "Hold on, please," as she pressed keys—they made no sound, not even a faint clack—with astonishing rapidity. Hardly a moment passed before she told the caller, "Mr. Copley won't be able to speak to you until tomorrow. But he's read your memo and he's interested. Okay? Great. I'll tell him." She hung up and pointed to a cabinet beside her computer terminal. It housed a printer that whirred softly. "A log of the call, and my notes on what was said, comes out automatically. Saves me hours of work," she commented as she reached for the sheet of paper. Something on the phone's display caught her eye. "Mr. Copley wants to talk to you on that phone," she pointed to a plain extension by the couch.

It wasn't beeping or ringing, but I picked up. Copley spoke without introduction, "Andy said he's got a half hour. He'll meet you on the basketball court. That's behind the main building. Laura'll tell you how to get there."

"Thank you. And when should I call to give you a report?" I asked.

That earned me a moment of silence. "A report?"

"Well," I lowered my voice, although it wasn't quiet enough to prevent Laura from overhearing. "I assume you're interested in knowing what Andy tells me. I owe you that much for all your help."

There was another silence before he conceded, "I would be interested. I may be out by the time you're done. Why don't you call from reception and Laura will figure it out?"

Following Laura's directions, I took the mirrored elevator down to the lobby, walked around it to unmarked double doors and stepped into the backyard of Minotaur. There was a halfhearted attempt at a garden amounting to four wood benches arranged around an abstract black metal sculpture. The bushes were scraggly. No flowers were in bloom. A path led away to the right, turning behind one of the beige concrete lab buildings. Making the turn, I came upon a basketball hoop attached to the back wall. It was the sole recreational structure. The path did continue toward the pond, as if it might be used for running, but there was something improvised and tired about the basketball hoop, as if it were attached to a suburban home to amuse the kids years ago, and they were now grown and gone away.

I found Andy Chen there, in dungarees and sneakers, his shirt off, wearing big round glasses with gold-colored frames. He stood to the right of the basket, taking twelve-foot jump shots. He missed one as I approached, gathered the ball, and missed another. He noticed me as he caught the rebound.

"Hi," he said. He was nearly six feet tall and painfully skinny. His chest was a boy's, hairless and flat. His large oval face needed his frail neck and skinny body to fill out to be proportionate. "You're Dr. Neruda?"

We shook hands. "Thanks for seeing me."

"No problem." At most, he was twenty-four years old. His voice was high and sweet, as if puberty still awaited him. "Okay if I keep shooting?"

"Sure. I'll rebound."

"Pessimist," he commented and took another shot.

The ball bounced way off the rim to the left and I had to trot to fetch it. I passed it to him. I introduced myself briefly, explaining I had been Gene's shrink, that I hadn't seen him for the last year—my usual version. He listened while concentrating on his shooting. He missed each time, often coming close, and always reacted calmly. Even when the ball spun all round the inner lip of the rim and popped out, he showed no frustration.

"Gene was my boss," he said. He held on to the ball to talk for a while. He kept his eyes on the basket, though. "I was the youngest on the Black Dragon team, but he put me in the fire right away. Gave me a lotta responsibility. I owe him a lot." He shot and missed everything.

I chased the ball, threw him a long pass. I called out, "Why don't you try from a different angle?"

He smiled, ignored my advice, and shot again. Another miss. He got the rebound this time; I was still off the court.

"Gene told me . . ." I had to pause for breath as I returned. It was hot in the sun. My hair was damp. Not Andy's. His mop of straight black hair was as unaffected and unmoving as a wig. "Gene used to say," I continued, "he wasn't all that great as an innovator, that his real skill was managing all the geniuses who worked under him."

"Don't know what that means." He shot. The ball thudded off the backboard right into my hands. Andy turned away from his target to look at me. "We're not inventing microprocessors. We just assemble what the geniuses invent. He was as good at that as anybody."

"But how you assemble them amounts to inventing them, doesn't it?"

He asked for the ball with his hands. I passed it. He measured another shot. "Maybe. I don't think that's genius anyway." He shot and missed again. The ball hit the side of the rim and returned to him in two bounces. "Gene was pretty good at basic design. As good as me. Maybe less sure of himself." He lifted the ball to shoot, then lowered it. "Yeah, that's the difference. He was a little slow to make a leap. Like with Centaur. He had the first instinct for Centaur and kind of let it go. Somehow it became Stick's . . ." Andy cut off that thought and covered the interruption by dribbling.

"What's Centaur?"

He returned his attention to the basket, raising the ball. "Our portable PC. That's what I'm working on. I can't talk about it much, but that's what Gene put me in charge of after Black Dragon. He concentrated on Unicorn, our mainframe. That was a disaster. I told him it was going to be a disaster." He shot. The ball thudded on the front of the rim and fell off lamely, as if it weighed a thousand pounds. "What a brick," he commented.

I gathered the ball and said, as I passed it, "It was Stick's idea for him to concentrate on Unicorn, right?" This was a pure guess. Gene hadn't discussed the details of his work in our handful of phone conversations during the previous year.

"Yeah," Andy laughed at a private thought, so my pass bounced off his hands. He quickly gathered it. "I guess I should ask you if what I say is going to be repeated. Nah," he shot again, missed again. I didn't move for the ball, nor did he. It bounced until reaching the grass, where it rested, a dimpled pumpkin in the sun. "Stick knows what I think. That's why he likes me. I'm not scared of him."

"Do you think it was fair to fire Gene?"

"I got his job, you know."

"I know," I said. "Do you think it was fair?"

"No." Andy's expressive face certainly belied the racist cliché of Chinese inscrutability: he frowned, looked down and his lips trembled. He trotted onto the grass, picked up the basketball, and dribbled awkwardly back to the same spot. He stared at the basket and let it fly. For the first time, the pumpkin went right through the hoop. "Gene taught me that," he said, eyes still on the rim.

"How to shoot?"

"No," he said and smiled at me. "To keep trying no matter what."

I walked over to Andy. Although his brow was dry, his hair unmussed, the large glasses were spotted by perspiration. "He was very proud of you," I said softly.

"He didn't give me a hard time," Andy said, his expression impassive. "Everybody does, sooner or later. Gene never gave me a hard time. Not even when I got his job. He said, 'Congratulations. You deserve it.' He must've hated me. Must have wanted to kill me. But he sure didn't show it."

I allowed a silence, a respectful silence to prevail for a while. Voices drifted from the parking lot while we stood and looked at each other solemnly. Finally I said, "I first met Gene when he was fifteen. While he was coming to me, he discovered how much he loved computers. I've never had a chance to see where he worked. I know you're all a little paranoid about who goes in—"

"I'm in his office," Andy interrupted. "They gave me his office. I didn't want . . ." He sighed, held up a finger to signal I should wait. He walked over to the basket, picked up a green polo shirt I hadn't noticed, neatly folded on the ground. He put it on in what seemed like a single movement. "Come on," he said.

We entered West Building through one of the rear emergency doors. This wasn't surreptitious, merely Andy's normal route to the court. The half-hour practice shooting was a ritual, he told me, when he was stuck on something or just bored. Contrary to the central glass building's cold elegance, and my own expectation of what a computer lab would be like, the halls and open central rooms for the technicians were sloppy and old-fashioned. They were drearily lit by fluorescent ceiling panels; the gray or green or black metal work tables were arranged without a pattern; the springs in the swivel chairs were often broken, their upholstery ripped; and everywhere were empty paper cups of coffee, crumpled cans of soda or fruit drinks, balled-up bags from McDonald's or crushed boxes from Pizza Hut. Even the odd personal possession was either old-tech or dilapidated: a radio with its antenna snapped off halfway and tinfoil balled at the end; a dusty plant, the edges of its drooping leaves black with disease; an attaché case with its handles amputated. The biggest surprise was the computers themselves. Few were housed in cases. Most were open circuit boards stacked into jumbles, thin wide gray cables crossing every which way, connecting them. The keyboards were stained by coffee. I noticed a dented one lying askew under a table, although still connected by a long curlicued cable.

"Welcome to Centaur team," Andy said. "It's messy 'cause we kick out the cleaners when we're on a deadline." They worked without a set schedule, some staying all night, sleeping all day, others arriving at dawn, leaving at four in the afternoon. The key men, like Andy, were there at least twenty hours of the day's twenty-four. And they were all men. Boys really, living in a barracks. Gene, I knew, had spent most of his waking life since college in this hellhole, or another just like it: the windows closed to preserve the machines from dust and changes of temperature, the venetian blinds shutting out the sun and the moon, presumably to thwart industrial spies armed with binoculars, but really to block out the temptation of daytime or the desolation of night. They exchanged colds, they shared a deathly pallor, they addressed each other with the rude, exasperated familiarity of siblings. That last quality of their lives was illustrated immediately.

As we neared his office, Andy was accosted by a fat, prematurely balding man I later learned was named Tim. Dirty blond hair draped from the hairless center of his head in tangled clumps. His torn stretched jeans hung well below his navel, the distended hole appearing quizzically whenever he raised his arms. "What did you do to the IO board?" he demanded. "It's fucked."

Andy ignored him, going into his cheerless office. Tim followed him so closely, I was cut off and entered last. Gene's old work place was medium-sized, furnished with another of those metal tables. It was covered by a jumble of circuit boards and wires in no apparent order, as if someone had dropped a computer from the ceiling and we were looking at the smashed result. There were no files, no cabinets, no posters, no photographs, no personal possessions, except for an expensive chess set, lying on the once white linoleum floor, the pieces in a complicated position that I recognized as arising from a dynamic line of the Sicilian Defense. A terminal connected to Black Dragon stood in the corner under the covered window.

Andy mumbled a reply to Tim's complaint. Tim answered in incomprehensible computer talk, working himself up into a scary rage, his fair skin reddening. His blue and white rugby shirt climbed higher with the gesticulation of his thick arms, until it settled on a ridge above his ballooning stomach and he appeared to be a comical belly dancer in male drag. While Tim ranted, Andy looked down at the dissected computer on his desk, his glasses gradually slipping to the end of his nose, showing no reaction.

"You fuck with my shit again and I'll break your head!" Tim shouted at the conclusion of his monologue, the first sentence I understood. He breathed loudly through his nose for several seconds, waiting. Andy, eyes on the machine, chewed his lips, apparently in deep thought. Finally, Andy reached into the jumble of boards, pulled off a cable from a raised ridge of copper wires, removed a circuit board smaller than his hand, moved it to the top one (later I was told that was the motherboard) and plugged it into the right corner. He yanked another cable from below and connected it to the tiny circuit. "Piggyback," he said. "That clears the serial for a modem."

"We're doing an internal modem!" Tim screamed. And I mean screamed, so desperately that I reacted involuntarily, saying, "Whoa. Take it easy."

They ignored me. Andy shook his head. "Modem's frying the board."

" 'Cause the chips are shit!" Tim screamed again. His face was splotchy with red dots of rage. "Fucking Japanese shit!"

"Shit is what we've got. So start eating it." Andy looked up at him for the first time. He pushed his glasses up to the bridge of his nose. "Piggyback," he said softly.

Tim pulled his shirt down over his belly. Until then, I thought he was unaware of the exposure. He dropped to his wide knees to stare at the new arrangement. He rubbed his bloodshot eyes and squinted.

Groaning, a hand on the floor to power himself, he got to his feet. He looked at Andy. "I ain't doing fuck-all until you tell the softies." He walked out without waiting for an answer.

I laughed nervously, unsettled by Tim. Andy still didn't seem bothered; he was focused on the prototype. "The softies?" I asked.

"Programmers. Operating software. He's right. They might throw a shit fit and cry behind my back to Stick. If he takes their side . . ." Andy fell into his chair. The sudden drop propelled a white curl of stuffing into the air. Andy caught it, quick to protect the exposed boards.

"It's wasted effort?" I tried to finish his sentence.

"Worse," Andy said, carefully disposing the tiny feather into a plastic trash container that was filled to the brim by Coke cans. "It's wasted time. We're late. We're designing, debugging and programming all at once. Doesn't make sense. Gotta do it in stages." He opened his hands to encompass the boards. "And it's too big. You need a truck to carry this thing." He laughed. Naturally, and with good humor, he laughed at the prototype.

"You handle stress well."

"Thanks. But maybe I'm just cracking up. Anyway, this was Gene's office. Pretty fancy for a VP, huh?"

"Are you a VP?"

"No. It's a bullshit title," he said with contempt. He seemed immediately embarrassed and added apologetically, "Meant something to Gene, I guess."

"More money?"

Andy looked down modestly. "Not necessarily."

"You make more than Gene did," I said, not a question.

"I don't know what Gene made," Andy said. He covered his mouth with his left hand and looked at me as if checking whether I believed him. I didn't. His mannerisms and answers had been straightforward until this conversation about salary.

"Did Gene have to stay in this office?"

"No. He liked it here. So do I." He relaxed again, the hand uncovering his mouth, smiling easily. "Seems incredible to you? We're nerds, Doctor. As kids, we were unpopular. As teenagers, we were hated. But here—this is home. We're safe here." Andy leaned forward, peering into his tower of circuits and wires. His glasses began another slide. "That's why Gene didn't move to the Glass Tower."

"Would Tim scream at Gene like that?"

Andy peeked over his glasses at me. "You trying to make me feel bad?"

"I'm trying to understand why losing all this would make him want to stop living."

Andy cocked his head, eyes straying to the fluorescent panel thoughtfully. "I never saw Gene lose his temper. He killed his wife, didn't he? I mean he finally lost his temper—big-time. And *then* he killed himself. Right?"

"Did Tim scream at Gene like that?" I asked again. Andy ignored my question for the second time, leaning back in his chair. His glasses remained stuck on the end of his nose. "Did *you* scream at him?" I asked.

Andy laughed, again easily, enjoying the thoughts my question provoked. He swiveled in his chair, head thrown back, chuckling. When his amusement died out, he adjusted his glasses and then commented, "If someone fucked up, Gene came in and fixed it. He covered everybody's ass. And he listened." Andy straightened, sobering up. "He listened to everybody. He listened too much. He wasted time, he gave everybody too much slack. Part of the reason Tim screams at me is because Gene didn't make the command chain clear. I've only been boss for six weeks. Some people haven't accepted it." He nodded at me earnestly. "They will."

"I'm supposed to report to Stick what I find out from talking to you."

Andy nodded as if that were a banal fact. "Me too."

"I'm not going to," I said. "You said something important, at least, important to a nutty shrink like me. It explains Gene's grief at being fired. That's what I came for. I'm not going to share it with Copley. And I'm certainly not going to tell him you're in trouble—"

Andy shifted his weight forward abruptly. The spring squealed faintly and his chair thudded to an upright position. "I'm not in trouble—"

"—But I have a piece of advice for you," I cut him off. "I know you think you're shrewder than Gene, and maybe you think you're stronger too. I made a mistake with Gene, I see that now. I assumed he would be rewarded for years of service. I assumed a talented man would always be valuable to a company. You see, my uncle was a businessman and he remained loyal to the people who did good work, well past their prime. My uncle wasn't a sentimental man. That wasn't why he was loyal. He knew that loyalty inspires the younger ones to work hard. Stick doesn't believe that."

"Nobody believes that anymore. This is the nineties. Haven't you heard of downsizing?" Andy stood up. "Listen, I'm not in trouble." He pointed to the smashed machine. "This may look like a mess to you, but it's normal—"

Again, I interrupted. "I didn't mean with the machine. I know nothing about it. I mean you can't handle these men and you're scared. You're still a kid. You miss Gene. He controlled their egos so you could be the star. Now you're having to do both jobs at once and you're floundering."

Andy stared at me through his spotted glasses, eyes half-closed. Their Asian slant lent the look a cold withdrawn aspect. In fact, he was furious. "I can build this machine alone," he said in a whisper. He wasn't attempting to conceal the remark. He was so clenched with anger he couldn't give it volume. "I don't need them."

"You're wrong," I said. "You told me so yourself. They're your family. They make you feel safe. You need them as badly as they need you."

Andy was still. He watched me watch him for a while. A man with a high squeaky voice entered behind me, talking without introduction, something about access time to the hard drive.

Andy greeted him with a shout, "Not now!"

"We can't piggyback—"

"Tell Tim to go home and stop causing trouble," Andy said. "Get out and close the door."

"Fuck you," said the voice, but the door shut in a moment. Andy continued to stare at me through the glistening spots on his glasses. Finally, he turned, moving to the black terminal by the window. He flipped a button and it whirred, the monitor flashing awake. Rather than pull his chair over, he squatted on his haunches and typed at Black Dragon's keyboard. "Come here."

I moved beside him. A heading across Dragon's screen said, COPLEY'S OUT BOX. Below was a list of dates and subjects. A bar of white color skipped down them, stopping at, "RE: Kenny Termination." The screen blipped. The text of a memo from Copley to Minotaur's comptroller appeared: "Since Gene Kenny is no longer an employee, the no-interest loan on his residence can be called as of July 1st, provided he is notified at least four weeks in advance. Do it today and confirm to my box." The date of Stick's memo was May 10th, two days before Gene's suicide.

"Do you know what that means?" Andy asked, twisting to look at me.

"I sure do. Was the letter sent?"

Andy typed more, got a menu heading, COPLEY'S IN BOX. He highlighted a return memo. The comptroller reported that a letter had been mailed to Gene's home address (although he hadn't lived there for a year) return receipt requested. It was signed by Cathy on May 11th, the day before she died.

Andy pressed a pair of buttons. The memo disappeared and the screen turned blue. He typed a command—ERASE: Dragonslayer search—and hit the Enter key. The screen responded: Search erased, Dragonslayer. He leaned forward and turned off the terminal. "The machines Gene built made Stick the owner of this company. When Copley started here, he was just a drone like us." Andy sprung up from his squat. "Stick'll give you money if you hold a gun to his head, but he won't share his power. Never his power. I'm not a fool. I know who I'm dealing with. Gene didn't."

"How were you able to show me those memos?"

Andy smiled. He pushed his glasses up, although they were already in place. "I gotta get to work."

"Could Gene invade the system like that?"

Andy shook his head no. "I told you, I'm not a fool. Unless the Prince of Darkness rips the Dragon network out, I'm in this company to stay."

"The Prince of Darkness," I repeated, amused.

"That's what we call him." Andy returned to his chair and focused on his troublesome prototype. "That's what everybody calls him. Except for Gene. He told me that making up nicknames for authority figures just shows you're really scared." Andy glanced at me, smiling. "He get that insight from you?"

"Probably."

Andy put his nose right up to a circuit board, peering through his dirty glasses at a jumble of cables. "Now why aren't you happy, my little hard drive?" he asked in a Transylvanian accent. He continued to play Dracula, while he added to me, "Nice to meet you, Dr. Neruda. I'd appreciate it if you went out the way we came in. What the Prince of Darkness doesn't know can't hurt us."

CHAPTER FIVE

Final Analysis

WHEN I APPEARED IN THE MAIN LOBBY, WITH AN AIR OF INNOCENCE, I didn't have to ask to phone Laura. The receptionist greeted me as I approached. "Dr. Neruda? Mr. Copley is looking for you. Here," she handed me a phone, "I'll get his assistant."

"Hello, Doctor," Laura said cheerfully, as if we were old friends.

"Call me Rafe," I said. "I'm a shrink. We're not real doctors."

She chuckled. "Oh, you shouldn't give up your title so easily. Let me get him."

"Dr. Neruda?" Stick came on instantly. "Did you bring your tennis racquet to New York?"

He had a knack for being surprising. "My tennis racquet?" I repeated dully.

"Edgar mentioned you're a player. I have a doubles game tonight. Our fourth has dropped out, our backup is out of town, and I hate playing Canadian."

Without thinking, I answered truthfully. "I haven't played in years."

"Oh." Copley's disappointment, even disapproval, went unconcealed. "Forget it."

I recovered. "But I doubt I've forgotten how to win. I sure knew how to beat Edgar's ass." Saying that so embarrassed me, I turned my back to the receptionist, hoping she wouldn't hear.

Copley was quiet for a moment. "That's what he said," he commented in a low voice. "You know, we don't throw our racquets or anything, but we take tennis pretty seriously. How rusty are you?"

"If I hit for a half hour before we start, I'll be fine. Do they have a pro there? He can warm me up."

Copley jumped on this notion, proposing a variation. He said the game was at the Wall Street Racquet Club (he claimed that my being in Manhattan was why he thought of me) and he would get there at six, an hour before the doubles, to hit with me. He could use the practice, he said, not bothering to make that fib convincing. I was being checked out. And not as a permanent tennis partner, I assumed.

Should he send a car for me? he asked. I declined. Did I have my racquet? I decided against telling him I no longer owned a tennis racquet. I said I hadn't brought it and would rent one from the courts. Oh no, he said, he'd arrange to have my model there. What did I normally play with? I couldn't believe I was being caught in such a silly lie. I retreated into the dignity of poverty, assuming a hurt tone. I said firmly, "I can't allow you to buy me a racquet. I'll rent one at the courts."

He wasn't done with that issue, however. At the very least, he wanted Laura to call the courts to make sure they had my model for rent. (Probably if they didn't, he would then have bought it.) At last, I found a way out. "You know, I'd rather play with a strange racquet. I've noticed it improves my concentration. I get so interested in observing how the new racquet plays that I focus better."

"Huh," he said, impressed. "That's a great marketing idea for tennis. Buy a new racquet every week and win."

"That's me. Always trying to get the economy going."

He said, "Anyway, Laura tells me it'll have to be a Wilson. That's all they have to rent." There hadn't been a break in our conversation. The magic phone was at work again.

"A Wilson will be fine," I said.

Our date was set. In the excitement of its arrangement, Copley forgot to ask, or seemed to, about my talk with Andy.

There are places in New York where limousines congregate, their long and squat dark shapes almost blending with the city's black gutters. They line up outside expensive restaurants from TriBeCa to Elaine's, park at the right Broadway show on the right night, queue beside the Garden during the playoffs, are almost always present at Lincoln Center, and also, I discovered that evening, at the Wall Street Racquet Club.

There were half a dozen docked by the sleek East River, in the shadows of the giant glowing green bubbles that cover Piers 13 and 14. The bubbles aren't Martian spaceships, but protection for synthetic clay tennis courts, rented at hourly rates that, with twice-a-week use in a year, could cost you enough to build your own. The lockers are made of wood, the showers are multi-headed, there are redwood-lined saunas, the help is soft-spoken, and the customers complain the facilities are second-rate.

I arrived early to inspect the choice of rental racquets so my ignorance wouldn't be revealed to Copley. When I played tennis regularly most people owned wood racquets. The few who used metal were seeing doctors for tennis elbow. I knew there wouldn't be any wood racquets, but I was surprised there were no metal ones either. The technology had moved on to composite plastic and graphite models. They are dramatically lighter than the old woodies: it's like picking up a tin frying pan instead of an iron skillet. I rejected the grotesque oversized head and wide-body types. They seemed like jokes to me, so large I couldn't imagine how a player would know if he was hitting near the sweet spot. A pro gossiping with two clerks heard me make that comment. He said that with the oversize heads I didn't have to worry about finding the sweet spot. The new racquets were so forgiving, even a ball struck near the edge of the frame has power. "Of course if you hit it in the sweet spot," he added, not joking, "the ball will go long."

"You mean, it rewards mediocrity," I said.

The two clerks laughed and then covered their mouths as if I had broken a taboo.

The pro nodded and winked at me. He suggested I try the Wilson pro staff model, the closest to the width and thickness of the antique woodies. "This is what Stefan Edberg uses. It's still got plenty of power," he commented dryly.

Before making the trip downtown, I had stopped by Paragon on Union Square and, with some difficulty, bought plain white shorts. I couldn't find a single plain shirt, so I wore one of my white polos. I had wrongly assumed the dress code at a place called the Wall Street Racquet Club would be white. In fact, I saw no other player in white. Copley showed up in a black and purple nylon matching outfit: black warm-up jacket with purple piping over a black shirt with a purple lightning bolt; black warm-up pants with zippers up the legs so they could be pulled off over his sneakers to reveal black shorts with purple piping.

"You changed already?" he said as a greeting.

"I came like this."

"Do you have a change of clothes?" His tone was curt and commanding, as if I were his child.

For a yes, I showed him my bag.

"Here," he gestured for me to give it to him. "I'll put it in my locker." He turned to the clerk. "We have Court One?"

"Yes, Mr. Copley," the clerk said, although Stick hadn't announced himself.

Copley disappeared into the lockers briefly. Returning, he led me onto the courts. When we passed through the rotating doors into the bubbles, my ears popped. Along with the roar of air-conditioning (outside the temperature had reached ninety-five) it felt as if we were in a jet. "How did it go with Andy?" Copley asked. He put his large tennis bag on a wood bench to the side of the net and opened it. He followed the serious tennis player's equipment recommendation to the letter: he brought two identical wide-body racquets for alternating use to maintain equal string tension in case one broke during play. (It was no surprise, by the way, that he hadn't offered me his spare racquet. Copley wasn't the sort of person who would allow another man to handle his phallus, even a spare phallus.) I didn't answer his question, apparently preoccupied by stretching my legs. He opened two cans of soft-surface balls for us to rally. I was nervous. I had played a lot of tennis as a teenager, but that was a long time ago. Stick watched me, bent over, moaning as I failed to touch my toes. When I didn't answer right away, he tried again. "You talked to Andy?"

I straightened and nodded. I arched to the left, my right hand reaching toward the opposite shoulder, like an ungainly ballerina.

"And? Was it helpful?"

"It was okay," I said doubtfully, as if it weren't.

"He was helpful?"

Again, I seemed reluctant to answer. I nodded and said, "You'll have to be patient with me for the first fifteen minutes or so. I haven't hit a ball in a while."

He dropped his chin a little and stared up, from the shadow of the bony ledge of his brow, into my eyes. The look was insistent, as if he were trying to instill confidence. He handed me three of the new balls. "We'll hit and get the rust out."

He stretched a little on his side before stroking the first ball to me. I hardly bothered to hit it back hard, merely tried to meet the ball cleanly.

My swing was late. I put so little weight into it, I expected my shot not to clear the net. Instead, the ball fled from my strings and carried over to the service line. The power in the racquet was astonishing. Stick leaned into my shot. His reply was past me before I knew it. I hit the next two balls into the bottom of the net. The light racquet had me out in front. Copley made no effort to help me. He stepped into every ball, his form graceful, a picture from a primer for topspin tennis: full shoulder turn, racquet face closed, sweeping from low to high. He used topspin to keep the shots in court, but he was also meeting the ball on the rise, his follow-through relatively level. He wasn't rallying, he was hitting winners.

After ten minutes of humiliation—my shots returned out of my reach to the corners, or my balls sailing long, nearly to the back wall—I abandoned hitting with topspin. I tried the old slice forehand, a shot that I knew (from watching professional tennis) had died out with the new technology of the racquets. Instead of the characteristic high bounce of a topspin stroke, my slice skipped away from Copley, staying low. Off-balance, he smashed it into the bottom of the net. He paused, stared at the mark on the clay where it had landed, and shook his head. He took out another ball and hit it at me. Again, I sliced into it, hard. Sure enough, it sailed out, although by no more than six inches; I couldn't take a full stride into the slice forehand with the lightweight racquet. In keeping with his behavior that we were playing rather than rallying, Copley didn't go for the ball. He did, however, pay careful attention to how it bounced on the surface and quickly looked up at me. Now he understood.

He gathered my errant ball, and, to my surprise, as if we were playing a game, avoided the new forehand I had displayed and hit to my backhand. I sliced it back defensively, again refusing to play a power game with him. My shot floated deep into his end of the court, nearly to the baseline. Copley had to wait for it. He prepared early, full shoulder turn, back foot raised slightly, head down. He put all his weight into his shot, trying to bang it back, although he was two feet behind the line. The ball smacked into the tape and fell on his side of the net.

He likes pace. From then on, I gave him mostly low, softly hit underspin. I used topspin only for variety. I tried to pace each reply differently. That didn't prevent Stick from hitting what would be the occasional winner (if we had been scoring) but he also mishit a lot, starting his swing early, stubbornly anticipating the bounce of each ball, trying to drive them with maximum power, rather than judging the movement of each shot and accepting what was given.

After a half hour, I was exhausted. I moved toward the net, intending to leave the court, calling out, "I need a drink."

"I've got water," Copley said, coming toward me. He appeared cooler and more rested than when we began. He unzipped his warm-up jacket. I admired his strong sinewy arms and bulging pecs. He was in superb shape, not merely for a fifty-five-year-old man, but for any age. I doubt most people, with his full head of hair and lean body, despite the lines of his craggy face, would have thought him more than forty-five. He opened another compartment of his enormous rectangular black and purple tennis bag. He gave me a bottle of spring water packaged in a clear plastic container. The brand was Glacéau. There were four more in his bag. The bottle didn't have a top that came off; instead, you had to lift a nub at the top and suck through it.

"Like mother's milk," I joked, but Copley didn't get it. Feeling foolish, I pulled the nipple out and fed. He said matter-of-factly, "You're playing like an old man."

I coughed a little, starting to talk before I finished swallowing. I looked embarrassed and shrugged. "I am an old man."

He frowned. "Come on. You're forty, right?"

"Thirty-nine," I said.

He shook his head. "I mean the old-fashioned forehand. You can't hit it hard."

"Not yet," I said and took another pull on the water, sucking so hard the middle of the bottle momentarily collapsed. Made me feel rather sympathetic to mothers. I put the bottle into a holder for drinks attached to the net. "I will," I said, trotting back to my side.

He lingered for a moment at the net. He wasn't finished with the conversation. He knew now that I hadn't played in more than a decade. "I'm ready," I called. He shrugged and returned to his backcourt. I tried driving the slice forehand, but Copley was correct. Too much speed and I couldn't clear the net; too much arc and it floated long. I could only rarely hit hard and be accurate. Also, he became accustomed to its low skipping motion. His replies to the underspin were more often good and getting deeper, harder to reach each time. Topspin allowed him to hit with all his strength and still keep the ball in play. Toward the end of our practice hour, he got bored, and stopped trying to hit winners. Only when he concluded that I wasn't a worthy adversary or a good potential partner, did he rally politely, sending the ball within easy reach and at less than full speed.

The other two men appeared at ten minutes before seven. They are unimportant to an understanding of Copley except in one respect. They were both ten years younger than Stick and his equals in business, one, the head of a software company, the other, a merger and acquisitions man at an investment banking firm. That surprised me. I expected his tennis partners would be the modern equivalent of courtiers, men motivated to lose to him, lawyers who worked for him, or perhaps a less successful friend. The head of the software company wore a skintight sky blue brace on his left knee. Copley introduced me and the software man said, "So you're the ringer, huh? Stick claims you haven't played in a while."

"He hasn't," Stick said calmly, no rancor. "Not since you were in college, I bet."

"Not since high school," I said.

"Great," the mergers and acquisitions man said to Copley. "He's your partner."

"What's wrong with your knee?" I asked the software man.

He blanched at the question and answered with his head down. "It's okay. I sprained it skiing last winter. Some jerk smashed into me. This is just a precaution."

We warmed them up. I hit my awkward self-conscious topspin to them, saving my underspin for the game, and kept my eyes on the side-to-side movement of Mr. Software. When he tried to push off quickly on the injured knee, there was a delay. He was stubborn, too. Although we were merely rallying, if I pulled a ball wide to his wounded side, he chased it. Mr. M&A seemed obsessed with beating Copley, clumsily trying to psyche him out. "Oh, you're hitting 'em too hard for me!" he called whenever Copley didn't whack the ball with every ounce of his strength. During one lull of ball gathering, he commented, "Are you doing something new with that backhand, Stick? It looks great."

"Nothing," Stick answered with a smile, "and you know it."

I had a pleasant surprise when we practiced our serves. Here the modern racquet helped me. The extra power meant that my softer, more accurate second serve had good pace, whereas their serves seemed no faster than what I remembered from opponents of my youth. Indeed, with the new power, I could place serves wide or down the middle and retain speed, a combination that wasn't possible in the old days for me. Stick, who had adopted a resigned air since our warm-up, was impressed. Hope returning, he whispered, as we moved to our positions to start the game, "You've got a good serve."

"We're going to win," I told him.

"They're good," he said. "Better than you."

"I'm smarter," I answered.

The flaw in playing this gambit with Stick was that I had to come through and I wasn't convinced I could. I needed a lot more practice, and perhaps more talent, to defeat these men. Besides, my partner Copley wasn't superior to our opponents. In fact, I felt he was slightly inferior. Mr. Software had a lot of variety to his shots and placed them well, relying less on raw power. His consistency and the fact that he played the net superbly are both keys to winning at doubles. Copley was aggressive at net, I discovered, but rarely hit a clean winning volley, since he refused to try for angles, insisting on trying to bang them past our opponents, which he failed at more often than not.

For the first four games, they held their two serves easily, smashing my feeble returns, and outhitting Stick, anticipating his passing shots as if they could read his swing. However, my height and reach helped me. Playing net while Copley served, I startled them with both my wingspan and my leap. Mr. M&A tried one lob. After I put it away, with an awkward but effective jump, he said, "That's the last time I try to go over your head." Also, my training with the more finesse game of wood helped at net. I had no trouble hitting drop volleys, or spinning them out of court. We held Stick's serve easily. As for the game on my serve, I was able, unlike with my ground strokes, to overpower them.

We were tied at two games all. It was soon apparent that, unfortunately, our opponents had been merely feeling us out. Beginning with the fifth game, they kept the ball away from me when I was at net and consistently hit to me when I was back, confident that my topspin ground strokes would be weak. They held their serves at love and broke Copley easily, partly because he stubbornly tried too hard to carry us by himself, and ended up overhitting. He also made mistakes while I was serving, driving what should have been two put-away volleys long. But we held my serve. We were now down five games to three, in immediate danger of losing the set.

Before receiving Mr. Software's first serve of the ninth game, I conferred with Copley in the backcourt. I whispered, "I'm going to hit with sidespin and underspin. I want to move him around on that knee."

"You think it's bothering him?"

"I think he won't protect it. Do you care if I test it?"

Stick frowned, as if I had insulted him. "Of course not."

Mr. Software had found my high, weak returns so easy to volley that he had been coming in behind his serve each time. He opened this game with a hard one to my backhand and followed it in. I replied with an abbreviated sidespin stroke, aiming to hit it at his feet and out wide. When he saw the low arc of my ball, he tried to stop. He tried to stop on the braced knee and it buckled as my shot passed him for a winner. He immediately stood, raising his knee off the ground. If I had blinked, I might not have noticed the collapse.

I rushed forward and stammered, "You—you okay?"

"Yeah, I'm okay. I've been passed before," he grumbled and rolled his eyes at his partner to highlight my foolishness.

When he moved to serve the second point to Stick, I didn't position myself at the net, instead playing back. This could be taken as an insult to Copley's ability to return Mr. Software's serve. And that's how Stick took it. "You should be up," he said.

"No I shouldn't," I answered insolently.

"Ready boys?" Mr. Software asked sarcastically.

Copley whacked the return hard. He made a good one, driving it across court to Software. Since I was back, Software took advantage. He hit a deep topspin shot to me. Although a groundstroke was called for, I floated a high lob over M&A, to force Software to have to run to the other side. He got to it easily, returning it to me, and I continued this old-womanish tactic, mooning balls over M&A each time, so that Mr. Software had to keep shifting laterally. He was stubborn and persisted in returning them to me. The play slowed down so much that M&A had the leisure to complain, "Cut it out, girls."

Finally, I hit my first underspin forehand, without much pace, almost a drop shot, about twelve feet in front of Software. He couldn't push off that knee fast enough to have a chance for it, but he tried anyway, and again his foot came down hard as he tried to reach, the knee buckling. This time he stayed down for a moment or two. He covered it by banging his racquet on the clay, as if the pose were frustration rather than physical weakness.

Copley was shrewd, as I expected. From then on, he stopped trying, for the most part, to hit winners and resorted to lobs or short balls at Mr. Software, keeping him on the run. Software lunged at balls as he tired, in pain I suspected, and made errors. We ran off four games quickly and won the set, seven to five. Not before, however, there was another clue to Mr. Software's immaturity about his infirmity. On the final and decisive point, although he had no hope of getting it, he recklessly chased a volley I had spun toward the alley into the netting that separates Court One and Court Two. He got tangled in the mesh, the right foot twisting, and he fell hard. We all rushed over to help. He brushed us off angrily, and insisted his ankle was okay. In fact, he was limping, wounded now in his left knee and his right foot. I suggested we quit for the night.

"Are you nuts?" Mr. Software said. "I'm just getting loose."

Copley frowned at me. "We play the best two out of three."

Taking a break, everybody sat on the bench, produced Glacéau bottles and sucked. I fell into a reverie. Was this a class difference? In Washington Heights, when we played touch football or basketball, the kind of strategy I had adopted against Mr. Software, including the meanness of the last few points, where I had deliberately varied the height and pace to force him into abrupt stops and starts, was considered fair play. Under the boards in basketball, we gathered rebounds with our sharp elbows out, whacking noses and foreheads until someone decided he'd had enough and let the sharpest elbow prevail. But an admission of injury and defeat was allowed and respected. No, this wasn't a matter of class. I knew from Albert that code was gone from the streets. Was it also gone from the penthouse?

For the second set, I resumed a losing strategy of hitting at Mr. M&A and returning serves to Mr. Software with topspin. Relieved by the reappearance of my feeble groundstrokes, Mr. Software strode into them. He hit two lovely winners down the line. He was certainly the best player on the court. Soon, we were behind three games to love.

Copley brought the balls for me to serve the fourth game. We were at the rear of our court. He turned his back to our opponents. Laying the balls on my racquet, Stick spoke through his thin lips so they hardly moved. "Cut it out."

"Cut what out?" I said.

"Play to win."

"He'll get hurt."

"Bullshit."

"He's out of control."

"That's his problem. Are you scared to win, Doctor?" Copley moved into position at the net. So be it, I decided. I spun a serve out wide to Mr. Software. He couldn't move quickly in that direction, nor, once he made the return, could he, with alacrity, get back into position for the rest of the point. His reply was short and slow. Three-quarters of an open court were available to Copley for a winning volley. Instead, at point-blank range, he punched the ball at Mr. M&A, who tried to cover up, but got smacked in the groin. It must have smarted. Mr. M&A pretended it didn't.

Copley and I blooped balls or floated them out of Mr. Software's reach, presenting him the choice of cutting back and forth to try to salvage a win, or allowing us our sneaky triumph. We won five straight games to come to within four points of victory when it happened. Mr. Software, knowing that a lazy lob of mine over his left shoulder was merely the prelude to a series of them, tried to end the point quickly with a twisting leap. He reached the ball, but came down with his foot going in one direction and his thigh in another. The knee crumpled. While he lay on the ground, Copley smashed a groundstroke at Software's head. He missed by an inch and then pretended surprise at the spectacle of his fallen opponent. That ended our friendly game of doubles.

Mr. Software had a comfortable limo to drive him home and, although he had to be helped to it, I was sure he had no worse than a twisted knee. What happened was far from horrible or ugly, yet a mild despair overcame me, a nauseating reminder of my childhood as a performing machine for my uncle.

After we watched our opponents limp into their chariots, Copley said, with an open look of admiration, "I see what Edgar meant about you knowing how to win."

"I need a shower," I said.

"You know, you should get into better shape." Copley's tone was a new one: avuncular. "You're perspiring too much. You're a fine athlete. Gotta maintain the machine."

"I sweat whether I'm in shape or not," I told him. "Remember, I'm a spic."

Copley laughed hard, stopping in his tracks to put his hands on his hips. He laughed too hard to suit me. I asked him what he did to keep fit. He gave me the details while we stripped in the locker room. Actually, while I stripped. He dawdled with his undressing so that I was naked and inside one of the multi-headed showers when he removed his black and purple outfit. I was convinced the delay was deliberate. Sure enough, he came out with a towel wrapped around him and angled himself in the shade of his locker door to put on his underpants; only then did he turn my way while talking. The precious jewels were kept from the vulgar gaze throughout.

An explication of Stick's regimen—swimming two miles a day and workouts on machines every other day—preoccupied us until he was dressed in chinos, a black polo shirt and, to my surprise, sandals. The kind of handmade soft brown leather sandals I used to wear in the early seventies. Copley asked if I wanted some pasta. "We need carbos," he said.

In his limo, heading north, he asked again about my meeting with Chen, in a different way. "What did you think of Andy?"

"Brilliant kid."

"He is."

"But he's a kid," I commented.

"They're all kids, really. Even when they're forty."

"Building machines keeps them boys?" I asked. "Still playing with their Legos?"

Stick nodded. "In a way. I guess that's a shrink's point of view. Did he answer your lingering questions about Gene?"

"Yes. Andy's very loyal and grateful to Gene, but it slipped through that Gene was burned out, feeling overwhelmed, out of his depth. You weren't kidding when you said that was a hazard of your business. Things are pretty grim down there."

"Grim?" Even in the dim light of the limo, I could see a flicker of irritation on Stick's face. "I don't think it's grim. More like a playroom, isn't it? Or summer camp?"

"They're not playing," I said firmly, but without emphasis, as if it had no importance to me. "They're fighting for survival."

"For survival?" He chuckled. "Aren't you exaggerating just a little?"

Adopting a casual and pompous tone, I delivered a monologue chock-full of popular psychology jargon. I talked about limits and the need for authority. I talked about structure: rewards and punishments; incentives and security. I talked about how loyalty to a consistent parent figure or an appropriate substitute, such as a corporation, can empower and build self-esteem. I said his young employees all had the same base psychological profile. (Stick didn't question how I could know that.) They are emotionally retarded, I said, fearful to ask for what they want, or worse, walled off from their emotions, suffocated by their mothers, rejected or squashed by their fathers as inadequate Oedipal competition—an outright contradiction, by the way, but the sort of all-encompassing generalization that is commonly made by popular psychologists. My rambling speech continued while we entered Il Cantinori, an expensive restaurant on Tenth Street off University Place. We had both ordered and consumed ziti with mussels, sun-dried tomatoes and yellow peppers by the time I finished my Dr. Joyce Brothers imitation.

"How do you think Andy is doing?" Stick asked. "What's your impression of his management skills?"

"Okay," I said, lowering my eyes and my voice.

"You know," he leaned forward, caressing a glass of white wine in both hands. "We've got a lot riding on our people. Andy's in a position to help himself and the company. He's also in a position to hurt himself and the company."

I nodded. But offered nothing.

"What's your opinion of his state of mind?"

"I spent less than an hour with him. Can't really say."

Copley leaned back and sipped his wine reflectively. He returned the glass lazily, sliding it onto the table. He cocked his head, locking his fingers together. "This afternoon I was thinking about you and Gene. He was doing very well, for himself and for us, up until about a year, year and a half ago. That's when he stopped seeing you, right?"

I nodded.

Copley flexed the fingers outward, cracking them. "Don't be shy, Doctor. Tell me your opinion of Andy's state of mind."

I paused and stared off thoughtfully for a moment. "Andy's a prodigy, right? I mean, even for a computer whiz, he's a prodigy?"

"Bachelor degree at seventeen. Graduate degree, age twenty. Could've had his pick of jobs. Apple, IBM. Microsoft, for that matter. I think he's as good at programming as engineering. Tell you the truth, he's something of an underachiever. You could have knocked me over with a feather when he said yes to our offer."

"I understand him choosing a young company, an underdog, if you don't mind my calling Minotaur an underdog."

"Not at all. We are underdogs. We try harder."

"Well, that would appeal to Andy. Prodigies are lone wolves. They're usually resented by other children while growing up, and often resented by adults, too. It's hard to deal with, the spectacle of a child doing something better than most of us could ever hope to. Hostility toward prodigies is understandable and easy to dismiss as envy if you have a sound ego and some life experience. But that hostility is directed at a child, who, also naturally enough, expects praise and love for his abilities. So prodigies learn to work alone, or at least as outsiders. Often they also learn to hide what they can do, to underachieve, as you call it. Unfortunately, this can sometimes lead to self-sabotage."

"Self-sabotage?"

"Yes, self-sabotage. As opposed to self-destructiveness. The distinction might seem academic, but it's significant to me. Self-sabotage isn't an act of self-punishment. Rather, it's an act of self-protection."

"You mean, they unconsciously fail so people won't resent them?"

"Very good." I raised my wine glass and toasted him. "I shouldn't be surprised. A man who runs a large successful company must have a delicate feel for psychology." Copley shook his head, about to shrug off my compliment. I prevented him by continuing, "I don't know enough about the structure of Andy's family relations. For example, his Oedipal dynamic. Was Gene a substitute father figure? If so, defeating him, taking Gene's job, might be very troubling, especially since Andy's victory is the Oepidal nightmare: Gene died." I stared up at Il Cantinori's excellent restoration of an elaborate tin ceiling and mused, almost mumbling, "Perhaps there is an element of self-destructiveness. Andy might be unconsciously punishing himself for his triumph."

"Punishing himself how, Doctor?"

I returned my attention to him, with a startled look, as if woken from a reverie. "Please, call me Rafe. I feel uncomfortable being addressed as Doctor."

"Okay. I'm sorry, Rafe, but I have to insist you be more specific. I've got a fiduciary responsibility to Minotaur stockholders. If Andy is psychologically unstable it could fuck up a lot more than just his life."

"Oh, I don't think it's *that* serious." I smiled at him, a forced artificial smile, and looked at my watch. "I'm sorry, but I'm leaving early in the morning. I should be getting to bed. And you have a long ride home. Luckily, you don't have to drop me off. I'm staying six blocks from here, so I won't need a ride." I twisted in my chair to look for our waiter. He saw me, I made a writing motion, and he nodded.

Turning back, I found Copley's dark eyes on me. "They have great desserts here," he said in an ominous tone.

"I'm full."

"Well, we're always full, aren't we?" Copley slapped his nonexistent belly as though he were pounding an enormous bass drum. "That's no reason to stop eating."

"Were you overweight as a child?" I asked. The question was absurdly posed: presumptuous, pompous, and grave. It should have gotten a laugh.

Instead, Copley stared at me. He cocked his head after a moment and drawled, "Yeah. I was a fat kid."

I nodded as if that were obvious. "Not for long, I bet."

"Soon as I hit puberty, I made sure to get rid of it."

"Exceptional," I commented in a schoolteacher's tone.

He grinned. "Exceptional?"

"Very rare for that cycle to be broken in adolescence. Shows enormous strength of character."

"You believe in concepts like strength of character?"

The waiter appeared. "No dessert?"

"We'll have two decaffeinated cappuccinos," Copley said and added to me, "Okay?"

"Sure," I agreed. The waiter left.

"You believe in innate qualities?" he asked. "Genetically encoded personality traits?"

"Of course. It's just that it's impossible to know exactly where heredity leaves off and environment begins. Or, for that matter, how much one distorts or influences the other. That's why we often treat the whole family unit, especially in child psychology."

"Hmmm," Copley considered this carefully. He smoothed his hair down and commented, "A company is like a family."

"Yes!" I leaned toward him, excited. "That's just what I was thinking when Andy showed me your labs. This is a family. That was the flaw with how I treated Gene—" I caught myself. I covered my mouth, embarrassed. "Please," I said, "don't blame Andy for showing me around."

Stick, who had been staring intently with a thin-lipped smile, broke out laughing. "Don't worry. I don't mind. I'm sure you're not an industrial spy. Anyway, I knew. Andy told me he gave you a tour."

"Really?" I stroked my chin thoughtfully. I understood why Freud grew a beard. Without one, the gesture doesn't quite work. "And yet he seemed so frightened about you finding out. That's fascinating . . . You really are their father. It's an unfair burden on you. To be an effective manager you can't also be an emotional support. That's why . . . I see now . . ." I trailed off, pensively.

"What?" Copley asked. I looked at him absentmindedly. "What are you thinking?"

"Well, I didn't understand, at first, why a man like you, who doesn't really know computers . . ." I let that go and shrugged, "I mean, you don't really have any creative ability, so why are you running a company that has to reinvent itself every year or so? In theory, someone like Gene or Andy ought to be CEO, not a salesman like you. That's your background, isn't it? You were head of sales for Flashworks, right?"

The amusement and self-assurance were gone from Copley's face and body language. He sat stiffly now, eyelids half-closed, waiting, warily, for me to go on.

"But it's leadership, isn't it?" I continued. "In fact, now that I think about it, this isn't an uncommon pattern in today's complex world. Presidents, for example, especially in this century, are rarely men of exceptional intelligence. And that has long been the case with armies. The era of brilliant tactical generals also being the political leader faded once we got past Napoleon. I think the skill you possess, the father-figure who can bring the best out of his brilliant children, is underrated. It isn't intellectual genius or creative genius as we understand it, but rather a kind of emotional—No!" I snapped my fingers, excited. "No, it's a genius of character. That's where your will, the strength of purpose that allowed you to get rid of the weight as you entered adolescence, comes in. It's a talent, an intelligence." I shook a finger at him. "What perhaps you don't appreciate is the extent of your emotional impact on people."

"You're wrong," he said mildly.

"Really?" I was cheerfully curious. He nodded. "Tell me. I know this must all seem silly to you, but it's important to me. I think there may be a major theoretical book in this notion of character intelligence."

Copley smiled again, relaxing. He was amused (understandably) by my pedantic manner. "I know the effect I have on people. It's calculated. What you're talking about may be a secret to psychiatrists, but it's no secret in American business. Management skills are key in today's competitive environment. Technical skills, what you call creative ability, are so specialized that you can't expect them to be combined with leadership. Andy, for example, barely has time to dress himself, much less keep track of the marketplace."

"Yes, yes, of course," I said, bursting with enthusiasm. Our decaffeinated cappuccinos had arrived. I drained half of mine in a gulp and leaned over the table, excited. "But I don't think even you appreciate the emotional leadership you provide. We live in a world where the family has deteriorated, community has disintegrated, religion is merely a sentiment. Today's extended family, today's community, today's moral leadership is provided by business. And today's corporate manager, unfairly, has become father, community leader, and priest—all wrapped into one. The psychological implications of your role are enormous."

Copley raised a hand to his smoothed-back hair and checked that it was in place. I finished my cappuccino, leaned back, and watched the pensive, calculating Copley, stroking his eyebrows. His fingers eventually trailed down his starved face, enjoying the accomplishment of his thinness, thinking hard, thinking himself into my trap.

Stick was slow to take the bait. Was the delay caused by a protective intuition he chose to ignore? He waited until he paid the check. (He had scoffed at my offer to split it.) "You think Andy's under too much pressure, don't you?"

"No," I said quickly, too quickly. "This is silly. I hardly know him."

"Give me a break, Rafe. Stop holding back. I'll take what you have to say with a grain of salt." He stood up. "Let's walk to where you're staying. I'll have the car follow us."

The streets were wet. It had rained lightly sometime during our meal. The temperature must have dropped twenty degrees. He asked for Susan's address and gave it to the driver. We strolled toward Fifth Avenue. "Let's hear your best guess about Andy."

"It's only a guess."

"Understood. Come on."

"He's going to fail. I can't identify, as I said earlier, whether it's punishment or neurotic self-protection, but he's isolating himself from his co-workers, developing symptoms of paranoia, and he's pressing. I don't know enough about computers to have any idea if he's actually done harm to the design yet, but he will, unless either his guilt or his vulnerability is relieved. I know you have a successful company, and I don't wish to insult you, but the atmosphere down there is dangerous. Morale is astonishingly low. I made a mistake with Gene that you're repeating with Andy."

Copley stopped walking. I pretended not to notice until I had gone ahead a few steps. "What's that?" he asked, not catching up.

I walked back to him. "You've put Andy in a role he's not fit for."

"And just how did *you* do that with Gene?" Copley asked, daring me.

I took the dare. "I encouraged Gene to go after your job."

For a moment, Copley's stone face seemed to have truly become stone. "What?" he barked.

"Surely you knew. I made a mistake. I decided that because Gene was responsible for creating all your products he should be aiming to run the company. Look, you asked me to be blunt. If you'd rather—"

"No!" Copley's tone was too loud. "I'm sorry," he mumbled, a hand touching his face again, fingers caressing his sunken cheeks. The hand came away. "Go on."

"Everybody at your company knows Gene was its creative heart. For God's sake, even your goddamn telephone was designed by Gene."

"Who told you that?" Copley asked.

"Nobody had to. He was its emotional leader. Who put up the basketball net for Andy? I bet that was Gene, too." Copley nodded, slowly. I continued, "Every machine your men design today is first tested theoretically on what?"

"Black Dragon."

"You told me Dragon was Andy's design. That was an exaggeration, wasn't it? Gene built it."

"He couldn't have done it without Andy."

"And who hired Andy?"

"I did."

"On whose recommendation?"

"Anyone would have hired Andy. I told you, we didn't expect him to accept our offer."

"Why do you think he accepted? Because of you? Who interviewed him? Who showed him the labs? Who talked to him about what he'd be doing? Gene."

Copley nodded. "I knew it," he said to himself. He grinned at me and repeated, "I knew it."

"Knew what?" I didn't conceal my irritation. My obsequious manner had vanished.

"I knew he was after my job."

"Not your job. I misspoke. He wanted a partnership. I told him he deserved it."

"That's why he had an affair with Halley."

"No," I said. "He loved her."

"Of course he loved her. But he thought I would let him have a piece of the company if he was her husband."

"No. That's your vanity talking. Maybe part of his attraction to her was because she was your daughter. But that wasn't opportunism. That was true respect for you. Gene loved you as much as he loved her." I came close, pushing my face at his. In the body language of popular psychology: I invaded his personal space. "They all know. You deliberately destroyed Gene and they know it. That's going to cost you."

Copley stepped back. Not a movement of surrender. He stiffened. "You want revenge."

"Revenge?" I laughed. "For what?"

"You're crazy if you think—"

I cut him off. "Revenge for my mistake? I don't blame you."

"I'm not a stupid man, Doctor. You said that I destroyed Gene."

"I can't blame you for your essential nature. That's a basic principle of psychiatry. No. *I* misjudged the situation. I thought you were merely a salesman living off Gene's talent. I didn't understand you are a leader. Gene was happy as your second lieutenant. He needed your guidance, just as Andy needed Gene's supervision. It's your character to be a leader, that's your genius. Of course, when he mutinied, you crushed him. You had no choice."

Stick turned away, squinting at the damp streets. He talked to them, thinking aloud, "And you expect me to believe that's what you'll report to Edgar?" He looked at me fast, as if to catch me at something. "That it was your fault?"

Edgar. I had forgotten Edgar was my leverage. That's why Copley was anxious. For a moment, I had hoped it was guilt, but no, he reacted entirely out of self-preservation. "I came for my own purpose. I'm just what you think I am. A harmless academic. You said it yourself, I don't want to win. Good night." I turned and walked briskly.

Copley reached my side effortlessly, with the silent tread of a predator. Of course, he was also wearing sandals. "Let's rewind the tape. I apologize. I didn't mean to offend you."

"You always think in terms of power and manipulation," I said, continuing to walk. "Both are foreign to my character. I came only for knowledge."

"I'd like your help." Copley put his hand on my arm and stopped me. "You said yourself that the corporate family would be a good subject for a book. I could use your observations while you're doing research. Obviously, I overreacted to Gene. I know Andy's in over his head. I like to win—you're right. But there are lots of ways to win."

A wave of people came out of a building, exiting from a party. They were loud and cheerful. One of the men stumbled into Copley. He was a beefy college kid. Nevertheless, Copley easily pushed him off.

The kid lurched our way again, coming between us. "Sorry," he shouted, exhaling beer.

"No problem," Copley said. One of his friends led him off. "How about it?" Stick asked with a smile. The interruption had given him time to put on a cheerful face.

"I don't understand."

"I want you to work for me," he said. "As a consultant. It'll be good research for your book and hopefully you'll improve morale and teach me to be a better boss."

"Work . . . for . . . you?" I spoke slowly, as if I were learning a foreign language.

"As a consultant. Any schedule you like. No obligation other than you tell me what you think. Just as straight and tough as tonight."

Of course I didn't comply right away. I waited through the weekend, calling from Baltimore on Monday to say yes. A quicker agreement, I feared, might have implied I had expected Stick's offer all along.

CHAPTER SIX

Transference

THROUGHOUT THE SUMMER I ESTABLISHED MYSELF AS A MEMBER OF THE Minotaur family. An odd figure to be sure, the maiden aunt, or perhaps the mildly retarded cousin, but certainly I acquired the invisibility of a familiar face, the benign appearance of the predictable. I visited the labs three days a week. Not that I was idle on the subject the rest of the time. I researched Copley and his company thoroughly.

Stick had reason to fear what I might say to Edgar, at least if he believed I could influence Edgar's opinion of his management. The leveraged buyout that elevated Copley from a mere employee to majority owner was accomplished with loans guaranteed by Levin & Levin, in exchange for options that, in essence, left Edgar in a position to take control of Minotaur at his whim. Some of the above was public information, some not. Molly Gray, a partner in Brian Stoppard's firm, on retainer to Edgar for such deals, confided to me that there was a private side agreement, a shadow clause she called it, whose provisions allowed Edgar to hold Stick's personal holdings in Minotaur hostage should profits falter. Molly explained that the secret agreement was legal, although its exercise, under certain conditions, might not be.

She didn't reveal the private deal right away. A week after briefing me on the public information, she invited me to dinner at her apartment to meet her husband, Stefan Weinstein. He is an eminent psychiatrist, on the board of New York Psychoanalytic and a trustee of Freud's archives. He had read some of my books and knew of my work with children. He was flattering about both. That must have influenced Molly to violate her client's confidentiality, although I think her difficult personal history was the deciding factor. Molly and Stefan adopted a girl whose mother, a close friend, had been murdered by the child's father. Molly appeared to be deeply affected when I told her Gene's story and the fate of his son, Pete.

"There wasn't a pattern of battering?" Stefan asked.

"No," I said. "His abusive behavior took the form of sexual and emotional withdrawal. It turned outward because of other factors. For Gene, in general, anger was always severely repressed, until . . ."

Stefan finished for me, "Until it wasn't."

"Until, abruptly, it wasn't," I agreed. "I'm afraid I've come to the conclusion that I wasn't sufficiently vigilant."

Stefan raised a brow. "Well," he mumbled. "You said he hadn't been seeing you regularly—"

"You feel responsible," Molly interrupted.

"Yes. I saw the potential for its evolution, but I didn't allow for it. Even in his irrational rage, Gene was repressed. He hit the wrong person."

"What?" Stefan chuckled. "What do you mean? He was myopic?" Throughout all this, Molly observed me closely, eyes glistening.

"Well, Cathy, his wife, was certainly an obstacle, but she wasn't . . ." I trailed off. There was a limit to what I wanted to reveal. "It's complicated."

"The person he wanted to kill is at Minotaur," Molly said. "That's why you're hanging out there."

"No," I lied. "I'm trying to understand my mistake. I'm afraid there are similar patterns in place for the people who work there now."

Stefan frowned. "What are you saying? You think this is some sort of psychological industrial hazard? Make computers and kill your wife?"

"Something like that." I smiled. "No, I mean I believe I can reconstruct my error with Gene through a better understanding of his life. The best I can do is observe the people he dealt with."

"I see," Stefan said, in a tone that implied he didn't. Molly, however, understood. Or, she saw through me and approved anyway. Whatever the reason, she wanted to help. When Stefan left the room to take a phone call, she revealed the shadow clause.

For two weeks I commuted between Baltimore and New York, sleeping on Susan's foldout couch. Stefan made things more comfortable for me after that, finding an apartment I could sublet on Central Park West between Seventy-fourth and Seventy-fifth Streets. The owner was a psychologist taking the traditional August shrink's vacation; luckily, in her calendar, August began in June and ended with Labor Day. We made a barter arrangement. The fee was caring for her calico cat, named Sally Rogers, in honor of the character on *The Dick Van Dyke Show*.

I made sure to be in New York for the two social events Edgar invited me to. I attended a Mets game in his private box, correctly assuming Stick would be there; and I was his guest at a UJA benefit dinner at the Waldorf. Copley, it turned out, hadn't been invited. But he heard I was, and that suited my purposes even better. It convinced Copley I enjoyed a degree of intimacy with Edgar that was barred to him. In fact, when alone with me, Edgar's attitude about my consulting job with Minotaur was sarcastic. "Do you always figure out a way to get paid for your research?" he teased. Whatever Copley might fear, Edgar obviously didn't think I had insights into the business that he needed to hear.

A month into my job as a consultant, Stick invited me to a barbecue on July 4th. That provided my introduction to his wife of twenty-seven years, Mary Catharine, an Italian-American born and raised in Boston. Halley's small stature, olive skin and dark hair came from her; otherwise they didn't appear related. Mary Catharine's light brown eyes were watery. Her neck was compressed into a shapeless torso, chin either weak or disappeared by the thickening of her face. Her people were working-class. She met Copley when he was at Harvard Business School. She waited tables at the pizzeria, around the corner from his bachelor apartment. I suspected (and later confirmed by the date of Halley's birth, seven months following their wedding) that the marriage was precipitated by a pregnancy.

Mary Catharine was an alcoholic. When I deliberately arrived forty-five minutes early, I smelled it on her breath. She excused herself to change for the barbecue. She reappeared in a half hour, wearing a bright yellow pants suit. A minty odor had replaced the boozy one. Twice during the party, I noticed her fiddle with something in a pocket and slip what I eventually discovered was a Tic-Tac into her mouth. Her drinking was camouflaged in other ways. She offered to refresh a different guest's drink every ten minutes or so, often when their glasses were merely half-empty. Each time, when she returned with her guest's refill, she had made a new drink for herself. During the two hours before burgers and hot dogs were served, I counted eight gin and tonics. To the casual eye, it would have seemed no more than two or three; and her behavior, although increasingly gay and friendly, was another confirmation of alcoholism—she didn't appear drunk.

Stick knew, of course. She annoyed him at one point, interrupting a pompous monologue he was delivering into the cleavage of the pretty wife of his vice-president in charge of domestic sales, Jack Truman. "Stick, honey," she said, blocking off his view of the Great Divide. "You don't have to convince Amy you're a great man. I bet when Jack comes home he neglects her to sing your praises."

"Thanks for the hint, dear," he answered. "You know what I need? Another drink. Why don't you get one for me?" he said, handing her his glass. "If you've left any gin for the rest of us," he added with a pleasant smile.

"Baby, I've only been sucking the limes," she answered, jiggling the yellow expanse of her behind luridly. "Practice makes perfect, right?" She laughed harshly in her husband's face, although her puzzling remark seemed to wound only herself. I was not surprised that Stick hadn't divorced this overweight, unhappy, and socially inferior woman for what magazines call a trophy wife. Nor was I surprised by his guests, my introduction to the second-rate men who worked on the business side of Minotaur. They were sycophants, frightened of Stick, intimidated by Halley, and annoyed by their dependence on the engineers working in the labs—a frustrated envy that was expressed as contempt.

While I stood with Jack Truman at the edge of Stick's flagstone patio, chewing our corn on the cob, he asked me about the nature of my consulting job this way: "So you're checking out Geek Heaven. I'd love to read your report. Always wanted to know if those guys have personal lives."

"Geek Heaven?" I asked with a smile.

"Sorry. They're brilliant. God bless 'em. What would we do without 'em?" Jack lowered his voice. "But they're weird, right?"

"That's why Stick's got me down there," I winked. "He wants to make sure they aren't chopping up prostitutes and stuffing them into suitcases."

Jack threw his head back and cackled. He finished with a sigh, commenting, "That's funny." He poked me with his elbow and turned away from the patio toward the pool. I shifted my position as well. He whispered, "Do you know about Gene Kenny? Used to be head of R&D? He seemed like the most normal nerd in Geek Heaven. But he cracked up. You know what he did?"

I recovered quickly from the surprise that neither Stick nor Halley, or any of the engineers, bothered to gossip with the marketers enough for him to know I was Gene's doctor. That evidently he didn't know Halley had an affair with Gene wasn't a surprise; I had discovered only Andy Chen was clever enough to suspect. I shook my head no.

Now I had surprised Jack. "Really? I figured that's why Stick brought in a head shrinker." He inclined his head toward the lawn, a signal to move with him. We stepped off the flagstones onto the grass, as if somehow this placed our conversation in a more discreet zone. Not that Jack relied entirely on the lawn's sound-dampening. He spoke through clenched teeth. "Kenny raped and killed his ex-wife. Then he smothered his baby boy and hung himself." Jack shuddered. "About two months ago." He studied me. "Nobody said anything to you?"

"Stick told me Kenny committed suicide, but not Andy or the other nerds, as you call them."

"They're okay. I didn't mean anything. You know, they say," he dropped his already low voice to a whisper, "that's why Centaur's so late. Gene destroyed the prototype when he flipped. We had to start from scratch."

"What are you boys whispering about?" Halley called, approaching us with a platter of watermelon and cantaloupe.

"You, of course," I said. "We were wondering why someone so glamorous and intelligent wants to work in a nerdy business like computers."

"Nerdy business?" Jack repeated with a nervous laugh.

"It's simple," Halley said, picking up a piece of cantaloupe with her free hand. "Don't tell my mother I used my fingers." She popped the square into her mouth and chewed. Jack and I watched solemnly while she consumed it. "Excuse me," she mumbled with a full mouth. She swallowed. "Dad's the only person who'd hire me. It's shameless nepotism." She offered the platter to me. "The cantaloupe's good."

Jack cleared his throat. "Now, that's not true, Hal. Don't give the doctor a wrong impression." He edged in front of me and used his fork to slide several pieces of watermelon onto his plate. "She had a terrific job at Time-Warner," he told me. He said to Halley, "And I happen to know it was for double what we pay you." Back to me. "She's brought us tons of contacts. We switched agencies 'cause of Hal. Wales & Simpson has been great." He commented to her, "I think the campaign for Centaur looks fantastic. You're doing great, Hal."

"I guess that's why," she said to me. "I work here for all the good feedback. But you're neglecting me, Doctor. Dad brings you on board to study us and I haven't seen you at all. Aren't I worth studying?"

"Please, I beg you, call me Rafe."

"Well, okay, if you're going to beg me. I haven't seen you at all, Rafe."

"That's right," Jack moved next to her, bumping her slightly. "We feel neglected," he said.

"You should be glad," I answered. "If I show my face in your office, you're in trouble." For a moment, they took this hard, mouths open, stupefied. "I'm kidding." I laughed. Jack tried a smile. Only a corner of his lips cooperated. Halley, however, really did smile appreciatively. "Seriously," I said. "Stick's just being nice to me. I'm doing research on the psychodynamics of . . ." I slapped Jack on the shoulder, rather hard. "Nerds. I'm a child psychologist and those are basically kids down there in Geek Heaven. It's really got nothing to do with the business. Your father's being most cooperative."

"I love my father," Halley said. "But he's no Mother Teresa. If he put you down there, he expects to get something out of it."

"Hal's right." Jack was earnest and also bothered by how to dispose of his watermelon pits. He modestly turned his head to spit them into his right hand, but was reluctant to drop them on his plate. He clutched them in his fist. "Stick told me you're doing wonders for their morale. He said you've calmed things down a lot. Efficiency's way up."

That was a complete fiction. I had been there for a month. There was no progress on Centaur; the main board continued to slow down when communicating with peripherals. It's true I had become chummy with the machine makers. I had gathered the basic material of their lives, established trust, and begun some reforms of their work environment. So far, there was no effect. They continued to shriek and pout at each other. Andy's exercise of his authority was halfhearted; he tended to deal with everything on his own and that wasted resources. At least half of the team was busy with concepts that Andy had privately decided to abandon. "Well," I said, "efficiency is up and Centaur's doing great, but I don't think I had much to do with it." I indicated my plate's gnawed cob, an untouched hill of potato salad, and a smear of ketchup—the last, all that remained of a hamburger. "Excuse me, I'm going for seconds."

In fact, I left my plate near the barbecue and walked into the glassed-in porch, aiming for Mary Catharine, who was at the bar, refreshing someone's drink and making another for herself. "This is a lovely house," I said to her back as she rattled ice cubes.

"Thank you," she said. "Do you need another drink?"

"No, I'm fine. Are there four bedrooms?" I asked.

"Three and a study. Want a tour?"

"Love it," I said softly and gently touched her arm.

She peered at me through woozy eyes, confused for a moment. I smiled at her comfortingly. She shook her head as if to clear it, stepped back and attempted a perky smile that came out slightly crooked. "Let's do it." She left the drink she was making for a guest on the bar, took her own, and walked us into a formal dining room.

"When did you move here?" I asked.

Mary Catharine explained what I already knew, about Stick's move from Flashworks in Massachusetts to Minotaur in Westchester. The furniture looked coordinated, as if bought in a single spree, probably by a decorator. She confirmed my assumption while we climbed to the second floor. "I threw out everything five years ago and started fresh," she said.

That would have been around the time of the death of their second born, Michael. The rooms were tasteful but impersonal, color drained from the objects, beige or black furniture, white drapes, a few books, and abstract paintings that appeared to have been selected to fit the wall space and not intrude on the eye. There were no personal things until we reached the master bedroom. On the right side of the bed, near the wall, was a long built-in dresser for her clothes, its surface covered by photos in silver frames. A similar dresser on the other side of the room for Stick was free of objects. "My family," she explained, when I bent over to inspect the people in the pictures. I asked after each of them. She interrupted twice to say, "This has gotta be boring," but was easily encouraged to continue.

"They remind me of my father's family," I said about the faded pictures of her grandparents and their siblings when they were young: dressed up in their Sunday best, the ladies in big hats, men standing stiff, eyes wary, mouths shut tight. Mary Catharine told me their stories, especially proud of one great-aunt, the family black sheep. Great-Aunt Gina had walked out on her husband and three sons to live out west with a strange woman. Their ultimate fate was unknown. "Mama never admitted she was a lesbian. She'd say they were radicals. She said this woman turned Aunt Gina into an anarchist, a bomb-throwing anarchist. I asked her what this other woman did. You know, like how they met and stuff. Who were they throwing bombs at? I expected to hear something about Sacco and Vanzetti. Mama said, 'She was the local librarian.'" Mary Catharine flopped onto the king-size bed and laughed. Her eyes watered. She took a gulp of her drink. The glass was nearly empty. "You know those wild librarians. Always throwing bombs and corrupting the local mothers. Finally, one day, when I was all grown up, she was visiting me . . . I think." She took another gulp. "Yeah, that's right. Mama was a guest in my own house. I said to her, 'Mama, Aunt Gina was a dyke.' You know what? She slapped me. I couldn't believe it. I was a mother myself. She slapped me like I was a kid. I expected—" she belched loudly. She didn't excuse herself; indeed, she didn't seem aware of her eruption. She sipped the last of her drink and continued. "I was waiting for her to bring out a bar of soap."

"Your mother used to wash your mouth out with soap?"

"Oh, yeah. All the Italian mothers did. Especially if you cursed Jesus. You'd get half a bar of soap for that. Enough to do the laundry for a week. I was a bad girl. I was a lot of trouble." She tried her drink again; only ice was left.

"Who's this?" I lifted a small framed photograph of a ten-year-old boy in a blue blazer, a white shirt, and a red tie. There were others, with an older Michael, that I could have chosen, but they weren't solo portraits.

Mary Catharine smiled at the picture and gestured for it with her free hand. I brought it over, sitting next to her on the bed. She looked wistful. "My son, Michael. When he was little."

"Is he married?" I asked.

She shook her head. "He's dead," she said without a quaver.

"I'm sorry. When did that happen?"

"Stupid," she said quietly to herself.

"Excuse me?"

"Nineteen eighty-six. In Aspen. He died skiing . . ." She tried once again to drink from her glass. She frowned at its emptiness: there was nothing left to wash out her mouth. "Avalanche," she said.

"I'm sorry. I didn't—"

"Stick never brings it up. I tell him. It's embarrassing for people to just, you know . . ." She waved at the photo.

"Put their foot in their mouths?"

"Well, that's the thing. It's not their fault, they don't know.

Everybody asks those kind of, you know, chitchat questions—'How many children do you have?' " She laughed bitterly. "What do you say? I had two. Now I'm down to one. Half of one. Halley used to be my best girl, but you know what happens once they have hormones." She belched again. This time she noticed. "Jesus. I'm sorry. It's those burgers, they give me gas. I tell Stick, you know, bring these things up ahead of time, so people don't feel they hurt your feelings. But you know what? I hate that too. Everybody walking on egg shells. Nothing works." She nodded at the window. "All those men and their . . . what do you call them? Wives!" She laughed. "That's right, wives. They . . . I don't know. They never talk about anything. You know? Hours and hours and hours, chitchat, this and that, but later you think, what did anybody say? I swear to God, I don't know the first thing about these people. In my old neighborhood, you knew everything. Or a lot anyway. We didn't know about lesbians though," she said and laughed. She stood up with a groan.

I rose, moving ahead of her to be in front of the dresser. Michael's school picture hovered between us. Very quietly, but insistently, I asked, "Why was it stupid?"

"What?" She looked up at me, eyes unfocused.

I nodded at the boy in the blazer. "You said it was stupid. You mean, how he died?"

She nodded and swallowed hard. "He'd been warned. He knew it was dangerous. You weren't supposed to ski that trail, that slope . . . I don't know what you call it. I don't ski. I never did. It's Stick's thing." She returned the photo to the dresser. She ran a finger across the top of the frame and backed off, squinting at the window. "He knew he wasn't supposed to."

I waited for her to add more. She continued to squint out the window. There was another belch. She suppressed this one; only her shoulders heaved, the sound muffled. "We'd better go back to the party," she said.

As we moved to the door, I commented, "It was something Stick had done? Skiing in an avalanche zone?"

She nodded, hardly interested in my inquiry and not at all concerned about the intimacy. "Stupid," she commented and then asked brightly, "You want another drink?"

"Sure," I said.

"Smart cookie," she commented.

"Did Michael always try to keep up with his father?" I asked as we descended the stairs.

"Of course. They both do. But Halley's a girl, so it's different. It was hard on Stick. He was really close to Mikey. Mikey was his little twin." We reached the bottom of the stairs and silently walked through the living room, the dining room and onto the glassed-in porch. When she arrived at the bar, she turned to me with a triumphant smile, "Good shrink stuff, huh?"

"Good shrink stuff?" I repeated quizzically.

She laughed at me. "Gin and tonic?" she asked.

"Sure," I said.

"You see, I'm a good host. I give my guests everything they want," she commented, turning her back on me and reaching into the ice bucket.

"No, you didn't," I said.

She paused, a hand full of cubes. For a moment, I wasn't sure she was going to acknowledge my comment. She dropped the ice, leaned on the bar, and twisted to look at me. "What did you say?"

"You didn't tell me what I want to know."

"What do you want to know?" she said. For the first time the words were slurred.

"Just how hard did he push?"

"Who?" Her eyes closed halfway.

"Stick. How hard did he push? How hard did Michael have to work for Stick to respect him?"

She shut her eyes and seemed to taste something, her lips moving. She took in a lot of air, opened her eyes wide and sighed. "Stick went down it the day before."

"He skied the dangerous slope the day before?"

"Yep. You want to let me make you this drink?"

"I don't want the drink."

"I do." She faced the bar and reached for the gin. "Yeah, he tried to get Mikey to go with him. Mikey said he didn't want to. So Stick went on his own. Afterwards, he bugged Mikey, telling him he was too cautious. All night Stick bragged about the virgin snow. The fucking virgin snow. 'Should've been out there,' he kept saying."

"You were there?"

"Sure. Halley was there, too. It was a family trip." Her drink was fixed. She sipped it and turned to me.

"And Halley teased him also, of course," I commented. "Big sister and all."

Mary Catharine waved her hand dismissively, swallowing hard. "She didn't mean anything. Mikey didn't care what she said. Yep," she sipped again. "All night we all sat around the condo listening to Stick talk about pushing the limit or testing the envelope . . . I can't remember the goddamn cliché."

"So he went to prove himself to his father?"

"It's not Stick's fault. Mikey knew better. He wasn't a baby. I told him, 'Don't let your father get your goat.' I was drinking hot toddies. That's a wicked drink. Gives you a bitch of a hangover. In the morning Mikey was gone." She pointed toward the patio doors. "I'm going back to the chitchat. You coming?"

"Sure," I said, walking with her.

"So what do you think?" she asked as the sun shone directly on our faces and the charcoal smoke filled our nostrils. Stick was about three feet to our right, bent over the grill to turn a second round of burgers. "You're an expert," she raised her voice a little. "You think maybe I'm a lesbian like my Aunt Gina?" Stick straightened, stepped back from the barbecue, and stared at us. The spatula was poised in midair, a greasy sword. "Just kidding, honey," she said and laughed. She called to one of the guests, "Jeff, I forgot your drink! Wait there. Don't move." She returned to the glassed-in porch.

A couple of Copley's regional sales managers were beside him at the barbecue grill. Stick moved away from them, stepping over to me, still armed with a spatula, and said quietly, "She's uncomfortable at parties and drinks too much."

"She drinks too much all the time," I said with no energy to the contradiction, as if I were talking about someone he didn't know.

His stone face didn't react. He said, "I've tried to get her into treatment."

"Probably better if it comes from someone else. She's rebelling against you and there are early symptoms of paranoia about you as well." I leaned closer to his ear. "By the way, I pretended to be ignorant about Gene with Jack Truman. There are wild rumors circulating. Are they deliberate? Did you float the one about Gene destroying a Centaur prototype?"

Stick gave me one of his hard looks, a scrutiny I had become used to during the six meetings we'd had so far about Andy and his team. No matter how many times I showed no disapproval or judgment of his management, he continued to check my reaction, as if he couldn't believe his good luck. I returned the stare of his dark eyes calmly and added, "It was a clever stroke." I nodded at the pair of sales directors; they were pretending not to strain to hear our conversation. "Provides a comforting explanation. I didn't contradict it."

Stick nodded, eyes still brilliant and unblinking. He asked, "We have a Wednesday meeting, right?" I nodded. "I'd better turn the burgers," he said, returning to the grill.

I stayed for another hour and a half, long enough to be confident that Mary Catharine's drinking meant she would remember little of our conversation and to reassure Stick that nothing I had seen or heard altered my loyalty. I evaded Halley, always flirtatious and friendly when I couldn't avoid contact, but quick to move on pointedly, paying court to the other women. She talked to the men while I gossiped with their wives. I noticed she kept her eye on me, obviously puzzled that I found these suburban women and their ratings of schools, nannies and malls, as well as their worries about aging parents, overworked husbands and fading beauty to be more fascinating than the male talk: golf, off-color jokes, how to make better use of focus groups, and which frequent flyer program is superior. What I hoped she would conclude is that I found the other women more interesting than she, in particular her mother.

When I announced my departure at four-thirty, explaining I wanted to leave early because I was worried about traffic heading into Manhattan to see the fireworks display, it was obvious I had succeeded. Halley said, "Could I get a ride with you?"

"You're not staying?" her mother asked. "I thought you were sleeping over, honey."

"I forgot, Mom. I've got to write an evaluation of Wales & Simpson's print campaign." She looked at me. "I came on the train. Do you mind? I'd like to avoid Grand Central on July 4th. It's probably a nightmare."

I frowned, but said, "Not at all."

"Bet he doesn't mind," Jack Truman said and cackled. His wife made a face. I had listened sympathetically to her concern about her eight-year-old son's reading problems. I urged her not to take the advice of the pediatrician who was pushing Ritalin to treat her boy. He had diagnosed the sort of biochemical attention deficit disorder that afflicted her son only when it came to homework, not when he read hint books on how to improve his score at video games. Before departing, in view of Halley and Jack, I kissed Amy Truman on the lips. Then I hugged Mary Catharine close, whispering, "Thank you for the tour of the house." She goggled at me. The gin had already erased our talk. All that remained for her was an impression of my friendliness.

"Everybody likes you so much," Halley said, once we were swaying back and forth on the Saw Mill's curves, heading for Manhattan.

"Don't sound so surprised."

"Oh, I don't blame them. I mean, you made a great impression. It was sweet of you to talk to my mother and the other ladies." Halley said "the other ladies" with a trace of sarcasm.

"Tell me something. How come there was no help?"

"Help?"

"Well, your father did the barbecuing and your mother tended bar."

"It's what they're both good at." Halley laughed to herself. "Dad likes to fry meat and Mom likes to drink."

I said nothing.

She laughed again, this time self-consciously. "That was mean," she said. "No, it's a tradition. When Daddy started with Flashworks and we didn't have much money to entertain, he'd throw a July 4th party. He could keep it informal. You know, not spend too much money and still have the businesspeople over. A cheap way to network."

"But today was a small select group, right? Nowhere near all the business executives of the company."

"Right," Halley agreed. "Now he only invites his favorites. Getting an invitation is virtually like getting a promotion. That's why the ladies were all gussied up."

Halley was dressed for an informal afternoon: white shorts, pale pink polo shirt, and black penny loafers. Of course, she wore makeup and time had been spent to give her long shimmering black hair its elegant shape. Her bare arms and legs were tan. Her narrow feet were pale. Once in my car, she slipped them out of her shoes and raised them to the edge of the seat, hugging her knees.

"They're so retro," she said, meaning the wives. "I feel sorry for them."

"Why?"

"Why? You know. Stuck out there in suburbs, raising kids."

"They seem quite happy to me."

"They do? Probably you're right. Actually, the truth is, I don't feel sorry for them. I mean, they took the easy way out. It's not like it was for my mother—she didn't have much choice. If they were guys, you'd call them wimps."

"A couple of them work." I named two women who had jobs.

"Oh, yeah?" Halley said. "Good for them. I didn't know."

"Actually, I thought the women were first-rate. It's the old story. You get a group of men and women together and my sex always runs a distant second. I guess your father's saved all the talent for the technical side."

"Oh, I don't agree. They're first-rate guys. Jack Truman's a great salesman. He came up with the direct mail idea that made us a major player in PCs. We're really starting to hurt IBM now. Going direct's allowed us to undersell them by thirty percent. It's gonna help us on Centaur too. I think we can price Centaur at fifty percent of Toshiba's laptops."

"I didn't know," I said sheepishly. "I assumed the direct sales idea came from your father."

"Well, he approved it. But it was Jack Truman's idea. Dad was going crazy trying to raise capital to go the Radio Shack route, or fighting IBM in the retail stores, which is their turf. I mean, how could Jack hope to compete with a tenth of Big Blue's sales force and one one thousandth of their budget? He saw that a lot of computer buyers were reading magazines to get tips on how the hell the machines work and he figured, hey, these people are sophisticated, they know we're all using the same chips, we run the same software. So we started selling peripherals through the mags and it wasn't that big a leap to selling whole machines. We're really gonna test it with Centaur. No retail at all, except maybe for a discounter."

"Are people going to feel comfortable spending a few thousand dollars on something they've never held in their own hands?"

"Well, that's the challenge with this campaign. I think the way to go is not to reassure them."

"*Not* to reassure them?"

"Right. Make it seem snobby. You know, hip. We'll sell them self-esteem. Like, 'I'm not an unsophisticated jerk who needs to spend twice as much for some salesman in an overpriced retail store to hold my hand.' I mean, realistically, at first we have to aim at second- or third-generation buyers, people who already feel savvy. Then let them promote the machine for us. I mean, if the one guy in your office who knows portables and laptops has a Centaur, then you'll feel safe buying one. Eventually, you're gonna feel stupid *not* calling our 800 number and ordering."

"Very clever. Psychologically very subtle."

"Marketing is *all* psychology." She leaned toward me and teased,

"That's why Daddy should have you working with us, not in Geek Heaven."

"I'll suggest it," I said, glancing at her. She winked at me. "So this sales approach with Centaur was Jack Truman's?"

"No," Halley said. She touched my arm, smiled when I glanced at her, and then pointed to herself. "It was mine. I mean, direct order in general was his. But going all direct with Centaur and going cutting edge with ads is mine."

"Funny," I said somberly.

"Funny?" she asked.

I didn't seem to have heard. I nodded at the road and furrowed my brows.

She released her feet from under her and stretched, sliding them back into the penny loafers. She twisted in my direction. "You said something was funny."

"Oh. Nothing."

She made one of her noises of multiple feeling, at once annoyed and amused. "It is *not* nothing. What's funny?"

"Just that—you know, sometimes it seems like there's no need for your father."

"No need for my father," she repeated incredulously. "What, for God's sakes, do you mean?"

"Well, the guys in the labs build the machines and you and Jack figure out how to sell them. Your father's obviously a brilliant man and he picked you all, but who needs him now?" I paused. Hearing nothing from her, I mused, "Unless that's the answer—that he's a coach of a collection of star players."

She didn't say anything. I slowed for the final toll to enter Manhattan. After I paid and got back to full speed, as we scooted underneath the George Washington Bridge, Halley said, "Are you going to watch the fireworks?"

"I haven't decided. Are they on the East Side or the West Side this year?"

"East Side."

"I don't know," I said. "How about you? Oh, that's right. You have work to do."

"I'll be done by nine. The fireworks are at nine-thirty."

"Okay, I'll pick you up at nine," I said. She nodded. We were silent until I stopped at her apartment on Seventy-sixth, only a block from my sublet. She opened the door, one penny loafer going out, the other still inside.

"See you at nine," I said.

She twisted back. "He's not just a coach," she said. "Without Daddy, nobody'd know the difference between a great idea and a lousy one. He's the star." She smiled cheerfully. "See you at nine."

CHAPTER SEVEN

Anima

HALLEY KNEW WHERE WE SHOULD GO FOR THE BEST VIEW OF THE FIRE-works. They closed the East River Drive from Eighteenth to Fifty-ninth Streets to allow pedestrians on it; she said the farther down we went, the better our angle. We took a cab to the Twenty-third Street entrance and walked onto the highway with streams of people: families, gangs of teenagers, gay and straight couples. We passed hawkers of flags, noise-makers, and sparklers. I stopped to buy a box of sparklers.

"You're kidding," Halley said, but she complied when I put one in her hand and lit it. At first she was too self-conscious to hold the sparkler high and wave. She had changed into a pale blue cotton dress, very short, showing off the full length of her slim tanned legs. The sparks flowed over her neck and chest. She winced and turned her head to the side. Putting a hand on her elbow, I lifted and moved her arm. "Be patriotic," I said.

Halley took over. I watched, following the white of her underarm up to the brown of her forearms, her pretty face flickering in the light. She was my very own animated Statue of Liberty.

A little boy, with kinky hair and dark skin, planted himself in front of her and said, *"Abuela! Mira,"* to a fat old woman holding his hand.

I said to her, *"Le doy uno? No son peligrosos."*

I lit a sparkler for the boy. He zigzagged back and forth across the highway's white lines, startling people with his bloom of sparks. His grandmother shouted at him, smiled at me, and waddled off in pursuit.

Halley's sparkler sputtered out. "You speak Spanish?" she asked. It flared again briefly, a last gasp. She was left with a withered burnt stub.

I nodded, removed the dead sparkler, and gave her another. I didn't light it. "Let's get to the water."

That was hard. People had gathered hours in advance. Halley was aggressive, however, and, in her short clingy dress, she also caused some men to make way without their intending to, especially when they realized she had me in tow. She pushed us all the way to the edge of the water.

I lit her sparkler. This time she raised it high on her own. I covered her forearm with my hand and stroked toward her shoulder. The skin was soft, the muscles firm. She watched my hand gravely. I let go. "Throw it," I said, nodding at the water. She obeyed. The sparkler's flight was cheered by our immediate neighbors. It arched up, a tiny firework, and nosedived into the water.

"We made our own fireworks," I said.

Her arm was still raised. She draped it around my neck and got up on tiptoe. She aimed her mouth at mine. She kissed me quickly, a light touch of her moist lips, and hung there as if contemplating the taste, checking her appetite for more. Her black eyes peered into mine, half her face disappeared by the shadow of the crowd. There was a cheer and muffled boom. "It's starting," she whispered. I bent my head and pressed, pushing her full lips apart with mine. She opened wide for me, while all around us the sky blossomed with colors.

The display was going strong when we unlocked. A woman to my left smiled when I met her eyes. As I turned toward the water, a man on my right winked at me. Halley put her arm around my waist and we watched. I was glad we didn't have to walk just then, pleasantly surprised to find my body reacting to a mere kiss with the enthusiasm of an adolescent.

We stood still until the show was over and left silently with the satisfied crowd. When we reached First Avenue I hailed a cab. As it stopped for us, I said, "Your apartment?"

She nodded. Inside, she twisted away from me to face the window while leaning her head against the crook of my shoulder. Her right arm rested on my thigh. I was wearing beige Bermuda shorts. Her fingers lightly stroked my skin above the knee, playing with the hairs. Against her elbow, she could feel my excitement at her touch.

Going crosstown in the seventies we stopped at a red light. She sat up, turned, held my face with both her hands, and kissed me again, parting her lips slightly. Then she resumed her place, fingers petting me. And it was just like being petted—the languid touch of an owner.

We were crossing Central Park when I said softly, "How long have you been having an affair with Jack?"

Her fingers closed on my thigh, not tight, more like holding on. We were out of the park before she answered with a question. "Do you care?"

"I'm not jealous, if that's what you mean."

She sat up and opened her purse. We were half a block from her building. "Sure you are," she said with good humor.

"I'll get this," I said.

"No," she took out money, told the driver which was her awning, and said to me, "I told you. I don't fall in love. So there's nothing to be jealous about."

I got out first, holding the door while she paid the cabby. At the corner I saw a trio of teenagers scatter. A moment later a trash can blew up. Or at least, it rattled and fell over, a cloud of smoke floating across the pavement.

"What was that?" Halley said, popping out of the taxi.

"A cherry bomb. I hope."

"Let's get inside," she said, taking my arm and pretending to run as we entered the building. We discussed the rowdy gangs of kids with the doorman on our way to the elevator. He was saying something about them losing fingers and hands if they weren't careful when the doors closed.

"Were you guessing about Jack?" Halley asked with a playful smile. "Or did you really know?"

"You were comfortable with him." I watched our ascent on the bank of lights. Eleven. Twelve. Fourteen—it was a superstitious building. "You're not really comfortable with a man unless you're having sex with him." At fifteen a faint bell rang and we stopped. The door opened. I put my back against it and made way for her.

Halley stared for a moment. She shook her head, then walked out. As she passed me, she commented, "And you say you're not jealous."

"How long?" I asked, following her to the end of the hallway, the corner apartment.

"We're not having an affair. There was a . . ." she searched in her purse for a key while also searching for the right word, ". . . an encounter a few months ago. That's all." She found the key and put it in. She asked, "Seriously. How did you know?" She unlocked the door, swung it open, stepped in, then turned back with a sudden worry, "He didn't tell you?"

"No." I entered after her, shivering at the refrigerator cold of her air-conditioning. The apartment was a one-bedroom with a sweeping view of Central Park, thanks to the low height of the adjoining building. Two walls of windows, forming the L-shaped living and dining rooms, were unadorned. A round butcher block table stood in the L next to the utility kitchen. A pair of cream-colored couches filled the living area. There was a machine-made Oriental, mostly red, and an old steamer trunk served as a coffee table. Walking around, my sweaty polo shirt chilling me, I was surprised to discover the living room's rear wall covered by bookcases. There were a few serious works of nonfiction, survivors from college days. Two whole shelves were devoted to plays, from her flirtation with acting. A new group of books on marketing and sales were allotted one shelf, there was a handful of modern novels, as well as a collection of classic and modern romantic fiction, but what fascinated me was that there were three shelves of popular books on self-help and psychology, ranging from New Age inspirationals to my own book on incest. I didn't have to investigate to find my work. While I answered her question, "I knew because of Jack's body language. I knew because you used the same nickname for the labs—Geek Heaven. I knew because he pretended in front of his wife that your coming home with me was somehow sexual, which I'm sure he thought was a good cover for him and incidentally gave expression to his genuine jealousy . . ."

Halley interrupted my monologue by removing a worn edition of my book from the shelves. "It turns out I've been a fan of yours for years." The copy was eight years old, the first paperback edition. "I discovered it after our dinner together. When you told me about your life I had this nagging feeling . . ." Halley flipped through the pages. "I bought it on an impulse and read it feverishly one weekend. I think I was in college. It's terrible, isn't it? You read something you find fascinating and you don't remember the author's name."

My pleasure at her literary praise was almost as keen as from her kiss. I wondered if her aim was also more lethal. "You found the subject of incest fascinating?"

"Well, the way you handled it. I read it again after our dinner. I started it that night and took it with me on a trip. Knowing you were an incest victim yourself, I was really impressed you could come up with those insights." She wandered away with my book, returning it to the shelves. With her back to me, she continued, "Incredible objectivity. It's truly brilliant," she said, sliding the book home.

I needed to sit down. I chose the cream-colored couch facing the windows.

"What should I read next?" she asked, moving toward the kitchen. "Do you want something to drink?"

"Did Gene notice it?" I asked.

"Gene?" she repeated as if she had never heard of him. "Oh, you mean when he was here . . . No. And he never told me your name, so . . ." She entered the kitchen, calling, "I'm getting some Evian. Do you want a glass?"

I was thirsty, very thirsty now that I thought about it. "No thanks," I said. "I'm fine."

"I'm going to read everything you've written," she said from the kitchen. "Tell you the truth, I'm a little scared of reading about the child abuse cases. They must be so sad." She appeared with a tall glass of water. She paused in front of me, kicking off her penny loafers. I watched her pale feet. "My father hit my brother once. Just once." She sat next to me, pulling her legs under her, angling my way. She sipped from her glass and leaned forward to put it on the steamer trunk. The movement opened her dress enough for me to see she wasn't wearing a bra. And I noticed as well that her breasts didn't require support. It had been fourteen years since I had been this close to making love to a twenty-six-year-old body, when I was twenty-six myself. The cliché "Youth is wasted on the young" came to mind. I wanted to laugh. "He slapped Mikey once," Halley was saying. "No big deal, but I burst into tears. My brother didn't do anything. He sat still, with his cheek turning red. I was inconsolable. Daddy had to buy me a ice cream cone to calm me down."

"Because you wanted the attention," I said. "You recognized that your father's slap was a sign that he cared more about your brother than you."

Halley leaned back, sitting sideways, facing me, an arm going behind my head. Her body carried some of the odors of our day—the barbecue, the humid streets, the crowded riverbank—and mixed with her perfume. All of her was talking to me: her heat and her longing. The commitment and concentration of the performance was impressive. "Is that what I was doing?" she asked. "I didn't care about my brother at all?"

Her eyes were serious, but a faint smile briefly played on her lips before she settled into a thoroughly earnest pose.

"Why do you and your father avoid each other when you're in public? I know you're close. So why the act?"

Halley lowered her eyes, disappointed. The hand behind my head stroked my neck, again a petting touch, and then departed. "Why are you so angry at me?" She looked up with a little girl's face, lips turned down in a pout, eyes wide and helpless. "Because I'm not sorry enough about Gene?" When I didn't answer, she looked off toward the book shelves. "I'm not a hypocrite, that's all. I'm not going to act weepy and say all those fake things people say when someone dies. I liked Gene, but he wanted more than I could give him. I'm not a wife, I'm not a girl-friend. What was I supposed to do, live some kind of lie so he wouldn't be miserable? He would have been miserable anyway because he'd know it was a lie and he'd never stop pushing me and pushing me until I hated him."

"You already hated him, didn't you?"

"That's really mean." She returned her attention to me. "Are you being so mean because you like me?"

"I'm in love with you," I said calmly. "But I'm not being mean and you know it. Gene was annoying you. He had served his purpose and he wouldn't be disposed of gracefully. That got so annoying you started to hate him. Isn't that the truth?"

Halley slid closer, her elbow capturing my neck, rising on her knees so she was a little above my head. "Could we go back to what you said before you went back to being mean?" She brought her lips close, eyes on mine, while hers smiled. "Did you say you were in love with me?" She rested her free hand on my thigh, fingers sliding up the lip of my Bermuda shorts. Her fingers were cool from holding the glass.

"Take your dress off," I said quietly. For a moment, she didn't react. "Take your dress off," I repeated. This time her eyes flickered. She moved closer, lips aiming for mine.

I averted my head. Her nose landed awkwardly against my cheek. She made the best of it, resting cheek on cheek, her mouth to my ear. "Let's go to the bedroom," she whispered.

"Don't pretend you need a romantic setting." I removed the hand that had by now completely infiltrated my shorts and shifted my position away from the arm behind my head, departing also from her cheek and the length of her body. Halley was left alone in the awkward position of aborted seduction—on her knees, facing the wall, embracing air. "Take the dress off," I said softly.

She frowned, thought about it for a few seconds. Abruptly, she stood up, arms arching to the back of her neck, undoing a clasp and then unzipping. She had to give the dress a tug to loosen it past the tight fit on her hips. Then it dropped suddenly. Breasts glowed white against the tanned skin. Her panties were white so the two zones were fluorescent.

Before she moved back onto the couch, I hooked the front of her panties with my index finger. "This too," I said and let go. The elastic snapped gently against her flat belly.

She put her hands on her hips, as self-assured naked as clothed. "What about you, fella?"

"We'll see," I commented in a bored, almost stern tone. "Hurry up."

"I'm cold," she said in a little voice, hands crossing over her belly.

I stood up—I could by now without difficulty or embarrassment—and took her hand. "You need a bath," I said, towing her through the brief hall and into her bedroom where I assumed the bathroom was located. I was a little amused—though not surprised—to find that her queen-sized bed was girlish: pink bed ruffles, a pair of stuffed animals wedged between pink pillows with lace trim. I released her hand, entered the bathroom alone, flipped on the lights, moved to the tub, sat on its rim, and turned on the hot and cold faucets. I tested the mix until the temperature was as hot as it could be this side of scalding. Resting in the corner were three bottles: shampoo, conditioner, and a pink one—bubble bath for children. I shut the drain, not looking to see what she was up to, and waved for her to enter. "Come on. Let's get you cleaned up. You had a messy day." I didn't hear a response. I picked up the pink bottle. "You want bubbles tonight?" I asked.

She came up behind me, hands resting on my shoulder. She whispered in my ear, "Yes, Daddy."

I poured two cupfuls of pink liquid under the faucet's waterfall. A cloud of suds appeared. I stirred them into the shallow pool already forming in the tub. I shifted to face her. Her panties were at eye level, the deep hole of her navel a Cyclops eye, questioning me. I hooked her panties on both sides, widening them away from her hips. "Let's get out of these."

She alternated using my shoulders for support as she stepped out of them, first the pale right foot, then the left. The hairs of her pubis were silky and fine, very black against a triangle of bleached skin. One thin wisp ascended up, ending well before the tan line. I brushed the surface lightly with the length of my thumb. "You're getting to be a big girl," I said. She watched me with wide innocent eyes.

I stood up, holding her left hand with my right. I tapped her white ass with my free hand. "Okay, step in."

She tried her right foot, arching up at the first touch of water. "It's hot," she complained.

"You're cold from the air-conditioning. You'll get used to it."

She leaned all her weight on my hand. I nearly staggered, but managed to keep my balance. She immersed all of one foot, saying, "Ow, ow, ow," while bringing the other in. She stood in the water for a moment.

"I'll make it cooler," I said, bending forward to adjust the water.

"Thanks, Daddy," she said, coming close to watch me. Her thigh and silky hairs brushed against my cheek.

"It's cooler now," I said looking up at her.

She was peering down at her dark left nipple, holding it between her thumb and finger. "It's hard," she said.

Lightly, I slapped the back of her hand. "Don't play with yourself."

She smiled mischievously. "The other isn't," she said, gesturing at the soft right nipple.

I cupped water in my palms and bathed a leg. "Mmmmm," she said. I gathered more and massaged the other with liquid. The bubbles lingered on her thighs. I brushed up toward her black hill, finally cupping it with all the fingers of my left hand, holding her as if it were a handle.

"I'm wet inside too," she said, which was obvious.

"Lie down," I said and eased her backwards into the water, supporting the neck until her head rested against the sloping porcelain. She shut her eyes. I got up.

"You're going?" she called out in a panic.

"Hush," I said. I turned off the harsh fluorescent light over the medicine cabinet and the recessed white lamp in the ceiling. From the bedroom window, a square of amber from New York's street lamps lit her upper half.

I sat on the edge of the tub, gathering bubbles with my fingers and meticulously cleaned her feet, her calves, her thighs, her stomach, her flanks, her underarms, her neck, leaving the best for last. I discovered what was ticklish, what was eager, what liked me to be rough, what liked me to be gentle.

As her excitement mounted, she raised a soapy hand, fingers probing for the lip of my shorts. I lifted them off disdainfully. "Keep your hands to yourself," I said.

"Please," she said in a whisper.

"I'll go if you don't behave yourself," I answered.

"Have a bath with me, Daddy," she moaned. I cupped her neck in my right palm and invaded her with the left hand. She planted her feet on either side of the faucet and arched her middle. "I can't," she pleaded. "I want you inside."

I leaned over, pressing my cheek against hers, my mouth to her ear. "Let yourself go," I whispered, my thumb on the quickening pulse in her throat to check on the work of my other hand.

"I can't like this," she said desperately.

I watched shadows move across the amber light on the tile, learning the rhythm of this woman. Around once slow, quickly across. Side to side. Up and down. Pause. Hard on the nub . . .

"Let me touch you," she begged.

"No," I said. Around and around. Pause. Depart. Let her think you've quit until her belly asks for more. Then fast and rougher.

Her warm dripping hand came up to grab my thigh. I stopped pleasing her, pulling her fingers from my skin, and pushed her hand into the water. "Lift your behind," I said harshly. She obeyed. I pinned her hand beneath her. "You're not clean yet," I said.

"Let me kiss you," she said, her lips blindly touching my face, searching for my mouth.

"Let go," I said. I tightened my grip on her neck to keep her head still and searched with my middle finger for the pressure point at its base, applying a light but persistent touch. She relaxed, passive again. I resumed playing the instrument, stroking her thighs, stomach, and around her breasts before I returned to her sex.

My eyes adjusted to the amber light until even that seemed bright. I listened to the bubbles subside while she whispered, "I can't . . . Please . . . I can't. Please . . . Let me touch you."

I took her earlobe between my teeth and bit lightly. I whispered, "But this isn't for you, my little baby. This is what I want."

"You want me like this?" she asked plaintively. I changed rhythm. She moaned in a deeper tone.

"This is for me."

She trembled, breathing rapidly as if she were having a fast and shallow orgasm. I didn't believe in it. She was eager to be rid of the attention. "Oh God, oh God, oh God," she said and then exhaled loudly to signal it was over. She whispered, "Thank you."

"You're a bad little girl," I said. "Don't try to fool Daddy." I slid the tip of my pinky into her other, dry hole. She was startled, then curious. With the rest of my hand I continued to play the central chord, as if I were at work on the crescendo of a Beethoven sonata.

She looked surprised as she felt a true orgasm begin. Her reactions were quite different than during her mock ecstasy. She arched against both ends of the tub, body rigid, no breathing, then a sudden release, sagging down into the water and up again taut, an irregular undulation. She cycled that way more than a dozen times—fighting and losing, fighting and losing to herself.

As she surrendered to the climax, pushing against both rims, she levitated out of the water. When I believed the momentum was too strong for her to stop it, I whispered, "Gene loved you. He loved you so much he preferred to die than live without you."

She turned her face to me, eyes glazed, listening hungrily while she grunted with pleasure. At the peak, as her body shuddered, her breaths deep, slow and long, I said, "He died for you."

She bucked so violently I was drenched. I left the bathroom immediately.

I paused briefly in her living room to take another look at the eight-year-old copy of my book. I found what I was looking for on the inside of the back cover. I ignored her puzzled calls asking for me and left for my sublet. My clothes dried quickly on the hot streets.

CHAPTER EIGHT

Last Chance

I DIDN'T RETURN THE MESSAGES HALLEY LEFT DURING THE FOLLOWING two days. She appeared in the lab—much to the surprise of my fellow geeks—on Wednesday morning and asked to see me in my office. "I want your opinion on the ad copy," she said in public, namely in front of Andy Chen and two others standing nearby. "See if we're brainwashing the consumer right," she added with a smile. "I could use your expertise."

Tim Gallent, the overweight debugger with a habit of screaming at Andy, said, "Whoa. No kidding, Doc. You brainwash people?"

"Every day," I said. "I don't have an office," I told Halley.

"Come to mine." She turned halfway, not sure if I would obey.

I didn't seem to have a choice—how could I explain a rude refusal to Andy and the others? I tried a compromise. "Andy, may we use your office?" I asked.

"*Mi casa es su casa,*" Andy said. He didn't look happy. I'm sure he felt he had a right to see the ad copy for the machine he was building.

I led the way into Gene's old office. The significance would be lost on her. I knew from Andy that Halley had been to the labs only once, her first week on the job, well before Gene had been promoted.

Still, Halley should have been impressed by my changes. At this point in my tenure, I had convinced Andy to allow the maintenance crews in to clean during the three days a week I was there, with a promise that I would supervise them. Andy trusted me to make sure the staff didn't disturb work in progress. I arranged for them to vacuum and dust in two shifts, accommodating the odd hours of the technicians. I had dealt with the office furniture bureaucracy. The broken chairs and desks were replaced. I bought as many plants as the guys would tolerate. I convinced Stick that spies were unlikely to be crouched with binoculars in the woods across the road and thus the shades could be opened. I arranged with two of the cleaning staff—Rose and Fred—to do so each morning; the technicians couldn't be trusted to remember. Since the windows had to remain shut, I was reduced to buying air filters and dehumidifiers, not without a lot of worry and memos from different divisions, including one called Technical Integrity, claiming that I was somehow going to destroy every microchip in the building. I found a lab in California which used the same method to freshen their sealed-air supply; that silenced Technical Integrity. So far, no disaster had occurred. Joe Stein's mother would have been proud of me. The place still wasn't spotless and it was far from beautiful, but the air was breathable, there was some light, and the leafy green plants were a reminder that the world has parts not made of metal and plastic.

As for Andy's office, now the chess set, the prototype and his Black Dragon terminal rested on different tables. I brought in a separate desk for the rare occasions he used paper. I requisitioned a small refrigerator and stocked it with Coke. I discovered he liked apples and sharp cheddar cheese; a supply of both was maintained. Since Andy was a Michael Jordan fan, on the wall opposite his desk I hung a poster depicting the Chicago star making a twisting layup between two mammoth defenders.

Halley entered, ignorant of my domestic touches, opened a large manila envelope and pulled out several pages of elaborate typefaces. "These are rough," she said. "I hate most of them. There's one that may be it."

"I don't know a goddamn thing about advertising," I said.

"You can read and you can react," she said. "That's all I need."

I proved to her I had no feel for promotion. The one I liked (We made Centaur Fast, Flexible and Smart. All you have to do is make a Lap.) was among her least favorite. The leading candidate was—Don't Take Your Troubles Home From The Office . . . Take The Solution.

"It's banal," I said. "And sort of pompous."

Halley smiled as she returned the papers to the envelope. "Well, you're right about one thing. We're not there yet." She closed the clasp. "Are you gay?" she asked casually. She brought her head up, in the style of a television detective, to catch my reaction.

I laughed. "That's a little weak, Halley."

"You just like to play mind games, is that it?"

"That's my job."

"What I want to know is—are they for your entertainment or mine?"

"It's really quite simple, Halley. I meant to talk to you about it. Do you want to do that now?"

She looked at the pint-size refrigerator, at the Staunton chess pieces frozen in mid-game, and finally at the guts of the prototype, still a crashed mess of boards and wires. "Well, we could find a more romantic spot." She smiled. "Or at least a bathroom."

I checked my watch. "I have a meeting with your father in a half hour—"

"What was that shit you pulled—saying you love me?" she interrupted. The words were angry; her tone, however, was merely annoyed. "I mean," she leaned one hand on Andy's desk, the other on her hip, "especially for a brilliant psychiatrist, that was pretty primitive manipulation."

"I do love you," I said. Halley straightened, blinking at me. "But, unfortunately, you're mentally ill and I'm not into that. I don't have the shrink's disease of having relationships with potential patients. Not that I would treat you anyway."

Halley's lovely full lips, her pink lipstick iridescent against the tan, opened into a broad, amazed smile. She turned to the wall as if there were someone there to share her amusement. She came back to me, both hands on her hips, let out one of her noises of multiple feelings, and repeated with utter skepticism, "I'm mentally ill?"

"You're a classic narcissist."

"At least I'm a classic," Halley mumbled.

I ignored her sarcasm. "I noticed you had one of Alice Miller's books on your shelves, so I know you won't misunderstand my use of the term. Almost nothing you do or say is genuine. You're constantly making up personas to win the love of whomever you're dealing with. Mostly, of course, you're focused on men because of your unresolved incestuous desires for Stick. Quite a nickname for someone with your fixation. Both phallic and punitive." I waved that digression away. "Your quest is hopeless, Halley—making yourself into the perfect fantasy for all these men to impress your father. What you really want, the only thing that will really satisfy you, is if Daddy falls in love with you. I guess you're so far gone that you might even actually want him to fuck you. To feel him quaking in your arms, groaning in ecstasy, vulnerable and in your control. But that's never going to happen. He doesn't love you. He doesn't love anyone. You said you were incapable of love, but you were really thinking of your father. You're very much in love and he's taking advantage of it. He's got every man in Minotaur by the balls—so to speak—thanks to you. Of course that's your murdered self all over again. The real Halley is dead—there are only pretty reflections to mesmerize us. You can't get Daddy to fuck you, so you help him fuck others."

Halley was still. She didn't appear alarmed or upset. She nodded once or twice during my speech, not in agreement, to indicate she was following me. "I don't want to fuck my father. I know why you think . . ." She smiled gently, as if regretting that she had to embarrass me. "I played along with your little fantasy because I thought—" She stopped, catching herself.

I finished for her, "Because you thought that would make me addicted to you—like Gene, like Jack, like who knows how many others. I knew that's what you thought. But it wasn't my fantasy, Halley. It was yours."

Once again, as she had so often, Halley surprised me with her will and her essential inner strength. There were many reactions she might have had—all of them genuine. There were many false reactions she might have chosen—all of them useless. Instead, she cocked her head, eyes brilliant, and asked coolly, "And what is *your* fantasy? You say I'm an expert at supplying them. So tell me, what do you like?"

I nodded, impressed. "You should have been a therapist. You always throw people back on themselves." I felt this was my last chance to reach her. I walked over, resting my hands on her shoulders. I shook her gently. "Okay. No games. Listen to me. You can be helped. You're very bright and you're young. There's really no limit to what you can accomplish. I know you must feel guilty, somewhere, about the harm you've caused, to your brother, to Gene, and possibly many others. But that really wasn't in your control, although you think you're in control all the time." Halley listened to me, chin up to meet my eyes, lips shut, face impassive. I believed she was interested. I was convinced most of her, the best of her, wished to hear me. "I can get you the names of many good doctors. There's nothing to be afraid of. You won't be anybody's fool. You won't turn into a victim. You won't be hurt and alone again, the way he made you feel as a little girl. You can find her—there's a real Halley in there—and she's even stronger than this one."

She lifted her arm. That eased my hand off her shoulder. She touched my cheek with her fingers, stroking me. "You have a beautiful face," she commented. "Tell me. Is that the same speech you made to Gene?" She backed away. There was not a trace of malice in her expression or in her voice. "I really don't need help, Doctor. Maybe you're right. Maybe I do terrible things. But they don't make me feel terrible. I'm happy. And believe it or not, I can make you happy." She waved the manila envelope gently for a goodbye. "Give me a call if you feel like learning to enjoy life," she said and left.

I had no guide, no text I could follow after I took that risk and it failed. Twenty minutes later, the big door to Stick's office whooshed open for me to enter. I had to be prepared for the possibility that Halley had reported my diagnosis to him, although I doubted she actually would. (Especially if I was on the money.) Still, if she did, what were the consequences? My position was untenable—I wanted to treat these people and they didn't believe they were ill. Therapy depends on the patient desiring a cure. If I took Halley at her word (as you know, an Olympian feat for a shrink) I was sadly mistaken and she was a paragon of adjustment. My training, the accumulated knowledge of dozens of geniuses studying the human condition, had taught me she couldn't be happy. Yet she functioned. There were no symptoms of distress. Settling into the black leather chair across from Stick's country French table I had to allow for the possibility that she was right. I pronounced Gene cured and he committed suicide; I said she was mentally ill and she thrived. At what point did I have to admit that if it walks like a duck, quacks like a duck and looks like a duck, then, at the very least, it was going to be able to live its life as a duck?

"Well," Stick said, palms out, as if he were surrendering, "I have to hand it to you. I just got off the phone with Andy. They've licked the I/O slowdown and—" Stick shook his head. "Goddamn, Andy actually gave credit to somebody else. Tim Gallent—"

"Yes," I said, glad to be on neutral ground. Not that I felt safe. I knew Stick well enough so that I didn't relax because he appeared relaxed. Halley might have told him, anyway. His self-control was formidable. "They were rechecking it early this morning," I continued. "Apparently Tim beat it last night."

"That's the first time Andy's sounded like a real manager." Stick winked at me. "Maybe he'll come after my job next."

"No," I said in a rush. "Not in his personality. As I told you, he's a prodigy and he's adjusted by——"

Stick halted me with a raised hand. And with laughter. Deep, self-satisfied laughter. "Okay, okay. I was joking. I know Andy knows his place." He fixed me with a steady beam from his dark eyes. "And we'll both have to make sure we keep it that way. We don't want to repeat our mistakes, right?"

"Right," I agreed and lowered my eyes. Something was wrong with me. This interview, with a powerful man behind a desk, and me, a supplicant in the chair, insecure, carrying secrets, unable to meet his eyes—I had already lived this chapter in the story of my life and it shouldn't be happening at my age and with what I had learned. How would you answer your own challenge, Dr. Neruda? I asked myself. Are you happy?

"Rafe?" Stick knocked on the bleached wood of his desk. "Hello? I lost you there."

"I'm sorry." Get your head up: hold that gaze. "What were you saying?"

"Did you get a chance to form an opinion of Jack Truman at the barbecue—I saw you talked a little." Stick smiled and shrugged his shoulders. "You can't blame me, Rafe. You've done such wonders downstairs, I'm tempted to move you to the Glass Tower."

"His wife is worried about their son," I said. "She's getting bad advice from her pediatrician."

"Really?" Stick lowered his chin, pinched his nose with his fingers, then stroked his eyebrows, finally locking his hands together. He leaned back. "Something you can help with?"

"Um . . ." I was having trouble concentrating—all the beloved theories were dancing upside down in my head and I found the view of their ungainly thighs and flipped skirts grotesque. "It's simple really. The boy just needs an adequate reading tutor, mostly to calm the mother down." I cleared my throat, shifting to the edge of my chair, which was designed to keep the sitter angled slightly back, passive compared to the straight up-and-down look of Stick across the desk. "My guess is Jack's withdrawing from the family because he's got a crush on Halley. One possibility is that Amy Truman is blowing this up into a crisis to call her wayward husband back home. Another is that the boy has intuited the marital trouble and this is his distress signal." I waited for Stick to react. When he failed to, I continued, "But dealing with the child's reading block directly will suffice. For a family dysfunction, it's pretty routine. And Jack's tough. He won't come apart when Halley dumps him."

Stick cracked his knuckles. I winced. "She's close to dumping him?" he asked.

"You tell me," I said and stood up. I had to gain height on him, and freedom of movement.

"You're going?" Stick asked.

I moved aimlessly toward his windows. The parking lot was full below. Theodore Copley was in charge of every life down there. Not as a matter of objective fact. But that's what he must feel as he watched them arrive, docking at his desire, looking up as they entered his house of worship. He was a very little Westchester god to the world, but, all the same, from the perspective of this window he was God. "I feel restless, that's all."

"You want to go for a swim?" he asked. "I'm going to the gym after our meeting."

I watched a Federal Express van pause at the security gate on its way out. "I don't swim," I said, a silly lie, a private form of rejection, told because I wanted so badly to disassociate myself from him and everything he did.

"No kidding." Stick swiveled in my direction. "How did that happen? Didn't you go to summer camp?"

"I was a poor kid. I grew up in the city."

"But you were a ward of your uncle, right? He was a friend of Edgar's father? Wasn't he—"

I interrupted, "—Not until I was a teenager. Uncle didn't want me to go to a regular camp. Mostly I took advanced courses offered to bright high school kids during the summer. You know, at colleges."

"So you never learned?"

"I'm a little frightened of the water," I said. "Don't want to go back to the womb, I guess." I shrugged, smiled at Stick, and returned to my chair.

"You know how my father taught me to swim?" Stick asked. I shook my head. "We vacationed in a cabin in Maine, on a pond. A lake really, at least in size. A large pond. He told me he was going to teach me. He rowed me to the center of Walker Pond, where it was very deep. He took off my little life jacket and threw me in." Stick watched for my reaction as if he were the shrink and I the patient.

But that makes no sense. I *am* the doctor, I reminded myself. Perhaps I should look in my wallet, show my identification, call an ambulance, put him in a straitjacket and order electroshock. We could jolt those self-confident brain cells, make them misfire, and cure him of his efficiency.

"Why are you smiling?" Stick asked.

"What happened?" I asked. "When he threw you in, I mean."

"He rowed away. I don't know how far. Far enough. He said, 'You'd better swim, boy, or you'll drown.' He didn't have to say that. It was pretty obvious."

"What happened?"

"I swam. I started to go under and I gulped some water, but I swam."

Certainly I could institutionalize him for this. They wouldn't question my rationale: I'm admitting this patient for his overdeveloped will to live. I covered my face with both hands and rubbed. The skin tingled. I uncovered my face and asked Stick, "Did you believe him?"

"Believe him about what?"

"That he would let you drown?"

"The pond was muddy. If I went under I'm not sure he could have saved me. I remember there was some story about a twelve-year-old kid who got a cramp in deep water and—I think it was his father and his uncle . . . Anyway, two grown men couldn't find him, although they were right nearby. We all knew that story."

"How old were you?"

"I was six."

"So you believed him?"

Stick laughed. "Hey, I was in a panic. I didn't think about it. I just swam. He was right. He said I knew how, that I just had to do it." He watched me and waited. I was silent. Finally, he got to the point. First, however, he moved his eyes away from mine, staring down as he picked off something from his pants. "I guess nowadays that would be called child abuse."

"Are you asking me if *I* think it's child abuse?"

Stick, without raising his eyes, nodded—a remarkably shy and boyish manner for him to display.

I cleared my throat. "Well, my professional opinion is that the risk was out of proportion to the gain."

Stick didn't laugh. He spoke softly, "I think he did me a favor. I was a mama's boy. She let me get away with murder. If I complained about anything, I was given aspirin, tucked into bed, brought hot chocolate, and she'd read me stories—"

I interrupted, "You were an only child, of course."

"That's obvious?" he asked.

"Oh sure. Why didn't she have more children?"

"There were complications at my birth. Cord was around my neck and I was breech. We both almost died. She couldn't have any more children after me."

The story of every god: the terrible, unique birth that ravages. And its glorious product: the cherished creature snatched from death and forever invulnerable.

Stick locked his fingers together and flexed out. No cracking sound, thank goodness. "Anyway, she pampered me. I was turning into a little scaredy-cat. Father saved me from what she was doing to me. Who knows? If he didn't give me a shock, she might have turned me into a fag. Isn't that what happens to a mama's boy? He made me strong. I know you don't approve, but I think throwing me into the water saved my life."

"Well, he certainly put your life at issue."

Stick leaned forward, elbows on the table, hands out, staring right at me. "Look, I'm not down on what you do. I have to admit I thought it was all bullshit, but you're no fake. You can help people. I'm really interested in your opinion. Would you call what my father did child abuse?"

"Of course it's child abuse. That's not what's interesting about the story."

"No kidding." Stick smiled, delighted. "What's interesting?"

"Your strength, your will not merely to survive, but to triumph. I don't mean to offend you, but psychologically, your family dynamic is rather ordinary—and I could have guessed it from your personality. In fact, I'm sure there were many other earlier and probably more damaging incidents with your father that you don't remember—"

He interrupted, his voice harsh. "Come on. You don't know that."

"I know because you didn't expect him to save you. That's quite an extraordinary assumption for a six-year-old boy to make."

Stick's brows twitched. I waited for him to dispute me. When he didn't, I continued, "The reason you remember that story, apart from the fact that you nearly died, of course . . ." I smiled and Stick chuckled. We werc becoming buddies. "The reason you remember is that it was the day you first triumphed over your sadistic father."

Stick cocked his head, turning an ear to me as if hard of hearing. "Sadistic?"

"Oh yes. You had a pretty clear choice, didn't you? You could be the sickly incompetent baby to please your weak mother or you could copy your brutal father. You figured out that being your father was a better deal. Tell me, I'm curious, when was the first time you saw him hit your mother?"

Stick didn't move, not a muscle, head still cocked, ear to the ground, the pose of a waiting hunter. He breathed through his nose. When he spoke, his lips hardly moved. He said, "She told you?"

"Who's she?"

He made a noise. "My wife, of course."

"Nobody told me, Stick. You like to hurt people. You think that's love. You think it toughens people up. You think it's being a man. That doesn't come from watching cartoon shows, although there are people who will tell you it does. You may have seen your father hit your mother only once. Maybe the rest of the time all he did was yell or show disdain. Maybe he liked to scold her. Whatever the details, you couldn't be who you are and not have a cruel father."

"I'm disappointed." Stick finally changed position. He leaned back, glancing at his phone, and then came at me, head up, eyes glazed with indifference. "I guess I'm someone who can't be helped by what you fellows do."

I answered in a loud, friendly tone. "I'm surprised."

"Well . . ." Stick pressed two buttons on his phone, sending a message. "I've never been much of a fan of psychiatry."

"No, no," I stood up. "I should get going. I'm sure you have calls to make before you go for your daily swim. You enjoy that, don't you? Swimming two miles a day? What I meant was, I'm surprised you feel you need help."

I had confused him, made him self-aware. For a moment, he was frozen in my headlights, mouth open, eyes dull. "What?" he said, as if waking from a dream.

"I said, I'm surprised you feel you need help."

"I don't," he said. "I feel good."

"Do you?" I leaned my hands on his antique table, a lawyer bearing down on the witness. "The son you loved died young, your wife is an alcoholic, your daughter is obsessed with you and can't make a life for herself, you don't seem to have friends—just employees and business contacts. No one could blame you for feeling you need to talk about your isolation, about the terribly high price you've had to pay for being strong."

When I began the speech, mentioning Mike's death, I hit a nerve. His right arm waved, as if brushing a fly off. His eyes changed, lids closing halfway. His thin ungenerous lips, so different from his daughter's, disappeared altogether. He was seething, although I'm sure a casual observer would have thought it an exaggeration to say so. I straightened when finished with presenting the evidence and said softly, "I can find someone, someone you'll feel comfortable with, someone discreet, of course, with whom you can talk."

Here was the test. Surely he would explode. I couldn't expect him to burst into tears, but its mirror image—rage—was the human reaction. Certainly, now he would let go, and show me the boy's panic, abandoned in the muddy pond, flailing his little arms to keep his head above water.

Stick rubbed his eyebrows thoughtfully. He inhaled, pinched his nose with two fingers, let out a long stream of air, and then opened a hand to me. "I have a better idea. Why don't you talk to Jack Truman and help his kid out? Maybe Jack should talk to someone too—I know my daughter can be overpowering. Even to me. I can't restrain her. Anyway, I'm sure the Trumans will get more out of a therapist than I would." He pressed the floor button. The door whooshed open. "Thanks, Rafe, for the good work. Oh," he wagged a finger, "by the way, I read your memo. You can go ahead with the recreation area improvements. As you know, I'm a believer in exercise." He winked at me, pleased by the ironic followup that had occurred to him: "A healthy mind in a healthy body, right Doctor?"

Chapter Nine

Surrender

"HELLO!" JEFF, HALLEY'S ASSISTANT, CALLED AS I PASSED HER OFFICE. I waved, but didn't go in. I had already stopped to chat with Laura, Stick's secretary, on my way out of that disastrous interview and didn't feel up to more pleasantries. I did notice, however, that Halley's inner door was open, so I shouted, "Jack Truman this way?"

"Around the corner," Jeff answered. "Second door on the right, Dr. Neruda."

Father and daughter weren't unsettled, but obviously I was. Why bother to let her know my destination? Playing the part of the jealous lover? What was the point now?

I found Jack standing behind his seated secretary, reading over a letter she had typed. He looked up and grinned at me. "Hi there," he said. "Slumming?"

"Do you have a few minutes? Stick suggested I see you."

I might as well have shot him between the eyes. I had forgotten my joke at the barbecue that if I showed my face in his office he was in trouble. He stammered, "You're here to—you want to see me?"

"Nothing important. I can come back. I need your advice. I'll call you—"

"No, no. Come in. You got this straight, Kelly?" he mumbled to his secretary, waving me in without listening to her reply. He met me at the door to his inner office, taking my elbow. He maintained the grip all the way to the chair opposite his desk, presumably guiding me, although he seemed to want the physical contact, as if by hanging on he was in control of me. He also put his face too close, smiling so hard I wondered if the lines he was making around his mouth would be permanent. Once he put me where he wanted me, he retraced his steps to shut the door, talking in a loud cheerful tone for the benefit of his assistant, "Well, this is a pleasant surprise. But I'm happy to help. Always wanted to be a doctor myself." The door was shut and he maneuvered toward the desk. He kept up the noisy banter, "I heard about fixing up a rec area out back. That'll be terrific—"

I interrupted, "Okay, Jack, she can't hear us now."

He was halfway down to his chair. He hung in midair for a moment and then fell the rest of the way. Its cushion sighed.

"I apologize for my abrupt entrance. I should have phoned. Stick has nothing to do with my being here. It was my idea. Your wife, Amy—I don't know if she told you—"

"She thought you were great!" Jack eagerly leaned toward me, stomach pressed against the edge of his desk, chest arched over the top. He framed my face with his large hands, centering it as the target for his praise. He had the build of a football player—chunky legs, thick neck— and the jowls of a man who enjoys beer and red meat. "She said she bugged you for advice about little Billy's reading problem—I guess that happens to doctors all the time, right? You're trying to relax on a holiday and people want free advice. Seriously, she was grateful. Said you were really helpful. But it's nothing. I keep telling her, Billy's got my lousy genes. I was the last in my class to read."

I noticed a pair of bamboo fishing poles resting in the corner. On a shelf nearby there was a teak wood box with brass fittings that I guessed housed lures. "Fly-fishing?" I asked, gesturing to the wall.

"Yeah . . . You fly-fish?" he asked hopefully.

"No, but I know someone who does. Those are hand-crafted rods, right? Very expensive?"

"Yeah, I splurged . . ." He was embarrassed. "They're collectibles, actually. Hand-made by these great characters. Weird old guys. Cost a bundle. Amy might want to talk to you about how I prioritize my spending." He winked at me. We were also becoming buddies. "I brought them in to show off to a client who's a fly fisher. Great guy. I'm seeing him for lunch."

"Ever take Billy along on a fishing trip?"

Jack swallowed. "Guess I should, huh?" he asked meekly. "I was waiting until he was a little older. That wrong?"

Is this what it's like for Dr. Joyce Brothers? I wondered. Everywhere she goes, she's the maven, no topic beyond her expert generalization. "I was just curious," I said.

"No, seriously, what do you think? I feel guilty when I take off for the weekend and leave him behind."

"Take him when you think he'd enjoy it, I guess. I don't know. Seems like a good bonding thing for a father and son. Just don't throw him in the river for bait."

Jack's wide nose twitched. "We don't use live bait. That's why it's called fly-fishing."

"I was joking," I said.

"I knew that," he said, nodding.

"Amy told me your pediatrician has recommended Ritalin for Billy. That seems excessive for a reading problem."

"Un huh," he nodded vigorously.

I waited for him to add something. His nods slowed. He remained silent and showily attentive, like a prep school boy in the headmaster's office, waiting for advice he intended to agree to enthusiastically and then ignore. I noticed a plastic name plate resting against the back of his phone. MR. TRUMAN was in white letters against a black background and below it the joke—The Jack Stops Here. I pointed to it. "That's cute."

"Salesman humor," he said. He shrugged.

"So . . . ?" I smiled. "Is that all there is to it? He's not reading at age eight?"

"He reads a little. But he's way behind the other kids. He's lazy. That's all I think it is. Doesn't like reading, so he doesn't work at it. Our doctor didn't say he definitely needed this, uh . . ."

"Ritalin."

"Right. He just said it was an option if Billy's problem was, you know, that he couldn't pay attention. That's what the school says. He's disruptive—"

"Disruptive?" I said, straightening with a start, as if he had sent an electric shock through my chair.

"No!" he reached toward me with his right hand, reeling in the word. "Not disruptive. You know, just . . . He's a cutup in class. He's a handful. Like me. I was a handful. I'm gonna talk to him, straighten it out. I've been on the road a lot. Haven't put in the hours at home I should. I'm sorry Amy bothered you. We'll take care of it. It's no big deal."

"May I speak with her about it?" As far as Jack was concerned I seemed to have switched to a different language. He stared, mouth open. "That's why I dropped by. I wanted to suggest some tutors. I know a couple of good remedial reading people in this general area. We hired them at my old clinic. Sometimes, a little extra help gives a child confidence. Once you fall behind in school, it's embarrassing and that makes catching up even harder. But I didn't want to talk to Amy behind your back. And certainly not without your permission."

Jack nodded, this time long and slow movements up and down, as if, as headmaster, I had begun to rave and he was unsure whether to summon the nurse.

"This has nothing to do with work, Jack," I continued into his wary silence. "Nothing to do with Stick. There's no implied threat. I'm only here to help. You see, I know a lot about children, a lot about Ritalin, a lot about cutups in school. I'm sure Billy's fine and I want to make sure that nobody makes his little problem into a big one by overreacting. I doubt, for example, that he needs to be straightened out. Probably he just needs a little help and reassurance."

Jack pushed off from his desk, eyes straying to the bamboo poles, the false good cheer gone. "He hit a couple kids," he said quietly. "Gave one a real shiner. And he kicked one of his teachers—the dance teacher, for Chrissakes. She was teaching him the polka—" he laughed with resignation, but also from his belly, really amused. He sighed afterwards, rolled in his chair over to the poles, and picked up one. "Beautiful work, huh?" he said, rising. He came near me, turning the bamboo in the air to show off details that I'm afraid I couldn't appreciate. "I envy those guys. I mean they don't look like they've got much to envy—living in the sticks, cars falling apart in the yard—but it must be peaceful. And great to know that what you make is unique. I'm a salesman. I don't make anything, so . . ." He rested the pole across his arm, as if surrendering his sword to me.

"It's beautiful," I said.

Jack said softly, "Billy's disruptive." Jack returned the fishing pole to the corner. He pushed his chair to the desk, continuing in a quiet tone, "The school told us if he doesn't get under control next year, they can't—

you know, we'll have to move him." He sat down heavily. "It's a private school. Supposed to be the best—"

"Amy told me the school was good," I said. "Stick doesn't have to know anything about my helping out. Would you like me to talk to Amy, maybe have Billy see some of my colleagues? They deal with truly crazy kids—it'd be refreshing for them to see a fine young boy who's just acting up a bit."

"You think that's all it is?" Jack's green eyes, small against the puffiness of his face, looked openly into mine for the first time. The appeal was sweet. He may not have known how best to defend his son, but he wanted to.

"Probably," I said. "You can't really blame him. I'd kick anybody who tried to teach me how to polka."

We parted friends. My childish trick had also worked. As I came out of Jack's office, Halley nearly bowled me over. She reared back, eyebrows up, her apparently profound surprise expressed so promptly she failed to make it convincing. "Rafe! What are you doing here?" she asked.

"Gossiping," I said with a smile. "And you?"

She gestured to the same manila envelope she had shown me in Andy's office. "I was gonna get some feedback from Jack."

"Better hurry," I said, walking away. "He's going to lunch with a fly fisher."

"What?" she called.

But I didn't stop. I called Amy Truman that afternoon. We met for coffee in Tarrytown, an hour before she was due to fetch Billy from school. Jack had alerted her about my interest. Feeling she had his permission, she opened up completely. After ten minutes, and one prompt, she widened the discussion from the subject of Billy's woes. I liked her. She was a Louisiana native whom Jack met on a sales trip and courted for a year before they married. Her father was a doctor, her mother a music teacher. She had a degree in education and was working, when they courted, in the local public school in charge of the reading readiness program for kindergarten. That was part of the reason Billy's learning problems were especially humiliating and, of course, so apt an arena in which to rebel. Dealing with their two-year-old girl, Billy's problems and Jack's heavier travel schedule left her feeling overwhelmed. Naturally, she blamed herself for Billy's reading problems. "I pushed him too hard, tried to get him to read too early, and now see, I've gotten just the opposite of what I bargained for." With her strawberry blonde hair, her lively blue eyes, her trim figure and generous smile she should be keeping Jack interested but I was no longer in a shrink's office, blind and deaf to her world. I knew what she was up against. Her essential decency put her at a disadvantage. She mistakenly thought that by taking care of Jack's children and providing a safe port he would feel love and gratitude. Instead, he felt she was safe. Meanwhile, at Minotaur, Jack was supplied with danger and excitement and triumph too. Not poor grades and messy diapers, not the constricted talk of suburban shopping and PTA meetings, not the same easily conquered body that, to his touch, was probably thicker and flabbier than the one he had wooed on humid bayou nights. Anyway, she was a fish he had already caught.

Within forty minutes, she returned three times to the theme of how rarely she and Jack were alone together, what with all his traveling and Billy's troubles and their two-year-old girl. She complained about Jack's work and then scolded herself for complaining. After all, she mumbled shyly, this coming year was a big opportunity for Jack.

I took a guess, commenting, as if I knew, "You mean, the big promise Stick made to Jack about the future if Centaur goes well."

"So you know." She smiled and slapped the table. "See that? I told Jack. I told him Stick isn't blowing smoke. And, of course, you know about it. Jack tells me Stick really leans on you. He's very jealous. Says you get a private meeting twice a week. He's only got Mondays."

"Jack's right to be cautious," I said. "Promises are just promises."

She looked grave. And nodded earnestly. "Right, of course. I just meant, you know, I feel—I mean, Jack's done wonderful work for—"

"Jack's done a superb job. Stick knows that." I covered her hand with mine. Her pale blue eyes, at that moment washed out by the sunlight falling on them, looked at me without reserve. I let all of myself go out to her, copying my new teacher, beaming love and devotion without fear of embarrassment or rejection—or the scruple that it wasn't sincere. "Listen. You need to take care of yourself. Jack can handle his job. You need him to help with his children."

"Right," she nodded. "That's right."

"Men have a tendency to think that their work is all-important. That the people who love them should drop everything and help. That the job isn't just a job, it's the future, it's security, it's love, it's being a good person. But, you know, in the end, it *is* just a job and it's not gonna love him back." I slipped my fingers under her palm, and held her hand, squeezing a little. She returned the pressure. "If he doesn't start taking care of you he's a fool." I let go. She swallowed, her freckled cheeks flushed pink, and her pupils widened. "I'll get you a reading tutor and I want you to make an appointment with a family therapist." I wrote down the name of one I knew well on a napkin. I had confidence that Amy was conscientious enough about her family, and tough enough, to make Jack go with her and Billy for counseling. I suspected that was the only way to get a fly fisher into therapy. I gave her the napkin.

"Thanks," Amy said, carefully folding and putting it in her purse.

I reached for her hand. She gave it to me willingly. "You and Jack need to take care of your marriage and Billy will be all right. Know what I mean?"

Amy nodded, her mouth set, ready for a fight. "Yes," she nodded. "I think I do."

I winked. "Okay. I'm single, you know. Tell Jack if he won't show you a good time, I will."

She smiled. "I'll tell him, Doctor. I'll be sure to tell him that," she said and winked back at me.

After she left, I used the coffee shop's phone booth to report to Stick that I had recommended a good reading tutor to the Trumans, that their son's problem was trivial, and that I was impressed by Jack's loyalty to the company. I emphasized to my boss—because that's what Theodore Copley had become, I realized, in spite of the fact that I provided less than full disclosure of my actions on his behalf—that he shouldn't let on to Jack I had performed this service at his prompting. "He would be alarmed," I said.

"Well, we don't want that," my fearless leader said. "We want Jack to feel relaxed. He's doing a terrific job. By the way, Rafe, is Thursday night okay for you to play doubles?" I had become his regular partner against a variety of opponents, usually business competitors.

"Sure," I said.

"Great. Seven at Wall Street. One other thing. I'm sending down the hotel brochure for the fall retreat."

"Fall retreat?"

"Yeah. Did I mention it to you? This is something we tried last year and we're gonna do it again. Just the top people, the weekend after Labor Day. This is the new hot thing in the corporate culture. Your friend Edgar is a big believer. He got me into it. And he recommended this place in Vermont. Green Mountain? You know it?"

"I'm afraid I don't know it. Or anything about something called a retreat."

"Retreat makes it sound grim. Really we just go to a resort, no families, have bull sessions in the A.M., let people sound off, play a little golf and tennis in the afternoon and kick back in the evenings. I don't normally include the techies, but I'm considering inviting Andy. Maybe Timmy also. Or is he too weird? Take a look at the brochure. This place has so-called session leaders to get us to open up. But I have an idea and I sounded out Edgar about it. He agrees with me that it would be better if you led our morning meetings. What Green Mountain offers sounds like low-rent group therapy and I can't believe they've got anybody as qualified as you. Also, take a look at the tentative list of invitees. Let me know what you think. Whoops," he said, "gotta call coming in from my man in Paris—" That would be Didier Lahost, the head of his recently acquired French division.

"One other thing," I called desperately into the pay phone. I didn't continue immediately. I was distracted by the thought that I might be in the same phone booth Gene had used to call me toward the end of his therapy, during those months that he was too busy to see me because of the Black Dragon deadline. Gene claimed calling from his office was dangerous, that he needed to keep his therapy a secret. I remembered what I used to think of his caution: a neurotic's shame disguised as a paranoia; a self-absorbed man suffering from grandiosity, elevating his banal problems into a state secret. No, this wasn't the same phone booth, I concluded, remembering that Gene had told me he called from the International House of Pancakes a mile from the labs so he could pretend he was there for a quick lunch if someone spotted him. I remembered because I wondered who would eat pancakes for lunch.

"Well?" Stick roused me from my long pause. "What is it? I've gotta catch Didier before he goes to sleep. It's almost eleven in Paris."

"Your wife. What we discussed briefly at the barbecue? I want to see her and gently recommend she do something about her drinking. I could escort her to an AA meeting. Or perhaps—is she religious at all? Her priest might suggest it."

The phone was dead. He'd hung up.

"Stick?" I cried out. He couldn't be this cold. He couldn't want my services for the sole purpose of manipulating employees.

"Yes?" He was there after all.

"I mean, even if only for Mary Catharine's physical health, something should be done. At her age, if she continues at this rate, she won't live much longer."

No sound. No background noise. No breathing. No faint whoosh. Where was he? Had he hit the mute button? Was he typing messages to Laura?

"Stick?" I called again.

"That's not your area," he said. "I know it's a little confusing, because of Halley and all that. But your relationship with Halley is personal."

"I don't have a relationship—"

He talked over me, "That's your business. As I told you, I don't believe psychiatry can help everybody—"

I interrupted, "I'm not proposing psychiatry. AA isn't—"

"It's not your area, Rafe. You do respect my privacy, don't you?"

"Yes. Of course. I'm trying—"

"I don't think it's fair to use your position to intrude on family matters. Not quite ethical, is it?"

"I'm speaking as a friend."

"Don't bullshit me, Rafe. We're not friends," he said, his tone stern and grim. Then he chuckled. "We may be great tennis partners, but we're not friends. See you on the court Thursday."

It was hot in the phone booth. Outside, the temperature was nearing a hundred and the humid air not only seemed visible, it felt chewable. Sweat streamed from my forehead. In Tampa, Francisco used to say to me, "That's our peasant Gallego blood. Our brains boil and makes our heads soft."

There were no papers or notes I had left at Minotaur that I would need. I walked to my car, reflecting I could return to Baltimore, ask the institute to say I was away if anyone phoned, and essentially disappear from Stick and Halley.

Want to run away? I asked myself.

Time to see Susan and talk it over, I answered. By the time I reached Greenwich Village she should be finished with her last session of the day.

Driving to the city, I exited at Riverdale without making a conscious decision. I'll just drive by, I explained it to myself. But I braked to a full stop at the entrance to my former clinic. Two vans were parked, one from the Bronx shelter, the other from Yonkers. The Yonkers driver, Walter, was looking under the hood of his vehicle. The hedges around the dormitory addition needed to be trimmed. I drove into the lot.

At the sound of my car door shutting, Walter looked up. I entered too quickly for him to react. Inside the clinic, on the left, Group B's door was open. I heard the trill of a boy giggling. Downstairs in the basement, the kitchen should be preparing dinner for the resident patients. I sniffed. Nothing. I was disappointed. I would have liked nothing better than to eat with everybody. It was a hot day. Maybe they were planning a barbecue in the backyard. Sometimes, after having ice cream or watermelon for dessert, they would play volleyball until the late summer sun went down. The kids always insisted Diane and I stay for the game.

I walked into the reception area, Sally's station, guarding the private offices. I greeted Sally with a question, "Is Diane free for a . . ."

I didn't finish the sentence. Sally scooted out from behind her desk and hugged me. Someone else patted me on the back—that turned out to be Gregory, one of the live-in counselors.

I tried to say I was just dropping in, but by then, an eleven-year-old girl whom I had treated peeked in and said, "Dr. Rafe's back!" She called into the hallway and soon three more children I used to treat appeared, smiling, saying things I couldn't really hear . . .

I sat down on a metal chair by the wall, leaned forward, hands covering my face, and cried. Sally seemed more astonished about that than by my sudden appearance. "Shh," she said to the others, shooing them away. "Give him time," she whispered. Her hand landed on my shoulder. "What's wrong? Are you okay?"

"Diane. I want to see—" I said and choked on my tears. I rubbed my eyes, feeling foolish. I breathed deeply, trying to calm down. My right hand was trembling. A cold inner voice told me: you're hysterical.

When Diane came in, from somewhere else, not her office, I was still sniffling, looking silly I'm sure. I was amazed by her appearance. She had straightened and dyed her hair a dull red color. She was also very thin, her face pinched. And something else was different, something I couldn't identify.

"What's the matter?" she said, meaning, I think, to sound concerned. Her general anger at me, however, lent it a scolding tone.

"Will you do me a favor?" I asked. My voice broke, my eyes watered. I stopped talking in order to gain control.

Sally, hanging in the background, whispered, "Should I leave?"

"Come to my office," Diane said, still sounding irritated, although she tugged at my arm gently.

Ashamed, I kept a hand shielding my eyes while I allowed her to tow me. She parked me in front of a new couch and shut the door. I stood, staring at the fabric. Was the couch new or had she merely re-covered it? I looked around and noticed that the room had been rearranged, the desk reoriented from between the windows to float in the center.

"Sit," she said. I didn't move. "Come on," she said. "You're scaring the shit out of me." I sat. She pulled an armchair, also new, over from near her desk so she would be only a foot away. She sat forward, leaning her elbows on her knees. "If you're in trouble, I'm sorry, but I really don't want to see you. I'm not over it, okay? And I don't want to start up again." Suddenly, her eyes brimmed with tears. "I'm just not made that way. I can take a lot but once I'm gone, I'm gone. You know what I'm saying? I don't care if you're sorry. You know, you were wrong. I'm nailing that motherfucker. His research was shit. Even he's admitting that the Stanford group's replication of his crappy study was kosher."

She was babbling as far as I was concerned. "Stanford?" I mumbled.

"Yes! Haven't you seen the Stanford data? They replicated Samuel and showed the kids are influenced at less than thirty percent—"

"Diane, stop—"

"No, I can't stop. That's why I don't want to see you, because I know I can't stop. These last four months have been like death. I really feel— I mean really feel—like you stepped on my heart. I know, I know. In two years I'll be laughing about you. But I won't take the chance of you hurting me again. Fuck love." She brushed away a flip of hair that wasn't there. Her new style was straight back. She sighed. "I'm sorry. Okay," she sighed. "What do you want?"

"What is that color?" I asked.

"What color?"

"Your hair? That's not a real color."

For a moment she stared. "Get the fuck out of here," she said and stood up.

I keened, head in my hands, and begged, "Don't do this to me, please." I was blubbering again. "Just let me talk. You're my colleague, you're my friend, you're the only one—" I breathed fast to stop the tears and then took one sustained inhalation to make more words, "You're the only one I can talk this out with. Okay? Susan can't help me—she's, she's . . ."

"Second-rate?" Diane said. "When did you find that out?" I looked up, wiping my eyes. Diane had sat down again, only sideways, her legs over the armrest. She muttered to the window, "Listen to me. Now I'm pissed off at poor Susan. She did her best with you. You're just a hard case. A hard-ass motherfucker who has the gall to come in here and cry." She turned to me. "Where do you get off crying?"

"You won't help me," I said.

She swung her legs to the floor and slapped her newly skinny thigh. "Help you with what!"

"I've met two people who are sick." I took a breath, relaxing a little as I began my report. Talking would help. "One of them is at ease only if he's putting people under stress. He promises rewards for loyalty and sacrifice, finds a weakness, and when the person is no longer useful, even if they're not a real threat, he hurts them as badly as he can. He tries to break anyone he can unless they're totally passive—"

Diane, nodding wearily as if she were bored, interrupted, "It's called sadism. What is this? A quiz?"

"Right. He's a sadist. A psychological sadist. Nothing overt. Nothing illegal. He's not a crude torturer—he doesn't use his fists, or his cock, or a belt. Every family member has been affected. His son was goaded into a thinly disguised suicide. His wife is alcoholic. His daughter is—"

Diane interrupted, "A sexless, passive—"

I stopped her. "No."

"Okay, she's a prostitute. She's a drug addict who fucks abusive men. Do I get the dishwasher and the trip to Hawaii?"

"No. She's a narcissist. She's strong. She has great inner strength. So she found a defense against him by murdering her real self before he could. She's become a heartless mirage. She transforms herself into a dream figure for every man she encounters who seems worth the trouble to have them fall in love with her. She wins them like trophies and presents them to Daddy in a bizarre symbolic act of incest."

Diane smirked. "Was she foolish enough to go after you?"

I nodded. "She even bothered to pretend to have bought my book on incest and read it years ago—"

"Is that an assumption? Your book was a bestseller."

"Not an assumption. I fell for it at first. But later, I had a moment alone to check. On the back page I saw the remnant of a new sticker from a second-hand bookstore."

"Which one?"

"The Strand."

"Kind of ironic, no?"

"Ironic?" I asked.

"We used to go there. Remember, Rafe? On Sundays we'd have bagels in bed and walk in the Village?" Diane turned her head and frowned at the door. "So how was she? A true narcissist should be a great lover—at least in the beginning. Totally devoted to your pleasure, huh? Must have been the blowjob of your life."

I didn't answer. I couldn't admit what I had done, that I had played an unscrupulous trick to confirm my diagnosis. Diane, of all people, would have had reason to be appalled.

"That good, eh?" Diane got up, walked to her desk, and opened a drawer. "Okay, here's your moment of triumph." She came out with a pack of Camel Lights, removing one and lighting it. "Yes, you've got me smoking again. You not only broke my heart, you've got my lungs." She took a long drag. "The worst thing is, you can't smoke anywhere in this fucking self-righteous world. Every asshole on earth thinks they have the right to live forever." She exhaled a foul cloud toward me. "God. I had an interview with Lisa Dorfman's father—a court-ordered interview to determine if he was rehabilitated enough to have visitation. Remember what he did to her? Fucked her up the ass in front of her baby sister and then put her in a tub of scalding water? So I light up a cigarette and Mr. Dorfman asks me to put it out. Second-hand smoke is dangerous, he says, I'm putting his health at risk. I should have put it out in his eye." She took another drag, lids shutting halfway with pleasure. "What do you want?" she asked and exhaled another cloud.

"They're happy."

"Who's happy? Oh. You mean the sadist and the narcissist? You know that would make a good name for a heavy metal group." She picked up a square glass ashtray, returned to the chair, and balanced the ashtray on her knee. She tapped it with her cigarette. "They're happy? What do you mean—happy?"

"I mean, they have all the symptoms of their diseases, except one. They're not unhappy. They function well. They don't mind the emptiness of their emotional lives. They see everyone else as weak. They are content. They are in homeostasis."

"God bless us, every one," Diane said, taking another drag. She squinted at the window, chin up, and blew out a long thin stream. "So? Mazel tov, they're happy. Who are they, anyway? How do you know them?"

"The narcissist is Halley."

Diane shook her head, bewildered. "Halley?"

"My former patient, Gene Kenny? She's the woman he left his wife for. And the sadist, her father, was his boss."

"*Was* his boss?"

"You don't know," I said, realizing my mistake. "It was after we split up."

"Split up? Is that how you think of it? Jesus Christ. That's a masterpiece of understatement." She pressed her cigarette out. "Wait a minute." She twisted and tried to slide the ashtray onto her desk. "What the hell—" she couldn't reach, so she stood up to put it there while talking, "—are you doing? Making contact with a patient's—?"

"He's dead," I said. "He killed his wife and committed suicide two months ago."

Diane sat on the edge of her desk. She gaped at me. "No."

"Halley dumped him. Copley, her father, fired him two weeks later. His wife was threatening to move out of state with their son. He had no job and lost their one asset, the house. Well, Gene didn't know the house was gone. I'm not sure exactly what happened, but . . ." I waved a hand in disgust. "That's bullshit. I know exactly what happened. Copley and Halley had decided Gene was getting too big for his britches. He was asking for a piece of the company and he had the loyalty of the whole creative team. They had a new kid genius Copley thought could replace him. Between the two of them, they knew Gene's situation, they knew how to make it as bad as possible, because just beating him down wasn't enough. What if he went to a competitor? Although, that wasn't it. What they did wasn't practical—that wasn't the real reason. What they did had the vicious irrationality of madness." I was talking to myself, I realized. I tried to focus on Diane's blank, still-amazed face. "That night, the night he murdered Cathy and killed himself, that was the night Gene realized how much they wanted to hurt him. Cathy confronted him with a letter calling in the loan on the house, exposing the fact that he'd been fired, that he had no way of stopping her from moving, and that he couldn't meet the next support payments. In a flash he understood Halley was in a league with her father, he understood that for years his life had been an elaborate con game, that he had thrown away his marriage, his child, and his career for nothing. He was a fool as far as they were concerned, a ridiculous man. All his life he had lived in fear of making demands and I pushed him past that fear. I cured him." I laughed bitterly. Diane was staring at the carpet, kneading an eyebrow. "I told him if he asserted himself with his boss, he'd be rewarded for his years of service. I told him his fears that Halley didn't love him were neurotic. I not only sent him into a battle he wasn't fit for, worst of all, I stripped away his one puny defense, his tortoise shell. He was safe. Don't you see? Diane, are you listening?" She looked up. "He wasn't getting what he was worth at the company because he knew, instinctively, that kept him safe. He didn't allow himself to fall in love with a beautiful, self-assured woman like Halley because he knew he couldn't survive her rejection. He didn't defy his wife because he knew he couldn't survive her anger. He was miserable, sure. He was being taken advantage of, sure. But he was safe."

Diane pushed off from her desk. She returned to the chair, pulled her legs under her, and sat on her haunches. "It didn't make sense to you, so you arranged to meet them, is that what happened?"

"You're wearing contacts," I said. "That's why you look so different."

"Yes! Yes, you got it. I'm on the prowl. I want everything to be different. I don't want anything to remind me of you. Not even when I look in the mirror."

"I'm sorry."

"Yeah, yeah, you're real sorry. What do you want me to say? That you're responsible for Gene's suicide? That you shouldn't cure neurotics because maybe their illness protects them?"

"Yes. Say that, if that's what you think it means."

"Jesus," Diane whispered to herself. "This is your insane perfectionism. Your God-complex."

"Are you saying you don't think what I've discovered is true? Copley and his daughter are mentally ill. If you believe the DSM III, if you believe everybody from Jesus to Freud to Phil Donahue, these people are sick. They should be miserable, they should be—"

Diane kicked out her legs and stood up. "They're mean. That's all. They're shitty people. Deal with it. Grow up." She waved at the door. "Go!" I didn't move. She stamped her foot. "I can't believe you came here to talk to me about this crap! That can't be why you're here. I don't think this is my vanity talking. You can't be here to talk about these creeps."

"Diane! Goddamnit! Listen to me!" She backed away, startled. Had I yelled that loudly? *I* was on my feet, I realized, and I was advancing on her. I swallowed, took a breath and also stepped away from her. I made an effort to speak calmly. "You have a first-rate mind. Use it. Reach for something bigger than just mechanistic technique." She breathed through her nostrils, her arms crossed protectively; but her eyes were waiting, prepared to listen. So I continued, "We divide the world into two groups—the well-adjusted and the dysfunctional. These people aren't serial killers. They're not sociopaths. On the contrary, they honor society and society honors them. They are well-adjusted but they have none of the healthy relationships that all the theorists maintain are the basis of being well-adjusted. No real love to sustain them, no true intimacy. And yet they function. They function at a high level. What do we call their psychological condition? We don't have a category for it."

Diane's shoulders slumped. Her arms uncrossed and drooped. She shut her eyes. "Sure we do."

"We do?" I was encouraged. Her tired voice meant she was taking me seriously.

Diane leaned against her desk and rubbed her eyes.

I whispered, "Are you going to tell me?"

She uncovered her eyes. They were red and she looked at me hopelessly. Despite the forceful words, her voice was enervated. "I'll tell you, if you promise you won't debate it. That after you hear what I think, whether you agree or not, you'll get the fuck out of my office, you'll get the fuck out of my clinic, and you'll get the fuck out of my life."

So that was the price. I didn't understand her equation. And I didn't care, as long as I got to hear its sum. "I promise."

"This is really what I think. Ph.D. and all."

"Okay." I felt profoundly relieved. No matter what she said, I would have something, something I could take with me. Something to discard or accept—that didn't matter—I would have something to anchor me again to the world.

Diane said, "We've had a word for it from the beginning of human history. What you're describing—these self-serving, heartless, destructive and perfectly respectable people—they're evil. And there's not a goddamn thing we can do about them."

CHAPTER TEN

The Banality of Evil

STICK PROVIDED THE ANSWER. I DISAPPEARED FROM MINOTAUR FOR three days, leaving a message with Laura that I couldn't make the tennis date, offering no explanation. I retreated to Baltimore. From there, I checked on Pete Kenny, who, according to David Cox, the child psychologist in Arizona, was doing better than expected.

"Perhaps he's strong," I said.

"Well, I guess that's part of it . . ." Cox reacted to my comment doubtfully. "He's getting a lot out of the sessions. He's articulate about his feelings, about how much he misses his Mommy and Daddy. Also, his grandmother is very loving. Not smart, but loving."

"He needs inner strength," I insisted. "He needs your help, of course, and he's fortunate his grandmother is doing her job, but, in the end, unless he's strong that won't be enough." I told him I would pay Pete's bills even if he doubled him to four sessions a week and that he should continue to tell Grandma the therapy was free.

For three days I focused on the new problem Diane's remark had defined for me. She had used the word evil as a form of surrender: less a description than a pejorative; not a diagnosis, but a despairing judgment. She had been clever and helpful in not applying it to the obviously ill or sociopathic: serial killers, rapists, child abusers. She had been right to reserve evil for Stick and Halley, my sane, respectable and thoroughly legal twosome, as opposed to everybody's favorite target for the appellation: monster tyrants of history. Hitler and Stalin are the prime examples of our century, although humanity has provided a constant supply, and our century has many more than merely that dynamic duo. But Hitler and Stalin, from all reports, were profoundly unhappy men. Only a willfully blind psychiatrist would declare them to have lived in homeostasis. There is a simple measurement that can be taken: Hitler and Stalin were less content and more paranoid as their power grew. Their appetites increased by what they fed on, craving more enemies and more killings to maintain the same level of comfort, rejecting opportunity after opportunity to preserve themselves and their power, destroying not only those who opposed them, but those who longed to help them. They were obviously ill. The question is, what do we call the hundreds, indeed hundreds of thousands of people, who obeyed fervently and worked passionately to help them? The Silent Majority? The Good Germans? Stalinists? Conformists? I don't mean concentration camp guards or Bebe Rebozo. I don't mean those who did wrong and looked the other way for the base purpose of gain or survival. I mean those who were happy to live in an unjust world, who function as well under Hitler as they do under Bill Clinton.

The presence of harmful function without anxiety or disorder, without stress on personality or mood—to call that psychological condition evil is not merely a judgment. It is a clear description and supplies the missing piece to a puzzle of psychology. Many practitioners have noted that it isn't unusual for a patient to emerge from therapy as a less likable person. That's a hint there *is* such a thing as too successful an adaptation to emotional conflict. Freud's essential view of human beings (and this, more than anything, is what provokes so much hostility to him) is that we are savage animals who require at least sublimation, if not repression, to prevent our unconscious desires from having sway. In his view, social adaptation restrains us from our true desires: to rip food from the mouths of our starving companions, to rape our neighbors' wives, to kill our fathers, to worship the moon with blood on our fangs, to live for the satiation of our animal appetites, relishing the moment-to-moment satisfaction of our mouths and genitalia. Sometimes the bondage of these unacceptable instincts causes neurotic conflict (and supplies Woody Allen with comedy): the wish to sleep with your mother appearing as a fear of elevators; the longing to eat your father's flesh surfacing as a horror of clams on the half-shell. Freud's many reinterpreters adopted a less harsh understanding of human nature, allowing for kinder and more altruistic ids. But they still posit emotional conflict as the cause of psychological dysfunction.

That view of humanity is supposed to catch everyone, from Gene Kenny to Adolf Hitler, in the net of psychology. Not Stick and Halley Copley, however. They don't appear on our radar because we don't recognize their outline. They are not in conflict. The equation is one-sided: they don't need love and victory, only victory; they don't need peace and pleasure, only pleasure. Truly, this makes labeling them evil a definition, not a swear word to vent our disapproval.

But how to treat them? They would not volunteer and society does not see them as ill. Indeed, their absence of conflict, their freedom from neurosis, makes them attractive, drawing nervous moths to immolation in their brilliant fire.

Frankly, I was stuck. I became desperate enough by the third day that, while idly going over the new chapters prepared by Amy Glickstein on Joseph's experimental neuroleptic drugs, I considered spiking Halley's Evian or Copley's herbal tea (he had recently given up caffeine) with a psychotropic. Perhaps an antidepressant would heighten their unnaturally low levels of anxiety. Perhaps drugging this natural Prozac pair with Prozac would push their legal acts of self-preservation into a murderous mania. Unfortunately, then I would be a poisoner, not a healer. I wouldn't have proved they suffered from a psychological condition susceptible to cure, any more than I believed Joseph had cured depression by chemical manipulation.

Edgar Levin broke through the barricade of the Prager Institute's switchboard and also my reverie. I hadn't included him on the list of those to be told I wasn't there. I could have declined the call anyway, but I was curious.

"Well, Rafe," Edgar said to my hello. "I've got to hand it to you. I didn't think anybody could make Stick Copley nervous and confused but you've done it."

"And how have I managed this miracle?"

"Apparently he doesn't know where the hell you are or why you've disappeared. I called him this morning to find out if you'd agreed to manage his retreat sessions. First he tried to fake it, but when I asked him to transfer me to you, out came the truth. So I called my brother in Hollywood and he called your cousin Julie to get your number."

"Julie knew my number?"

"Yeah. Is that a surprise? So what's the story? You got the info you wanted for your book and you're outta there?"

"Just taking a break."

"Do me a favor, okay? Either in or out. This is a businessman you're dealing with. They think a yes is yes and a no is no. Subtlety's not their strong point. He's got to know if he can rely on you."

"I see." I lapsed into thought.

It must have been a long pause, because Edgar laughed and said, "Hey, Rafe! I'm a busy man. I'm the biggest boy on my block. You can't keep me waiting on the phone. The American economy will collapse."

"Whose idea was it, Edgar?"

"Idea?"

"I'm sorry. I mean, to ask me to lead this fall retreat thing? You or Stick?"

"I like the retreats. I like an intimate management team. Happy families and all that. But, and this is one of the reasons I think Stick is a good manager, the encounter group leaders at these places are pathetic. Stick thought you might come up with better techniques. If you do, I'll package you on a video, and we'll make infomercials. My brother can produce it—*Dr. Neruda's Five Keys to Success.*"

I was baffled. "Infomercial?" I asked.

Edgar chuckled. "Don't worry. I was kidding. Are you having second thoughts about spending so much time in corporate land?"

"Something like that."

"Come up to New York tomorrow. Stick invited me to lunch with the head of our new European division. You should join us."

"Didier Lahost?"

"Yeah, some name like that. A French businessman. What a nightmare. I'm going to be bored out of my mind. Come along and entertain me. It'll give you time to think and you can tell Stick your decision face-to-face."

"I don't want to crash a meeting."

"Ain't no meeting, just a how-do-you-do. The food'll be good anyway. We're eating at the Carnegie Deli. I love taking Frogs to eat Jew food."

"There *are* delis in Paris," I said.

"What do you want to bet Monsieur Lahost has never darkened their door?"

Another look at Copley wouldn't hurt, I decided. I told Edgar to expect me and then dialed Stick. While I did, I wondered why Julie had my number. Perhaps her mother was worse; she had a mild stroke six months ago. I should call her and perhaps visit my cousins in Great Neck. I hadn't seen them since Sadie's funeral three years ago. This isolation from the world was silly—I was no superman. I needed my family.

"Well hello, stranger," Laura returned my greeting with a happy note of welcome. "We've been trying to find you. Hold on."

Stick's stern voice was there immediately. "Where are you?"

"Don't take that tone with me," I said. "I'm not your employee. I don't have to account to you for my whereabouts and my time." I was surprised by my anger and momentarily ashamed. But why hold anything back? This man wasn't my patient.

For a moment there was nothing but that weird absolute silence—not a hint of electronic contact. Then, very softly, Stick said, "I *am* paying you to be a consultant."

"Every penny has gone back into Minotaur. I can show you the receipts. I bought furniture and plants so your labs wouldn't resemble an unfinished basement."

He stayed in a low key. "You've done a fine job. Centaur's testing fifty percent faster than our competition. Jack's looking more relaxed, too. Said to me this morning he was bringing the family along when he makes his West Coast swing."

"How was your doubles game?"

"I canceled it. What about this Saturday? We could play at my country club."

"I'll tell you tomorrow. Edgar invited me to your lunch at the Carnegie Deli."

Another silence. I waited. Finally Stick said in a normal volume, "Good. I'd like to know your opinion of Didier."

"Okay. Also, I haven't decided if I want to stay on long enough to lead your retreat sessions. I'll let you know about that tomorrow."

Stick remained in neutral. "I need to know one way or the other," he said coolly. "To make plans." I said nothing. He waited until the silence was uncomfortable and continued, "Would you consider a full-time position with a meaningful salary, say . . . one hundred K?"

"No," I answered immediately. "Our financial arrangement is satisfactory. I'll let you go, Stick. It's time for your daily swim."

"What? Oh." He sounded enervated. "No, I've changed my exercise program. I'm doing machines now."

For a moment, I had no words. Was he teasing me? Worried he was playing a game, I asked sheepishly, "You've dropped the two-mile swim?"

"Yeah . . ." His voice was weary and sad.

I didn't draw a breath. I couldn't believe it was happening. I was almost frightened to ask—what if his gym was having trouble with the pool filter? "Why?"

"Too boring. And it's not challenging enough. I'd have to swim longer to get the same benefit I can in half the time on the machines. I thought we discussed this. I thought I told you I was giving it up."

"Probably you did. Okay, Stick. See you tomorrow." A chill actually ran down my back. I shook my shoulders to be rid of it. I considered whether he could be this clever. No. There was no way he could know what it meant to me.

In the tradition of listening to the patient for answers, Copley had provided the solution to the problem of his condition: our conversation about his father had had an effect. Three days before, I had gently suggested the association in his office. I commented after Stick's story of being thrown in the pond that he must enjoy his daily swim. At the time I hardly thought the remark was subtle. Surely Stick didn't need me to explicate that the reason he relished swimming briskly for two miles was its reminder of triumph over his sadistic father. His conscious mind had missed my point, but not his subconscious. What once was an enjoyable reenactment had become predictable, its emotional power sapped by awareness. The effect was similar to traditional therapy's—only in reverse. Neurotic patterns can be broken by bringing the original motivation to the surface. Copley's swim had lost its pleasure by awakening that frightened little boy: it no longer made him feel strong. An effective adaptation had been spoiled by self-knowledge.

I wasn't sure, of course. Perhaps it was a coincidence. Perhaps it wouldn't work with behavior driven by less painful memories. Another question: was the subtlety important? Confronting Stick's and Halley's psyches with open analysis seemed to have failed miserably, but had it softened him up for the penetration of my quieter observation? Also, why did Stick think he had already told me he was giving up his daily swim? Had he been talking to me in his head? That would be an indication of transference. I noted that my mean tone, my angry reaction to being questioned, seemed to cow him. Could I effect a transference of his sadistic relationship with his father to me and replay his childhood so that he emerged as a neurotic? If I interfered with his successful adaptation to the pain of childhood, could I create conflict where now there was none?

A few hours later, when I decided to drive to the city, I was excited. Why not? If talking therapy can make an ineffective neurotic into a functioning well-adjusted person, shouldn't it also work in reverse?

I phoned Mary Catharine. After I reminded her of who I was, we had a long talk. Although she seemed to have no memory of our conversation in her bedroom, she was far enough along in her drinking day—this was just after lunch—to be easily drawn into reminiscences of Halley's childhood.

I searched for the book she told me about at the mall next to the institute, bought a copy, and went to the supermarket—where I found only half of what I needed to complete the treatment. I was unable to find an important aid for Halley's sense memory. To my surprise, I discovered from the assistant manager that the manufacturer doesn't sell it during the summer. I decided to take a chance on the slow-moving inventories of New York's delis.

I departed for the city. I arrived late, almost ten o'clock, thanks to a violent summer thunderstorm. The decaying West Side Highway became a black river and the street's potholes were muddy ponds. I crawled for an hour and a half from the George Washington Bridge to Central Park West in the seventies, a distance of five or six miles. There were no parking spaces so I used the garage opposite my sublet. The driving rain had stopped. At last, I felt smart again—sure enough, I found one box of what I needed in an all-night Korean grocery store. I walked the block to her apartment building. I announced myself to the same doorman who had assured us the cherry bombers were going to lose fingers.

He told Halley my name, said, "Hold on," and offered me the intercom, explaining, "She wants to talk to you." Its receiver was no different than an old-fashioned phone's.

"Rafe?" Halley's voice crackled as they always do on intercoms—as if coming over a shortwave radio.

"Yes."

"What's . . . ? You're here to see me?"

"I'm here to tuck you in," I said and winked at the doorman. He smiled slyly, then looked away, as if he shouldn't be listening, even if I didn't mind. "I have Malomars," I said.

She came in loud. "What?"

"Ma-lo-mars," I said slowly. "I have Malomars and hot chocolate."

That got me a puzzled look from the doorman. The storm hadn't cooled things off. The reverse, in fact. The city air was as thick as steam—the sidewalks seemed to be boiling the rain.

She was at her door when I came out of the elevator, hair wet, dressed in a large white men's T-shirt that reached her knees. She watched my approach with her head tilted, black eyes wide and unafraid. I pulled the box of Malomars out from the grocery bag. "Good," I said, handing them to her. "You've had your bath."

She took the yellow box in both hands, staring at it as if it couldn't be real. With her head down, she was no taller than my stomach. Cradling the bag in my left arm, I ran my right hand over the top of her damp hair, gathering it. I tugged gently. "Put this in a ponytail," I said.

She raised her eyes. They narrowed. She stepped back, breaking my hold, the door opening wider, yet still blocking the way. She asked, "Is this game for you or for me?"

I reached into the bag and showed her a box of Nestle's mix. "Hot chocolate, Malomars, and a bedtime story. You know how I like to read bedtime stories," I said.

She stamped her foot. "Just tell me!" Annoyed at herself for that display, she shut her eyes, took a breath through her nostrils—their flare was quite pretty—and said softly, "I don't care. I just want to know."

I let the Nestle's box slip back into the bag, stepped into the doorway and looked down at her. "I love you," I said. And then a whisper, "This is for me."

I heated the milk in a pot on the stove, shunning the microwave, noisily stirring the sides with a metal spoon. I hadn't covered this point with her mother; that was how I remember Grandma Jacinta made hot chocolate. I would listen from the next room to the slow scrape of metal on metal and anticipate the sweet taste. There wasn't a brown mug like the one Mary Catharine had described, but the white mugs Halley owned were large and would feel heavy in her hands. I put four Malomars on a plate, poured the hot chocolate, and brought the drink and cookies to her bedroom. On the way, I got the book I had brought from my raincoat.

Halley, her hair braided into a tail that draped down her right shoulder, was propped up by two pillows in bed, clutching a small stuffed white bear.

She sipped the hot chocolate and said, "Mmmmm." She took a bite of a Malomar.

"Don't you want to dip it?" I asked.

"It'll be messy."

"You've been a good girl. You can dip." I opened the book, *Goodnight Moon*, holding it in my left hand, and began: "In the great green room, there was a telephone, and a red balloon." She dunked half the Malomar, spread her lips over the melting chocolate shell and sucked at the gooey interior. I slid my right hand under the covers and ran the tips of my fingers up her thigh.

I left an hour later. The procedure took ninety minutes. Double a normal therapy session, but I had been slowed down by her initial resistance, and this was, after all, our first one.

She complained that I didn't allow her to touch me. In the early throes of orgasm, she asked to see my penis—using a child's words, of course: "Can I see your thing?" I said no, that she was dirty.

As she climaxed, when I leaned over to whisper in her ear, she yelled, "Don't say it!" I assume she meant my blunder during the bath adventure of reminding her that Gene died for her—although the bath scene had a different goal than my new one and therefore I can't say it was a blunder. This time, as her belly undulated against my arm, I whispered, "You're a good girl," over and over until she was finished.

After I left her room, she called for me plaintively three times. Waiting in her foyer, ready to hurry out if I heard her leave the bed, I didn't hear (nor did I expect to so early in the treatment) the tears, the sobs of abandonment, that I believed would mean we had achieved a breakthrough.

The next day, I arrived late at the Carnegie Deli. There was a line spilling out the door waiting for tables. I didn't see Edgar or Stick so I joined its end. A short man in an expensive three-piece came up to me. "Dr. Neruda?" I nodded. "Mr. Levin's waiting for you inside. Follow me."

He led me through a narrow path between jammed tables, and around waiters carrying plates of towering sandwiches above their heads. A pastrami and corned beef came within an inch of my nose. "You're too tall," the pale, sweating waiter told me. "Sit down already."

Edgar, Stick, and Didier Lahost had been seated in the closest thing to a private table, all the way in the left rear corner, against two mirrored walls and with no one to the right because of the kitchen door. Even so, we were crowded in, bumped repeatedly, and of course the noise was deafening.

"Edgar, this is a ridiculous place to get acquainted with someone. Hello, Monsieur," I added to Didier, and began an imitation of my father, a model for me of how to be charming. I was, at once, curious about the stranger, teasing toward the powerful presence of Edgar and apparently intimate about my life. I treated Stick as if he were my child, talking about him in the third person, sometimes answering for him. I asked Didier if his name was Alsatian. They hadn't bothered to inquire about his history and he was glad to tell it. When he mentioned that his mother was Spanish, he and I were off. She turned out to be an Asturian, the neighboring province to my grandfather's, Galicia, and the birthplace of my Uncle Pancho. I told the story of Francisco abducting me from Uncle Bernie—delighting Edgar, naturally, since this now encompassed Great Neck gossip. I was very lucky in the coincidence of a Spanish connection with Didier. That made it easier to isolate Stick, dimming his light before Edgar, and exacerbating his mild paranoia (a presenting symptom of sadism) into a frenzy.

Our cheerful conversation lasted for more than two hours, past three o'clock, when the popular Carnegie emptied out considerably and we could lower our voices. Edgar used a cellular phone to cancel a meeting, saying he was having too good a time listening to me spill the beans about Bernie.

"I hope the meeting wasn't important, Edgar," I said. "Buying the Empire State Building?"

"Just the West Side," he said. "Listen, Didier, what about Spain? Shouldn't we move into that market?"

"Well, we do have . . . That is, earlier, you know, the old company, had pretty good sales there," Didier said.

"Didier," Edgar said. "You should have Rafe come over to Paris and consult. Stick can tell you how helpful he's been to him."

"Yes?" Didier said, looking at Stick.

"Oh yeah," Stick had to clear his throat. He hadn't gotten a word in for over an hour. "Terrific."

"You're a psychiatrist?" Didier asked me doubtfully.

Edgar nudged him with an elbow. Didier was startled. "He's figured out how to make those misfits in the labs happy. What's up, anyway, Rafe? You bored with us? Stick wants you to work full-time. You done with your research? Lost interest in us greedy capitalists?"

I smiled at Edgar and then glanced at Stick. I searched for nervousness. His stern gaunt face showed nothing, merely a steady watchful gaze. He's dangerous, I thought. He's a different breed than Halley. In the final analysis, her narcissism was a defense against an unloving father; his sadism was a counterattack.

"If you are a capitalist," Didier asked me, "you should be greedy, no?"

"Absolutely," I said. "Anything else would be neurotic."

"Now there's a book for you to write," Edgar said to me. "For a while there in the eighties, greed was developing a good reputation. But what we need is a first-rate psychological defense of greed."

"History's on your side, Edgar," I said. "Don't worry."

"So what's the verdict, Rafe?" Edgar insisted, his eyes straying to Stick. "Are you going to continue consulting for us?"

"He's consulting for me," Stick said softly. "It was my idea." He stared at Edgar.

Good for you, I thought. You're not really scared of the great Edgar Levin. You're using him, and if you're given the chance, you'll beat him too.

"I'm glad we had this lunch," I said, interrupting their staring contest. "Before I decide whether to stay on and lead the fall retreat, I'd like you, Edgar, to answer a question as carefully and precisely as you can."

He whistled. "Wow. This sounds good. What is it?"

"You've made a big bet on Stick's management abilities, is that right?"

"Medium-sized bet."

"Congratulations, Edgar."

"On making money? That doesn't sound like you, Rafe."

"Congratulations on the scale of your world. Here's my question. What if—remember, this is hypothetical—what if I told you that I believed Minotaur could run just as well, perhaps better, without Stick?" Didier, who was facing me, opened his eyes very wide. I didn't check on Stick's reaction. I smiled pleasantly at Edgar and continued, "That he isn't responsible for creating their products or how they are marketed?"

Edgar tried to lean back. He bumped his bald spot against the mirrored wall. The breezy blustering rich boy was gone. He frowned at me with the disgust of a commander-in-chief confronted by a deserter. "That's your question?"

"Assuming you believed me, what would you do?"

"I don't run Minotaur," Edgar said, winking at Stick. "I'm just an investor."

"If you could," I insisted. "Are you scared of answering truthful—?"

Edgar cut that off. "Nothing," he said grimly.

"Take your time, Edgar."

"I don't need time. If it ain't broke, don't fix it. Just because I don't need a man, you think I should fire him? Jesus, you haven't fallen for this downsizing crap, have you? If you fired every American who isn't obviously necessary half the country would be unemployed."

"I don't believe you. You're not taking my question seriously. Let me ask it another way. Granting my premise—entirely hypothetical of course—that Stick doesn't contribute to how Minotaur's products are made or sold, what use is he?"

Edgar laughed. "Maybe you should withdraw your offer, Stick."

At my elbow I heard Copley's low tones, barely above a mumble, "It's an interesting question. I don't mind him asking."

Didier shook his head. "This is strange," he commented.

"Well, Edgar? You promised an answer."

"You're right. Let's see . . . He is useful . . ." he paused, thinking, and then came out with an answer as if it had just occurred to him, "because he's greedy."

"No joking, Edgar."

"I'm not joking. As you would say, he's all id. Stick came to me for the money to take over from bozos who were too chicken to take on IBM and Toshiba toe-to-toe. If you're right and he's got no talent, then his coming to me is even more impressive—imagine having the balls to ask to run a company with someone else's money when you really don't have any skill at making or selling its product? The people under him at Minotaur may be talented but they're not greedy. Or, at least, I don't know that they're greedy."

I slapped the table. I was pleased that all three of them jumped. "Well. Then I'm in for the fall retreat. And I've got a basis for a psychological defense of greed, Edgar. I may write that book for you after all. Thanks a lot." I put my hand on Stick's bony shoulder. I squeezed. "I've got my mandate. I should head back to the labs to get started." I squeezed harder.

He didn't wince although it must have hurt—I'm not that weak. He looked at my fingers and smiled as if their presence was a delight. "Tennis on Saturday?" he asked. "There's a round-robin tournament at my club and I'm allowed a guest for a partner."

I let go. His eyes closed halfway, showing relief. "Definitely," I said. "Together we'll crush them."

CHAPTER ELEVEN

Countertransference

THE GREATEST SURPRISE OF THIS TREATMENT WAS THAT IT WAS BOTH RAPID and effective. The difficulties of its unorthodox nature, such as how to create the regular, defined sessions of psychotherapy, were easily surmounted. I had already established a twice-weekly meeting with Stick, supposedly to debrief him on employee morale. In addition, we had the doubles game one night a week and I became a regular on Saturdays at his country club in Westchester. Each of these four weekly encounters had the shape of a therapeutic hour. It was a simple matter to feed Copley's sadistic tendency to paranoia, as opposed to exploring its irrationality.

A typical exchange would go like this: "Andy is excited about presenting Centaur at the convention," I said and frowned.

"Of course," Stick commented.

"I guess it's because he has many old friends he'll get a chance to catch up with." I maintained the frown.

"*Old* friends?"

I laughed. "He *is* a little young to have old friends. Do you have many friends in the business?"

"Not many."

"How about George Jellick? He hired you at Flashworks? Do you get together?" This was a reminder of Copley's betrayal of a boss. Stick had left Jellick's company abruptly, taking with him the training and sales contacts he had acquired and raiding Flashworks for half the staff of engineers, including Gene, and several key marketers, Jack Truman being one.

"Jellick's retired," Stick said. "Who is Andy excited about seeing?"

"Are the names important?"

"I'd like to know."

"I'll find out. I guess it's natural that there's a lot of socializing between rival companies at the conventions. Much of it seems to be competitive, not really friendly. There's one reunion Andy isn't looking forward to—with a buddy from college who's made millions designing video games. Andy says he used to be brilliant at programming. He regrets going into machine design. 'It's a dead end,' he says."

The next day, much to Andy's dismay, Stick announced he would be attending the convention. Andy had looked forward to being the sole representative.

Intensifying Stick's innate pattern of excessive vigilance led naturally to exploring his anal fears of aging and weakness, and also to probing his homophobic modesty—another symptom of sadism. I took tennis lessons to sharpen my game and bought myself a new racquet. For a while I concentrated on playing my best. Stick became accustomed to our beating the men he found for opponents. Within a few weeks, I had sufficient control to contrive that we lose the second set in a way that seemed to imply Stick was tiring. Playing the net behind his serve it was a simple matter, by not poaching as aggressively as usual, or by making my volleys an easier get for our opponents, to arrange that our defeats seemed to happen because his serve was less effective.

Three losses of this kind and Stick complained. "After we get one win under our belts, we stop concentrating."

I said, "I don't think that's the reason."

He was in a shower stall at the Wall Street Racquet Club, talking to me by shouting over the noise of the running water. I was toweling off. He dawdled when undressing, waiting until I was in a stall before he stripped. He always brought his own kelly green towel with him to the club, although they supplied clean white ones, not as large or as thick as his, but sufficient. I assumed this was a mild version of the sadist's fear of germs. There were hooks on the outside of the shower door to hang a towel, but he always entered with his lower half wrapped up, to conceal his privates all the way, despite the fact that carrying the towel inside meant it would get wet. "What did you say?" he called.

"I know why we're losing the second set," I said, moving beside the stall door. "You're getting tired. Your serves lose power and I can't get as clean a volley on their returns."

"Bullshit," he said.

I said nothing. When the silence had lasted long enough to be uncomfortable, I yanked the shower door open.

Stick backed against the tiles, chest smeared with soap, eyes blinking from the rain of water. I stared at his genitals (of course, there was nothing remarkable about them, they were of normal size) and said, "Is my sweatband in here?"

"You didn't use this shower," he complained.

"Sorry," I slammed the stall door. I had seen the secret, so I made my judgment, "I'm pretty sure you're getting tired in the second set. Maybe it's my volleying, but I think your serve is too short."

He chose not to continue the argument. He liked to eat after playing and that same evening afforded an opportunity for further infiltration of his subconscious. He showed a rare curiosity about my work with children. Appearing to ramble, I told a story about a boy who was anally abused. I didn't have to invent it; unfortunately, my work provided many examples. I used Jeffrey Y., from one of my published case histories, who was repeatedly sodomized by his father and his uncle.

Stick's one question about Jeffrey Y.'s case was revealing, although not a surprise. "Do they usually end up becoming homosexual?" he asked.

I told a half-truth. "Once a boy has been anally stimulated, especially between the ages of five and ten, there's a good chance he will continue to want," and here I was deliberately crude, "to be fucked up the ass."

He surprised me, not for the first time, and it was a warning that I had to be careful with him. I had provoked him, anyway, that night with the shower stall invasion. He stared into my eyes; his looked black and dead. He said, "Halley told me your mother had sex with you when you were a boy. What does that do to a man?"

He meant to devastate me with this sideways revelation that Halley had told him my "secret." Of course my incest story came from my first dinner with her, not our recent encounters. I was taken aback, nevertheless. It was another reminder that I shouldn't underestimate the depth of their connection. I don't know how well I covered with my face, but my spoken answer was quick and effective. "It makes you a very confident man. It's every boy's dream, after all."

[I hope I don't have to explain why the above is a ridiculous lie. If

Copley was enough of a scholar to check, he would have known from my book on incest that I was full of it. The latter didn't overly worry me: in reverse therapy, if I may so label my new technique, Stick discovering I was untrustworthy might work to our advantage. He was probing for my weakness. That is the dynamic of this new therapy for an unneurotic sadist. We repeat the ancient drama: Copley searches for a way to defeat me, hoping for the same ending rather than a new one; while I, instead of replacing the villain with a caring parent, play my role better than the original.]

"Every boy's dream?" he repeated, squinting and frowning. The lines of his face wrinkled with pain. I almost felt sorry for him.

"I never had any performance anxiety with girls, never worried about the size of my penis, and I never had to worry about competition with my father. I was a winner in the Oedipal game very early on, so I didn't have anything to prove."

He was disappointed at the result of his counterattack. He sipped his herbal tea. His eyes and attention wandered off, forgetting our battle. "I guess all boys worry about the size of their cock," he said quietly, more to himself.

"Not *all*. Not even the majority," I commented grimly. He looked up, startled. "Only the ones with small penises," I said. Stick winced. I laughed, reached over and kneaded his shoulder. He disliked male-to-male physical contact—for obvious reasons, given his father. I took every opportunity to invade that barrier. "Just a little shrink humor. Of course everybody does," I patted him. "It's natural."

I frustrated his bribes, threats, tests and ambushes of employees on the one hand, and I aided or provoked their ambitions and demands on the other. There were too many instances to catalogue; besides, they are repetitious. The examples I've provided should suffice. I ended Jack's obsession with Halley by reinforcing his wife, Halley being one of the ways Stick knew someone was safely in his grasp. I encouraged Andy's development as a manager, both with his own men and by introducing him to Jack and the other salesmen, just as I had once encouraged Gene to try for more responsibility, only this time— and this was also true in my defense of the Truman marriage—I had a diversion to keep them safe. The diversion was me. Copley was convinced I was the threat to his control of the company, by virtue of my relationship with Edgar, not Andy's growing confidence and maturity. Halley was convinced we were having a love affair; so was Stick and that meant I was under control. In this first, and most crucial stage of therapy, only by presenting myself as a potential victim could I hope to be their healer.

This brings us to an aspect of the treatment it is crucial I warn other practitioners about. Two dangers exist in reverse therapy that, although they have corollaries in traditional psychoanalysis, are more present and intense. The first should be familiar, namely countertransference: I had to struggle to avoid forming a real attachment to Halley and I had to be careful not to want to harm Stick. The second danger, which unfortunately I did not fully anticipate, is that, since the treatment moves toward disintegration of the patient's personality rather than greater control, caution must be taken not to push the patient into outright psychosis.

Halley was the tougher assignment in terms of countertransference. I don't mean to make a vulgar joke of it, but my sexual frustration alone would have tested the patience of a saint—the pleasure was all one-sided and it was a mockery of lovemaking. I don't suppose I need to explain how I found relief for my physical forbearance, and I won't pretend fondling Halley was all work. The emotional frustration was another matter. I underestimated its danger. Although I limited physical contact with Halley to two nights a week of incest fantasy and my role demanded, when we were in public, that I treat her with stiff formality, almost contempt, nevertheless I had to (in order to play the part of lover/father) telephone her every day and maintain a deep emotional connection.

The routine was rigid. I telephoned her apartment at seven-thirty every morning, greeting her in a loving voice, "Hello, little one. How did you sleep?" The daily conversations, once she came to expect them so she picked up instead of her machine, lasted roughly half an hour. On weekends they sometimes continued for an hour or more. They allowed me to monitor the residue of my interference with the sexual and emotional dynamics of her relationship with her father; more importantly, however, I repeated the assurances her narcissism demanded. She'd rustle the sheets, groan sleepily, and ask plaintively, "Do you love me?"

"I love you," I'd say.

"Then why aren't you here?" she'd whine.

"Because you don't love me," I'd say.

"But I do!" she answered on the second week of these morning calls.

The first week she tried teasing me with the reply, "Tough," but I would only laugh at that.

"You don't love anyone," I said.

"Maybe I love you," she said sweetly, playing the innocent music of a little girl. It was hard to remember that she was lying.

"If you love me," I said, "then you're going to have my babies and get fat. You're going to be covered with spit-up and men won't want you. If you give me a beautiful daughter, I won't bother to look at you. If you give me a strong son, I won't bother to talk to you."

For a moment there was no reply. Then I heard a thump—I decided later it was her feet landing on the floor as she got out of bed. She said in an efficient tone, "That's right," and hung up with a bang.

The next morning she picked up and answered my, "Hello, little one. How did you sleep?" by saying, "I have a guest, I'll call you later."

She tried to make me jealous for two weeks, either by not picking up or answering only to say she had company and couldn't talk. I ignored the taunts so thoroughly that (and maybe Stick proposed this or she intuited his desire) she appeared in the labs and invited Andy to lunch, using the ad campaign for Centaur as the excuse. She took him out twice more before giving up on him, probably when she figured out that Andy was gay. I half expected her male secretary to call him next, but evidently Halley was not a delegator—and besides, that would hardly have upset me.

During the jealousy resistance phase, one night she told the doorman not to allow me up for an incest session. That alarmed me, but it shouldn't have. The physical craving for so complete a physical satisfaction—a narcissistic ecstasy that no one else could or would supply her—was addictive. The next morning she answered my greeting with a grumpy, "I didn't sleep well."

"Is that my fault?" I asked.

"Yes," she said.

"You missed your bedtime story," I said.

"Come here now," she insisted.

"No. Thursday night."

"What's your phone number? You know, it's outrageous that no one can call you at home. If you won't give me your number, I'll get it from Laura."

That was the first time she tried to bring her father in as a greater authority figure than me. "Stick doesn't have this number. This isn't my home," I said. "And I don't really work for your company. I'm doing research."

"Come here," she groaned. "*I'll* read *you* a story," she added brightly. "I'm a good lover, you know."

"You're a great lover—but you're not sincere."

She whispered, "Let me make you happy."

"You don't want to make me happy," I said. "I'll be there Thursday. The next time you don't let me in will be the last time I'll come to see you." I hung up. There were no more cancellations.

Despite the unprecedented intimacy my daily feeding of her narcissism required, I was convinced that she was nothing more than a patient to me until an interruption in our work proved otherwise. In late August, Aunt Ceil, Julie's mother, suffered another stroke and died. Since my family was told by the institute that they didn't have my New York number, Edgar, of all people, informed me on their behalf and offered a ride in his limo to Great Neck. He had joint real estate investments with Jerry, Uncle Bernie's son-in-law, and would be attending the funeral. This was another reinforcement to Copley of my dangerous connection to the larger business world. I made sure to tell Stick who was providing my ride when I canceled our Thursday meeting.

I also warned Halley that I wouldn't be available to tuck her in and refused to discuss why although she was sure to learn the reason from Stick. When she said, "How about Friday?" I said softly, "No."

I can imagine what Stick fantasized Edgar and I would say to each other during the ride to temple. In fact, we reminisced about Great Neck High, the old men who played gin at the country club, and the toughness of his father and my uncle in business. Edgar launched into an anecdote about Bernie to illustrate. "You know," Edgar said, "when your uncle bought Home World he was having trouble with the Mafia hijacking trucks. Hijacking! The union drivers would pull over nicely at such and such a time in a rest stop and have a cup of coffee while goombahs would take their load. Then they'd call the cops. It was a regular thing, taking about ten percent off the top. That was fucking up his profit margin big-time. So supposedly Bernie goes to see the Godfather—who's drooling in a wheelchair in his mansion. Somehow Bernie knows him—"

I explained, "When they were kids they used to lead gangs against each other in the Bronx." I knew the story he was telling, but I was interested in his version.

"No kidding? That's for real?"

"That part is real," I assured him.

"So Bernie tells him . . ." Edgar started to laugh and he began again, "So Bernie, he brings this big hulking Jew with him," Edgar laughed again so hard that he paused, swallowed and continued, "Bernie says, 'This man here is on a leave from the Israeli Army. He needs work and he has lots of buddies from Tel Aviv who need work and if my trucks keep having trouble, they'll be riding in every one for me as security men. You know about the Israeli Army,' Bernie says. 'They're used to fighting Arab terrorists so they don't mind getting their hands dirty,'" Edgar smiled. "And that was why the Home World trucks made their rounds without losing any inventory. Now here's the payoff. Supposedly the big hulking Jew was a cantor from a synagogue in Texas." Edgar laughed. We were exiting the LIE, heading for Community Road. He looked through the smoked-glass window at a Mercedes flanking us. The driver was a jeweled woman with a deep tan. Beside her was an African-American nanny. In the back, a toddler sat beside an infant in a car seat. "God," he said to their comfortable domesticity, "I wish that story was true."

"It's true," I told him.

"Really? You're shitting me."

"I know it's a true story."

"Are you sure? You knew it? Why didn't you stop me?"

"I'm sure. I didn't stop you because I wanted to know if you had it right. And you don't. The hulking Jew wasn't a cantor. He was a colonel in the Mossad."

"You're shitting me," Edgar said.

"No. Uncle was good at matching men with jobs they were qualified for."

"Don't be a bleeding heart."

"Between the two of us, Edgar, you're the sentimental one." He was. He stayed beside me through our entrance at the temple and, despite gestures of invitation from men important to him in business, pulled me down the center aisle row after row. Twice I mumbled, "Here's good." Edgar insisted on our progress until we got to the front where Julie sat in a black dress, an arm around each of her children.

"I brought him," Edgar said to her.

She stood up. I had only a moment to see that her hair was cut very short, her skin looked five years younger than when we last saw each other, and that her warm brown eyes, calm before she saw me, were immediately wet. She was in my arms and that's when I knew something was wrong with me. Julie's strong back, the feel of her long body in my arms, had always, always and I thought forever, been both a thrill and a comfort. Although my mind told me to embrace her thoroughly, if only to express sympathy, my body revolted. My arms were stiff, my legs tense, and my belly reluctant to be flush with her.

"It's so good—" she said in my ear and tried to squeeze my unyielding chest. "It's so good to see you."

I pulled away as soon as I could, mumbling I was sorry. She wiped away a tear and smiled. "Here are my babies," she gestured to a handsome eleven-year-old curly-haired boy and a shy nine-year-old girl—my cousins, and I realized in a flash, the only heirs I was likely to have. Was I that alone? Not even to have been introduced to my future?

The listless ceremony began. Her dead father, Harry, was the loved parent; Ceil had been a critical and self-absorbed woman. Probably I was the only one who knew how little Julie liked her and felt loved by her. Not that the loss of her mother left her cold. On the contrary, she wept harder at this funeral than at her father's, out of guilt and regret.

But I wasn't the only one who knew what she was feeling, I reflected. I looked around for her husband and only then noticed he wasn't present.

When we rose to follow the casket to the grave, Julie gathered her children with one arm and reached for my hand with the other. "You're with us," she said. Her eyes were red and tears kept flowing, although her voice was strong and clear. As we led the way out with the other Rabinowitzes, between mumbled thanks to mumbled expressions of condolence, Julie whispered asides to me. I didn't prompt them and they were non sequiturs, as if I were a part of her mind. "I'm thinking of moving to New York," she said, a moment after being released from a hug by Cousin Aaron. Guiding her boy and girl into the limo parked behind the hearse, she thanked the rabbi for his eulogy, then said to me, "I'm getting a divorce," and ducked inside.

Confronted by her son's earnest face, I didn't feel I could follow up on that news. Julie put her daughter in her lap. Margaret leaned her head on her mother's breasts and closed her eyes. I looked at her boy, Brian. "He's very good at math," Julie told me, another non sequitur.

"And basketball," he told me.

"I bet," I said. He was tall. "Do you know why six is afraid of seven?" I asked.

Cousin Margaret lifted her head and giggled. Brian frowned at me. "That's old," he said.

"You're right," I agreed.

"What's old?" Julie said.

"Why is six afraid of seven?" I asked Julie.

Brian looked at his mother sideways and smiled. "She doesn't remember anything," he told me. "That's an old joke, Mom."

Margaret said, "You know why, Mommy."

"I don't," Julie said with a pout.

"Because seven ate nine!" Margaret said and laughed loud, showing a row of big and little teeth.

Following tradition, we buried Aunt Ceil both in symbol and fact, each of us in turn digging a shovelful of earth from a mound to the right of the grave and tossing it on the casket. Julie went first. She stabbed at the dirt and flipped the shovel over casually.

She turned to Brian, doubtful whether to offer him a turn. He had no doubt. He took the shovel confidently. He dropped a heaping load into the grave and whispered, "Goodbye Grandma." He looked to his little sister, pointing the handle at her. Margaret shrank from it.

"You don't have to, honey," Julie said.

"Let's do it together," I said. Margaret's hand seemed very little beside mine as we filled only the tip of the spade. We cleared it with a wave over the open earth. "Bye," Margaret said low and sadly. She ran into Julie's arms.

Staring down at the smears of brown on the shining black coffin, I thought—Even you, Ceil, will be missed.

While the rest each took a turn, I walked five feet to the right to stand at my mother's lonely grave, the sister they had killed, to put it as bluntly as I feel. Another fifteen feet to the left and north, was Papa Sam and his wife. Below them I looked at the other solo placement: Uncle Bernie was positioned at the center of the triangle of dead Rabinowitzes, still dominating them. His first and second wives were buried elsewhere. Only he and my mother would rest alone.

Julie's hand fell on my back, rubbing. Again, I tensed at her touch. She sensed it and stopped. I looked toward the open grave. Her children weren't in sight. The line waiting to use the shovel was shrinking.

"I want us to be together," she said in that oddly calm voice, despite the red eyes and stained face.

"What?" I felt stupid. I knew what she meant. "You mean ride back together?" I said obstinately.

She shook her head and frowned. "You know what I mean. There's no reason we can't."

"When did you—" I stopped because I understood why I didn't like her touch. I had to think more about the revelation, of course, but the obvious worry had at last penetrated. Perhaps the daily recital of "I love you" to Halley wasn't all medicine.

Someone called to us. "In a minute," Julie said. "When did I what? Decide? Always."

"Always? You said you were over it."

"You knew I was full of shit when I told you I didn't love you. You see my kids? Don't I have great kids?" I nodded. "I have everything but you. And I'm greedy. Rafe, I'm forty-five. I've already had my face done. My marriage was . . ." She reached for me, shyly, fingers lighting on the sleeve of my blue summer suit. "Anyway, why? I heard you don't—I mean . . . Are you with someone?"

"You're upset," I said.

"Of course I'm upset. My mother's dead. But I've been thinking about it for a . . . Since I knew my marriage was . . ." She tugged at my sleeve and looked down.

"When did you break up?"

"In reality a long time ago. You know me. It took four years to get up the nerve to tell him. I did it last January. I was chicken. Hurting the kids, and all that garbage. It's not garbage, but you know what I mean. It was an okay marriage . . . But I don't want okay." She watched me for a reaction and answered what she thought she saw in my face. "I didn't just think of this!" Julie looked away at someone whose approach I hadn't heard. She said, "Sit with them in the car. Rafe and I need a moment." She turned to me and rubbed at the short cropped hairs above her temple. "What do you think this is? 'Oh gee whiz, I'll be in New York, so I'll come on to Rafe?' "

"You have to give me some time, Julie. I'm in the middle of something important . . . Important work—"

"It doesn't have anything to do with your work. I'm sorry. I've gotten rude in my old age. You can do your work. I don't care. I'll move to New York or wherever you want. I can fail to get my movies made in Indiana just as well as in Hollywood."

I felt ashamed and nervous. Had I lost control with Halley? The thought of never seeing her smooth white breasts again, of never hearing her naughty girl's voice asking, "Do you love me?" seemed impossible. And to join Julie in middle age, growing old with a woman whose prime I had missed, seemed grotesque.

"Is it them?" Julie gestured contemptuously to the graves. "They don't care anymore." She leaned forward, mouth set angrily, and whispered, "They're dead."

"Not to me," I said and thought it was a lie.

Julie nodded to herself and insisted, "They really got to you."

"I'm sorry," I said.

"I'm sorry!" she said louder, topping me. To get away, she walked over Bernie's grave.

I stayed for only a short time at my uncle's old house, merely a polite appearance of sitting shiva, instead of the all-night visit I had intended. I expected Julie to be hurt or angry. If so, she didn't show it. She squeezed me tight, kissed me on both cheeks, on my lips, and finally on the tip of my nose. She said, "Call me."

I turned to leave. She resumed a conversation with Jerry about the Rabinowitz plot becoming crowded. I reached the double-height foyer, with its long sweeping staircase, and paused on the spot where Julie had tried to defend me from my angry mother the night I found the *Afikomen*. I heard Julie say loudly, "What we all need is an exorcist." The room laughed.

My early departure meant I was back at the sublet in time to go to Halley's for our regular session. I had told her I wouldn't be able to. Perhaps a surprise appearance would make it all the more effective and I would at last hear grief when I deserted her.

Was effectiveness what I sought? Or consummation?

Probably the reader will be amused that this was when I realized my new method might be impractical. Unless psychiatrists were willing to give up their personal lives how could they imitate it? The obvious to an outsider became clear to me: I was as much on a personal mission as I was engaged in a scientific quest.

At nine-thirty, an hour before I usually appeared to announce myself to Halley's doorman, I tried to make notes, read, watch television. I microwaved and then rapidly ate a whole bag of Paul Newman's popcorn, hoping the deafening crunch in my head would silence my nagging desire. I had the night off. I could be myself. So—who was I?

Nothing could distract me. I couldn't divert my mind from the new questions I planned to ask as I slipped a hand under her pale pink sheets. Who was more addicted, Halley or me? Was her cure fatal to me?

Ten-thirty. Time for me to go, if I was going.

Accept the worst hypothesis, I decided. That was Joseph's technique, I had learned from Amy Glickstein's chapters. Presume that I could cure Halley only by infecting myself. With luck I might escape—but accept the worst as inevitable. Was neutralizing her worth it?

That August night was clear. As I walked, a bright new moon peeked out from behind the tall buildings. Between the squat brownstones it seemed to be a friendly lamppost.

"Goodnight, moon," I said aloud as I turned the corner to Halley's building. "Goodnight air," I mumbled to the amber streetlights. And to a wailing ambulance, as the doorman opened the way for me, I whispered, "Goodnight noises, everywhere."

CHAPTER TWELVE

The Second Danger

BY LABOR DAY I WAS SO DEEPLY INVOLVED WITH HALLEY THAT I DARED not test how important she was to me. I had her complete trust—she confided everything, no matter how ugly or trivial. That was as thrilling as the convulsions of her narcissistic ecstasies. Every day, I learned more about her self-murder and the temptress she had created to live.

And I had cornered Stick. The once separated and distrustful units of Hyperion were communicating without clearing everything through him; their feeling of independence grew unhindered while he was busy probing for a way to hurt me. I was fully committed to my enterprise, prepared either to cure them or lose myself in their whirlpool of illness. I faced this truth on August 30th, thanks to the banal need to find another place to stay in New York. Susan helped me there. An old friend in the Village, a writer, got a teaching job in the Midwest. I agreed to a six-month sublet at eight hundred a month and moved my few possessions down to a studio apartment on 33 East Ninth Street. More than two weeks later, on September 17th, I left for Vermont the night before Stick and the others to prepare for the retreat. My intention, because of the intense level of the countertransference, was to provoke a crisis, in the hope we could achieve a breakthrough.

The Green Mountain resort had no mountain in view. Instead, the five-story stone hotel overlooked a golf course. Behind it were six tennis courts, a heated swimming pool, and, about a quarter mile away, a large cabin for the "encounter sessions." The cabin was set on the western border of a man-made pond. The pond and its immediate environs existed solely for use by retreaters. Rowboats were available. They could cross to the sandy beach on its northern shore where a swimming area was marked off by a string of red and white striped buoys. In its center floated a wood platform and an eight-foot diving board. The pond was stocked. The east shore was set aside for fishing with the understanding that every catch must be thrown back. Also, there was a camping area, with two discreet outhouses, in a meadow ringed by pines and cedars hidden away off the east shore, if retreaters decided that a night under the stars would be helpful.

Ten rooms in the stone building were booked for me, Stick, Halley, Andy Chen, Jack Truman, Tim Gallent, Jonathan Stivik, the operating system programmer, two regional sales managers—Carl Hanson and Joe Gould—and the only other woman besides Halley, Martha Klein. Martha worked under Halley as the market researcher for Centaur and the rest of the new PC line.

I shooed away Green Mountain's retreat leaders, declined their offers of foam bats (to strike people with as a "playful acting out of aggression"), their New Age music tapes for meditating nude ("Body awareness can strip away hierarchical stereotypes and build self-esteem," I was told), and also their "cooperative tasks," basically scavenger hunts designed to require team effort for success. However, I did accept exclusive use of the cabin, the pond and its amenities.

At eleven o'clock Friday morning, I lingered over room service breakfast. The others were due in the late afternoon. The room was pleasantly furnished, as if it were a rustic inn, with a four-poster bed and plain pine furniture. I mulled over how to make use of the encounter meetings since I had rejected their gimmicks. I had the television tuned to ESPN, listening with one ear to their college football forecast show for Saturday's games. After a long silence, Albert had gotten a message to me and we had talked by phone for over an hour. He was excited. His college coach had been tough on him, he said, especially about his fitness. (The coach didn't really mean fitness, he meant his bulk. He wanted Albert—at seventeen, already six foot three and two hundred and fifty pounds of muscle—to get even bigger.) Nevertheless, Albert would be starting tomorrow at middle linebacker, a great honor for a freshman. "It's happening for me, Rafe. It's happening," Albert said, the thrill in his voice obviously exciting me too, since I was now watching a mind-numbing hour-long sports show on the off-chance I would hear Albert's name mentioned. I was disappointed that I wouldn't be able to attend the game, or see it for that matter, since I would be busy with the group all day Saturday.

There was a knock at the door. I assumed the maid wanted to clean. I shut off the television and answered it. Halley walked into my arms, on tiptoe, mouth puckered, reaching for my lips.

Gently, but firmly, I pulled on her long shimmering hair to keep her off. Since July 4th, I had, of course, not permitted embraces or kisses. A chubby teenage chambermaid, pushing a service cart out of the room across the hall, looked at us. I smiled at her, put my cheek against Halley's and whispered, "Stop this right now or I'll throw you out."

Halley let go and walked around me into the room. I shut the door. She was in jeans, a pink polo shirt, feet bare in black penny loafers. She flopped onto the four-poster bed and said, "I guess I'll have to fuck Jack."

"You told me that was over." Weeks ago, she confessed they had had many more than the one encounter she originally claimed.

"He'll want to. Every trip I've taken with Jack he gets horny. He leaves home promising himself he'll be good, but I talk him out of it. You know what he likes? He likes to order room service while I'm giving him a blowjob."

"Are you enjoying talking dirty to me?"

She lay down, hands behind her head. She kicked off her shoes. One dribbled onto a throw rug. The other tipped on its side, the cream-colored interior looking at me. "You said I had to be honest or you wouldn't be nice to me."

"I said as long as you were honest I would love you."

She ignored that. "I've been in meetings all week preparing the pitch for our 800 operators. I'm ready to scream. All I could think about driving here was your lovely hands, your big brown eyes, and that I'll probably get to see your buns in a teeny-tiny bathing suit. You really believe in this retreat?" she asked without a transition.

"I doubt much can be accomplished in two days. Less than that, really. Just two mornings."

"So what are you going to do to us?" She sat up and pulled her legs under her. "Finger painting? Oh, I know. We'll close our eyes, fall backwards and see if we catch each other."

"No. The nearest hospital is fifteen miles."

She smiled. "My room is next door. We have three nights."

"No," I said.

"You know what the Great White Father wants?" That was the nick-name for Stick she used with her lovers. I understood the contempt ex-pressed didn't mean she was disloyal to him in action or thought—Gene and others, unfortunately for them, did not. Her use of it inspired a thought for the sessions and I considered asking her to leave.

"No," I said. "What does Stick want?"

She kicked at the shoe on the bed. It tumbled down, bumped into its twin and rolled off the rug onto the pine floor. "He thinks I should get to know Edgar."

That stopped me from sending her away. "He puts it to you that bluntly?" I asked.

"What?" She looked up. "What do you mean? Oh . . . No, that's not what he says, you pig. He says I should move in his quote, circle, un-quote. He says Edgar would be happy to include me in his glamorous New York social life." She set her jaw to copy Stick's stern face and barely moved her lips to imitate his ominous style of talking, " 'You'd make lots of good contacts, Hal.' "

"What he really wants is for you to have an affair with Edgar."

"That's ridiculous. Edgar can buy any piece he wants. And he already has a trophy wife."

"Your father has a higher opinion of you than that."

Halley winked at me. "Do you?"

"Do I think Edgar would have an affair with you?"

"No!" She frowned. "Do you have a higher opinion of me than that?"

"Than what?"

"Than . . ." Halley shook her head. "You're confusing me."

"Do I have a higher opinion of you than that you're more than a tro-phy wife or a piece of ass?"

"That's it."

"Is that what you think of yourself?"

"That's what men think of me."

I shook my head and commented quietly, "You hate yourself."

She watched me. Her black eyes seemed to cross a little. She dropped a hand down to her right foot and squeezed her big toe. "Let's get mar-ried," she said in her deep, absolutely earnest voice.

I stood up, offering my hand. "Okay. We can do it right now. Burlington's only a half hour away. We'll go to their city hall and see if they'll waive the waiting period."

"I mean it," she said.

"So do I. We can pack up and fly to Vegas." I beckoned with my hand. "Come on."

"You would really marry me?"

"Of course."

Halley kicked her legs over the edge of the bed, hands on its edge, staring at the small throw rug. She thought for a moment. "Where would we live?"

"We would live where you want. We would do everything exactly the way you want it."

She looked up, her high brow shining above the dark eyes. "You mean I'd get to have real sex with you?"

"No."

"Even if we were married?"

"That would stay the same."

"Why?"

"You don't want real lovemaking."

She sneered, "Oh, *I* don't want it." I said nothing, my hand still offered in marriage. She studied my fingers, smiled and asked in a sweet tone, "What do you do afterwards? Go home and masturbate?"

I lowered my hand and sat down. "Is that what you imagine?"

"Do you wish I was really a little girl? Is that what you did at your clinic—molest little girls?"

"You're the only girl I've ever read bedtime stories to."

She straightened, arched her back and made one of her composite noises. Mostly, I heard disgust. "You're just a sick motherfucker who likes to play power games," she said.

"I love you," I said.

"You're scared to really love me."

"I love you," I said.

"When Didier was here he asked me to become his mistress."

"You told me."

"He said I should move to Paris and we'd run the European division together."

"King Didier and Queen Halley."

"You're laughing, but he means it."

"What did Stick think of that offer?"

"I—" She shut her mouth and pushed off the bed as if she were a gymnast dismounting, landing on the balls of her feet, arms akimbo. "I haven't told him yet." She walked slowly, watching her feet as she put one in front of the other, to the window. "The pool looks nice," she said, her mouth against the glass. It fogged up. "Let's go swimming."

"It's been almost a week. Why haven't you told Stick?"

Halley turned my way. "I could run the European division."

"I know."

"You know what my friend, Paula Robeson at IBM, told me? Their head of marketing got a sneak peek at the Centaur 800 ads and flipped out. They think we're going to—"

"You told me this morning."

"I did? Oh, right . . ." She leaned on the window frame, studying her feet. "You know everything," she said softly.

"I love you," I said.

She shut her eyes, pressed her full lips together, and said between clenched teeth, "Stop saying it."

"Why? It's the—"

She held on to the window frame and stamped her feet, shouting, "I'm ugly!"

"*You're* ugly?"

"I mean—*it's* ugly."

"Loving you is ugly?"

"It's a lie!" She came over to my chair and dropped to her knees, hands in her lap. She was praying to me. "I know when a man loves me. He wants *me*. He wants me to tell him how great he is, he wants to tell me how scared he is, he wants to hear that he's too nice—'You should be stronger, people are taking advantage of you,'" she talked with perfect sincerity in her deep voice to an invisible lover.

"Flattery disguised as criticism," I said. "It's an excellent technique."

She reached for my knee shyly, touching lightly with two fingers. "You're a genius," she said softly. "I mean a real genius. I'm not flattering you."

"Don't touch me," I said.

She pulled back as if burned. Her eyes seemed to cross and she snapped, "I hate you."

"I'm glad," I answered gently, as if she had presented me with an endearment.

"You don't care what I feel."

"Yes I do."

"You don't care what I say."

"You can say anything you want. That doesn't mean I don't care."

"You don't care what I do."

"I want you to do what you want."

Still on her knees, with no transition, she said angrily, "I can make Jack leave his wife if I want."

"I'm sure you can," I answered.

She stood up, hands on her hips, and challenged me, "I know what you did."

"What's that?"

"You told him to take his family on the West Coast trip."

"I never discussed that with Jack. I recommended a reading tutor for his son, that's all."

"I can't fuck them anymore!" she shouted and turned her back. She bent over—giving her ass to me—and picked up the penny loafers. "It's too goddamn boring." She straightened and carried them in one hand toward the door. "Get your bathing suit on. I want to go swimming." She looked at me over her shoulder and flowing raven hair, resting a hand on the doorknob.

"I'll sit by the pool and watch you. I have to make notes for the sessions."

"What is it? You're covered with a disgusting rash?"

"You want me to put on my bathing suit?"

"Yes." She hissed the *s*.

"Okay."

"Oh goody," she mocked. She opened the door, eyes still on me. She paused. "I just want you to know I could do it."

"Do what?"

"Get Jack to leave his insipid wife."

"I know you can get rid of rivals. The oldest child is very good at dealing with siblings."

She let go of the doorknob and frowned. "What does that mean?"

"When my father remarried he got his new wife pregnant. I was with him in Spain, remember? I told you?"

"Yeah . . ." Her mouth hung open, eyes glazed. I was talking to her subconscious, a kind of shallow hypnotism.

"That's why I ran away and testified against him. Remember? I told you I got him exiled from the U.S. I ruined his life because he had the nerve to replace me. I was the one and only heir. I had to be that or I would be nothing at all."

Halley put her back against the door. It shut quietly. She slid down until she was on the floor. "What does that . . . ?" She frowned, put on one of the penny loafers angrily, the leather snapping against skin. "What does that have to do with Mr. and Mrs. Truman?"

"It was an illusion. Not what I wished, but what I *did*. Do you understand?"

She put on her other shoe, this time fitting it on her foot gently. "I don't have the slightest idea what you're talking about."

"I didn't kill my brother, but I know what it feels like to wish he was dead."

She stared. Her mouth trembled. "You bastard," she whispered.

"It's not your fault, Halley. All you wanted was to be the most important person in the world to your father. But that's impossible. So now you want to be the most important person alive to everyone you meet. I guess most people would think that's a crazy ambition, but it isn't really, it's just a waste of your time. I know you can get Jack to want you so badly he'll sacrifice anything. I know it, you know it, Stick knows it. Even Jack knows it. So what's the point? Do *you* want him? If you want him, then there's a point."

Halley bent over, as if she were doing a stretching exercise, forehead pressed to the pine floor. She put both hands down and pushed up, hopping to her feet. Her mouth was set, talking tight. She was imitating Stick again, only this time it wasn't conscious mimicry. "I didn't do what you think. Okay? I didn't do anything to Mikey." She turned to the door ready to go, then wheeled back, adding, "I'm not a heartless bastard like you. I don't know what Gene told you—he really loved me so I could talk to him, I could tell him things about Mikey and Dad and he wouldn't throw it back at me so ugly—so many fucking ugly words! You asshole! I can't believe you said that to me." This was the closest I had seen her come to genuine rage. She forgot her self-possession. Her shoulders were hunched, her brow wrinkled, her beautiful lips in a snarl.

I was calm and unmoved. I said matter-of-factly, "All I'm saying is that they're no match for you. Of course you can do what you want with Jack, of course you can pretend to become Didier's mistress and end up running Europe. You could also run the U.S. and Japan. Even Stick is not your equal. That's why I'm surprised he suggested you get to know Edgar. I thought he was smarter than that." I slapped my thighs and stood up. "Well, I guess we should change and go down to the pool."

"You know, you're a sexist. That's all. That's all it is. You don't think I can accomplish anything unless I take a man into my bed."

I smiled, stood up, crossed to her, put my hands on her shoulders, turning her to the door. She jerked back stubbornly and called out, like a kid in the schoolyard, "Sexist pig, sexist pig . . ."

"You're not taking them to your bed, Halley. Come on. That's not what you do."

"They don't fall in love with me! That's romantic bullshit men use as an excuse—"

I laughed over the rest of her tirade, opened the door and pushed her out, saying, "*I* know you don't have to fuck them to get ahead. You're the one who doesn't." She peered at me from the hall, listening skeptically. "*I* know you don't have to make them love you. *You* don't." I patted her on the head. "I love you," I said, casually closing my door. "Meet you at the pool."

The conversation was satisfying—the less I gave her a real human being to play upon, the more she reacted to me with real feelings. But the toll on me seemed worse every day. I took three Tylenol (after all, I'm a big man) for my headache—the same sort of migraine-like pain I had been suffering from after the incest sessions. Those I attributed to mere physical frustration; if so, why did a talk session provoke one? The pain was nauseating. I bent over the bowl, but nothing happened. I drank some water and felt a little better. I put on the nylon shorts I used for tennis; actually, they were sold as a bathing suit. There was something worrisome about wearing them, and it concerned me that I was so drained from the scene with Halley I couldn't make the association. The shorts were a hideous turquoise and black—perhaps I was reminded of Stick's space-age tennis outfits. I also put on a white polo shirt. I was hardly less dressed than when I wore shorts and a work shirt to the office, so I expected Halley to be disappointed.

She was. By the time I met her at the pool, her anger had vanished, of course. She had recollected her false self. Anyone seeing her, small, slim and brown, hair slick, walking out of the shallow end, and greeting me—"Come in! The water's great."—would have thought we were the best of friends. In fact, we had no audience. There was a couple sunning by the deep end, but they seemed to be asleep.

"I'm gonna sit here and watch you," I said.

She stood in a foot of water. She kicked some at me. "Oh come on. Don't be a scaredy cat."

I reclined on a white plastic lounge chair, and flipped my legal pad. "I've got work to do."

She pouted and slunk backwards into the water, lewdly rocking her hips. "At least take off your shirt," she called.

I ignored her. She began to do laps, slowly, savoring each stroke, the way she did everything, with tantalizing concentration and grace. I stared at the pad. The sun glared off the yellow paper and hurt my head, which was still throbbing. I decided that, since only nine people were coming to the retreat, there was no point in dividing them. The question was whether I could accomplish what I wanted with Stick in a group that large. Also, wouldn't it be better to remove Halley? She might defend him at a crucial moment. But she was also on the verge of challenging him, my ultimate goal. She still hadn't informed him of Didier's offer, not significant because of the offer itself, merely her new secrecy. If she had really kept it secret. She was still capable of lying to me . . .

The tedium of checking and rechecking every word for manipulations tired me out. I drifted off, although my dream began at the pool, with Halley swimming, so I didn't know at first.

She was in a yellow pants suit. I meant to shout that she shouldn't be wearing her mother's clothes in the water; instead I said, "I'm in a bathing suit."

Then I knew I was dreaming because Halley was out of the pool, kneeling beside me at the white plastic lounge chair. She had an enormous version of my penis in her mouth. Her lips were distended as they widened to swallow the gigantic phallus. Her eyes watched me and crossed. "You're a kosher pig," she said, although talking should have been impossible.

"That's not mine," I said, meaning the penis.

A phone rang and Albert answered, telling the caller I wasn't available. He told me to sleep and tiptoed out, shutting the door gently. It was night. I felt a cool breeze—I knew that was real—but in the dream the breeze was a relief because it was dark and close in the room. My mother was painting the walls of Andy Chen's office, painting them a bright white that was fluorescent in the gloom. I was a very little boy, on the floor, looking up at her. There was a red X on her back. She glanced my way with a loving smile, an enchanting look that made me long for her to be real. She commented, "Remember, you don't know."

"How did you paint the X?"

"You don't know how to drown," she said and pointed the thick bristles of the brush at her face. A drop of white paint dripped onto her eye.

"No!" I cried out to stop her from painting her face because then she would disappear. And she did. I had become Francisco; he was chatting with Halley and the sleeping poolside couple, only we were on Grandma's porch in Tampa, "Well," Francisco asked, "what does political action mean in the context of physical bravery or cowardice? I am brave as to principle, a coward in kindergarten. I'm scared of my father."

Halley said, very clearly, "He's sleeping."

That's real, my conscious voice yelled to me. Wake up. That's real.

"What's he got planned?" Stick said.

You're in trouble. Get up. I pushed against the heavy chlorinated water of the dream, dragging me down to cool sleep. I jerked to the surface. Panting, I broke the skin of consciousness, blinking at the shadow staring down at me. "What?" I cried, terrified.

The head answered, "Sorry to wake you, Rafe. I just checked in."

The dream was over. That was Stick's head. Halley, wrapped in a large brown towel, was in a chair. Next to her, on a small table, was a glass of iced tea. She had a paperback mystery in her hand. "You slept for three hours," she said.

Stick moved out of the sun. "I'll change into my trunks," he said. "I'm looking forward to tomorrow's sessions. Sorry I woke you."

I nodded. I watched him wander toward Green Mountain's stone building. My mouth was dry, the throbbing in my head gone, although at my temples there were remnants of pain.

Halley said, "You want some coffee?" I nodded. She waved to a man at a small refreshment stand that had been closed when we arrived. There were four people at the pool, one in the water, two talking, another reading the *Times*. The attendant started toward us. Halley called, "A pot of coffee," and he wheeled back to his bar.

"Thanks," I said and rubbed my face.

"Why didn't you tell me you don't know how to swim?" Halley asked.

That was it. That was the surface message of the dream. The bathing suit and my mother's warning. I had told Stick an idiotic lie that I couldn't swim and I almost gave it away unintentionally. I was too groggy to think it through. Should I reveal I had lied? Would that be fruitful? And did I hear right? Was he changing to swim? That wasn't good. I didn't care for him to resume his daily ritual of triumph over his father on the eve of the encounter session.

"Can't you admit it when you don't know how to do something?" Halley fanned herself with the paperback. She had put on dark sunglasses. It hurt my sleepy eyes to look at her. She glowed in a rectangle of the late afternoon sun while I was in a shadow thrown by a wing of the stone hotel. In fact, I felt chilled because the air was dry and cool, hinting at the coming autumn.

I wanted to say (I should say, my id wanted me to say)—I know how to swim, you stupid bitch. I can do everything better than your asshole father. A slice of me was rotting—infected by them. That was why I had summoned an image of myself as my mother in the dream. The dream was a warning that my ego was disintegrating in the countertransference; I was, to put it in laymen's terms, losing my objectivity. My reaction to Halley's taunt was that of a lover: emotionally invested in the competition with her father, rather than merely using it for the therapy.

Halley put her book on the glass table and picked up the iced tea. "I can teach you how to swim," she said. She sipped.

"Who taught you?" I asked in a croaky voice. The pool attendant was coming with a tray. Thank goodness. I needed coffee.

"I learned at summer camp," she said.

"You're lucky Stick didn't teach you," I said and laughed.

"Why?" she asked. The coffee was there so I ignored her. I drank two cups in a row. She watched me through the black lenses. Black eyes through black glass, I thought, and decided it was time to begin, time to push for a breakthrough before I had nothing left for leverage. "Really," she said, at last, her voice soft and loving. "I'd really like to teach you. At least let me give you that. We could do it right here. The pool doesn't get any deeper than four feet."

I cleared my throat. Behind her, in the distance, I saw Stick appear from the stone building, a towel draped over one shoulder, wearing a navy blue bathing suit the length of bermuda shorts, his feet in hippie leather sandals. "I told Edgar the other day . . ." I cleared my throat again. "Excuse me. I told Edgar that if Centaur is a success it's to your credit on the marketing side and Andy Chen's on the creative. I also told him you're more qualified to run Minotaur than Stick. He was intrigued. So maybe it isn't such a bad idea for you to socialize with him."

Halley was in the middle of raising her glass to lips. She missed a little when I said she was more qualified than her father to run Minotaur. She tried to center the glass as she tipped it to her mouth. That didn't work. Some tea dribbled down a corner and off her chin. She caught that with her hand, leaned forward with a jerk, and more tea sloshed out onto her towel. "You're kidding," she started.

I nodded toward Stick. "He's coming. And I'm not kidding. You could easily become Edgar's mistress. You'd dazzle him—with your cleverness, your energy, and yes, with your body and expert lovemaking—he'd give you anything you want. I told you, Halley. I love you. I'm going to make sure you don't sell yourself short."

"Hey, Rafe," Stick called as he reached the border of the pool's tiles. "How are the courts here?"

"Hard surface. Pretty fast, I think."

He reached us. Halley was still, her black eyeglasses fixed on me. He draped a towel on the chair next to his daughter. "Maybe we'll hit before dinner."

I rubbed the underside of my right thigh. Earlier in the week I had strained the hamstring going for a volley. "You know this still feels tender. Maybe I'd better rest it."

"You should do some laps," he said. "That'll help it recuperate."

Now he had surprised Halley. She jerked her head at him. "But, Daddy, you said . . ." she started and then stopped.

He ignored her. So did I.

"I can't swim, Stick, remember?" Since I was going on the attack, I decided to maintain the lie. Restoring a feeling of superiority might relax his vigilance.

"Oh, that's right," he said, pretending to recall. "But you're so coordinated, such a good athlete. Come in. I'll teach you the crawl. I'm sure you'll get it in a few minutes."

"No thanks. I think I'll go up to the room. We'll play tennis on Sunday." I stood up.

"Really, Rafe," Stick stepped in front of me. His hands were on his hips. He breathed in sharply, inflating his impressive pecs. "A grown man should know how to swim."

"But Stick," I put a hand on his bare shoulder. He tried not to show tension at my touch. I scanned down, openly studying his puffed-up chest. I said quietly, "God, you're in great shape." I hurried on, raising my eyes to his, and squeezed his shoulder, "I thought you understood— I'm not a grown man. I'm just a very self-confident ten-year-old."

I left them together. Whether or not Halley told him my lie that I had recommended her to Edgar as a future manager of Minotaur, the crisis would come soon. Either she would completely accept me as her new father figure—to the extent of choosing her next lover and marking Stick as someone we were going to get out of the way—or she would inform Stick that I was really the deadly foe he feared and he would be forced to act.

I didn't go to my room. I took the elevator to the second floor and stood by a hallway window with a view of the pool. When I reached my observation post, Stick still hadn't gone into the water. He stood beside a seated Halley, not looking at her. She peered across him toward the refreshment stand. But they were talking. That is, Stick was doing most of the talking. Halley occasionally answered briefly.

"Don't tell him," I whispered, and it's still an open question for me whether this was the doctor or Rafe talking. "Make the leap, my beautiful little girl. It's time to leave home."

Chapter Thirteen

Breakthrough

I WROTE WORDS ON A BLACKBOARD WHILE THEY POURED COFFEE (THERE was herbal tea for Stick) and grumbled about the fact that I had removed all the chairs from the cabin. Outside, at eight-thirty it was still cool, although the sun shimmered on Green Mountain pond and there wasn't a cloud in the sky. Jack had his eyes on the east end, the fishing and camping side.

Earlier, during our seven-thirty A.M. phone session, Halley told me, "Well, you win, you bastard. Last night, I gave Jack every opportunity to invite me to his bed. You've put him back into the big bosom of his 'adorable little family,'" she finished with a poor imitation of Amy Truman's Southern accent.

"He's small fish," I said. "You're going for the Great White Shark— Edgar and the company he'll give you to run."

"You're crazy."

"No. Remember, I'm the doctor."

"I don't use sex to get ahead."

"That's true," I said. It was true. Her love affairs weren't practical; at least, not to her. "But it isn't sex I'm talking about. That's merely the way Edgar will get to know you. Maybe he won't even bother to go to bed with you."

"I still say you're crazy," she said. "No one can run Minotaur better than my father."

I couldn't tell, frankly, if that meant she had betrayed my lie to her father. My guess was no, since she pretended, in order to hear more encouragement, to believe my proposal wouldn't work.

On the blackboard, I wrote the words: NERD. THE GLASSHOLES. GEEK HEAVEN. PRINCE OF DARKNESS. SOFTHEAD. BEER BRAINS. LEECH. By now, the mumbling and giggling about how to get comfortable on the cabin floor stopped. When I turned to face them, I had their full attention. "You've all heard the cliché that life is really just high school. Well, for a lot of people life often *is* high school, but it isn't meant to be. Adults are supposed to understand that differences in taste, appearance, behavior and abilities are the natural order. Adults are supposed to have learned, in high school, that when human beings are successful, they used these differences to their advantage. Teenagers have a good excuse for dividing into cliques and making up mean nicknames for the cliques they don't belong to. Adolescents are discovering who they are. Their hold on identity is tenuous. To know who they are, often first they have to know who they are not. But a mature person, to put it in business terms—a winner—is someone who has confidence in his or her identity and who isn't afraid of differences. I'm not talking about racism or religious tolerance or other sorts of general tribal identity. I'm talking about confidence within the tribe. You have formed a unit to forage for food and shelter and, for better or worse, the personnel of Minotaur are your only resource. The words up here are a sample of the high school nicknames used secretly within your tribe. Their existence proves you are not a mature group. They prove you are losers."

Tim Gallent, whose long stringy blond hair was washed and combed for the first time since I had met him, laughed. A nervous whinny, actually, that continued to escalate in both pitch and volume. His eyes were wide and they moved desperately back and forth from Andy to me. Andy was seated on the floor beside him. They made quite a contrast: Andy's bowl of black hair and pale face; Tim's mane of blond hair and florid skin; Andy's long skinny legs folded neatly under him; Tim's wide thighs pushing his stumpy legs away from a big belly. Andy mumbled something to Tim, who immediately covered his mouth with his hand. Muffled giggles continued, though subsiding. As for the others, most of them watched me like penitent children. The exceptions were: Jack, whose green eyes regarded me with interest and no alarm; Halley, head tilted, smirking at me as if we were sharing a joke; and Stick, who sipped his herbal tea without any affect—he might have been watching a dull television show.

"If people want to laugh, or yell, or throw up, pee on the floor, that's okay," I said. "I'm not a member of your tribe. You don't owe me loyalty or respect. Go ahead and laugh, Tim."

He removed the hand from his mouth and lowered his head. "Sorry."

"What for? I know that the chief of your tribe is here and that he can cast you out into the wilderness. You know that he has asked me to lead you in these sessions. So you might think in dealing with me you are dealing with him. But that's not true. I have an understanding with the Prince of Darkness. Isn't that right?" I asked Stick.

He had put himself at the rear. Tim covered his mouth again. Martha Klein and Jonathan Stivik turned to look at their boss. Halley lifted her eyes to the ceiling, her smirk broadening to a smile. The rest stared ahead, but too stiffly, obviously wanting to look.

Stick put his mug of tea on the floor and cleared his throat. "I guess you're talking to me, Rafe. That's good. I've always wanted to be a prince."

There was polite laughter. I continued, "The Prince of Darkness knows I'm going to make you all say things that are taboo in the normal rules of the tribe. If he doesn't like the result—well, let me ask you, Prince, who will you blame?"

"I'm going to blame you, Witch Doctor," Stick answered and this time there was loud, genuine laughter.

I smiled. "Very good." I turned and wrote WITCH DOCTOR on the blackboard while I continued, "This morning we're all going to use our high school names. But first," I faced them again, "since these names aren't of your own choosing, the Witch Doctor will tell you who you are." I pointed at Jack. "Stand up, Glasshole."

Timmy laughed again, this time normally.

Jack stood up. He was on the other side of the room and a little behind so he had to step forward and turn to catch Tim's eye. He asked, "Are you enjoying yourself in Geek Heaven?"

Andy bent over, laughed and smacked the floor. "Geek Heaven," he repeated. "It's us!" he said and laughed.

I had them get up one by one and accept a pejorative. A couple of alternates were cheerfully suggested that I agreed to, but I resisted outright invention, insisting on those they had actually used before, with one exception. Stick and Halley were the last two on the floor. "Get up, Prince of Darkness," I told Copley. That left Halley alone and unnamed. Her smirk was long gone. She looked small, young, and surrounded.

"Well," I asked the group, "what do we call her?"

It became obvious that she didn't have a nickname they all used. That didn't surprise me, since she presented a different persona to each one. "Glassholette," Tim offered and laughed, but the others didn't join him or clap to show approval.

I peered at her. "I don't think so." I scanned the group. Jack seemed to want to talk. "Yes?"

"Queen of Darkness," he said solemnly, green eyes on me alone. He swallowed afterwards. I knew that he had been brave and I winked at him.

"Is that how the tribe thinks of Halley?" I asked. I noted that, although this ordeal would bring most people to the verge of tears, Halley's black eyes were calm, eerily abstracted, and her body, in a half-lotus, remained still and at ease. A defense certainly, but to call Halley's emotional shield a "defense" is to forget that the armor of a tank is there to protect its gun, not the passenger. She wasn't wounded. I didn't imagine for a moment she could be by this group. I looked at Martha, who had shown little apprehension about the game. "What do you call her, Leech?"

Martha was a big-boned fleshy woman, overweight by modern standards, although realistically she couldn't keep her broad shoulders and wide hips free of fat unless she were to starve. She also had the misfortune of a pug nose, too small for the scale of her broad forehead and wide mouth. "Miss Halley."

"Miss Halley?" I nodded sagely. "You mean you're her slave?"

Martha laughed, a good incautious laugh, from the belly. "I sure am."

"And she's just the useless self-centered daughter of the plantation owner?"

Martha frowned. She put her hands on her hips and stared down at the small dark girl on the floor. "No," she admitted.

"Maybe you're a sexist, Leech," I said, touching Martha on the shoulder to make it clear that I wasn't really scolding her. I addressed the others. "Let's pretend Halley is the Prince's son, not a daughter. I know that's hard with Halley, but let's say she were just as attractive, only she was a handsome young son. What would you call her?"

Jonathan Stivik said, "That's easy. Prince Hal."

Andy and Gould laughed appreciatively—presumably fans of Shakespeare. "Prince Hal?" I asked the group. Everyone but Stick and Halley nodded.

"Sure," Andy said. "They're family."

"Stand up, Prince Hal," I said. "I want you to form a line in this way. From right to left, arrange yourselves according to how insulting, how personally degrading, is your nickname. The most despised on the right, the most honored on the left."

This caused some hilarity. Martha (Leech) and Carl Hanson (Beer Brains) kept circling each other, fighting to be the low person. Stick helped by immediately taking the top spot and so did Halley, standing beside him at number two, although according to business title she was below Jack, Joe Gould and Hanson. Tim and Andy were confused. Jack watched them hesitate and then steered Andy (Geek Genius) by the arm next to Halley at the number three position and moved himself to fourth. Jonathan (Softhead) revealed his high self-esteem by taking number five. Gould (Cash Cretin), although he was presumably the equal of Hanson, took number six.

Martha grabbed Hanson to stop him from getting below her one more time and called to me, "Will you tell him a leech is the lowest form of life?"

"At least you are a form of life," Hanson argued. "I'm a fermented potato."

"Martha's right," I said. "But she's not low man." I looked at Tim, bewildered now that his colleague Andy was in the line and he couldn't stand beside him. "You are, Nerd." I grabbed his chunky arm and moved him toward Martha.

This was my first break. Tim jerked his arm out of my grasp, stepped back, shoulders hunched and head down like an angry bull. "No," was all he said, but it was definite.

"Think about it, Nerd. All the others have something good in their names. Two of them are Princes. I'm a Doctor. He's a Genius, even if he's a Geek. Jack has glass in his name. That ties him to the Glass Tower, which is the seat of power. Jonathan's Softhead, but at least he's got a head. Gould is the Cash Cretin, but he's got money. Carl not only has Brains, he has Beer and Martha is a Leech, but that means she gets blood out of people. You're just Nerd. You're harmless. In fact, they don't even single you out. You're just one of dozens of nerds. You don't really have a name all to yourself."

Tim backed away another step. His face was redder, his jaw out, and he breathed fast, through his nose. Someone mumbled, "Take it easy." I think that was Jack.

"Get at the end of the line," I said sternly.

"They're nothing," Tim answered in a rush and then shut up.

"They don't think so. They think you're nothing."

Tim pointed a thick finger at Jack. "Everybody in the Glass Tower is a Glasshole. Not just him. He doesn't have his own name." He pointed to Jonathan. "All the programmers are Softheads."

"He's *The* Glasshole. He's *The* Softhead. Are you *The* Nerd?"

Tim's jaw trembled. "Yes," he stammered.

"No," I was sorrowful. "*The* Nerd is Andy. He's the Geek Genius, the head nerd. The Nerd of nerds. You're replaceable. You're a worker bee, a nothing."

Tim spoke very very softly—a hunted whisper. "They need me."

"They don't think so."

From behind me, Andy said, "Yes, we do." Jack also said something encouraging.

"Shut up," I told them without looking. I advanced on Tim. He was a few inches shorter than me and much wider. We were almost nose-to-nose. His frantic, noisy breathing sounded like the sniffling of a weepy child. There was a streak of red in his left eye, a burst blood vessel. A drop of sweat from his receding hairline trailed down, heading for his nose. "They're being kind," I told him. "Kind to the nerd. Kind to the big baby nerd."

Tim put his fat palms on my chest and shoved me. Martha, I think, gasped. I stumbled back. Tim shouted, "They're nothing!" He shuffled sideways, almost as if he were dancing, and screamed, "I make the machines! They're nothing! They got nothing without me. Me! I'm the one! He's—" Tim, his face bright red, slid and hopped up to Andy. "He's not a genius! Without me, he's a retard!" He skipped down the startled line and stuck a finger at Jonathan. "Softhead!" he tried to laugh scornfully, but the sound was more like a choke. "If he was any good he'd be at Nintendo! I cleaned up the protocols for him. You dumb fuck," he added and then skipped backwards.

"So the tribe dies without you," I said.

"I'm the fucking hunter. I get the meat." Tim banged his thick hands together. They made a shattering sound, like the report of a gun. "They die without me."

There was an embarrassed silence. I allowed it to settle until we could all hear Tim's noisy breathing and the soft lapping of the pond against the rowboats docked outside our cabin. "Make a new line. You're at the head since you've had the courage to name yourself." I walked over and touched him on both shoulders as if I were knighting him. He straightened. "You are the Hunter."

Thus, I said, inspired by Tim's example, we would rechristen the tribe. Jonathan, stung by Tim's attack, immediately argued that he was the Scout, since he checked the proposed machine designs by running simulations on Black Dragon. The others, without much enthusiasm, nodded. Tim, his face returning to his usual florid color instead of cardiac arrest red, said nothing.

I announced that a new title had to be accepted by the previously named, and in turn, by each of the newly baptized. "So it's up to you," I said to Tim. "Is Jonathan the Scout?"

Emboldened by his triumph, Tim said, "No. Andy's the Scout. He sees what's ahead and I go and get it."

I ordered Tim and Jonathan into one of the boats. I told them to row to the east shore, sit in the meadow and discuss it. We would wait for them on our shore and think about what we thought our names should be.

We followed them outside and watched as they traveled across. There was some snickering because they weren't very good at it, moving in a zigzag. Gould called, "If you don't row together, you'll sink together."

Martha arranged herself on the ground to be in the sun. Jack asked if he could fetch a rod from the hotel and do some casting. "No," I said. Andy asked if he was the Scout, as Tim had said. "No," I said. "He doesn't get to name you."

"Who does?" he asked.

"I don't know yet," I answered.

Stick maneuvered by my side and mumbled, "This could take all day."

"And all night," I said.

"Really we're here to relax," he continued in a whisper.

"You asked me to do this. You and Edgar said you were interested in what I would come up with. Have you changed your mind?"

"Well . . ." He gestured for me to walk with him, away from the others. Although pretending not to be, they were aware of us.

I raised my voice. "If you have something to say, Prince, say it so everybody can hear."

Halley and Martha twisted to look. Jack, standing under a broad maple for shade, turned our way. Andy was on the cabin porch, behind

Stick, but listening. Gould and Hanson were over by the rowboats, hold-ing oars; they weren't facing us, but their backs were stiff and they were quiet.

Stick snorted. The sun was on his lined gaunt face, his prominent fore-head shadowing his eyes. He put his hands in the same Bermuda shorts he had worn yesterday to the pool. "Okay," he mumbled. "Forget it."

"No," I persisted in a loud annoyed tone. "Everybody here has been told you put me in authority. If that's not true, then this is even more of a farce than you say it is—"

"I didn't say it was a farce," he complained. He raised his hand. "Enough. I made a mistake."

"I want you to tell everyone what's on your mind. Do you think I'm wasting your time?"

"I'm disappointed," he said, taking his hands out of his pockets, turn-ing away to the porch. He noticed Andy staring at him. Stick frowned, put a sandal on the cabin's granite step, and rocked on the foot.

"Disappointed by what?"

Stick took a long breath. He exhaled it as a sigh. "Doesn't seem very original, that's all." He kicked the step with his heel, walked up to the porch, and sat on its banister.

"Original?" I was openly scornful. "What do you know about psy-chology? Your idea of psychology is to promise people raises."

It was Hanson (I think, my back was to him) who couldn't help but laugh—a very abbreviated laugh to be sure.

"I can cancel this," Stick said, not in a threatening tone, an idle com-ment.

"Then we can name you Quitter," I said. "Or maybe Welcher. How about Indian Giver?"

"I don't believe in it, that's all."

"Oh!" I opened my arms and swiveled a half turn as I spoke each sen-tence, eventually taking them all in. "You don't believe in it. So it must be worthless. There's no doubt! If you don't believe it, who will?" I ap-peared to have lost control.

"Nobody believes in it." Stick got calmer in answer to my show of temper. He swung a leg, his leather sandal brushing the porch deck. He nodded toward the far shore. "We can humor poor Tim and call him Hunter, but we all know he's . . ." Stick paused. He turned from the meadow to look at us. He saw me, of course, arms still out, sneering at him, but he also realized the group was listening.

"He's what?" I demanded. "Garbage? Something you can throw out whenever you want?"

"No, of course not. Don't play games. I never said anything like that." Stick stood up, stretched. "As long as we're waiting by the pond, let's take advantage of it. Jack, go ahead and get a rod. I'll get towels and—"

"Scared to finish the conversation, aren't you?" I asked.

Stick's thin lips disappeared altogether. He had come down to the granite step to give his orders and got stuck there.

"Make up your mind, Prince," I said. "Who's in charge? You told them I was. You promised them I was. Are you taking it back? Were you lying?"

Abruptly, Stick dropped his head in mock surrender and laughed. "Okay, you're right. In for a penny, in for a pound." He sat down on the step. "I apologize, Witch Doctor." He was positively charming. "You're in charge."

"Good. Then finish your sentence. Tim is . . . what? If he's not the Hunter, what is he?"

That sustained the tension he wanted to slacken. Stick glanced at Halley, saw only an impassive young woman, squinted at the sky and appeared to think. "He's a nerd," he said at last. No one laughed. Stick was surprised. After a moment of awkward silence, *he* tried a laugh, but it was more of a cackle. "I'm joking," he added, lamely.

"Maybe that's what we'll call you," I answered. "The Joker."

A heavy silence followed. Human silence, that is. A loon called across the pond. Breezes rustled the maple above Jack's head and rippled the water. I moved to the step, used it to help stretch my tight hamstring, and then sat down next to Stick. He stared at his sandals, smoothing his slick hair with both hands. I kept my eyes on him until he met them. His were dead, to prove to me that I hadn't hurt him. Eventually, Gould and Hanson resumed their discussion of proper rowing technique in low voices. Martha groaned, rolled on her side, and said to Halley, "I know what I want my name to be."

Halley smiled. She appeared completely at ease. "What's that?"

"Mama Cass."

"Oh, Martha—"

"Leech."

"Sorry. You're not fat, Leech."

"I wasn't talking about being fat, Miss—excuse it, I mean Prince Hal. I was talking about my beautiful singing voice."

Meanwhile, Jack had idly strolled toward the porch. He asked Andy, who was backed against the cabin's door, "Do you fish?"

"No."

"You'd like it. Great for thinking through a problem . . ."

With three conversations going, I whispered into Stick's ear in a rush, "I have to be the one to attack you. I'm acting out their secret resentments." I looked at the others to check if anyone heard or noticed. They hadn't.

Stick whispered, "You're doing too good a job."

I squeezed his shoulder. He suffered the contact, although he had to purse his lips to endure it. "Okay," I called. "Everybody back in the cabin while we're waiting." There were protests—the day was sunny and mild, couldn't we stay outside? I was stern and herded them in.

I told Martha to sit in front of the blackboard and ordered the others to face her.

"Since we're going to have to rename everyone, maybe we'd better learn more about each other. I'm going to ask you questions, Martha. If you don't want to answer a question, just say, 'No,' or, 'No Comment,' or, 'Fuck off.' If you want to answer partially, then answer partially. Understood?"

"Fuck off," Martha said and there was long sustained laughter from everyone, including Stick.

"Okay, you've got the idea. How many diets have you tried, Martha?"

I had picked her because I was sure she would be facile at intimacies, even if they were mostly banal. She was. My questions merely asked for the surface of personal truth, convinced the core would be exposed anyway because of the earlier flexing of emotion. I had misbehaved, so had Tim. Our extravagance would encourage them to spend more of themselves than was typical. Martha, in fact, eventually made a deeply felt speech about the death of her father. By then, all of them had asked her questions, except, of course, for Stick.

I had moved Gould to the inquisition spot when we heard a voice calling from the pond. We rushed out to the cabin porch. Jonathan and Tim were in the rowboat, going in a circle for the most part, since Jonathan kept abandoning his oar to call, "I'm Trans . . ." and the rest was too faint to understand.

"He's a transistor?" Gould asked.

Hanson yelled, "Pick up your oar or you'll never get here!"

Eventually, they were close enough for us to hear, "I'm Translator."

"Translator?" Martha called, openly skeptical.

"I make sure that man and machine can talk," Jonathan explained.

Stick turned his back to the others. He rolled his eyes to show his contempt.

"The point is they worked it out," I said.

"If I were you," he mumbled, "I would break for lunch."

I didn't. I did provide lunch (prearranged to arrive in picnic baskets that were discreetly left at the head of the pond's path to the hotel) but no break. I sent Martha across with Jonathan, returned Gould to his inquisition, and we proceeded in that manner, until all had been rechristened except for Halley, Stick, and me, and all had been questioned but for me and Stick. The sun crossed above and behind the cabin. The northern part of Green Mountain pond was dyed amber by the late afternoon sun when I sent Halley across to be named by Andy—but I am getting ahead of myself.

The naming of Andy had been the one of a series of events that was important. The inquisitions and baptisms inevitably created an atmosphere of intimacy and friendliness among them. Stick's moody withdrawal was ignored. Probably they assumed the whole day, in the end, was an unimportant exercise and that I would pay for his annoyance. They couldn't help, however, learning that they were capable of being at ease with each other—it was Stick who couldn't.

Martha was named Scout, since that was the true meaning of market research. Gould was named Warrior (salesmen go out into the world, after all) and he insisted Hanson accept the same name—as opposed to his earlier attempt to stand higher in the line. Hanson took Jack to the meadow and stuck the first pin in Stick by naming Jack Warrior King. He explained that Jack had to take on IBM, Toshiba, and Compaq nationally—he was the face of war Hyperion presented to the world. Halley looked at her father when we were told. The others applauded. I sent Andy off with Jack and they wounded Stick again when Jack explained he had called Andy the Creator, since without him the tribe had nothing to sell.

During Andy and Jack's absence, Halley faced the rest of the circle and put on a performance. I should say, half a performance. In all her incarnations there was some truth. She had noticed how moved they were by Martha's grief, and anyway I had stirred the pot about her brother the day before, so they heard a convincing speech telling of the loss of Mikey. She portrayed herself as a loving older sister with a brilliant, but impetuous brother. They heard she was shocked by the loss of his energy and optimism. There were no lies, only omissions. The battle she had fought to replace him as her father's favorite and the lack of guilt about her victory were expunged, replaced with tearful mumbles that she should have known he would try to ski the dangerous slope. Martha hugged her and said it was crazy to blame herself. Halley erased any hint that she had helped to provoke Mikey, not only that fateful night, but over and over for years.

Halley's choice of identity was admirable in a perverse way. In a sense, she was coming to her father's rescue. He couldn't even fake having a heart. By telling them of their family tragedy (the details of which were a mystery to them all) she made his lack of feeling appear to be wounded reserve. She's not as dangerous as Stick, I thought to myself, but she's shrewder.

Unfortunately for Halley, and for Stick, she merely succeeded in making him more uncomfortable. He didn't want them to think of him as human. He wanted to be feared and he was clever enough to see they no longer did, at least not as long as I was present.

Copley faced the circle last, while Andy took Halley to the meadow to name her. When I asked him to move in front of the blackboard, he tried a small rebellion. "Isn't it your turn?" he teased me.

"No, Prince."

Stick nodded, a wan smile on his face. He walked to the front and opened his hands to show he was ready. Everybody else had sat on the floor. "Sit down," I said.

"Sure." He grinned to show he was a good sport. He squatted without a groan, settled on his behind and pulled both feet underneath him.

"Did you hope Mike would work with you at Minotaur?" was my first question.

Stick answered without hesitation or complaint. "He wasn't interested in computers. He was still finding himself when he had his accident."

"Did his death have anything to do with Halley coming into the company?"

Stick blinked at me. I don't think this had occurred to him. His skill at using people involved only a partial ability to understand them. He could see weakness, not necessarily motivation. "Um . . ." he hesitated. "Let's see . . . Halley asked if there was a job—I mean, she was very qualified. She worked for Time Warner—"

"It wasn't your idea that she come in?"

Stick scanned the others. They were fascinated. I hadn't lied to him. I was able to act out their fantasies: be angry, ask intrusive questions, give him orders. "No," he said. "I was glad she wanted to. But it was her idea."

"Do you think she wanted to work with you because, with Mike gone, she needed to be closer to you?"

Martha made a sympathetic sound. I saw Jack nod to himself. I was filling in Halley's self-portrait for them, painting her nepotistic presence in a new light.

Stick frowned, lowered his head and mumbled, "I guess . . ."

"And maybe she thought you needed her help?"

He looked at me from under his heavy brow. He ran his hands over his slicked-down hair. "Well . . . I guess Halley would know the answer to that."

I allowed a silence. He was uncomfortable. I don't know if he understood that his blank emotions would impress the others unfavorably. A man who was so incurious and unempathetic about his own daughter was hardly someone to run to for aid and comfort. Finally, I said, "You took a big chance with the leveraged buyout, right?"

"I don't think it was a big—" he stopped, lowered his hands. "I'm a risk-taker."

"You needed a first-rate marketer?"

"Always do."

"And you were probably distracted when Mike died. It must have been hard to go to work."

"No," he said with the bluntness of a child.

"Hmmm," Martha made that noise without knowing.

"I took a week off," he said, apparently apologizing.

"Was it a comfort to go back to work?"

Stick nodded gratefully. "Right."

"Who's going to succeed you?"

"Pardon me?"

"When you decide to retire, or, I guess with all the expansion, you might hire someone to run the day-to-day operations—"

"No," Stick interrupted. I waited. He glanced at Jack. "I'm not—"

I interrupted. "Remember the rules. If you don't want to answer just say 'Fuck you.'"

"I'm happy to answer. There's no plan for that. The company's bigger, but it's nothing I can't handle."

"Oh, I didn't mean you couldn't handle it. I meant, at your age, don't you think about taking more time for yourself and your family?"

"Really, Rafe—"

"Witch Doctor."

"Really, Witch Doctor, I'm a little young to be thinking about retirement."

"So you have no plans for a successor. No one you're grooming to take your place?"

He chuckled. "No."

"I was talking about it with Edgar," I said. "You know, what he would do if you dropped dead—" Someone made a noise at this phrase. I repeated it, "If you dropped dead, you know, who was qualified to take over?"

"Probably lots of people," Stick said. He tried a smile at his employees. "Probably everybody in this room."

He was lying, of course, and they knew it, but I doubt they cared. They weren't my target, anyway. I had accomplished what I wanted and shifted to questions he was glad to answer, namely how he got started as a salesman for Flashworks and moved up the ladder. By the time we heard the creaky noise of oars rowing, signaling that Andy and Halley were coming back, everyone was stupefied, the fatigue of the day showing, especially on Stick. His voice was hoarse, his eyes rheumy.

We gathered on the porch. All of the cabin was in shadow and most of the pond as well. The sun had disappeared behind the banks of pines screening us from the hotel. Above our heads the sky was tinged red and the eastern horizon showed the black edge of night.

Halley and Andy rowed in silently. No one spoke until the boat scraped to a stop on our side.

"Well?" Martha demanded, hands on her wide hips.

Halley peered at her father, her tanned face dappled by red light filtered through the evergreens. Her expression was unreadable. I was behind everyone, standing on the porch. Andy looked at me, a silent question. I nodded for him to proceed.

"We had a disagreement," Andy said.

"I don't like my name," Halley explained quietly.

"What is it?" Tim asked. He had been bold and sure of himself since being renamed.

"Peacemaker," Andy said.

"Well, that's nice," Jonathan said.

"Yeah," Jack agreed. "I like it."

"I don't know what it means," Halley said.

"When there's fighting inside the tribe, you make the peace," Andy said.

I clapped my hands. "Okay. It's almost dinnertime. Stick, I want you to row to the other side and wait for me. I'm going to talk to the others about your name and I'll come over to tell you."

Stick actually said, "Huh?" He was exhausted. He rubbed his forehead as if his head hurt. I know mine did.

"Well, no single person can be expected to name you. And if I ask people to discuss it in front of you they'll be self-conscious."

"It's late," Stick said, dropping the hand, palm turned out to me in a plea for reason.

"Won't take long, Prince."

For a moment, I thought he would balk. Or rather, turn on his sandals and make for the hotel. I could hardly have tackled him. But he had endured so much, ten hours of my nonsense to prove to them he was a good sport, how could he blow it now with only one more inning of my silly game to be played?

"Better not," he grumbled, unable to resist making a threat. He pushed the boat off land, got in nimbly, and rowed with power and grace. He must have crossed the pond twice as fast as anyone else.

I watched him all the way. The others waited with me. Once on the far shore, Stick stared at us, as if annoyed we hadn't moved. Finally, he disappeared into the trees. I waved them into the cabin.

"Well?" I asked immediately, before they settled on the floor. They looked bedraggled, their rumps dirty from sitting on grass and the pine floor, hair askew, eyes bleary, shirts wrinkled and hanging out. Halley stood with her arms crossed, rubbing herself, as if she felt chilled. With the sun down, the air had the bite of fall. Mosquitoes were appearing in greater numbers. Tim slapped at his legs and arms to kill them, hitting himself so hard it made me wince.

"I have a can of OFF in my room," Martha commented wistfully.

"Well?" I repeated. "Any suggestions?"

"He's the Chief, right?" Jack asked.

"I'll tell you what," I said. "You think up a name privately and come and whisper it in my ear. I'll sit here by the door. Then you can go to your rooms, relax, get drunk, have dinner, whatever. If there's a common theme I'll tell Stick. Otherwise I'll tell him he's the Chief."

"Then I'm done," Jack said brightly.

"If that's really your suggestion and not just public relations," I said.

"It's easy for me," Halley said. She came over, hands lightly gripping my arms, and got up on tiptoe. She whispered, "I'm going to my room to take a bubble bath."

"Thank you," I said, straightening. "You're dismissed."

"No fair," Jonathan complained, although he hadn't heard. He meant that she was done so quickly.

"Bye," Halley said and left.

"How come we don't get to give you a new name, Witch Doctor?" Martha asked.

"Come on, no fooling around," I said. "It's late."

"Well, I'm staying with Chief," Jack said.

"Okay," I said casually and dismissed him. This cued them not to work at it and they didn't. I could feel their disappointment that I was abandoning the game when it could be most challenging. Tim tried a little by whispering, "Sitting Bull," but Gould and Hanson both copied Jack, saying, "Chief." Martha was sarcastic, offering, "Geronimo," and Jonathan, embarrassed to be last, said, "I don't have anything."

"Okay," I told him gently. "I've got it. You can go."

A half moon appeared in the deep blue, almost black sky as I walked around the perimeter of the pond. My sore hamstring could use the exercise and walking would give Stick more time to think, more time to be tired and worried and angry. Besides, I wanted to return in the rowboat with him. A fly circled my head, following me as I followed the shore. Once in the woods, I lost him. The lower branches of the evergreens that segregated pond from meadow were trimmed up to the height of my head; the bed of dark pink needles crunched underfoot. I pushed away a gray limb the groundskeepers had missed and emerged into the clearing. The noise of my approach, in the quiet of the evening, had Stick on his feet to greet me. I stopped and listened to a bird call, in a low guttural note, for a mate.

"So?" Stick asked, walking up to me.

"Let's sit down," I said.

"You can tell me in the boat," he said with a laugh that was more of a groan. He passed me, heading for the pines.

"I'm afraid I have no choice, Stick," I said and wandered farther out into the meadow. Tall wild flowers, their colors dimmed to gray by nightfall, brushed against my bare legs. I itched all over. I imagined that

I must have a dozen bites by now. "After today . . ." I said loud, voice ringing, thanks to the acoustics of the surrounding trees. I had silenced the lonely bird. ". . . After the exhibition you put on today I have no choice but to recommend to Edgar that he protect his investment by firing you." My back was to him. For all I knew, he had ducked into the tunnel of pines and departed in his rowboat.

A violent rustle of feet trampling flowers warned me. I had turned halfway when I felt his cold fingers on my forearm. "What the fuck are you talking about? I put up with this shit all day—"

I interrupted, "Edgar can replace you with Andy and Halley. Jack will accept being passed over for her." I pulled my arm free. In the bowl of the clearing, no light reached his face. All I could see was a shadow breathing rapidly and shallowly. "You're not a leader, Stick. And they don't need you for anything else. If you can't supply leadership, you're just a leech. That's the name they gave you, by the way. They didn't expect me to tell it to you, of course. Halley suggested I give you the name 'Chief' so your feelings wouldn't be hurt. She said that, after all, they owe you for giving them their start."

"You idiot." The shadow's head bobbed, arms moving up and down, as if he were trying to fly. "I control the company. You don't know shit about business." He laughed scornfully. "You're really a fool. You don't know anything about the real world."

I reached for his shoulder.

He ducked away and growled, "You touch me and I'll punch your fucking face in."

"But you want me to touch you, Theodore," I said softly and then raised my voice to a neutral matter-of-fact level—a doctor giving him the bad news as coolly as possible. "I know all about the shadow agreement with Edgar. I admit he had to explain it twice. It was hard for an academic like me to understand. But I know that you don't control Minotaur. You shouldn't be too upset. The settlement of your shares will leave you a rich man. You get five million. Isn't that right? And three years of nominal consulting at three hundred and fifty thousand a year. By then you'll be old enough to retire."

He backed away. "He can't . . . I'll sue. It's not—"

"Legal?" I picked up his train of thought. "Well, I gather that's a gray area. And if you do prove the secret clause about your shares is illegal then, of course, you go to jail also." I moved close to the dark of his shape, close enough to see his mouth was open. I added, quietly, "I think you should accept the money without a fuss and take time to explore your homosexuality." I patted his rigid arm. "For your sake, I'll keep that part to myself. Edgar is a fag-hater."

For a while, I don't know how long, perhaps thirty seconds, perhaps ten—it felt like a lifetime—there was no talk. There were sounds: the high whine of crickets, the bird resuming its call for love, a breeze infiltrating the woods so the trees leaned against the dark sky. And Stick's breathing, too, as he stood, a scarecrow in the field, stiff and still. I smelled a sweet musty odor—was that his fear or the pine floor only ten feet away?

"I'm not gay myself," I said with regret. "Or I'd explore it with you. I know you have fantasies about me."

At last, he moved. He shook his head and there was a long hiss of exhaled air.

"I can reassure you about one thing," I said before he spoke. "Halley will understand."

Now there was laughter, deep and scornful. Stick turned and walked into the woods, heading for the rowboat, apparently unimpressed.

I had lost. I couldn't believe it. There was always the chance of failure, of course, but evidently I had felt supremely confident. I was beaten and I was amazed.

I rubbed my face. The skin felt rough and hot. I licked my lips. They tasted salty. My legs were cold and stiff. And once Stick was gone, I felt uneasy. It was so dark I could no longer see through the black trees to the gray water.

I rushed through the woods to the pond shore. The rowboat was still beached. I hurried over and stared into it, wondering if he was lying down. I jumped when Stick's voice came at me, deep and amused, from behind. "Where's yours?"

"What?" was all I could manage out of the shock.

He had been standing against one of the tree trunks. He moved beside me. "Your rowboat. Where is it?"

"I walked."

"Get in," he said. "I'll take you across."

I looked at the pond, black on our side, gray in the middle thanks to a slight shimmer of silver from the half moon. You couldn't see the green cabin on the far shore, only a black mass. In the distance, stars shone through the trees—but they were really lights from the hotel.

"Since Hal is part of your recommendation to Edgar," Stick continued in a confident voice, "I thought we'd have dinner with her and discuss your evaluation of my leadership abilities."

Was there any point in going on with the charade? I didn't think so. A mosquito buzzed right into my ear, as loud as a helicopter. I slapped at it and succeeded only in deafening myself.

"She told me your little secret, you know," he said, a whisper in my ringing ear.

That was a crushing blow. So Halley had reported my suggestion at the pool. I had not only failed with him, I had failed with her. I looked at Stick, not bothering to conceal my despair. But he probably couldn't see it anyway. To me, he was only a shape, no features.

"She told me about your sick little sex game," he continued. "How would you like that to get out?"

I was surprised again. My relief came out undisguised, "That's *it*?"

"How do you think it would look for everybody to know that the great child psychiatrist likes to play Daddy gives his little girl a bath?"

I laughed with real pleasure. "That's really it, Stick?"

"That's it, Doctor. So maybe you'd better rethink what you tell Edgar."

"Oh, we play many more sick games than just Daddy gives his little girl a bath. Hasn't she told you? Don't you have all the details, or is she starting to hold out on you?"

"She's . . ." He paused, then he snorted. "What the fuck are you talking about?"

I chuckled. "Nothing. You go ahead. You tell the world about my sick games and I'll tell Edgar about your management. It's a fair trade, Stick. My so-called reputation for your career. I accept."

Stick moved close. At that range, I could see the grooves of his stern face, his thin lips hardly moving as he mumbled, "I'm not kidding, Rafe."

I leaned in, breathing on his mouth. "Nor am I, Stick. If that's the best you can do, you're finished."

I held my ground. He was the one to step back. "I don't believe—" he began and shook his head, dismissing that thought.

"I'm going back," I said. I moved as if I planned to return along the shore.

"Wait—" he called.

"I'm tired and I'm cold and we're finished, Leech." Again, I moved as if to walk.

"Okay!" he cried. It *was* a cry. "What do you want? What do I have to do?"

I faced the pond and stared out, pensively. "There's a lot of work for you to do. You've got to deal with your personal problems, your fears, your family life. I suppose if you went into therapy . . ." I kicked at the pond's fringe of muddy sand. "It's hard to believe you'd really work at it, Stick. If I could—"

"Look—" he stepped forward, then stopped as if he didn't have a right to approach me. "Are they expecting us?"

"Not really. I told them to go back to their rooms, have dinner and relax."

"Can we—?" He gestured, hands out, pleading, "How about we have dinner in my room? We'll talk and work something out. I know you're right. I—" he lowered his head, ashamed. "I need help."

I said nothing. The bird no longer called, but an owl asked the world to identify itself. It was cold and the mosquitoes were feasting on my bare legs. I slapped at one on my thigh, scratched, and said with a sigh, "Well, I'm willing to talk about it."

"Great. Thanks." He nodded at the boat. "I'll row you across."

"I'd rather walk," I said and slapped the back of my neck.

"You'll get eaten alive." He bent over, both hands on the rowboat. "Get in. I'll push off." He shifted it from side to side, loosening the sand's grip.

I shrugged, took a step, and said loud, over the scraping noise, "Is there a lifejacket in there?"

"What?" he asked.

"Nothing," I mumbled. I stepped into the boat, stumbling on its first bench. I lost my balance.

"Whoa," he said. I caught myself by grabbing hold of the side, twisted and flopped onto the second bench.

He pushed. The boat floated out onto the water, turning aimlessly. Stick didn't move.

"Aren't you getting in?" I asked plaintively.

He strolled casually into the pond, in no hurry, although the water had been chilly even during the height of the day. "I was thinking of swimming across," he said.

I rose partway, as if to stand. "Then I'm getting out." The boat rocked, turning so I was horizontal to the shore, and continued to drift farther out onto the water. "Oh . . ." came out of me. I remained stuck in a crouch, desperately holding the sides of the boat.

He laughed and sloshed toward the boat. "Take it easy. Can't you row across?"

"I don't want to," I whined.

"Okay, okay," he said, a hand catching the prow. The water was up to his waist. "Sit down. Didn't anybody ever tell you not to rock the boat?"

"Are you getting in?"

"Yes," he hissed, annoyed. "Sit down."

I did, my hands gripping the sides, arms rigid. The boat tipped violently as he put his right foot in. I moaned. He took his time bringing up the left foot and steadying the boat. He sat facing me. "Okay," he said. "I'll have you across in no time."

"Good," I said.

"You can relax," he said, unlocking the oars. He used one to straighten us and then rowed gracefully twice. We were immediately twenty feet from shore. The pond was silver-black, its border of trees swaying shadows. Some moonlight reached his face, enough for me to see a crescent of his features: hooded eyes, long nose, thin lips. "Really, you can relax," he said, slowing down, rowing, pausing to let us drift, dragging an oar to keep us straight, then using both for one powerful row. We were well into deep water. "Let go of the sides," he said.

"I don't want to," I complained in a little voice, but I obeyed.

He nodded his approval. "Why did you walk?" he asked.

I cleared my throat. "Um. What sort of therapy would you be comfortable with? A group or private?"

"You're afraid of the water," he said, raising the oars. The boat drifted, circling gradually in the stirred pond.

I said, "Everybody's afraid of something, Stick."

"Yes, you proved that." He rested the oars on the side, fitting them into hooks. "But some things it's silly to be afraid of." He stood up and rocked the boat gently.

I shut my eyes. "Cut it out."

He shifted his weight from side to side more violently. Water lapped in. "I'll do what you want, Rafe. I'll go into therapy. Really." He rocked us again. Water soaked my sneakers. "But first I want to see you swim." He stopped, standing over me. "Get out of the boat."

I said firmly, "No."

He rocked us again, the angle steeper. For a second, my face was perpendicular to the black water. I held on tight and screamed, "Stop it!"

He sat. The water covered my feet. "Get out or I'll swamp us." He slipped forward, capturing my legs between his knees. "I'm going to teach you how to swim."

I shook my head.

"Yes," he insisted. "You hang on to the side and kick your legs. Then, when you tell me you're ready, you'll let go and swim." He parted his knees, freeing my legs. A cold hand gripped my upper arm and urged me out. "Come on. You're better off doing it that way than if I dumped us both into the water."

I turned my head toward the far shore and called desperately, "Halley!"

He slapped me. Slapped me so hard, my head rang and the skin burned.

"Don't . . ." I mumbled.

He yanked my arm and I tipped over. I grabbed the oar locked onto the side. My face was pointed at the water. In a calm even voice, he said, "Get out or I'll hit you again."

I shifted my legs past his, moving to the edge in a crouch, hands gripping the boat. "I can't . . ."

He put a hand on my back and urged. "Put your legs over the side."

I put my right leg over, my left braced against the oar, my ass half on the bench, half on the side. The black water was cold. At its touch, my sore hamstring seized. "My leg feels tight," I said, felt his hand on my back again, and my world spun over.

There were several rapid impressions: my left leg burned, scraping wood as it went into the air, my face was suffocated, my heart stopped at the shock of icy submersion and then beat wildly.

You're in the water, my head informed me, while my body panicked, struggling to orient itself. Don't breathe, I reminded myself, as I somersaulted underwater and came up, gasping.

Stick grabbed my right forearm and pulled me to the boat. "Help," I gurgled.

"Take it easy," Stick's irritated voice told me. I gripped the side with both hands. My left leg felt hot, bleeding in the water I was sure. My right leg was taut, warning it might cramp. I pulled on the boat with my fingers, raising my chest free of the pond. The boat swayed.

Stick banged my hands with his fist and I let go, sinking. He grabbed me by the hair to raise my head. I yelled and swallowed some water. My right leg contracted—pain drew it up and then pain forced it open, only to be greeted by more pain. I *was* cramping. "Don't do that!" he shouted. "Just hold on."

My fingers desperately grabbed the side of the boat, barely keeping my head above water. I couldn't straighten my right leg and I couldn't not straighten it—it hurt too much either way. "Okay," I gasped. "Experiment's over. I've got a cramp. I can't do this." I found an angle, knee bent halfway, where the muscle's contraction didn't cause agony.

"Start kicking," Stick said.

"I know how to swim," I told him. "I was tricking you—my leg's cramping. I can't—Let me in." I pulled to raise myself and he banged my left hand against the wood. I yelped, let go. That stretched me to my full length, reduced to the anchor of my right hand. I yelped again because my thigh felt as if it was tearing in half. "Let me up, Stick! I wanted to see how far you'd go. I can swim, but I've got a cramp."

He snorted. "That's a pretty stupid lie for a Ph.D."

I reached for the boat with my left hand and took hold with my fingers. Bending it gradually, I tried to relax the right leg. The severe pain was gone—it felt numb. But there was no strength and I knew if I tried to flex it the agony would return.

"Listen," I said in a rushed gasp. "I knew—so I lied. I can. Really. I can swim. But I've got a cramp. You have to let me up."

"Un huh." Stick leaned back, his cruel face dissolving into a shadow. "Now you just kick nice and easy and get used to the water. When you're relaxed, you let go and swim. The most important thing is not to be afraid to put your face in the water. If you need to breathe, you just turn your head to the side." He pantomimed the actions, a shadow turning its head to the side. He brought an arm up and said, "You bring your arm through the water, keeping your fingers cupped . . . All the way through and back. Try to keep your elbow high." He stopped the demonstration, sat facing me, and leaned toward me. He pulled gently, teasing me, lifting the index finger of my right hand. "Why don't you let go with one hand?"

I didn't react to his sadism. I flexed my leg gradually to see if I could move it enough to avoid the paralyzing contractions. I had roughly fifty percent mobility. If I could remember not to extend it fully, I might be able to swim.

He pulled my middle finger off and then whacked the remaining digits. I was stretched away from the boat, clinging with only the tips of my left hand. I put my right arm into the water, through and out. "See?" I said. "I can swim."

"Just one more and you're there," he said. He pulled at the pinky of my left hand.

I twisted to look. We were nearer to the east shore.

Stick pried off another finger.

"Stick, are you paying attention to yourself—"

"Keep moving your arm," he pulled at the middle finger.

"You're excited," I said. Water slid into my mouth. I spit it out. "Do you have an erection?"

He smashed my left hand and I slipped down. I sank without a struggle. I couldn't risk flailing for effect with my crippled leg. We were deep, he hadn't made a mistake about that. Well before I felt the bottom, I rolled onto my left side, keeping my half-bent right leg still, using a side stroke to propel me beneath the boat. I hoped—the pond was too dark to see through for orientation. Something, I was sure it was a fish, slithered along my chest. I hadn't had time to gasp air, but I wanted to swim underwater for as long as possible.

My lungs ached while I repeated in my brain, over and over, "Don't use your right leg." When I surfaced smoothly, I rolled onto my back. I had succeeded in passing underneath the boat and beyond it toward the east shore. The pond was quiet for a while and then I heard a big splash, followed by more noise of someone moving in the water. Stick called, "Rafe!" A moment later the rowboat groaned and I heard him grunt. I assumed that he was climbing back in.

I floated with only my eyes and mouth out of the water, arms stroking well below the surface, in no hurry to reach safety.

Finally my right foot felt the bottom and I eased myself quietly into shallow water until I could lean on my arms and lift my head enough to look across the pond.

Stick was crouched in the rowboat, facing the other way, peering at the black surface. He had an oar dipped into the water, moving it slowly back and forth. He called, "Rafe!" abruptly. I started, thinking he knew I was alive. But he didn't. He continued to stare intently where I had disappeared. In a little while, he said it again, "Rafe?" only this time he made a sad sound.

Since his back was to me I rose and quickly moved onto the shore. At the noise of my breaking the water, Stick turned. I was in the shadow of the woods by then.

"Rafe?" he called, this time with a desperate hope.

I slid behind the trees and waited, rubbing my right leg until I could stretch it out. Stick shifted to the side of the boat facing me and dove into the water. While he was submerged, I hurried through the evergreens. When I had run half the distance to the cabin, I stopped, peering toward the pond. I couldn't see through to make out what Stick was up to.

I maneuvered to bring myself out at the back of the cabin, carefully placing one foot after another with gentle pressure to keep the crackling forest quiet. I heard faint sounds that could have been Stick rowing on the pond. I was shivering by then.

I entered the cabin through the rear door and found the towels in a cabinet where I had stored them the night before, when I first decided to provide Stick with an opportunity to teach me how to swim. Through the window I saw Stick rowing slowly to shore. Before he reached it, I crossed to the pond side of the cabin and opened that door halfway. I maneuvered beside the frame, inside, out of sight.

I couldn't see his face as his boat came to a rest on the sand. He got out, moving very slowly, as if every bone in his body ached. He was wet. His slumped shoulders trembled uncontrollably. He faced the pond and stood there, shivering, looking at the still water.

I stepped into the open doorway and onto the porch. He didn't hear the squishy noise of my feet in the drenched sneakers. I waited for him to turn.

He made a noise through his teeth and dropped slowly to his knees. He must have crossed his arms because a hand appeared on each shoulder. He cried out, "Rafe!" with rage and then bent forward all the way until his head touched the earth.

The trees echoed with his cry. In the ringing aftermath, I answered calmly, "Are you sorry, Stick?"

"Ah!" he screamed and rolled to the ground.

I ran up to him as he tried to right himself. I bent over him as he scrambled, crawling from me. I said into his terrified face, "That's who you are!" I pointed to the black water. "That's you! That's the real man!"

"No!" He kicked at me with both legs, backing away on his elbows and his ass, so scared he pushed himself into the pond.

I kept pace, stepping between his legs, finally bending down to say, "What are you?"

"I didn't mean—I tried to—"

"What are you!" I shouted into his trembling mouth.

"I'm bad!" he cried out desperately and shook his head from side to side as if he were denying his own testimony, but he wasn't. He was rapturously feeling the truth of it. "I'm bad," he called again, this time to the dark sky.

"You're dangerous," I told him.

He gasped and shut his mouth. He looked at me meekly.

"Aren't you?" I asked softly.

Water lapped at his chest. He asked cautiously, "Are you alive?"

"That doesn't matter, Stick. You murdered me whether I'm alive or not."

His chin trembled and at last the miracle happened. He cried. Like a scared boy, he blubbered, "I'm bad."

"Yes," I agreed.

His chest quaked and he sobbed again. "I'm bad," he said in a high little voice.

"You want to hurt people."

He nodded his head up and down and sniffled.

"We're going to have to watch you, watch you very carefully."

He nodded. I offered a hand. He took it. I pulled him up. There was a rank smell coming from him, the smell of a frightened animal.

"There was no danger here tonight from me, Stick. I can't do anything to hurt you. Do you understand?"

"I think so," he said in a whisper.

"There was no danger except from you."

"I know," he said in a little voice.

"I have a towel for you." I turned my back and went to the porch. I brought him a dry towel. He hadn't moved, he was still in two feet of water. "Come on out," I coaxed.

He walked to me, arms folded across his chest, shivering and sniffling. I put the towel around his shoulder. He hugged it. He lowered his head and whispered, "I'm sorry."

"You're not sorry, Stick, you're just scared. I'll ask you again. What are you?"

He rubbed his wet face with a corner of the towel and took a deep breath. He looked at me frankly. "I'm bad," he said calmly.

"Okay," I told him. "At least that's a start."

CHAPTER FOURTEEN

The Last Conflict

AFTER THE NIGHT ON THE POND, THERE REMAINED ONE OBSTACLE FOR ME to surmount with Halley, and I knew months, perhaps years, might pass before the time came to face it.

Stick's progress was smooth. Three months later, he drove Mary Catharine to an AA meeting. He waited outside to take her home—and to make sure she sat through it. Centaur was a great success. Stick put what would have been Gene's bonus into a trust fund for Pete Kenny. Under Andy Chen's supervision (he was named VP in charge of product development), Tim and Jonathan inaugurated a software line that, as of this writing (summer 1994), became Minotaur's most profitable division, protecting it from the laptop and PC price-cutting catastrophes of the past two years. Today, Jack Truman is manager of the company. Theodore Copley, although still its titular head and owner, functions as a consultant, approving future plans, representing Minotaur to its board and the public at large. He keeps himself aloof from day-to-day personnel decisions. This is entirely voluntary on his part. He wishes to avoid the temptation to hurt people.

The night I "drowned"—we did have dinner in his room—and during many more conversations over the following months, I learned that his childhood and adolescence had been a series of cruelties similar to the story of how he was taught to swim. He remembered the details gradually. Part of his adaptation (a copy of neurosis and another proof that his condition qualifies as a disorder) had been to repress the memories. My assumption that his father taunted him about his sexuality had been correct. He was called girlie if he dropped a ball or reacted with pain to a fall—both commonplace taunts. He was savagely teased for being a little fat boy, also a cliché. A less well known sadism to me, although I had intuited this wound, was his father's snide remarks about the size of his prepubescent penis. A particularly traumatic event occurred when Stick was six. His father observed him walking hand in hand with his closest male friend and forbade him from seeing the boy ever again because, "they were acting like little fags." (Stick didn't know what that meant. He found out during adolescence when the implication was especially upsetting.) Although his father slapped his mother on a regular basis, he was rarely hit. Stick recalled two spankings and a vicious punch in the stomach and his father's most brutal language was always delivered in private. I can't say the abuse was severe or that unusual for a man of his generation. Perhaps the disguised nature of his father's sadism, its apparent respectability, was what made Stick's successful adaptation possible. After Stick admitted to himself he was afraid he was homosexual, he was able to discover he wasn't, and there followed great relief, a relief that allowed him to give up some of his sadistic impulses, in particular toward his wife and daughter.

I don't mean to imply that Stick was cured. For one thing, a complete "cure" of emotional conflict seems to me an illusion that blinds itself both to the power of instinct and the real world. Stick was born with an aggressive, selfish nature that cannot be fundamentally altered and we live in a society that, despite its public claims, admires and rewards ruthless individual behavior. What was accomplished was the creation of self-consciousness. Guilt, some might call it, although I believe the result with Stick is closer to the idea implicit in the word responsibility. He came to understand that his resistance to pain and loneliness, his relish of competition, is not shared by many. He learned patience in the face of the simple although annoying truth that most people who are thrown into cold water sink rather than swim.

Halley's "cure" seemed to proceed, if at all, with the stubbornness of normal therapy. Six months after the fall retreat, by the time Stick severed his end of their metaphorical incest, she had already transferred her fixation to me. Under the guise of reporting what Gene, Jack, Didier (and others) felt about his management, she used to give Stick explicit accounts of her lovemaking. To make clear what has already been implied, since our "games" were satisfying her Electra complex, she stopped that behavior after our first encounter. Nevertheless, in April of 1992, when Stick told her he no longer wanted to hear about her affairs, she was rocked.

She hunted for me immediately, although it was during work hours, something she avoided. (She concealed our intimacy from others, just as she had pretended not to be friendly with her father.) She found me out back, watching the work on the new recreational area. They were laying a full basketball court, putting up a volleyball net on the grass, and carving a true running path for jogging enthusiasts.

I was on the grass, under the new volleyball net, watching as they put down a layer of blacktop for the basketball court. The smell had driven all but the workmen away. Halley appeared in a navy blue suit and high heels. She had to circle around to reach me. Her right foot gave out on the soft earth at the border and she twisted her ankle slightly. She kicked off her shoe angrily, bent over and rubbed. I got up and went to her. "Did you hurt yourself?"

I was astonished when she turned her face to me. There were tears in her black eyes, the first I had ever seen. "You know I'm not all right." She tried to walk, stumbled because the other foot was still in a high heel shoe. She kicked that one off too. Her stocking feet were getting dirty.

"Here," I said, putting an arm around her. "I'll help you onto the grass."

"You can't do this," she said bitterly and I knew she didn't mean my physical act of charity.

"Do what?"

"You know." She hopped while I held her. We reached the grass and I helped her sit down. She brushed dirt off the bottom of her feet. "Get my shoes," she said, glancing up. She squinted against the tears. Her mouth was tight as if she were also fighting unhappy words. "I'm going to quit. If he thinks I won't, he's kidding himself."

I fetched her shoes. She checked the heel of the one she had twisted. It was all right. "I really don't know what you're talking about," I told her.

"He—" she nodded at the top floor of the Glass Tower, "he doesn't want to hear my, quote unquote gossip, anymore." She stared at the machine while it rolled over steaming tar. Perhaps inspired, she shut her eyes, squeezing back the tears. "He doesn't even know I've already stopped telling him."

"Yes he does."

She frowned at my interruption and ignored it. "He said if I have anything to tell him I should do it in the Friday marketing meeting." She played one of her notes of feeling. There was a sad chord to its bitterness. "Fuck him. I can get another job like *that*." She snapped her fingers.

"Why don't you?"

She raised her head, slowly, eyes clearing. She pursed her lips, stretched her legs, and thought for a while. When she settled her gaze on me, she had regained her self-possession: a pretty young woman taking a break from the office to flirt casually with a co-worker. "The Great White Father says I'm in love with you," she smiled at me sweetly.

"But we know that's impossible, right?"

Her innocent, charming smile didn't fade when she answered, "I told him he's scared of you."

"That was probably the most provocative thing you could say to him."

Her smile disappeared. "He hates me," she commented. She leaned back on her hands, looking up at the sky.

"No," I said. "He just doesn't love you. He's not capable of love."

She called to the blue air, "It's the same thing."

"Where would you like to work?" I asked.

She coughed. "I—uh—" She coughed again and then couldn't stop. I suspected her suppressed tears were the cause. She leaned forward and I pounded her back twice. She got them under control. "You know Mom's quit drinking before," she gasped out as they ended.

"Not the same," I said.

"Why?" she asked, elongating the word like a child playing at keeping a conversation going.

"I bet she never admitted she was an alcoholic. She just did it on her own, right? For a week or two? This time she's been on the wagon for four months."

Halley didn't answer. She watched me, her black eyes big and solemn.

"She has your father's support—instead of teasing her, undermining her resolve," I continued.

"I called Edgar," she blurted out.

"Good," I said. "He'll help you find work that's worthy of your talents."

"I'm going to fuck him," she informed me without rancor or challenge, merely a promise.

"From what I know of men like Edgar that'll probably speed up the process. Although he'd help you anyway."

"I don't want a job. He's worth, what? Six hundred million? He can keep me until I get pregnant. Then he'll leave his wife."

I nodded and waited.

She rotated on her behind, legs under her, elbows on her knees, and faced me. "I was glad Mikey died." She rocked back and watched me.

I nodded.

"That's what you want me to say," she told me.

"If it's the truth."

Her eyes strayed up to the volleyball net. "I felt like shit for a while, but then I realized I was glad. That's why I told Gene I loved him."

I nodded. "Because you wanted to be able to love."

"Right," she agreed.

"So really you were just trying to be a better person when you told him you loved him?"

"It made him happy and I . . . I believed it, too. Even *I* believed it for a while." She tilted her head and she regarded me, waiting.

"Bullshit," I said.

"No," she shook her head.

"All of it. Pure bullshit," I said. "What's bothering you is that your father is paying attention to your mother instead of you."

Halley smiled. Head tilted, arms hugging her knees, eyes bright, she smiled as if I had just complimented her. The roller reached the border of the court and started beeping, a steady insistent noise to warn that it was moving backwards. She held my attempt at an impassive gaze while her eyes were lively and interested. When the roller stopped beeping and turned to press another section flat, she asked, "Do you love me?"

"More than ever," I said.

She rocked forward, patted my arm, then reached for her shoes. I watched her small feet fit into them. I knew the details of every pore of her body and all its incarnations: the birthmark above her left hip, the puffed look of her belly bloated by menstruation, the quizzical stare of her wet knees breaking the water of her bath, her hair down and long to play the cool adventuress, her hair bound in a ponytail for girlish comfort. I knew, as well, every turn of her quick competitive mind, furiously constructing disguises. She stood up and nothing remained of the pain she had brought to show me. She stared at the roller squeezing moisture from the black ground. "Dr. Neruda's playground for gifted children," she said and laughed.

She left. I waited until the layer was finished. I checked my watch, saw that it was almost ten-thirty, and walked to the parking lot. Stick appeared. It was time for him to take Mary Catharine to her AA meeting. Afterwards they would have lunch. He flipped the keys to his Lexus back and forth while he walked my way, not surprised by my presence. "She told you," he said, not a question.

"Was it difficult?"

"It was my fault," he said, stating a fact. His gaunt face stared at the low gray body of his car.

"Yes," I agreed.

"I encouraged her."

"Yes," I said.

"She's done great work. The whole 800 scheme was really . . . She put it together." He looked at me, smiling slightly. "They're all copying it. Including Big Blue. With all those fucking salesmen."

"Are you proud of her?"

He stared down at the keys and flipped them over. They struck his knuckles. "Yep," he said and flipped them back against his palm. "She deserves to be promoted more than Jack."

"That's true."

"Is she going to leave?" he mumbled.

"My guess is, she's calling Edgar now. She claims she's going to be his second wife."

He nodded and opened his door. He moved between it and the car, one foot inside, ready to mount his horse. "She's trying to piss you off."

"Predictable," I said. "So you told her you were promoting Jack?"

"That's what we agreed, right?"

I nodded.

He got himself in, and looked through the windshield. He didn't close the door. "I thought you said she told you."

"In her way. She complained about your asking her to keep her love life to herself."

He reached for the door. "She's a real loss to the company."

I helped shut it while saying, "But you'll get a daughter back."

I turned to leave. He started the car and lowered his window to say,

"Rafe?" I faced him. He frowned and stared ahead. I leaned on the door and waited. The stone face didn't move.

"What is it, Stick?"

His lips barely moved. "You don't love her?" he asked and looked at me.

"No. If I did, it would be a disaster for her."

"Poor Hal," he said. He pressed a button and his window rolled up. I backed away and he drove off. He was hurting his daughter, hurting her more keenly than anyone else could, and, although he hadn't hesitated to do the deed, he didn't seem to get much pleasure from it. We *had* made progress.

Halley resigned a week later to work for Edgar in his recently formed media subsidiary, Levin Entertainment, which included his brother's production company, Channel 8—the independent New York broadcast station that he was transforming into a cable superstation—and the Catalogue Channel, a slightly upscale copy of the Home Shopping Network. During our seven-thirty-in-the-morning phone calls, I heard how thrilled she was by the day-to-day progress of her new career. For her, the job was really centered around captivating Edgar, the target I (her new father) had set for her.

Edgar took Halley's job inquiry seriously right from the start. Stick had recommended her highly and confirmed her story that she was the one who wanted to leave Minotaur. Nevertheless, Halley insisted Edgar was only interested in her sexually. "He's got very few women working for him and I bet he's fucked all of them."

"Could be," I conceded. "But he wants you for a job that you're qualified for anyway—mass media marketing."

"He should be hiring someone from the Home Shopping Network. That would kill two birds with one stone—hurting them while getting himself started."

"Did you suggest that to him?" I asked.

"Yes." She didn't linger in her bed these days for our talks. She roved while dressing. There was a rush of water, followed by the sound of pouring. "Was that a mistake?"

"Are you making coffee?"

"Yes. Did I make a mistake?"

"It was good advice. That should prove to him you're the right choice."

"Good," she said. Over the next month I was introduced each morning, by phone, to her new world. Our night sessions continued, on Monday and Thursday. They were strictly ritualized with no variation: a bath on Monday, a bedtime story on Thursday. Only during the throes of orgasm did she complain that she couldn't touch me and she was obviously insincere. She was convinced that I was what I seemed to be: a loving mirror in which she could see a true reflection. My headaches, of course, grew worse. No matter what I tried—long walks; midnight exercise at, ironically, The Workout; or, to be blunt, masturbation—nothing relieved my frustration. I wondered about an absurdity: if I had a real relationship going that I could return to after my sessions with Halley, would that be easier? My guess was yes—except for the minor detail that no healthy woman would accept my behavior.

I had a more immediate problem. By May, Halley was settled at Levin Entertainment. My presence at Minotaur was no longer required—Stick had gone too far in relinquishing power and he showed no sign of wishing to return to his former behavior. Besides, a weekly phone call kept him satisfied and well-monitored. I had even found him a doubles partner who relished winning as much as he. It was time to terminate— allow Andy, Jack, Tim, Jonathan and Stick to function on their own. If I returned to Baltimore, however, I couldn't maintain my sessions with Halley and that would be disastrous. In a year, all I had accomplished with her was a transference of her fixation from Stick. Where could I go in New York, be useful, and still available to Halley? There seemed to be only one choice.

Since it might not be easy to pull off, I waited until Halley left on a week-long trip to the West Coast—a key experience since Edgar was going along and she expected to begin their affair. "He wants me," she told me during a morning phone session two days before they left. "He booked us onto the same floor of the Four Seasons." She confessed to some nervousness about having sex with Edgar.

"Why?" I asked innocently, hoping she would make the leap without a push.

"I haven't had sex—" she laughed. "Real sex, I mean, since Jack. That's almost six months." She crunched toast.

"You forgot Didier."

"Oh Didier, right." She swallowed. "That's still almost six months. But you're right." She sipped coffee. There was a pause, then the test. "Do you love me?"

Once again, no progress. "I love you," I said and noted with grim amusement that my temples had begun to throb.

They left for California Sunday night. We would miss our morning call for the first time in eight months, since by eight A.M. New York time, I drove to Riverdale, and I expected to be busy by ten-thirty when she woke up in L.A. The clinic's lot was filled. Four shelter vans occupied all the visitor spots. I parked on the street. Naturally, I didn't recognize most of the kids gathered in the hall. One of the full-time counselors saw me and blurted out, "Rafe?"

I nodded and hurried into Sally's room. She had a phone halfway to her ear, a finger poised to hit buttons. She stared at me, frozen in position.

"Hello," I said and pointed to my old office. The door was ajar. I could see my desk, but the rest of the furniture was different. "Does anyone work in there?"

Sally followed my hand, peering as if she had just noticed that office existed. "Uh . . ." Sally glanced at Diane's office. The door was shut. She hung up and said, "Um . . ."

"It's good to see you, Sally," I said and smiled.

"Good to see you, Rafe," she answered softly.

I nodded at my old office. "What's it being used for?"

"A spare interview room. Vaughn uses it sometimes to talk with kids alone—but he prefers to write up reports in his dorm bedroom."

"Who's Vaughn?"

She seemed embarrassed by my ignorance. "One of—a new counselor."

"Okay," I said. "I'll be using it from now on. I'll tell Vaughn to kick me out when he needs it. Do you have a schedule sheet and the Child Welfare waiting list?" Sally glanced at Diane's closed door again before she handed me the schedule and list in slow motion.

"Thanks," I said and entered my old office. Diane had removed all my books. I knew that—they were stored in boxes in the basement. My personal things—photographs, degrees—were in Baltimore. I shut the door and sighed with relief.

It was annoying that my Knoll desk chair was gone, that my supply of blank lined notebooks had also been confiscated, but the view of the clinic's backyard was a comfort. I looked over the new requests from Child Welfare, checked the schedule and noted that, as usual, the clinic was overloaded. Twelve kids from the Bronx would have to be rejected for outpatient care. The previous week I had spoken with the Prager Institute director, promising him a major work for their money, warning that it might not be available for publication and would have to be sealed and stored in their archives. Actually, that detail seemed to please him. I told him I would need to remain in New York for further research. He agreed to extend my grant for another year. Diane wouldn't have to compensate me; I could see patients all day at no cost to her.

I read the preliminary interviews of kids on the waiting list and, using a felt-tip pen—my Mont Blanc was still at Hyperion—checked off the most urgent cases.

Diane opened my door at eight twenty-five. She must have left her office to head to Group Room A for her eight-thirty and heard the news from Sally. She stood on the sill. I didn't look up.

"What are you doing?" she demanded.

I raised my head and offered the circled list of children I wanted to see. Her hair was still that odd red color, only longer, another new style, this one combed back on the left side and flipped to the right. She seemed lopsided to me. She was still wearing contacts, but she had gained her weight back. "I want to work," I answered. "You don't need to pay me. Here are the kids I think you should schedule for me." I stood up and extended the sheet. "With your approval, of course."

Diane stepped in. She hooked the door with her foot and kicked it shut. "What?" she complained.

"You need another therapist. A utility shrink." I tried a smile but received no encouragement. "I don't expect any authority. Use me to fill in the gaps." I shook the paper.

Diane frowned at the floor. Abruptly, she walked over and took the sheet, pretending to study it to avoid my eyes.

"Where's my chair?"

"I took it," she mumbled.

"This one'll kill my back," I said. Getting no response, I added, "I'll buy another one."

Her head was still down. I ducked to see her eyes. She met mine from under her brows. They were cold and enraged. She offered the sheet. "I can't call for these kids unless I know you're here to stay."

I took it from her. "I'm here as long as you want me."

She turned to the window. The blinds were open halfway and sunlight striped her. She communed with herself for a moment that was excruciating for me to endure. "Stay out of my way."

"I will."

She looked at me. "I don't want you in the staff meetings."

I nodded. She mumbled, "Only 'cause I need another body," and then left.

Sally made the calls and I managed to see three children that afternoon. I collected my few possessions from Minotaur in the evening and avoided the temptation to return the message from Halley on my voice mail. We had kept calls to a strict morning schedule since the previous fall, and trips shouldn't alter the pattern.

I missed our phone sessions all week because I had patients in New York when Halley woke in L.A. I stayed hidden in my office, seeing the children, writing up reports for Diane, and leaving without so much as a peek into the group rooms, or the basement cafeteria. I declined invitations to join the pickup basketball game Vaughn had organized for every afternoon at five. That's when I left for my sublet in the Village, proceeding directly through Sally's office to the hallway, out to the lot and into my car, walking with blinders on. Altogether, I saw Diane three times: twice on the way to the coffee pot in Sally's office and once coming out of the hall bathroom. We exchanged nods without a word.

I hardly slept Friday, the night of Halley's return flight. I was up hours before our regular Saturday call at eight A.M. It rang four times and Halley's machine answered. "This is Rafe," I said after the beep and waited.

She didn't pick up. That was a long day and night for me. I napped for a few hours in the afternoon and then had trouble falling asleep, staying up until three in the morning. Thus I was dizzy and bleary-eyed at eight A.M. on Sunday when I dialed Halley's number.

"Hello?" she answered, very hoarse, obviously asleep.

"I woke you," I said.

"Hmmmm," she answered.

"Should I call tomorrow?"

"Give me a minute," she said. From the faint sounds, I think she went to the bathroom. She came back, her voice stronger, and said, "Let me make coffee."

"Should I call back?"

"No. I'll take you with me." I walked electronically through her hall and into the kitchen. We fetched coffee from the freezer, found a filter paper, and began measuring. While doing that she asked, "Where did you go? They said you've left Minotaur."

"I'm working at my old clinic, seeing kids again."

"Why?" she asked in her child's tone—all innocence.

"Sabbatical's over. Time for me to get back to my work."

"The book's done?"

"I have more writing to do. How was L.A.?"

She cleared her throat. I heard her pour water into the coffee machine. "The business was great. We're all set up to premiere in September. I was a big hit with everybody including . . ." She let it hang and then dropped the bomb, "Your cousin Julie."

I knew I was in trouble, but I kept my voice cool. "How did you meet her?"

"She's producing a movie for Edgar—or, for Alex, Edgar's brother. But you know him. They certainly all know you. Especially Julie."

I tried to ignore her suggestive tone. "And how did it go with Edgar? Did you get him into your bed?"

"*His* bed." She laughed, a deep throaty noise. "He was the one with the suite." The refrigerator door opened and shut. "I want to see you."

"You'll see me Monday night."

"No," she said firmly. "I want to see you today."

It was my turn to become the curious child. "Why?" I asked gently.

"Because you're a liar." She was matter of fact. Remarkably composed, in fact. "I've been really stupid. I can't believe what a jerk I've been. Anyway . . ." She sipped something. Presumably the first brewed cup of coffee. "If you want to see me ever again it had better be today."

My heart was pounding. She called herself stupid, but I was the one who felt like an idiot. I should have anticipated the possibility that she would meet Julie. I don't know how I could have controlled that encounter; nevertheless, I ought to have made an attempt. In retrospect, it would have been more sensible to aim Halley at someone other than Edgar. But Edgar was the ideal lure; he represented a more powerful male than Stick—in the dynamic of Minotaur he was the Holy Spirit.

"Well . . . ?" she demanded into my silence.

So the crisis had come—and not of my making, thus I was not only unprepared, I didn't know for sure which illusion had been dissolved. "Where should we meet?"

"You want to come here?" she asked.

"No," I said. No matter how much damage had been done, her home must remain the exclusive location of our incest rituals, unpolluted by reality.

"It's a nice day. Why don't we walk in the park?"

"Okay," she said in mild tone. The background chord of triumph was unmistakable, however. "I need an hour to take a bath," she said and laughed, a laugh that frightened me. It resonated with a strange combination of delight and despair.

"I'll meet you outside your building." It was too early to phone Julie. Besides, how would talking to her help? Assuming Halley had gained my cousin's complete confidence—and knowing my charming little narcissist, I *had* to assume that—what could she have learned the she didn't already know in some form or other? The answer: that Julie and I had had a love affair. And perhaps some details about the clinic. But probably nothing about Diane and me—unless Julie had heard through family gossip. Before Aunt Sadie died, during happier times for Diane and me, she knew we were more than colleagues. I didn't think Julie had been in close touch with Sadie, but Sadie might have told Aunt Ceil, who . . . By the time I reached Halley's building, although clouds had covered what seemed to be a promising morning for New York, they had lifted for me. I could guess now what Halley must be feeling. My surmise didn't relax me about the outcome, but at least I was prepared.

Halley emerged from her building wearing black jeans and an oversized workshirt with the sleeves rolled above her elbows. Accompanying the clouds was a cool wet breeze blowing off the park. She peered up and said, "It's going to rain."

"Let's risk it," I said and turned.

She came up beside me. Her raven hair had been dried and combed into a thick mane that reached halfway down the blue shirt. She had a light pink shade of lipstick on. Her already dark skin was a deeper shade thanks to the West Coast. She didn't say anything while we walked to the corner, crossed to the park, walking along its border toward an entrance.

"Well?" I said. "Why did you call me a liar?"

"I'm a fool, but you're sick." She brushed her high forehead with a hand as if hair had fallen across it. None had. She twisted my way, slowing, almost walking backwards. "I still can't figure out what you think you're doing. I guess I'm stupid too."

I stopped, backed up to the park's stone wall, and leaned against it. The sky was heavy with clouds. The cars on Central Park West passed in a hurry, as if racing to be home before the storm. "Did you sleep with Edgar?"

"None of your business," she answered.

I smiled. "How was it?"

Halley's beautiful mouth hung open. She looked away, peering at the swaying trees. I felt a drop of rain on my head. She returned her eyes to me and they were slightly crossed. "That's what you were trying to do? Fuck me up so I couldn't have sex?"

I beamed at her. "And could you?"

She stepped up to me, almost touching, and snapped, "He couldn't keep his hands off me. He loved it."

By now I was grinning. I seemed to struggle in order not to laugh as I asked, "And how was it for *you?*"

For the second time since I'd known her, I saw tears fill her eyes. "I did it for you. I played that sick game for you."

Still grinning, I shook my head from side to side. "I didn't lie to you, Halley. I told you—it isn't my fantasy, it's yours."

She shut her eyes and stamped a foot, shouting, "Just tell me the truth!"

"What truth?" I whispered. Another drop fell on my head. The gray pavement behind her was spotted by rain.

"Did your loudmouth cousin—" she started to say, talking at the ground. She inhaled and looked up at me. She hadn't been able to control the tears. Her eyes continued to fill. She arched up on tiptoe and pressed her lips on mine. My elbows were resting on the stone wall. She put her arms around my chest and hugged my stiff body. She tried to push her tongue through my sealed mouth. Failing to break through, she broke off and said, "Kiss me back!"

I shook my head grimly from side to side. There was hardly any gray pavement left. Dark spots of rain had blackened the sidewalk.

"Is she telling the truth?" Halley complained, her mouth trembling. "Did you live with her—?"

She stopped because I was nodding.

"And with that other woman—at your clinic?"

I nodded.

"Are you going back to her? Is that why you're working there?"

I nodded and asked her wounded face, "You couldn't feel anything while he fucked you. Is that it?"

She put her hands on my waist—my arms were still resting on the wall, refusing to give her anything. She said softly, "I'm going to say something to you and I mean it. I really mean it." So far, the rain wasn't falling hard enough through the leaves of a tall maple over our heads for much to penetrate. A drop hit her forehead and trailed down her sagging cheek. She shut her eyes and swallowed. "I love you," she said, as if she were praying.

I said nothing.

She opened her eyes. They weren't crossed or red. They were clear and innocent.

With a clatter the rain came hard and fast, rattling through the leaves and wetting us. "I don't love you," I said.

She pulled at me with her small hands. "You're lying."

"You were just research for my book," I explained.

"I'll get him to marry me," she pleaded, the shape of her hair dissolving in the rain. "And then that's it—we're finished."

I nodded.

"No more phone calls. No more hearing everything about me," she said, her face shiny from the water.

"No more," she said in a little girl's voice.

"It's over anyway, Halley. There never *was* anything to end."

Her drenched face contorted. She slid up my chest, eyes shut, her lips parting to take mine. I felt her fingers grab at my groin. She didn't kiss me. She screamed, "She said you love to fuck!"

She didn't have a hold on anything vital, just the hump of fabric on my jeans' zipper. Nevertheless, I couldn't control my instinctive reaction. I pushed her. She staggered. But her fingers kept their grip on the bunch of material at my groin. She shouted into the noise of battered leaves, "She said you're a real hot Latin—"

I didn't hear the rest, because when I pried her hand off my jeans, she spun away and the words were lost on the wind and rain. I backed off, toward the avenue.

Halley was in a crouch by the stone wall, the oversized workshirt glued to her shoulders, hair drowned. Her hands were out, fingers arched into claws, and she yelled, "I'll cut it off!"

I turned and walked away fast. I didn't hear an attempt to follow. I doubt I could have through the storm. I kept my eyes forward until I reached the IND subway entrance and then looked back. No Halley.

Sunday night was far from pleasant for me. I tried Edgar at his home shortly after nine-thirty. He told me to wait, he had to switch phones. When he first greeted me, I heard in the background what I assumed was his wife and two sons playing Monopoly. A boy shouted, "Yes! That's four railroads!"

"God, you were right," Edgar said when he came back on. "She was great."

"And the business meetings?"

"Oh *that*. Hey, Rafe, man does not live by profits alone." He laughed. "She's terrific at the work too. For one hundred fifty thousand a year, she's a real bargain."

"I'm glad it's working out," I said.

"You really never had a taste?" Edgar asked.

I ignored him. "How does it feel to be home, Eddie?"

He chuckled at my dig. "Feels great to be home," he said. "Now I can get some rest."

I feel asleep after five A.M. I was up at seven and phoned her at seven-thirty. I got nothing: no machine, no Halley. I gave up after fifteen rings.

I was almost useless with the children in the morning sessions. For my lunch break, I lay down on the cheap sofa Diane had moved into my office. It was too short. My feet hung over the edge. But I slept. I dreamt I heard Halley ask, "Do you love me?" when cold fingers landed on a dangling ankle. I jerked up, heart racing, gasping for air.

"Sorry!" Diane said, backing away from the couch. "I'm sorry. I didn't mean to startle you. Your two o'clock is here and Sally didn't know if she should wake you."

I shifted to sit, head in my hands, panting, waiting for my heart to slow and my breathing to relax. The back of my shirt was soaked through. While I calmed down I peered through my fingers at Diane, who once again looked different. "You're wearing your glasses?" I asked, answering my own question, and uncovering my face.

Diane doesn't blush, but she might as well have. She lowered her eyes and adjusted the frames with a hand. "Contacts are too much trouble," she mumbled. She moved to the door. "Do you want me to cancel your session?"

I stood up. "No, I'll get some coffee and I'll be all right." I walked to my desk for the cup I had left there. I expected Diane to be gone when I turned around. I was surprised to see her, back against the door, watching me.

"What?" I asked.

"Did you change your mind?"

"Change my mind?" I was groggy anyway, but I doubt that even if I were completely alert I would have known what she meant.

"About Samuel."

"Samuel?" I shook my head to clear it. "What about Samuel?"

She sighed and spoke slowly to control her irritation. "Is that why you're back? Did you change your mind about Samuel's study?"

"Oh." I understood and felt silly not to have. I laughed. I straightened and tried to look serious. "Yes," I answered solemnly. "I've done some research and come to a conclusion about Phil Samuel."

Diane, quite interested, nodded for me to go on.

"He's an asshole," I said.

Diane blinked at me. I glanced at my watch. "I think I'd better have another cup of coffee and get to my patient. If you want, I'd be glad to have dinner sometime and discuss it."

She left slowly, without a word, apparently in a daze.

I left the clinic at five, reached the Village a little after six, and ate alone in a Chinese restaurant. I was unhappy. I longed to reach a conclusion that would allow me to give up Halley's therapy, but my task seemed inescapable.

I arrived at Halley's building at ten-thirty, the regular time for the Monday night bath. She knew the rules: if she weren't available, I would never return. Her doorman, the same one who, ten months before, had dire predictions for the cherry bomb thrower's fingers, waved me in without buzzing her. He hadn't announced me for months.

I paused outside her door. Was I really up to it? There couldn't be a break in my front and she was more dangerous than ever, now that she knew my end of our sessions was a performance. She knew that somewhere there was a real man for her to seduce.

And there was my own resolve to consider. Because, after all, I had to admit that I was lost in the countertransference. I knew then I did love her. And I knew the primitive Rafe, the wishing animal, believed in a miracle, believed our two false selves could embrace and manufacture real happiness.

I rang her doorbell and waited. There was no answer.

I wasn't sure if I should ring again—wasn't that already displaying too much desire on my part? Luckily, I gave her the benefit of the doubt and rang again.

I heard nothing for at least a minute. I had turned to go when Halley called through the door, "Rafe?" She sounded weak and scared. She called a little louder, "Is that you?"

"It's time for your bath," I said.

"Oh . . ." she said faintly. The top lock turned. "I didn't think you were coming . . ." The bottom lock tumbled and the door opened an inch or two. "I have to—I'm in the bathroom," she whispered.

When I pushed the door and stepped in, she was gone. I heard water filling the tub in the distance. From my vantage point at the foyer I could see most of the living room. Piles of books were on the floor by the shelves. About half had been taken down. All of the self-help books, the New Age books, and her collection of my work were in one towering stack near the hall to her bedroom. (After the fall retreat, she had bought more of my books and read them, eager to tell me I was brilliant, but I didn't respond to the flattery and she eventually dropped that approach to my ego.) The plays were also piled together, a small stack. The largest by far, crowding the front door, were the books on marketing. I didn't linger by them because my eye was attracted to the couch.

All the cushions were off, piled on the steamer trunk coffee table. There seemed to be something on the bare bottom of the couch. To see what, I had to move to it. There were five of Halley's suits in a row, jackets neatly folded over skirts. I was about to turn away when I noticed loose threads near the lapel of the navy blue jacket. I lifted it and gasped as it came apart.

The sleeves fell off; two cuts running from each lapel to the pockets billowed open. They were fine, apparently made by a razor. I saw the skirt had also been meticulously cut in two places. I lifted a pale pink jacket from the next pile. The arms fell off and the body opened like an origami paper animal.

"Halley!" I called, alarmed. No answer. The tub water was still running. "Halley!" I called again, dropped the clothes and moved quickly toward the hall to her bedroom. I glanced at the kitchen and stopped again. The sink was full of bottles.

I stepped in and saw they were makeup containers—it looked as if every cosmetic she owned was in there. Each one was smashed, half-submerged in a dull brown mess, the color they had formed when mixed together.

I hurried toward her bedroom. I was relieved to see the bed wasn't destroyed. The stuffed animals were snuggled peacefully between the pink pillows. Entering, though, I found the room hadn't entirely escaped. The mirrored doors of her bedroom closet were gone. Only the blank cardboard backing was left and written in black felt-tip pen across one door was the word: LITTLE. On the other, GIRL. Two cartons were on the floor, neatly filled by shards of glass.

I looked no farther. "Halley," I called to the bathroom door.

"I'm ready, Daddy," she called in a hoarse but cheerful voice.

I don't know exactly what horror I expected, but opening the door was hard. I was scared, scared enough for part of me to argue that I should run away, that whatever had happened, the job was done, and it was too late to regret the doing.

But I opened it. The lights were out as they would be for our ritual. A lamp from her bedroom provided a shaft of illumination that showed me the bath was full of bubbles, puffy white clouds overflowing the rim. Halley was submerged with only her head exposed. In the shadow I cast, I couldn't see her face.

I flipped both light switches, the fluorescent one above the sink and the recessed light. I don't think I actually screamed—the yell was inside my head. It seemed to me the floor was covered with blood. The sink was full of glass from the medicine cabinet mirror. There was a razor resting next to the cold water faucet. Two bloody palm prints were on its rim. Later, I discovered what seemed to be a blood-soaked floor was merely a trail of spots and one footprint by the tub. At the time my eyes went right to her.

The mounds of white bubbles were pristine except for a floating pool of blood trailing off her chin. She turned her head my way, slowly, squinting at the light and I saw the source. Beginning right below each eye were two symmetrical cuts made by the razor, like a trail of tears, that opened her cheeks down to the jaw line.

"It's too bright," she said faintly. "Turn them off."

I left them on, of course. I hurried to the tub and reached into the water to pull her arms out. The wrists were untouched. She complained, "I don't want to get out," as I lifted her to make sure the rest of her was okay.

"Keep your head back," I said and went into the bedroom to make two calls, the first for an ambulance and another to Stefan Weinstein, asking him to meet us at Bellevue to admit her.

"Is she a suicide?" he asked.

I considered explaining that she was in no mortal danger, that technically this was self-mutilation, not suicide, but I didn't. I answered, "Yes."

"Don't be angry," she said when I reentered the bathroom.

"I'm not angry," I said as I searched the cabinet for gauze, Band-Aids—anything. It was empty. The wastebasket under the sink was also empty; she hadn't dumped anything there. I pulled two white hand towels from the rack and applied them to the cuts.

"Ow!" she complained and fought me, shaking her head.

"Stop!" I yelled. "They'll bleed more."

"It hurts!" she whined.

"Lie still. Put your head back." I held the towels firmly, more concerned about stopping the flow than infection. The blood immediately soaked through in lines matching the cuts and began to spread. "When did you do this?"

She rested her head on the sloping porcelain and looked at me. I didn't need a medical degree to see in her blank eyes that she was in shock. She whispered to me, "Now I'm safe."

"You'll be fine," I reassured her.

She tried to smile, but the cuts and the pressure of the towels made it more of a grimace. "No," she told me. "You're stupid."

"When did you do this, Halley?"

She shut her eyes. Her chin slackened, her lips parted. She seemed to have passed out. But she hadn't. She whispered, "Now we're both safe."

Postscript
POINTS OF TECHNICAL INTEREST

I DON'T HAVE AS MUCH TIME TO COMPLETE THIS MANUSCRIPT AS I WOULD like. An urgent case calls me away from the evenings I have devoted to writing it. However, given the dangers in the crude techniques I worked out for Theodore and Halley Copley, I wanted to be sure to provide a rough record before continuing my research into what I've somewhat whimsically labeled Evil Disorder.

Obviously, the ending with Halley was not a desirable one. The misfortune that the final crisis was provoked by an outside source, namely her encounter with Julie, was handled poorly. I was precipitate in landing the blow that everything we shared was fake; that I was not a loving incestuous Daddy, but merely a mirror; a mirror that, like her false reflections, provided an addictive fantasy. The success of the trauma therapy with Stick at the pond had misled me. I should have taken into account that Halley's disorder, despite the superficial appearance of an attack on others, was always self-directed, a series of self-murders. To block her meant she would turn entirely against herself and not, as Stick had, against me. The pale, almost invisible scars she bears today on her face, following two rounds of reconstructive surgery, and the deeper scars she bears forever within, are my fault and my responsibility. The promise I made to myself after Gene's death, to write a book of my failures, has been kept. Despite the success with Stick, and the fact that Halley is no longer a danger to others, I can hardly point to her as a triumph.

Stefan Weinstein treated Halley during the thirty-day stay at Bellevue for observation. He was waiting at the emergency entrance when we arrived in the ambulance. He stayed with me during her surgery. I was frightened. Stefan insisted I take a sedative and I agreed. Considering both our prejudices against drugs, that proves I was in a bad state. My guilt, and the full realization of what I had lost, unnerved me so much I told him the details of my dealings with Halley. (I don't regret having taken the risk of admitting my manipulative behavior and not because it proved to be no risk. It helped him treat her effectively, and I owed poor Halley at least that.) I was not in immediate professional danger, since, as far as medical and legal ethics go, I was not treating her, and thus my actions couldn't be labeled as malpractice. Stefan was angry and questioned my mental stability, which did imply a professional threat.

I did not explain my motive or my logic. He knows nothing of why I played the role of an incestuous father. I went along with his assumption that I was suffering from a breakdown, caused by the stress of leaving the clinic and the shock of Gene's death. Given Stefan's bias as a traditional Freudian, I couldn't inform him of my diagnosis of Halley; and certainly I couldn't admit that my intention *had* been, in his terms, to make her neurotic—or, in my terms, to disrupt her successful adaptation as a narcissist. I agreed to see Dr. Richard Goodman, a psychiatrist he recommended, as a patient. Only a few sessions were required for me to convince Dr. Goodman that I had had an episode, an episode brought to an end by the shock of Halley's mutilation and understood thanks to his analysis.

The patient Stefan treated in Bellevue regressed to childhood. For weeks, Halley spoke with a little girl's lisp and claimed not to recognize her mother and father when they visited. (There was a residual benefit to her psychosis. Stick felt responsible and his own desire for reform was reinforced.) I saw her only three times. After that, Stefan asked me not to visit. Although she showed no distress in my presence, chatting lucidly about Minotaur and Levin Entertainment, she would weep uncontrollably after I left. Stefan concluded that my visits were sustaining what I insisted was her delusion that I was her lover. (Of course, he didn't agree that was a delusion. Again, one hand was tied behind my back in these arguments, since I couldn't explain my reason for insisting we were not and had never been lovers.)

Shortly after my last visit to Bellevue, I met with Stick and Mary Catharine to help them select a private psychiatric hospital for Halley to complete her recovery.

The sober Mary Catharine was even more frank than the drunk. "I was a rotten mother," she told me boldly. Stick kept his head down. "Soon as she started sprouting tits I wanted to kill her. And he was no help," she nodded at her penitent husband. "Kept barging into her room without knocking hoping to get a peek."

He took me aside later and whispered, "I want you to know. I never touched her."

"I know that, Stick," I said, almost feeling sorry enough to tell him the truth.

"They say she keeps talking about Daddy touching her, but it's not true."

"I've told them that, Stick. You don't have to worry."

Almost two years have passed. Halley wrote four letters to me immediately after her release from Bellevue that I should append to this, although my personal things aren't with me at the moment, and for safety's sake, pending the outcome of my next case, I am filing this manuscript immediately in the Prager archives. Her letters won't reveal much, but they meant a great deal to me. She wrote that I was the first man she truly loved and she added, poignantly, that now she knows how Gene must have felt. Today, Halley is back at work for Edgar. Their relationship, he tells me, and he's trustworthy about such things, has been strictly professional since her release. He said her whole manner was changed when she returned to the job. She became cool, sometimes abrasive in her dealings. Just as effective, but much less popular. To avoid arousing Stefan, I have neither seen nor spoken with her since Bellevue.

A month ago, Edgar reported that Halley is engaged to be married to a Pakistani, a resident in thoracic surgery at New York Hospital, who plans to practice in the States. Edgar added that today Halley is a devout Muslim and one of his most valued employees which proves, he joked, that peace in the Middle East will last.

That last detail, her conversion to her fiancé's religion, worried me sufficiently to ask whether Halley and her husband had made definite plans to be married. "Their plans are definite," Edgar said. "I have an invitation to the wedding." I was relieved. She might have acquired a false faith to woo her betrothed, but that is a quite normal form of self-murder for the sake of love. Stefan Weinstein is to be complimented in restoring Halley to stability, but some credit must be given to my treatment that she did not revert to her old, destructive self.

As for my condition? I plead guilty that in my invention of a new treatment for Halley, I failed to protect myself. I loved her. But that wasn't a destructive experience. Indeed, I believe I resolved my two most difficult and troubling conflicts. I can, at last, bring to fruition my construction of these case histories: in the expiation of my failure with Gene I found relief from the guilt of my betrayal of my father; in the impersonation of incest with Halley, I was able to forgive my mother. I loved my little girl just as my mother must have loved her little boy. That, of course, is not rational—but why should a cure make more sense than the illness?

I married Diane six months ago. As I'm sure any professional would guess, she loves me today with complete confidence in my feelings for her. Since my "admission" to her and others that I had been suffering from an emotional crisis when I handed the tape to Phil Samuel, her sympathy hasn't wavered. Absence may not make the heart grow fonder, but repentance certainly does. By the way, my repentance is perfectly sincere. Although Diane may not know everything I am doing these days, my commitment to her has no reservations. When I saw cousin Julie at this past Seder I couldn't keep my eyes off her, but not for the old reason. I could no longer recognize why she had been, for so many years, the lost prize of my youth.

Five months ago Diane accompanied me to Tampa to bury Pepín. They called me after messages left for my father at his number in Havana weren't returned. A handful of senile or doddering relatives came to the service that I arranged. Baffled by Pepín's atheism and embarrassed by the funeral director's startled look when I informed him of Grandpa's irreligion, I arranged for a Methodist minister to speak. He babbled so much nonsense at the funeral home I told him to keep it short and sweet at the grave.

Diane rode with me to the burial at the Centro Asturiano de Tampa Memorial Park Cemetery. It was over and we were walking back to the car when a taxi appeared and a tall, very thin, bald man got out. He was in a long white Cuban dress shirt, a *guayabera*, and his skin was so tanned, at a distance he might have been taken for a black. It was Francisco, of course. Diane and I waited for him to reach us. I noticed he limped. He stopped in front of me and demanded, "Is it over?"

"We tried to reach you."

"I was in France," he said, staring into my eyes. "Meeting with a publisher for a book on Fidel." His eyes were set farther back than I remembered, sunken compared to his high cheeks. He swayed, as if he were dizzy. I put a hand on his shoulder. He peered past me toward the graves. "What happened?" he asked.

"We just finished—"

He cut me off. "How did he die?"

"In his sleep. Heart failure. As peacefully as it could happen."

My father's old face looked frightened for a moment. "Show me," he said.

I moved aside. He walked with me. The path was uneven. Because of his limp, he stumbled, and I put my arm through his. He clutched it tight against him, with all his old strength and command. He allowed me to guide him to his father's grave.

He stood and stared at the coffin without a flinch or a tear. After a long silence, he said, "A world is gone."

He didn't talk in the car or argue at the hotel while I got him a room. He nodded in reply when I asked if he wanted something to eat. Diane said she'd go up to the room to take a nap. We went to the hotel coffee shop and Francisco ordered a hamburger. "They only know how to make them in the States," he told me.

He asked a few questions, whether Diane and I had children. "Not yet," I told him.

"I would like a grandson," he said. "I don't want you to be the last of the Nerudas." I wasn't sure if that was meant as a criticism.

"You're forgetting Cuco."

He shook his head. "He can't have children. He had testicular cancer and the treatment made him sterile."

"Is he all right?"

"Yes. The operation was done a year ago. He's in complete remission. He's made a fantastic recovery. But he couldn't come with me. There's . . . These days, in Cuba—" Embarrassed, Francisco waved away the beloved country's woes. "He couldn't take the time."

"Give him my love."

Francisco nodded. "He said to say hello."

"You plan to continue to live in Cuba?" I asked.

"I will die there," he said in his dramatic voice that could transform melodrama into a reasonable comment.

"I have something to apologize for," I said.

He shut his eyes, irritated. "Not this."

"No," I said and touched his thin arm. "You misunderstand. The last time I saw you, I told you I didn't think I could change the world and it made you angry. You were right to be angry. I was wrong. I apologize."

Francisco sat up straight, his head back as if to gain perspective on me. "You can't mean that," he said finally.

"I do. It's wrong for a son to say that to his father. Whether or not I can change the world, for your sake I have to try."

He seemed embarrassed and he busied himself with the last french fry on his plate. In a moment I knew why. A tear rolled down my cheek. I wiped it away and soon he was telling me Fidel was going to survive despite the fact that he was utterly alone and at the mercy of the United States. I didn't believe a word he said, but I listened happily to the music of his resonant voice. When he left the next morning, he embraced me at the airport and kissed Diane, telling her, "Give me a grandson," so earnestly that she had to look away.

I've tried to go over this text in the past few weeks. I know it requires revision and supplemental data, mostly to quell academic quibbles. Unfortunately, a recent visit to Albert prevents further work at the moment. Albert called and asked for my help two weeks ago. He has been benched by his coach in an effort to intimidate him into taking steroids and has gotten into other trouble thanks to a teammate. I believe I may have identified another example of Evil Disorder and will spend most of the next six months as an advisor to the football program.

There are other points which ought to be covered, such as how I managed to form a "friendship" with Phil Samuel despite my marriage to Diane. Phil, it turns out, provides an interesting instance of this newly defined illness within my own profession. I must leave the bracketed portions—possible footnotes—and other loose ends untied until I have completed these investigations.

During the past year, I have formed a company, Neruda Consulting, that advertises itself as a help to corporations who wish to adjust to the shifting demands of the modern business world. Edgar, believing this is some sort of magic cure for corporate healing such as I performed at Minotaur, has backed me financially and is, of course, an invaluable salesman of our service. During the past year, I have prepared a questionnaire for our clients to circulate among their employees. I will return to this manuscript after dealing with Albert's nemesis and releasing the information I've gathered about Phil Samuel's behavior toward his female graduate students. By then, I should have identified more cases and be able to proceed with refining my treatment for Evil Disorder. Diane understands that I feel I can no longer limit myself to working with children. I am forty-two years old and yet I feel my life has just begun. I look forward to expanding my new practice and I welcome other professionals to the cause.

DATE DUE
